"Truly breathtaking. . . . A sensual feast."
—*San Francisco Chronicle*

"Orringer's writing is glorious."
—*The Oregonian*

"One of the best books of the year."
—Junot Diaz

"An unforgettable, important work. . . . Extraordinary."
—*The Miami Herald*

"Heartbreaking—and inspiring."
—*Chicago Sun-Times*

"Brilliant. . . . Remarkably accomplished."
—*The Washington Post Book World*

"You don't so much read it as live it." —Simon Schama

"Dazzling. . . . A story simultaneously epic and intimate."
—*Entertainment Weekly*

Praise for Julie Orringer's

THE
Invisible Bridge

"To bring an entire lost world—its sights, its smells, its heartaches, raptures and terrors—to vivid life between the covers of a novel is an accomplishment; to invest that world, and everyone who inhabits it, with a soul, as Julie Orringer does in *The Invisible Bridge*, takes something more like genius."

—Michael Chabon, author of
The Amazing Adventures of Kavalier & Clay

"What begins as a jewel-box romance soon breaks open into a harrowing saga of war. Orringer . . . conveys a piercing sense of what it means to be fated by one's blood." —*Vogue*

"The word 'epic' seems inadequate to describe Julie Orringer's phenomenal first novel, *The Invisible Bridge*. You don't so much read it as live it. . . . Profoundly moving. . . . This is one that cries for you to linger over it, page by enthralling page."

—*Financial Times*

"Engrossing. . . . *The Invisible Bridge* follows Hungarian architecture student Andras Lévi and his older lover, Klara Morgenstern, through some of the most fraught and consequential years of twentieth-century history, but Orringer never seems out of her depth." —*Time Out New York*

"Powerful. . . . So mesmerizing that in spite of the book's heft, its ending comes too soon." —*The Miami Herald*

"*The Invisible Bridge* is dense with a master's intelligence. . . . The stuff of classic novels." —*Kansas City Star*

"With *The Invisible Bridge*, Julie Orringer has built a large novel in the grand old style, and out of that rubble made something new and beautiful." —*The Onion*'s A. V. Club

"Orringer has a gift for re-creating distant times and places: a Paris suffused with the scent of paprikas and the sounds of American jazz, the camraderies and cruelties of the work camps. The ticking clock of history keeps it urgent and moving forward, and the result is, against all odds, a Holocaust page-turner." —*New York* magazine

"Orringer's great achievement here is to give us the Holocaust anew, to remind us of the scale of what was lost and to cherish what survived." —*Seattle Post-Intelligencer*

"A Tolstoy-esque novel of the Holocaust, one that tracks the passage of quotidian life and the flutter of the human heart against the implacable roll of history. . . . The love story that unfolds in Orringer's pages is as romantic as *Doctor Zhivago* and the seamless, edifying integration of truckloads of historical and topical research." —*Newsday*

"As rich in historical detail as it is human in its cast of sympathetic characters. . . . Speaks to the power of love and the steadfastness of the heart." —*O, The Oprah Magazine*

"Awe-inspiring. [Orringer's] research is painstaking and deftly woven into the body of her work—never academic, yet consistently learned." —*The Oregonian*

"Andras's Europe is fully realized: its cornices and cobblestones, its frigid winters and chance meetings in cafés." —*Bookforum*

"A work of impressive scope and powerful depth." —*BookPage*

"In a field as crowded with artistic representations as the Holocaust, it's easy to assume that there is nothing new to say. Julie Orringer reminds us that there always is, so long as there are individual stories to tell. . . . Brilliant. . . . Orringer covers the darkest matters with a tender authority while imbuing her characters with the subtle, endless dimensions of love and suffering. . . . Gripping, fresh, and worth remembering . . . this novel will endure." —*Forward* magazine

"A fine first novel. . . . Has much to say about war, and how it affects individuals indiscriminately, changing their dreams."
—*The Dallas Morning News*

"The sheer joy of storytelling fills each moment of Orringer's novel. Like Tolstoy and Eliot's work, it transports us completely into its world—that of young Andras, his friends, family and loves—and a landscape of war and redemption. Thrilling, tender, and terrifying; a glorious reminder of how books can change our lives. It is the novel of the year."
—Andrew Sean Greer, author of *The Story of a Marriage*

Julie Orringer

THE
Invisible Bridge

Julie Orringer is the author of the award-winning short-story collection *How to Breathe Underwater*, which was a *New York Times* Notable Book. She is the winner of *The Paris Review*'s Discovery Prize and the recipient of fellowships from the National Endowment for the Arts, Stanford University, and the Dorothy and Lewis B. Cullman Center for Scholars and Writers at the New York Public Library. She lives in Brooklyn, where she is researching a new novel.

www.julieorringer.com

ALSO BY JULIE ORRINGER

How to Breathe Underwater

THE
Invisible Bridge

THE
Invisible Bridge

A NOVEL

Julie Orringer

Vintage Books
A Division of Random House, Inc.
New York

FIRST VINTAGE BOOKS EDITION, JANUARY 2011

Copyright © 2010 by Julie Orringer

All rights reserved. Published in the United States by Vintage Books,
a division of Random House, Inc., New York, and in Canada
by Random House of Canada Limited, Toronto.
Originally published in hardcover in the United States by Alfred A. Knopf,
a division of Random House, Inc., New York, in 2010.

Owing to limitations of space, all acknowledgments for permission to reprint
previously published material may be found at the end of the volume.

The Library of Congress has cataloged the Knopf edition as follows:
Orringer, Julie
The invisible bridge / Julie Orringer.—1st ed.
p. cm.
1. Architecture students—Fiction. 2. Jews—Hungary—Fiction. 3. Brothers—
Fiction. 4. Jews—Persecutions—Fiction. 5. World War,
1939–1945—Europe—Fiction. 6. Budapest (Hungary)—Fiction. 7. Paris
(France)—Fiction. I. Title.
PS3615.R59168 2010
813'.6—dc22 2009046498

Vintage ISBN: 978-1-4000-3437-6

Book design by Robert C. Olsson

www.vintagebooks.com

Printed in the United States
24 26 28 30 29 27 25 23

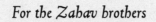

For the Zahav brothers

O tempora! O mores! O mekkora nagy córesz.
O the times! O the customs! O what tremendous tsuris.

—from *Marsh Marigold,*
a Hungarian Labor Service newspaper,
Bánhida Labor Camp, 1939

From Bulgaria thick wild cannon pounding rolls,
It strikes the mountain ridge, then hesitates and falls.
A piled-up blockage of thoughts, animals, carts, and men;
whinnying, the road rears up; the sky runs with its mane.
In this chaos of movement you're in me, permanent,
deep in my consciousness you shine, motion forever spent
and mute, like an angel awed by death's great carnival,
or an insect in rotted tree pith, staging its funeral.

—Miklós Radnóti, from "Picture Postcards,"
written to his wife during his death march from Heidenau, 1944

It is
as though I lay
under a low
sky and breathed
through a needle's eye.

—W. G. Sebald,
from *Unrecounted*

CONTENTS

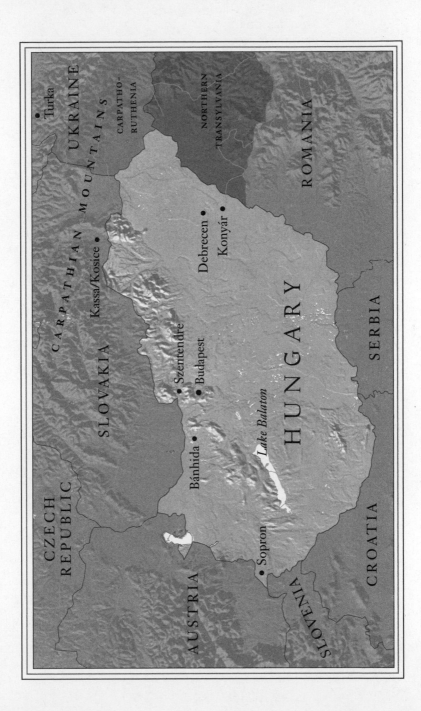

PART ONE

The Street of Schools

CHAPTER ONE

A Letter

LATER HE WOULD TELL her that their story began at the Royal Hungarian Opera House, the night before he left for Paris on the Western Europe Express. The year was 1937; the month was September, the evening unseasonably cold. His brother had insisted on taking him to the opera as a parting gift. The show was *Tosca* and their seats were at the top of the house. Not for them the three marble-arched doorways, the façade with its Corinthian columns and heroic entablature. Theirs was a humble side entrance with a red-faced ticket taker, a floor of scuffed wood, walls plastered with crumbling opera posters. Girls in knee-length dresses climbed the stairs arm in arm with young men in threadbare suits; pensioners argued with their white-haired wives as they shuffled up the five narrow flights. At the top, a joyful din: a refreshment salon lined with mirrors and wooden benches, the air hazy with cigarette smoke. A doorway at its far end opened onto the concert hall itself, the great electric-lit cavern of it, with its ceiling fresco of Greek immortals and its gold-scrolled tiers. Andras had never expected to see an opera here, nor would he have if Tibor hadn't bought the tickets. But it was Tibor's opinion that residence in Budapest must include at least one evening of Puccini at the Operaház. Now Tibor leaned over the rail to point out Admiral Horthy's box, empty that night except for an ancient general in a hussar's jacket. Far below, tuxedoed ushers led men and women to their seats, the men in evening dress, the women's hair glittering with jewels.

"If only Mátyás could see this," Andras said.

"He'll see it, Andráska. He'll come to Budapest when he's got his baccalaureate, and in a year he'll be sick to death of this place."

Andras had to smile. He and Tibor had both moved to Budapest as soon as they graduated from gimnázium in Debrecen. They had all grown up in Konyár, a tiny village in the eastern flatlands, and to them, too, the capital city had once seemed like the center of the world. Now Tibor had plans to go to medical college in Italy, and Andras, who had lived here for only a year, was leaving for school in Paris. Until the news from the École Spéciale d'Architecture, they had all thought Tibor would be the first to go. For the past three years he'd been working as a salesclerk in a shoe store on Váci utca, saving money for his tuition and poring over his medical textbooks at night as desperately as if he were trying to save his own life. When Andras had moved in with him a year earlier, Tibor's departure had seemed imminent. He had already passed his exams and submitted his application to the medical school at Modena. He thought it might take six months to get his acceptance and student visa. Instead the medical college had placed him on a waiting list for foreign students, and he'd been told it might be another year or two before he could matriculate.

Tibor hadn't said a word about his own situation since Andras had learned of his scholarship, nor had he shown a trace of envy. Instead he had bought these opera tickets and helped Andras make his plans. Now, as the lights dimmed and the orchestra began to tune, Andras was visited by a private shame: Though he knew he would have been happy for Tibor if their situations had been reversed, he suspected he would have done a poor job of hiding his jealousy.

From a door at the side of the orchestra pit, a tall spindling man with hair like white flames emerged and stepped into a spotlight. The audience shouted its approval as this man made his way to the podium. He had to take three bows and raise his hands in surrender before they went quiet; then he turned to the musicians and lifted his baton. After a moment of quivering stillness, a storm of music rolled out of the brass and strings and entered Andras's chest, filling his ribcage until he could scarcely breathe. The velvet curtain rose to reveal the interior of an Italian cathedral, its minutiae rendered in perfect and intricate detail. Stained-glass windows radiated amber and azure light, and a half-completed fresco of Mary Magdalene showed ghostly against a plaster wall. A man in striped prison garb crept into the church to hide in one of the dark chapels. A painter came in to work on the fresco, followed by a sexton bent upon making the painter tidy up his brushes and dropcloths before the next service. Then came the opera diva Tosca, the model for Mary Magdalene, her carmine skirts swirling around her ankles. Song flew up and hovered in the painted dome of the Operaház: the clarinetlike tenor of the painter Cavaradossi, the round basso of the fugitive Angelotti, the warm apricotty soprano of the fictional diva Tosca, played by the real Hungarian diva Zsuzsa Toronyi. The sound was so solid, so tangible, it seemed to Andras he could reach over the edge of the balcony and grab handfuls of it. The building itself had become an instrument, he thought: The architecture expanded the sound and completed it, amplified and contained it.

"I won't forget this," he whispered to his brother.

"You'd better not," Tibor whispered back. "I expect you to take me to the opera when I visit you in Paris."

At the intermission they drank small cups of black coffee in the refreshment salon and argued over what they'd seen. Was the painter's refusal to betray his friend an act of selfless loyalty or self-glorifying bravado? Was his endurance of the torture that followed meant to be read as a sublimation of his sexual love for Tosca? Would Tosca herself have stabbed Scarpia if her profession hadn't schooled her so thoroughly in the ways of melodrama? There was a bittersweet pleasure in the exchange; as a boy, Andras had spent hours listening to Tibor debate points of philosophy or sport or literature with his friends, and had pined for the day when he might say something Tibor would find witty or incisive. Now that he and Tibor had become equals, or something like equals, Andras was leaving, getting on a train to be carried hundreds of kilometers away.

"What is it?" Tibor said, his hand on Andras's sleeve.

"Too much smoke," Andras said, and coughed, averting his eyes from Tibor's. He was relieved when the lights flickered to signal the end of the intermission.

After the third act, when the innumerable curtain calls were over—the dead Tosca and Cavaradossi miraculously revived, the evil Scarpia smiling sweetly as he accepted an armload of red roses—Andras and Tibor pushed toward the exit and made their way down the crowded stairs. Outside, a faint scattering of stars showed above the wash of city light. Tibor took his arm and led him toward the Andrássy side of the building, where the dress-circle and orchestra-floor patrons were spilling through the three marble arches of the grand entrance.

"I want you to have a look at the main foyer," Tibor said. "We'll tell the usher we left something inside."

Andras followed him through the central doorway and into the chandelier-lit hall, where a marble stairway spread its wings toward a gallery. Men and women in evening dress descended, but Andras saw only architecture: the egg-and-dart molding along the stairway, the cross-barrel vault above, the pink Corinthian columns that supported the gallery. Miklós Ybl, a Hungarian from Székesfehérvár, had won an international competition to design the opera house; Andras's father had given him a book of Ybl's architectural drawings for his eighth birthday, and he had spent many long afternoons studying this space. As the departing audience flowed around him, he stared up into the vault of the ceiling, so intent upon reconciling this three-dimensional version with the line drawings in his memory that he scarcely noticed when someone paused before him and spoke. He had to blink and force himself to focus upon the person, a large dovelike woman in a sable coat, who appeared to be begging his pardon. He bowed and stepped aside to let her pass.

"No, no," she said. "You're just where I want you. What luck to run into you here! I would never have known how to find you."

He struggled to recall when and where he might have met this woman. A diamond necklace glinted at her throat, and the skirt of a rose silk gown spilled from beneath her pelisse; her dark hair was arranged in a cap of close-set curls. She took his arm and led him out onto the front steps of the opera house.

"It was you at the bank the other day, wasn't it?" she said. "You were the one with the envelope of francs."

Now he knew her: It was Elza Hász, the wife of the bank director. Andras had seen her a few times at the great synagogue on Dohány utca, where he and Tibor went for an occasional Friday night service. The other day at the bank he'd jostled her as she crossed the lobby; she'd dropped the striped hatbox she was carrying, and he'd lost his grip on his paper folder of francs. The folder had opened, discharging the pink-and-green bills, and the money had fluttered around their feet like confetti. He'd dusted off the hatbox and handed it back to her, then watched her disappear through a door marked PRIVATE.

"You look to be my son's age," she said now. "And judging from your currency, I would guess you're off to school in Paris."

"Tomorrow afternoon," he said.

"You must do me a great favor. My son is studying at the Beaux-Arts, and I'd like you to take a package for him. Would it be a terrible inconvenience?"

A moment passed before he could respond. To agree to take a package to someone in Paris would mean that he was truly going, that he intended to leave his brothers and his parents and his country behind and step into the vast unknown of Western Europe.

"Where does your son live?" he asked.

"The Quartier Latin, of course," she said, and laughed. "In a painter's garret, not in a lovely villa like our Cavaradossi. Though he tells me he has hot water and a view of the Panthéon.

Ah, there's the car!" A gray sedan pulled to the curb, and Mrs. Hász lifted her arm and signaled to the driver. "Come tomorrow before noon. Twenty-six Benczúr utca. I'll have everything ready." She pulled the collar of her coat closer and ran down to the car, not pausing to look back at Andras.

"Well!" Tibor said, coming out to join him on the steps. "Suppose you tell me what that was all about."

"I'm to be an international courier. Madame Hász wants me to take a box to her son in Paris. We met at the bank the other day when I went to exchange pengő for francs."

"And you agreed?"

"I did."

Tibor sighed, glancing off toward the yellow streetcars passing along the boulevard. "It's going to be awfully dull around here without you, Andráska."

"Nonsense. I predict you'll have a girlfriend within a week."

"Oh, yes. Every girl goes mad for a penniless shoe clerk."

Andras smiled. "At last, a little self-pity! I was beginning to resent you for being so generous and coolheaded."

"Not at all. I could kill you for leaving. But what good would that do? Then neither of us would get to go abroad." He grinned, but his eyes were grave behind his silver-rimmed spectacles. He linked arms with Andras and pulled him down the steps, humming a few bars from the overture. It was only three blocks to their building on Hársfa utca; when they reached the entry they paused for a last breath of night air before going up to the apartment. The sky above the Operaház was pale orange with reflected light, and the streetcar bells echoed from the boulevard. In the semidarkness Tibor seemed to Andras as handsome as a movie legend, his hat set at a daring angle, his white silk evening scarf thrown over one shoulder. He looked at that moment like a man ready to take up a thrilling and unconventional life, a man far better suited than Andras to step off a railway car in a foreign land and claim his place there. Then he winked and pulled the key from his pocket, and in another moment they were racing up the stairs like gimnázium boys.

Mrs. Hász lived near the Városliget, the city park with its storybook castle and its vast rococo outdoor baths. The house on Benczúr utca was an Italianate villa of creamy yellow stucco, surrounded on three sides by hidden gardens; the tops of espaliered trees rose from behind a white stone wall. Andras could make out the faint splash of a fountain, the scratch of a gardener's rake. It struck him as an unlikely place for Jewish people to live, but at the entrance there was a mezuzah nailed to the doorframe—a silver cylinder wrapped in gold ivy. When he pressed the doorbell, a five-note chime sounded from inside. Then came the approaching click of heels on marble, and the throwing back of heavy bolts. A silver-haired housemaid opened the door and ushered him in. He stepped into a domed entrance hall with a floor of pink marble, an inlaid table, a sheaf of calla lilies in a Chinese vase.

"Madame Hász is in the sitting room," the housemaid said.

He followed her across the entry hall and down a vaulted corridor, and they stopped just outside a doorway through which he could hear the crescendo and decrescendo of women's voices. He couldn't make out the words, but it was clear that there was an argument in progress: One voice climbed and peaked and dropped off; another, quieter than the first, rose and insisted and fell silent.

"Wait here a moment," the housemaid said, and went in to announce Andras's arrival. At the announcement the voices exchanged another brief volley, as if the argument had something to do with Andras himself. Then the housemaid reappeared and ushered Andras into a large bright room that smelled of buttered toast and flowers. On the floor were pink-and-gold Persian rugs; white damask chairs stood in conversation with a pair of salmon-colored sofas, and a low table held a bowl of yellow roses. Mrs. Hász had risen from her chair in the corner. At a writing desk near the window sat an older woman in widow's black, her hair covered with a lace shawl. She held a wax-sealed letter, which she set atop a pile of books and pinned beneath a glass paperweight. Mrs. Hász crossed the room to meet Andras and pressed his hand in her large cold one.

"Thank you for coming," she said. "This is my mother-in-law, the elder Mrs. Hász." She nodded toward the woman in black. The woman was of delicate build, with a deep-lined face that Andras found lovely despite its aura of grief; her large gray eyes radiated quiet pain. He gave a bow and pronounced the formal greeting: *Kezét csókolom*, I kiss your hand.

The elder Mrs. Hász nodded in return. "So you've agreed to take a box to József," she said. "That was very kind of you. I'm sure you have a great deal to think about already."

"It's no trouble at all."

"We won't keep you long," said the younger Mrs. Hász. "Simon is packing the last items now. I'll ring for something to eat in the meantime. You look famished."

"Oh, no, please don't bother," Andras said. In fact, the smell of toast had reminded him that he hadn't eaten all day; but he worried that even the smallest meal in that house would require a lengthy ceremony, one whose rules were foreign to him. And he was in a hurry: His train left in three hours.

"Young men can always eat," said the younger Mrs. Hász, calling the housemaid to her side. She gave a few instructions and sent the woman on her way.

The elder Mrs. Hász left her chair at the writing desk and beckoned Andras to sit beside her on one of the salmon-colored sofas. He sat down, worrying that his trousers would leave a mark on the silk; he would have needed a different grade of clothing altogether, it seemed to him, to pass an hour safely in that house. The elder Mrs. Hász folded her slim hands on her lap and asked Andras what he would study in Paris.

"Architecture," Andras said.

"Indeed. So you'll be a classmate of József's at the Beaux-Arts, then?"

"I'll be at the École Spéciale," Andras said. "Not the Beaux-Arts."

The younger Mrs. Hász settled herself on the opposite sofa. "The École Spéciale? I haven't heard József mention it."

"It's rather more of a trade school than the Beaux-Arts," Andras said. "That's what I understand, anyway. I'll be there on a scholarship from the Izraelita Hitközség. It was a happy accident, actually."

"An accident?"

And Andras explained: The editor of *Past and Future*, the magazine where he worked, had submitted some of Andras's cover designs for an exhibition in Paris—a show of work by young Central European artists. His covers had been selected and exhibited; a professor from the École Spéciale had seen the show and had made inquiries about Andras. The editor had told him that Andras wanted to become an architect, but that it was difficult for Jewish students to get into architecture school in Hungary: A defunct numerus clausus, which in the twenties had restricted the number of Jewish students to six percent, still haunted the admissions practices of Hungarian universities. The professor from the École Spéciale had written letters, had petitioned his admissions board to give Andras a place in the incoming class. The Budapest Jewish community association, the Izraelita Hitközség, had put up the money for tuition, room, and board. It had all happened in a matter of weeks, and at every moment it seemed as if it might fall through. But it hadn't; he was going. His classes would begin six days from now.

"Ah," said the younger Mrs. Hász. "How fortunate! And a scholarship, too!" But at the last words she lowered her eyes, and Andras experienced the return of a feeling from his school days in Debrecen: a sudden shame, as if he'd been stripped to his underclothes. A few times he'd spent weekend afternoons at the homes of boys who lived in town, whose fathers were barristers or bankers, who didn't have to board with poor families—boys who slept alone in their beds at night and wore ironed shirts to school and ate lunch at home every day. Some of these boys' mothers treated him with solicitous pity, others with polite distaste. In their presence he'd felt similarly naked. Now he forced himself to look at József's mother as he said, "Yes, it's very lucky."

"And where will you live in Paris?"

He rubbed his damp palms against his knees. "The Latin Quarter, I suppose."

"But where will you stay when you arrive?"

"I imagine I'll just ask someone where students take rooms."

"Nonsense," said the elder Mrs. Hász, covering his hand with her own. "You'll go to József's, that's what you'll do."

The younger Mrs. Hász gave a cough and smoothed her hair. "We shouldn't make commitments for József," she said. "He may not have room for a guest."

"Oh, Elza, you're a terrible snob," said the elder Mrs. Hász. "Mr. Lévi is doing a service for József. Surely József can spare a sofa for him, at least for a few days. We'll wire him this afternoon."

"Here are the sandwiches," said the younger, visibly relieved by the distraction.

The housemaid wheeled a tea cart into the room. In addition to the tea service there was a glass cake stand with a stack of sandwiches so pale they looked to be made of snow. A pair of scissorlike silver tongs lay beside the pedestal, as if to suggest that sandwiches like these were not meant to be touched by human hands. The elder Mrs. Hász took up the tongs and piled sandwiches onto Andras's plate, more than he would have dared to take for himself. When the younger Mrs. Hász herself picked up a sandwich without the aid of silverware or tongs, Andras made bold to eat one of his own. It consisted of dilled cream cheese on soft white bread from which the crusts had been cut. Paper-thin slices of yellow pepper provided the only indication that the sandwich had originated from within the borders of Hungary.

While the younger Mrs. Hász poured Andras a cup of tea, the elder went to the writing desk and withdrew a white card upon which she asked Andras to write his name and travel information. She would wire József, who would be waiting at the station in Paris. She offered him a glass pen with a gold nib so fine he was afraid to use it. He leaned over the low table and wrote the information in his blocky print, terrified that he would break the nib or drip ink onto the Persian rug. Instead he inked his fingers, a fact he apprehended only when he looked down at his final sandwich and saw that the bread was stained purple. He wondered how long it would be until Simon, whoever that was, appeared with the box for József. A sound of hammering came from far off down the hallway; he hoped it was the box being closed.

It seemed to please the elder Mrs. Hász to see that Andras had finished his sandwiches. She gave him her grief-etched smile. "This will be your first time in Paris, then."

"Yes," Andras said. "My first time out of the country."

"Don't let my grandson offend you," she said. "He's a sweet child once you get to know him."

"József is a perfect gentleman," said the younger Mrs. Hász, flushing to the roots of her close-set curls.

"It's kind of you to wire him," Andras said.

"Not at all," said the elder Mrs. Hász. She wrote József's address on another card and gave it to Andras. A moment later, a man in butler's livery entered the sitting room with an enormous wooden crate in his arms.

"Thank you, Simon," said the younger Mrs. Hász. "You may leave it there."

The man set the crate down on the rug and retreated. Andras glanced at the gold clock on the mantel. "Thank you for the sandwiches," he said. "I'd better be off now."

"Stay another moment, if you don't mind," said the elder Mrs. Hász. "I'd like to ask you to take one more thing." She went to the writing desk and slid the sealed letter from beneath its paperweight.

"Excuse me, Mr. Lévi," said the younger. She rose and crossed the room to meet her mother-in-law, and put a hand on her arm. "We've already discussed this."

"I won't repeat myself, then," said the elder Mrs. Hász, lowering her voice. "Kindly remove your hand, Elza."

The younger Mrs. Hász shook her head. "György would agree with me. It's unwise."

"My son is a good man, but he doesn't always know what's wise and what is not," said the elder. She extricated her arm gently from the younger woman's grasp, returned to the salmon-colored sofa, and handed the envelope to Andras. Written on its face was the name C. MORGENSTERN and an address in Paris.

"It's a message for a family friend," said the elder Mrs. Hász, her eyes steady on Andras's. "Perhaps you'll think me overcautious, but for certain matters I don't trust the Hungarian post. Things can get lost, you know, or fall into the wrong hands." She kept her gaze fixed upon him as she spoke, seeming to ask him not to question what she meant, nor what matters might be delicate enough to require this degree of caution. "If you please, I'd rather you not mention it to anyone. Particularly not to my grandson. Just buy a stamp and drop this into a mailbox once you get to Paris. You'll be doing me a great favor."

Andras put the letter into his breast pocket. "Easily done," he said.

The younger Mrs. Hász stood rigid beside the writing desk, her cheeks bright beneath their patina of powder. One hand still rested on the stack of books, as though she might call the letter back across the room and have it there again. But there was nothing to be done, Andras saw; the elder Mrs. Hász had won, and the younger now had to proceed as though nothing out of the ordinary had happened. She composed her expression and smoothed her gray skirt, returning to the sofa where Andras sat.

"Well," she said, and folded her hands. "It seems we've concluded our business. I hope my son will be a help to you in Paris."

"I'm certain he will," Andras said. "Is that the box you'd like me to take?"

"It is," said the younger Mrs. Hász, and gestured him toward it.

The wooden crate was large enough to contain a pair of picnic hampers. When Andras lifted it, he felt a deep tug in his intestines. He took a few staggering steps toward the door.

"Dear me," said the younger Mrs. Hász. "Can you manage?"

Andras ventured a mute nod.

"Oh, no. You mustn't strain yourself." She pressed a button in the wall and Simon reappeared a moment later. He took the box from Andras and strode out through the front door of the house. Andras followed, and the elder Mrs. Hász accompanied him to the driveway, where the long gray car was waiting. Apparently they meant to send him home in it. It was of English make, a Bentley. He wished Tibor were there to see it.

The elder Mrs. Hász put a hand on his sleeve. "Thank you for everything," she said.

"It's a pleasure," Andras said, and bowed in farewell.

She pressed his arm and went inside; the door closed behind her without a sound. As the car pulled away, Andras found himself twisting backward to look at the house again. He searched the windows, unsure of what he expected to see. There was no movement, no curtain-flutter or glimpse of a face. He imagined the younger Mrs. Hász returning to the drawing room in wordless frustration, the elder retreating deeper behind that butter-colored façade, entering a room whose overstuffed furniture seemed to suffocate her, a room whose windows offered a comfortless view. He turned away and rested an arm on the box for József, and gave his Hársfa utca address for the last time.

CHAPTER TWO

The Western Europe Express

HE TOLD TIBOR about the letter, of course; he couldn't have kept a secret like that from his brother. In their shared bedroom, Tibor took the envelope and held it up to the light. It was sealed with a clot of red wax into which the elder Mrs. Hász had pressed her monogram.

"What do you make of it?" Andras said.

"Operatic intrigues," Tibor said, and smiled. "An old lady's fancy, coupled with paranoia about the unreliability of the post. A former paramour, this Morgenstern on the rue de Sévigné. That's what I'd bet." He returned the letter to Andras. "Now you're a player in their romance."

Andras tucked the letter into a pocket of his suitcase and told himself not to forget it. Then he checked his list for the fiftieth time, and found that there was nothing left to do now but to leave for Paris. To save the taxi fare, he and Tibor borrowed a wheelbarrow from the grocer next door and wheeled Andras's suitcase and József's enormous box all the way to Nyugati Station. At the ticket window there was a disagreement over Andras's passport, which apparently looked too new to be authentic; an emigration officer had to be consulted, and then a more exalted officer, and finally an über-officer in a coat peppered with gold buttons, who made a tiny mark on the edge of the passport and reprimanded the other officers for calling him away from his duties. Minutes after the matter had been settled, Andras, fumbling with his leather satchel, dropped his passport into the narrow gap between the platform and the train. A sympathetic gentleman offered his umbrella; Tibor inserted the umbrella between platform and train and slid the passport to a place where he could retrieve it.

"I'd say it looks authentic now," Tibor said, handing it over.

The passport was smudged with dirt and torn at one corner where Tibor had stabbed it with the umbrella. Andras replaced it in his pocket and they walked down the platform to the door of his third-class carriage, where a conductor in a red-and-gold cap ushered passengers aboard.

"Well," Tibor said. "I suppose you'd better find your seat." His eyes were damp behind his glasses, and he put a hand on Andras's arm. "Hold on to that passport from now on."

"I will," Andras said, not making a move to board the train. The great city of Paris awaited; suddenly he felt lightheaded with dread.

"All aboard," the conductor said, and gave Andras a significant look.

Tibor kissed Andras on both cheeks and drew him close for a long moment. When they were boys going off to school, their father had always put his hands on their heads and said the prayer for travel before he let them on the train; now Tibor whispered the words under his breath. *May God direct your steps toward tranquility and keep you from the hands of every foe. May you be safe from all misfortune on this earth. May God grant you mercy in his eyes and in the eyes of all who see you.* He kissed Andras again. "You'll come back a worldly man," he said. "An architect. You'll build me a house. I'm counting on it, do you hear?"

Andras couldn't speak. He let out a long breath and looked down at the smooth concrete of the platform, where travel stickers had adhered in multinational profusion. Germany. Italy. France. The tie to his brother felt visceral, vascular, as though they were linked at the chest; the idea of boarding a train to be taken away from him seemed as wrong as ceasing to breathe. The train whistle blew.

Tibor removed his glasses and pressed the corners of his eyes. "Enough of this," he said. "I'll see you before long. Now go."

* * *

Sometime after dark, Andras found himself looking out the window at a little town where the street signs and shop signs were all in German. The train must have slipped over the border without his knowing it; while he had been asleep with a book of Petőfi poems on his lap, they had left the landlocked ovulet of Hungary and entered the larger world. He cupped his hands against the glass and looked for Austrians in the narrow lanes, but could see none; gradually the houses became smaller and farther apart, and the town dwindled into countryside. Austrian barns, shadowy in moonlight. Austrian cows. An Austrian wagon, piled with silver hay. In the far distance, against a night-blue sky, the deeper blue of mountains. He opened the window a few inches; the air outside was crisp and smelled of woodsmoke.

He had the strange sensation of not knowing who he was, of having traveled off the map of his own existence. It was the opposite of the feeling he had every time he traveled east between Budapest and Konyár to see his parents; on those trips to his own birthplace there was a sense of moving deeper into himself, toward some essential core, as if toward the rice-sized miniature at the center of the Russian nesting doll his mother kept on the windowsill in her kitchen. But who might he imagine himself to be now, this Andras Lévi on a train passing westward through Austria? Before he'd left Budapest, he had scarcely considered how ill-equipped he was for an adventure like this one, a five-year course of study at an architectural college in Paris. Vienna or Prague he might have managed; he had always gotten high marks in German, which he'd studied since the age of twelve. But it was Paris and the École Spéciale that wanted him, and now he would have to get by on his two years of half-forgotten French. He knew little more than a smattering of food names, body parts, and laudatory adjectives. Like the other boys at his school in Debrecen, he had memorized the French words for the sexual positions that appeared on a set of old photographs passed along from one generation of students to another:

croupade, les ciseaux, à la grecque. The cards were so old, and had been handled so thoroughly, that the images of intertwined couples were visible only as silver ghosts, and only when the cards were held at a particular angle to the light. Beyond that, what did he know of French—or, for that matter, of France? He knew that the country bordered the Mediterranean on one side and the Atlantic on another. He knew a little about the troop movements and battles of the Great War. He knew, of course, about the great cathedrals at Reims and at Chartres; he knew about Notre-Dame, about Sacré-Coeur, about the Louvre. And that was all, give or take a fragmentary fact. In the few weeks he'd had to prepare for the trip, he'd tortured the pages of his antiquated phrase book, bought cheap at a used bookstore on Szent István körút. The book must have predated the Great War; it offered translations for phrases like *Where might I hire a team of horses?* and *I am Hungarian but my friend is Prussian.*

Last weekend when he'd gone home to Konyár to say good-bye to his parents, he'd found himself confessing his fears to his father as they walked through the orchard after dinner. He hadn't meant to say anything; between the boys and their father was the tacit understanding that as Hungarian men, they were not to show any sign of weakness, even at times of crisis. But as they passed between the apple rows, kicking through the knee-high stems of wild grass, Andras felt compelled to speak. Why, he wondered aloud, had he been singled out for recognition among all the artists in the show in Paris? How had the École Spéciale admissions board determined that *he*, in particular, deserved their favor? Even if his pieces had shown some special merit, who was to say he could ever produce work like that again, or, more to the point, that he'd succeed at the study of architecture, a discipline vastly different from any he'd undertaken before? At best, he told his father, he was the beneficiary of misplaced faith; at worst, a simple fraud.

His father threw his head back and laughed. "A fraud?" he

said. "You, who used to read aloud to me from Miklós Ybl when you were eight years old?"

"It's one thing to love an art and another to be good at it."

"There was a time when men studied architecture just because it was a noble pursuit," his father said.

"There are nobler pursuits. The medical arts, for example."

"That's your brother's talent. You've got your own. And now you've got time and money to court it."

"And what if I fail?"

"Ah! Then you'll have a story to tell."

Andras picked up a fallen branch from the ground and switched at the long grass. "It seems selfish," he said. "Going off to school in Paris, and at someone else's expense."

"You'd be going at my expense if I could afford it, believe me. I won't have you think of it as selfish."

"What if you get pneumonia again this year? The lumber-yard can't run itself."

"Why not? I've got the foreman and five good sawyers. And Mátyás isn't far away if I need more help."

"Mátyás, that little crow?" Andras shook his head. "Even if you could catch him, you'd be lucky to get any work out of him."

"Oh, I could get work out of him," his father said. "Though I hope I won't have to. That scapegrace will have trouble enough graduating, with all the foolery he's gotten into this past year. Did you know he's joined some sort of dance troupe? He's performing nights at a club and missing his morning classes."

"I've heard all about it. All the more reason I shouldn't be going off to school so far away. Once he moves to Budapest, someone's got to look after him."

"It's not your fault you can't go to school in Budapest," his father said. "You're at the mercy of your circumstances. I know something of that. But you do what you can with what you've got."

Andras understood what he meant. His father had gone to

the Jewish theological seminary in Prague, and might have become a rabbi if it hadn't been for his own father's early death; a series of tragedies had attended him through his twenties, enough to have made a weaker man surrender to despair. Since then he'd experienced a reversal of fortune so profound that everyone in the village believed he must have been particularly pitied and favored by the Almighty. But Andras knew that everything good that had come to him was the result of his own sheer stubbornness and hard work.

"It's a blessing you're going to Paris," his father said. "Better to get out of this country where Jewish men have to feel second-class. I can promise you that's not going to improve while you're gone, though let's hope it won't get worse."

Now, as Andras rode westward in the darkened railway carriage, he heard those words in his mind again; he understood that there had been another fear beneath the ones he'd spoken aloud. He found himself thinking of a newspaper story he'd read recently about a horrible thing that had happened a few weeks earlier in the Polish town of Sandomierz: In the middle of the night the windows of shops in the Jewish Quarter had been broken, and small paper-wrapped projectiles had been thrown inside. When the shop owners unwrapped the projectiles, they saw that they were the sawn-off hooves of goats. *Jews' Feet*, the paper wrappings read.

Nothing like that had ever happened in Konyár; Jews and non-Jews had lived there in relative peace for centuries. But the seeds were there, Andras knew. At his primary school in Konyár, his schoolmates had called him Zsidócska, little Jew; when they'd all gone swimming, his circumcision had been a mark of shame. One time they held him down and tried to force a sliver of pork sausage between his clenched teeth. Those boys' older brothers had tormented Tibor, and a younger set had been waiting for Mátyás when he got to school. How would those Konyár boys, now grown into men, read the news from Poland? What seemed an atrocity to him might seem to them like justice, or permission. He put his head against the cool glass of the window and stared into the unfamiliar landscape, surprised only by how much it looked like the flatland country where he had been born.

In Vienna the train stopped at a station far grander than any Andras had ever seen. The façade, ten stories high, was composed of glass panes supported by a gridwork of gilded iron; the supports were curlicued and flowered and cherubed in a design that seemed better suited to a boudoir than a train station. Andras got off the train and followed the scent of bread to a cart where a woman in a white cap was selling salt-studded pretzels. But the woman wouldn't take his pengő or his francs. In her insistent German she tried to explain what Andras must do, pointing him toward the money-changing booth. The line at the booth snaked around a corner. Andras looked at the station clock and then at the stack of pretzels. It had been eight hours since he'd eaten the delicate sandwiches at the house on Benczúr utca.

Someone tapped him on the shoulder, and he turned to find the gentleman from Nyvgafi Station, the one who had let Tibor use his umbrella to retrieve Andras's passport. The man was dressed in a gray traveling suit and a light overcoat; the dull gold of a watch chain shone against his vest. He was barrel-chested and tall, his dark hair brushed back in waves from a high domed forehead. He carried a glossy briefcase and a copy of *La Revue du Cinema*.

"Let me buy you a pretzel," he said. "I've got some schillings."

"You've been too kind already," Andras said.

But the man stepped forward and bought two pretzels, and they went to a nearby bench to eat. The gentleman pulled a monogrammed handkerchief from a pocket and spread it over his trouser legs.

"I like a fresh-made pretzel better than anything they serve in the dining car," the man said. "Besides, the first-class passengers tend to be first-class bores."

Andras nodded, eating in silence. The pretzel was still hot, the salt electric on his tongue.

"I gather you're going on past Vienna," the man said.

"Paris," Andras ventured. "I'm going there to study."

The man turned his deep-lined eyes on Andras and scrutinized him for a long moment. "A future scientist? A man of law?"

"Architecture," Andras said.

"Very good. A practical art."

"And yourself?" Andras asked. "What's your destination?"

"The same as yours," the man said. "I run a theater in Paris, the Sarah-Bernhardt. Though it might be more correct to say the Sarah-Bernhardt runs me. Like a demanding mistress, I'm afraid. Theater: Now, there's an impractical art."

"Must art be practical?"

The man laughed. "No, indeed." And then: "Do you go to the theater?"

"Not often enough."

"You'll have to come to the Sarah-Bernhardt, then. Present my card at the box office and tell them I sent you. Say you're a *compatriote* of mine." He extracted a card from a gold case and handed it to Andras. *NOVAK Zoltán, metteur en scène, Théâtre Sarah-Bernhardt.*

Andras had heard of Sarah Bernhardt but knew little about her. "Did Madame Bernhardt perform there?" he asked. "Or"— more hesitantly—"does she still?"

The man folded the paper wrapper of his pretzel. "She did," he said. "For many years. Back then it was called Théâtre de la Ville. But that was before my time. Madame Bernhardt is long dead, I'm afraid."

"I'm an ignoramus," Andras said.

"Not at all. You remind me of myself as a young man, off to

Paris for the first time. You'll be fine. You come from a fine family. I saw the way your brother looked out for you. Keep my card, in any case. Zoltán Novak."

"Andras Lévi." They shook hands, then returned to their railway cars—Novak to the first-class wagon-lit, Andras to the lesser comforts of third class.

It took him another two days to get to Paris, two days during which he had to travel through Germany, into the source of the growing dread that radiated across Europe. In Stuttgart there was a delay, a mechanical problem that had to be fixed before the train could go on. Andras was dizzy with hunger. He had no choice but to exchange a few francs for reichsmarks and find something to eat. At the exchange counter, a gap-toothed matron in a gray tunic made him sign a document affirming that he would spend all the exchanged money within the borders of Germany. He tried to enter a café near the station to buy a sandwich, but on the door there was a small sign, hand-lettered in Gothic characters, that read *Jews Not Wanted*. He looked through the glass door at a young girl reading a comic book behind the pastry counter. She must have been fifteen or sixteen, a white kerchief on her head, a thin gold chain at her throat. She raised her eyes and smiled at Andras. He took a step back and glanced down at the reichsmark coins in his hand—on one side an eagle with a wreathed swastika in its claws, on the other the mustachioed profile of Paul von Hindenburg—then back over his shoulder at the girl in the shop. The reichsmarks were nothing more than a few drops of blood in the country's vast economic circulatory system, but suddenly he felt desperate to be rid of them; he didn't want to eat the food they could buy him, even if he found a shop where *Juden* were not *unerwünscht*. Quickly, making sure no one saw what he was doing, he knelt and dropped the coins into the echoing mouth of a storm drain. Then he returned to the train without having eaten anything, and rode hungry through the final hundred kilometers of Germany. From the platform of every small-town German station, Nazi flags fluttered in the slipstream of the train. The red flag spilled from the topmost story of buildings, decorated the awnings of houses, appeared in miniature in the hands of a group of children marching in the courtyard of a school beside the tracks. By the time they crossed the border into France, Andras felt as though he'd been holding his breath for hours.

They passed through the rolling countryside and the little half-timbered villages and the interminable flat suburbs and finally the outer arrondissements of Paris itself. It was eleven o'clock at night before they reached the station. Struggling with his leather satchel, his overcoat, his portfolio, Andras made his way down the aisle of the train and out onto the platform. On the wall opposite, a mural fifty feet high showed serious young soldiers, their eyes hooded with determination, leaving to fight the Great War. On another wall hung a series of cloth banners that depicted a more recent battle—a Spanish one, Andras guessed from the soldiers' uniforms. The overhead loudspeakers crackled with French; among the travelers on the platform, the low buzz of French and the lilt of Italian crossed the harsher cadences of German and Polish and Czech. Andras scanned the crowd for a young man in an expensive overcoat who seemed to be looking for someone. He hadn't asked for a description or a photograph of József. It hadn't occurred to him that they might have trouble finding each other. But an increasing number of passengers filled the platform, and Parisians ran to greet them, and József failed to appear. Amid the crush Andras caught a glimpse of Zoltán Novak; a woman in a smart hat and a fur-collared coat threw her arms around him. Novak kissed the woman and led her away from the train, and porters followed with his luggage.

Andras retrieved his own suitcase and the enormous box for József. He stood and waited as the crowd became even more dense and then began to dissipate. Still no brisk-looking young man stepped forward to conduct him into a life in Paris. He sat down on the wooden crate, suddenly lightheaded. He needed a place to sleep. He needed to eat. In a few days' time he was supposed to appear at the École Spéciale, ready to begin his studies. He looked toward the row of doors marked SORTIE, at the lights of cars passing on the street outside. A quarter of an hour rolled by, and then another, without any sign of József Hász.

He reached into his breast pocket and pulled out the heavy card on which the elder Mrs. Hász had written her grandson's address. This was all the direction he had. For six francs Andras recruited a walrus-faced porter to help him load his luggage and József's enormous box into a taxi. He gave the driver József's address and they rushed off in the direction of the Quartier Latin. As they sped along, the taxi driver kept up a steady stream of jocose French, of which Andras understood not a word.

He was hardly aware of what they passed on the way to József Hász's. Fog tumbled in billows through the light of the streetlamps, and wet leaves blew against the windows of the cab. The gold-lit buildings spun by in a rush; the streets were full of Saturday night revelers, men and women with their arms slung loosely around each other. The cab sped over a river that must have been the Seine, and for an instant Andras allowed himself to imagine that they were passing over the Danube, that he was back in Budapest, and that in a short time he'd find himself home at the apartment on Hársfa utca, where he could climb the stairs and crawl into bed with Tibor. But then the taxi stopped in front of a gray stone building and the driver climbed out to unload Andras's luggage. Andras fumbled in his pocket for more money. The driver tipped his hat, took the francs Andras offered, and said something that sounded like the Hungarian word *bocsánat*, I'm sorry, but which Andras later understood to be *bon chance*. Then the cab pulled away, leaving Andras alone on a sidewalk of the Quartier Latin.

CHAPTER THREE

The Quartier Latin

JÓZSEF HÁSZ'S BUILDING was of sharp-edged sandstone, six stories with tall casements and ornate cast-iron balconies. From the top floor came a blast of hot jazz, cornet and piano and saxophone dueling just beyond the blazing windows. Andras went to the door to ring the bell, but the door had been propped open; in the vestibule a cluster of girls in close-fitting silk dresses stood drinking champagne and smoking violet-scented cigarettes. They gave him hardly a glance as he dragged his luggage inside and pushed it against the wall. With his heart in his throat he stepped forward to touch one of the girls on the sleeve, and she turned a coy eye toward him and raised a painted brow.

"József Hász?" he said.

The girl raised one finger and pointed toward the very top of the oval staircase. "*Là-bas,*" she said. "*En haut.*"

He dragged his luggage and the massive box into the lift, and took it as high as it would go. At the top, he stepped out into a crush of men and women, of smoke and jazz; the entirety of the Latin Quarter, it seemed, had assembled at József Hász's. Leaving his luggage in the hall, he stepped in through the open door of the apartment and repeated the question of Hász's name to a series of drunken revelers. After a labyrinthine tour of high-ceilinged rooms he found himself standing on a balcony with Hász himself, a tall, loose-limbed young man in a velvet smoking jacket. Hász's large gray eyes rested on Andras's in an expression of champagne-tinged bemusement, and he asked a question in French and raised his glass.

Andras shook his head. "I'm afraid it's got to be Hungarian for now," he said.

József squinted at him. "And which Hungarian are you, exactly?"

"Andras Lévi. The Hungarian from your mother's telegram."

"What telegram?"

"Didn't your mother send a telegram?"

"Oh, God, that's right! Ingrid said there was a telegram." József put a hand on Andras's shoulder, then leaned in through the door of the balcony and shouted, "Ingrid!"

A blond girl in a spangled leotard pushed out onto the balcony and stood with one hand on her hip. A rapid French exchange ensued, after which Ingrid produced from her bosom a folded telegram envelope. József extracted the slip, read it, looked at Andras, read it again, and fell into a paroxysm of laughter.

"You poor man!" József said. "I was supposed to meet you at the station two hours ago!"

"Yes, that was the idea."

"You must have wanted to kill me!"

"I might still," Andras said. His head was throbbing in time with the music, his eyes watering, his insides twisting with hunger. It was clear to him he couldn't stay at József Hász's, but he could hardly imagine venturing out now to find another place to spend the night.

"Well, you've done well enough without me so far," József said. "Here you are at my place, where there's enough champagne to last us all night, and plenty of whatever else you like, if you take my meaning."

"All I need is a quiet corner to sleep in. Give me a blanket and put me anywhere."

"I'm afraid there's no quiet corner here," József said. "You'll have to have a drink instead. Ingrid will get you one. Follow me." He pulled Andras into the apartment and placed him under the care of Ingrid, who produced what must have been the last clean champagne flute in the building and poured Andras a tall sparkling glassful. The bottle sufficed for Ingrid herself; she toasted Andras, gave him a long smoky kiss, and pulled him into the front room, where the pianist was faking his way through

"Downtown Uproar" and the partygoers had just started to dance.

In the morning he woke on a sofa beneath a window, his eyes draped in a silk chemise, his head a mass of cotton wool, his shirt unbuttoned, his jacket rolled beneath his head, his left arm stinging with pins and needles. Someone had put an eiderdown over him and opened the curtains; a block of sunlight fell across his chest. He stared up at the ceiling, where the floral froth of a plaster medallion curled around the fluted brass base of a light fixture. A knot of gold branches grew downward from the base, bearing small flame-shaped bulbs. *Paris*, he thought, and pushed himself up on his elbows. The room was littered with party detritus and smelled of spilled champagne and wilted roses. He had a vague recollection of a prolonged tête-à-tête with Ingrid, and then of a drinking contest with József and a broad-shouldered American; after that he could remember nothing at all. His luggage and the crate for József had been dragged inside and stacked beside the fireplace. Hász himself was nowhere to be seen. Andras rolled from the sofa and wandered down the hall to a white-tiled bathroom, where he shaved at the basin and bathed in a lion-footed tub that dispensed hot water directly from the tap. Afterward he dressed in his only clean shirt and trousers and jacket. As he was searching for his shoes in the main room, he heard a key in the lock. It was Hász, carrying a pastry-shop box and a newspaper. He tossed the box on a low table and said, "Up so soon?"

"What's that?" Andras said, eyeing the ribbon-tied box.

"The cure for your hangover."

Andras opened the box to find half a dozen warm pastries nestled in waxed paper. Until that moment he hadn't allowed himself to realize how desperately hungry he was. He ate one chocolate croissant and was halfway through another before he thought to offer the box to his host, who refused, laughing.

"I've been up for hours," József said. "I've already had my breakfast and read the news. Spain's a wreck. France still won't send troops. But there are two new beauty queens competing for the title of Miss Europe: the dark and lovely Mademoiselle de Los Reyes of Spain, and the mysterious Mademoiselle Betoulinsky of Russia." He tossed the newspaper to Andras. Two sleek ice-cold beauties in white evening gowns gazed from their photographs on the front page.

"I like de Los Reyes," Andras said. "Those lips."

"She looks like a Nationalist," József said. "I like the other." He loosened his orange silk scarf and sat back on the sofa, spreading his arms across its curving back. "Look at this place," he said. "The maid doesn't come until tomorrow morning. I'll have to dine out today."

"You ought to open that box. I'm sure your mother sent you something nice for dinner."

"That box! I forgot all about it." He brought it from across the room and pried open the top with a butter knife. Inside were a tin of almond cookies; a tin of rugelach; a tin into which an entire Linzer torte had been packed without a millimeter to spare; a supply of woolen underclothes for the coming winter; a box of stationery with the envelopes already addressed to his parents; a list of cousins upon whom he was supposed to call; a list of things he was supposed to procure for his mother, including certain intimate ladies' garments; a new opera glass; and a pair of shoes made for him by his shoemaker on Váci utca, whose talents, he said, were unparalleled by those of any cobbler in Paris.

"My brother works at a shoe store on Váci utca," Andras said, and mentioned the name of the shop.

"Not the same one, I'm afraid," József said, a hint of condescension in his tone. He cut a slice of the Linzer torte, ate it, and pronounced it perfect. "You're a good man, Lévi, dragging this cake across Europe. How can I repay the favor?"

"You might tell me how to set up a life here," Andras said.

"Are you sure you want to take instruction from me?" József said. "I'm a wastrel and a libertine."

"I'm afraid I've got no choice," Andras said. "You're the only person I know in Paris."

"Ah! Lucky you, then," József said. As they ate slices of Linzer torte from the tin, he recommended a Jewish boarding-house and an art-supply store and a student dining club where Andras might get cheap meals. He didn't dine there himself, of course—generally he had his meals sent up from a restaurant on the boulevard Saint-Germain—but he had friends who did, and found it tolerable. As for the fact that Andras was enrolled at the École Spéciale and not the Beaux-Arts, it was regrettable that they wouldn't be schoolmates but probably just as well for Andras; József was a notoriously bad influence. And now that they had solved the problem of setting up Andras's life in Paris, didn't he want to come out to the balcony to have a smoke and look at his new city?

Andras allowed József to lead him through the bedroom and through the high French doors. The day was cold, and the previous night's fog had settled into a fine drizzle; the sun was a silver coin behind a scrim of cloud.

"Here you are," József said. "The most beautiful city on earth. That dome is the Panthéon, and over there is the Sorbonne. To the left is St.-Etienne-du-Mont, and if you lean this way you can see a sliver of Notre-Dame."

Andras rested his hands on the railing and looked out over an expanse of unfamiliar gray buildings beneath a cold curtain of mist. Chimneys crowded the rooftops like strange alien birds, and the green haze of a park hovered beyond a battalion of zinc mansards. Far off to the west, blurred by distance, the Tour Eiffel melted upward into the sky. Between himself and that landmark lay thousands of unknown streets and shops and human beings, filling a distance so vast as to make the tower look wiry and fragile against the slate-gray clouds.

"Well?" József said.

"There's a lot of it, isn't there?"

"Enough to keep a man busy. In fact, I've got to be off again in a few minutes. I've got a lunch appointment with a certain Mademoiselle Betoulinsky of Russia." He winked and straightened his tie.

"Ah. You mean the girl in sequins from last night?"

"I'm afraid not," József said, a slow smile coming to his face. "That's another mademoiselle altogether."

"Maybe you can spare one for me."

"Not a chance, old boy," József said. "I'm afraid I need them all to myself." And he slipped through the balcony door and returned to the large front room, where he wrapped the orange silk scarf around his neck again and put on a loose jacket of smoke-colored wool. He caught up Andras's satchel and Andras took the suitcase, and they brought everything down in the lift.

"I wish I could see you to that boardinghouse, but I'm late to meet my friend," József said once they'd gotten everything out to the curb. "Here's the cab fare, though. No, I insist! And come around for a drink sometime, won't you? Let me know how you're getting on." He clapped Andras on the shoulder, shook his hand, and went off in the direction of the Panthéon, whistling.

Madame V, the proprietress of the boardinghouse, had a few useless words of Hungarian and plenty of unintelligible Yiddish, but no permanent place for Andras; she managed to communicate that he could spend the night on the couch in the upstairs hallway if he liked, but that he'd better go out at once to look for other lodgings. Still in a haze from the night at József's, he ventured out into the Quartier Latin amid the artfully disheveled students with their canvas schoolbags, their portfolios, their bicycles, their stacks of political pamphlets and string-tied bakery boxes and market baskets and bouquets of flowers. Among them he felt overdressed and provincial, though his clothes were the same ones in which he had felt elegant and urban a week earlier in Budapest. On a cold bench in a dismal little plaza he combed his phrase book for the words for *price*, for *student*, for *room*, for *how much*. But it was one thing to understand that *chambre à louer* meant *room for rent*, and quite another to ring a doorbell and inquire in French about the *chambre*. He wandered from Saint-Michel to Saint-Germain, from the rue du Cardinal-Lemoine to the rue Clovis, re-cursing his inattentiveness in French class and making tiny notes in a tiny notebook about the locations of various *chambres à louer*. Before he could muster the courage to ring a single bell, he found himself utterly exhausted; sometime after dark he retreated to the boardinghouse in defeat.

That night, as he tried to find a comfortable position on the green sofa in the hallway, young men from all across Europe argued and fought and smoked and laughed and drank until long past midnight. None of the men spoke Hungarian, and none seemed to notice that there was a new man in their midst. Under different circumstances Andras might have gotten up to join them, but now he was so tired he could scarcely turn over beneath the blanket. The sofa, a spindly, ill-padded thing with wooden arms, seemed to have been designed as an instrument of torture. Once the men had gone to bed at last, rats emerged from the wainscoting to conduct their predawn scavengery; they ran the length of the hallway and stole the bread Andras had saved from dinner. The smells of decaying shoes and unwashed men and cooking grease followed him into his dreams. When he woke, sore and exhausted, he decided that one night had been enough. He would go out into the quartier that morning and inquire at the first place that advertised a room for rent.

On the rue des Écoles, near a tiny paved square with a spreading chestnut tree, he found a building with that now-familiar sign in the window: *chambre à louer*. He knocked on the red-painted door and crossed his arms, trying to ignore the rush of anxiety in his chest. The door swung open to reveal a short, square, heavy-browed woman, her mouth bent sideways into a scowl; on the bridge of her nose rested a pair of thick black-rimmed spectacles that made her eyes look tiny and faraway, as though they belonged to another, smaller person. Her wiry gray hair was flattened on one side, as if she had just been sleeping in a wing chair with her head on the wing. She put a fist on her hip and stared at Andras. Summoning all his courage, Andras forcefully mispronounced his need and pointed to the sign in the window.

The concierge understood. She beckoned him into a narrow tiled hall and led him up a spiral staircase with a skylight at the top. When they could go no higher, she took him down the hall to a long narrow garret with an iron bed against one wall, a crockery basin on a wooden stand, a farm table, a green wooden chair. Two dormer windows looked out onto the rue des Écoles; one of them was open, and on the windowsill sat an abandoned nest and the remnants of three blue eggs. In the fireplace there was a rusted grate, a broken toasting fork, an ancient crust of bread. The concierge shrugged and named a price. Andras searched his mind for the names of numbers, then cut the price in half. The concierge spat on the floor, stomped her feet, railed at Andras in French, and finally accepted his offer.

So it began: his life in Paris. He had an address, a brass key, a view. His view, like József's, included the Panthéon and the pale limestone clock tower of St.-Étienne-du-Mont. Across the street was the Collège de France, and soon enough he would learn to use it as a marker for his building: *34 rue des Écoles, en face du Collège de France.* Down the block was the Sorbonne. And farther away, down the boulevard Raspail, was the École Spéciale d'Architecture, where classes would begin on Monday. Once he had cleaned the room from top to bottom and unpacked his clothes into an apple crate, he counted his money and made a shopping list. He went down to the shops and bought a glass jar full of red currant jam, a box of cheap tea, a box of sugar, a mesh strainer, a bag of walnuts, a small brown crock of butter, a long baguette, and, as a single extravagance, a tiny nugget of cheese.

What a pleasure it was to fit his key to the lock, to open the door to his private room. He unloaded his groceries onto the windowsill and laid out his drawing supplies on the table. Then he sat down, sharpened a pencil with his knife, and sketched his view of the Panthéon onto a blank postal card. On its reverse he wrote his first message from Paris: *Dear Tibor, I am here! I have a desperate garret; it's everything I hoped for. On Monday I start school. Hurrah! Liberté, egalité, fraternité! With love, Andras.* All he lacked was a stamp. He thought he might borrow one from the concierge; he knew there was a postbox around the corner. As he tried to picture exactly where it was, what came to mind instead was the recollection of an envelope, a wax seal, a monogram. He had forgotten the promise he'd made to the elder Mrs. Hász. Her missive to C. Morgenstern on the rue de Sévigné still waited in his suitcase. He dragged the case out from beneath the bed, half fearing that the letter would be gone, but it was there in the pocket where he'd put it, the wax seal intact. He ran downstairs to the concierge's apartment and, with the help of his phrase book and a series of urgent gestures, begged a pair of stamps. After a search, he located the *boîte aux lettres* and slipped Tibor's card inside. Then, imagining the pleasure of some silver-haired gentleman when the next day's mail arrived, he dropped Mrs. Hász's letter into the anonymous dark of the box.

CHAPTER FOUR

École Spéciale

TO GET TO SCHOOL he had to cross the Jardin du Luxembourg, past the elaborate Palais, past the fountain and the flowerbeds teeming with late snapdragons and marigolds. Children sailed elegant miniature boats in the fountain, and Andras thought with a kind of indignant pride of the scrapwood boats he and his brothers had sailed on the millpond in Konyár. There were green benches and close-clipped limes, a carousel with painted horses. On the far side of the park was a cluster of what looked to Andras like neat brown dollhouses; when he got closer he could hear the hum of bees. A veiled beekeeper bent toward one of the hives, waving his canister of smoke.

Andras walked down the rue de Vaugirard, with its art-supply shops and narrow cafés and secondhand bookstores, then down the wide boulevard Raspail with its stately apartment buildings. Already he felt a little more Parisian than he had when he'd first arrived. He had his apartment key on a cord around his neck, a copy of *L'Oeuvre* under his arm. He had knotted his scarf the way József Hász had knotted his, and he wore the strap of his leather bag slung diagonally across his chest, in the manner of the students of the Latin Quarter. His life in Budapest—the job at *Past and Future*, the apartment on Hársfa utca, the familiar sound of the streetcar bell—seemed to belong to another universe. With an unexpected pang of homesickness, he imagined Tibor sitting at their usual sidewalk table at their favorite café, within sight of the statue of Jókai Mór, the famous novelist who had escaped the Austrians during the 1848 revolution by disguising himself in his wife's clothing. Farther east, in Debrecen, Mátyás would be drawing in his notebook as his classmates studied Latin declensions. And what about Andras's parents? He must write to them tonight. He touched the silver watch in his pocket. His father had had it restored just before Andras had left; it was a fine old thing, its numbers painted in a spidery copperplate script, its hands a deep blue iridescent metal. The workings still functioned as well as they had in Andras's grandfather's time. Andras remembered sitting on his father's knee and winding the watch, taking care not to tighten the spring too far; his father had done the same thing when he was a boy. And here was that same watch in Paris in 1937, a time when a person might be transported a distance of twelve hundred kilometers in a flash of days, or a telegram sent across a wire network in a matter of minutes, or a radio signal transmitted instantaneously through thin air. What a time to study architecture! The buildings he designed would be the ships in which human beings would sail toward the horizon of the twentieth century, then off the map and into the new millennium.

He found he had walked past the gates of the École Spéciale and now had to retrace his steps. Young men streamed in through a pair of tall blue doors at the center of a gray neoclassical building, the name of the school cut into the stone of its cornice. The École Spéciale d'Architecture! They had wanted him, had seen his work and chosen him, and he had come. He ran up the front steps and in through those blue doors. On the wall of the entryway was a plaque with gold bas-relief busts of two men: Emile Trélat, who had founded the school, and Gaston Trélat, who had succeeded his father as director. Emile and Gaston Trélat. Names he would always remember. He swallowed twice, smoothed his hair, and entered the registrar's office.

The young woman behind the desk seemed a figure from a dream. Her skin was the color of dark-stained walnut, her close-cropped hair as glossy as satin. Her gaze was friendly, her dark-fringed eyes steady on his own. It didn't occur to him to try to speak. Never before had he seen a woman so beautiful, nor had he ever encountered in real life a person of African descent. Now this gorgeous young black Frenchwoman asked him a question he couldn't understand, and he mumbled one of his few French words—*désolé*—and wrote his name on a slip of paper, which he pushed across the desk. The young woman thumbed through a stack of thick envelopes in a wooden box and extracted one with his name, Lévi, printed across the top in precise block capitals.

He thanked her in his awkward French. She told him he was welcome. He might have continued to stand there and stare if a group of students hadn't come in at that moment, calling greetings to her and leaning over the desk to kiss her cheeks. *Eh, Lucia! Ça va, bellissima?* Andras slipped past the others, holding his envelope against his chest, and went out into the hall. Everyone had gathered under the glass roof of a central atrium where studio assignments had just been posted. He sat down on a low bench there and opened his envelope to find a list of classes:

COURS	PROFESSEUR
Histoire d'Architecture	A. Perret
Les Statiques	V. Le Bourgeois
Atelier	P. Vago
Dessinage	M. Labelle

All matter-of-fact, as though it were perfectly natural for Andras to study those subjects under the tutelage of famous architects. There was a long list of required texts and materials, and a small white card handwritten in Hungarian (by whom?) indicating that Andras, due to his scholarship status, would be permitted to purchase his books and supplies on the school's credit at a bookstore on the boulevard Saint-Michel.

He read and reread the message, then looked around the atrium, wondering who could have been responsible for that piece of communication. The crowd of students provided no clue. None of them looked even vaguely Hungarian; they were all hopelessly, perfectly Parisian. But in one corner a trio of uncertain-looking young men stood close together and scanned the room. He could tell at a glance that they were first-year students, and the names on their folders suggested they were Jewish: Rosen, Polaner, Ben Yakov. He raised a hand in greeting, and they nodded, a kind of tacit recognition passing between them. The tallest of them waved him over.

Rosen was lanky, freckled, with unruly red hair and the vague beginnings of a goatee. He took Andras by the shoulder and introduced Ben Yakov, who resembled the handsome French film star Pierre Fresnay; and Polaner, small and light-boned, with a neat, close-shorn head and tapering hands. Andras greeted everyone and repeated his own name, and the young men's conversation continued in quick French as Andras tried to pick up a thread of meaning. Rosen seemed to be the leader of the group; he led the conversation, and the others listened and responded. Polaner seemed nervous, buttoning and unbuttoning the top button of his antique-looking velvet jacket. The handsome Ben Yakov eyed a group of young women; one of them waved, and he waved in return. Then he leaned in toward Polaner and Rosen to make what could only have been a suggestive joke, and the three of them laughed. Though Andras found himself struggling to follow the men's talk, and though they had hardly addressed him at all, he felt an acute desire to know them. When they went to look at the studio lists, he was glad to find they were all in the same group.

After a short time the students began to move out into the stone-walled courtyard, where tall trees overshadowed rows of wooden benches. One student carried a lectern to a small paved area at the front, and the others sat down on the benches. From beyond the stone courtyard walls came the rush and hum of traffic. But Andras was here inside, sitting beside three men whose names he knew; he was one of these students, and he belonged on this side of the wall. He tried to take note of the feeling, tried to imagine how he might write about it to Tibor, to Mátyás. But before he could put the words together in his mind, a door opened in the side of the building and a man strode out. He looked as though he could have been a military captain; he wore a long gray cloak lined in red, and sported a short triangular beard with wax-curled moustaches. His eyes were narrow and fierce behind rimless pince-nez. In one hand he carried a walking stick, and in the other what looked like a jagged gray rock. Any other man, it seemed to Andras, would have had to bow under the weight of the thing, but this man crossed the courtyard with his back straight and his chin set at a martial angle. He stepped up to the lectern and set the rock down upon it with a hollow thud.

"Attention," he bellowed.

The students fell silent and came to attention, their backs straightening as if they had been pulled by invisible strings. Quietly, a tall young man in a frayed work shirt slid onto the bench beside Andras and bent his head toward Andras's ear.

"That's Auguste Perret," the young man said in Hungarian. "He was my teacher, and now he'll be yours."

Andras looked at the young man in surprise and relief. "You're the one who wrote the note in my packet," he said.

"Listen," the man said, "and I'll translate."

Andras listened. At the lectern, Auguste Perret lifted the jagged rock in both hands and asked a question. The question, according to Andras's translator, was whether anyone knew what this building material was. You there, in front? Concrete, that was correct. Reinforced concrete. By the time they finished their five years at the school, all of them would know everything there was to know about reinforced concrete. Why? Because it was the future of the modern city. It would make buildings that surpassed in height and strength anything that had been built before. Height and strength, yes; and beauty. Here at the École Spéciale we were not *seduced* by beauty, however; leave that to the sons of privilege at *that other school*. That school was a gentlemen's institution, a place where boys went to play at the art of *dessinage;* we at the École Spéciale were interested in real architecture, buildings that people could inhabit. If our designs were beautiful, so much the better; but let them be beautiful in a manner that belonged to the common man. We were here because we believed in architecture as a democratic art; because we believed that form and function were of equal importance; because we, the avant-garde, had shrugged off the bonds of aristocratic tradition and had begun to think for ourselves. Let anyone who wanted to build Versailles stand now and go through that gate. *That other school* was only three Métro stops away.

The professor paused, his arm flung toward the gate, his eyes fixed on the rows of students. *"Non?"* he shouted. *"Pas un?"*

No one moved. The professor stood statuelike before them. Andras had the sense of being a figure in a painting, paralyzed for all eternity by Perret's challenge. People would admire the painting in museums centuries from now. Still he would be sitting on the bench, inclined slightly toward this man with the cape and the white beard, this general among architects.

"He gives this speech every year," the Hungarian man next to Andras whispered. "Next he'll talk about your responsibility to the students who will come after you."

"Les étudiants qui viennent après vous," the professor went on, and the Hungarian translated. Those students were relying upon you to study assiduously. If you did not, they, too, would fail. You would be taught by those who came before you; at the École Spéciale you would learn collaboration, because your life as an architect would involve close work with others. You might have your own vision, but without the help of your colleagues that vision wasn't worth the paper it was drawn upon. In this school, Emile Trélat had instructed Robert Mallet-Stevens, Mallet-Stevens had instructed Fernand Fenzy, Fernand Fenzy had instructed Pierre Vago, and Pierre Vago would instruct you.

At that, the professor pointed into the audience, and the young man beside Andras stood up and made a polite bow. He strode to the front of the assembly, took his place beside Professor Perret at the lectern, and began addressing the students in French. Pierre Vago. This man who had been translating for Andras—this rumpled-looking young man in an inkstained work shirt—was the P. VAGO of Andras's class schedule. His studio leader. His professor. A Hungarian. Andras felt suddenly faint. For the first time it seemed to him he might have a chance of surviving at the École Spéciale. He could hardly concentrate on what Pierre Vago was saying now, in his elegant, slightly accented French. Pierre Vago had indeed been the one who'd written the Hungarian note in Andras's manila envelope. Pierre Vago, it occurred to Andras, was probably the one man responsible for his being there at all.

"Hey," Rosen said, pulling Andras's sleeve. *"Regardes-toi."*

In the excitement, Andras's nose had begun to bleed. Red spots glistened on his white shirt. Polaner looked at him with concern and offered a handkerchief; Ben Yakov went pale and turned away. Andras took the handkerchief and pressed it against his nose. Rosen made him tip his head back. A few people turned to see what was going on. Andras sat bleeding into the handkerchief, not caring who was looking, happier than he'd ever been in his life.

Later that day, after the assembly, after Andras's nosebleed had stopped and he'd traded his own clean handkerchief for the one he'd bled upon, after the first meeting of the studio groups, and after he'd exchanged addresses with Rosen, Polaner, and Ben Yakov, Andras found himself in Vago's cluttered office, sitting on a wooden stool beside the drafting table. On the walls were sketched and printed plans, black-and-white watercolors of beautiful and impossible buildings, a scale drawing of a city from high above. In one corner was a heap of paint-stained clothes; a rusted, twisted bicycle frame leaned against the wall. Vago's bookshelves held ancient books and glossy magazines and a teakettle and a small wooden airplane and a skinny-legged junk sculpture of a girl. Vago himself leaned back in his swivel chair, his fingers laced behind his head.

"So," he said to Andras. "Here you are, fresh from Budapest. I'm glad you came. I didn't know if you'd be able to make it on such short notice. But I had to try. It's barbarous, those prejudices about who can study what, and when, and how. It's not a country for men like us."

"But—forgive me—are you Jewish, Professor?"

"No. I'm a Catholic. Educated in Rome." He gave his *R* a deep Italianate roll.

"Then why do you care, sir?"

"Shouldn't I care?"

"Many don't."

Vago shrugged. "Some do." He opened a folder on his desk. There, in full color, were reproductions of Andras's covers for *Past and Future:* linoleum prints of a scribe inking a scroll, a father and his boys at synagogue, a woman lighting two slender candles. Andras saw the work now as if for the first time. The subjects seemed sentimental, the compositions obvious and childish. He couldn't believe this was what had earned his admission to the school. He hadn't had a chance to submit the portfolio he'd used for his applications to Hungarian architectural colleges—detailed drawings of the Parliament and the Palace, measured renderings of the interiors of churches and libraries, work he'd slaved over for hours at his desk at *Past and Future.* But he suspected that even those pieces would have seemed clumsy and amateurish in comparison to Vago's work, the crisp plans and gorgeous elevations pinned to the walls.

"I'm here to learn, sir," Andras said. "I made those prints a long time ago."

"This is excellent work," Vago said. "There's a precision, an accuracy of perspective, rare in an untrained artist. You've got great natural skill, that's apparent. The compositions are asymmetrical but well balanced. The themes are ancient but the lines are modern. Good qualities to bring to your work in architecture."

Andras reached for one of the covers, the one that showed a man and boys at prayer. He'd carved the linoleum original by candlelight in the apartment on Hársfa utca. Though he hadn't considered it at the time—and why not, when it was so clear now?—this man in the tallis was his father, the boys his brothers.

"It's fine work," Vago said. "I wasn't the only one who thought so."

"It's not architecture," Andras said, and handed the cover back to Vago.

"You'll learn architecture. And in the meantime you'll study French. There's no other way to survive here. I can help you, but I can't translate for you in every class. So you will come here every morning, an hour before studio, and practice your French with me."

"Here with you, sir?"

"Yes. From now on we will speak only French. I'll teach you all I know. And for God's sake, you will cease to call me 'sir,' as if I were an army officer." His eyes assumed a serious expression, but he twisted his mouth to the left in a French-looking moue. "*L'architecture n'est pas un jeu d'enfants*," he said in a deep, reso-nant voice that matched exactly, both in pitch and tone, the voice of Professor Perret. "*L'architecture, c'est l'art le plus sérieux de tous.*"

"*L'art le plus sérieux de tous,*" Andras repeated in the same deep tone.

"*Non, non!*" Vago cried. "Only I am permitted the voice of Monsieur le Directeur. You will please speak in the manner of Andras the lowly student. *My name is Andras the Lowly Student,*" Vago said in French. "If you please: repeat."

"My name is Andras the Lowly Student."

"I shall learn to speak perfect French from Monsieur Vago."

"I shall learn to speak perfect French from Monsieur Vago."

"I will repeat everything he says."

"I will repeat everything he says."

"Though not in the voice of Monsieur le Directeur."

"Though not in the voice of Monsieur le Directeur."

"Let me ask you a question," Vago said in Hungarian now, his expression earnest. "Have I done the right thing by bringing you here? Are you terribly lonely? Is this all overwhelming?"

"It *is* overwhelming," Andras said. "But I find I'm strangely happy."

"I was miserable when I first got here," Vago said, settling back in his chair. "I came three weeks after I finished school in Rome, and started at the Beaux-Arts. That school was no place for a person of my temperament. Those first few months were awful! I hated Paris with a passion." He looked out the office window at the chill gray afternoon. "I walked around every day, taking it all in—the Bastille and the Tuileries, the Luxembourg, Notre-Dame, the Opéra—and cursing every stick and stone of it. After a while I transferred to the École Spéciale. That was when I began to fall in love with Paris. Now I can't imagine living anyplace else. After a time, you'll feel that way too."

"I'm beginning to feel that way already."

"Just wait," Vago said, and grinned. "It only gets worse."

In the mornings he bought his bread at the small boulangerie near his building, and his newspaper from a stand on the corner; when he dropped his coins into the proprietor's hand, the man would sing a throaty *Merci*. Back at his apartment he would eat his croissant and drink sweet tea from the empty jam jar. He would look at the photographs in the paper and try to follow the news of the Spanish Civil War, in which the *Front Populaire* was losing ground now against the *Nationalistes*. He wouldn't allow himself to buy a Hungarian expatriate paper to fill in the blanks; the urgency of the news itself eased the effort of translation. Every day came stories of new atrocities: teenaged boys shot in ditches, elderly gentlemen bayoneted in olive orchards, villages firebombed from the air. Italy accused France of violating its own arms embargo; large shipments of Soviet munitions were reaching the Republican army. On the other side, Germany had increased the numbers of its Condor Legion to ten thousand men. Andras read the news with increasing despair, jealous at times of the young men who had run away to fight for the Republican army. Everyone was involved now, he knew; any other view was denial.

With his mind full of horrific images of the Spanish front, he would walk the leaf-littered sidewalks toward the École Spéciale, distracting himself by repeating French architectural terms: *toit, fenêtre, porte, mur, corniche, balcon, balustrade, souche de cheminée.* At school he learned the difference between stereobate and stylobate, base and entablature; he learned which of his professors secretly preferred the decorative to the practical, and which were adherents to Perret's cult of reinforced concrete. With his statics class he visited the Sainte-Chapelle, where he learned how thirteenth-century engineers had discovered a way to strengthen the building using iron struts and metal supports; the supports were hidden within the framework of the stained-glass windows that spanned the height of the chapel. As morning light fell in red and blue strands through the glass, he stood at the center of the nave and experienced a kind of holy exaltation. No matter that this was a Catholic church, that its windows depicted Christ and a host of saints. What he felt had less to do with religion than with a sense of harmonious design, the perfect meeting of form and function in that structure. One long vertical space meant to suggest a path to God, or toward a deeper knowledge of the mysteries. Architects had done this, hundreds of years ago.

Pierre Vago, true to his word, tutored Andras every morning for an hour. The French he'd learned at school returned with speed, and within a month he had absorbed far more than he'd ever learned from his master at gimnázium. By mid-October the lessons were nothing more than long conversations; Vago had a talent for finding the subjects that would make Andras talk. He asked Andras about his years in Konyár and Debrecen—what he had studied, what his friends had been like, where he had lived, whom he'd loved. Andras told Vago about Éva Kereny, the girl who had kissed him in the garden of the Déri Museum in Debrecen and then spurned him coldheartedly; he told the story of his mother's only pair of silk stockings, a Chanukah gift bought with money Andras had earned by taking on his fellow students' drawing assignments. (The brothers had all been competing to get her the best gift; she'd reacted with such childlike joy when she'd seen the stockings that no one could dispute Andras's victory. Later that night, Tibor sat on Andras in the yard and mashed his face into the frozen ground, exacting an older brother's revenge.) Vago, who had no siblings of his own, seemed to like hearing about Mátyás and Tibor; he made Andras recite their histories and translate their letters into French. In particular he took an interest in Tibor's desire to study medicine in Italy. He had known a young man in Rome whose father had been a professor of medicine at the school in Modena; he would write a few letters, he said, and would see what could be done.

Andras didn't think much about it when he said it; he knew Vago was busy, and that the international post traveled slowly, and that the gentleman in Rome might not share Vago's ideas about educating young Hungarian-Jewish men. But one morning Vago met Andras with a letter in hand: He had received word that Professor Turano might be able to arrange for Tibor to matriculate in January.

"My God!" Andras said. "That's miraculous! How did you do it?"

"I correctly estimated the value of my connections," Vago said, and smiled.

"I've got to wire Tibor right away. Where do I go to send a telegram?"

Vago put up a hand in caution. "I wouldn't send word just yet," he said. "It's still just a possibility. We wouldn't want to raise his hopes in vain."

"What are the chances, do you think? What does the professor say?"

"He says he'll have to petition the admissions board. It's a special case."

"You'll tell me as soon as you hear from him?"

"Of course," Vago said.

But he had to share the preliminary good news with someone, so he told Polaner and Rosen and Ben Yakov that night at their student dining club on the rue des Écoles. It was the same club József had recommended when Andras had arrived. For 125 francs a week they received daily dinners that relied heavily upon potatoes and beans and cabbage; they ate in an echoing underground cavern at long tables inscribed with thousands of students' names. Andras delivered the news about Tibor in his Hungarian-accented French, struggling to be heard above the din. The others raised their glasses and wished Tibor luck.

"What a delicious irony," Rosen said, once they'd drained their glasses. "Because he's a Jew, he has to leave a constitutional monarchy to study medicine in a fascist dictatorship. At least he doesn't have to join us in this fine democracy, where intelligent young men practice the right of free speech with such abandon." He cut his eyes at Polaner, who looked down at his neat white hands.

"What's that about?" Ben Yakov said.

"Nothing," Polaner said.

"What happened?" asked Ben Yakov, who could not stand to be left out of gossip.

"I'll tell you what happened," Rosen said. "On the way to school yesterday, Polaner's portfolio handle broke. We had to stop and fix it with a bit of twine. We were late to morning lecture, as you'll recall—that was us, coming in at half past ten. We had to sit in the back, next to that second-year, Lemarque—that blond bastard, the snide one from studio. Tell them, Polaner, what he said when we slid into the row."

Polaner laid his spoon beside the soup bowl. "What you *thought* he said."

"He said *filthy Jews*. I heard it, plain as day."

Ben Yakov looked at Polaner. "Is that true?"

"I don't know," Polaner said. "He said something, but I didn't hear what."

"We both heard it. Everyone around us did."

"You're paranoid," Polaner said, the delicate skin around his eyes flushing red. "People turned around because we were late, not because he'd called us filthy Jews."

"Maybe it's all right where you come from, but it's not all right here," Rosen said.

"I'm not going to talk about it."

"Anyway, what can you do?" said Ben Yakov. "Certain people will always be idiots."

"Teach him a lesson," Rosen said. "That's what."

"No," Polaner said. "I don't want trouble over something that may or may not have happened. I just want to keep my head down. I want to study and get my degree. Do you understand?"

Andras did. He remembered that feeling from primary school in Konyár, the desire to become invisible. But he hadn't anticipated that he or any of his Jewish classmates would feel it in Paris. "I understand," he said. "Still, Lemarque shouldn't feel"—he struggled to find the French words—"like he can *get away* with saying a thing like that. If he did say it, that is."

"Lévi knows what I mean," Rosen said. But then he lowered his chin onto his hand and stared into his soup bowl. "On the other hand, I'm not at all sure what we're supposed to do about it. If we told someone, it would be our word against Lemarque's. And he's got a lot of friends among the fourth- and fifth-years."

Polaner pushed his bowl away. "I have to get back to the studio. I've got a whole night's worth of work to do."

"Come on, Eli," Rosen said. "Don't be angry."

"I'm not angry. I just don't want trouble, that's all." Polaner put on his hat and slung his scarf around his neck, and they watched him make his way through the maze of tables, his shoulders curled beneath the worn velvet of his jacket.

"You believe me, don't you?" Rosen said to Andras. "I know what I heard."

"I believe you. But I agree there's nothing we can do about it."

"Weren't we talking about your brother a moment ago?" Ben Yakov said. "I liked that line of conversation better."

"That's right," Rosen said. "I changed the subject, and look what happened."

Andras shrugged. "According to Vago, it's too early to celebrate anyway. It may not happen after all."

"But it may," Rosen said.

"Yes. And then, as you pointed out, he'll go live in a fascist dictatorship. So it's hard to know what to hope for. Every scenario is complicated."

"Palestine," Rosen said. "A Jewish state. That's what we can hope for. I hope your brother does get to study in Italy under Mussolini. Let him take his medical degree under Il Duce's nose. Meanwhile you and Polaner and Ben Yakov and I will get ours in architecture here in Paris. And then we'll all emigrate. Agreed?"

"I'm not a Zionist," Andras said. "Hungary's my home."

"Not at the moment, though, is it?" Rosen said. And Andras found it impossible to argue with that.

For the next two weeks he waited for news from Modena. In statics he calculated the distribution of weight along the curved underside of the Pont au Double, hoping to find some distraction in the symmetry of equations; in drawing class he made a scaled rendering of the façade of the Gare d'Orsay, gratefully losing himself in measurements of its intricate clock faces and its line of arched doorways. In studio he kept an eye on Lemarque, who could often be seen casting inscrutable looks at Polaner, but who said nothing that could have been construed as a slur. Every morning in Vago's office he eyed the letters on the desk, looking for one that bore an Italian postmark; day after day the letter failed to arrive.

Then one afternoon as Andras was sitting in studio, erasing feathery pencil marks from his drawing of the d'Orsay, beautiful Lucia from the front office came to the classroom with a folded note in her hand. She gave the note to the fifth-year monitor who was overseeing that session, and left without a look at any of the other students.

"Lévi," said the monitor, a stern-eyed man with hair like an explosion of blond chaff. "You're wanted at the private office of Le Colonel."

All talk in the room ceased. Pencils hung midair in students' hands. Le Colonel was the school's nickname for Auguste Perret. All eyes turned toward Andras; Lemarque shot him a thin half smile. Andras swept his pencils into his bag, wondering what Perret could want with him. It occurred to him that Perret might be involved with Tibor's chances in Italy; perhaps Vago had enlisted his help. Maybe he'd exerted some kind of influence with friends abroad, and now he was going to be the one to deliver the news.

Andras ran up the two flights of stairs to the corridor that housed the professors' private offices, and paused outside Perret's closed door. From inside he could hear Perret and Vago speaking in lowered voices. He knocked. Vago called for him to enter, and he opened the door. Inside, standing in a shaft of light near one of the long windows that overlooked the boulevard Raspail, was Professor Perret in his shirtsleeves. Vago leaned against Perret's desk, a telegram in his hand.

"Good afternoon, Andras," Perret said, turning from the window. He motioned for Andras to sit in a low leather chair beside the desk. Andras sat, letting his schoolbag slide to the floor. The air in Perret's office was close and still. Unlike Vago's office, with its profusion of drawings on the walls and its junk sculptures and its worktable overflowing with projects, Perret's was all order and austerity. Three pencils lay parallel on the

Morocco-topped desk; wooden shelves held neatly rolled plans; a crisp white model of the Théâtre des Champs-Élysées stood in a glass box on a console table.

Perret cleared his throat and began. "We've had some disturbing news from Hungary. Rather disturbing indeed. It may be easier if Professor Vago explains it to you in Hungarian. Though I hear your French has advanced considerably." The martial tone had dropped from his voice, and he gave Andras such a kind and regretful look that Andras's hands went cold.

"It's rather complicated," Vago said, speaking in Hungarian. "Let me try to explain. I received word from my friend's father, the professor. A place came through for your brother at the medical college in Modena."

Vago paused. Andras held his breath and waited for him to go on.

"Professor Turano sent a letter to the Jewish organization that provides your scholarship. He wanted to see if money could be found for Tibor, too. But his request was denied, with regrets. New restrictions have been imposed this week in Hungary: As of today, no organization can send money to Jewish students abroad. Your Hitközség's student-aid funds have been frozen by the government."

Andras blinked at him, trying to understand what he meant.

"It's not just a problem for Tibor," Vago continued, looking into Andras's eyes. "It's also a problem for you. In short, your scholarship can no longer be paid. To be honest, my young friend, your scholarship has never been paid. Your first month's check never arrived, so I paid your fees out of my own pocket, thinking there must have been some temporary delay." He paused, glancing at Professor Perret, who was watching as Vago delivered the news in Hungarian. "Monsieur Perret doesn't know where the money came from, and need not know, so please don't betray surprise. I told him everything was fine. However, I'm not a rich man, and, though I wish I could, I can't pay your tuition and fees another month."

An ice floe ascended through Andras's chest, slow and cold. His tuition could no longer be paid. His tuition had never been paid. All at once he understood Perret's kindness and regret.

"We think you're a bright student," Perret said in French. "We don't want to lose you. Can your family help?"

"My family?" Andras's voice sounded thready and vague in the high-ceilinged room. He saw his father stacking oak planks in the lumberyard, his mother cooking potato paprikás at the stove in the outdoor kitchen. He thought of the pair of gray silk stockings, the ones he'd given her ten years earlier for Chanukah—how she'd folded them into a chaste square and stored them in their paper wrapping, and had worn them only to synagogue. "My family doesn't have that kind of money," he said.

"It's a terrible thing," Perret said. "I wish there were something we could do. Before the depression we gave out a great many scholarships, but now . . ." He looked out the window at the low clouds and stroked his military beard. "Your expenses are paid until the end of the month. We'll see what we can do before then, but I'm afraid I can't offer much hope."

Andras translated the words in his mind: *not much hope.*

"As for your brother," Vago said, "it's a damned shame. Turano wanted very much to help him."

He tried to shake himself from the shock that had come over him. It was important that they understand about Tibor, about the money. "It doesn't matter," he said, trying to keep his voice steady. "The scholarship doesn't matter—for Tibor, I mean. He's been putting money away for six years. He's got to have enough for the train ticket and his first year's tuition. I'll cable him tonight. Can your friend's father hold the place for him?"

"I'd imagine so," Vago said. "I'll write to him at once, if you think it's possible. But perhaps your brother can help you, too, if he's got some money put away."

Andras shook his head. "I can't tell him. He hasn't saved enough for both of us."

"I'm dreadfully sorry," Perret said again, coming forward to shake Andras's hand. "Professor Vago tells me you're a resourceful young man. Perhaps you'll find a way through this. I'll see what I can do on our side."

This was the first time Perret had touched him. It was as though Andras had just been told he had a terminal disease, as though the shadow of impending death had allowed Perret to dispense with formalities. He clapped Andras on the back as he led him to the door of the office. "Courage," he said, giving Andras a salute, and turned him out into the hall.

Andras went down through the dusty yellow light of the staircase, past the classroom where his Gare d'Orsay drawing lay abandoned on the table, past the beautiful Lucia in the front office, and through the blue doors of the school he had come to think of as his own. He walked down the boulevard Raspail until he reached a post office, where he asked for a telegraph blank. On the narrow blue lines he wrote the message he'd composed on the way: POSITION SECURED FOR YOU AT MEDICAL COLLEGE MODENA, GRATIAS FRIEND OF VAGO. OBTAIN PASSPORT AND VISAS AT ONCE. HURRAH! For a moment, in a fog of self-pity, he considered omitting the HURRAH. But at the last moment he included it, paying the extra ten centimes, and then walked out onto the boulevard again. The cars continued to speed by, the afternoon light fell just as it always fell, the pedestrians on the street rushed by with their groceries and drawings and books, all the city insensible to what had just taken place in an office at the École Spéciale.

Unseeing, unthinking, he walked the narrow curve of the rue de Fleurus toward the Jardin du Luxembourg, where he found a green bench in the shade of a plane tree. The bench was within sight of the bee farm, and Andras could see the hooded beekeeper checking the layers of a hive. The beekeeper's head and arms and legs were speckled with black bees. Slow-moving, torpid with smoke, they roamed the beekeeper's body like cows grazing a pasture. In school, Andras had learned that there were bees who could change their nature when conditions demanded it. When a queen bee died, another bee could become the queen; that bee would shed its former life, take on a new body, a different role. Now she would lay eggs and converse about the health of the hive with her attendants. He, Andras, had been born a Jew, and had carried the mantle of that identity for twenty-two years. At eight days old he'd been circumcised. In the schoolyard he'd withstood the taunts of Christian children, and in the classroom his teachers' disapproval when he'd had to miss school on Shabbos. On Yom Kippur he'd fasted; on Shabbos he'd gone to synagogue; at thirteen he'd read from the Torah and become a man, according to Jewish law. In Debrecen he went to the Jewish gimnázium, and after he graduated he'd taken a job at a Jewish magazine. He'd lived with Tibor in the Jewish Quarter of Budapest and had gone with him to the Dohány Street Synagogue. He'd met the ghost of Numerus Clausus, had left his home and his family to come to Paris. Even here there were men like Lemarque, and student groups that demonstrated against Jews, and more than a few anti-Semitic newspapers. And now he had this new weight to bear, this new tsuris. For a moment, as he sat on his bench at the Jardin du Luxembourg, he wondered what it would be like to leave his Jewish self behind, to shrug off the garment of his religion like a coat that had become too heavy in hot weather. He remembered standing in the Sainte-Chapelle in September, the holiness and the stillness of the place, the few lines he knew from the Latin mass drifting through his mind: *Kyrie eleison, Christe eleison.* Lord, have mercy, Christ, have mercy.

For a moment it seemed simple, clear: become a Christian, and not just a Christian—a Roman Catholic, like the Christians who'd imagined Notre-Dame and the Sainte-Chapelle, the Mátyás Templom and the Basilica of Szent István in Budapest. Shed his former life, take on a new history. Receive what had been withheld from him. Receive mercy.

But when he thought of the word *mercy*, it was the Yiddish

word that came to his mind: *rachmones,* whose root was *rechem,* the Hebrew word for womb. *Rachmones:* a compassion as deep and as undeniable as what a mother felt for her child. He'd prayed for it every year at synagogue in Konyár on the eve of Yom Kippur. He had asked to be forgiven, had fasted, had come away at the end of Yom Kippur with a sense of having been scraped clean. Every year he'd felt the need to hold his soul to account, to forgive and be forgiven. Every year his brothers had flanked him in synagogue—Mátyás small and fierce on his left, Tibor lean and deep-voiced on his right. Beside them was their father in his familiar tallis, and behind the women's partition, their mother—patient, forbearing, firm, her presence certain even when they could not see her. He could no sooner cease being Jewish than he could cease being a brother to his brothers, a son to his father and mother.

He stood, giving a last look to the beekeeper and his bees, and set off across the park toward home. He was thinking now not of what had happened but of what he was going to have to do next: find a job, a way of making the money it would take to stay in school. He wasn't French, of course, but that didn't matter; in Budapest, thousands of workers were paid under the table and no one was the wiser. Tomorrow was Saturday. Offices would be closed, but shops and restaurants would be open—bakeries, groceries, bookshops, art-supply stores, brasseries, men's clothiers. If Tibor could work full-time in a shoe store and study his anatomy books at night, then Andras could work and go to school. By the time he had reached the rue des Écoles, he was already framing the necessary phrase in his head: I'm looking for a job. In Hungarian, *Állást keresek.* In French, *Je cherche . . . je cherche . . .* a job. He knew the word: *un boulot.*

CHAPTER FIVE

Théâtre Sarah-Bernhardt

THAT FALL the Sarah-Bernhardt was presenting *The Mother*, a new play by Bertolt Brecht, at nine o'clock every night but Monday. The theater was located at the direct center of the city, in the place du Châtelet. It offered five tiers of luxurious seating and the thrilling awareness that Miss Bernhardt's voice had filled *this space*, had caused *that chandelier* to shiver on its chain. Somewhere inside the theater was the cream-and-gilt-paneled dressing room with the gold bathtub in which the actress had reputedly bathed in champagne. On the first Saturday in November the cast had been called for an unscheduled rehearsal; Claudine Villareal-Bloch, the Mother of the title, had suffered an acute attack of vocal strain that everyone tacitly attributed to her new affair with a young Brazilian press attaché. Into these vaguely embarrassing circumstances, Madame Villareal-Bloch's understudy had been called at the last moment to take over the part. Marcelle Gérard paced her dressing room in a fury, wondering how Claudine Villareal-Bloch could have dared to spring this trick upon her; it seemed an intentional humiliation. Madame Villareal-Bloch knew that Madame Gérard, chafed by her position as understudy, had failed to prepare. That very morning in rehearsal she'd forgotten her lines and had stammered in the most unprofessional manner. In his office down the hall, Zoltán Novak drank Scotch neat and wondered what would happen to him if the play could not go forward, if Marcelle Gérard froze onstage as she had at that morning's rehearsal. The minister of culture himself was scheduled to attend the following night's performance; that was how popular the new Brecht play had become, and how dire the current situation was. If public embarrassment resulted tomorrow night, the blame would fall to Novak, the Hungarian. Failure was not French.

Desperately, desperately, Zoltán Novak wanted to smoke. But he couldn't smoke. The previous night, when he'd learned of Madame Villareal-Bloch's illness, his wife had hidden his cigarettes, knowing he might tend toward excess; she had made him swear not to buy more, and vowed that she would sniff his clothes for smoke. As he paced his office in a state of nicotine-deprived anxiety, the production assistant came in with a list of urgent messages. The properties manager was missing a set of workers' shovels from the third scene; should they do the scene without them, or buy new shovels? Madame Gérard's name had been misspelled in the program for tomorrow night (Guérard, a minor mistake), and did he want the whole lot reprinted? Finally, there was a boy downstairs looking for a job. He claimed to know Monsieur, or at least that was what he seemed to be saying—his French was imperfect. What was his name? Something foreign. Lévi. Undrash.

Buy new shovels for the workers. Leave the programs as they were—too expensive to reprint. And no, he didn't know a Lévi Undrash. Even if he did, God help him, the last thing he had for anyone right now was a job.

Andras had planned to arrive at school on Monday morning with triumphant news for Professor Vago: He had found a job, had arranged to pay his tuition, and would therefore remain at school. Instead he found himself trudging down the boulevard Raspail in twig-kicking frustration. All weekend he had scoured the Latin Quarter in search of work; he had inquired at front doors and back doors, in bakeshops and garages; he had even dared to knock on the door of a graphic design shop where a young man sat working in his shirtsleeves at a drafting table. The man had stared at Andras with a kind of bemused contempt and told him to stop in again once he'd earned his degree. Andras had walked on, hungry and chilled by rain, refusing to capitulate. He had crossed the Seine in a fog, trying to imagine who he might call upon for help; when he looked up he saw that he'd walked all the way to the place du Châtelet. It occurred to him then that he might present himself at the Théâtre Sarah-Bernhardt and ask to see Zoltán Novak, who had, after all, invited Andras to stop by. He could go that very moment; it was half past seven, and Novak might be at the theater before the show. But at the Sarah-Bernhardt he'd been turned away—politely, regretfully, and with a great deal of rapid, sympathetic French—by a young man who claimed to have spoken directly to Novak, who hadn't recognized Andras's name. Andras had spent the rest of that evening and all the next day searching for work, but his luck hadn't improved. In the end he'd found himself back at home, sitting at the table by the window, holding a telegram from his brother.

UNBELIEVABLE NEWS! THANKS FOREVER TO YOU & VAGO. WILL APPLY STUDENT VISA TOMORROW. MODENA. HURRAH! TIBOR

He would have given anything to see Tibor, to tell him what had happened and hear what he thought Andras should do. But Tibor was twelve hundred kilometers away in Budapest. There was no way to ask or receive advice of that kind by telegram, and a letter would take far too long. He had, of course, told Rosen and Polaner and Ben Yakov at the student dining club that weekend; their anger on his behalf had been gratifying, their sympathy fortifying, but there was little they could do to help. In any case, they weren't his brother; they couldn't have Tibor's understanding of what the scholarship meant to him, nor what its loss would mean.

At seven o'clock in the morning the École Spéciale was deserted. The studios were silent, the courtyard empty, the amphitheater an echoing void. He knew he could find a few students asleep at their desks if he looked, students who had stayed up all night drinking coffee and smoking cigarettes and working on drawings or models. Sleepless nights were commonplace at the École Spéciale. There were rumors of pills that sharpened your mind and allowed you to stay up for days, for weeks. There were legends of artistic breakthroughs occurring after seventy-two waking hours. And there were tales of disastrous collapse. One studio was called *l'atelier du suicide*. The older students told the younger about a man who'd shot himself after his rival won the annual Prix du Amphithéâtre. In that particular studio, on the wall beside the chalkboard, you could see a blasted-out hollow in the brick. When Andras had asked Vago about the suicide, Vago said that the story had been told when he was a student, too, and that no one could confirm it. But it served its purpose as a cautionary tale.

A light was on in Vago's office; Andras could see the yellow square of it from the courtyard. He ran up the three flights and knocked. There was a long silence before Vago opened the door; he stood before Andras in his stocking feet, rubbing his eyes with an inky thumb and forefinger. His collar was open, his hair a wild tangle. "You," he said, in Hungarian. A small word, salted with a grain of affection. *Te.*

"Me," Andras said. "Still here, for now."

Vago ushered him into the office and motioned him to sit down on the usual stool. Then he left Andras alone for a few minutes, after which he returned looking as if he'd washed his face in hot water and scrubbed it with a rough towel. He smelled of the pumice soap that was good for getting ink off one's hands.

"Well?" Vago said, and seated himself behind the desk.

"Tibor sends his deepest thanks. He's applying for his visa now."

"I've already written to Professor Turano."

"Thank you," Andras said. "Truly."

"And how are you?"

"Not very well, as you can imagine."

"Worried about how you're going to pay your tuition."

"Wouldn't you be?"

Vago pushed back his chair and went to look out the window. After a moment he turned back and put his hands through his hair. "Listen," he said. "I don't feel much like teaching you French this morning. Why don't we take a field trip instead? We've got a good hour and a half before studio."

"You're the professor," Andras said.

Vago took his coat from its wooden peg and put it on. He pushed Andras through the door ahead of him, followed him down the stairs, and steered him through the blue front doors of the school. Out on the boulevard he fished in his pocket for change; he led Andras down the stairs of the Raspail Métro just as a train flew into the station. They rode to Motte-Picquet and transferred to the 8, then changed again at Michel-Ange Molitor. Finally, at an obscure stop called Billancourt, Vago led Andras off the train and up onto a suburban boulevard. The air was fresher here outside the city center; shopkeepers sprayed the sidewalks in preparation for the morning's business, and window-washers polished the avenue's glass storefronts. A line of girls in short black woolen coats stepped briskly along the sidewalk, led by a matron with a feather in her hat.

"Not far now," Vago said. He led Andras down the boulevard and turned onto a smaller commercial street, then onto a long residential street, then onto a smaller residential street lined with gray duplexes and sturdy red-roofed houses, which yielded suddenly to a soaring white ship of an apartment building, triangular, built on a shard of land where two streets met at an acute angle. The apartments had porthole windows and deep-set balconies with sliding-glass doors, as if the building really were an ocean liner; it lanced forward through the morning behind a prow of curving windows and milk-white arcs of reinforced concrete.

"Architect?" Vago said.

"Pingusson." A few weeks earlier they had gone to see his work in the design pavilion at the International Exposition; the fifth-year student who had been their guide had declaimed about the simplicity of Pingusson's lines and his unconventional sense of proportion.

"That's right," Vago said. "One of ours—an École Spéciale man. I met him at an architecture convention in Russia five years ago, and he's been a good friend ever since. He's written some sharp pieces for *L'Architecture d'Aujourd'hui*. Pieces that got people to read the magazine when it was just getting off the ground. He's also a hell of a poker player. We've got a regular Saturday night game. Sometimes Professor Perret pays us a visit—he can't play worth a damn, but he likes to talk."

"I can imagine that," Andras said.

"Well, now, this Saturday night, guess what the talk was about?"

Andras shrugged.

"Not a guess?"

"The Spanish Civil War."

"No, my young friend. We talked about you. Your problem. The scholarship. Your lack of funds. Meanwhile, Perret kept pouring champagne. A first-rate '26 Canard-Duchêne he received as a gift from a client. Now, Georges-Henri—that's Pingusson—he's an uncommonly intelligent man. He's responsible for a lot of very fine buildings here in Paris and has a houseful of awards to show for them. He's an engineer, too, you know, not just an architect. He plays poker like a man who knows numbers. But when he drinks champagne, he's all bravado and romance. Around midnight he threw his bankbook on the table and told Perret that if he, Perret, won the next hand, then he—Pingusson, I mean—would pitch in for your tuition and fees."

Andras stared at Vago. "What happened?"

"Perret lost, of course. I don't think I've ever seen him beat Pingusson. But the champagne had already done its work. He's a smart one, our Perret. In the end, smarter than Pingusson."

"What do you mean?"

"Afterward, we're all standing on the street trying to get a cab. Perret's sober as an owl, shaking his head. 'Terrible shame about the Lévi boy,' he says. 'Tragic thing.' And Georges-Henri, drunk on champagne—he practically goes to his knees on the sidewalk and begs Perret to let him stand you a loan. Fifty percent, he says, and not a centime less. 'If the boy can come up with the other half,' he says, 'let him stay in school.' "

"You can't be serious," Andras said.

"I'm afraid so."

"But he came to his senses the next morning."

"No. Perret made him put it in writing that night. He owes Perret, in any case. The man's done him more than a few favors."

"And what kind of security does he want for the loan?"

"None," Vago said. "Perret told him you were a gentleman. And that you'd earn plenty once you graduated."

"Fifty percent," Andras said. "Good God. From Pingusson." He looked up again at the curving profile of the building, its soaring white prow. "Tell me you're not joking."

"I'm not joking. I've got the signed letter on my desk."

"But that's thousands of francs."

"Perret convinced him you were worth helping."

He felt his throat closing. He was not going to cry, not here on a street corner at Boulogne-Billancourt. He scuffed the sole of his shoe against the sidewalk. There had to be a way to come up with the other half. If Perret had worked magic for him, if he had made something for him out of nothing, if he considered him a gentleman, the least Andras could do was to meet the challenge of Pingusson's loan. He would do whatever he had to do. How long had he spent looking for a job? A few days? Fourteen hours? The city of Paris was a vast place. He would find work. He had to.

* * *

There were times when a good-natured ghost seemed to inhabit the Théâtre Sarah-Bernhardt, times when a play should have fallen apart but didn't. On the evening of Marcelle Gérard's début as the Mother, all had seemed poised for disaster; an hour before curtain Marcelle appeared in Novak's office and threatened to quit. She wasn't ready to go on, she told him. She would embarrass herself in front of her public, the critics, the minister of culture. Novak took her hands and implored her to be reasonable. He knew she could perform the role. She had been flawless in the audition. The part had gone to Claudine Villareal-Bloch only because Novak hadn't wanted to show favoritism toward Madame Gérard. Their affair may have been long past now, but people still talked; he'd been afraid that word would get back to his wife at a time when things were already delicate between them. Marcelle understood that, of course; hadn't they discussed it when the decision had been made? He would never have considered allowing her to go on tonight if he didn't think she would be perfect. Her fears were normal, after all. Hadn't Sarah Bernhardt herself overcome a paralyzing bout of stage fright in her 1879 portrayal of Phèdre? He knew without a doubt that as soon as Marcelle set foot onstage she would become Brecht's vision of the role. She must know it too. Didn't she? But when he'd finished, Madame Gérard had pulled her hands away and retired to her dressing room without a word, leaving Novak alone.

Perhaps it was the earnest force of his worry that called Sarah Bernhardt's ghost out of the walls of the theater that night; perhaps it was the collective worry of the cast and crew, the lighting men, the ushers, the costumers, the janitors, the coat-check girl. Whatever the reason, by the time the nine o' clock hour struck, Marcelle Gérard's hesitation had vanished. The minister of culture sat in his box, tippling discreetly from a silver flask; Lady Mendl and the honorable Mrs. Reginald Fellowes were with him, Lady Mendl with peacock feathers in her hair, Daisy Fellowes resplendent in a Schiaparelli suit of jade-green silk. The war in Spain had made communist theater fashionable in France. The house was packed. The lights dimmed. And then Marcelle Gérard stepped onto the stage and spoke as if in the plum-toned voice of Sarah Bernhardt herself. From his place in the wings, Zoltán Novak watched as Madame Gérard called forth a rendition of *The Mother* that put Claudine Villareal-Bloch's love-addled performances to shame. He breathed a sigh of relief so pleasurable, so deep, he was glad his wife had denied him the chest-constricting comfort of his cigarettes. With any luck, he had left his consumption behind for good. The time he'd spent back home in Budapest at the medicinal baths had flushed the blood and pain from his lungs. The play had not failed. And his theater might survive after all—who knew—despite the long red columns in its ledger books and the debts that increased persistently each week.

He found himself in such an expansive mood, once he'd received the praise of the minister of culture after the show and had passed his compliments along to the blushing, breathless Marcelle Gérard, that he accepted and drank two glasses of champagne, one after the other, there in the dressing-room hallway. Before he left, Marcelle called him into her inner sanctum and kissed him on the mouth, just once, almost chastely, as if everything were forgiven. At midnight he pushed through the stage door into a fine sharp mist. His wife would be waiting for him in the bedroom at home, her hair undone, her skin scented with lavender. But he hadn't moved three steps in her direction before someone rushed him from behind and grabbed his arm, making him drop his briefcase. There had been a spate of muggings outside the theater of late; he was generally cautious, but tonight the champagne had made him careless. Acting upon instincts he'd developed in the war, he swung around and struck his assailant in the stomach. A dark-haired young man fell gasping to the curb. Zoltán Novak stooped to pick up the briefcase, and it was only then that he heard what the boy was gasping.

Novak-úr. Novak-úr. His own name, with its Hungarian honorific. The young man's face seemed vaguely familiar. Novak helped him to his feet and brushed some wet leaves from his sleeve. The young man touched his lower ribs gingerly.

"What were you thinking, coming up behind someone like that?" Novak said in Hungarian, trying to get a better look at the boy's face.

"You wouldn't see me in your office," the young man managed to say.

"Should I have seen you?" Novak said. "Do I know you?"

"Andras Lévi," the young man gasped.

Undrash Lévi. The boy from the train. He remembered Andras's bewilderment in Vienna, his gratitude when Novak had bought him a pretzel. And now he'd punched the poor boy in the stomach. Novak shook his head and gave a low, rueful laugh. "Mr. Lévi," he said. "My deepest apologies."

"Thanks ever so much," the young man said bitterly, still nursing his rib.

"I knocked you clear into the gutter," Novak said in dismay.

"I'll be all right."

"Why don't you walk with me awhile? I don't live far from here."

So they walked together and Andras told him the whole story, beginning with how he'd gotten the scholarship and lost it, and finishing with the offer from Pingusson. That was what had brought him back here. He had to try to see Novak again. He was willing to perform the meanest of jobs. He would do anything. He would black the actors' shoes or sweep the floors or empty the ash cans. He had to start earning his fifty percent. The first payment was due in three weeks.

By that time, they'd reached Novak's building in the rue de Sèvres. Upstairs, light radiated from behind the scrim of the bedroom curtains. The falling mist had dampened Novak's hair and beaded on the sleeves of his overcoat; beside him, Lévi shivered in a thin jacket. Novak found himself thinking of the ledger he'd closed just before he'd gone up to see the show. There, in the accountant's neat red lettering, were the figures that attested to the Sarah-Bernhardt's dire state; another few losing weeks and they would have to close. On the other hand, with Marcelle Gérard in the role of the Mother, who knew what might happen? He knew what was going on in Eastern Europe, that the drying up of Andras's funds was only a symptom of a more serious disease. In Hungary, in his youth, he'd seen brilliant Jewish boys defeated by the numerus clausus; it seemed a crime that this young man should have to bend, too, after having come all this way. The Bernhardt was not a philanthropic organization, but the boy wasn't asking for a handout. He was looking for work. He was willing to do anything. Surely it would be in the spirit of Brecht's play to give work to someone who wanted it. And hadn't Sarah Bernhardt been Jewish, after all? Her mother had been a Dutch-Jewish courtesan, and of course Judaism was matrilineal. *He* knew. Though he had been baptized in the Catholic church and sent to Catholic schools, his own mother had been Jewish, too.

"All right, young Lévi," he said, laying a hand on the boy's shoulder. "Why don't you come by the theater tomorrow afternoon?"

And Andras turned such a brilliant and grateful smile upon him that Novak felt a fleeting shock of fear. Such trust. Such hope. What the world would do to a boy like Andras Lévi, Novak didn't want to know.

CHAPTER SIX

Work

THE MOTHER had twenty-seven actors: nine women, eighteen men. They worked six days a week, and in that time they performed seven shows. Backstage they had few moments to spare and an astonishing number of needs. Their costumes had to be mended and pressed, their lapdogs walked, their letters posted, their voices soothed with tea, their dinners ordered. Occasionally they needed the services of a dentist or a doctor. They had to run lines and take quick restorative naps. They had to cultivate their offstage romances. Two of the men were in love with two of the women, and the two beloved women each loved the wrong man. Notes flew between the enamored parties. Flowers were sent, received, destroyed; chocolates were sent and consumed.

Into this mayhem Andras descended ready to work, and the assistant stage manager set him to it at once. If Monsieur Hammond broke a shoelace, Andras was to find him another. If the bichon frisé who belonged to Madame Pillol needed to be fed, Andras was to feed him. Notes had to be transmitted between the director and the principals, between the stage manager and the assistant stage manager, between the offstage lovers. When the displaced Claudine Villareal-Bloch arrived at the theater to demand her role back, she had to be appeased with praise. (The fact was, the assistant stage manager told Andras, Villareal-Bloch had been dismissed for good; Marcelle Gérard was making a killing in the role. The Bernhardt was selling out its seats every night for the first time in five years.) It was unclear to Andras how anything had been accomplished backstage at the Sarah-Bernhardt before he was hired. By the time the performance began on his first day of work, he was too exhausted even to watch from the wings. He fell asleep on a sofa he didn't know was needed for the second act, and was jostled awake when two stagehands hoisted it to move it onstage. He scrambled off just as the actors were leaving the stage after the first act, and found himself the recipient of countless requests for aid.

That night he stayed until long after the performance was over. Claudel, the assistant stage manager, had told him he must always remain until the last actor had gone home; that night it was Marcelle Gérard who lingered. At the end of the evening he stood outside her dressing room, waiting for her to finish talking to Zoltán Novak. He could hear the thrill in Madame Gérard's rapid French through the dressing-room door. He liked the sound of it, and felt he wouldn't mind if there were something he could do for her before he left for the evening. At last Monsieur Novak emerged, a look of vague trouble creasing his forehead. He seemed surprised to see Andras standing there.

"It's midnight, my boy," he said. "Time to go home."

"Monsieur Claudel instructed me to stay until all the actors had gone."

"Aha. Well done, then. And here's something for your dinner, an advance against your first week's pay." Novak handed Andras a few folded bills. "Get something more substantial than a pretzel," he said, and went off down the hall to his office, rubbing the back of his neck.

Andras unfolded the bills. Two hundred fifty francs, enough for two weeks' dinners at the student dining club. He gave a low whistle of relief and tucked the bills into his jacket pocket.

Madame Gérard emerged from her dressing room, her broad face pale and plain without her stage makeup. She carried a brown Turkish valise, and her scarf was knotted tight as if to keep her warm during a long walk home. But Claudel had said that Madame Gérard must have a taxi, so Andras asked her to wait at the stage door while he hailed one on the quai de Gesvres. By now the autograph-seekers had all gone. Madame Gérard had signed more than a hundred autographs at the stage door after the show. Andras held her arm as she walked to the curb. He could feel that her tweed coat had worn thin at the elbow. She paused at the open door of the cab and met his eyes, her scarf framing her face. She had a wide arched brow with narrow eyebrows; her strong bones gave her a look of nobility that would have suited her in the role of a queen, but served her equally well in the role of the proletarian Mother.

"You're new here," she said. "What is your name?"

"Andras Lévi," said Andras, with a slight bow.

She repeated his name twice, as if to commit it to memory. "A pleasure to meet you, Andras Lévi. Thank you for seeing about the car." She climbed inside, drew her coat around her legs, and closed the door.

As he watched the cab make its way down the quai de Gesvres toward the Pont d'Arcole, he found himself replaying the brief script of their conversation. In his mind he heard her saying *très heureux de faire votre connaissance*, which meant *örülök, hogy megismerhetem* in Hungarian. How was it that he seemed to have heard an echo of *örülök* beneath her *très heureux*? Was everyone in Paris secretly Hungarian? He laughed aloud to think of it: all the Right Bank women in their fur coats, the theatergoers in their long cars, the jazz-loving art students in their fraying jackets, all nursing a secret hunger for paprikás and peasant bread as they ate their bouillabaisse and baguettes. As he walked across the river he felt a rising lightness at the center of his chest. He had a job. He would earn his fifty percent. New pencils lay sharp on his worktable, and it seemed not impossible that he might finish his drawings of the d'Orsay before morning.

He worked all night without pause and managed to stay awake through his morning classes. Then he fell asleep in a corner of the library and didn't wake for hours. When he did, he found a note pinned to his lapel in Rosen's handwriting: *Meet us at the Blue Dove at 5, you lazy ass.* Andras sat up and dug his knuckles into his eyes. He pulled his father's watch from his pocket and checked the time. Four o'clock. In three hours he would have to be back at work. All he wanted was to go home to his bed. He shuffled out into the hall and went to the men's room, where he found that his upper lip had been inked with a Clark Gable–style moustache while he slept. Leaving the moustache in place, he combed his hair with his fingers and tugged his jacket straight.

The Blue Dove Café was a good half-hour walk up the boulevard Raspail and across the Latin Quarter. Andras was the first to arrive; he took a table at the back, near the bar, and ordered the cheapest thing on the menu, a pot of tea. The tea came with two butter biscuits with an almond pressed into the center of each. That was why students liked the Blue Dove: It was generous. In the Latin Quarter it was a rarity to receive two biscuits with a pot of tea, much less almond biscuits. By the time he'd finished the tea and eaten the biscuits, Rosen and Polaner and Ben Yakov had arrived. They unwound their scarves and pulled chairs up to the table.

Rosen kissed Andras on both cheeks. "Gorgeous moustache," he said.

"We thought you were dead," said Ben Yakov. "Or at least in a coma."

"I was nearly dead."

"We took bets," Ben Yakov said. "Rosen bet you'd sleep all night. I bet you'd meet us here. Polaner abstained, because he's broke."

Polaner blushed. Of the three of them he came from the wealthiest family, but his family's kingdom was a garment business in Kraków and his father had no idea how much things really cost in Paris. Every month he sent Polaner not quite enough to keep him clothed and fed. Acutely aware of his growing debt to his father, Polaner couldn't bear to ask him for more. As a child of privilege he had never worked, and seemed never to consider taking a job as a possible means to ease his situation. Instead he ordered hot water at cafés and patched his shoes with thick pasteboard left over from model-building and saved extra bread from the student dining club.

With his pocket full of bills, Andras knew it was his turn to buy everyone a drink. They all had tiny glasses of whiskey and soda, the drink of American movie stars. They cursed the Hungarian government and its attempt to remove Andras from their company, and then toasted his new role as the courier of actors' love notes and the walker of actors' dogs. When the whiskey-and-sodas were gone, they ordered another large pot of tea.

"Ben Yakov has an assignation tonight," Rosen announced.

"What do you mean, an assignation?" Andras said.

"A rendezvous. A meeting. Possibly romantic in nature."

"With whom?"

"Only with the beautiful Lucia," Rosen said, and Ben Yakov laced his fingers and flexed them in mute glory. A hush fell over the table. They all revered Lucia, with her deep velvet voice and her skin the color of polished mahogany. At night, alone in their beds, they had all imagined her stepping out of her dress and slip, standing naked before them in their darkened rooms. By day they had been shamed by her talent in studio. She didn't just work in the office; she was a fourth-year student, one of the best in her class, and it was rumored that Mallet-Stevens had particularly praised her work.

"Cheers to Ben Yakov," Andras said, raising his cup.

"Cheers," said the others. Ben Yakov raised a hand in mock modesty.

"Of course, he'll never tell us what happens," Rosen said. "Ben Yakov's affairs are his own."

"Unlike Monsieur Rosen's," said Ben Yakov. "Monsieur Rosen's affairs belong to everyone. If only your ladies knew!"

"It's the city of love," Rosen said. "We should all be making love." He used the vulgar word for it, *baiser*. "What's wrong, Polaner? Do I offend?"

"I'm not listening," Polaner said.

"Polaner is a gentleman," said Ben Yakov. "Gentlemen *ne baisent pas*."

"On the contrary," said Andras. "Gentlemen are great *baiseurs*. I've just finished reading *Les Liaisons Dangereuses*. It's full of gentlemen *baisent*."

"I'm not sure you're qualified to enter this conversation," Rosen said. "At least Polaner had a *petite amie* back home. His Krakovian bride-to-be, isn't that right?" He pushed Polaner's shoulder, and Polaner blushed again; he'd mentioned a few letters from the girl, the daughter of a woolens manufacturer whom his father expected him to marry. "He's done it all before, whether he likes to talk about it or not," Rosen said. "But you, Andras, you've never done it."

"That's a lie," Andras said, though it was true.

"Paris is full of girls," Rosen said. "We should arrange an assignation for you. One of a professional nature, I mean."

"With whose money?" Ben Yakov said.

"Didn't artists at one time have benefactors?" Rosen said. "Where are our benefactors?" He stood and repeated the question at full volume to the room at large. A few of the other patrons raised their glasses. But there was not a prospective benefactor among them; they were all students, with their pots of tea and two biscuits, their left-leaning newspapers, their threadbare coats.

"At least I have a job," Andras said.

"Well, save up, save up!" Rosen said. "You can't stay a virgin forever."

At work he ran from one task to another like a sous-chef assisting in the preparation of a twelve-course meal, each task ending just as another was beginning, all of it under the mounting pressure of time. Claudel, the assistant stage manager, was Basque and had a temper that often expressed itself in the throwing of props, which would then have to be fixed before they were needed onstage. As a result the props-master had quit, and the props had fallen into disrepair. Claudel terrorized the prompters and the stagehands, the assistant director and the wardrobe mistress; he even terrorized his own superior, the stage manager himself, Monsieur d'Aubigné, who was too afraid of Claudel's wrath to complain to Monsieur Novak. But particularly Claudel terrorized Andras, who made a point of being close at hand. Andras knew he didn't mean any harm. Claudel was a perfectionist, and any perfectionist would have been driven mad by the confusion of the Bernhardt backstage. Messages got lost, the masterless props lay about at random, parts of costumes were misplaced; no one ever knew how long it was until curtain or the end of intermission. It seemed a miracle that the show could be performed at all. His first week there, Andras built pigeonholes for the exchange of notes between stage manager, assistant stage manager, director, cast, and crew; he bought two cheap wall clocks and hung them in the wings; he knocked together a few rough shelves, lined up the props upon them, and marked each spot with the act and scene in which the prop was to be used. Within a few days, a sense of tranquility began to emerge backstage. Whole acts would pass without an outburst from Claudel. The stagehands commented upon the change to the stage manager, who commented upon the change to Zoltán Novak, and Novak congratulated Andras. Emboldened by his success, Andras asked for and received seventy-five francs a week to stock a table with coffee and cream and chocolate biscuits and jam and bread for everyone backstage. Soon his mailbox was stuffed with notes of gratitude.

Madame Gérard in particular seemed to have taken a special interest in Andras. She began to call upon him not only to perform her errands, but also for his company. After the show, when the rest of the actors had gone, she liked to have him sit in her dressing room and talk to her while she removed her makeup. Her démaquillage took so long that Andras came to suspect that she dreaded going home. He knew she lived alone, though he didn't know where; he imagined a rose-colored flat papered with old show posters. She spoke little about her own life, except to tell him that he'd guessed her origins correctly: She had been born in Budapest, and her mother had taught the young Marcelle to speak both French and Hungarian. But she required Andras to speak only French to her; practice was the best way to master the language, she said. She wanted to hear about Budapest, about the job at *Past and Future*, about his family; he told her about Mátyás's penchant for dancing, and about Tibor's impending departure for Modena.

"And does Tibor speak Italian?" she asked as she rubbed cold cream into her forehead. "Has he studied the language?"

"He'll learn it faster than I learned French. In school he won the Latin prize three years running."

"And is he eager to leave?"

"Quite eager," Andras said. "But he can't go until January."

"And what else interests him besides medicine?"

"Politics. The state of the world."

"Well, that's excusable in a young man. And beyond that? What does he do in his spare time? Does he have a lady friend? Will he have to leave someone behind in Budapest?"

Andras shook his head. "He works night and day. There's no spare time."

"Indeed," said Madame Gérard, swiping at her cheeks with a pink velvet sponge. She turned a look of bemused inquiry upon Andras, her eyebrows raised in their narrow twin arcs. "And what about you?" she said. "You must have a little friend."

Andras blushed profoundly. He had never discussed the subject with any adult woman, not even his mother. "Not a trace of one," he said.

"I see," said Madame Gérard. "Then perhaps you won't object to a lunch invitation from a friend of mine. A Hungarian woman I know, a talented instructress of ballet, has a daughter a few years younger than you. A very handsome girl by the name of Elisabet. She's tall, blond, brilliant in school—gets high marks in mathematics. Won some sort of citywide math competition, poor girl. I'm certain she must speak some Hungarian, though she's emphatically French. She might introduce you to some of her friends."

A tall blond girl, emphatically French, who spoke Hungarian and might show him another side of Paris: He could hardly say no to that. In the back of his mind he could hear Rosen telling him he couldn't stay a virgin forever. He found himself saying he'd be delighted to accept the invitation to lunch at the home of Marcelle Gérard's friend. Madame Gérard wrote the name and address on the back of her own calling card.

"Sunday at noon," she said. "I can't be there myself, I'm afraid. I've already accepted another invitation. But I assure you you've got nothing to fear from Elisabet or her mother." She handed him the card. "They live not far from here, in the Marais."

He glanced at the address, wondering if the house were in the part of the Marais he had visited with his history class; then he experienced a sharp mnemonic tug and had to look again. *Morgenstern*, Madame Gérard had written. *39 rue de Sévigné.*

"Morgenstern," he said aloud.

"Yes. The house is at the corner of the rue d'Ormesson." And then she seemed to notice something strange about Andras's expression. "Is there a problem, my dear?"

He had a momentary urge to tell her about his visit to the house on Benczúr utca, about the letter he'd carried to Paris, but he remembered Mrs. Hász's plea for discretion and recovered quickly. "It's nothing," he said. "It's been a while since I've had to appear in polite company, that's all."

"You'll do splendidly," said Madame Gérard. "You're more of a gentleman than most gentlemen I know." She stood and gave him her queenly smile, a kind of private performance of her own authority and elegance; then she drew her Chinese robe around her and retreated behind the gold-painted lindens of her dressing screen.

* * *

That night he sat on his bed and looked at the card, the address. He knew that the world of Hungarian expatriates in Paris was a finite one, and that Madame Gérard was well connected within it, but he felt nonetheless that this convergence must have some deeper meaning. He was certain his memory was correct; he hadn't forgotten the name Morgenstern, nor the street name rue de Sévigné. It thrilled him to think he would find out if Tibor had been right when he'd guessed that the letter had been addressed to the elder Mrs. Hász's former lover. When he arrived at the Morgensterns', would he encounter a silver-haired gentleman—the father-in-law, perhaps, of Madame Morgenstern—who might be the mysterious *C*? How were the Hászes of Budapest connected with a ballet teacher in the Marais? And how would he refrain from mentioning any of this to József Hász the next time they met?

But in the days that followed, he found he had little time to think about the approaching visit to the Morgensterns'. Only a month remained before the end of the term, and in three weeks' time there would be a critique of the students' fall projects. His project was a model of the Gare d'Orsay, built from his measured drawing; he'd finished the plans but had yet to begin the model itself. He would have to buy materials, study topographical maps so he could build the base, make templates for the forms of the model, cut out the forms, draw the arched windows and clock faces and all the stone detailing, and assemble them into the finished piece. He spent the week in studio surrounded by his plans. At night, after work, he was consumed with preparations for a statics exam, and in the afternoons he attended a series of lectures by Perret on the ill-fated Fonthill Abbey, a nineteenth-century faux cathedral whose tower had collapsed three times due to poor design, hasty construction, and the use of shoddy materials.

By Saturday afternoon when he arrived at work, the only mystery in his mind was how he had managed to reach the day before the luncheon without having had his only white shirt laundered, and without having set aside a few francs for a gift for his hostess. After confessing the problem of his attire to Madame Gérard, he found himself in the workshop of the wardrobe mistress, Madame Courbet, who had constructed all the workers' clothes and military uniforms required for *The Mother*. While the revolution unfolded onstage, Madame Courbet had turned her attention to a different struggle: She was sewing fifty tutus for a children's dance recital that was to take place at the Bernhardt that winter. Andras found her sitting amid a storm of white tulle and tiny silk flowers, her sewing machine beating its mechanical thunder at the center of that snowy cumulus. She was a sparrowlike woman past fifty, always dressed in impeccably tailored clothes; today her green wool dress was frosted with icy-looking fibers, and she held a spool of silver-white thread between her fingers. She removed her rimless spectacles to look at Andras.

"Ah, young Monsieur Lévi," she said. "And is it another complaint from Monsieur Claudel, or has someone else split a seam?" She twisted her mouth into a wry moue.

"It's something for me, actually," he said. "I'm afraid I need a shirt."

"A shirt? Are you to have a walk-on in the play?"

"No," he said, and blushed. "I need a shirt for a luncheon tomorrow."

"I see." She lay down the thread and crossed her arms. "That's not my usual line."

"I hate to disturb you when you're already so busy."

"Madame Gérard sent you, didn't she."

Andras confessed that she had.

"That woman," said Madame Courbet. But she got up from her little chair and stood in front of Andras, looking him up and down. "I wouldn't do this for just anyone," she said. "You're a good young man. They hound you to death here and pay you almost nothing, but you've never been short with me. Which is more than I can say for certain people." She took a tape measure from a table and strapped a pincushion to her wrist. "Now, a gentleman's shirt, is it? You'll want a plain white oxford, of course. Nothing fancy." With a few deft movements she measured Andras's neck and shoulders and the length of his arm, then went to a wardrobe cabinet marked CHEMISES. From it she extracted a fine white shirt with a crisp collar. She showed Andras how the shirt contained a special pocket inside for a tube of fake blood; in one play, a man had to be stabbed night after night by his wife's jealous lover, and Madame Courbet had had to make an endless supply of shirts. From a drawer marked CRVT she selected a blue silk tie decorated with partridges. "It's an aristocrat's tie," she said, "a rich man's tie done up from a scrap. Look." She turned the tie over to show him how she'd sewn the silk remnant onto a plain cotton backing. Andras put it on along with the shirt, and she pinned the shirt for a swift alteration. At the end of the evening she gave him the finished shirt, wrapped in brown paper. "Don't let anyone else know where you got this," she said. "I wouldn't want the word to get out." But she pinched his ear affectionately as she sent him on his way.

As he was leaving, he had a sudden inspiration. He went to the grand front entrance of the theater, where Pély, the custodian, was sweeping the marble floor with his push broom. As usual, Pély had set the previous week's flower arrangements in a row inside the front doors; in the morning they would be picked up by the florist, vases and all, and replaced with new ones. Andras tipped his cap at Pély.

"If no one's using these flowers," he said, "may I?"

"Of course! Take them all. Take as many as you like."

Andras gathered a staggering armload of roses and lilies and chrysanthemums, branches with red berries, faux bluebirds on green twigs, feathery bunches of fern. He would not arrive empty-handed at the Morgensterns' on the rue de Sévigné; no, not he.

CHAPTER SEVEN

A Luncheon

IT HAD BEEN only a few weeks since Andras had studied the architecture of the Marais with Perret's class. They had taken a special trip to see the Hôtel de Sens, the fifteenth-century city palace with its turrets and leonine gargoyles, its confusion of rooflines, its cramped and cluttered façade. Andras had expected Perret's lecture to be a stern critique, a disquisition on the virtues of simplicity. But the lesson had been about the strength of the building, the fine craftsmanship that had allowed it to endure. Perret moved his hand along the stonework of the front entrance, showing the students what care the masons had taken in cutting the voussoirs of the Gothic arches. As he spoke, a pair of Orthodox men had appeared on the street, leading a group of schoolboys in yarmulkes. The two groups of students had stared at each other as they passed. The boys whispered to each other, looking at Perret in his military cloak; a few lagged behind as if to hear what Perret might say next. One boy snapped a salute, and his teacher delivered a reprimand in Yiddish.

Now Andras passed behind the Hôtel de Sens, past the manicured topiary gardens and the raised beds planted with purple kale for winter. Hefting his load of flowers, he sidestepped through the traffic on the rue de Rivoli. In the Marais the streets had an inside feel, almost as if they were part of a movie set. In *Cinescope* and *Le Film Complet*, Andras had seen the miniature cities built inside cavernous sound-stages in Los Angeles; here, the pale blue winter sky seemed like the arching roof of a studio, and Andras half expected to see men and women in medieval costume moving between the buildings, trailed by megaphone-wielding directors, by cameramen with their rafts of complicated equipment. There were kosher butchers and Hebrew bookshops and synagogues, all of them with signs written in Yiddish, as though this were a different country within the city. But there was no anti-Semitic graffiti of the kind that regularly appeared in the Jewish Quarter in Budapest. Instead the walls were bare, or plastered with advertisements for soap or chocolate or cigarettes. As Andras entered the tall corridor of the rue de Sévigné, a black taxi roared past, nearly knocking him off his feet. He steadied himself, shifted his vast bouquet from one arm to the other, and checked the address on the card Madame Gérard had given him.

Across the street he could see a windowed shop front with a wooden sign cut into the form of a child ballerina, and beneath it the legend ÉCOLE DE BALLET—MME MORGENSTERN, MAÎTRESSE. He crossed the street. A set of demi-curtained windows ran along both sides of the corner building, and when he stood on his toes he could see an empty room with a floor of yellow wood. One wall was lined from end to end with mirrors; polished wooden practice barres ran along the others. A squat upright piano crouched in one corner, and beside it stood a table with an old-fashioned gramophone, its glossy black morning-glory horn catching the light. A diffuse haze of dust motes hovered in the midday silence. Some remnant of movement, of music, seemed revealed in that tourbillon of dust, as if ballet continued to exist in that room whether a class was being conducted there or not.

The building entrance was a green door set with a leaded glass window. Andras rang the bell and waited. Through the sheer panel that covered the window, he could see a stout woman descending a flight of stairs. She opened the door and put a hand on her hip, giving him an appraising look. She was red-faced, kerchiefed, with a deep smell of paprika about her, like the women who brought vegetables and goat's milk to sell at the market in Debrecen.

"Madame Morgenstern?" he said, with hesitation; she didn't look much like a ballet mistress.

"Hah! No," she said in Hungarian. "Come in and close the door behind you. You'll let in the cold."

So he must have passed her inspection; he was glad, because the smells coming from inside were making him dizzy with hunger. He stepped into the entry, and the woman continued in a rapid stream of Hungarian as she took his coat and hat. What an enormous lot of flowers. She would see if there was a vase upstairs large enough to hold them. Lunch was nearly ready. She had prepared stuffed cabbage, and she hoped he liked it, because there was nothing else, except for spaetzle and a fruit compote and some sliced cold chicken and a walnut strudel. He should follow her upstairs. Her name was Mrs. Apfel. They climbed to the second floor, where she directed him to a front parlor decorated with worn Turkish rugs and dark furniture; she told him to wait there for Madame Morgenstern.

He sat on a gray velvet settee and took a long breath. Beneath the heady smell of stuffed cabbage there was the dry lemony tang of furniture polish and a faint scent of licorice. On a small carved table before him was a candy dish, a cut-glass nest filled with pink and lilac sugar eggs. He took an egg and ate it: anise. He straightened his tie and made sure the cotton backing wasn't showing. After a moment he heard the click of heels in the hall-way. A slim shadow moved across the wall, and a girl entered with a blue glass vase in her hands. The vase bristled with a wild profusion of flowers and branches and fake bluebirds, the daylilies beginning to darken at their edges, the roses hanging heavy on their stems. From behind this mass of fading blooms the girl looked at Andras, her dark hair brushed like a wing across her forehead.

"Thank you for the flowers," she said in French.

As she set the vase on the sideboard, he saw she wasn't a girl at all; her features had the sharper angles of an adult woman's, and she held her back straight as if from decades of ballet train-ing. But she was lithe and small, her hands like a child's on the blue glass vase. Andras drank in a flood of embarrassment as he watched her arrange the bouquet. Why had he brought so many half-dead flowers? Why the bluebirds? Why all those branches? Why hadn't he just bought something simple at the corner market? A dozen daisies? A sheaf of lupines? How much could it have cost? A couple of francs? The wood nymph smiled back at him over her shoulder, then came to shake his hand.

"Claire Morgenstern," she said. "It's a pleasure to meet you at last, Mr. Lévi. Madame Gérard has had many kind things to say about you."

He took her hand, trying not to stare; she looked decades younger than he'd imagined. He'd envisioned her as a woman of Madame Gérard's age, but this woman couldn't have been more than thirty. She had a quiet, astonishing beauty—fine bones, a mouth like a smooth pink-skinned fruit, large intelligent gray eyes. Claire Morgenstern: So this was the *C.* of the letter, not some elderly gentleman who had once been Mrs. Hász's lover. Her large gray eyes were Mrs. Hász's eyes, the quiet grief he saw there a mirror of the expression he'd seen in the older woman's eyes. This Claire Morgenstern had to be Mrs. Hász's daughter. A long moment passed before Andras could speak.

"The pleasure to make your acquaintance," he said in rushed and stilted French, knowing he'd gotten it wrong as soon as he said it. Belatedly he remembered to rise, and though he struggled for the right words, found himself continuing in the same vein. "Thank you for the invitation of me," he stammered, and sat down again.

Madame Morgenstern took a seat beside him on a low chair. "Would you rather speak Hungarian?" she asked in Hungarian. "We can, if you like."

He looked up at her as if from the bottom of a well. "French is fine," he said, in Hungarian. And then in French, again, "French is fine."

"All right, then," she said. "You'll have to tell me what Hungary is like these days. It's been years since I was there, and Elisabet has never been."

As if she'd been conjured by the mention of her name, a tall stern-looking girl entered the room, carrying a pitcher of iced tea. She was broad-shouldered like the swimmers Andras had admired at Palatinus Strand in Budapest; she gave him a look of impatient disdain as she filled his glass.

"This is my Elisabet," said Madame Morgenstern. "Elisabet, this is Andras."

Andras couldn't make himself believe that this girl was Madame Morgenstern's daughter. In Elisabet's hands, the tea pitcher looked like a child's toy. He drank his tea and looked from mother to daughter. Madame Morgenstern stirred her tea with a long spoon, while Elisabet, having set the pitcher on a table, threw herself into a wing chair and checked her wristwatch.

"If we don't eat now I'll be late for the movie," she said. "I'm supposed to meet Marthe in an hour."

"What movie?" Andras said, searching for a thread of conversation.

"You wouldn't be interested," Elisabet said. "It's in French."

"But I speak French," Andras said.

Elisabet gave him a dry smile. "May-juh-pargl-Fronsay," she said.

Madame Morgenstern closed her eyes. "Elisabet," she said.

"What?"

"You know what."

"I just want to go to the movies," Elisabet said, and knocked her heels dully against the rug. Then she tilted her chin toward Andras and said, "Lovely tie."

Andras looked down. His tie had flipped over as he'd leaned forward to take his glass of tea, and now the cotton backing faced the world, while the gold partridges flew unseen against his shirtfront. Hot with shame, he turned it around and stared into his tea.

"Lunch is served!" said the red-faced Mrs. Apfel from the doorway, pushing back her kerchief. "Come now, before the cabbage gets cold."

There was a proper dining room, with polished wooden china cabinets and a white cloth on the table: echoes of the house on Benczúr utca, Andras thought. But there were no exsanguinated sandwiches here; the table was heavy with platters of stuffed cabbage and chicken and bowls of spaetzle, as though there were eight of them eating instead of three. Madame Morgenstern sat at the head of the table, Andras and Elisabet across from each other. Mrs. Apfel served the stuffed cabbage and spaetzle; Andras, grateful for the distraction, tucked his napkin into his collar and began to eat. Elisabet frowned at her plate. She pushed the cabbage aside and began eating the spaetzle, one tiny dumpling at a time.

"I hear you're interested in mathematics," Andras said, speaking to the top of Elisabet's lowered head.

She raised her eyes. "Did my mother tell you that?"

"No, Madame Gérard did. She said you won a competition."

"Anyone can do high-school mathematics."

"Do you think you'll want to study it in college?"

Elisabet shrugged. "If I go to college."

"Darling, you can't live on spaetzle," Madame Morgenstern said quietly, looking at Elisabet's plate. "You used to like stuffed cabbage."

"It's cruel to eat meat," Elisabet said, and leveled her eyes at Andras. "I've seen how they butcher cows. They stick a knife in the neck and draw it downwards, like this, and the blood pours out. My biology class took a trip to a *shochet*. It's barbaric."

"Not really," Andras said. "My brothers and I used to know the kosher butcher in our town. He was a friend of our father's, and he was quite gentle with the animals."

Elisabet watched him intently. "And can you explain to me

how you gently butcher a cow?" she said. "What did he do? Pet them to death?"

"He used the traditional method," Andras said, his tone sharper than he'd intended. "One quick cut across the neck. It couldn't have hurt them for more than a second."

Madame Morgenstern set her silverware down and put a napkin to her mouth as if she felt ill, and Elisabet's expression became slyly triumphant. Mrs. Apfel stood in the doorway holding a water pitcher, waiting to see what would happen next.

"Go on," Elisabet said. "What did he do then, after he made the cut?"

"I think we're finished with this subject," Andras said.

"No, please. I'd like to hear the rest, now that you've started."

"Elisabet, that's enough," Madame Morgenstern said.

"But the conversation's just getting interesting."

"I said it's enough."

Elisabet crumpled her napkin and threw it onto the table. "I'm finished," she said. "You can sit here with your guest and eat meat. I'm going to the cinema with Marthe." She pushed her chair back and stood, nearly upsetting Mrs. Apfel and the water pitcher, then went off down the hall and knocked around in a distant room. A few moments later her heavy footsteps echoed on the stairs. The door of the dance studio slammed and its mullioned window jingled.

At the dining table, Madame Morgenstern lowered her forehead onto her palm. "I apologize, Monsieur Lévi," she said.

"No, please," he said. "It's fine." In fact, he wasn't at all sorry to have been left alone with Madame Morgenstern. "Don't be upset on my account," he said. "That was a terrible topic of conversation. *I* apologize."

"There's no need," Madame Morgenstern said. "Elisabet is impossible at times, that's all. I can't do anything with her once she's decided she's angry at me."

"Why should she be angry at you?"

She gave a half smile and shrugged. "It's complicated, I'm afraid. She's a sixteen-year-old girl. I'm her mother. She doesn't like me to have anything to do with her social affairs. And I mustn't remind her that we're Hungarian, either. She considers Hungarians an unenlightened people."

"I've felt that way, too, at times," Andras said. "I've spent a lot of time lately struggling to be French."

"Your French is excellent, as it turns out."

"No, it's terrible. And I'm afraid I did nothing to dispel your daughter's notion that Magyars are barbarians."

Madame Morgenstern hid a smile behind her hand. "You were rather quick with that business about the butcher," she said.

"I'm sorry," Andras said, but he'd started to laugh. "I don't think I've ever spoken about that over lunch."

"So you really did know the butcher in your town," she said.

"I did. And I saw him at his work. But Elisabet was right, I'm afraid—it was awful!"

"You must have grown up—where? Somewhere in the countryside?"

"Konyár," he said. "Near Debrecen."

"Konyár? That's not twenty kilometers from Kaba, where my mother was born." A shade passed over her features and was gone.

"Your mother," he said. "But she doesn't live there anymore?"

"No," Madame Morgenstern said. "She lives in Budapest." She fell silent for a moment, then turned the conversation back to Andras's history. "So you're a Hajdú, too. A flatlands boy."

"That's right," he said. "My father owns a lumberyard in Konyár." So she wouldn't talk about it, wouldn't discuss the subject of her family. He had been on the verge of mentioning the letter—of saying *I've met your mother*—but the moment had passed now, and there was a kind of relief in the prospect of talking about Konyár. Ever since he'd arrived in Paris and had mastered enough French to answer questions about his origins, he'd been telling people he was from Budapest. What would anyone have known of Konyár? And to those who would have known, like József Hász or Pierre Vago, Konyár meant a small and backward place, a town you were lucky to have escaped. Even the name sounded ridiculous—the punchline of a bawdy joke, the sound of a jumping jack springing from a box. But he really was from Konyár, from that dirt-floored house beside the railroad tracks.

"My father's something of a celebrity in town, to tell the truth," Andras said.

"Indeed! What is he known for?"

"His terrible luck," Andras said. And then, feeling suddenly brave: "Shall I tell you his story, the way they tell it at home?"

"By all means," she said, and folded her hands in anticipation.

So he told her the story just as he'd always heard it: Before his father had owned the lumberyard, he had suffered a string of misfortunes that had earned him the nickname of Lucky Béla. His own father had fallen ill while Béla was at rabbinical school in Prague, and had died as soon as he returned home. The vineyard he inherited had succumbed to blight. His first wife had died in childbirth, along with the baby, a girl; not long after, his house had burned to the ground. All three of his brothers were killed in the Great War, and his mother had given in to grief and drowned herself in the Tisza. At thirty he was a ruined man, penniless, his family dead. For a time he lived on the charity of the Jews of Konyár, sleeping in the Orthodox shul at night and eating what they left for him. Then, at the end of a drought summer, a famous Ukrainian miracle rabbi arrived from across the border and set up temporary quarters in the shul. He studied Torah with the local men, settled disputes, officiated at weddings, granted divorces, prayed for rain, danced in the courtyard with his disciples. One morning at dawn he came upon Andras's father sleeping in the sanctuary. He'd heard the story of this unfortunate, this man whom all the village said must be suffering from a curse; they seemed to regard him with a kind of gratitude, as if he'd drawn the attention of the evil eye away from the rest of them. The rabbi roused Béla with a benediction, and Béla looked up in speechless fear. The rabbi was a gaunt man with an ice-white beard; his eyebrows stood out from the curve of his forehead like lifted wings, his eyes dark and liquid beneath them.

"Listen to me, Béla Lévi," the rabbi whispered in the half-light of the sanctuary. "There's nothing wrong with you. God asks the most of those he loves best. You must fast for two days and go to the ritual bath, then accept the first offer of work you receive."

Even if Lucky Béla had been a believer in miracles, his misfortunes would have made him a skeptic. "I'm too hungry to fast," he said.

"Practice at hunger makes the fast easier," the rabbi said.

"How do you know there's not a curse on me?"

"I try not to wonder how I know. Certain things I just know." And the rabbi made another blessing over Béla and left him alone in the sanctuary.

What more did Lucky Béla have to lose? He fasted for two days and bathed in the river at night. The next morning he wandered toward the railroad tracks, faint with hunger, and picked an apple from a stunted tree beside a white brick cottage. The proprietor of the lumberyard, an Orthodox Jew, stepped out of the cottage and asked Béla what he thought he was doing.

"I used to have a vineyard," Béla said. "When I had a vineyard, I would have let you pick my grapes. When I had a house I would have welcomed you to my house. My wife would have given you something to eat. Now I have neither grapes nor house. I have no wife. I have no food. But I can work."

"There's no work for you here," the man said, gently, "but come inside and eat."

The man's name was Zindel Kohn. His wife, Gitta, set bread and cheese before Lucky Béla. With Zindel and Gitta and their five small children, Lucky Béla ate; as he did, he allowed himself to imagine for the first time that the rest of his life might not be shaped by the misery of his past. He could not have imagined that this house would become his own house, that his own children would eat bread and cheese at this very table. But by the end of the afternoon he had a job: The boy who worked the mechanical saw at Zindel Kohn's lumberyard had decided to become a disciple of the Ukrainian rabbi. He had left that morning without notice.

Six years later, when Zindel Kohn and his family moved to Debrecen, Lucky Béla took over the lumberyard. He married a black-haired girl named Flóra who bore him three sons, and by the time the oldest was ten, Béla had earned enough money to buy the lumberyard outright. He did a fine business; people in Konyár needed building materials and firewood in every season. Before long, hardly anyone in Konyár remembered that Lucky Béla's nickname had been given in irony. The history might have been allowed to fade altogether had it not been for the return of the Ukrainian rabbi; this was at the height of the worldwide depression, just before the High Holidays. The rabbi spent an evening at Lucky Béla's house and asked if he might tell his story in synagogue. It might help the Jews of Konyár, he said, to be reminded of what God would do for his children if they refused to capitulate to despair. Lucky Béla consented. The rabbi told the story, and the Jews of Konyár listened. Though Béla insisted his good fortune was due entirely to the generosity of others, people began to regard him as a kind of holy figure. They touched his house for good luck when they passed, and asked him to be godfather to their children. Everyone believed he had a connection to the divine.

"You must have thought so yourself as a child," Madame Morgenstern said.

"I did! I thought he was invincible—even more so than most children think of their parents," Andras said. "Sometimes I wish I'd never lost the illusion."

"Ah, yes," she said. "I understand."

"My parents are getting older," Andras said. "I hate to think of them alone in Konyár. My father had pneumonia last year, and couldn't work for a month afterward." He hadn't spoken about this to anyone in Paris. "My younger brother's at school a few hours away, but he's caught up in his own life. And now my older brother's leaving, going off to medical school in Italy."

A shadow came to Madame Morgenstern's features again, as if she'd experienced an inward twist of pain. "My mother's getting older too," she said. "It's been a long time since I've seen her, a very long time." She fell silent and glanced away from the table at the tall west-facing windows. The late autumn light fell in a diagonal plane across her face, illuminating the tapered curve of her mouth. "Forgive me," she said, trying to smile; he offered his handkerchief, and she pressed it to her eyes.

He found himself fighting the impulse to touch her, to trace a line from her nape down the curve of her back. "Perhaps I've stayed too long," he said.

"No, please," she said. "You haven't even had dessert."

As if she'd been listening just beyond the dining-room door, Mrs. Apfel came in at that moment to serve the walnut strudel. Andras found that he had an appetite again. He was ravenous, in fact. He ate three slices of strudel and drank coffee with cream. As he did, he told Madame Morgenstern about his studies, about Professor Vago, about the trip to Boulogne-Billancourt. He found her easier to talk to than Madame Gérard. She had a way of pausing in quiet thought before she responded; she would pull her lips in pensively, and when she spoke, her voice was low and encouraging. After lunch they went back to the parlor and looked through her album of picture postcards. Her dancer friends had traveled as far as Chicago and Cairo. There was even a hand-colored postcard from Africa: three animals that looked like deer, but were slighter and more graceful, with straight upcurved horns and almond-shaped eyes. The French word for them was *gazelle*.

"Gazelle," Andras said. "I'll try to remember."

"Yes, try," she said, and smiled. "Next time I'll test you."

When the afternoon light had begun to wane, she rose and led Andras to the hallway, where his coat and hat hung on a polished stand. She gave him his things and returned his handkerchief. As she led him down the stairs she pointed out the photographs on the wall, images of students from years past: girls in ethereal clouds of tulle or sylphlike draperies of silk, young dancers under the transient spell of costumes and makeup and stage lights. Their expressions were serious, their arms as pale and nude as the branches of winter trees. He wanted to stay and look. He wondered if any of the photographs were of Madame Morgenstern herself when she was a child.

"Thank you for everything," he said when they'd reached the bottom of the stairs.

"Please." She put a slim hand on his arm. "I should thank you. You were very kind to stay."

Andras flushed so deeply at the pressure of her hand that he could feel the blood beating in his temples. She opened the door and he stepped out into the chill of the afternoon. He found he couldn't look at her to say goodbye. *Next time I'll test you.* But she'd returned his handkerchief as though their paths were unlikely to cross again. He spoke his goodbye to the doorstep, to her feet in their fawn-colored shoes. Then he turned away and she closed the door behind him. Without thinking, he retraced his steps toward the river until he had reached the Pont Marie. There he paused at the edge of the bridge and brought out the handkerchief. It was still damp where she'd used it to dry her eyes. As if in a dream, he put a corner of it into his mouth and tasted the salt she'd left there.

CHAPTER EIGHT

Gare d'Orsay

THAT NIGHT HE found it impossible to sleep. He couldn't stop reviewing every detail of his afternoon at the Morgensterns'. The shameful bouquet, and how doubly shameful it had looked when she'd carried it into the parlor in the blue glass vase. The moment when he'd realized that she must be the elder Mrs. Hász's daughter, and how it had flustered him to discover it— how he'd said *The pleasure to make your acquaintance* and *Thank you for the invitation of me.* How she'd held her back straight as though she were always dancing, until the moment at the table after Elisabet had gone—the way her back had curved then, showing the linked pearls of her spine, and how he'd wanted to touch her. The way she'd listened as he'd told his father's story. The close heat of her shoulder as she sat beside him on the sofa in the parlor, paging through the album of picture postcards. The moment at the door when she'd rested her hand on his arm. He tried to re-create an image of her in his mind—the dark sweep of hair across her brow, the gray eyes that seemed too large for her face, the clean line of her jaw, the mouth that drew in upon itself as she considered what he'd said—but he couldn't make the disparate elements add up to an image of her. He saw her again as she turned to smile at him over her shoulder, girlish and wise at the same time. But what was he thinking, what could he be thinking? What an absurdity for him to think this way about a woman like Claire Morgenstern—he, Andras, a twenty-two-year-old student who lived in an unheated room and drank tea from a jam jar because he couldn't afford coffee or a coffee cup. And yet she hadn't sent him away, she'd kept talking to him, he'd made her laugh, she'd accepted his handkerchief, she'd touched his arm in a confiding and intimate manner.

For hours he rolled over and over in bed, trying to put her

out of his mind. When the sky outside his window filled with a deep gray-blue light, he wanted to cry. *All night* he'd lain awake, and soon he would have to get up and go to class and then to work, where Madame Gérard would want to hear about the visit. It was Monday morning, the beginning of a new week. The night was over. The only thing he could do was to get out of bed and write the letter he had to write, the one he had to mail before he went to school that morning. He took an old piece of sketch paper and began a draft:

Dear Mme Morgenstern,
Thank you for the

For the what? For the very pleasant afternoon? How flat it would sound. How much that would make it seem like any ordinary afternoon. Whatever else it had been, it hadn't been that. What was he supposed to write? He wanted to express his gratitude for Madame Morgenstern's hospitality; that was certain. But underneath he wanted to send a coded message, to convey what he had felt and what he felt now—that a kind of electrical conduit had opened between them and ran between them still; that he'd taken her at her word when she'd suggested they might see each other again. He scratched out the lines he'd written and started again.

Dear Madame Morgenstern,
As absurd as it sounds, I've been thinking of you since we parted.
I want to take you into my arms, tell you a million things, ask
you a million questions. I want to touch your throat and unbut-
ton the pearl button at your neck.

And then what? What would he do, given the chance? For one brief delirious moment he thought of those old photographs that depicted the elaborate sexual positions, the silver images of entwined couples visible only when the cards were held at an angle to the light. He remembered standing in the changing room near the gymnastics hall with four other boys, each of them hunched over and holding a card, their gym shorts around their ankles, each in solitary agony as the silver couples flashed into and out of view. His card had shown a woman lying on a settee, her legs raised in a sharp *V*. She wore a Victorian-style gown that revealed her arms and shoulders and had fallen away from her legs entirely, leaving them bare as they strained toward the ceiling. A man bent over her, doing what even the Victorians did.

Flushed with shame and desire, he scratched out the lines again to begin another draft. He dipped his pen and wiped off the excess ink.

Dear Madame Morgenstern,
Thank you for your hospitality and for the pleasure of your company. My own accommodations are too poor to allow me to return your invitation, but if I may be of service to you in some other way, I hope you will not hesitate to call upon me. In the meantime I shall retain the hope that we will meet again.
                              Yours sincerely, ANDRAS LÉVI

He read and reread the draft, wondering if he should try to write in French instead of Hungarian; finally he decided he was likely to make an imbecillic error in French. He wrote a fair copy on a sheet of thin white paper, which he folded in half and sealed into an envelope before he could begin to reexamine every line. Then he mailed the letter at the same blue box where he'd posted the letter from her mother.

That week he was grateful for the hard, painstaking work of model-building. In the studio he cut a rectangle of thick pasteboard to serve as a base for the model, and he traced the footprint of the building onto the base in a thin pencil line. On another piece of pasteboard he drew the shapes of the building's four elevations, working meticulously from his measured drawing. His favorite tool was a ruler of near-transparent cellulose through which he could see the pencil lines that intersected the one he was drawing; that ruler, with its strict grid of millimeters, was an island of exactitude in the sea of tasks he had to complete, a strip of certainty in the midst of his uncertainty. Every piece of the model had to be made from sturdy material that could not be bought at a discount or substituted with flimsy stuff; everyone recalled what had happened during the first week of classes, when Polaner, trying to stretch his dwindling supply of francs, had used Bristol paper for a model, rather than pasteboard. In the middle of the critique, when Professor Vago had tapped the roof of Polaner's model with his mechanical pencil, one wall had buckled and sent the paper château to its knees. Pasteboard was expensive; Andras could not afford to make a mistake, neither in the ink drawing nor the cutting. It provided some comfort to work alongside Rosen and Ben Yakov and Polaner, who were building the École Militaire, the Rotonde de la Villette, and the Théâtre de l'Odéon, respectively. Even smug Lemarque provided a welcome distraction; he'd decided to build a model of the twenty-sided Cirque d'Hiver, and could be heard periodically swearing as he traced wall after wall onto pasteboard.

In statics class there was the clear plain order of math: the three-variable equation to calculate the number and thickness of steel rods per cubic meter of concrete, the number of kilograms a support column could bear, the precise distribution of pressure along the crown of an arch. At the front of the classroom, chalking his way through a maze of calculations on the chip-edged blackboard, stood the wildly untidy Victor Le Bourgeois, professor of statics, a practicing architect and engineer, who, like Vago, was said to be a close friend of Pingusson's. His disorder expressed itself in trousers torn at the knee, a jacket permanently grayed with chalk dust, a shaggy halo of ginger-colored hair, and a tendency to misplace the blackboard eraser. But when he began to trace the relationship between mathematical abstractions and tangible building materials, all the chaos of his person seemed to drop away. Willingly Andras followed him into the curved halls of calculus, where the problem of Madame Morgenstern could not exist because it could not be described by an equation.

At the theater there was the relief of being able to speak her name aloud to Madame Gérard. During intermission at the Tuesday night performance, Andras brought Madame a cup of strong coffee and waited by the door of her dressing room as she drank it. She looked up from under the graceful arch of her brows; she was stately even in the soot-stained apron and head kerchief of the Mother. "I haven't had word from Madame Morgenstern," she said. "How was your luncheon?"

"Quite pleasance," Andras said, and blushed. "Pleasant, I mean."

"Quite pleasant, he says."

"Yes," Andras said. "Quite." His French vocabulary seemed to have fled.

"Aha," said Madame Gérard, as if she understood entirely. Andras's blush deepened: He knew she must think that something had passed between himself and Elisabet. Something had, of course, though not at all what she must have imagined.

"Madame Morgenstern is very kind," he said.

"And Mademoiselle?"

"Mademoiselle is very . . ." Andras swallowed and looked at the row of lights above Madame Gérard's mirror. "Mademoiselle is very tall."

Madame Gérard threw her head back and laughed. "Very tall!" she said. "Indeed. And very strong-willed. I knew her when she was a little girl playing at dolls; she used to speak to them so imperiously I thought they would burst into tears. But you mustn't be scared of Elisabet. She's harmless, I assure you."

Before Andras could protest that he wasn't in the least afraid of Elisabet, the double bell sounded to signal the impending end of intermission. Madame had a costume change to complete, and Andras had to leave to finish his tasks before the third act began. Once the actors went on again, time slowed to a polar trickle. All he could think of was the letter he'd written and when a response might come. His letter might have been delivered by that afternoon's post, and she might have posted her own response today. Her letter could arrive as soon as tomorrow. It wasn't unreasonable to think she might invite him for lunch again that weekend.

The next night, when the play finally ended and Andras had finished his duties for the evening, he ran all the way home to the rue des Écoles. In his mind he could see the envelope glowing in the dark of the entryway, the cream-colored stationery, Madame Morgenstern's neat, even handwriting, the same handwriting in which she'd made the inscriptions beneath the postcards in her album. *From Marie in Morocco. From Marcel in Rome.* Who was Marcel, Andras wondered, and what had he written from Rome?

As he opened the tall red door with his skeleton key, he could already make out an envelope on the console table. He let the door swing behind him as he went for the letter. But it wasn't the cream-colored lilac-scented envelope he'd hoped for; it was a wrinkled brown envelope addressed in the handwriting of his brother Mátyás. Unlike Tibor, Mátyás rarely wrote; when he did, the letters were thin and informational. This one was thick, requiring twice the usual amount of postage. His first thought was that something had happened to his parents—his father had been injured, his mother had caught influenza—and his second thought was of how ridiculous he'd been to expect a letter from Madame Morgenstern.

Upstairs he lit one of his precious candles and sat down at the table. He slit the brown envelope carefully with his penknife. Inside was a creased sheaf of pages, five of them, the longest letter Mátyás had ever written to him. The handwriting was large and careless and peppered with inkblots. Andras scanned the first lines for bad news about his parents, but there wasn't any. If there had been, Andras thought, Tibor would have wired him. This letter was about Mátyás himself. Mátyás had learned that Andras had arranged for Tibor to enter medical school in January. Congratulations to them both, to Andras for having successfully exploited his lofty connections, and to Tibor for getting to leave Hungary at last. Now he, Mátyás, would certainly have to remain behind, alone, heir by default to a rural lumberyard. Did Andras think it was easy, having to hear their parents talk about how exciting Andras's studies were, how well he was doing in his classes, how wonderful it was that Tibor could now study to become a doctor, what a fine couple of sons they were? Had Andras forgotten that Mátyás, too, might have hopes for his own studies abroad? Had Andras forgotten everything Mátyás had said on the subject? Did Andras think Mátyás was going to give up on his own plans? If he did, he'd better reconsider. Mátyás was saving money. If he saved enough before he graduated, he wouldn't bother with his bac. He would run away to America, to New York, and go on the stage. He'd find a way to get by. In America all you needed was determination and the willingness to work. And once he left Hungary, it would be up to Andras and Tibor to worry about the lumberyard and their parents, because he, Mátyás, would never return.

At the end of the last page, written in a calmer hand—as if Mátyás had set the letter aside for a time, then come back to finish it once his anger had burned out—was a remorseful *Hope you're well*. Andras gave a short, exhausted laugh. Hope you're well! He might as well have written "Hope you die."

Andras took up a sheet of paper from the desk. *Dear Mátyás*, he wrote. *If it makes you feel any better, I've been wretched a hundred times since I've been here. I'm wretched right now. Believe me when I tell you it hasn't all been wonderful. As for you, I haven't the slightest doubt that you will finish your bac and go to America, if that's what you want (though I'd much rather you came here to Paris). I don't expect you to take over for Apa, and neither does Apa himself. He wants you to finish your studies.* But Mátyás was right to raise the question, right to be angry that there was no easy solution. He thought of Claire Morgenstern saying of her own mother, *It's been a long time since I've seen her, a very long time.* How her expression had clouded, how her eyes had filled with a grief that seemed to echo the grief he'd witnessed in her mother's features. What had parted them, and what had kept Madame Morgenstern away? With effort he turned his thoughts back to his letter. *I hope you won't be angry with me for long, Mátyáska, but your anger does you credit: It's evidence of what a good son you are. When I finish my studies I'll go back to Hungary, and may God keep Anya and Apa in health long enough for me to be of service to them then.* In the meantime he would worry about them just as his brothers did. *In the meantime I expect you to be brilliant and fearless in all things, as ever! With love, your ANDRAS.*

He posted the reply the next morning, hoping that the day would bring word from Madame Morgenstern. But there was no letter on the hall table that night when he returned from work. And why should he have expected her to write? he wondered. Their social exchange was complete. He had accepted Madame Morgenstern's hospitality and had sent his thanks. If he'd imagined a connection with her, he had been mistaken. And in any case he was supposed to have made a connection with her daughter, not with Madame Morgenstern herself. That night he lay awake shivering and thinking of her and cursing himself for his ridiculous hope. In the morning he found a thin layer of ice in the washbasin; he broke it with the washcloth and splashed his face with a burning sheet of ice-cold water. Outside, a stiff wind blew loose shingles off the roof and shattered them in the street. At the bakery the woman gave him hot peasant loaves straight from the oven, charging him as if they were day-old bread. It was going to be one of the coldest winters ever, she told him. Andras knew he would need a warmer coat, a woolen scarf; his boots would need to be resoled. He didn't have the money for any of it.

All week the temperature kept falling. At school the radiators emitted a feeble dry heat; the fifth-year students took places close to them, and the first-years froze by the windows. Andras spent hopeless hours on his model of the Gare d'Orsay, a train station already drifting into obsolescence. Though it still served as the terminus for the railways of southwestern France, its platforms were too short for the long trains used now. Last time he'd gone there to take measurements, the station had looked derelict and unkempt, a few of its high windows broken, a stippling of mildew darkening its line of arches. It didn't cheer him to think he was preserving its memory in cardboard; his model was a flimsy homage to a tatterdemalion relic. On Friday he walked home alone, too dispirited to join the others at the Blue Dove—and there on the entry table was a white envelope with his name on it, the response he'd waited for all week. He tore it open in the foyer. *Andras, you're very welcome. Please visit us again sometime. Regards, C. MORGENSTERN.* Nothing more. Nothing certain. *Please visit us again sometime:* What did that mean? He sat down on the stairs and dropped his forehead against his knees. All week he'd waited for this! *Regards.* His heart went on drumming in his chest, as if something wonderful were still about to happen. He tasted shame like a hot fragment of metal on his tongue.

After work that night he couldn't bear the thought of going home to his tiny room, of lying down in the bed where he'd now spent five sleepless nights thinking about Claire Morgenstern. Instead he wandered toward the Marais, drawing his thin coat closer around him. It cheered him to take an unfamiliar path through the streets of the Right Bank; he liked losing his way and finding it again, discovering the strangely named alleyways and lanes—rue des Mauvais Garçons, rue des Guillemites, rue des Blancs-Manteaux. Tonight there was a smell of winter in the air, different from the Budapest smell of brown coal and approaching snow; the Paris smell was wetter and smokier and sweeter: chestnut leaves turning to mash in the gutters, the sugary brown scent of roasted nuts, the tang of gasoline from the boulevards. Everywhere there were posters advertising the ice-skating rinks, one in the Bois de Boulogne and another in the Bois de Vincennes. He hadn't imagined that Paris would get cold enough for skating, but both sets of posters proclaimed that the ponds were frozen solid. One depicted a trio of spinning polar bears; the other showed a little girl in a short red skirt, her hands in a fur muff, one slender leg extended behind her.

In the rue des Rosiers a man and a woman stood beside one of these posters and kissed unabashedly, their hands buried inside each other's coats. Andras was reminded of a game the children used to play in Konyár: Behind the baker's shop there was a wall of white stone that was always warm because the baker's oven was on the other side, and in the wintertime the boys would meet there after school to kiss the baker's daughter. The baker's daughter had pale brown freckles scattered across her nose like sesame seeds. For ten fillér she would press you up against the wall and kiss you until you couldn't breathe. For five fillér you could watch her do it to someone else. She was saving for a pair of ice skates. Her name was Orsolya, but they never called her that; instead they called her Korcsolya, the word for ice skates. Andras had kissed her once, had felt her tongue explore his own as she held him up against the warm wall. He couldn't have been more than eight years old; Orsolya must have been ten. Three of his friends from school were watching, cheering him on. Halfway through the kiss he'd opened his eyes. Orsolya, too, was open-eyed, but absent, her mind fixed else-where—perhaps on the ice skates. He'd never forgotten the day he came out of the house to see her skating on the pond, the sil-ver flash at her soles like a teasing wink, a steely goodbye-forever to paid kissing. That winter she'd nearly died of cold, skating in all weather. "That girl will go through the ice," Andras's mother had predicted, watching Orsolya tracing loops in an early March rain. But she hadn't gone through the ice. She'd survived her winter on the millpond, and the next winter she was there again, and the one after that she'd gone away to secondary school. He could see her now, a red-skirted figure through a gray haze, untouchable and alone.

Now he made his way though the grotto of medieval streets toward the rue de Sévigné, toward Madame Morgenstern's building. He hadn't decided to come here, but here he was; he stood on the sidewalk opposite and rocked on his heels. It was near midnight, and all the lights were out upstairs. But he crossed the street and looked over the demi-curtains into the darkened studio. There was the morning-glory horn of the phonograph, gleaming black and brutal in a corner; there was the piano with its flat toothy grimace. He shivered inside his coat and imagined the pink-clad forms of girls moving across the yellow plane of the studio floor. It was bitterly, blindingly cold. What was he doing out here on the street at midnight? There was only one explanation for his behavior: He'd gone mad. The pressure of his life here, of his single chance at making a man and an artist of himself, had proved too much for him. He put his head against the wall of the entryway, trying to slow his breathing; after a moment, he told himself, he would shake off this madness and find his way home. But then he raised his eyes and saw what he hadn't known he'd been looking for: There in the entryway was a slim glass-fronted case of the kind used to post menus outside restaurants; instead of a menu, this one held a white rectangle of cardstock inscribed with the legend *Horaire des Classes.*

The schedule, the pattern of her life. There it was, printed in her own neat hand. Her mornings were devoted to private lessons, the early afternoons to beginning classes, the later afternoons to intermediate and advanced. Wednesdays and Fridays she took the mornings off. On Sundays, the afternoons. Now, at least, he knew when he might look through this window and see her. Tomorrow wasn't soon enough, but it would have to be.

All the next day he tried to turn his thoughts away from her. He went to the studio, where everyone gathered on Saturdays to work; he built his model, joked with Rosen, heard about Ben Yakov's continuing fascination with the beautiful Lucia, shared his peasant bread with Polaner. By noon he couldn't wait any longer. He went down into the Métro at Raspail and rode to Châtelet. From there he ran all the way to the rue de Sévigné; by the time he arrived he was hot and panting in the winter chill. He looked over the demi-curtains of the studio. A crowd of little girls in dancing clothes were packing their ballet shoes into canvas satchels, holding their street shoes in their hands as they lined up at the door. The covered entrance to the studio was crowded with mothers and governesses, the mothers in furs, the governesses in woolen coats. A few little girls broke through the cluster of women and ran off toward a candy shop. He waited for the crowd at the door to clear, and then he saw her just inside the entryway: Madame Morgenstern, in a black practice skirt and a close-wrapped gray sweater, her hair gathered at the nape of her neck in a loose knot. When all the children but one had been collected, Madame Morgenstern emerged from the entryway holding the last girl's hand. She stepped lightly on the sidewalk in her dancing shoes, as if she didn't want to ruin their soles on the paving stones. Andras had a sudden urge to flee.

But the little girl had seen him. She dropped Madame Morgenstern's hand and took a few running steps toward him, squinting as if she couldn't quite make him out. When she was close enough to touch his sleeve, she stopped short and turned back. Her shoulders rose and fell beneath the blue wool of her coat.

"It's not Papa after all," she said.

Madame Morgenstern raised her eyes in apology to the man who wasn't Papa. When she saw it was Andras, she smiled and tugged the edge of her wrapped sweater straight, a gesture so girlish and self-conscious that it brought a rush of heat to Andras's chest. He crossed the few squares of pavement between them. He didn't dare to press her hand in greeting, could hardly look into her eyes. Instead he stared at the sidewalk and buried his hands in his pockets, where he discovered a ten-centime coin left over from his purchase of bread that morning. "Look what I found," he said, kneeling to give the coin to the little girl.

She took it and turned it over in her fingers. "You found this?" she said. "Maybe someone dropped it."

"I found it in my pocket," he said. "It's for you. When you go to the shops with your mother, you can buy candy or a new hair ribbon."

The girl sighed and tucked the coin into the side pocket of her satchel. "A hair ribbon," she said. "I'm not allowed candy. It's bad for the teeth."

Madame Morgenstern put a hand on the girl's shoulder and drew her toward the door. "We can wait by the stove inside," she said. "It's warmer there." She turned back to catch Andras's eye, meaning to include him in the invitation. He followed her inside, toward the compact iron stove that stood in a corner of the studio. A fire hissed behind its isinglass window, and the little girl knelt to look at the flames.

"This is a surprise," Madame Morgenstern said, lifting her gray eyes to his own.

"I was out for a ramble," Andras said, too quickly. "Studying the quartier."

"Monsieur Lévi is a student of architecture," Madame Morgenstern told the girl. "Someday he'll design grand buildings."

"My father's a doctor," the girl said absently, not looking at either of them.

Andras stood beside Madame Morgenstern and warmed his hands at the stove, his fingers inches from her own. He looked at her fingernails, the slim taper of her digits, the lines of the bird-like bones beneath the skin. She caught him looking, and he turned his face away. They warmed their hands in silence as they waited for the girl's father, who materialized a few minutes later: a short mustachioed man with a monocle, carrying a doctor's bag.

"Sophie, where are your glasses?" he asked, pulling his mouth into a frown.

The little girl fished a pair of gold-rimmed spectacles from her satchel.

"Please, Madame," he said. "If you can, be sure she wears them."

"I'll try," Madame Morgenstern said, and smiled.

"They fall off when I dance," the girl protested.

"Say goodbye, Sophie," the doctor said. "We'll be late for dinner."

In the doorway, Sophie turned and waved. Then she and her father were gone, and Andras stood alone in the studio with Madame Morgenstern. She stepped away from the stove to gather a few things the children had left behind: a stray glove, a hairpin, a red scarf. She put all the things into a basket which she set beside the piano. *Objets trouvés.*

"I wanted to thank you again," Andras said, when the silence between them had stretched to an intolerable length. It came out more gruffly than he'd intended, and in Hungarian, a low rural growl. He cleared his throat and repeated it in French.

"Please, Andras," she said in Hungarian, laughing. "You wrote such a lovely note. And there was no need to thank me in the first place. I'm certain it wasn't the most pleasant afternoon for you."

He couldn't tell her what the afternoon had been like for him, or what the past week had been like. He saw again in his mind the way she'd smiled and tugged at her sweater when she'd recognized him, that involuntary and self-conscious act. He crushed his cap in his hands, looking at the polished studio floor. There were heavy footsteps on the floor above, Elisabet's, or Mrs. Apfel's.

"Have we put you off for good?" Madame Morgenstern asked. "Can you come again tomorrow? Elisabet will have a friend here for lunch, and maybe we'll go skating in the Bois de Vincennes afterward."

"I don't have skates," he said, almost inaudibly.

"Neither do we," she said. "We always rent them. It's lovely. You'll enjoy it."

It's lovely, you'll enjoy it, as if it were really going to happen. And then he said yes, and it was.

CHAPTER NINE

Bois de Vincennes

THIS TIME, when he went to lunch on the rue de Sévigné, he didn't wear a costume tie and he didn't bring a bushel of wilting flowers; instead he wore an old favorite shirt and brought a bottle of wine and a pear tart from the bakery next door. As before, Mrs. Apfel laid out a feast: a layered egg-and-potato *rakott krumpli*, a tureen of carrot soup, a hash of red cabbage and apples with caraway, a dark peasant loaf, and three kinds of cheese. Madame Morgenstern was in a quiet mood; she seemed grateful for the presence of Elisabet's friend, a stout heavy-browed girl in a brown woolen dress. This was the Marthe with whom Elisabet had gone to the movies the week before. She kept Elisabet talking about goings-on at school: who had made a fool of herself in geography class and who had won a choir solo and who was going to Switzerland to ski during the winter holidays. Every now and then Elisabet threw a glance at Andras, as if she wanted him to take note of the fact that the conversation excluded him. Outside, a light snow had begun to fall. Andras couldn't wait to get out of the house. It was a relief when the pear tart was cut and eaten, when they could put their coats on and go.

At half past two they rode the Métro to the Bois. When they emerged from the station, Elisabet and Marthe hurried ahead, arm in arm, while Madame Morgenstern walked with Andras. She spoke about her students, about the upcoming winter pageant, about the recent cold snap. She was wearing a close-fitting red woolen hat shaped like a bell; the loose ends of her hair curled from its edge, and snowflakes gathered on its crown.

Inside the snowy Bois, between the barren elms and oaks and frosted evergreens, the paths were full of men and women carrying skates. From the lake came the shouts and calls of skaters, the scrape of blades on ice. They came to a break in the trees, and before them lay the frozen lake with its small central islands, its fenced banks crowded with Parisians. On the ice, serious-looking men and women in winter coats moved in a slow sweep around the islands. A warming house with a scalloped glass entryway stood on a shallow rise. According to a sign lettered in red, skates could be rented there for three francs. Elisabet and Marthe led their little group into the warming house and they waited in line at the rental counter. Andras insisted on renting skates for all of them; he tried not to think about what those twelve vanished francs would mean to him in the coming week. On a damp green bench they exchanged their shoes for skates, and soon afterward they were staggering downhill on a rubber path toward the lake.

Andras stepped onto the ice and cut a chain of arcs toward the larger of the two islands, testing the edge and balance of the blades. Tibor had taught him to skate when he was five years old; they had skated every day on the millpond in Konyár, on blades their father had made from scrapwood edged with heavy-gauge wire. As schoolboys in Debrecen they had skated at an outdoor rink on Piac utca, a perfect manmade oval artificially cooled by underground pipes and groomed to a glassine smoothness. Andras was light and nimble on skates, faster than his brothers or his friends. Even now, on these dull rental blades, he felt agile and swift. He cut between the skaters in their dark woolen coats, his jacket fluttering behind him, his cap threatening to fly from his head. If he had paused to notice, he might have seen young men watching him with envy as he sped by; he might have seen the girls' curious glances, the elderly skaters' looks of disapproval. But he was aware only of the pure thrill of flying across the ice, the quick exchange of heat between his blades and the frozen lake. He made a circuit around the larger island, coming up behind the women at top speed, then slipped between Madame Morgenstern and Elisabet so neatly that they both stopped and gasped.

"Do you mind watching where you're going?" Elisabet said in her curt French. "You could hurt someone." She took Marthe's arm and the two of them pushed past him. And Andras was left to skate with Madame Morgenstern through a drifting tulle of snow.

"You're quick on your feet," she said, and gave him a fleeting smile from beneath the bell of her hat.

"Maybe on the ice," Andras said, blushing. "I was never very good at sports."

"You look as if you knew something about dancing, though."

"Only that I'm not very good at that, either."

She laughed and skated ahead of him. In the gray afternoon light, the lake brought to mind the Japanese paintings Andras had seen at the International Exposition; the evergreens spread their dark feathers against a wash of sky, and the hills were like doves huddled together for warmth. Madame Morgenstern moved easily on the ice, her back held straight, her arms rounded, as though this were just another form of ballet. She never stumbled against Andras or leaned on him as they circled the lake; even when she hit a sprig of evergreen and lost her balance, she skipped onto the other blade without a glance at him. But as they cleared the far end of the smaller island a second time, she drifted to his side.

"My brother and I used to skate in Budapest," she said. "We used to go to the Városliget, not far from our house. You know the beautiful lake there, by the Vajdahunyad Castle?"

"Oh, yes." He'd never been able to afford the entry fee while he'd lived in Budapest, but he and Tibor had gone many times to watch the skaters at night. The castle, an amalgam of a thousand years of architectural styles, had been built for a millennial celebration forty years earlier. Romanesque, Gothic, Renaissance, and Baroque elements melted into one another along the length of the building; to walk along that strange façade was to pass through centuries. The castle was lit from below, and there was always music. Now he imagined two children, Madame Morgenstern and her brother—József Hász's father?—casting their own dark shadows across the lighter shadow of the castle.

"Was your brother a good skater?" he asked.

Madame Morgenstern laughed and shook her head. "Neither of us was very good, but we had a good time. Sometimes I would invite my friends to come along. We would link hands and my brother would lead us along like a string of wooden ducks. He was ten years older, and far more patient than I would have been." She pressed her lips together as she skated on, tucking her hands into her sleeves. Andras kept close beside her, catching glimpses of her profile beneath the low brim of her hat.

"I can teach you a waltz, if you'd like," he said.

"Oh, no. I can't do anything fancy."

"It's not fancy," he said, and skated ahead to show her the steps. It was a simple waltz he'd learned in Debrecen as a ten-year-old: three strokes forward, a long arc, and a turn; three strokes backward, another arc, another turn. She repeated the steps, following him as he traced them on the ice. Then he turned to face her. Drawing a breath, he put a hand at her waist. Her arm came around him and her gloved hand found his hand. He hummed a few bars of "Brin de Muguet" and led her into the steps. She hesitated at first, particularly at the turns, but soon she was moving as lightly as he might have imagined, her hand firm against his hand. He knew that Rosen and Polaner and Ben Yakov would have laughed to see him dancing like this in front of everyone, but he didn't care. For a few moments, the length of the song in his head, this light-footed woman in her bell-shaped hat was pressed close against him, her hand closed inside his hand. His mouth brushed the brim of her hat, and he tasted a cold damp veil of snowflakes. He could feel her breath against his neck. She glanced up at him and their eyes caught for an instant before he looked away. He reminded himself that anything he felt for her was hopeless; she was an adult woman with a complicated life, a profession, a daughter in high school. The waltz ended and went silent in his head. He let his arms fall from her body, and she moved away to skate at his side. They skated twice around the island before she spoke again.

"You make me homesick for Hungary," she said. "It's more than sixteen years since I was there. Elisabet's lifetime." She scanned the ice, and Andras followed her gaze. They could see the green and brown of Elisabet's and Marthe's coats far ahead. Elisabet pointed to something on the shore, the black shape of a dog leaping after a smaller, fleeter shape.

"Sometimes I think I might go back," Madame Morgenstern said in a half whisper. "More often, though, I think I never will."

"You will," Andras said, surprised to find his voice steady. He took her arm, and she didn't pull away. Instead she removed a hand from her coat sleeve and let it rest upon his arm. He shivered, though he could no longer feel the cold. They skated that way in silence for the time it took to circle the islet once more. But then a voice reached them from across the ice, resonant and familiar: It was Madame Gérard, calling his name and Madame Morgenstern's. *Andráska. Klárika.* The Hungarian diminutives, as though they were all still in Budapest. Madame Gérard came gliding toward them in a new fur-collared coat and hat, followed by three other actors from the theater. She and Madame Morgenstern embraced, laughed, remarked on the beauty of the snow and the number of people on the frozen lake.

"Klárika, my dear, I'm very glad to see you. And here's Andráska. And that must be Elisabet up ahead." She smiled slyly and gave Andras a wink, then called Elisabet and Marthe back to the group. When they complained of the cold, she invited everyone for hot chocolate at the café. They sat together at a long wooden table and drank chocolate from crockery mugs, and it was easy for Andras to let everyone else talk, to let their conversation join the conversations of other skaters in the crowded warming house. The rising feeling he'd had just before Madame Gérard had arrived had already begun to dissipate; Madame Morgenstern seemed once again impossibly far away.

When they were finished with the chocolate, he retrieved their shoes from the rental desk, and afterward they walked together along the path toward the edge of the Bois. He kept looking for his chance to take Madame Morgenstern's elbow, to let the others go on ahead while the two of them walked behind. Instead it was Marthe who dropped back to walk with Andras. She was purposeful and grim in the deepening cold.

"It's hopeless, you know," she said. "She wants nothing to do with you."

"Who?" Andras said, alarmed to think he'd been so transparent.

"Elisabet! She wants you to stop looking at her all the time. Do you think she likes being looked at by a pathetic Hungarian?"

Andras sighed and glanced up ahead to where Elisabet was now walking with Madame Gérard, her green coat swinging around her legs. She stooped to say something to Madame, who threw her head back and laughed.

"She's not interested in you," Marthe said. "She's already got a boyfriend. So there's no need to come to the house again. And you don't have to waste your time trying to charm her mother."

Andras cleared his throat. "All right," he said. "Well, thank you for telling me."

Marthe gave a businesslike nod. "It's my duty as Elisabet's friend."

And then they had reached the edge of the park, and Madame Morgenstern was beside him again, her sleeve brushing his own. They stood at the entrance to the Métro, the rush of trains echoing below. "Won't you come with us?" she said.

"No, come with us!" Madame Gérard said. "We're taking a cab. We'll drop you at home."

It was cold and growing dark, but Andras couldn't bear the thought of a ride on the crowded Métro with Elisabet and Marthe and Madame Morgenstern. Nor did he want to crowd into a cab with Madame Gérard and the others. He wanted to be alone, to find his way back to his own neighborhood, to lock himself into his room.

"I think I'll walk," he told them.

"But you'll come again for lunch next Sunday," Madame Morgenstern said, looking up at him from under the brim of her hat, her skin still illuminated with the rush of skating. "In fact, we're hoping you'll make a habit of it."

How else could he have replied? "Yes, yes, I'll come," he said.

CHAPTER TEN

Rue de Sévigné

AND SO ANDRAS became a fixture at Sunday lunches on the rue de Sévigné. Quickly they established a pattern: Andras would come and exchange pleasantries with Madame Morgenstern; Elisabet would sit and scowl at Andras, or make fun of his clothes or his accent; when she failed to whip him up as she'd done at the first lunch, she'd grow bored and go out with Marthe, who had cultivated her own towering scorn for Andras. Once Elisabet had gone he would sit with Madame Morgenstern and listen to records on the phonograph, or look at art magazines and picture postcards, or read from a book of poetry to practice his French, or talk about his family, his childhood. At times he tried to bring up the subject of her own past—the brother whom she hadn't seen in years, the shadowy events that had resulted in Elisabet's birth and had brought Madame Morgenstern to Paris. But she always managed to evade that line of conversation, turning his careful questions aside like the hands of unwelcome dance partners. And if he blushed when she sat close beside him, or stammered as he tried to respond after she'd paid him a compliment, she gave no sign that she'd noticed.

Before long he knew the precise shape of her fingernails, the cut and fabric of every one of her winter dresses, the pattern of lace at the edges of her pocket handkerchiefs. He knew that she liked pepper on her eggs, that she couldn't tolerate milk, that the heel of the bread was her favorite part. He knew she'd been to Brussels and to Florence (though not with whom); he knew that the bones of her right foot ached when the weather was wet. Her moods were changeable, but she tempered the darker ones by making jokes at her own expense, and playing silly American tunes on the phonograph, and showing Andras droll photos of her youngest students in their dance exhibition costumes. He knew that her favorite ballet was *Apollo*, and that her least favorite was *La Sylphide*, because it was overdanced and so rarely done with originality. He considered himself shamefully ignorant on the subject of dance, but Madame Morgenstern seemed not to care; she would play ballets on the phonograph and describe what would be happening onstage as the music crested and ebbed, and sometimes she rolled up the sitting-room rug and reproduced the choreography for him in miniature, her skin flushing with pleasure as she danced. In return he would take her on walks around the Marais, narrating the architectural history of the buildings among which she made her life: the sixteenth-century Hôtel Carnavalet, with its bas-reliefs of the Four Seasons; the Hôtel Amelot de Bisseuil, whose great medusa-headed carriage doors had once opened regularly for Beaumarchais; the Guimard Synagogue on the rue Pavée, with its undulating façade like an open Torah scroll. She wondered aloud how she'd never taken note of those things before. He had pulled away a veil for her, she said, revealed a dimension of her quartier that she would never have discovered otherwise.

Despite the reassurance of the standing invitation, he lived in the fear that one Sunday he'd arrive at Madame Morgenstern's to find another man at the table, some mustachioed captain or tweed-vested doctor or talented Muscovite choreographer— some cultivated forty-year-old with a cultural fluency that Andras could never match, and a knowledge of the things that gentlemen were supposed to know: wines, music, ways to make a woman laugh. But the terrifying rival never appeared, at least not on Sunday afternoons; that fraction of the Morgenstern week seemed to belong to Andras alone.

Outside the household on the rue de Sévigné, life went on as usual—or what had come to seem usual, within the context of his life as a student of architecture in Paris. His model progressed toward completion, its walls already cut from the stiff white pasteboard and ready for assembly. Despite the fact that it was now as large as an overcoat box, he'd begun carrying the model to and from school each day. This was due to a recent spate of vandalism, directed only, it seemed, at the Jewish students of the École Spéciale. A third-year student named Jean Isenberg had had a set of elaborate blueprints flooded with ink; a fourth-year, Anne-Laure Bauer, had been robbed of her expensive statics textbooks the week before an exam. Andras and his friends had so far escaped unscathed, but Rosen believed it was only a matter of time before one of them became a target. The professors called a general assembly and spoke sternly to the students, promising severe consequences for the perpetrators and imploring anyone with evidence to come forth, but no one volunteered any information. At the Blue Dove, Rosen advanced his own theory. Several students were known to belong to the Front de la Jeunesse and a group called Le Grand Occident, whose professed nationalism was a thin cover for anti-Semitism.

"That weasel Lemarque is a Jeunesse stooge," Rosen said over his almond biscuits and coffee. "I'd bet he's behind this."

"It can't be Lemarque," Polaner said.

"Why not?"

Polaner flushed slightly, folding his slim white hands in his lap. "He helped me with a project."

"He did, did he?" Rosen said. "Well, I think you'd better watch your back. That little *salopard* would just as soon slit your throat as bid you bonjour."

"You won't make friends by setting yourself against everyone," said the politic Ben Yakov, whose chief preoccupation seemed to be to get as many people as possible to admire him, both male and female.

"Who cares?" said Rosen. "This isn't a tea party we're talking about."

Andras quietly agreed with Rosen. He'd had his misgivings about Lemarque ever since the ambiguous incident with Polaner at the beginning of the year. He'd watched Lemarque after that, and had found it impossible to ignore the way Lemarque looked at Polaner, as if there were something compelling and repellent about him at once, or as if his disgust with Polaner gave him a kind of pleasure. Lemarque had a way of sidling up to Polaner, of finding excuses to talk to him in class: Could he borrow Polaner's pantograph? Could he see Polaner's solution to this difficult statics problem? Was this Polaner's scarf that he'd found in the courtyard? Polaner seemed unwilling to consider that Lemarque could have anything but friendly motives. But Andras didn't trust Lemarque, nor the slit-eyed students who sat with him at the student cantina, smoking a German brand of cigarettes and wearing buttoned-up shirts and surplus military jackets, as if they wanted to be ready to fight if called upon. Unlike the other students, they kept their hair clipped close and their boots polished. Andras had heard some people refer to them disparagingly as *la garde*. And then there were the ones who wore subtler signs of their politics: the ones who seemed to look directly through Andras and Rosen and Polaner and Ben Yakov, though they passed each other in the halls or in the courtyard every day.

"What we need to do is infiltrate those groups," Rosen said. "The Front de la Jeunesse. The Grand Occident. Go to their meetings, learn what they're planning."

"That's brilliant," Ben Yakov said. "They'll find us out and break our necks."

"What do you think they're planning, anyway?" Polaner said, beginning to grow angry. "It's not as though they're going to mount a pogrom in Paris."

"Why not?" Rosen said. "Do you think they haven't considered it?"

"Can we talk about something else, please?" Ben Yakov said.

Rosen pushed his coffee cup away. "Oh, yes," he said. "Why don't you tell us about your latest conquest? What could possibly be more important or more urgent?"

Ben Yakov laughed off Rosen's slight, which infuriated Rosen all the more. He stood and threw money on the table, then slung his coat over his shoulder and made for the exit. Andras grabbed his own hat and followed; he hated to see a friend leave in anger. He caught up with Rosen on the corner of Saint-Germain and Saint-Jacques, and they stood together on the corner and waited for the light to change.

"You don't think I'm speaking nonsense, do you?" Rosen said, his hands deep in his pockets, his eyes fixed on Andras.

"No," Andras began, trying to find the words in French for what he wanted to say. "You're just trying to think a few chess moves ahead."

"Oh," said Rosen, brightening. "Are you a chess player?"

"My brothers and I used to play. I wasn't very good. My older brother mastered a book of defenses by a Russian champion. I couldn't do a thing against him."

"Couldn't you read the book yourself?" Rosen said, and grinned.

"Maybe if he hadn't hidden it so well!"

"I suppose that's all I'm doing, then. Trying to find the book."

"You won't have to look very hard," Andras said. "There are posters for those Front de la Jeunesse meetings all over the Latin Quarter."

They had reached the Petit Pont at the foot of rue Saint-Jacques, and they crossed it together in the twilight. The towers of Notre-Dame caught the last rays of the setting sun as they entered the Place du Parvis Notre Dame and walked toward the cathedral. They stopped to look at the grim saints who flanked the portals, one of whom held his own severed head in his hand.

"Do you know what I want to do when I grow up?" Rosen said.

"No," Andras said. "What?"

"Move to Palestine. Build a temple of Jerusalem stone." He paused and looked at Andras as if daring him to laugh, but Andras wasn't laughing. He was thinking of some photographs of Jerusalem that had been printed in *Past and Future*. The buildings had a kind of geologic permanence, as if they hadn't been made by human hands at all. Even in the black-and-white photos their stones seemed to radiate gold light.

"I want to make a city in the desert," Rosen said. "A new city where an old one used to be. In the shape of the ancient city, but composed of all-new buildings. Perret's reinforced concrete is perfect for Palestine. Cheap and light, cool in the heat, ready to take on any shape." He seemed to be seeing it in the distance as he spoke, a city in the rippling dunes.

"So you're a dreamer," Andras said. "I never would have guessed."

Rosen smirked and said, "Don't let the others know." They looked up again at the tops of the towers as the line of gold narrowed to a filament. "You'll do it, won't you?" he said. "Come to one of these Jeunesse meetings? Then we'll see what they're plotting."

Andras hesitated. He tried to imagine what Madame Morgenstern might think of an act like that, an infiltration. He envisioned narrating it to her on one of their Sunday afternoons: his daring, his bravery. His foolishness? "And what if someone does recognize us?" he said.

"They won't," Rosen said. "They won't be looking for us among them."

"When do they meet?"

"That's my good man, Lévi," Rosen said.

They decided to infiltrate a recruitment session for Le Grand Occident, reasoning that the meeting would be full of unfamiliar faces. It was to take place that Saturday at an assembly hall on rue de l'Université in Saint-Germain. But first there were the end-of-term critiques to get through. Andras had finished his Gare d'Orsay at last, staying up two nights straight to do it; on Friday morning it stood white and inviolate on its pasteboard base. He knew it was good work, the product of long study, of many hours of painstaking measurement and construction. Rosen and Ben Yakov and Polaner had put in their time, too, and there on the studio tables stood their ghost-white versions of the École Militaire, the Rotonde de la Villette, and the Théâtre de l'Odeon. They were to be evaluated in turn by their peers, by their second- and third- and fourth-year superiors, by their fifth-year studio monitor, Médard, and finally by Vago himself. Andras thought himself seasoned by the relentless friendly criticism of his editor at *Past and Future;* he'd had some critiques earlier that fall, none of them as bad as what his editor had regularly delivered.

But when the critique of his d'Orsay began, the commentary took a savage turn almost at once. His lines were imprecise, his methods of construction amateurish; he had made no attempt whatever to replicate the building's front expanse of glass or to capture what was most striking about the design—the way the Seine, which flowed in front of the station, threw light against its high reflective façade. He'd made a dead model, one fourth-year student said. A shoebox. A coffin. Even Vago, who knew better than anyone how hard Andras had worked, criticized the model's lifelessness. In his paint-flecked work shirt and an incongruously fine vest, he stood over the model and gazed at it with undisguised disappointment. He drew a mechanical pencil from his pocket and tapped its metal end against his lip.

"A dutiful reproduction," he said. "Like a Chopin polonaise played at a student recital. You've hit all the notes, to be sure, but you've done so entirely without artistry."

And that was all. He turned away and moved on to the next model, and Andras fell into an oubliette of humiliation and misery. Vago was right: He had replicated the building without inspiration; how had he ever seen the model otherwise? It was little consolation that the other first-year students fared just as badly. He couldn't believe how confident he'd been half an hour earlier, how certain that everyone in the room would proclaim his work evidence of what a fine architect he would turn out to be.

He knew that the school had a tradition of difficult end-of-term critiques, that few first-year students survived with pride intact. It was the school's version of an initiation ritual, an annealing that prepared the students for the deeper and more subtle humiliations that would occur when the work under discussion was of their own design. But this critique had been much harsher than he'd imagined—and, what was worse, the comments had seemed justified. He'd worked as hard as he could and it hadn't been enough, not nearly, not by miles. And his humiliation was linked, in a way he found it impossible to articulate, to the idea of Madame Morgenstern and his relation to her—as though by building a fine replica of the Gare d'Orsay he might have had greater claim upon her affections. Now he couldn't give her an honest account of the day's events without revealing himself to be a prideful fool. He left the École Spéciale in a vile mood, a mood tenacious enough to stay with him through the night and the next morning; it was still with him when he went to meet Rosen for their infiltration.

The meeting hall was just around the corner from the palatial Beaux-Arts, a few blocks east of the Gare d'Orsay. Andras didn't ever want to see that building again. He knew that the critiques he'd received had been accurate; in his zeal to replicate each detail of the building he had failed to grasp its whole, to understand what made the design distinct and alive. This was a classic first-year mistake, Vago had told him on his way out. But if that were the case, why hadn't Vago cautioned him against it when he'd started? Rosen, too, now claimed a towering hatred for the subject of his model, the École Militaire. They scowled at the sidewalk in companionate symmetry as they made their way down the rue de l'Université.

Since the meeting they were attending was just a recruitment session, there was no need for secrecy or disguise; they arrived with the rest of the attendees, most of whom looked to be students. At a lectern on a low stage at the front of the room, a whip-thin man in an ill-fitting gray suit declared himself to be Monsieur Dupuis, "Secretary to President Pemjean himself," and clapped his hands for order. The gathering fell silent. Volunteers walked along the aisles, handing out special supplementary sections of a newspaper entitled *Le Grand Occident*. The Secretary to President Pemjean Himself announced that this supplement set forth the beliefs of the organization, which the governing members would now read aloud to the assembly. A half-dozen grim-looking young fellows gathered on the stage, their copies of the supplement in hand. One by one they read that Jews must be removed from positions of influence in France, and that they should cease to exercise authority over Frenchmen; that Jewish organizations in France must be dissolved, because, while masquerading shamelessly as Jewish welfare agencies, they were working to achieve global domination; that the rights of French citizenship must be taken away from all Jews, who must henceforth be regarded as foreigners—even those whose families had been settled in France for generations; and that all Jewish goods and belongings should become the property of the state.

As each of the tenets was read, there were brief cracklings of applause. Some of the assembled men shouted their approval, and others raised their fists. Still others seemed to disagree, and a few began to argue with the supporters.

"What about the Jews whose brothers or fathers died for France in the Great War?" someone shouted from the balcony.

"Those Zionists died for their own glory, not for the glory of France," the Secretary to the President Himself called back. "Israelites can't be trusted to serve France. They must be forbidden to bear arms."

"Why not let *them* die, if someone has to die?" another man called.

Rosen curled his hands around the back of the seat in front of him, his knuckles going white. Andras didn't know what he would do if Rosen started shouting.

"You're here because you believe in the need for a pure France, for the France our fathers and grandfathers built," the Secretary to the President continued. "You're here to lend your strength to the cleansing of France. If you're not here for that purpose, please depart. We need only the most patriotic, the most true-hearted among you." The Secretary waited. There was a quiet rumble among the assembly. One of the six young men who had read the tenets shouted, *"Vive la France!"*

"You will become part of an international alliance—" the Secretary began, but his words disappeared under a sudden staccato din, a wooden clapclacking that rendered his words unintelligible. Then, just as abruptly as it had begun, the noise ceased. The Secretary cleared his throat, straightened his lapels, and began again. "You will become part—"

This time the noise was even louder than before. It came from every part of the hall. Certain members of the audience had gotten to their feet and were spinning wooden noisemakers on sticks. As before, after a few moments of loud hard clatter, they stopped.

"I welcome your enthusiasm, gentlemen," the Secretary continued. "But, if you please, wait until—"

The noise exploded again, and this time it did not cease. The men with noisemakers—there were perhaps twenty or thirty of them among the assembly—pushed into the aisles and spun their instruments as hard and as loud as they could. These were Purim noisemakers, Andras saw now—the wooden graggers used at synagogue during the reading of the story of Esther, whenever the villain Haman's name occurred in the text. He glanced at Rosen, who had understood, too. The Secretary banged on his lectern. The six grim-faced men onstage stood at attention, as if awaiting an order from the Secretary. More men pushed out of the rows and into the aisles, bearing large banners that they unrolled and held high so the audience could see them. *Ligue*

Internationale Contre l'Antisemitisme, read one. *Stop the French Hitlerians,* said another. *Liberté, Egalité, Fraternité,* read a third. The men holding the banners sent up a cheer, and an angry roar burst from the audience. The thin Secretary to the President flushed a surprising purple. Rosen let out a whoop and pulled Andras into the aisle, and the two of them helped to hoist one of the banners. One member of the Ligue, a tall broad-shouldered man in a tricolor neckerchief, produced a megaphone and began to shout, "Free men of France! Don't let these bigots poison your minds!"

The Secretary growled an order at the six stern-faced young men, and in another moment all was chaos in the assembly hall. The seats emptied. Some audience members pulled at the banners, others pursued the men with the noisemakers. The six men who had read the beliefs of the organization went after the man with the megaphone, but other men defended him in a ring as he continued to urge *Fraternité! Egalité!* The Secretary disappeared behind a curtain at the back of the stage. Men shoved Andras from behind, kicked at his knees, elbowed him in the chest. Andras wouldn't let go of the banner. He raised the pole high and shouted *Stop the French Hitlerians.* Rosen was no longer at his side; Andras couldn't see him in the crowd. Someone tried to take the banner and Andras wrestled with the man; someone else grabbed him by the collar, and a blow caught him across the jaw. He stumbled against a column, spat blood onto the floor. All around him, men shouted and fought. He shoved his way toward an exit, feeling his teeth with his tongue and wondering if he'd have to see a dentist. In the vestibule he found Rosen grappling with a massive bald man in work overalls. As though he meant to fight Rosen himself, Andras caught him around the waist and wrenched him away, sending Rosen shoulder-first into a wall. The man in overalls, finding his arms empty, charged back into the fray of the auditorium. Andras and Rosen staggered out of the building, past streams of policemen who were rushing up the steps to break up the riot. When they'd gotten clear of the crowd, they tore down the rue de Solférino, all the way to the quai d'Orsay, where they cast themselves down on a pair of benches and lay panting.

"So we weren't the only ones!" Rosen said, touching his ribs with his fingertips. Andras felt the inside of his lip with his tongue. His cheek still bled where his teeth had cut it, but the teeth were intact. At the sound of quick footsteps he looked up to see three members of the Ligue running down the street, their banners flapping. Other men chased them. Policemen chased the others.

"I'd love to see the look on that secretary's face again," Rosen said.

"You mean the Secretary to the President Himself?"

Rosen put his hands on his knees and laughed. But then an ambulance rushed down the street in the direction of the assembly hall, and a few moments later another followed. Not long afterward, more Ligue members passed; these looked pale and stricken, and they dragged their banners on the sidewalk and held their hats in their hands. Andras and Rosen watched them in silence. Something grave had happened: Someone from the Ligue had been hurt. Andras took off his own hat and held it on his lap, his adrenaline dissolving into hollow dread. Le Grand Occident wasn't the only group of its kind; there had to be dozens of similar meetings taking place all over Paris that very minute. And if meetings like that were taking place in Paris, then what was going on in the less enlightened cities of Europe? Andras pulled his jacket tighter around himself, beginning to feel the cold again. Rosen got to his feet; he, too, had become quiet and serious.

"Far worse things are going to happen here," he said. "Wait and see."

On the rue de Sévigné the next day, Madame Morgenstern and Elisabet sat in silence as Andras described the incidents of the past forty-eight hours. He told them about the critique, and how far his work had fallen in his own estimation; he told them what had happened at the meeting. He produced a clipping from that morning's *L'Oeuvre* and read it aloud. The article described the disrupted recruitment session and the melee that followed. Each group blamed the other for initiating the violence: Pemjean took the opportunity to point out the deviousness and belligerence of the Jewish people, and Gérard Lecache, president of the Ligue Internationale Contre l'Antisemitisme, called the incident a manifestation of Le Grand Occident's violent intent. The newspaper abandoned all pretense of journalistic objectivity to praise the Maccabean bravery of the Ligue, and to accuse Le Grand Occident of bigotry, ignorance, and barbarism; two members of the Ligue, it turned out, had been beaten senseless and were now hospitalized at the Hôtel-Dieu.

"You might have been killed!" Elisabet said. Her tone was acidic as usual, but for an instant she gave him a look of what seemed like genuine concern. "What were you thinking? Did you imagine you'd take on all those brutes at once? Thirty of you against two hundred of them?"

"We weren't part of the plan," Andras said. "We didn't know the LICA was going to be there. When they started making noise, we joined in."

"Ridiculous fools, all of you," Elisabet said.

Madame Morgenstern fixed her gray eyes upon Andras. "Take care you don't get in trouble with the police," she said. "Remember, you're a guest in France. You don't want to be deported because of an incident like this."

"They wouldn't deport me," Andras said. "Not for serving the ideals of France."

"They certainly would," Madame Morgenstern said. "And that would be the end of your studies. Whatever you do, you must protect your status here. Your presence in France is a political statement to begin with."

"He'll never last here, anyway," Elisabet said, the moment of concern having passed. "He'll fail out of school by the end of the year. His professors think he's talentless. Weren't you listening?" She peeled herself from the velvet chair and slouched off to her bedroom, where they could hear her knocking around as she got ready to go out. A few moments later she emerged in an olive-green dress and a black wool cap. She'd braided her hair and scrubbed her cheeks into a windy redness. Pocketbook in one hand, gloves in the other, she stood in the sitting-room doorway and gave a half wave.

"Don't wait up for me," she told her mother. Then, as an apparent afterthought, she arrowed a look of disdain in Andras's direction. "There's no need to come next weekend, Champion of France," she said. "I'll be skiing with Marthe in Chamonix. In fact, I wish you'd desist altogether." She slung her bag over her shoulder and ran down the stairs, and they heard the door slam and jingle behind her.

Madame Morgenstern lowered her forehead into her hand. "How much longer will she be like this, do you think? You weren't like this when you were sixteen, were you?"

"Worse," Andras said, and smiled. "But I didn't live at home, so my mother was spared."

"I've threatened to send her to boarding school, but she knows I don't have the heart. Nor the money, for that matter."

"Well," he said. "Chamonix. How long will she be there?"

"Ten days," she said. "The longest she's been gone from home."

"Then I suppose it'll be January before I see you again," Andras said. He heard himself say it aloud—*maga*, the singular Hungarian *you*—but by that time it was too late, and in any case Madame Morgenstern hadn't seemed to notice the slip. With the excuse that it was time for him to go to work, he got up to take his coat and hat from the rack at the top of the stairs. But she stopped him with a hand on his sleeve.

"You're forgetting the Spectacle d'Hiver," she said. "You'll come, won't you?"

Her students' winter recital. He knew it was next week, of course. It was to take place at the Sarah-Bernhardt on Thursday evening; he was the one who had designed the posters. But he hadn't expected to have any excuse to attend. He wasn't scheduled to work that night, since *The Mother* would already have closed for the holidays. Now Madame Morgenstern was looking at him in quiet anticipation, her hand burning through the fabric of his coat. His mouth was a desert, his hands glacial with sweat. He told himself that the invitation meant nothing, that it fell perfectly within the bounds of their acquaintance: as a friend of the family, as a possible suitor of Elisabet, he might well be asked to come. He mustered a response in the affirmative, saying he'd be honored, and they executed their weekly parting ritual: the coat-rack, his things, the stairs, a chaste goodbye. But at the threshold she held his gaze a moment longer than usual. Her eyebrows came together, and she held her mouth in its pensive pose. Just as she seemed about to speak, a pair of red-jacketed schoolgirls ran down the sidewalk chasing a little white dog, and they had to move apart, and the moment passed. She raised a hand in farewell and stepped inside, closing the door behind her.

CHAPTER ELEVEN

Winter Holiday

THAT YEAR, in her studio on the rue de Sévigné, Claire Morgenstern had taught some ninety-five girls between the ages of eight and fourteen, three of the oldest of whom would soon depart for professional training with the Ballet Russe de Monte Carlo. She had been preparing the children for the Spectacle d'Hiver for two months now; the costumes were ready, the young dancers schooled in the ways of snowflakes, sugarplums, and swans, the winter-garden scenery in readiness. That week Andras's advertising poster appeared all over town: a snowflake child in silhouette against a starry winter sky, one leg extended in an arabesque, the words *Spectacle d'Hiver* trailing the upraised right hand like a comet tail. Every time he saw it—on the way to school, on the wall opposite the Blue Dove, at the bakery—he heard Madame Morgenstern saying *You'll come, won't you?*

By Wednesday, the evening of the dress rehearsal, he felt he couldn't wait another day to see her. He arrived at the Sarah-Bernhardt at his usual hour, carrying a large plum cake for the coffee table. The corridors backstage were thronged with girls in white and silver tulle; they surged around him, blizzardlike, as he slipped into the backstage corner where the coffee table was arranged. With his pocketknife he cut the plum cake into a raft of little pieces. A group of girls in snowflake costumes clustered at the edges of the curtain, waiting for their entrance. As they tiptoed in place, they cast interested glances at the coffee table and the cake. Andras could hear a stage manager calling for the next group of dancers. Madame Morgenstern—Klara, as Madame Gérard called her—was nowhere to be seen.

He watched from the wings as the little girls danced their snowflake dance. The girl whose father had come late was among that group of children; when she ran back into the wings after her dance, she called to Andras and showed him that she had a new pair of glasses, this one with flexible wire arms that curled around the backs of her ears. They wouldn't fall off while she danced, she explained. As she kicked into a pirouette to demonstrate, he heard Madame Morgenstern's laugh behind him.

"Ah," she said. "The new glasses."

Andras allowed himself a swift look at her. She was dressed in practice clothes, her dark hair twisted close against her head. "Ingenious," he said, trying to keep his voice steady. "They don't come off at all."

"They come off when I *want* them to," the girl said. "I take them off *at night*."

"Of course," Andras said. "I didn't mean to suggest you wore them *always*."

The girl rolled her eyes at Madame Morgenstern and raced to the coffee table, where the other snowflakes were devouring the plum cake.

"This is a surprise," Madame Morgenstern said. "I didn't expect to see you until tomorrow."

"I have a job here, in case you've forgotten," Andras said, and crossed his arms. "I'm responsible for the comfort and happiness of the performers."

"That cake is your doing, I suppose?"

"The girls don't seem to object."

"I object. I don't allow sweets backstage." But she gave him a wink, and went to the table to take a piece of plum cake herself. The cake was dense and golden, its top studded with halved mirabelles. "Oh," she said. "This is good. You shouldn't have. Take some for yourself, at least."

"I'm afraid it wouldn't be professional."

Madame Morgenstern laughed. "You've caught me at a rather busy time, I'm afraid. I've got to get the next group of girls onstage." She brushed a snow of gold crumbs from her hands, and he found himself imagining the taste of plum on her fingers.

"I'm sorry I disturbed you," he said. He was ready to say *I'll be off now*, ready to leave her to the rehearsal, but then he thought of his empty room, and the long hours that lay between that night and the next, and the blank expanse of time that stretched into the future beyond Thursday—time when he'd have no excuse to see her. He raised his eyes to hers. "Have a drink with me tonight," he said.

She gave a little jolt. "Oh, no," she whispered. "I can't."

"Please, Klara," he said. "I can't bear it if you say no."

She rubbed the tops of her arms as if she'd gotten a chill. "Andras—"

He mentioned a café, named a time. And before she could say no again, he turned and went down the backstage hallway and out into the white December evening.

The Café Bédouin was a dark place, its leather upholstery cracked, its blue velvet draperies lavendered with age. Behind the bar stood rows of dusty cut-glass bottles, relics of an earlier age of drinking. Andras arrived there an hour before the time he'd mentioned, already sick with impatience, disbelieving what he'd done. Had he really asked her to have a drink with him? Called her by her first name, in its intimate-seeming Hungarian form? Spoken to her as though his feelings might be acceptable, might even be returned? What did he expect would happen now? If she came, it would only be to confirm that he'd acted inappropriately, and perhaps to tell him she could no longer admit him to her house on Sunday afternoons. At the same time he was certain she'd known his feelings for weeks now, must have known since the day they'd gone skating in the Bois de Vincennes. It was time for them to be honest with each other; perhaps it was time for him to confess that he'd carried her mother's letter from Hungary. He stared at the door as if to will it off its hinges. Each time a woman entered he leapt from his chair. He shook his father's pocket watch to make sure nothing was loose, wound it again to make sure it was keeping time. Half an hour passed, then another. She was late. He looked into his empty whiskey glass and wondered how long he could sit in this bar without having to order a second drink. The waiters drifted by, throwing solicitous glances in his direction. He ordered another whiskey and drank it, hunched over his glass. He had never felt more desperate or more absurd. Then, finally, the door opened again and she was before him in her red hat and her close-fitting gray coat, out of breath, as if she'd run all the way from the theater. He leapt from his chair.

"I was afraid I'd miss you," she said, and gave a sigh of relief. She took off her hat and slid onto the banquette across from him. She wore a snug gabardine jacket, closed at the collar with a neat silver pin in the shape of a harp.

"You're late," Andras said, feeling the whiskey in his head like a swarm of bees.

"The rehearsal finished ten minutes ago! You ran out before I could tell you what time I could come."

"I was afraid you'd say you wouldn't see me at all."

"You're quite right. I shouldn't be here."

"Why did you come, then?" He reached across the table for her hand. Her fingers were freezing cold, but she wouldn't let him warm them. She slid her hand away, blushing into the collar of her jacket.

The waiter arrived to ask for their orders, hopeful that the young man would spend more money now that his friend had arrived. "I've been drinking whiskey," he said. "Have a whiskey with me. It's the drink of American movie stars."

"I'm not in the mood," she said. Instead she ordered a Brunelle and a glass of water. "I can't stay," she said, once the waiter had gone. "One drink, and then I'll go."

"I have something to tell you," Andras said. "That's why I wanted you to come."

"What is it?" she said.

"In Budapest, before I left, I met a woman named Elza Hász."

Madame Morgenstern's face drained of color. "Yes?" she said.

"I went to her house on Benczúr utca. She'd seen me exchanging pengő for francs at the bank, and wanted to send a box to her son in Paris. There was another woman there, an older woman, who asked me to carry something else. A letter to a certain C. Morgenstern on the rue de Sévigné. About whom I must not inquire."

Madame Morgenstern had gone so pale that Andras thought she might faint. When the waiter arrived a moment later with their drinks, she took up her Brunelle and emptied half the glass.

"I think you're Klara Hász," he said, lowering his voice. "Or you were. And the woman I met was your mother."

Her mouth trembled, and she glanced toward the door. For a moment she looked as if she might flee. Then she sank back into her seat, a tense stillness coming over her body. "All right," she said. "Tell me what you know, and what you want." Her voice had thinned to a whisper; she sounded, more than anything, afraid.

"I don't know anything," he said, reaching for her hand again. "I don't want anything. I just wanted to tell you what happened. What a strange coincidence it was. And I wanted you to know I'd met your mother. I know you haven't seen her in years."

"And you carried a box for my nephew József?" she said. "Have you spoken to him about this? About me?"

"No, not a word."

"Thank God," she said. "You can't, do you understand?"

"No," he said. "I don't understand. I don't know what any of this means. Your mother begged me not to speak to anyone about that letter, and I haven't. No one knows. Or almost no one—I did show it to my brother when I came home from your mother's house. He thought it must be a love letter."

Klara gave a sad laugh. "A love letter! I suppose it was, in a way."

"I wish you'd tell me what this is all about."

"It's a private matter. I'm sorry you had to be involved. I can't make direct contact with my family in Budapest, and they can't send anything directly to me. József can't know I'm here. You're certain you haven't told him anything?"

"Nothing at all," Andras said. "Your mother mentioned that specifically."

"I'm sorry to make such a drama of it. But it's very important that you understand. Some terrible things happened in Budapest when I was a girl. I'm safe now, but only as long as no one knows I'm here, or who I was before I came here."

Andras repeated his vow. If his silence would protect her, he would keep silent. If she had asked him to sign his pledge in blood upon the gray marble of the café table, he would have taken a knife to his hand and done it. Instead she finished her drink, not speaking, not meeting his eyes. He watched the silver harp tremble at her throat.

"What did my mother look like?" she asked finally. "Has her hair gone gray?"

"It's shot with gray," Andras said. "She wore a black dress. She's a tiny person, like you." He told her a few things about the visit—what the house had looked like, what her sister-in-law had said. He didn't tell her about her mother's grief, about the expression of entrenched mourning he had remembered all this time; what good could it have done? But he told her a few things about József Hász—how he'd given Andras a place to stay when he'd first come to town, and had advised him about life in the Latin Quarter.

"And what about György?" she asked. "József's father?"

"Your brother."

"That's right," she said, quietly. "Did you see him, too?"

"No," Andras said. "I was there only for an hour or so, in the middle of the day. He must have been at work. From the look of the house, though, I'd say he's doing fine."

Klara put a hand to her temple. "It's rather difficult to take this in. I think this is enough for now," she said, and then, "I think I'd better go." But when she stood to put on her coat, she swayed and caught the edge of the table with her hand.

"You haven't eaten, have you?" Andras said.

"I need to be someplace quiet."

"There's a restaurant—"

"Not a restaurant."

"I live a few blocks from here. Come have a cup of tea. Then I'll take you home."

And so they went to his garret, climbing the bare wooden stairs to the top of 34 rue des Écoles, all the way to his drafty and barren room. He offered her the desk chair, but she didn't want to sit. She stood at the window and looked down into the street, at the Collège de France across the way, where the clochards always sat on the steps at night, even in the coldest weather. One of them was playing a harmonica; the music made Andras think of the vast open grasslands he'd seen in American movies at the tiny cinema in Konyár. As Klara listened, he lit a fire in the grate, toasted a few slices of bread, and heated water for tea. He had only one glass—the jam jar he'd been using ever since his first morning at the apartment. But he had some sugar cubes, pilfered from the bowl at the Blue Dove. He handed the glass to Klara and she stirred sugar into her tea with his one spoon. He wished she would speak, wished she would reveal the terrible secret of her past, whatever it was. He couldn't guess the details of her story, though he suspected it must have had something to do with Elisabet: an accidental pregnancy, a jealous lover, angry relatives, some unspeakable shame.

A draft came through the ill-fitting casement, and Klara shivered. She handed him the glass of tea. "You have some too," she said. "Before it gets cold."

His throat closed with a spasm of emotion. For the first time, she'd addressed him with the familiar *te* instead of the formal *maga*. "No," he said. "I made it for you." For you: *te*. He offered it to her again, and she closed her hands around his own. The tea trembled between them in its glass. She took it and set it down on the windowsill. Then she moved toward him, put her arms around his waist, tucked her dark head under his chin. He raised a hand to stroke her back, disbelieving his luck, worrying that this closeness was ill-gotten, the product of his revelation and her stirred emotions. But as she shivered against him he forgot to care what had brought them to that moment. He let his hand move along the curve of her back, allowed himself to trace the architecture of her spine. She was so close he could feel the jolt of her ribcage as she pulled a sharp breath; an instant later she moved away from him, shaking her head.

He lifted his hands, surrendering. But she was already retrieving her coat from the rack, winding her scarf around her neck, putting on the red bell-shaped hat.

"I'm sorry," she said. "I have to go. I'm sorry."

At seven o'clock the next evening he went to see the Spectacle d'Hiver. The Sarah-Bernhardt was filled with the families of the dancers, an anxious chattering crowd. The parents had all brought ribboned cones of roses for their daughters. The aisles were draped with fir garland, and the theater smelled of rose and pine. The scent seemed to wake him from the haze in which he'd lived since the previous night. She was backstage; in two hours' time he would see her.

Violins began to play in the orchestra pit, and the curtain rose to reveal six girls dressed in white leotards and jagged points of tulle. They seemed to levitate above the silvered floorboards, their movements dreamlike and precise. It was the way *she* moved, he thought. She had distilled her sharpness, her fluidity, into these little girls, into the forming vessels of their bodies. He felt as if he were caught in a strange dream; something seemed to have broken in him the night before. He had no idea how to behave in a situation like this. Nothing in his life had prepared him for it. Nor could he imagine what she might have been thinking—what she must think of him now, after he'd touched her that way. He would have liked to run backstage that moment and get it over with, whatever was going to happen.

But at intermission, when he might really have gone back-stage, he was hit by a wave of panic so deep and cold he could hardly breathe. He went downstairs to the men's washroom, where he locked himself into a stall and tried to slow his racing pulse. He leaned his forehead against the cool marble of the wall. The voices of men all around him had a soothing effect; they were fathers, they sounded like fathers. He could almost imagine that when he came out, his own father would be wait-ing. Lucky Béla, though sparing with words of advice, would tell him what to do. But when he came out, no one he knew was waiting; he was alone in Paris, and Klara was upstairs.

The lights flickered to signal the end of the intermission. He went up and took his seat again just as the house fell into dark-ness. A few rustling moments, and then blue lights glowed from the lighting bar beneath the catwalk; a high cold string of wood-wind notes climbed from the orchestra pit, and the snowflakes drifted out to begin their dance. He knew Klara was standing just behind the stage-left curtain. She was the one who had sig-naled the musicians to begin. The girls danced perfectly, and were replaced by taller girls, and after that taller girls still, as if the same girls were growing older backstage during the moments when the lights dimmed. But at the end of the show they all came onstage to bow, and they called out for their teacher.

She came out in a simple black dress, an orange-red dahlia

pinned behind her ear, like a girl in a Mucha painting. First she made her révérence to the young dancers, then to the audience. She acknowledged the musicians and the conductor. Then she disappeared into the wings again, allowing the girls to reap the glory of their curtain calls.

Andras sensed the return of his panic, heard its millipedal footsteps drawing closer. Before it could take him again he slid out of his row and ran backstage, where Klara was surrounded by a mass of rouged, tulle-skirted girls. He couldn't get anywhere near her. But she seemed to be looking for him, or for someone in particular; she let her gaze drift over the heads of the little girls and move toward the darker edges of the wings. Her eyes flickered past him and returned for an instant. He couldn't tell if her smile had darkened just at that moment, or if he had imagined it. In any case, she'd seen him. He took off his hat and stood twisting its brim until the crowd around her began to subside. As the parents rushed backstage to bestow bouquets on their children, he cursed himself for failing to bring flowers. He saw that many of the parents had brought roses for her as well as for their daughters. She would have a cartload of bouquets to bring home, none of them from him. The father of the bespectacled little Sophie had brought a particularly large sheaf of flowers for Madame—red roses, Andras noted. He saw her cordially refuse countless invitations to celebratory post-performance dinners; she claimed she was exhausted and must have her rest. It was nearly an hour before the little girls had all gone home with their families, leaving Klara and Andras alone backstage. He had twisted his hat entirely out of shape by then. Her arms were full of flowers; he couldn't embrace her or even take her hand.

"You didn't have to wait," she said, giving him a half-reproachful smile.

"You've got a lot of roses there" was what he managed to say.

"Have you had dinner?"

He hadn't, and he told her so. In the prop room he found a basket for her flowers. He loaded it and covered it with a cloth to protect the roses from the cold. As he helped her into her coat, he received a wondering look from Pély, the custodian, who had already begun to sweep up the evening's snowfall of sequins and rose petals. Andras raised his hat in farewell and they went out through the backstage door.

She took his arm as they walked along, and let him lead her to a whitewashed café near the Bastille. It was a place he'd passed many times in his walks around Paris; it was called Aux Marocaines. On the low tables were green bowls of cardamom pods. On the walls, wooden racks held Moroccan pottery. Everything seemed to be built on a small scale, as if made for Klara. He could afford to buy her dinner there, though just barely; a week earlier he had received a Christmas bonus from Monsieur Novak.

A waiter in a fez seated them shoulder to shoulder at a corner table. There was flatbread and honey wine, a piece of grilled fish, a vegetable stew in a clay pot. As they ate they talked only about the performance, and about Elisabet, who had departed with Marthe for Chamonix; they talked about Andras's work, and about his examinations, which he'd passed with top marks. But he was always aware of her heat and movement beside him, her arm brushing his arm. When she drank, he watched her lips touch the rim of the glass. He couldn't stop looking at the curve of her breasts beneath her close-wrapped dress.

After dinner they had strong coffee and tiny pink macaroons. Still, neither of them had mentioned what had happened the previous night—not their conversation about her family, nor what had passed between them afterward. A time or two Andras thought he saw a shadow move across her features; he waited for her to reproach him, to say she wished he'd never told her that he'd met her mother and sister-in-law, or that she hadn't meant to give him a mistaken impression. When she didn't, he began to wonder if she meant for them to pretend it had never happened. At the end of the meal he paid the bill, despite her protests; he helped her into her coat again and they walked toward the rue de

Sévigné. He carried the heavy basket of flowers, thinking of the ridiculous bouquet he'd brought to that first Sunday lunch. How ignorant he'd been of what was about to befall him, how unprepared for everything he'd experienced since—the shock of attraction, the torment of her closeness on Sunday afternoons, the guilty pleasure of their growing familiarity, and then that unthinkable moment last night when she'd closed her hands around his hands—when she'd put her arms around his waist, her head against his chest. And what would happen now? The evening was almost over. They had nearly reached her house. A light snow began to fall as they rounded the corner of her street.

At the doorstep her eyes darkened again. She leaned against the door and sighed, looking down at the roses. "Funny," she said. "We've done the winter show every December for years, but I always feel this way afterward. Like there's nothing to look forward to. Like *everything's* finished." She smiled. "Dramatic, isn't it?"

He let out a long breath. "I'm sorry if—last night," he began.

She stopped him with a shake of her head and told him there was nothing to apologize for.

"I shouldn't have asked about your family," he said. "If you'd wanted to talk about it, you would have."

"Probably not," she said. "It's become such a habit with me, keeping everything secret." She shook her head again, and he experienced the return of a memory from his early childhood— a night he'd spent hiding in the orchard while his brother Mátyás lay in bed, gravely ill with fever. A doctor had been called in, plasters applied, medicines dispensed, all to no effect; the fever rose and rose, and everyone seemed to believe Mátyás would die. Meanwhile, Andras hid in the branches of an apple tree with his terrible secret: He himself had passed the fever along, playing with Mátyás after their mother told him he must keep away at all costs. If Mátyás died, it would be his fault. He had never been so lonely in his life. Now he touched Klara's shoulder and felt her shiver.

"You're cold," he said.

She shook her head. Then she took her key from her little purse and turned to unlock the door. But her hand began to tremble, and she turned back toward him and raised her face to him. He bent to her and brushed the corner of her mouth with his lips.

"Come in," she said. "Just for a moment."

His pulse thundering at his temples, Andras stepped in after her. He put a hand at her waist and drew her toward him. She looked up at him, her eyes wet, and then he lifted her against him and kissed her. He closed the door with one hand. Held her. Kissed her again. Took off his thin jacket, unbuttoned the glossy black buttons of her coat, pushed it from her shoulders. He stood in the entryway with her and kissed her and kissed her— first her mouth, then her neck at the margins of her dress, then the hollow between her breasts. He untied the black silk ribbon at her waist. The dress fell around her feet in a dark pool, and there she was before him in a rose-colored slip and stockings, the red-gold dahlia in her hair. He buried his hands in her dark curls and drew her to him. She kissed him again and slid her hands under his shirt. He heard himself saying her name; again he touched the bead-row of her spine, the curve of her hips. She lifted herself against him. It couldn't be true; it was true.

They went upstairs to her bedroom. He would remember it as long as he lived: the way they moved awkwardly through the doorway, his persistent certainty that she would change her mind, his disbelief as she lifted the rose-colored slip over her head. The quick work she made of his embarrassing sock braces, his poorly darned socks, his underclothes worn to transparency. The shallow curves of her dancer's body, the neat tuck of her navel, the shadow between her legs. The cool embrace of her bed, her own bed. The softness of her skin. Her breasts. His certainty that it would all be over in an embarrassing flash the instant she touched him with her hand; his wild concentration on anything else as she did it. The word *baiser* in his mind. The unbearable thrill of being able to touch her. The shock of the heat inside her. It could have all ended then—the city of Paris, the world, the universe—and he wouldn't have cared, would have died happy, could have found no heaven broader or more drenched with light.

Afterward they lay on the bed and he stared at the ceiling, at its pattern of pressed flowers and leaves. She turned onto her side and put a hand on his chest. A velvety drowsiness pinned him to the bed, his head on her pillow. Her scent was in his hair, on his hands, everywhere.

"Klara," he said. "Am I dead? Are you still here?"

"I'm still here," she said. "You're not dead."

"What are we supposed to do now?"

"Nothing," she said. "Just lie here for a little while."

"All right," he said, and lay there.

After a few minutes she removed her hand from his chest and rolled away from him, then got out of bed and went off down the hall. A moment later he heard the thunder of running water and the low roar and hiss of a gas heater. When she reappeared in the bedroom doorway, she was wearing a dressing gown.

"Come have a bath," she said.

She didn't have to coax him. He followed her into the white-tiled bathroom, where water steamed into the porcelain tub. She let the dressing gown drop and climbed into the water as he stood watching, speechless. He could have stood there all night while she bathed. Her image burned itself into his retinas: the small, high breasts; the twin wings of her hips; the smooth plane of her belly. And now, in the electric light of the bathroom, he saw something he hadn't noticed before: a crescent-shaped scar with faint stitch-marks, just above the neat dark triangle of her hair. He stepped forward to touch her. He ran his hand along her belly, down to the scar, and brushed it with his fingers.

"She was a difficult birth," Klara said. "In the end, a cesarean. She was too much for me, even then."

Andras had an unbidden vision of Klara as a fifteen-year-old, straining upward on a metal table. The image hit him like a train. His knees seemed to liquefy, and he had to brace himself against the wall.

"Come in with me," she said, and gave him her hand. He climbed into the bathtub and sank down into the water. She took the cloth and washed him from head to toe; she poured shampoo into her hands and massaged it into his scalp. Then they made love again, slowly, in the bathtub, and she showed him how to touch her, and he concluded that his life was over, that he would never want to do anything else in this lifetime. Then he washed her as she had washed him, every inch of her, and then they staggered to bed.

Nothing in his life had prepared him to imagine that a series of days might be spent the way they spent the next ten days. Later, in the darkest moments of the years that followed, he would come back again and again to those days, reminding himself that if he died, and if death led him into formless silence instead of into some other brighter life, he would still have experienced those days with Klara Morgenstern.

The Brecht play had gone dark for the holidays; Elisabet would be in Chamonix until the second of January. The studio was closed; school was out until after the new year; Andras's friends had gone home for the duration. Mrs. Apfel had gone to her daughter-in-law's cottage in Aix-en-Provence. Even the signs advertising meetings of anti-Jewish organizations had ceased to appear. At all hours of the day, the streets were filled with people out shopping or on their way to parties. Klara had been invited to half a dozen parties herself, but she cancelled all her engagements. Andras went to his cold attic for some articles of clothing and his sketchbooks, locked the door behind him, and decamped to the rue de Sévigné.

They went on an expedition for provisions: potatoes for potato pancakes, cold roast chicken, bread, cheese, wine, a cake packed with currants. At a music shop on rue Montmartre they bought records for five francs apiece, comic operettas and American jazz and ballets. With their arms full and their pockets empty, they returned to Klara's apartment and set up house. Chanukah began that night. They made potato pancakes, filling the kitchen with the rich smell of hot oil, and they lit candles. They made love in the kitchen and in the bedroom and once, awkwardly, on the stairs. The next day they went skating at the other skating pond, the one at the Bois de Boulogne, where they were unlikely to see anyone they knew. The skaters at the park wore bright colors against the gray of the afternoon; there was a marked-off patch at the center of the ice where the more adroit among them executed spins. Andras and Klara skated until their lips were blue with cold. Every night they bathed together; every morning they woke and made love. Andras received an astonishing education in the ways a human being could experience pleasure. At night, when he woke and thought of Klara, it amazed him that he could turn over and curl himself around her. He surprised her with his knowledge of cookery, gained from watching his mother. He could make *palacsinta*, thin egg pancakes, with chocolate or jam or apple filling; he could make *paprikás burgonya* and spaetzle, and red cabbage with caraway seeds. They slept long and gloriously in the afternoons. They made love in the middle of the day on Klara's white bed while freezing rain fell outside. They made love late at night in the dance studio, on rugs they'd dragged down from upstairs. One time, on the way home from a café, they made love against the wall in an alleyway.

They celebrated New Year's Eve at the Bastille, with thousands of other cheering Parisians. Afterward they drank a bottle of champagne in the sitting room and ate a feast of cold paté and bread and cheese and cornichons. Neither of them wanted to sleep, knowing that the next day would be the last of that string of impossible days. When dawn broke, instead of going to bed they put on coats and hats and went walking by the river. The sun cast its gold light onto the buttresses of Notre-Dame; the streets were full of cabs taking drowsy revelers home to their apartments. They sat on a bench in the dead garden at the eastern tip of Île St.-Louis and kissed each other's freezing hands, and Andras dredged from his mind a Marot poem he'd learned with Professor Vago:

D'Anne qui luy jecta de la Neige

Anne (par jeu) me jecta de la Neige
Que je cuidoys froide certainement;
Mais estoit feu, l'experience en ay-je;
Car embrasé je fuz soubdainement.
Puis que le feu loge secretement
Dedans la Neige, où trouveray je place
Pour n'ardre point? Anne, ta seule grace
Estaindre peult le feu que je sens bien,
Non point par Eau, par Neige, ne par Glace,
Mais par sentir un feu pareil au mien.

And when she protested against sixteenth-century French after a night of sleeplessness and drinking, he whispered another version into her ear, a spontaneous Hungarian translation of that hot exchange between the poet Marot and his girlfriend: as a game Anne threw snow at him, and it was cold, of course. But what he felt was heat, because he found himself in her arms. If fire dwelt secretly in snow, how could he escape burning? Only Anne's mercy could control the flame. Not with water, snow, nor ice, but with a fire like his own.

When he woke that afternoon, Klara lay fast asleep beside him, her hair tangled on the pillows. He got up, pulled on his trousers, washed his face. His head throbbed. He cleaned up the remnants of the previous night's sitting-room picnic, made coffee in the kitchen, drank a slow black cup and rubbed his temples. He wanted Klara to be awake, to be with him, but he didn't want to wake her. So he refilled his cup and roamed the apartment by himself. He walked through the empty dining room, where they'd had their first lunch together; he walked through the sitting room, where he'd seen her for the first time. He took a long look at the bathroom with its miraculous hot-water heater, where they'd spent long hours bathing. Finally, in the hall, he paused before Elisabet's bedroom. Their travels through the rooms had never taken them there, but now he pushed the door open. Elisabet's room was surprisingly neat; her dresses hung in a limp row in the open wardrobe. Two pairs of brown shoes were ranged under-neath: a caramel-colored pair on the left, a chestnut-colored pair on the right. On the dresser there was a wooden music box with tulips painted on the lid. A silver comb stood upright between the bristles of a silver brush. An empty perfume flask glowed yellow-green. He opened the top dresser drawer: grayish cotton underwear and grayish cotton brassieres. A few handkerchiefs. Some frayed hair ribbons. A broken slide rule. A tube of epoxy rolled tight all the way to its tip. Six cigarettes bound with a strip of paper.

He closed the drawer and sat down in the little wooden chair beside the bed. He looked at the yellow coverlet, at the rag doll keeping watch over the silent room, and considered how furious Elisabet would be if she knew what had happened in her absence. Though there was some small hint of triumph in the feeling, there was also a sense of fear; if she found out, he knew she wouldn't stand for it. He couldn't know what effect her anger might have upon her mother, but at the very least he knew that Klara's ties to Elisabet were far stronger than her tenuous ties to him. The scar on her belly reminded him of it every time they made love.

He turned and left the little room, and went to Klara where she lay sleeping on the tumbled bed. She had curled herself around the pillow he'd been using. She was naked, her legs tan-gled in the eiderdown. In the silvery northern light of the winter afternoon, he could see the hairline creases at the corners of her eyes, the faint signs of her age. He loved her, wanted her, felt himself stirring again at the sight of her. He knew he would be willing to give his life to protect her. He wanted to take her to Budapest and heal whatever terrible hurt had occurred there, see her walk into the drawing room of that house on Benczúr utca and put her hands into her mother's hands. His eyes burned at the thought that he was only twenty-two, a student, unable to do anything of substance for her. The lives they'd been leading those past ten days hadn't been their real lives. They hadn't worked, hadn't taken care of anyone but themselves, hadn't had much need for money. But money was an ever-present woe for him. It would be years before he'd have a steady income. If his studies went as planned, it would be another four and a half years before he became an architect. And he'd lived long enough already, and had faced enough difficulty, to know that things seldom went as planned.

He touched her shoulder. She opened her gray eyes and looked at him. "What is it?" she said. She sat up and held the eiderdown against herself. "What's happened?"

"Nothing's happened," he said, sitting down beside her. "I've just been thinking about what's to happen after."

"Oh, Andras," she said, and smiled drowsily. "Not that. That's my least favorite subject at the moment."

This was the way it had gone, anytime either of them had introduced the topic over the past week or so; they had turned it aside, allowed it to drift away as they drifted into another series of pleasures. It was easy enough to do; their real lives had come to seem far less real than the one they were leading together on the rue de Sévigné. But now their time was nearly finished. They couldn't avoid the subject any longer.

"We have six more hours," he said. "Then our lives begin again."

She slipped her arms around him. "I know."

"I want to have everything with you," he said. "A real life.

God help me! I want you beside me at night, every night. I want to have a child with you." He had not yet said these things aloud; he could feel the blood rushing to his skin as he spoke.

Klara was silent for a long moment. She dropped her arms, sat back against the pillows, put her hand in his. "I have a child already," she said.

"Elisabet's not a child." But those vulnerable shoes at the bottom of the closet. The painted box on the dresser. The hidden cigarettes.

"She's my daughter," Klara said. "She's what I've lived for these sixteen years. I can't just take up another life."

"I know. But I can't not see you, either."

"Perhaps it would be best, though," she said, and looked away from him. Her voice had fallen almost to a whisper. "Perhaps it would be best to stop with what we've had. Our lives may spoil it."

But what would his life be without her, now that he knew what it was to be with her? He wanted to weep, or to take her by the shoulders and shake her. "Is that what you've thought all along?" he said. "That this was a lark? That when our lives began again it would be over?"

"I didn't think about what would happen," she said. "I didn't want to. But we've got to think about it now."

He got out of bed and took his shirt from a chair. He couldn't look at her. "What good will that do?" he said. "You've already decided it's impossible."

"Please, Andras," she said. "Don't go."

"Why should I stay?"

"Don't be angry at me. Don't leave like that."

"I'm not angry," he said. But he finished dressing, then retrieved his suitcase from beneath the bed and began to pack the few articles of clothing he'd brought from the rue des Écoles.

"There are things you don't know about me," she said. "Things that might frighten you, or change the way you felt."

"That's right," he said. "And there's a great deal you don't know about me. But what does that matter now?"

"Don't be cruel to me," she said. "I'm as unhappy as you are."

He wanted to believe that it was true, but it couldn't have been; he'd laid himself open before her and she'd withdrawn from him. He put his last few things in the suitcase and snapped the latches, then went into the hallway and took his coat from the rack. She followed him to the top of the stairs, where she stood barefoot and bare-shouldered, the sheet wrapped around her as though she were a Greek sculpture. He buttoned his coat. He couldn't believe he was going to walk down the stairs and through the door, not knowing when he'd see her again. He put a hand to her arm. Touched her shoulder. Tugged a corner of the sheet so that it fell from her body. In the dim hallway she stood naked before him. He couldn't bear to look at her, couldn't bear to touch or kiss her. And so he did what a moment before had seemed unimaginable: He descended the stairs, past the eyes of all those child dancers in their ethereal costumes, opened the door, and left her.

PART TWO

Broken Glass

CHAPTER TWELVE

What Happened at the Studio

CLASSES BEGAN the first Monday of January with a two-day charrette. Within a span of forty-eight hours they had to design a freestanding living space of fifty meters square, with a movable wall, two windows, a bath, a galley kitchen. They would submit a front elevation of the building, a floor plan, and a model. Forty-eight hours, during which anyone who cared about the project wouldn't eat a meal or sleep or leave the studio. Andras took the project like an oblivion drug, felt the crush of time in his veins, willed it to make him forget his ten days with Klara. He bent over the plane of his worktable and made it the landscape of his mind. The Gare d'Orsay critique had left its imprint; he vowed that he would not be humiliated before the rest of the class, before that smug Lemarque and the ranks of the upperclassmen. Toward the end of his thirtieth waking hour he looked at his design and found that what he'd drawn was his parents' house in Konyár, with a few details changed. One bedroom, not two. An indoor bath instead of the tin tub and outhouse. A modern indoor kitchen. One external wall had become a movable wall; it could be opened in summer to let the house communicate with the garden. The façade was plain and white with a many-paned window. On his second sleepless night he drew the movable wall as a curve; when it was open it would make a shady niche. He drew a stone bench in the garden, a circular reflecting pool. His parents' house made over into a country retreat. He feared it was absurd, that everyone would see it for what it was: a Hajdú boy's design, rude and primitive. He turned it in at the last minute and received, to his surprise, an appreciative nod and a paragraph of closely written praise from Vago, and the grudging approval of even the harshest fifth-year students.

At the Bernhardt they struck the set of *The Mother* and held auditions for Lope de Vega's *Fuente Ovejuna*. Though Zoltán Novak pleaded, Madame Gérard would not take a role in the new play; she'd already been offered the role of Lady Macbeth at the Théâtre des Ambassadeurs, and Novak couldn't pay her what they would. Andras was grateful for her impending departure. He couldn't look at her without thinking of Klara, without wondering whether Madame Gérard knew what had happened between them. The day before she departed for the Ambassadeurs he helped her box up her dressing room: her Chinese robe, her tea things, her makeup, a thousand fan letters and postcards and little presents. As they worked she told him about the members of the new company she would join, two of whom had been featured in American films, and one of whom had appeared with Helen Hayes in *The Sin of Madelon Claudet*. He found it difficult to pay attention. He wanted to tell her what had happened. He had told no one; even to have told his friends at school would have reduced it somehow, made it seem a superficial and fleeting liaison. But Madame Gérard knew Klara; she would know what it meant. She might even be able to offer some hope. So he closed the dressing-room door and confessed it all, omitting only the revelation about the letter.

Madame Gérard listened gravely. When he'd finished, she got to her feet and paced the green rug in front of the dressing-room mirror as if bringing a monologue to mind. At last she turned and put her hands on the backrest of her makeup chair. "I knew it," she said. "I knew, and I ought to have said something. When I saw you at the Bois de Vincennes, I knew. You didn't care at all for the girl. You looked only at Klara. I'll admit," and she turned her eyes from him, laughing ruefully to herself, "old as I am, I was a little jealous. But I never thought you'd act upon your feelings."

Andras rubbed his palms against his thighs. "I shouldn't have," he said.

"It's well she ended it," Madame Gérard said. "She knew it wasn't right. She invited you into her house thinking you might be a friend to her daughter. You should have stopped going once you knew you didn't care for Elisabet."

"It was too late by then," he said. "I couldn't stop."

"You don't know Klara," Madame Gérard said. "You can't, not after a few Sunday lunches and a week-long affair. She's never made any man happy. She's had ample chance to fall in love—and, if you'll pardon me, with grown men, not first-year architecture students. Don't imagine she hasn't had plenty of suitors. If she ever does take a man seriously, it'll be because she wants to get married—that is to say, because she wants someone to ease her life, to take care of her. Which you, my dear, are in no position to do."

"You don't have to remind me of that."

"Well, someone must, apparently!"

"But what now?" he demanded. "I can't pretend it didn't happen."

"Why not? It's over between the two of you. You said as much yourself."

"It's not over for me. I can't put her out of my mind."

"I'd advise you to try," Madame Gérard said. "She can't be any good to you."

"That's all, then? I'm supposed to forget her?"

"That would be best."

"Impossible," he said.

"Poor darling," Madame Gérard said. "I'm sorry. But you'll get over it. Young men do." She turned again to her packing, loading her gold and silver makeup sticks into a box with dozens of little drawers. A private smile came to her mouth; she rolled a tube of rouge between her fingers and turned to him. "You've joined an illustrious club, you know, now that Klara's thrown you over. Most men never make it that far."

"Please," he said. "I can't bear to hear you speak of her that way."

"It's the girl's father, you know. I think she must still be in love with him."

"Elisabet's father," he said. "Is he here in Paris? Does she still see him?"

"Oh, no. He died many years ago, as I understand it. But death isn't a bar to love, as you may learn someday."

"Who was he?"

"I'm afraid I don't know. Klara keeps her history close."

"So it's hopeless, then. I'm supposed to let it go because she's in love with a dead man."

"Allow it to be what it was: a pretty episode. The satisfaction of a mutual curiosity."

"That wasn't what it was to me."

She tilted her head at him and smiled again, that terrible all-knowing smile. "I'm afraid I'm the wrong person to dispense advice about love. Unless you'd like to be disabused of your romantic notions."

"You'll excuse me, then, if I leave you to your packing."

"My dear boy, no excuse needed." She rose, kissed him on both cheeks, and turned him out into the hall. There was no choice for him but to go back to his work; he did it in mute consternation, wishing he had never confided in her.

There was one great source of relief, one astonishing piece of news that had arrived in a telegram from Budapest: Tibor was coming to visit. His classes in Modena would start at the end of January, but before he went to Italy he would come to Paris for a week. When the telegram arrived, Andras had shouted the news aloud into the stairwell of the building, at a volume that had brought the concierge out into the hall to reprimand him for disturbing the other tenants. He silenced her by kissing her on the brow and showing her the telegram: Tibor was coming! Tibor, his older brother. The concierge voiced the hope that this older brother would beat some manners into Andras, and left him in the hall to experience his delight alone. Andras hadn't mentioned Klara in his letters to Tibor, but he felt as if Tibor knew—as if Tibor had sensed that Andras was in distress and had decided to come for that reason.

The anticipation of the visit—three weeks away, then two, then one—got him from home to school, and from school to work. Now that *The Mother* was finished and Madame Gérard gone, afternoons at the Sarah-Bernhardt passed at a maddening crawl. He had arranged everything so well backstage that there was little to do while the actors rehearsed; he paced behind the curtain, subject to an increasing fear that Monsieur Novak would discover his superfluity. One afternoon, after he'd overseen the delivery of a load of lumber for the set of *Fuente Ovejuna*, he approached the head carpenter and offered his services as a set builder. The head carpenter put him to work. During the afternoon hours Andras banged flats together; after hours he studied the design of the new sets. This was a different kind of architecture, all about illusion and impression: perspective flattened to make spaces look deeper, hidden doors through which actors might materialize or disappear, pieces that could be turned backward or inside out to create new tableaux. He began to mull over the design in bed at night, trying to distract himself from thoughts of Klara. The false fronts that represented the Spanish town might be put on wheels and rotated, he thought; their opposite sides could be painted to represent the building interiors. He made a set of sketches showing how it might be done, and later he redrew the sketches as plans. His second week as assistant set builder he went to the head carpenter and showed him the work. The carpenter asked him if he thought he had a budget of a million francs. Andras told him it would cost less than building the two sets of flats that would be required to make separate exteriors and interiors. The head carpenter scratched his head and said he'd consult the set designer. The set designer, a tall round-shouldered man with an ill-trimmed moustache and a monocle, scrutinized the plans and asked Andras why he was still working as a gofer. Did he want a job that would pay three times what he was making now? The set designer had an independent shop on the rue des Lombards and generally employed an assistant, but his most recent one had just finished his coursework at the Beaux-Arts and had taken a position outside the capital.

Andras did want the job. But Zoltán Novak had saved his life; he couldn't very well walk out on the Sarah-Bernhardt. He accepted the man's business card and stared at it all that night, wondering what to do.

The next afternoon he went to Novak's office to lay the situation before him. There was a long silence after he knocked, then the sound of male voices in argument; the door flew open to reveal a pair of men in pinstriped suits, briefcases in hand, their faces flushed as though Novak had been insulting them in the vilest terms. The men clapped hats onto their heads and walked out past Andras without a nod or glance. Inside the office Novak stood at his desk with his hands on the blotter, watching the men recede down the hallway. When they'd disappeared, he came out from behind the desk and poured himself a tumbler of whiskey from the decanter on the sideboard. He looked over his shoulder at Andras and pointed to a glass. Andras raised a hand and shook his head.

"Please," Novak said. "I insist." He poured whiskey and added water.

Andras had never seen Novak drinking before dusk. He accepted the tumbler and sat down in one of the ancient leather chairs.

"*Egészségedre,*" Novak said. He lifted his glass, drained it, set it down on the blotter. "Can you guess who that was, leaving?"

"No," Andras said. "But they looked rather grim."

"They're our money men. The people who've always managed to persuade the city to let us keep our doors open."

"And?"

Novak sat back in his chair and laced his hands into a mountain. "Fifty-seven people," he said. "That's how many I have to fire today, according to those men. Including myself, and you."

"But that's everyone," Andras said.

"Precisely," he said. "They're closing us down. We're finished until next season, at least. They can't support us any longer, even though we've posted profits all fall. *The Mother* did better than any other show in Paris, you know. But it wasn't enough. This place is a money-sink. Do you know what it costs to heat five stories of open space?"

Andras took a swallow of whiskey and felt the false warmth of it move through his chest. "What will you do?" he said.

"What will *you* do?" Novak said. "And what will the actors do? And Madame Courbet? And Claudel, and Pély, and all the others? It's a disaster. We're not the only ones, either. They're closing four theaters." He sat back in his chair and stroked his moustache with one finger, his eyes moving over the bookshelves. "The fact is, I'm not sure what I'll do. Madame Novak is in a delicate condition, as they say. She's been pining for her parents in Budapest. I'm sure she'll take this as a sign that we should return home."

"But you'd rather stay," Andras said.

Novak released a sigh from the broad bellows of his chest. "I understand how Edith feels. This isn't our home. We've scratched out our little corner here, but none of it belongs to us. We're Hungarians, in the end, not French."

"When I met you in Vienna, I thought no man could look more Parisian."

"Now you see how green you were," Novak said, and smiled sadly. "But what about you? I know you've got your school fees to pay."

Andras told him about the offer of an assistantship with the set designer, Monsieur Forestier, and how he'd just been coming to ask Novak's advice on the matter.

Novak brought his hands together, a single beat of applause. "It would have been a terrible shame to lose you," he said. "But it's an excellent chance, and well timed. You've got to do it, of course."

162 · JULIE ORRINGER

"I can't thank you enough for what you've done," Andras said.

"You're a good young man. You've worked hard here. I've never regretted taking you on." He drained the rest of his drink and pushed the empty glass across the desk. "Now, would you fill that again for me? I've got to go break the news to the others. You'll come to work tomorrow, I hope. There'll be a great deal to do, getting this place closed down. You'll have to tell Forestier I can't release you until the end of the month."

"Tomorrow, as usual," Andras said.

He went home that evening with a frightening sense of vacancy in his chest. No more Sarah-Bernhardt. No more Monsieur Novak. No more Claudel, or Pély; no more Marcelle Gérard. And no more Klara, no more Klara. The hard white shell of his life punctured and blown clean. He was light now, hollow, an empty egg. Hollow and light, he drifted home through the January wind. At 34 rue des Écoles he climbed the flights and flights of stairs—how many hundreds of them were there?—feeling he didn't have the energy to look at his books that night, nor even to wash his face or change for bed. He wanted only to lie down in his trousers and shoes and overcoat, pull the eiderdown over his head, ride out the hours before dawn. But at the top of the stairs he saw a line of light coming from beneath his own door, and when he put a hand on the doorknob he found it unlocked. He pushed the door open and let it swing. A fire in the grate; bread and wine on the table; in the single chair with a book in her hands, Klara.

"*Te*," he said. You.

"And you," she said.

"How did you get in?"

"I told the concierge it was your birthday. I said I was planning a surprise."

"And what did you tell your daughter?"

She looked down at the cover of her book. "I told her I was going to see a friend."

"What a shame that wasn't true."

She got to her feet, crossed the room to him, put her hands on his arms. "Please, Andras," she said. "Don't speak to me that way."

He moved away from her and took off his coat, his scarf. For what felt like a long time he couldn't say anything more; he went to the fireplace and crossed his arms, looking down into a faltering pyramid of bright coals. "It was bad enough, not knowing whether or not I'd see you again," he said. "I told myself we were finished, but I couldn't convince myself it was true. Finally I confided in Marcelle. She was kind enough to tell me I wasn't alone in my misery. She said I belonged to an illustrious club of men you'd thrown over."

Her gray eyes darkened. "Thrown over? Is that what you feel I've done to you?"

"Thrown over, jettisoned, sent packing. I don't suppose it matters what you call it."

"We decided it was impossible."

"You decided."

She went to him and moved her hands over his arms, and when she looked up into his face he saw there were tears in her eyes. To his horror his own eyes began to burn. This was Klara, whose name he'd carried with him from Budapest; Klara, whose voice came to him in his sleep.

"What do you want?" he said into her hair. "What am I supposed to do?"

"I've been miserable," she said. "I can't let it go. I want to know you, Andras."

"And I want to know you," he said. "I don't like secrecy." But he knew as he said it that what was hidden made her all the more attractive; there was a kind of torment in her unknowability, in the rooms that lay beyond the ones in which she entertained him.

"You'll have to be patient with me," she said. "You'll have to let me trust you."

"I can be patient," he said. He had drawn her so close that the sharp crests of her pelvis pressed against him; he wanted to reach into her body and grab her by the bones. "Claire Morgenstern," he said. "Klárika." She would ruin him, he thought. But he could no sooner have sent her away than he could have dismissed geometry from architecture, or the cold from January, or the winter sky from outside his window. He bent to her and kissed her. Then, for the first time, he took her into his own bed.

When he stepped into the world the next morning it was a transformed place. The dullness of the weeks without her had fallen away. He had become human again, had reclaimed his own flesh and blood, and hers. Everything glittered too brilliantly in the winter sun; every detail of the street rushed at him as if he were seeing it for the first time. How had he never noticed the way light fell from the sky onto the bare limbs of the lindens outside his building, the way it broke and diffused on the wet paving stones and needled whitely from the polished brass handles of the doors along the street? He savored the bracing slap of his soles against the sidewalk, fell in love with the cascade of ice in the frozen fountain of the Luxembourg. He wanted to thank someone aloud for the fine long corridor of the boulevard Raspail, which conducted him every day along its row of Haussmann-era buildings to the blue doors of the École Spéciale. He adored the empty courtyard awash with winter sunlight, its green benches empty, its grass frozen, its paths wet with melted snow. A speckle-breasted bird on a branch pronounced her name exactly: Klara, Klara.

He ran upstairs to the studio and looked among the drawings for the new set of plans he'd been working on with Polaner. He thought he might spend a few minutes on them before he had to report to Vago for his morning French. But the plans weren't there; Polaner must have taken them home with him. Instead he picked up the textbook of architectural vocabulary he would study that morning with Vago, and ran downstairs again for a stop at the men's room. He pushed open the door into echoing dark and fumbled for the light switch. From the far corner of the room came a low wheezing groan.

Andras turned on the light. On the concrete floor, against the wall beyond the urinals and the sinks, someone was curled into a tight *G*. A small form, a man's, in a velvet jacket. Beside him a set of plans, crumpled and boot-stomped.

"Polaner?"

That sound again. A wheeze sliding into a groan. And then his own name.

Andras went to him and knelt beside him on the concrete. Polaner wouldn't look at Andras, or couldn't. His face was dark with bruises, his nose broken, his eyes hidden in purple folds. He kept his knees tight against his chest.

"My God," Andras said. "What happened? Who did this?"

No response.

"Don't move," Andras said, and staggered to his feet. He turned and ran out of the room, across the courtyard, and up the stairs to Vago's office, and opened the door without knocking.

"Lévi, what on earth?"

"Eli Polaner's been beaten half to death. He's in the men's room, ground floor."

They ran downstairs. Vago tried to get Polaner to let him see what had happened, but Polaner wouldn't uncurl. Andras pleaded with him. When Polaner dropped his arms from his face, Vago took a sharp breath. Polaner started to cry. One of his lower teeth had been knocked out, and he spat blood onto the concrete.

"Stay here, both of you," Vago said. "I'm going to call an ambulance."

"No," Polaner said. "No ambulance." But Vago had already gone, the door slamming behind him as he ran into the court-yard.

Polaner rolled onto his back, letting his arms go limp.

Beneath the velvet jacket his shirt had been torn open, and something had been written on his chest in black ink.

Feygele. A Jewish fag.

Andras touched the torn shirt, the word. Polaner flinched.

"Who did it?" Andras said.

"Lemarque," Polaner said. Then he mumbled something else, a phrase Andras could only hear halfway, and couldn't translate: *"J'étais coin . . ."*

"Tu étais quoi?"

"J'étais coincé," Polaner said, and repeated it until Andras could understand. They'd caught him in a trap. Tricked him. In a whisper: "Asked me to meet him here last night. And then came with three others."

"Meet him here at night?" Andras said. "To work on those plans?"

"No." Polaner turned his blackened and swollen eyes on him. "Not to work."

Feygele.

It took him a moment to understand. Meet at night: an assignation. So this, and not the girl back in Poland, the would-be fiancée who had written him those letters, was what had prevented him from showing interest in women here in Paris.

"Oh, God," Andras said. "I'll kill him. I'll knock his teeth down his throat."

Vago came through the door of the men's room with a first-aid box. A cluster of students crowded into the doorway behind him. "Go away," he shouted back over his shoulder, but the students didn't move. Vago's brows came together into a tight *V.* "Now!" he cried, and the students backed away, murmuring to each other. The door slammed. Vago knelt on the floor beside Andras and put a hand on Polaner's shoulder.

"An ambulance is coming," he said. "You'll be all right."

Polaner coughed, spat blood. He tried to hold his shirt closed with one hand, but the effort was beyond him; his arm fell against the concrete floor.

"Tell him," Andras said.

"Tell me what?" said Vago.

"Who did this."

"Another student?" Vago said. "We'll bring him before the disciplinary council. He'll be expelled. We'll press criminal charges."

"No, no," Polaner said. "If my parents knew—"

Now Vago saw the word inked across Polaner's chest. He rocked back onto his heels and put a hand to his mouth. For a long time he didn't speak or move. "All right," he said, finally. "All right." He moved the shreds of Polaner's shirt aside to get a better look at his injuries; Polaner's chest and abdomen were black with bruises. Andras could hardly bear to look. Nausea plowed through him, and he had to put his head against one of the porcelain sinks. Vago pulled off his own jacket and draped it over Polaner's chest. "All right," he said. "You'll go to the hospital and they'll take care of you. We'll worry about the rest of this later."

"Our plans," Polaner said, touching the crumpled sheets of drafting paper.

"Don't think about that," Vago said. "We'll fix them." He picked up the plans and handed them carefully to Andras, as though there were any chance they could be salvaged. Then, hearing the ambulance bell outside, he ran to direct the attendants to the men's room. Two men in white uniforms brought a stretcher in; when they lifted Polaner onto it, he fainted from the pain. Andras held the door open as they carried him into the courtyard. A crowd had gathered outside. The word had spread as the students arrived for morning classes. The attendants had to push their way through the crowd as they carried Polaner down the flagstone path.

"There's nothing to see," Vago shouted. "Go to your classes." But there were no classes yet; it was only a quarter to eight. Not a single person turned away until the attendants had gotten Polaner into the ambulance. Andras stood at the courtyard door, holding Polaner's plans like the broken body of an animal. Vago put a hand on his shoulder.

"Come to my office," he said.

Andras turned to follow him. He knew this was the same courtyard he'd crossed earlier that morning, with the same frosted grass and green benches, the same paths bright-wet in the sun. He knew it, but now he couldn't see what he had seen before. It astonished him to think the world could trade that beauty for this ugliness, all in the space of a quarter hour.

In his office, Vago told Andras about the other cases. Last February someone had stenciled the German words for *filth* and *swine* onto the final projects of a group of Jewish fifth-year students, and later that spring a student from Côte d'Ivoire had been dragged from the studio at night and beaten in the cemetery behind the school. That student, too, had had an insult painted on his chest, a racial slur. But not one of the perpetrators had been identified. If Andras had any information to volunteer, he would be helping everyone.

Andras hesitated. He sat on his usual stool, rubbing his father's pocket watch with his thumb. "What will happen if they're caught?"

"They'll be questioned. We'll take disciplinary and legal action."

"And then their friends will do something worse. They'll know Polaner told."

"And if we do nothing?" Vago said.

Andras let the watch drop into the hollow of his pocket. He considered what his father would tell him to do in a situation like this. He considered what Tibor would tell him to do. There was no question: They would both think him a coward for hesitating.

"Polaner mentioned Lemarque," he said. It came out as a

whisper at first, and he repeated the name, louder. "Lemarque and some others. I don't know who else."

"Fernand Lemarque?"

"That's what Polaner said." And he told Vago everything he knew.

"All right," said Vago. "I'm going to talk to Perret. In the meantime"—he opened his architectural vocabulary book to the page that depicted the inner structures of roofs, with their vertical *poinçons*, their buttressing *contre-fiches*, their riblike *arbalétriers*—"stay here and study," he said, and left Andras alone in the office.

Andras couldn't study, of course; he couldn't keep the image of Polaner from his mind. Again and again he saw Polaner on the floor, the word inscribed on his chest in black ink, the plans crumpled beside him. Andras understood desperation and loneliness; he knew how it felt to be thousands of kilometers from home; he knew how it felt to carry a secret. But to what depths of misery would Polaner have had to descend in order to imagine Lemarque as a lover? As a person with whom he might share a moment of intimacy in the men's room at night?

Not five minutes passed before Rosen burst into Vago's office, cap in hand. Ben Yakov stood behind him, abashed, as though he'd tried and failed to prevent Rosen from tearing upstairs.

"Where's that little bastard?" Rosen shouted. "Where is that weasel? If they're hiding him up here, I swear to God I'll kill them all!"

Vago ran down the hall from Perret's office. "Lower your voice," he said. "This isn't a beer hall. Where's who?"

"You know who," Rosen said. "Fernand Lemarque. He's the one who whispers *sale Juif*. The one who put up those posters for that Front de la Jeunesse. You saw them: *Meet and Unite, Youth of France*, and all that rubbish, at the Salle des Sociétés Savantes, of all places. They're anti-parliament, anti-Semitic, anti-everything.

He's one of their little stooges. There's a whole group of them. Third-years, fifth-years. From here, from the Beaux-Arts, from other schools all over the city. I know. I've been to their meetings. I've heard what they want to do to us."

"All right," Vago said. "Suppose you tell me about it after studio."

"After studio!" Rosen spat on the floor. "Right now! I want the police."

"We've already contacted the police."

"Bullshit! You haven't called anyone. You don't want a scandal."

Now Perret himself came down the hall, his gray cape rolling behind him. "Enough," he said. "We're handling this. Go to your studio."

"I won't," Rosen said. "I'm going to find that little bastard myself."

"Young man," Perret said. "There are elements of this situation that you don't understand. You're not a cowboy. This is not the Wild West. This country has a system of justice, which we've already put into play. If you don't lower your voice and conduct yourself like a gentleman, I'm going to have you removed from this school."

Rosen turned and went down the stairs, cursing under his breath. Andras and Ben Yakov followed him to the studio, where Vago met them ten minutes later. At nine o'clock they continued with the previous day's lesson, as if designing the perfect *maison particulier* were the only thing that mattered in the world.

At the hospital that afternoon, Andras and Rosen and Ben Yakov found Polaner in a long narrow ward filled with winter light. He lay in a high bed, his legs propped on pillows, his nose set with a plaster bridge, deep purple bruises ringing his eyes. Three broken ribs. A broken nose. Extensive contusions on the upper body and legs. Signs of internal bleeding—abdominal swelling, unstable pulse and temperature, blood pooling beneath the skin. Symptoms of shock. Aftereffects of hypothermia. That was what the doctor told them. A chart at the foot of Polaner's bed showed temperature and pulse and blood-pressure readings taken every quarter hour. As they crowded around the bed, he opened his swollen eyes, called them by unfamiliar Polish names, and lost consciousness. A nurse came down the ward with two hot-water bottles, which she tucked beneath Polaner's sheets. She took his pulse and blood pressure and temperature and recorded the numbers on his chart.

"How is he?" Rosen asked, getting to his feet.

"We don't know yet," the nurse said.

"Don't know? Is this a hospital? Are you a nurse? Isn't it your job to know?"

"All right, Rosen," Ben Yakov said. "It's not her fault."

"I want to speak to that doctor again," Rosen said.

"I'm afraid he's making his rounds at the moment."

"For God's sake! This is our friend. I just want to know exactly how bad it is."

"I wish I could tell you myself," the nurse said.

Rosen sat down again and put his head in his hands. He waited until the nurse had gone off down the ward. "I swear to God," he said. "I swear to God, if I catch those bastards! I don't care what happens to me. I don't care if I do get kicked out of school. I'll go to jail if I have to. I want to make them regret they were born." He looked up at Andras and Ben Yakov. "You'll help me find them, won't you?"

"Why?" Ben Yakov said. "So we can bash their skulls in?"

"Oh, pardon me," Rosen said. "I suppose you wouldn't want to risk having your own pretty nose broken."

Ben Yakov got up from his chair and took Rosen by the shirt-front. "You think I like seeing him like this?" he said. "You think I don't want to kill them myself?"

Rosen twisted his shirt out of Ben Yakov's grasp. "This isn't just about *him*. The people who did this to him would do it to us." He took up his coat and slung it over his arm. "I don't care if you come with me or not. I'm going to look for them, and when I find them they're going to answer for what they did." He jammed his cap onto his head and went off down the ward.

Ben Yakov put a hand to the back of his neck and stood looking at Polaner. Then he sighed and sat down again beside Andras. "Look at him. God, why did he have to meet Lemarque at night? What was he thinking? He can't be—what they said."

Andras watched Polaner's chest rise and fall, a faint disturbance beneath the sheets. "And what if he were?" he said.

Ben Yakov shook his head. "Do you believe it?"

"It's not impossible."

Ben Yakov set his chin on his fist and stared at the railing of the bed. He had ceased for the moment to resemble Pierre Fresnay. His eyes were hooded and damp, his mouth drawn into a crumpled line. "There was one time," he said, slowly. "One day when we were going to meet you and Rosen at the café, he said something about Lemarque. He said he thought Lemarque wasn't really an anti-Semite—that he hated himself, not Jews. That he had to put on a show so people wouldn't see him for what he was."

"What did you say?"

"I said Lemarque could go stuff himself."

"That's what I would have said."

"No," Ben Yakov said. "You would have listened. You'd have had something intelligent to say in return. You would have asked what made him think so."

"He's a private person," Andras said. "He might not have said more if you'd asked."

"But I knew something was wrong. You must have noticed it too. You were working on that project with him. Anyone could tell he hadn't been sleeping, and he was so quiet when Lemarque was around—quieter than usual."

Andras didn't know what to say. He'd been consumed with thoughts of Klara, with his anticipation of Tibor's visit, with his own work. He was aware of Polaner as a constant presence in his life, knew him to be guarded and circumspect, even knew him to brood at times; but he hadn't considered that Polaner might possess private woes as monumental as his own. If the affair with Klara had been difficult, how much harder might it have been for Polaner to nurse a secret attraction to Lemarque? He had spent little time imagining what it might be like to be a man who favored men. There were plenty of girlish men and boyish women in Paris, of course, and everyone knew the famous clubs and balls where they went to meet: Magic-City, the Monocle, the Bal de la Montagne-Sainte-Geneviève; but that world seemed remote from Andras's life. What hint of it had there been in his own experience? Things had gone on at gimnázium—boys cultivated friendships that seemed romantic in their intrigues and betrayals; and then there were those times when he and his classmates would stand in a row, their shorts around their ankles, bringing themselves off together in the semidark. There was one boy at school whom everyone said loved boys—Willi Mandl, a lanky blond boy who played piano, wore white embroidered socks, and had been glimpsed one afternoon in a secondhand store dreamily fondling a blue silk reticule. But that was all part of the fog of childhood, nothing that seemed to bear upon his current life.

Now Polaner opened his eyes and looked at Andras. Andras touched Ben Yakov's sleeve. "Polaner," Andras said. "Can you hear me?"

"Are they here?" Polaner said, almost unintelligibly.

"We're here," Andras said. "Go to sleep. We're not going to leave you."

CHAPTER THIRTEEN

Visitor

ANDRAS HADN'T BEEN back to the Gare du Nord since he'd arrived from Budapest in September. Now, in late January, as he stood on the platform waiting for Tibor's train, it amazed him to consider the bulk of ignorance he'd hauled to Paris those few months ago. He'd known almost nothing about architecture. Nothing about the city. Less than nothing about love. He had never touched a woman's naked body. Hadn't known French. Those SORTIE signs above the exits might as well have said YOU IDIOT! The past days' events had only served to remind him how little he still knew of the world. He felt he was just beginning to sense the scope of his own inexperience, his own benightedness; he had scarcely begun to allay it. He'd hoped that by the time he saw his brother again he might feel more like a man, like someone conversant with the wider world. But there was nothing more he could do about that now. Tibor would have to take him as he was.

At a quarter past five the Western Europe Express pulled into the station, filling that glass-and-iron cavern with the screech of brakes. Porters lowered the steps and climbed down; passengers poured forth, men and women haggard from traveling all night. Young men his age, sleepless and uncertain-looking in the wintry light of the station, squinted at the signs and searched for their baggage. Andras scanned the faces of the passengers. As more and more of them passed without a sign of Tibor, he had a moment of fear that his brother had decided not to come after all. And then someone put a hand on his shoulder, and he turned, and there was Tibor Lévi on the platform of the Gare du Nord.

"Fancy meeting you here," Tibor said, and pulled Andras close.

A carbonated joy rose up in Andras's chest, a dreamlike sense of relief. He held his brother at arm's length. Tibor scrutinized Andras from head to toe, his gaze coming to rest on Andras's hole-ridden shoes.

"It's a good thing you have a brother who's a shoe clerk," he said. "Or was one. Those filthy oxfords wouldn't have lasted you another week."

They retrieved Tibor's bags and took a cab to the Latin Quarter, a trip Andras found surprisingly brief and direct, and he grasped how profoundly his first Parisian cab driver had cheated him. The streets flashed past almost too quickly; he wanted to show Tibor everything at once. They flew down the boulevard de Sébastopol and over the Île de la Cité, and were turning onto the rue des Écoles in what felt like an instant. The Latin Quarter crouched beneath a haze of rain, its sidewalks crowded with umbrellas. They rushed Tibor's bags through the drizzle and dragged them upstairs. When they reached Andras's garret, Tibor stood in the doorway and laughed.

"What?" Andras said. He was proud of his shabby room.

"It's exactly as I imagined," Tibor said. "Down to the last detail."

Under his gaze the Paris apartment seemed to come fully into Andras's possession perhaps for the first time, as if his seeing it made it continuous with the places Andras had lived before, with the life he had led before he climbed onto a train at Nyugati Station in September. "Come in," Andras said. "Take off your coat. Let me make a fire."

Tibor took off his coat, but he wouldn't let Andras make the fire. It couldn't have mattered less that this was Andras's apartment, nor that Tibor had been traveling for three days. This was how it had always been between them: The older took care of the younger. If this had been Mátyás's apartment and Andras had been there to visit, Andras would have been the one cracking the kindling and piling the paper beneath the logs. In a few minutes Tibor had conjured a steady blaze. Only then would he take off his shoes and crawl into Andras's bed.

"What a relief!" he said. "It's been three days since I slept lying down." He pulled the coverlet over himself and in another moment he was asleep.

Andras set up his books on the table and tried to study, but found he couldn't concentrate. He wanted news of Mátyás and his parents. And he wanted news of Budapest—not of its politics or its problems, which anyone could read about in the Hungarian dailies, but of the neighborhood where they'd lived, the people they knew, the innumerable small changes that marked the flow of time. He wanted, too, to tell Tibor what had happened to Polaner, whom he'd seen again that morning. Polaner had looked even worse than before, swollen and livid and feverish. His breath had grated in his throat, and the nurses had bent over him with dressings for his bruises and doses of fluids to raise his blood pressure. A team of doctors gathered at the foot of his bed and debated the risks and benefits of surgery. The signs of internal bleeding persisted, but the doctors couldn't agree whether it was best to operate or whether the bleeding would stop on its own. Andras tried to decode their quick medical patter, tried to piece through the puzzle of French anatomical terms, but he couldn't grasp everything, and his fear prevented him from asking questions. It was horrible to think of Polaner cut open, and even worse to think of the bleeding unstinted inside him. Andras had stayed until Professor Vago arrived to take over the watch; he didn't want Polaner to wake and find himself alone. Ben Yakov hadn't made an appearance that morning, and no one had heard from Rosen since he'd left the hospital in search of Lemarque.

Now he forced himself to look at his textbook: a list of statics problems swarming in an antlike blur. He willed the numbers and letters into an intelligible order, penciled neat columns of figures onto a clean sheet of graph paper. He calculated the force vectors acting upon fifty steel rods in a load-bearing wall of reinforced concrete, located the points of highest tension along a cathedral buttress, estimated the wind sway of a hypothetical steel structure twice as tall as the Eiffel Tower. Each building with its quiet internal math, the numbers floating within the structures. An hour passed as he made his way through the list of problems. At last Tibor groaned and sat up in bed.

"Orrh," he said. "Am I still in Paris?"

"I'm afraid so," Andras said.

Tibor insisted on taking Andras to dinner. They went to a Basque restaurant that was supposed to serve good oxtail soup. The waiter was a broad-shouldered bully who banged the plates onto the tables and shouted curses at the kitchen. The soup was thin, the meat overcooked, but they drank Basque beer that made Andras feel flushed and sentimental. Here was his brother at last, here they were together, dining in a foreign city like the grown men they'd become. Their mother would have laughed aloud to see them together in this mannish restaurant, leaning over their mugs of ale.

"Be honest," Andras said. "How's Anya? Her letters are too cheerful. I'm afraid she wouldn't tell me if something were wrong."

"I went to Konyár the weekend before I left, " Tibor said. "Mátyás was there too. Anya's trying to convince Apa to move to Debrecen for the winter. She wants him close to a good doctor if he gets pneumonia again. He won't go, of course. He insists he won't get sick, as though he had any control over that. And when I take Anya's side, he asks me who I think I am to tell him what to do. You're not a doctor yet, Tibi, he says. And he shakes his finger at me."

Andras laughed, though he knew it was a serious matter; they both knew how ill their father had been, and how their mother relied on him. "What will they do?"

"Stay in Konyár, for now."

"And Mátyás?"

Tibor shook his head. "A strange thing happened the night

before I left. Matyás and I went walking out to the rail bridge above that creek, the one where we used to catch minnows in the summer."

"I know the one," Andras said.

"It was a cold night to be out walking. The bridge was icy. We never should have been up there in the first place. Well, we stood there for a while looking at the stars, and we started talking about Anya and Apa, about what Mátyás might have to do if something happened to them, and he was angry at me, you know—I was leaving him to handle everything alone, he said. I tried to tell him they'd be fine, and that if anything truly bad happened, you and I would come home, and he said we'd never come home, that you were gone for good and that I would be soon. We were having this argument above that frozen creek, and then we heard a train coming."

"I don't know if I want to hear the end of this."

"So Mátyás says, 'Stay on the bridge. Stand here beside the tracks, on the crossties. See if we can keep our balance when the train comes by. Think you can? Not scared, are you?' The train's coming fast now. And you know that bridge, Andras. The ties give you about a meter on each side of the tracks. And it's maybe twenty meters above the creek. So he jumps onto the ties between the rails and stands there facing the train. It's coming on. The light from the headlamp's already on him. I'm shouting at him to get off, but he's not going anywhere. 'I'm not afraid,' he says. 'Let it come.' So I run at him and put him over my shoulder like a sack of sawdust, and I swear to God, the bridge was iced so badly I nearly fell and killed us both. I got him off and threw him in the snow. The train came by about a second later. He stood up laughing like a madman afterward, and I got up and hit him across the jaw. I wanted to break his neck, the little idiot."

"I *would* have broken his neck!"

"Believe me, I wanted to."

"He didn't want you to go. He's all alone there now."

"Not exactly," Tibor said. "He's got quite a life in Debrecen. Nothing like our school days. He and I made it up the next day, and I went back there with him on the way to Budapest. You should see what he's been doing at that nightclub where he performs! He ought to be in movies. He's like Fred Astaire, but with back handsprings and somersaults. And they pay him to do it! I might be happy for him if I didn't think he's completely lost his mind. He's inches from being kicked out of school, you know. He's failing Latin and history and barely sliding by in his other classes. I'm sure he'll quit as soon as he saves enough for a ticket out of Hungary. Anya and Apa know it, too."

"You didn't tell them about that bridge business, did you?"

"Are you joking?"

They signaled to the waiter for another round of drinks. While they waited, Andras asked about Budapest and their old Hársfa utca and the Jewish Quarter.

"It's all much the same as when you left," Tibor said. "Though everyone's increasingly worried that Hitler's going to drag Europe into another war."

"If he does, the Jews will get the blame. Here in France, at least."

The waiter returned, and Tibor took a long, thoughtful drink of Basque beer. "Not as much *fraternité* or *égalité* as you once thought, is there?"

Andras told him about the meeting of Le Grand Occident, and then about what had happened to Polaner. Tibor took off his glasses, wiped the lenses with his handkerchief, and put them on again.

"I was talking to a man on the train who'd just been in Munich," he said. "A Hungarian journalist sent to report on a rally there. He saw three men beaten to death for destroying copies of a state-sponsored anti-Jewish newspaper. Insurgents, the German press called them. One of them was a decorated officer from the Great War."

Andras sighed and rubbed the bridge of his nose. "With

Polaner the situation's personal," he said. "There are questions about his relationship with one of the men who did it."

"It's just the same brand of hatred writ small," Tibor said. "Horrible any way you look at it."

"I was a fool to think things would be different here."

"Europe's changing," Tibor said. "The picture's getting bleaker everywhere. But it hasn't all been grim for you here, I hope."

"It hasn't." He looked up at Tibor and managed a smile.

"What's that about, Andráska?"

"Nothing."

"Are you harboring secrets? Have you got some intrigue going on?"

"You'll have to buy me a stronger drink," Andras said.

At a nearby bar they ordered whiskey, and he told Tibor everything: about the invitation to the Morgensterns', and how he'd recognized the name and address from the letter; how he'd fallen in love with Klara, not Elisabet; how they'd failed to keep the attraction at bay. How Klara had told him nothing about what had brought her to Paris, or why her identity had to be kept a secret. When he'd finished, Tibor held on to his glass and stared.

"How much older is she?"

There was no way around it. "Nine years."

"Good God," Tibor said. "You're in love with a grown woman. This is serious, Andras, do you understand?"

"Serious as death."

"Put down that glass. I'm talking to you."

"I'm listening."

"She's thirty-one," Tibor said. "She's not a girl. What are your intentions?"

A tightness gathered in Andras's throat. "I want to marry her," he said.

"Of course. And you'll live on what?"

"Believe me, I've thought about that."

"Four and a half more years," Tibor said. "That's how long it'll take you to get your degree. She'll be thirty-six. When you're her age, she'll be nearly forty. And when you're forty, she'll be—"

"Stop it," Andras said. "I can do the math."

"But have you?"

"So what? So what if she's forty-nine when I'm forty?"

"What happens when you're forty and a thirty-year-old woman starts paying attention to you? Do you think you'll stay faithful to your wife?"

"Tibi, do you have to do this?"

"What about the daughter? Does she know what's going on between you and her mother?"

Andras shook his head. "Elisabet detests me, and she's terrible to Klara. I doubt she'd take kindly to the situation."

"And József Hász? Does he know you've fallen in love with his aunt?"

"No. He doesn't know his aunt's whereabouts. The family doesn't trust him with the information, whatever that means."

Tibor laced his fingers. "Good God, Andras, I don't envy you."

"I was hoping you'd tell me what to do."

"I know what I'd do. I'd break it off as soon as I could."

"You haven't even met her."

"What difference would that make?"

"I don't know. I was hoping you might want to. Aren't you even curious?"

"Desperately," he said. "But I won't participate in your undoing. Not even as a spectator." And he called the waiter over and requested the bill, then firmly changed the subject.

In the morning Andras brought Tibor to the École Spéciale, where they met Vago at his office. When they entered, Vago was sitting behind his desk and talking on the telephone in his particular manner: He held the mouthpiece between his cheek and shoulder and gesticulated with both hands. He sketched the shape of a flawed building in the air, then erased it with a sweep of his arm, then sketched another building, this one with a roof that *seemed flat* but was *not flat*, to allow for *drainage*—and then the conversation was over, and Andras introduced Tibor to Vago at last, there in the room where he had been the subject of so many morning conversations, as though the talking itself had caused Tibor to materialize.

"Off to Modena," Vago said. "I envy you. You'll love Italy. You won't ever want to go back to Budapest."

"I'm grateful for your help," Tibor said. "If I can ever repay the favor . . ."

Vago waved the idea away. "You'll become a doctor," he said. "If I'm lucky, I won't need your favors." Then he gave them the news from the hospital: Polaner was holding steady; the doctors had decided not to operate yet. Of Lemarque there was still no sign. Rosen had kicked down the door of his rooming house the day before, but he was nowhere to be found.

Tibor sat through the morning classes with Andras. He heard Andras present his solution to the statics problem about the cathedral buttress, and he let Andras show him his drawings in studio. He met Ben Yakov and Rosen, who quickly exhausted the few words of Hungarian they'd learned from Andras; Tibor bantered with them in his sparse but fearless French. At noon, over lunch at the school café, Rosen talked about his trip to Lemarque's rooming house. He looked depleted now; his face had lost its angry flush, and his russet-colored freckles seemed to float on the surface of his skin. "What a rathole," he said. "A hundred cramped dark rooms full of smelly men. It stank worse than a prison. You could almost feel sorry for the bastard, living in a place like that." He paused to give a broad yawn. He'd been up all night at the hospital.

"And nothing?" Ben Yakov said. "Not a trace of him?"

Rosen shook his head. "I searched the place from basement to attic. Nobody had seen him, or at least they claimed they hadn't."

"And what if you'd found him?" Tibor asked.

"What would I have done, you mean? At the time, I would have choked him to death with my bare hands. But I would have been a fool to do it. We need to know who his accomplices were."

The student café began to clear. Doors opened and slammed all around the atrium as students filtered into the classrooms. Tibor watched them go, his eyes grave behind his silver-rimmed glasses.

"What are you thinking about?" Andras asked him in Hungarian.

"Lucky Béla," Tibor said. "*Ember embernek farkasa.*"

"Speak French, Hungarians," Rosen said. "What are you talking about?"

"Something our father used to say," Andras said, and repeated the phrase.

"And what does that mean, in the parlance of the rest of the world?"

"*Man is a wolf to man.*"

That night they were supposed to go to a party at József Hász's on the boulevard Saint-Jacques. It was to be the first time Andras would spend an evening at József's since the beginning of his liaison with Klara. The idea made him anxious, but József had invited him in person a week earlier; a few of his paintings were to appear in a student show at the Beaux-Arts, which Andras must be sure to miss because it would be a terrible bore, but after the opening there would be drinks and dinner at József's. Andras had demurred on the basis that Tibor would be in town and that he couldn't burden József with another guest, but that had only made József insist all the more: If Tibor were in Paris for the first time, he couldn't miss a party at József Hász's.

When they arrived, the company was already drunk. A trio of poets stood on the sofa and shouted verse in three-part cacophony while a girl in a green leotard performed acts of contortion on the Oriental rug. József himself presided over the card table, winning at poker while the other players scowled at their dwindling piles of money.

"The Hungarians have arrived!" József said when he saw them. "Now we'll have a real game. Pull up a chair, men! Play cards."

"I'm afraid we can't," Andras said. "We're broke."

József dealt a hand with dazzling speed. "Eat, then," he said. "If you're broke, you're probably hungry. Aren't you hungry?" He didn't look up from his cards. "Visit the buffet."

On the dining table was a raft of baguettes, three wheels of cheese, pickles, apples, figs, a chocolate torte, six bottles of wine.

"Now that's a welcome sight," Tibor said. "Free dinner."

They made sandwiches of figs and cheese and took them to the large front room, where they watched the contortionist become a circle, a bell, a Spanish knot. Afterward she posed erotically with another girl, while a third girl took photographs with an ancient-looking camera.

Tibor watched in a mesmeric trance. "Does Hász have parties like this often?" he asked, following the girls with his eyes as they shifted to a new pose.

"More often than you'd imagine," Andras said.

"How many people live in this apartment?"

"Just him."

Tibor let out a low whistle.

"There's hot water in the bathroom, too."

"Now you're exaggerating."

"No, I'm not. And a porcelain tub with lion feet. Come see."

He led Tibor down the hall toward the back of the apartment

and paused at the bathroom door, which stood open just enough to show a sliver of white porcelain. A glow of candles emanated from within. Andras opened the door. There, blinking against the glare from the hallway, was a couple standing against the wall, the girl's hair disheveled, the top buttons of her shirt undone. The girl was Elisabet Morgenstern, one hand raised against the light.

"Pardon us, gentlemen," the man said in American-accented French, each word delivered with drink-soaked languor.

Elisabet had recognized Andras at once. "Stop looking at me, you stupid Hungarian!" she said.

Andras took a step backward into the hall, pulling Tibor along with him. The man gave them a wink of drunken triumph and kicked the door closed.

"Well," Tibor said. "I suppose we'd better examine the plumbing later."

"That might be best."

"And who was that darling girl? She seems to know you."

"That darling girl was Elisabet Morgenstern."

"*The* Elisabet? Klara's daughter?"

"The."

"And who was the man?"

"Someone awfully brave, that's for sure."

"Does József know Elisabet?" Tibor said. "Do you think the secret's out between them?"

Andras shook his head. "No idea. Elisabet does seem to live her own life outside the house. But József's never mentioned a secret cousin, which I'm certain he would have, as much as he loves to gossip." His temples began to pound as he wondered what exactly he had discovered, and what he would tell Klara.

They wove their way back to the sofa and sat down to watch the guests play charades; a girl appropriated Andras's coat and wore it over her head like a hood while she stooped to pick invisible flowers. The others called out the titles of films Andras had never seen. He needed another glass of wine, and was ready to get up and look for one when Elisabet's lover staggered into the room. The man, blond and broad-shouldered and wearing an expensive-looking merino jacket, tucked his shirt into his trousers and smoothed his hair. He raised a hand in greeting and sat down on the couch between Andras and Tibor.

"How are we, gentlemen?" he asked in his languid French. "You're not having nearly as much fun as I am, from the look of it." He sounded like the Hollywood stars who did commercials for Radio France. "That girl's quite a firecracker. I met her on a ski vacation over Christmas, and I'm afraid I've become addicted to her."

"We were just leaving," Andras said. "We'll be on our way now."

"No, sir!" the blond American crowed. He put an arm across Andras's chest. "No one goes! We're staying all night!"

Down the hall came Elisabet, shaking drops of water from her hands. She'd hastily rearranged her hair and misbuttoned her blouse. When she reached the front room, she beckoned to Andras with a single urgent sweep of her hand. Andras got up from the sofa and excused himself with a half bow, then followed Elisabet down the hall. She led him to József's bedroom, where a deluge of coats had overflowed the bed and pooled on the floor.

"All right," she said, crossing her arms over her chest. "Tell me what you saw."

"Nothing!" Andras said. "Not a thing."

"If you tell my mother about Paul, I'll kill you."

"When would I tell her, now that you've banished me from your house?"

Elisabet's look became shrewd. "Don't play innocent with me," she said. "I know you haven't spent the past two months hoping I'd fall in love with you. I know what's going on between you and my mother. I could see how she looked at you. I'm not a fool, Andras. She might not tell me everything, but I've known her long enough to be able to tell when she's got a lover. And you're just her type. Or one of her types, I should say."

Now it was his turn to show a self-conscious flush; *I could see how she looked at you.* And how he must have looked at her. How could anyone have failed to see it? He glanced down at the hearth; a silver cigarette case lay among the ashes, its monogram obscured. "You know she wouldn't want you to be here," he said. "Does she know you know József Hász?"

"That idiot who lives here, you mean? Why, is he some sort of notorious criminal?"

"Not exactly," Andras said. "He can throw a rather rough party, that's all."

"I just met him tonight. He's some friend of Paul's from school."

"And you met Paul in Chamonix?"

"I don't see where that's any business of yours. And I mean it, Andras, you can't tell my mother about any of this. She'll lock me in my room for life." She tugged at her shirt, and when she saw she'd buttoned it wrong, pronounced an unladylike curse.

"I won't tell," he said. "Upon my honor."

Elisabet scowled at him, seeming to doubt his trustworthiness; but behind her hard look there was a flash of vulnerability, a consciousness that he held the key to something that mattered to her. Andras wasn't certain whether it was Paul himself she loved, or whether it was simply the freedom to carry on a life beyond her mother's scrutiny, but in either case he understood. He spoke his pledge again. Her tight-held shoulders relaxed a single degree, and she let out a truncated sigh. Then she fished a pair of coats from the pile on the bed, brushed past him into the hall, and returned to the front room, where Paul and Tibor were still watching the charades.

"It's late, Paul," Elisabet said, throwing his coat onto his lap. "Let's go."

"It's early!" Paul said. "Come sit here with us and watch these girls."

"I can't. I have to get home."

"Come to me, lioness," he said, and took her wrist.

"If I have to go home alone, I will," she said, and pulled away.

Paul got up from the sofa and kissed Elisabet on the mouth. "Stubborn girl," he said. "I hope this gentleman wasn't rude to you." He gave Andras a wink.

"This gentleman has the deepest respect for the young lady," Andras said.

Elisabet rolled her eyes. "All right," she said. "That's enough." She shrugged into her coat, gave Andras a last warning look, and went to the door. Paul snapped a salute and followed her into the hallway.

"Well," Tibor said. "I think you'd better sit down and tell me what that was all about."

"She begged me not to tell her mother that I saw her with that man."

"And what did you say?"

"I swore I'd never tell."

"Not that you'd have the opportunity anyway."

"Well," Andras said. "It seems Elisabet has figured out what's going on between her mother and me."

"Ah. So the secret's out."

"That one is, anyway. She seemed not at all surprised. She said I was her mother's type, whatever that means. But she doesn't seem to have any idea that József's her cousin." He sighed. "Tibor, what in God's name am I doing?"

"That's just what I've been asking you," Tibor said, and put an arm around Andras's shoulders. A moment later József Hász appeared, three glasses of champagne in his hands. He passed them each a glass and toasted their health.

"Are you having fun?" he said. "Everyone must have fun."

"Oh, yes," Andras said, grateful for the champagne.

"I see you've met my American friend Paul," József said. "His father's an industrial chieftain. Automobile tires or some such thing. That new girlfriend of his is a little sharp-tongued for my taste, but he's wild about her. Maybe he thinks that's just the way French girls act."

"If that's the way French girls act, you gentlemen are in trouble," Tibor said.

"Here's to trouble," József said, and they drained their glasses.

The next day Andras and Tibor walked the long halls of the Louvre, taking in the velvet-brown shadows of Rembrandt and the frivolous curlicues of Fragonard and the muscular curves of the classical marbles; then they strolled along the quais to the Pont d'Iéna and stood beneath the monumental arches of the Tower. They circumnavigated the Gare d'Orsay as Andras described how he'd built his model; finally they backtracked to the Luxembourg, where the apiary stood in silent hibernation. They sat with Polaner at the hospital as he slept through the nurses' ministrations; Polaner, whose terrible story Andras hadn't yet told Klara. They watched him sleep for nearly an hour. Andras wished he'd wake, wished he wouldn't look so pale and still; the nurses said he was better that day, but Andras couldn't see any change. Afterward they walked to the Sarah-Bernhardt, where Tibor lent a hand with the closing-down. They stowed the coffee things and folded the wooden table, cleared the actors' pigeonholes of ancient messages, shuttled stray props to the prop room and costumes to the costume shop, where Madame Courbet was folding garments into her neatly labeled cabinets. Claudel gave Andras a half-full box of cigars—a former prop—and apologized for having told him so many times to burn in hell. He hoped Andras could forgive him, now that they'd both been cast upon the whims of fate.

Andras forgave him. "I know you didn't mean any harm," he said.

"That's a good boy," Claudel said, and kissed him on both cheeks. "He's a good boy," he told Tibor. "A darling."

Monsieur Novak met them in the hallway as they were on their way out. He called them into his office, where he produced three cut-crystal glasses and poured out the last of a bottle of Tokaji. They toasted Tibor's studies in Italy, and then they toasted the eventual reopening of the Sarah-Bernhardt and the three other theaters that were closing that week. "A city without theater is like a party without conversation," Novak said. "No matter how good the food and drink are, people will find it dull. Aristophanes said that, I believe."

"Thank you for keeping my brother out of the gutter," Tibor said.

"Oh, he would have found a way without me," Novak said, and put a hand on Andras's shoulder.

"It was your umbrella that saved him," Tibor said. "Otherwise he would have missed his train. And then he might have lost his nerve."

"No, not him," Novak said. "Not our Mr. Lévi. He would have been all right. And so will you, my young man, in Italy." He shook Tibor's hand and wished him luck.

It was dark by the time they left. They walked along the quai de Gesvres as the lights of the bridges and barges shivered on the water. A wind tore through the river channel, flattening Andras's coat against his back. He knew Klara was in her studio at that hour, teaching the final segment of her evening class. Without telling Tibor where they were going he steered them down the rue François Miron in the direction of the rue de Sévigné. He traced the route he hadn't walked in weeks. And there on the corner, its light spilling into the street, was the dance studio with its demi-curtains, its sign that said MME. MORGENSTERN, MAÎTRESSE. The faint sound of phonograph music reached them through the glass: the slow, stately Schumann she used for the end-of-class révérences. This was a class of intermediate girls, slender ten-year-olds with downy napes, their shoulder blades like small sharp wings beneath the cotton of their leotards. At the front of the room Klara led them through a series of sweeping curtseys. Her hair was gathered into a loose roll at the base of her neck, and she wore a practice dress of plum-colored viscose, tied at the waist with a black ribbon. Her arms were supple and strong, her features tranquil. She needed no one; she had made a life, and here it was: these end-of-day révérences, her own daughter upstairs, Mrs. Apfel, the warm rooms of the flat she'd bought for herself. And yet from him, from Andras Lévi, a twenty-two-year-old student at the École Spéciale, she seemed to want something: the luxury of vulnerability, perhaps; the sharp thrill of uncertainty. As he watched, his heart seemed to go still in his chest.

"There she is," he said. "Klara Morgenstern."

"God," Tibor said. "She's beautiful, that's for certain."

"Let's see if she'll have dinner with us."

"No, Andras. I'm not going to do it."

"Why not?" he said. "You came here to see how I live, didn't you? This is it. If you don't meet her, you won't know."

Tibor watched as Klara lifted her arms; the children lifted their arms and swept into low curtseys.

"She's tiny," Tibor said. "She's a wood nymph."

Andras tried to see her as Tibor was seeing her—tried to see her for the first time. There was something fearless, something girlish, about the way she moved her body, as if part of her remained a child. But her eyes held the look of a woman who had seen one lifetime pass into another. That was what made her like a nymph, Andras thought: the way she seemed to embody both timelessness and the irrevocable passage of time. The music reached its end, and the girls rushed for their satchels and coats. Tibor and Andras watched them leave. Then they met Klara at the studio door, where she stood shivering in her practice dress.

"Andras," she said, reaching for his hand. He was relieved that she seemed glad to see him; he hadn't known how she'd react to his coming to the studio. But there was nothing wrong with his stopping in as he passed through the Marais, he told himself; it was an ordinary thing, something an acquaintance might have done.

"This is a surprise," she said. "And who's this gentleman?"

"This is Tibor," Andras said. "My brother."

Klara took his hand. "Tibor Lévi!" she said. "At last. I've been hearing about you for months." She glanced over her shoulder, up the stairs. "But what are the two of you doing here? I know you haven't come to take a lesson."

"Have dinner with us," Andras said.

She laughed, a little nervously. "I'm hardly dressed for it."

"We'll have a drink and wait for you."

She put a hand to her mouth and glanced over her shoulder again. From the apartment came the sound of quick footsteps and the rustle of outdoor garments. "My inscrutable daughter is dining out with friends tonight."

"Come, then," Andras said. "We'll keep you company."

"All right," she said. "Where will you be?"

Andras named a place that served bouillabaisse with slabs of thick brown bread. They both loved it; they'd been there during their ten days together in December.

"I'll be there in half an hour," Klara said, and ran upstairs.

The restaurant had once been a smithy, and still smelled faintly of cinders and iron. The smelting ovens had been converted to cooking ovens; there were rough-hewn wooden tables, a menu full of cheap dishes, and strong apple cider served in earthenware bowls. They sat down at one of the tables and ordered drinks.

"So that was your Klara," Tibor said, and shook his head. "She can't be the mother of that girl we met at the party last night."

"I'm afraid so."

"What a disaster! How did she come by that child? She must have been little more than a girl herself at the time."

"She was fifteen," Andras said. "I don't know anything about the father, except that he's long dead. She doesn't like to talk about any of it."

She came in just as they were ordering a second round of drinks. She hung her red hat and her coat on a hook beside the table and sat down with them, tucking a few damp strands of hair behind her ear. Andras felt the heat of her legs close to his own; he touched the folds of her dress beneath the table. She raised her eyes to him and asked if anything were wrong. He couldn't tell her, of course, what was most immediately wrong: that Tibor objected to their liaison, at least in theory. So he told her instead what had happened to Polaner at the École Spéciale.

"What a nightmare," she said when he'd finished, and put her forehead into her hands. "That poor boy. And what about his parents? Has someone written to them?"

"He asked us not to. He's ashamed, you know."

"Of course. My God."

The three of them sat in silence, looking at their bowls of cider. When Andras glanced at Tibor it seemed to him that his brother's look had softened; it was as though, in the shadow of what had happened to Polaner, it had become an absurdity, a luxury, to hold an opinion about the rightness or wrongness of love. Tibor asked Klara about the class she'd been teaching, and she asked what he thought of Paris and whether he'd have time to see Italy before school began.

"There won't be much time to travel," Tibor said. "Classes start next week."

"And what will you study first?"

"Anatomy."

"You'll find it fascinating," she said. "I did."

"You've studied anatomy?"

"Oh, yes," she said. "In Budapest, as part of my ballet training. I had a master who believed in teaching the physics and mechanics of the human body. He made us read books with anatomical drawings that disgusted most of the girls—and some of the boys, too, though they tried not to show it. And one day he took us to the medical school at Budapest University, where the students were dissecting cadavers. He had one of the professors show us all the muscles and tendons and bones of the leg and the arm. Then the back, the spine. Two girls fainted, I remember. But I loved it."

Tibor looked at her with reluctant admiration. "And do you think it improved your dancing?"

"I don't know. I think it helps my teaching. It helps me explain things." She became pensive for a moment, touching the stitched edge of her napkin. "You know, I have some of those anatomy books at home. More than I need or use. I should make you a gift of one of them, if you've got room in your luggage."

"I couldn't," Tibor said, but a familiar covetousness had come into his eyes. Their father's mania for old books had become their own; Tibor and Andras had spent hours at the used bookstores in Budapest, where Tibor had taken down one ancient anatomy book after another and showed Andras in color-plated detail the shy curve of a pancreas, the cumular cluster of a lung. He pined for those gorgeous tomes he could never afford, not even at the used booksellers' prices.

"I insist," Klara said. "You'll come by after dinner and choose one."

And so, after the bouillabaisse and another round of cider, they went to the rue de Sévigné and climbed the stairs to Klara's apartment. Here was the sitting room where he'd seen her for the first time; here was the nest-shaped bowl with its candy eggs, the gray velvet sofa, the phonograph, the amber-shaded lamps—the intimate landscape of her life, denied him for the past month. From one of the bookshelves she extracted three large leather-bound anatomy books. She laid them on the writing desk and opened the gold-stamped covers. Tibor unfolded the leaves of illustrations to reveal the mysteries of the human body in four-color ink: the bones with their woven sheaths of muscle, the spiderweb of the lymphatic system, the coiled snake of the intestines, the small windowed room of the eye. The heaviest and most beautiful of all the volumes was a folio copy of *Corpus Humanum*, printed in Latin and inscribed for Klara in the bold angular script of her ballet master, Viktor Romankov: *Sine scientia ars nihil est. Budapest 1920.*

She took that volume from Tibor and replaced it in its leather box. "This is the one I want to give you," she said, laying it in his arms.

He flushed and shook his head. "I couldn't possibly."

"I want you to have it," she said. "For your studies."

"I'll be traveling. I wouldn't want to damage it." He held it toward her again.

"No," she said. "Take it. You'll be glad to have it. I'll be glad to think of it in Modena. It's a small thing, considering what you've had to do to get there."

Tibor looked down at the book in his hands. He raised his eyes to meet Andras's, but Andras wouldn't look at him; he knew that if he did, this would become a matter of whether or not Tibor approved of what existed between Andras and Klara. So he kept his own gaze fixed on the fireplace screen, with its faded scene of a horse and rider in a shadowy wood, and let Tibor's desire for that gorgeous folio make the decision for him. After another moment of hesitation, Tibor made gruff avowals of his gratitude and let Klara wrap the book in brown paper.

On Tibor's final day in Paris, he and Andras rode the thundering Métro to Boulogne-Billancourt. The afternoon was warm for January, windless and dry. They walked the long quiet avenues, past the bakeries and greengrocers and haberdashers, out toward the neighborhood where Pingusson's white ocean-liner building cut through the air as though en route to the sea. Andras told the story of the poker game wherein Perret's loss had been transformed into a scholarship; then he led his brother farther along the rue Denfert-Rochereau, where buildings by Le Corbusier and Mallet-Stevens and Raymond Fischer and Pierre Patout stood radiating their austere, unadorned strength. In the months since his first visit here, Andras had returned again and again to this small cluster of streets where the living architects he admired most had built small-scale shrines to simplicity and beauty. One morning not long ago he had come upon Perret's Villa Gordin, a blocklike and vaguely Japanese-looking house built for a sculptor, with a bank of reflective windows offset by two rectangles of perpendicularly laid bricks. Perret might have built anything he liked on any empty piece of land in Paris, but had chosen to do this: to create a work of Spartan simplicity, a human-sized space for an artist on a tiny street where a person could work and be alone. The building had become Andras's favorite in Boulogne-Billancourt. They sat down on the curb across the street and he told his brother about the Latvian-born sculptor who lived there, Dora Gordin, and about the airy studio Perret had designed for her at the back of the house.

"Remember those huts you used to build in Konyár?" Tibor said. "Your housing business?"

The housing business. The summer he turned nine, just before he'd started school in Debrecen, he had become a building contractor for the neighborhood boys. He had a monopoly on scrap wood, and could build a fort or clubhouse in half a day. Four-year-old Mátyás was his assistant. Mátyás would come along on the jobs and solemnly hand nails to Andras as Andras pounded the huts together. In return for his building services, Andras collected whatever the boys had to offer: a photograph of someone's father in a soldier's uniform, a fleet of tiny tin warplanes, a cat's skull, a balsa boat, a white mouse in a cage. That summer he had been the richest boy in town.

"Remember my mouse?" Andras said. "Remember what you used to call him?"

"Eliahu ha Navi."

"Anya hated that. She thought it was sacrilegious." He smiled and flexed his fingers against the cold curb. The shadows were lengthening, and the chill had made its way through the layers of his clothing. He was ready to suggest they keep walking, but Tibor leaned back on his elbows and looked up at the roof garden with its row of little evergreens.

"That was the year I fell in love for the first time," he said. "I never told you. You were too young to understand, and by the time you were old enough I was in love with someone else, Zsuzsanna, that girl I used to take to dances at gimnázium. But before her there was a girl named Rózsa Geller. Rózsika. I was thirteen, she was sixteen. She was the oldest daughter of the family I boarded with in Debrecen. The ones who moved away just before you came to school."

Andras caught an unfamiliar edge in Tibor's voice, almost a note of bitterness. "Sixteen," he said, and gave a low whistle. "An older woman."

"I used to watch her bathing. She used to bathe in the kitchen in a tin washtub, and my bed was on the other side of the curtain. That curtain was full of holes. She must have known I was watching."

"And you saw everything."

"Everything. She would stand there pouring water over herself and humming the Marseillaise."

"Why the Marseillaise?"

"She was in love with some French film star. He'd been in a lot of war movies."

"Pierre Fresnay."

"That's right, that was the bastard's name. How did you know?"

"That friend of mine, Ben Yakov, looks just like him."

"Hm. I'm glad I didn't know that when I met your friend."

"So what happened?"

"One day her father caught me watching. He beat me bloody. Broke my arm."

"You broke your arm playing football!"

"That was the official story. Her father said he'd turn me over to the police if I told the truth. They put me out of the house. I never saw her again."

"Oh, God, Tibor. I never knew."

"That was the idea."

"It's terrible! You were only thirteen."

"And she was sixteen. She knew better than to let it go on. She must have known I'd get caught eventually. Maybe she wanted me to get caught." He stood and brushed the dust from his trousers. "So you see, that's my experience with older women."

There was a motion behind one of the windows of the house, the shadow of a woman crossing a square of light. Andras stood up beside his brother. He imagined the sculptor coming to her window, seeing them loitering there as if they were waiting to catch a glimpse of her.

"I'm not thirteen," Andras said. "Klara's not sixteen."

"No, indeed," Tibor said. "You're adults. Which means the consequences may be graver if you get in over your heads."

"It's too late," Andras said. "I'm already in over my head. I don't know what'll happen. I'm at her mercy."

"I hope she'll show some mercy, then," Tibor said. And he used the Yiddish word *rachmones*, the same word that had called Andras back to himself three months earlier at the Jardin du Luxembourg.

The next morning they carried Tibor's bags to the Gare de Lyon, just as they'd carried Andras's bags to Nyugati Station when he'd left for Paris. Now it was Tibor going off to an unknown life in a foreign place, Tibor going off to study and work and navigate the dark passageways of a foreign language. The wind roared through the channels of the boulevards and tried to twist the suitcases from their hands; the previous day's warm weather was gone as though they'd only dreamed it. Paris was as gray as it had been the day Andras had arrived. He wished he had an excuse to keep Tibor with him another day, another week. Tibor was right, of course. It was a foolish thing Andras had done, getting involved with Klara Morgenstern. He'd already ventured into dangerous terrain, had found himself edging along a dwindling path toward a blind corner of rock. He didn't have the shoes for this, nor the provisions, nor the clothing, nor the foresight, nor the mental strength, nor the experience. All he had was a kind of reckless hope—something, he imagined, not unlike the hope that had sent fifteenth-century explorers hurtling off the map. Having pointed out how ill-equipped Andras was, how could Tibor now let him go on alone? How could he step onto a train and speed off to Italy, even if medical school waited at the other end? His role had always been to show Andras the way when the way was obscure—at times, in their boyhood, quite literally, his hand was Andras's only guide in the dark. But now they had reached the Gare de Lyon; there was the train itself, black and impassive on its tracks.

"All right, then," Tibor said. "Off I go."

Stay, Andras wanted to say. "Good luck," he said.

"Write to me. And don't get in trouble. Do you understand?"

"I understand."

"Good. I'll see you before long."

Liar, Andras wanted to say.

Tibor put a hand on Andras's sleeve. He looked as if he meant to say something more, a few final words in Hungarian before he boarded a train full of Italian- and French-speakers, but he was silent as he glanced off toward the vast mouth of the station and the tangle of tracks that lay beyond it. He stepped up onto the train and Andras handed him his leather satchel. His silver-rimmed glasses slid down the bridge of his nose; he pushed them back with his thumb.

"Write me when you get there," Andras said.

Tibor touched his cap and disappeared into the third-class car, and was gone.

When the train had left the station, Andras went back through the SORTIE doors and walked out into a city that no longer contained his brother. He walked on benumbed feet in the new black Oxfords his brother had brought him from Hungary. He didn't care who passed him on the street or where he was going. If he had stepped off the curb into the air instead of down into the gutter, if he had climbed the void above the cars and between the buildings until he was looking down at the rooftops with their red-clay chimney pots, their irregular curving grid, and if he had then kept climbing until he was wading through the slough of low-lying clouds in the winter sky, he would have felt no shock or joy, no wonder or surprise, just the same leaden dampness in his limbs. His feet led him farther from his brother, westward across town to the boulevard Raspail, all the way to the École Spéciale, and in through the blue doors of the courtyard.

The yard was full of students, all of them strangely silent, standing in head-bowed clumps of three and four. A heavy stillness hung in the air above the yard. It had a palpable black presence, like a flock of crows frozen midflight. On a splintered bench in a corner Perret himself sat with his head in his hands.

This was what had happened: By way of the slow-moving provincial post, the news of Polaner's injuries had reached Lemarque in Bayeux, where he'd fled to his parents' farm after the attack. The letter, written by his accomplices, told him that Polaner lay in the hospital on the brink of death, bleeding from internal wounds: an account meant to hearten Lemarque, to show him that all had not been in vain, that the work of the beating had continued after the attack. Having received this letter, Lemarque had written two of his own. One he addressed to the directors of the school, claiming responsibility for what had happened and naming three other students, third- and fourth-year men, who had participated. The other he addressed to Polaner, a brief admission of remorse and love. Late at night, after he'd left both letters on the kitchen table, he'd hanged himself from a crossbeam in his parents' barn. His father had discovered the body that morning, cold and blue as the hibernal dawn itself.

CHAPTER FOURTEEN

A Haircut

IT WAS DECIDED—first in a late-night meeting at Perret's office, then later still at the Blue Dove—that Andras would be the one to break the news of Lemarque's death to Polaner. Perret believed it was his own responsibility as director of the school, but Vago argued that the delicacy of the situation called for special measures; it might be easier, he said, if the news were to come from a friend. Andras and Rosen and Ben Yakov agreed, and decided among themselves that Andras should be the one to give Polaner the letter. They would wait, of course, until the doctors considered him to be out of danger; there was reason to think that time might come soon. After a second week in the hospital the symptoms and aftereffects of internal bleeding had abated. Polaner's disorientation had passed, his bruising and swelling had receded; he could eat and drink again on his own. He would be in a weakened state for nearly a month, the doctors said, while he remade the blood that had been lost, but all agreed that he had moved back from the brink. That weekend, in fact, he appeared so well recovered that Andras dared to approach one of his doctors and explain in careful French about Lemarque. The doctor, a long-faced internist who had made Polaner's case his special project, expressed concern about the possible effects of the shock; but because the news could not be kept from Polaner forever, the doctor agreed that it might be better to tell him while he was still in the hospital and could be closely watched.

The next day, as Andras sat in the now-familiar steel chair beside the bed, he introduced the subject of the École Spéciale for the first time since the attack. Now that Polaner was mending so well, Andras said, the doctor thought he might consider a gradual return to his schoolwork. Could Andras bring him anything from the studio—his statics texts, his drawing tools, a sketchbook?

Polaner gave Andras a look of pity and closed his eyes. "I'm not going back to school," he said. "I'm going home to Kraków."

Andras laid a hand on his arm. "Is that what you want?"

Polaner let out a long breath. "It's been decided for me," he said. "They decided it."

"Nothing's been decided. You'll go back to school if you want."

"I can't," Polaner said, his eyes filling with tears. "How can I face Lemarque, or any of them? I can't go to studio and sit down at my table as if nothing happened."

There was no use waiting any longer; Andras took the letter from his pocket and put it into Polaner's hands. Polaner spent a long moment looking at the envelope, at his name written in Lemarque's sharp-edged print. Then he opened the letter and flattened the single sheet against his leg. He read the six lines in which Lemarque confessed himself and begged Polaner's pardon, both for the attack and for what he felt he must do. When he'd finished reading, he folded the note again and lay back against the pillow, his eyes closed, his chest rising and falling beneath the sheet.

"Oh, God," he said in a half whisper. "It's as though I killed him myself."

Before that moment Andras had believed that his hate for Lemarque had reached its limit, that with Lemarque's death his feelings had moved past hate toward something more like pity. But as he watched Polaner grieve, as he watched the familiar lines and planes of his friend's face crumple under the burden of the news, he found himself shaking with anger. How much worse that Lemarque's death had come with this confession of remorse and love! Now Polaner would always have to consider what had been lost, what might have been if the world had been a different place. Here was a cruelty beyond the attack and the death itself, a sting like that of certain fire nettles that grew on the Hajdú plain: Once the spine was in, it would work its way deeper into the wound and discharge its poison there for days, for weeks, while the victim burned.

He stayed with Polaner that night long past dark, ignoring the ward nurse's reminder that visiting hours were over. When she insisted, he told her she would have to call the police to get rid of him; eventually the long-faced doctor interceded on Andras's behalf, and he was allowed to stay all night and into the next morning. As he kept watch beside the bed, his mind kept returning to what Polaner had said at the Blue Dove in October: *I just want to keep my head down. I want to study and get my degree.* If it were in his power, he thought, he would not let Polaner's shame and grief send him home to Kraków.

Another week passed before Polaner left the hospital. When he did, it was Andras who brought him home to his room on the boulevard Saint-Germain. He watched over Polaner's injuries, kept him fed, took his clothes to the laundry, built up the fire in the grate when it burned low. One morning he returned from the bakery to find Polaner sitting up in bed with a drawing tablet angled against his knees; the coverlet was snowed with pencil shavings, the chair beside the bed strewn with charcoals. Andras said not a word as he deposited a pair of baguettes on the table. He prepared bread and jam and tea for Polaner and gave it to him in bed, then took a seat at Polaner's table. And all morning the noise of Polaner's pencil followed him through his own work like music.

Later that morning, Polaner stood before the mirror at the bureau and ran his hands over his stubble-shadowed chin. "I look like a criminal," he said. "I look like I've been in jail for months."

"You look a good deal better than you did a few weeks ago."

"It seems absurd to think about a haircut," he said, almost in a whisper.

"What's absurd about it?"

"I don't know. Everything. To begin with, I don't know if I

can sit in a barber's chair and carry on a barbershop conversation."

Andras stood beside Polaner at the mirror, regarding him in the glass. He himself looked neater than he had in weeks; Klara had given him a trim the night before, and had made him look something like a gentleman, though she liked his hair long.

"Look," Andras said. "Suppose I were to ask a friend to come and cut your hair. Then you wouldn't have to sit in a barber's chair and trade stories with the barber."

"What friend?" Polaner said, regarding Andras in the glass.

"A rather close friend."

Polaner turned from the mirror to look at Andras directly. "A lady friend?"

"*Exactement.*"

"What lady friend, Andras? What's been going on while I've been lying in bed?"

"I'm afraid this has been going on quite a while longer than that. Months, actually."

Polaner gave Andras a fleet, shy smile; for that moment, and for the first time since the news of Lemarque's death, he seemed to have slipped back into his own skin. "I don't suppose you'd like to tell me all about it."

"Now that I've mentioned it, I consider myself under an obligation."

Polaner gestured toward a chair. "Tell," he said.

The next night found Polaner seated on that same chair in the middle of the room, his shoulders draped in a tea towel, the mirror propped before him, while Klara Morgenstern ministered to him with scissors and comb and talked to him in her low hypnotic way. When Andras had spoken to her the night before, she had understood at once why she must do what he asked; she had cancelled her dinner plans to do it. Earlier that evening, on their way to Polaner's, she'd held Andras's hand with a kind of mute fervor as they crossed the Seine, her eyes downcast with what Andras imagined to be the memory of a similar grief. Now he stood near the fire and watched the locks of hair fall, silent with gratitude to this woman who understood the need to do this simple and intimate thing, to perform this act of restoration in an attic apartment on the boulevard Saint-Germain.

CHAPTER FIFTEEN

In the Tuileries

THAT SPRING, when he was not in class or tending Polaner or seeing Klara, Andras learned the design and construction of stage sets under the tutelage of Vincent Forestier. Monsieur Forestier had a studio on the rue des Gravilliers where he drafted designs and built his models; for months he had been desperately in need of a new apprentice to assist with the copying of plans, the detailed and painstaking work of model construction. Forestier was tall and heavy and mournful, with a perpetual haze of gray stubble and a habit of punctuating his utterances with shrugs of his broad shoulders, as if he himself didn't set much store by what he was saying. It turned out that he was also a quiet genius of design. With the strictest of financial constraints and the shortest of production times, he could produce palaces and city streets and shady glens in his own incomparable style. His stage sets often metamorphosed into one another: A fairy queen's bower might become a commandant's office in another theater on the other side of town, and then might serve a third tour of duty as a train compartment or a hermit's hut or a pasha's veil-draped bed. Andras's idea of making flats with interiors on one side and exteriors on the other was one of Forestier's lesser tricks. He made stage sets like puzzles, stage sets that could become three or four different interiors depending upon the order in which their panels were arranged; he was a master of optical illusion. He could make an actor seem to grow or shrink as he walked across a stage, could use a subtle shift of lighting to turn a nursery into a hall of horrors. Projections of hand-colored slides could suggest distant cities or mountains, ghostly presences, memories from a character's youth. A magic lantern made to spin by the heat of a candle could send flocks of birds rippling across a scrim. Any stage set might conceal trapdoors and rotating panels; every surface hid a mysterious interior that might hide another interior that might hide still another interior that bore a haunting resemblance to the exterior. Monsieur Forestier himself had a way of appearing and disappearing as if he were an actor within a set he'd designed; he would come in and assign Andras a task, and five minutes later he would have vanished as if into a wall, leaving Andras to puzzle through the difficulties of the design alone. After the tumult of the Sarah-Bernhardt, Andras found it solitary and at times lonely work. But at night, when he came home to his room, Klara might be waiting.

He rushed home every night hoping she'd be there; most often it was her ghost he embraced in the dark, the shadow presence that remained in his room when the real Klara was absent. It nearly drove him mad when days would pass between her visits. He knew, but didn't want to be reminded, that while he was going to school and working and taking care of Polaner, Klara was conducting her own life. She gave dinner parties, went to the cinema and the theater, to jazz clubs and gallery openings. He conjured images of the people she met at her friends' parties or entertained at her own—choreographers and dancers from abroad, young composers, writers, actors, wealthy patrons of the arts—and felt certain that her attention would turn away from him. If for three nights she failed to appear at the rue des Écoles, he would think, *Well, it's happened,* and spend the next day in a haze of despair. If he walked out alone he resented every couple he passed on the street; if he tried to distract himself with a film he cursed the jet-haired screen goddess who crept from her husband's train compartment to climb into her lover's moonlit couchette. If, at the end of such a night, he came home to the rue des Écoles to find a light on in his windows, he would climb the stairs telling himself she had only come to break it off for good. Then he'd open the door and find her sitting beside the fire, reading a novel or stitching the hem of a practice dress or making tea, and she would get to her feet and put her arms around his neck, and he would be ashamed he'd doubted her.

In mid-May, when the trees wore close-fitting green singlets and the breeze from the Seine was warm even at night, Klara appeared one Saturday evening in a new spring hat, a pale blue toque with a ribbon of darker blue. A new hat, that simple thing: It was nothing more than a scrap of fashion, a sign of the changing season. Surely she'd worn a variety of hats since the red bell of their first winter embraces; he could remember a camel-colored one with a black feather, and a green cap with some sort of leather tassel. But this decidedly vernal hat, this pale blue toque, reminded him, as the others hadn't, that time was passing for both of them, that he was still in school and she was still waiting for him, that what existed between them was an affair, gossamer and impermanent. He removed her dragonfly hatpin and hung the hat on the coat stand beside the door, then took both her hands and led her to the bed. She smiled and put her arms around him, saying his name into his ear, but he took her hands again and sat down with her.

"What is it?" she said. "What's wrong?"

He couldn't speak, couldn't begin to say what had made him melancholy. He couldn't find a way to tell her that her hat had reminded him that life was short and that he was no closer to being worthy of her than he'd ever been. So he took her into his arms and made love to her, and told himself he didn't care if there were never anything more between them than these late-night meetings, this circumscribed affair.

The hours passed quickly; by the time they'd pried themselves from the warmth of the bed and dressed, it was nearly three o'clock. They descended the five flights of stairs to the street, then walked to the boulevard Saint-Michel to hail a cab. They always said their goodbyes on the same corner. He'd grown to hate that patch of pavement for taking her away from him night after night. During the day, when its power to strip him of her was cloaked beneath the love-ignoring clamor of everyday life, it seemed a different place; he could almost believe it was like any other street corner, a place of no particular significance. But now, at night, it was his nemesis. He didn't want to see it—not the bookstore across the street, nor the fenced limes, nor the pharmacy with its glowing green cross: none of it. He turned with her instead down another street and they walked toward the Seine.

"Where are we going?" she said, smiling up at him.

"I'm walking you home."

"All right," she said. "It's a beautiful night." And it was. A May breeze came up the channel of the Seine as they crossed the bridges toward the Marais. The sidewalks were still full of men and women in evening clothes; no one seemed ready to give up the night. As they walked, Andras entertained the impossible fantasy that when they reached Klara's house they would climb the stairs together and move noiselessly down the hall to her bedroom, where they would fall asleep together in her white bed. But at Number 39 they found the lights ablaze; Mrs. Apfel ran downstairs at the sound of Klara's key and told her that Elisabet had not yet been home.

Klara's eyes widened with panic. "It's past three!"

"I know," Mrs. Apfel said, twisting her apron. "I didn't know where to find you."

"Oh, God, what could have happened? She's never been this late."

"I've been all over the neighborhood looking for her, Madame."

"And I've been out all this time! Oh, God. Three in the morning! She said she was just going to a dance with Marthe!"

A panicked hour followed, during which Klara made a series of telephone calls and learned that Marthe hadn't seen Elisabet all night, that the hospitals had admitted no one by the name of Elisabet Morgenstern, and that the police had received no report of foul play involving a girl of Elisabet's description.

When she'd hung up the phone, Klara walked up and down the parlor, her hands on her head. "I'll kill her," she said, and then burst into tears. "Where is she? It's nearly four o' clock!"

It had occurred to Andras that Elisabet was most likely with her blond American, and that the reason for her absence was in all probability similar to the reason for Klara's late return. He'd sworn to keep her secret; he hesitated to speak his suspicions aloud. But he couldn't watch Klara torture herself. And besides that, it might be dangerous to hesitate. He imagined Elisabet in peril somewhere—drink-poisoned in the aftermath of one of József's parties, or alone in a distant arrondissement after a dance-hall night gone wrong—and he knew he had to speak.

"Your daughter has a gentleman friend," he said. "I saw them together one night at a party. We might find out where he lives, and check there."

Klara's eyes narrowed. "What gentleman friend? What party?"

"She begged me not to tell you," Andras said. "I promised her I wouldn't."

"When did this happen?"

"Months ago," Andras said. "January."

"January!" She put a hand against the sofa as if to keep herself upright. "Andras, you can't mean that."

"I'm sorry. I should have told you sooner. I didn't want to betray Elisabet's trust."

The look in her eyes was pure rage. "What is this person's name?"

"I know his first. I don't know his last. But your nephew knows him. We can go to his place—I'll go up, and you can wait in the cab."

She took up her light coat from the sofa, and a moment later they were running down the stairs. But when they opened the door they found Elisabet on the doorstep, holding a pair of evening shoes in one hand, a cone of spun-sugar candy in the other. Klara, standing in the doorway, took a long look at her, at the shoes, the cone of candy; it was clear she hadn't come from an innocent evening with Marthe. Elisabet, in turn, cast a long look at Andras. He couldn't hold her gaze, and in that instant she seemed to understand that he had betrayed her; she turned an expression of startled outrage upon him, then pushed past him and her mother and ran up the stairs. A few moments later they heard her bedroom door slam.

"We'll talk later," Klara said, and left him standing in the entryway, having earned the furious contempt of both Morgensterns.

"I think you ought to know what kind of woman my mother is," Elisabet said.

She sat on a bench in the Tuileries and Andras stood before her; two days had passed since he'd last seen Klara, and no word had come from the rue de Sévigné. Then that afternoon, Elisabet had surprised him in the courtyard of the École Spéciale, causing Rosen and Ben Yakov to think she must be the mysterious woman he'd been seeing all that time—the woman they'd never met, whom he'd mentioned only in the vaguest terms during their conversations at the Blue Dove. When they emerged from studio and saw Elisabet standing in the courtyard, her cold eyes fixed upon Andras, her arms crossed over the bodice of her pale green dress, Rosen gave a whistle and Ben Yakov raised an eyebrow.

"She's an Amazon," he whispered. "How do you scale her in bed?"

Only Polaner knew this wasn't the woman Andras loved— Polaner, who, thanks to Andras's ministrations, and Klara's, and the unwavering friendship of Rosen and Ben Yakov, had returned to the École Spéciale and entered his classes again. Only Polaner was privy to the secret of Andras's relationship; though he had never met Elisabet, he knew as much about Klara's history and family as Andras did himself. So when this tall, powerful girl had appeared in the courtyard of the École Spéciale, shooting cold electric fire in Andras's direction, he guessed in an instant who she was. He distracted Rosen and Ben Yakov with a request for tea at the student café, seeing no other alternative but to leave Andras to his fate.

At the gates of the school, Elisabet turned and led Andras down the boulevard Raspail without a word. All the way to the Tuileries she stayed two steps ahead of him. She had drawn her hair into a tight ponytail; it beat a rhythm against her back as she walked. He followed her down Raspail to Saint-Germain, and they crossed over the river and into the Tuileries. She led him down paths awash in gold and lilac and fuchsia, through the too-fragrant profusion of May flora, until they reached what must have been the park's only dismal corner: a black bench in need of repainting, a deflowered flowerbed. Behind them swept the rush of traffic on the rue de Rivoli. Elisabet sat down, crossed her arms again, and gave Andras a hate-laced stare.

"This won't take long," she said. And then she told him he ought to know what kind of woman her mother was.

"I know what kind of woman she is," Andras said.

"You told her the truth about Paul and me. And now I'm going to tell you the truth about her."

She was angry, he reminded himself. She would do whatever she could to hurt him, would tell whatever lies it suited her to tell. In a sense, he owed it to her to listen; he had betrayed her, after all.

"All right," he said. "What do you want to tell me?"

"I suppose you think you're my mother's first lover since my father."

"I know she's led a complicated life," he said. "That's not news."

Elisabet gave a short, hard laugh. "Complicated! I wouldn't say so. It's simple, once you know the pattern. I've seen pathetic men fawning over her for as long as I can remember. She's always known what she wanted from them, and what she was worth. How do you think she got the apartment and the studio? By dancing her heart out?"

It was all he could do not to slap her. He dug his nails into the palms of his hands. "That's enough," he said. "I won't listen to this."

"Someone has to tell you the truth."

"Your mother doesn't take me for a fool, and neither should you."

"But you *are* a fool, you stupid fool! She's playing a game with you, using you to make another man jealous. A real man, an adult, one with a job and money. You can read about it yourself." She produced a sheaf of envelopes from her leather schoolbag. A masculine hand; Klara's name. She took out another sheaf, and another. Stacks and stacks of letters. She peeled an envelope from the top of the pile, extracted the letter, and began to read.

" 'My dear Odette.' That's what he calls her, his Odette, after the swan-princess in the ballet. 'Since last night I've done nothing but think of you. Your taste is still in my mouth. My hands are full of you. Your scent is everywhere in my house.' "

Andras took the letter from her hand. There were the lines she'd just read, in a familiar script; he turned it over to look for the signature. One initial: Z. The envelope bore a year-old postmark.

"Who do you think it is?" Elisabet said, her eyes fixed on his own. "It's your Monsieur Novak. Z is for Zoltán. She's been his mistress for eleven years. And when things go sour, as they do now and then, she takes up with idiots like you to drive him mad. He always comes back. That's how it works. Now you know."

A wave of hot needles rolled through him. He felt as though his lungs had been punctured, as though he couldn't draw a breath. "Are you finished?" he said.

She got up and smoothed the skirt of her pale green dress. "It might seem hard to take," she said. "But I can assure you it's no harder than what she's doing to me, now that she knows about

Paul." And she left him there in the Tuileries with Novak's letters.

He didn't go to work. Instead he sat on the bench in that dusty corner of the park and read the letters. The oldest was dated January 1927. He read about Klara's first meeting with Novak after a dance performance; he read about Novak's failing struggle to stay faithful to his wife, and then he read Novak's half-exultant self-castigation after his first tryst with Klara. There were cryptic references to places where they must have made love—an opera box, a friend's cottage in Montmartre, a bedroom at a party, Novak's office at the Sarah-Bernhardt; there were notes in which Novak pleaded for a meeting, and notes in which he begged her to refuse to see him the next time he asked. There were references to arguments involving crises of conscience on both sides, and then a six-month break in the regular stream of letters—a time when they must have been apart and she must have begun seeing someone else, because the next letters made angry mention of a young dancer named Marcel. (Was this the Marcel, Andras wondered, who'd written Klara those postcards from Rome?) Novak demanded that she break off the liaison with Marcel; it was absurd, he wrote, to think that that young salamander's feelings could ever match his own. And she must have done as he wished, because the letters from Novak picked up their steady pace again, and they were once again full of affectionate reference to the time he'd spent with Klara. There were letters in which he wrote about the dance studio and the apartment he'd found for her, dull letters about the technicalities of the real-estate transaction; desperate notes about how he would leave his wife and come to live with her on the rue de Sévigné—marry her and adopt Elisabet—and sober-toned notes about why he couldn't. Then another break, and more letters referring to another lover of Klara's, this one a writer whose plays had been performed at the Sarah-Bernhardt; one week Novak swore that this was the final straw, that he was finished with Klara forever, but the next week he begged her to come to him, and the following week it was clear that she had done so—*what sweet relief to have you again, what fulfillment of my wildest hopes.* Finally, in early 1937, it seemed his wife had learned from their lawyer that they owned a piece of property she hadn't known about; she'd confronted Novak, and he'd confessed. His wife had told him to make a choice. That was when he'd gone home to Hungary—to take a cure for a mild case of tuberculosis, as he'd told everyone, but also, in fact, to decide between his marriage and his mistress. It must have been on his way back from Hungary that Andras had met him at the train station. He'd come back full of remorse, ashamed at having wronged both Edith and Klara. He'd broken off his relations with Klara, and his wife had become pregnant. That piece of news had come in December. But the most recent letter was from just a few weeks ago, and concerned rumors that Klara had been seeing someone else— and not just anyone, but *Andras Lévi*, the young Hungarian whom Zoltán had hired at the Sarah-Bernhardt last fall. He demanded that she explain herself, and begged her to do so in person at a certain hotel, on a certain afternoon; he would be waiting for her.

Andras sat on the bench with the stack of letters beside him. That afternoon, two weeks earlier—what had he been doing? Had he been at work? At school? He couldn't remember. Had she cancelled her classes, gone to meet Novak? Was she with him this very instant? He had the sudden desire to choke someone to death. Anyone would do: that brocaded matron beside the fountain with her bichon frisé; that sad-looking girl beneath the limes; the policeman on the corner whose moustache seemed grotesquely like Novak's. He got to his feet, stuffed the letters into his bag, and walked back toward the river. It was dark now, a damp spring night. He stepped in front of cars that blared their horns at him, shouldered past men and women on the side-

walks, trudged through groups of clochards on the bridges. He
didn't know what time it was, and didn't care. He was exhausted.
He hadn't eaten anything and wasn't hungry. It was too late for
him to show up at Forestier's now, but he didn't want to go
home, either; there was a chance Klara might come to talk to
him, and he couldn't bear the thought of seeing her. He didn't
want to confront her about Novak; he was ashamed at having
read the letters, at having allowed Elisabet to do this to him. He
turned away and walked off down the rue des Écoles to the place
de la Sorbonne, where he sat at the edge of a fountain and listened to a one-legged accordionist playing the bitterest love
songs he had ever heard. When he couldn't stand another measure he fled to the Jardin du Luxembourg, where he fell into a
fretful sleep on an elm-shadowed bench.

He awoke some time later in a humid blue dawn, his neck in
a spasm from the way he'd slept. He remembered that some disaster had crushed him the night before; he could feel it rushing
toward his consciousness again. And there it was: Zoltán Novak,
the letters. He rubbed his eyes with thumb and forefinger and
blinked at the morning. Before him on the grass two tiny rabbits
browsed the clover. The first light of day came through the delicate endive leaves of their ears; they were so close he could hear
the snip and grind of their teeth. The park was otherwise silent,
and he was alone with what he knew about Klara and could not
unknow.

He was right: She'd been at his apartment the night before. In
fact she'd been looking for him all over town. He traced her
movements through a series of increasingly anxious notes, which
he received in reverse order. First the one she'd tacked to his
drawing table at the studio: *A, where can you be? I've looked everywhere. Come see me as soon as you get this. K.*; next the one she'd left
in the care of the good Monsieur Forestier, who was more worried than angry when Andras came to work looking like he'd

spent the previous night on a bench: *A, When you didn't come home I came here to look for you. Going to check at school. K.*; and finally, at the end of what felt like the longest day he'd ever lived, the note she'd left for him at home, on the table downstairs: *A, I've gone to look for you at Forestier's. Your K.* He climbed the five flights to his attic and opened the door. In the dark, there was the clatter of a chair falling over, and Klara's light tread on the floor, and then she was beside him. He lit a lamp and shrugged off his jacket.

"Andras," she said. "My God, what happened to you? Where have you been?"

"I don't want to talk," he said. "I'm going to bed." He couldn't look at her. Every time he did, he saw Novak's hands on her, his mouth on her mouth. *Your taste.* Nausea came at him in a towering wave, and he went to his knees beside the bed. When she put a hand on his shoulder he shrugged it away.

"What's wrong?" she said. "Look at me."

He couldn't. He stripped off his shirt and trousers and crawled into bed, his face to the wall. He heard her moving through the room behind him.

"You can't do this," she said. "We've got to talk."

"Go away," he said.

"This is crazy. You're acting like a child."

"Leave me alone, Klara."

"Not until you talk to me."

He sat up in bed, his eyes going hot. He wouldn't cry in front of her. Without a word, he got up and took the letters from his bag and threw them on the table.

"What are those?" she said.

"You tell me."

She picked up one of the letters. "Where did you get these?"

"Your daughter was kind enough to deliver them. It was her way of thanking me for telling you about Paul."

"What?"

"She thought I might want to know who else you were fucking."

"Oh, God!" she cried. "Unbelievable. She did this?"

" *'Your taste is still in my mouth. My hands are full of you. Your scent is everywhere in my house.'* " He peeled the letter off the pile and threw it at her. "Or this one: *'But for you, my life would be darkness.'* Or this: *'Thoughts of last night have sustained me through this terrible day. When will you come to me again?'* And this one, from two weeks ago: *". . . The Hotel St. Lazare, where I'll be waiting.'* "

"Andras, please—"

"Go to hell, Klara, go to hell! Get out of my house! I can't look at you."

"It's all in the past," she said. "I couldn't do it anymore. I never loved him."

"You were with him for eleven years! You slept with him three nights a week. You left two other lovers for him. You let him buy you an apartment and a studio. And you never loved him? If that's true, is it supposed to make me feel better?"

"I told you," she said, her voice flattened with pain. "I told you you didn't want to know everything about me."

He couldn't stand to hear another word. He was exhausted and hungry and depleted, his mind a scorched pot whose contents had burned away to nothing. He almost didn't care whether there was anything between Klara and Novak still, whether their most recent break was decisive or just one of many temporary breaks. The idea that she'd been with that man, Zoltán Novak, with his odious moustache—that he'd put his hands on her body, on her birthmarks and scars, the terrain that had seemed to belong to Andras alone, but which of course belonged only to Klara, to do with as she wished—he couldn't stand it. And then there were the others—the dancer, the playwright—and before them there had undoubtedly been others still. They seemed to become real to him all at once, the legions of her former lovers, those men who had preceded him in his knowledge of her. They seemed to crowd the room. He could see them in their ridiculous ballet costumes and their expensive overcoats and their decorated military jackets, with their good haircuts and bad haircuts and dusty or glossy shoes, their proud or defeated-looking shoulders, their grace, their awkwardness, their variously shaped spectacles, their collective smell of leather and shaving soap and Macassar oil and plain masculine desire. Klara Morgenstern: That was what they had in common. Despite what Madame Gérard had told him, he had thought himself unique in her life, without precedent, but the truth was that he was a foot soldier in an army of lovers, and once he'd fallen there would be others to replace him, and others after that. It was too much. He pulled the quilt over his shoulder and put an arm across his eyes. She said his name again in her low familiar voice. He remained silent, and she said it again. He wouldn't make a sound. After a while he heard her get up and put on her coat, and then he heard the door open and close. On the other side of the wall a pair of new neighbors began to make noisy love. The woman called out in a breathy contralto; the man grunted in basso. Andras ground his face into the pillow, wild with grief, thinking of nothing, wishing to God he were dead.

CHAPTER SIXTEEN

The Stone Cottage

BY THE NEXT MORNING he was dizzy with fever. Heat poured out of him and soaked the bed; then he was shaking with chills beneath his blanket and his jacket and his overcoat and three wool sweaters. He couldn't eat, couldn't get up for work, couldn't go to school. When he got thirsty he drank the cold remains of tea straight from the kettle. When he had to piss he used the chamber pot beneath the bed. On the morning of the second day, when Polaner came looking for him, he didn't have the strength to tell him to leave, though all he wanted was to be alone. Now it was Polaner who stepped into the role of nurse; he did it as though he'd done it all his life. He made Andras get out of bed and wash himself. He emptied the chamber pot, changed Andras's sheets. He boiled water and brewed strong tea; he sent the concierge for soup and made Andras eat it. When Andras was clean and dressed and lying exhausted on the freshly made bed, Polaner made him tell him exactly what had happened. He took it all in with careful attention, and judged the situation grave, though not hopeless. The important thing now, he said, was for Andras to get well. There were two projects to be finished for studio. If he couldn't get out of bed and get back to work, Polaner would suffer for it: They were team projects, and he and Andras were the team. Then there were exams to prepare for: statics and history of architecture. They would be given in ten days' time. If Andras failed, he would lose his scholarship and be sent home. There was also the small matter of Andras's job. For two days he'd sent no word to Monsieur Forestier.

Polaner said he would gather their things from the studio—Andras was too depleted from the fever to make the trip to the boulevard Raspail—and they would work on their projects all day. In the afternoon Polaner would go to the set-design studio with a note from Andras begging Monsieur Forestier's pardon. Polaner would offer to do Andras's copy work that night. In the meantime Andras would lay out a plan of study for the statics and the history exams.

He had never had a friend like Polaner, and would never have a better one as long as he lived. By the next day his job was secure, his final projects on their way to completion. They had to draw plans for a single-use building, a modern concert hall, and there were still problems to solve in the design: They had chosen a cylindrical shape for the exterior, and had to design a ceiling inside that would send the sound toward the audience without echo or distortion. When they were finished with the plans they would have to build a model. Arranging and rearranging cardboard forms consumed an entire day and night. Polaner didn't mention going home; he slept on the floor, and was there when Andras woke in the morning.

At half past ten, just as Polaner was getting ready to go home, they heard a rising tread on the stairs. It seemed to Andras as if someone were climbing his very spine, toward the black and painful cavern of his heart. They heard a key in the lock, and the door edged open; it was Klara, her eyes dark beneath the brim of her spring hat.

"I'm sorry," she said. "I didn't know you had company."

"Monsieur Polaner is on his way home," Polaner said. "Monsieur Lévi has had enough of me for now. I taxed his brain with architecture all night, though he was still recovering from a fever."

"A fever?" Klara said. "Has the doctor been here?"

"Polaner's been taking care of me," Andras said.

"I've been a poor doctor," Polaner said. "He looks like he's lost weight. I'll be off before I do any further damage." He put on his own spring hat, of such a fashionable shape and color that you could miss the place where he'd resewn the brim to the crown, and he slipped into the hall, closing the door quietly behind him.

"A fever," Klara said. "Are you feeling better now?"

He didn't answer. She sat down in the wooden chair and touched the cardboard walls of the concert hall. "I should have told you about Zoltán," she said. "This was a terrible way for you to find out. And there might have been worse ways. You worked together. Marcelle knew."

He hated to think of it, of Madame Gérard knowing all and seeing all. "It was a bad enough way to find out," he said.

"I want you to know it's over," Klara said. "I didn't see him two weeks ago, and I won't if he asks again."

"I'm sure you've said that every time."

"You have to believe me, Andras."

"You're still tied to him. You live in the house he bought you."

"He made the down payment for me," Klara said. "But I paid for the rest. Elisabet doesn't know the details of our finances. Perhaps she doesn't want to believe I support us. That would make it difficult for her to justify the way she behaves toward me."

"But you did love him," Andras said. "You still do. You took up with me to make him jealous, just as you did with those others. Marcel. And that writer, Édouard."

"It's true that when Zoltán turned away from me, I didn't sit home alone. Not for long, in any case. When he claimed to be moving on with his life, I moved on with mine. But I didn't care for Marcel or Édouard the way I cared for him, so I went back."

"So it's true, then," Andras said. "You do love him."

She sighed. "I don't know. Zoltán and I are very close, or we were, once. But we didn't give ourselves to each other. He couldn't, because of what he felt for Edith; and I didn't, also because of that. In the end I decided I didn't want to be someone's mistress for the rest of my life. And he decided we couldn't keep on with it if he and Edith were to have a child."

"And now?"

"I haven't seen him since we made those decisions. Since November."

"Do you miss him?"

"Sometimes," she said, and folded her hands between her knees. "He was a dear friend, and he's been a great help with Elisabet. She's fond of him, too, or was. He's the closest thing she's had to a father. When we decided to end it, she felt as though he'd left both of us. She blamed me for it. I think she hoped I was seeing him again, those nights when I was with you."

"And what now? What if he asks you again? You were together for eleven years, nearly a third of your life."

"It's finished, Andras. You're in my life now."

"Am I?" he said. "I thought you were finished with *me*. I didn't know if you could forgive me for keeping Elisabet's business from you."

"I don't know if I can," she said, without a hint of humor. "Elisabet had no right to put you in that position, but once she did, you should have told me immediately. The man is five years older than she is—a rich American, studying painting at the Beaux-Arts on a lark. Not someone who's likely to treat her kindly, or take her seriously. And worse than that, he knows my nephew."

"You can hardly hold that against him," Andras said. "I believe your nephew knows everyone between the ages of sixteen and thirty in the Quartier Latin."

"In any case, it's got to stop. I don't intend to let that young man prove himself dishonorable."

"And what about what Elisabet wants?"

"I'm afraid that's beside the point."

"But Elisabet won't see it that way. If you oppose her, she'll only become more resolved."

Klara shook her head. "Don't try to tell me how to raise that child, Andras."

"I don't claim to know how. But I do know how I felt at sixteen."

"I told myself that was why you'd kept her secret," Klara said. "I knew you felt a certain empathy with her, and I think it's rather sweet of you, actually. But you've got to imagine my position, too."

"I see. So you've put an end to things between Elisabet and Paul."

"I hope so," Klara said. "And I've punished her for showing you those letters." Her brow folded into a familiar set of creases. "She seemed rather pleased with herself when she saw how upset I was about that. She told me I had gotten what I deserved. I've placed her under a kind of house arrest. Mrs. Apfel is keeping watch while I'm gone. Elisabet is not to go out until she writes you a letter of apology."

"She'll never do it. She'll grow old and die first."

"That will be her decision," Klara said.

But he knew Elisabet wouldn't remain bound by Klara's house arrest for long, Mrs. Apfel notwithstanding. She'd soon find a way to escape, and he worried that when she did she'd leave no forwarding address. He didn't want to be responsible for that.

"Let me come tomorrow and speak to her," he said.

"I don't think there's any point."

"Let me try."

"She won't see you. She's been in a vicious mood."

"It can't have been as bad as my own."

"You know what she's like, Andras. She can be beastly."

"I know. But she's still just a girl, after all."

Klara gave a deep sigh. "And what now?" she said, looking up at him from her chair. "What do we do, after all this?"

He ran a hand over the back of his neck. The question had been in his mind. "I don't know, Klara. I don't know. I'm going to sit down here on the bed. You can sit beside me if you like."

He waited until she sat beside him, and then he continued. "I'm sorry about the way I spoke to you the other night," he said. "I acted as though you'd been unfaithful to me, but you haven't, have you?"

"No," she said, and put a hand on his knee, where it burned like a feverish bird. "What I feel for you would make that impossible. Or absurd, at the very least."

"How is that, Klara? What is it you feel for me?"

"It may take me some time to answer that question," she said, and smiled.

"I can't be what he was. I can't give you a place to live, or be anything like a father to Elisabet."

"I have a place to live," she said. "And Elisabet, though she's still a child in many ways, will soon be grown. I don't need now what I needed then."

"What do you need now?"

She drew in her mouth in her pensive way. "I'm not certain, exactly. But I can't seem to stand to be away from you. Even when I'm livid with anger at you."

"There's still a great deal I don't know about you." He stroked the curve of her back; he could feel the glowing coals of her vertebrae through her thin jersey.

"I hope there'll be time to learn."

He drew her down with him onto the bed, and she put her head on his shoulder. He ran his hand along the warm dark length of her hair and took its upturned ends between his fingers. "Let me talk to Elisabet," he said. "If we're to continue with this, I can't have her hate me. And I can't hate her."

"All right," Klara said. "You're welcome to try." She rolled over onto her back and looked up at the slope of the ceiling, with its water stains in the shape of fish and elephants. "I was terrible to my mother, too," she said. "It's foolish to pretend I wasn't."

"We're all terrible to our parents at sixteen."

"Not you, I'm sure," she said, her eyelids closing. "You love your parents. You're a good son."

"I'm here in Paris while they're in Konyár."

"That's not your fault. Your parents worked so you could go to school, and they wanted you to come here. You write to them every week. They know you love them."

He hoped she was right. It had been nine months since he'd seen them. Still, he could feel a fine cord stretched between them, a thin luminous fiber that ran from his chest all the way across the continent and forked into theirs. Never before had he lived through a fever without his mother; when he'd been sick in Debrecen she'd taken the train to be with him. Never had he finished a year at school without knowing that soon he'd be home with his father, working beside him in the lumberyard and walking through the fields with him in the evening. Now there was another filament, one that linked him to Klara. And Paris was her home, this place thousands of kilometers from his own. He felt the stirring of a new ache, something like homesickness but located deeper in his mind; it was an ache for the time when his heart had been a simple and satisfied thing, small as the green apples that grew in his father's orchard.

For the first time ever, he went to see József Hász at school. The Beaux-Arts was a vast urban palace, a monument to art for art's sake; it made the humble courtyard and studios of the École Spéciale look like something a few boys had thrown together in an empty lot. He entered through a floriated wrought-iron gate between two stern figures carved in stone, and crossed a sculpture garden packed with perfect marble specimens of kore and kouros, straight from his art history textbook, staring into the distance with empty almond-shaped eyes. He climbed the marble entry stairs of a three-story Romanesque building and found himself in a hallway teeming with young men and women, all of them dressed with careful offhandedness. A list of studio assignments bore József's name; a map told him where to look. He went upstairs to a classroom with a sloping north-facing ceiling made all of glass. There, among rows of students intent on their paintings, József was applying varnish to a canvas that at first glance seemed to depict three smashed bees lying close to the black abyss of a drain. Upon closer inspection, the bees turned out to be black-haired women in black-striped yellow dresses.

József didn't seem much surprised to see Andras at his painting studio. He raised a cool eyebrow and continued varnishing. "What are you doing here, Lévi?" he asked. "Don't you have projects of your own to finish? Are you slacking off for the day? Did you come to make me have a drink in the middle of the morning?"

"I'm looking for that American," Andras said. "That person who was at your party. Paul."

"Why? Are you dueling with him over his statuesque girlfriend?" He kicked the easel of the student across from him, and the student gave a shout of protest.

"You imbecile, Hász," said Paul, for that was who it was. He stepped out from behind the canvas with a paintbrush full of burnt umber, his long equine features tightened with annoyance. "You made me give my maenad a moustache."

"I'm sure it'll only improve her."

"Lévi again," Paul said, nodding at Andras. "You go to school here?"

"No. I came to talk to you."

"I think he wants to fight you for that strapping girl," József said.

"Hász, you're hilarious," Paul said. "You should take that act on tour."

József blew him a kiss and went back to his varnishing.

Paul took Andras's arm and led him to the studio door. "Sometimes I can stand that jackass and sometimes I can't," he said as they descended the stairs. "Today I can't, particularly."

"I'm sorry to interrupt you at studio," Andras said. "I didn't know where else to find you."

"I hope you've come to tell me what's going on," Paul said. "I haven't seen Elisabet for days. I assume her mother's keeping her at home after that late night we had. But maybe you've got more information." He gave Andras a sideways glance. "I understand you've got something going with Madame Morgenstern."

"Yes," Andras said. "I suppose you could say we've got something going." They had reached the front doors of the building and sat down outside on the marble steps. Paul searched his pocket for a cigarette and lit it with a monogrammed lighter.

"So?" he said. "What's the news, then?"

"Elisabet's been confined to her room," Andras said. "Her mother won't let her out until she apologizes to me."

"For what?"

"Never mind. It's complicated. The thing is, Elisabet won't apologize. She'd rather die."

"Why is that?"

"Well, I'm afraid I'm the one who blew the whistle on the two of you. When Elisabet was out late the other night, her mother was frantic. I had to tell her Elisabet might be with you. Now it's all out in the open. And her mother didn't take kindly to the idea of her having a gentleman friend."

Paul took a long draw of his cigarette and blew a gray cloud into the courtyard. "I'm relieved, to tell you the truth," he said. "The secrecy was getting a little stifling. I'm wild about the girl, and I hate"—he seemed to search his mind for the French phrase—"*sneaking around*. I like to be the guy in the white cowboy hat. Do you understand me? Are you a fan of the American western?"

"I've seen a few," Andras said. "Dubbed in Hungarian, though."

Paul laughed. "I didn't know they did that."

"They do."

"So you're here on a peace mission? You want to help us, now that you've mucked everything up?"

"Something like that. I'd like to act as a go-between. To earn Elisabet's trust again, if you will. I can't have her hate me forever. Not if her mother and I are going to keep seeing each other."

"What's the plan, then?"

"You can't pay a visit to Elisabet, but I can. I'm sure she'd want to hear from you. I thought you might want to send a note."

"What if her mother finds out?"

"I plan to tell her," Andras said. "I predict she'll come around to you eventually."

Paul took a long American drag on his cigarette, seeming to consider the proposition. Then he said, "Listen to me, Lévi. I'm serious about this girl. She's like no one else I know. I hope this isn't just going to make things worse."

"At the moment, I'm not sure they could get much worse."

Paul stubbed his cigarette against the marble step, then kicked it down into the dirt. "All right," he said. "Wait here. I'll go write a note." He got to his feet and offered Andras a hand up. Andras stood and waited, watching a pair of finches browse for seeds in a clump of lavender. He looked over his shoulder to make sure no one saw him, took out his pocketknife, and cut a sheaf of stems. A length of cotton string torn from the strap of his canvas satchel served to tie them. A few minutes later, Paul came downstairs with a kraft envelope in his hand.

"There's a note," Paul said, and handed it to him. "Good luck to us both."

"*Here goes nothing,*" Andras said. His sole English phrase.

When he arrived the next day at noon, Klara was teaching a private student. It was Mrs. Apfel who opened the door. Her white apron was stained with purple juice, and she had a pair of bruised-looking moons under her eyes, as though she hadn't slept in days. She gave Andras a tired frown; she seemed to expect nothing from him but more trouble.

"I'm here to see Elisabet," Andras said.

Mrs. Apfel shook her head. "You'd better go home."

"I'd like to speak to her," he said. "Her mother knows why I'm here."

"Elisabet won't see you. She's locked herself in her room. She won't come out. Won't even eat."

"Let me try," Andras said. "It's important."

She knit her ginger-colored eyebrows. "Believe me, you don't want to try."

"Give me a tray for her. I'll take it in."

"You won't have any better luck than the rest of us," she said, but she turned and led him up the stairs. He followed her into the kitchen, where a fallen blueberry cake stood cooling on an iron rack. He stood over it and breathed its scent as Mrs. Apfel made an omelet for Elisabet. She cut a fat slice of the cake and set it on a plate with a square of butter.

"She hasn't eaten a thing in two days," Mrs. Apfel said. "We're going to have to get the doctor here before long."

"I'll see what I can do," Andras said. He took the tray and went down the hall to Elisabet's room, where he knocked the corner of the tray twice against the closed door. From within, silence.

"Elisabet," he said. "It's Andras. I brought your lunch."

Silence.

He set the tray down in the hall, took Paul's envelope from his bag, pressed it flat, and slipped it under Elisabet's door. For a long while he heard nothing. Then a faint scraping, as though she were drawing the note closer. He listened for the rustle of paper. There it was. More silence followed. Finally she opened the door, and he stepped in and set the tray on her little desk. She gave the food a contemptuous glance but wouldn't look at Andras at all. Her hair was a dun-colored tangle, her face raw and damp. She wore a wrinkled nightgown and red socks with holes in the toes.

"Close the door," she said.

He closed the door.

"How did you get that letter?"

"I went to see Paul. I thought he'd want to know what had happened to you. I thought he might want to send you a note."

She gave a shuddering sigh and sat down on the bed. "What does it matter?" she said. "My mother's never going to let me leave the house again. It's all over with Paul." When she raised her eyes to him there was a look he'd never seen in them before: grim, exhausted defeat.

Andras shook his head. "Paul doesn't think it's all over. He wants to meet your mother."

Elisabet's eyes filled with tears. "She'll never meet him," she said.

She was exactly Mátyás's age, Andras thought. She would have cut her teeth when he'd cut his teeth, walked at the same time, learned to write during the same school year. But she was no one's sister. She had no age-mate in that house, no one she could think of as an ally. She had no one with whom to divide the intensity of her mother's scrutiny and love.

"He wants to know you're all right," Andras said. "If you write back to him, I'll take the note."

"Why would you?" she demanded. "I've been so hateful to you!" And she put her head against her knees and cried—not from remorse, it seemed to him, but from sheer exhaustion. He sat down in the desk chair beside the bed, looking out the window into the street below, where one set of posters touted the Jardin des Plantes and another set advertised Abel Gance's *J'accuse*, which had just opened at the Grand Rex. He would wait as long as she wanted to cry. He sat beside her in silence until she was finished, until she'd wiped her nose on her sleeve and pushed her hair back with a damp hand. Then he asked, as gently as possible, "Don't you think it's time to eat something?"

"Not hungry," she said.

"Yes, you are." He turned to the tray of food on the desk and spread the butter on the blueberry cake, took the napkin and laid it on Elisabet's knees, set the tray before her on the bed. A quiet moment passed; from below they could hear the triple-beat lilt of a waltz, and Klara's voice as she counted out the steps for her private student. Elisabet picked up her fork. She didn't set it down again until she'd eaten everything on the tray. Afterward she put the tray on the floor and took a piece of notepaper from the desk. While Andras waited, she scribbled something on a page of her school notebook with a blunt pencil. She tore it out, folded it in half, and thrust it into his hand.

"There's your apology," she said. "I apologized to you and to my mother, and to Mrs. Apfel for being so awful to her these past few days. You can leave it on my mother's writing desk in the sitting room."

"Do you want to send a note to Paul?"

She bit the end of the pencil, tore out a new piece of paper. After a moment she threw a glare at Andras. "I can't write it while you're watching me," she said. "Go wait in the other room until I call you."

He took the tray and the cleaned plates and brought them to the kitchen, where Mrs. Apfel stared in speechless amazement. He delivered the apology to Klara's writing table. Finally he went to the bedroom and set the little bunch of lavender in a glass on Klara's bedside table with a four-word note of his own. Then he went into the sitting room to wait for Elisabet's note, and to gather his thoughts about what he'd say to Klara.

In August, Monsieur Forestier closed his set design studio for a three-week holiday. Elisabet went to Avignon with Marthe, whose family had a summer home there; they wouldn't be back until the first of September. Mrs. Apfel went once again to her daughter's house in Aix. And Klara wrote a note to Andras, telling him to come to the rue de Sévigné with enough clothing for a twelve-day stay.

He packed a bag, his chest tight with joy. The rue de Sévigné, that apartment, those sunlit rooms, the house where he'd lived with Klara in December: Now it would be theirs again for nearly two weeks. He'd longed for that kind of time with her. In the first month after he'd found out about Novak, he had lived in a state of near-constant dread; despite Klara's reassurances, he could never shake the fear that Novak would call to her and she would go to him. The dread abated as July passed and there was no word from Novak, no sign that Klara would abandon Andras for his sake. At last he began to trust her, and even to envision a future with her, though the details were still obscure. He began to spend Sundays at her house again, and more pleasantly than in the past: His diplomacy with Elisabet had earned him her reluctant gratitude, and she could sit with him for an hour without insulting him or mocking his imperfect French. Though Klara had been furious at first when Andras had told her of his role as go-between, she had nonetheless been impressed with the change he'd brought about in Elisabet. He had made an earnest argument for Paul's merits, and finally Klara had relented and invited Elisabet's gentleman friend to lunch. Before long, a delicate peace had emerged; Paul had impressed Klara with his knowledge of contemporary art, his good-natured courtliness, his unfailing patience with Elisabet.

Now another milestone was approaching: the first time Andras would celebrate a birthday in Paris. In late August he would turn twenty-three. As he packed his suitcase he imagined drinking champagne with Klara on the rue de Sévigné, the two of them sweetly alone, a reprise of their winter idyll. But when he arrived at her house that morning there was a black Renault parked at the curb, its top folded down. Two small suitcases stood beside the car; a scarf and goggles lay on the driver's seat. Klara stepped out of the house, shading her eyes against the sun; she wore a motoring duster, canvas boots, driving gloves. She had gathered her hair into two bunches at the back of her head.

"What's this all about?" Andras said.

"Put your things in the trunk," Klara said, throwing him the keys. "We're going to Nice."

"To Nice? In this car? We're driving this car?"

"Yes, in this car."

He gave a shout, climbed over the car, and took her in his arms. "You can't have done this," he said.

"I did. It's for your birthday. We have a cottage by the sea."

Though he knew in theory that cars and cottages could be hired, it seemed almost impossible to believe that Klara had *in actuality* hired a car, and that, having the car in their possession, they could simply fill its tank with gas and drive to a cottage in Nice. No struggling with baggage in a train station, no crowded third-class rail carriage smelling of smoke and sandwiches and sweating passengers, no search for a cab or horse cart at the other end of the line. Just Andras and Klara in this tiny beetle-black car. And then a house where they would be alone together. What luxury; what freedom. They piled their suitcases into the car, and Klara put on her scarf and driving goggles.

"How do you know how to drive?" he asked her as they pulled away toward the rue des Francs-Bourgeois. "Do you know everything?"

"Nearly everything," she said. "I don't know Portuguese or Japanese, and I can't make brioche, and I'm a terrible singer. But I do know how to drive. My father taught me when I was a girl. We used to practice in the country, near my grandmother's house in Kaba."

"I hope you've driven more recently than that."

"Not often. Why? Are you afraid?"

"I don't know," Andras said. "Should I be?"

"You'll find out soon!"

From the rue du Pas de la Mule she turned onto the boulevard Beaumarchais and merged effortlessly into the traffic encircling the Bastille. She picked up the boulevard Bourdon; they crossed the Seine at Pont d'Austerlitz and shot off toward the south. Andras's cap threatened to fly away, and he had to hold it to his head with one hand. They motored through the seemingly endless suburbs of Paris (Who lived in these distant neighborhoods, these balconied three-story buildings? Whose washing was that on the line?) and then out into the gold haze and the rolling green pastures of the countryside. Sturdy sheep and goats stood in bitten-down grass. Beside a farmhouse, children beat at the exoskeleton of a rusted Citroën with sticks and spades. A clutter of chickens crowded into the roadway and Klara had to blast them with a *ga-zoo-bah!* from the Renault's horn. Tall feathery lindens whipped by, each with its fleeting rush of sound. For lunch they stopped beside a meadow and ate cold chicken and an asparagas salad and a peach tart that attracted yellowjackets. At Valence a thunderstorm overtook them and threw a hard slant of rain into the car before they could raise the roof; as they drove on, the windshield became so clouded with steam that they had to stop and wait for the storm to pass. It was nearly sunset when, after passing through a thirty-mile stretch of olive groves, they crested a hill and began to descend toward the edge of the earth. That was how it looked to Andras, who had never before seen the sea. As they drew closer it became a vast plain of liquid metal, a superheated infinity of molten bronze. But the air grew cooler with their approach, and the grasses along the road bent their seed pods in a rising wind. They reached a stretch of sand just as the red lozenge of the sun dissolved into the horizon. Klara stopped the car at an empty beach and turned off the motor. At the margin of the water, a pounding roar and a cataclysm of foam. Without a word they got out of the car and walked toward that ragged white edge.

Andras cuffed his pants and stepped into the water. When a wave rolled in, the ground slid away beneath his feet and he had to catch Klara's arm to keep from falling. He knew that feeling, that powerful and frightening tidal pull: It was Klara, her draw upon him, her inevitability in his life. She laughed and went to her knees in the waves, letting them wash over her body and render her blouse transparent; when she stood, her skirt was decorated with seaweed. He wanted to lay her down on the cooling stones and have her right there, but she ran back across the beach toward the car, calling for him to come.

After they'd driven through the town with its white hotels, its glittering curvelet of sea, they turned onto a road so rutted and rocky it threatened to disembowel the Renault. At the top of the road, a crumbling stone cottage stood in a tiny garden surrounded by gorse. The key was in a bird's nest above the door. They dragged their suitcases inside and fell onto the bed, too exhausted now to consider lovemaking or dinner preparations or anything besides sleep. When they awoke it was velvet dark. They fumbled for kerosene lanterns, ate the cheese and bread that had been intended for breakfast the next morning. A slow-moving fog obscured the stars. Klara had forgotten her nightgown. Andras discovered that he was allergic to some plant in the garden; his eyes burned, and he sneezed and sneezed. They spent a restless night listening to the door rattling against its jamb, the wind soughing between the window frame and the sill, the endless gripe and creak of nighttime insects. When Andras woke in the gray haze of early morning, his first thought was that they could simply get into the car and return to Paris if they wanted. But here was Klara beside him, a scattering of sand grains in the fine hair at her temple; they were at Nice and he had seen the Mediterranean. He went outside to shoot a long arc of asparagus-scented urine out over the back garden. Inside again, he curled against Klara and fell into his deepest sleep of the night, and when he awoke for the second time there was a block of hot sunlight in bed with him where she had been. God, he was hungry; he felt as if he hadn't eaten in days. From outside he heard the snick of gardening shears. Without bothering to don a shirt or trousers or even a pair of undershorts, he went out to find Klara removing a cluster of tall flowers that looked like close-crocheted doilies.

"Wild carrot," she said. "That's what made you sneeze last

night." She was wearing a sleeveless red cotton dress and a straw hat; her arms glowed gold in the sunlight. She wiped her brow with a handkerchief and stood to look at Andras in the doorway. "Au naturel," she observed.

Andras made a fig leaf of his hand.

"I think I'm finished gardening," she said, and smiled.

He went back to the bed, which lay in a windowed alcove from which he could see a slice of Mediterranean. Eons passed before she came in and washed her hands. He had forgotten how hungry he'd been when he first awakened. He had forgotten everything else in the world. She removed her shoes and climbed onto the bed, leaning over him. Her dark hair burned with absorbed sunlight, and her breath was sweet: She'd been eating strawberries in the garden. The red veil of her dress fell over his eyes.

Outside, three pygmy goats stepped out of the gorse and ate all the clipped flowers and a good many half-grown lettuces and an empty cardboard matchbook and Klara's forgotten handkerchief. They liked to visit this cottage; intriguing and unfamiliar things often appeared in the yard. As they sniffed the tires of the Renault, a burst of human noise from the cottage made them raise their ears: two voices calling out and calling out inside the house.

Far below the cottage, silent from that high vantage point, lay the town of Nice with its blinding white beaches. In Nice you could swim in the rolling sea. You could eat at a café by the beach. You could sleep in a rented lounge chair on the pebbled strand or stroll through the colonnade of a hotel. For five francs you could watch a film projected onto the blank wall of a warehouse. You could buy armloads of roses and carnations at a covered flower market. You could tour the ruins of Roman baths at Cemenelum and eat a picnic lunch on a hill overlooking the port. You could buy art supplies for half what they cost in Paris.

Andras bought a sketchbook and twelve good pencils with leads of varying density. In the afternoons, while Klara practiced ballet, he practiced drawing. First he drew their cottage until he knew every stone and every roof angle. Then he razed the cottage in his mind and began to plan the house they could build on that land. The land had a gentle slope; the house would have two stories, one of them invisible from the front. Its roofline would lie close to the hillside and be covered with sod; they would grow lavender thick and sweet in that layer of earth. He would build the house of rough-cut limestone. He would abandon the hard geometry of his professors' designs and allow the house to lie against the hillside like a shoulder of rock revealed by wind. On the sea-facing side, he would set sliding glass doors into the limestone. There would be a practice room for Klara. There would be a studio for himself. There would be sitting rooms and guest rooms, rooms for the children they might have. There would be a stone-paved area behind the house, large enough for a dining table and chairs. There would be a terraced garden where they would grow cucumbers and tomatoes and herbs, squashes and melons; there would be a pergola for grapes. He didn't dare to guess how much it might cost to buy a piece of land like that or to build the house he'd designed, or whether the building council of Nice would let him do it. The house didn't exist in a reality that included money or seaside zoning laws. It was a perfect phantom that became more clearly visible the longer they stayed. By day, as he walked the scrubby perimeter of the garden, he laid out those sea-lit rooms; by night, lying awake at Klara's side, he paved the patio and terraced the hillside for the garden. But he didn't show his drawings to Klara, or tell her what he was doing while she practiced. Something about the project made him cautious, self-protective; perhaps it was the vast gulf between the harmonious permanence the house suggested and the complicated uncertainty of their lives.

At the stone cottage they lived for the first time like husband and wife. Klara bought food in the village and they cooked together; Andras spoke to her about his plans for the next year, how he might work as an intern at the architecture firm that employed Pierre Vago. She told him of her own plans to hire an assistant teacher from the ranks of young dancers from abroad. She wanted to do for someone what Novak and Forestier had done for Andras. They talked as they dawdled along the road that led to town; they talked after sunset in the dark garden, sitting on wooden chairs they'd dragged out of the house. They bathed each other in a tin tub in the middle of the cottage floor. They set out vegetables and bread for the pygmy goats, and one of the goats gave them milk. They discussed the names of their children: the girl would be Adèle, the boy Tamás. They swam in the sea and ate lemon ices and made love. And on the flat dirt roads that ran along the beaches, Klara taught Andras to drive.

On his first day out he stalled and stalled the Renault until he was blind with rage. He jumped out of the car and accused Klara of teaching him improperly, of trying to make an ass of him. Without surrendering her own calm, she climbed into the driver's seat, gave him a wink, and drove off, leaving him fuming in the dust. By the time he'd walked the two miles back to the cottage, he was sunburned and contrite. The next day he stalled only twice; the day after that he drove without a stall. They followed the hillside road down to the Promenade des Anglais and drove along the sea all the way to Cannes. He loved the press of the curves, loved the vision of Klara with her white scarf flying. On their way back he drove more slowly, and they watched the sailboats drifting over the water like kites. He navigated the tricky hill up to the cottage without a stall. When they reached the garden, Klara got out and cheered. That night, the eve of his birthday, he drove her into town for drinks at the Hôtel Taureau d'Or. She wore a sea-green dress that revealed her shoulders, and a glittering hairpin in the shape of a starfish. Her skin had deepened to a dusky gold on the beach. Most beautiful of all were her feet in their Spanish sandals, her toes revealed in their shy brown beauty, her nails like chips of pink nacre. On the deck of the Taureau d'Or he told her he loved seeing her feet bare in public.

"It's so risqué," he said. "You seem thrillingly naked."

She gave him a sad smile. "You should have seen them when I was *en pointe* every day. They were atrocious. You can't imagine what ballet does to the feet." She turned her glass in careful rings on the wooden table. "I wouldn't have worn sandals for a million pengő."

"I would have paid two million to see you wear them."

"You didn't have two million. You were a schoolboy at the time."

"I'd have found a way to earn it."

She laughed and slipped a finger under the cuff of his shirt, smoothed the skin of his wrist. It was torture to be beside her all day like this. The more he had of her, the more he wanted. Worst of all were the times on the beach, where she wore a black maillot and a bathing cap with white racing stripes. She'd turn over on her rattan beach mat and there would be silvery grains of sand dusting her breasts, the soft rise of her pubis, the smooth skin of her thighs. He had spent most of their time on the beach shielding his erection from public view with the aid of a book or towel. The previous afternoon he'd watched her execute neat dives from a wooden tower at this very beach; he could see the tower now, ghostly in the moonlight, a skeleton standing in the sea.

"I think we ought to stay here always," he said. "You can teach ballet in Nice. I can finish my studies by correspondence."

A veil of melancholy seemed to fall over her features. She took a sip of her drink. "You're turning twenty-three," she said. "That means I'll be thirty-two soon. Thirty-two. The more I think about it, the more it begins to seem like an old woman's age."

"That's nonsense," Andras said. "The last Hungarian women's

swimming champion was thirty-three when she won her gold medal in Munich. My mother was thirty-five when Mátyás was born."

"I feel as if I've lived such a long time already," she said. "Those days when I wouldn't have worn sandals for a million pengő—" She paused and smiled, but her eyes were sad and far-away. "So many years ago! Seventeen years!"

This wasn't about him, he understood. It was about her own life, about how everything had changed when she'd become pregnant with her daughter. That was what had caused the veil to fall. When the waiter came she ordered absinthe for both of them, a drink she chose only when she was sad and wanted to be lifted away from the world.

But absinthe didn't have the same effect on him; it tended to play dirty tricks on his mind. He told himself it might be different here at Nice, at this dreamlike hotel bar overlooking the beach, but it wasn't long before the wormwood began to do its poisonous work. A gate swung open and paranoia elbowed through. If Klara was melancholy now, it wasn't because she'd lost her life in ballet; it was because she'd lost Elisabet's father. Her one great love. The single monumental secret she'd never told him. Her feelings for Andras were chaff by comparison. Even her eleven-year relationship with Novak hadn't been able to break the spell. Madame Gérard knew it; Elisabet herself knew it; even Tibor had guessed it in the space of an hour, while Andras had failed to recognize it for months and months. How absurd of him to have spent the summer worrying about Novak when the real threat was this phantom, the only man who would ever have Klara's heart. The fact that she could sit here in a sea-green dress and those sandals, calmly drinking absinthe, pretending she might someday be Andras's wife, and then allow herself to be pulled back to wherever she'd been pulled—by *him*, no doubt, that nameless faceless man she'd loved—made him want to take her by the shoulders and shake her until she cried.

"God, Andras," she said finally. "Don't look at me that way."

"What way?"

"You look as if you want to kill me."

Her limpid gray eyes. The glitter of the starfish in her hair. Her child-sized hands on the table. He was more afraid of her, of what she could do to him, than anyone he'd known in his life. He pushed back his chair and went to the bar, where he bought a pack of Gauloises, and then walked down to the beach. There was some comfort in picking up shells at the water's edge and skipping them into the surf. He sat down on the wooden slats of a deck chair and smoked three cigarettes, one after the other. He thought he might like to sleep on the beach that night, with the waves pounding the shore in the dark and the sound of the hotel band drifting down from the plein air ballroom. But soon his head began to clear and he realized he'd left Klara sitting alone at their table. The absinthe gate was closing. His paranoia retreated. He looked back over his shoulder, and there was the sea-green brushmark of Klara's dress disappearing into the saffron light of the hotel.

He raced up the beach to catch her, but by the time he got there she was nowhere to be seen. In the lobby, the desk clerk denied having seen a woman in green walk past; the doormen had seen her leave, but one of them thought she'd headed away from town and another thought she'd headed toward it. The car was still parked where they'd left it, at the outside corner of a dusty lot. It was quite dark now. He thought she wouldn't walk toward town, not in her current mood. He got into the car and drove at a crawl along the beach road. He hadn't gotten far before his headlights illuminated a sea-green flash against the roadside. She was walking swiftly, her sandals raising clouds of dust. She'd wrapped her arms around herself; he could see the familiar sweet column of her vertebrae rising out of the deep-cut back of her dress. He brought the car to a stop and jumped out to catch up with her. She gave him a swift glance over her shoulder and kept walking.

"Klara," he said. "Klárika."

She stopped finally, her arms limp at her sides. From around a curve in the road came a sweep of headlights; they splashed across her body as a roadster tore past and shot off toward the center of town, its passengers shouting a song into the night. When it had gone, there was nothing but the thrum and pound of waves. For a long time neither of them spoke. She wouldn't turn to face him.

"I'm sorry," he said. "I don't know why I left you sitting there."

"Let's just go home," she said. "I don't want to talk about this on the side of the road."

"Don't be angry."

"It's my fault. I shouldn't have brought up the past. It makes me miserable to think of it, and that must have been what made you get up and go down to the beach."

"It was the absinthe," he said. "It makes me crazy."

"It wasn't the absinthe," she said.

"Klara, please."

"I'm cold," she said, and put her arms around herself. "I want to get back to the house."

He drove them, feeling no satisfaction in his mastery of the road; when they got out of the car there was no celebration of his skill. Klara went into the yard and sat down in one of the wooden chairs they'd dragged outside. He sat down beside her.

"I'm sorry," he said. "I did a foolish thing, a selfish thing, leaving you there at the table."

She didn't seem to hear him. She'd retreated to some distant place of her own, too small to admit him. "It's been little more than torture for you, hasn't it?" she said.

"What are you talking about?"

"All of it. Our connection. My half-truths. Everything I haven't told you."

"Don't speak in those maddening generalizations," he said. "What half-truths? Do you mean what happened with Novak? I thought we'd moved past that, Klara. What else do you want to tell me?"

She shook her head. Then she put her hand to her eyes and her shoulders began to shake.

"What's happened to you?" he said. "I didn't do this. I didn't make this happen by walking down to the beach for a smoke."

"No," she said, looking up, her eyes lit with tears. "It's just that I understood something while you were down there."

"What is it?" he said. "If it has a name, tell me."

"I ruin things," she said. "I'm a ruiner. I take what's good and make it bad. I take what's bad and make it worse. I did it to my daughter and to Zoltán, and now I've done it to you. I saw how unhappy you looked before you left the table."

"Ah, I see. It's all your fault. You forced Elisabet to have the problems she's had. You forced Novak to deceive his wife. You forced me to fall in love with you. The three of us had no part in it at all."

"You don't know the half of what I've done."

"Then tell me! What is it? Tell me."

She shook her head.

"And if you don't?" he said. He got to his feet and took her by the arm, pulled her up beside him. "How are we supposed to go on? Will you keep me in ignorance? Will I learn the truth some-day from your daughter?"

"No," she said, almost too quietly to hear. "Elisabet doesn't know."

"If we're to be together, I have to know everything. You've got to decide, Klara. If you want this to continue, you'll have to be honest with me."

"You're hurting my arm," she said.

"Who was he? Just tell me his name."

"Who?"

"That man you loved. Elisabet's father."

She yanked her arm away. In the moonlight he could see the

fabric of her dress straining against her ribs and going smooth again. Her eyes filled with tears. "Don't ever grab me like that," she said, and began to sob. "I want to go home. Please, Andras. I'm sorry. I want to go home to Paris." She put her arms around herself, shivering as though she'd caught a fever in the cool Mediterranean night. Her starfish pin glittered like a beautiful mistake, a festive scrap torn from an ocean-liner ball, blown across the sea and caught by chance in the dark waves of her hair.

He could see it: She'd been overtaken by something that was like a disease, something that shook her frame and brought a pallor to her skin. He saw it in the way she huddled beneath the blankets in the cottage, the way she stared flat-eyed at the wall. She was serious about going home; she wanted to leave in the morning. For an hour he lay in bed with her, wide awake, until he heard her breath slide into the rhythm of sleep. He didn't have the heart to be angry at her anymore. If she wanted to go home, he'd take her home. He could gather their things that night and be ready to leave at dawn. Careful not to wake her, he crawled out of bed and began to pack their suitcases. It was good to have something concrete and finite to do. He folded her little things: the cotton dresses, her stockings, her underclothes, her black maillot; he replaced her necklaces and earrings in the satin envelope from which he'd seen her remove them. He tucked her ballet shoes into each other and folded her practice skirts and leotards. Afterward, he put on a jacket and sat alone in the garden. In the weeds beside the driveway, crickets sang a French tune; the song his crickets sang in Konyár had had different high notes, a different rhythm. But the stars overhead were the same. There was the damsel stretched on her rock, and the little bear, and the dragon. He had pointed them out to Klara a few nights earlier; she'd made him repeat them each night until she knew them as well as he did.

They drove back to Paris the next morning. He had helped

her get up and dress in the blue morning light; she had wept when she saw he'd packed all their things. "I've ruined this holiday for you," she said. "And today's your birthday."

"I don't care about that," he said. "Let's get home. It's a long drive."

While she waited in the car he locked the cottage and restored the key to the bird's nest above the door. For the last time he drove down the winding road toward Nice; the sea glittered as sun began to spill across its pailletted surface. He wasn't frightened on the road, not after the lessons she'd given him. He drove toward Paris as she sat silently and watched the fields and farms. By the time they'd reached the tangle of streets outside the city, she'd fallen asleep and he had to try to remember how they'd come. The streets had their own ideas; he lost an hour trying to find his way through the suburbs before a policeman directed him to the Porte d'Italie. At last he found his way across the Seine and up the familiar boulevards to the rue de Sévigné. By that time the sun was low in the sky; the dance studio lay in shadow, and the stairs were dark. Klara woke and rubbed her face with her hands. He helped her upstairs and got her into the nightgown she'd forgotten on the bed. She lay on her back and let the tears roll down her temples and onto the pillow.

"What can I do for you?" he asked, sitting beside her. "What do you need?"

"Just to be alone," she said. "Just to sleep for a while."

Her tone was strangely flat. This pale woman in the embroidered gown was the ghostly sister of the Klara he knew, the woman who'd raced from her house a week earlier in a duster and driving goggles. It seemed impossible to go home. He didn't intend to leave her in this fog. Instead he carried her things upstairs from the car, then made her a cup of the linden tea she drank when she had a headache. When he brought it in, she sat up in bed and extended a hand to him. He came to the bed and sat down beside her. She held his eyes with her eyes; a pink flush had spread across her chest. She laid her head on his shoulder and put her arms around his waist. He felt the rise and fall of her chest against his own.

"What a dreadful birthday you've had," she said.

"Not at all," he said, stroking her hair. "I've been with you all day."

"There's something for you in the dance studio," she said. "A birthday present."

"I don't need a present," he said.

"Nonetheless."

"You can give it to me another time."

"No," she said. "You should have it on your birthday, as long as we're back anyway. I'll come down with you." She got out of bed and took his hand. Together they went down the stairs and into the dance studio. Standing against one wall was a sheet-draped object the size and shape of an upright piano.

"My God," he said. "What is it?"

"Take a look," she said.

"I don't know if I dare."

"Dare."

He lifted the sheet by the corner and tugged it free. There, with its polished wooden drawing surface tilted toward the window, its steel base engraved with the name of a famous cabinetmaker, was a handmade drafting table as handsome and professional as Pierre Vago's. At the bottom of the drawing surface was a perfect groove for pencils; on the right side, a deep inkwell. A drafting stool stood beneath the table, its seat and brass wheels gleaming. His throat closed.

"You don't like it," she said.

He waited until he knew he could speak. "It's too good," he said. "It's an architect's table. Not something for a student."

"You'll still have it when you're an architect. But I wanted you to have it now."

"Keep it for me," he said. He turned to her and put a hand against her cheek. "If you decide we're going to be together, I'll take it home."

The color faded from her lips and she closed her eyes. "Please," she said. "I want you to take it now. It comes apart in two pieces. Take it in the car."

"I can't," he said. "Not now."

"Please, Andras."

"Keep it for me. Once you've had some time to think, you'll let me know if I should take it or not. But I won't take it as a memento of you. Do you understand? I won't have it instead of you."

She nodded, her gray eyes downcast.

"It's the best gift I've ever gotten in my life," he said.

And their holiday was at an end. September was coming. He could feel it as he walked home along the Pont Marie, carrying his bag with twelve days' worth of clothes. September was sending its first cool streamers into Paris, its red tinge of burning. The scent of it blew through the channel of the Seine like the perfume of a girl on the threshold of a party. Her foot in its satin shoe had not yet crossed the sill, but everyone knew she was there. In another moment she would enter. All of Paris seemed to hold its breath, waiting.

CHAPTER SEVENTEEN

Synagogue de la Victoire

HE WOULD HAVE given anything to spend Rosh Hashanah in Konyár that year—to go to synagogue with his father and Mátyás, to eat honey cake at his mother's table, to stand in the orchard and put a hand on the trunk of his favorite apple tree, the crown of which had always been his refuge when he was frightened or lonely or depressed. Instead he found himself in his attic on the rue des Écoles, nearing the end of his first year in Paris, waiting for Polaner to meet him so they could go to synagogue together on the rue de la Victoire. Four weeks had passed since he'd last spoken to Klara. And as the Jewish year drew to a close, all of Europe seemed to hang from a filament above an abyss. As soon as he had returned to consciousness after Nice, as soon as he'd read the letters waiting for him and made his way through the usual sheaf of newspapers, he'd been reminded that there were worse things happening in Europe than the refusal of Klara Morgenstern to reveal the essential secrets of her history. Hitler, who had flouted the Versailles treaty with his annexation of Austria that past spring, now wanted Czechoslovakia's border region, the mountain barrier of the Sudetenland, with its military fortifications, its armament plants, its textile factories and mines. *What do you think of the chancellor's newest mania?* Tibor had written from Modena. *Does he really believe Britain and France will stand idly by while he strips Central Europe's last democracy of all her defenses? It would be the end of free Czechoslovakia, we can be certain of that.*

From Mátyás there was a different note of indignation, a schoolboy's protest against Hitler's geographic revisionism: *How can he demand the "return" of the Sudetenland when it never belonged to Germany in the first place? Who does he think he's fooling? Every second-former knows that Czechoslovakia belonged to Austria-*

Hungary before the Great War. To that, Andras had written back that the Hungarian government itself was likely implicated in Hitler's plans, since Hungary would stand to regain its own lost territory if Germany took the Sudetenland; the word *return* was an incitement to anyone who felt that his country had been shortchanged at Versailles. *But at least you've been paying attention in school,* he wrote. *Maybe you'll get your baccalaureate after all.*

The Paris papers revealed more as the situation unfolded: On the twelfth of September, in his closing speech at the Nazi party rally in Nuremberg, Hitler brutalized the air with a fist and demanded justice for the millions of ethnic Germans living in the Sudetenland; he refused to stand idly by and see them oppressed by the Czech president Beneš and his government. A few days later, Chamberlain, who had never before set foot on an airplane, flew to Hitler's mountain retreat in Berchtesgaden to discuss what everyone was now calling the Sudeten crisis.

"He should never have gone," Polaner said, over a glass of whiskey at the Blue Dove. "It's a humiliation, don't you see? This old man who's never been on a plane before, made to travel to the remotest corner of Germany for a meeting with the Führer. It's a show of force on Hitler's part. The fact that Chamberlain went means he's frightened. I promise you, Hitler will see his advantage and take it."

"If anyone's making a show of force, it's Chamberlain," Andras said. "He went to Berchtesgaden to make a point: If Hitler attacks Czechoslovakia, Britain and France will go to any length to bring him down. That's what this is about."

But soon it became clear that Andras was wrong. The papers reported that Chamberlain had come out of the meeting with a list of demands from Hitler, and was now determined to persuade his own government, and France's, to meet the Führer's conditions in short order. French editorials argued in favor of the sacrifice of the Sudetenland if it meant preserving the peace that had been won at such staggering cost in the Great War; the opposing view seemed to belong to a few fringe communist and socialist commentators. A few days later, envoys from the French and British governments presented President Beneš with a proposal to strip the republic of its border regions, and demanded that the Czech government accept the plan without delay. Andras found himself spending all day combing the papers and listening to the red Bakelite wireless at Forestier's set-design studio, as if his constant attention might turn events in a different direction. Even Forestier put aside his design tools and mulled over the news with Andras. In response to the Anglo-French proposal, President Beneš had submitted a measured and scholarly memorandum reminding France that it had sworn to defend Czechoslovakia if it were threatened; a few hours after the memo was transmitted, the British and French foreign ministers in Prague pulled Beneš out of bed to insist he accept the proposal at once. Otherwise he would find himself facing Germany alone. The next day Andras and Monsieur Forestier listened in incredulous dismay as a commentator announced Beneš's acceptance of the Anglo-French plan. The entire Czech cabinet had just resigned in protest. Chamberlain would meet with Hitler again on the twenty-second of September, this time in Bad Godesberg, to arrange the transfer of the Sudetenland.

"Well, that's that!" Forestier said, his broad shoulders curling. "The last democracy of Central Europe kneels to Hitler at the urging of Britain and France. These are terrible times, my young Mr. Lévi, terrible times."

Andras had assumed then that the crisis was over, that a war had been averted, even if at a cruel price. But he arrived at Forestier's on the twenty-third of September to learn that the meeting in Bad Godesberg had yielded more demands still: Hitler wanted his troops to occupy the Sudetenland, and he required the Czech population of the area to vacate their homes and farms within a week, leaving behind everything they owned. Chamberlain brought home the new list of demands, which were promptly rejected by both the French and British governments. A military occupation was unthinkable, akin to surrendering the rest of Czechoslovakia without a fight.

The dreaded call-up has come, Andras had written to Tibor that morning, the eve of Rosh Hashanah. *The Czech military has been mobilized, and our Premier Daladier has ordered a partial mobilization of French troops as well.* Andras had watched it happen that morning: All over town, reservists left their shops and taxicabs and café tables and headed for points outside Paris where they would meet their battalions. When he went to send the letter to Tibor, there had been a crush at the postbox; every departing soldier seemed to have a missive to mail. Now he sat on his bed with his tallis bag in hand, waiting for Eli Polaner and thinking of his parents and his brothers and Klara and the prospect of war. At half past six Polaner arrived; they took the Métro to Le Peletier in the Ninth, and walked two blocks to the Synagogue de la Victoire.

This synagogue was not at all like the ornate Moroccan-style temple of Dohány utca, where Andras and Tibor had gone for High Holiday services in Budapest. Nor was it like the one-room shul in Konyár with its dark paneling and its wooden screen dividing the men's section from the women's. The Synagogue de la Victoire was a soaring Romanesque building of pale gold stone, with a grand rose window crowning the arched façade. Inside, slender columns rose toward a barrel-vaulted ceiling; a high clerestory deluged the space with light. Above the Byzantine-ornamented bimah, an inscription implored TU AIMERAS L'ETERNEL TON DIEU DE TOUT TON COEUR. By the time Andras and Polaner arrived, the service had already begun. They took seats in a pew near the back and unbuttoned their velvet tallis bags: Polaner's tallis was of yellowed silk with blue stripes, Andras's of fine-spun white wool. Together they said the blessing for donning the prayer shawls; together they draped the shawls over their shoulders. The cantor sang in Hebrew, *How good and sweet it is when brothers sit down together.* Again and again the familiar melody: one line low and somber like a work chant, the next climbing up into the arch of the ceiling like a question: Isn't it good for brothers to sit down together? Polaner had learned the melody in Kraków. Andras had learned it in Konyár. The cantor had learned it from his grandfather in Minsk. The three old men standing beside Polaner had learned it in Gdynia and Amsterdam and Prague. It had come from somewhere. It had escaped pogroms in Odessa and Oradea, had found its way to this synagogue, would find its way to others that had not yet been built.

For Andras, who had spent the past four weeks constructing a wall around the part of himself that concerned Klara Morgenstern, the melody had the effect of an earthquake. It began as a small tremor, just enough to make the wall tremble—yes, it was good when brothers sat down together, but it had been months, months, since he'd seen his own brothers—and then there was a jolt of unbearable homesickness for Konyár, and a second jolt of homesickness for the rue de Sévigné and for the deeper, more intimate home that was Klara herself. For the past four weeks he had immersed himself in the news of the world and turned his thoughts away from her; late at night, when it was no use to pretend that he had really put her out of his mind, he told himself that her silence alone could not be taken to mean that all was over. Though she hadn't contacted him, she hadn't sent back his letters or requested that he return the things she kept at his apartment, either. She hadn't given him reason to abandon hope altogether. But now, as the population of Paris fled to the countryside in anticipation of a bombardment, as the abstract possibility of war became a real and tangible thing, what was he supposed to make of her continued silence? Would she leave Paris without letting him know? Would she leave under the protection of Zoltán Novak, in a private car he had sent for her? At that very moment was she packing the same suitcase Andras had unpacked for her a few weeks earlier?

He pulled his tallis closer and tried to still his thoughts; there was some relief in repeating the prayers, some comfort in Polaner's presence and the presence of these other men and women who knew the words by heart. He said the prayer that listed the sins committed by the House of Israel, and the one in which he asked the Lord to keep his mouth from evil and his lips from speaking guile. He said the prayer of gratitude for the Torah, and listened to others sing the words written in the white-clad scrolls. And at the end of the service he prayed to be written into the Book of Life, as if there might still be a place in such a book for him.

After the service, he and Polaner walked across the river to the students' dining club, which had emptied over the summer, filled again as the schools prepared to reopen, and then emptied again with the threat of war. The server loaded Andras's plate with bread and beef and hard oily potatoes.

"At home, my mother would be serving brisket and chicken noodle soup," Polaner said as they took their plates to a table. "She would never let potatoes like these enter her kitchen."

"You can't blame the potato," Andras said. "It's hardly the potato's fault."

"It always begins with the potato," Polaner said, raising an eyebrow darkly.

Andras had to laugh. It seemed a miracle that Polaner could be sitting across the table from him after what had happened last January. Though much was wrong with the world, it could not be denied that Eli Polaner had recovered from his injuries and had been brave enough to return to the École Spéciale for a second year.

"Your mother must have hated to let you leave Kraków," Andras said.

Polaner unfolded his napkin and arranged it on his lap. "She's never glad to see me go," he said. "She's my mother."

Andras looked at him carefully. "You never told your parents what happened, did you?"

"Did you think I would?"

"You nearly died, after all."

"They'd never have let me come back," Polaner said. "They'd have shipped me off to some Freudian sanatorium for a talking cure, and you'd be lonely tonight, *copain.*"

"Lucky for me, then, that you didn't tell," Andras said. He had missed his friends, and Polaner in particular. He had imagined that by now they would all be dining at this club again, that soon they would be together in the studio, that they'd be meeting after classes at the Blue Dove to drink black tea and eat almond biscuits. He'd imagined himself narrating their exploits to Klara, making her laugh as they sat by the fire on the rue de Sévigné. But Rosen and Ben Yakov were home with their families, and he and Polaner were here alone together, and the École Spéciale had suspended the beginning of classes, as had all the other colleges of Paris. And he wasn't narrating anything to Klara at all.

As the Days of Awe between Rosh Hashanah and Yom Kippur began to unfold, he told himself he would likely hear from her soon. War seemed inevitable. At night there were practice blackouts; the few corner lamps that remained lit were covered with black paper hoods to cast their light downward. Departing families clotted the trains and raised a cacophony of car horns in the streets. Five hundred thousand more men were called to the colors. Those who stayed in Paris rushed to buy gas masks and canned food and flour. A telegram arrived from Andras's parents: IF WAR DECLARED COME HOME FIRST AVAIL TRAIN. He sat on his bed with the telegram in his hands, wondering if this were the end of everything: his studies, his life in Paris, all of it. It was the twenty-eighth of September, three days before Hitler's threatened occupation of the Sudetenland. In seventy-two hours his life might fall apart. It was impossible to wait any longer. He would go to the rue de Sévigné at once and demand to see Klara; he would insist that she let him escort her and Elisabet out of the city as soon as they could pack their bags. Before he could lose his nerve, he threw on a jacket and ran all the way to her house.

But when he reached the door, he found his way barricaded by Mrs. Apfel. Madame Morgenstern would see no one, she said. Not even him. And she had no plans to leave the city, as far as Mrs. Apfel knew. At the moment she was in bed with a headache and had asked particularly that she not be disturbed. In any case, hadn't Andras heard? There was to be a meeting at Munich the next day, a final effort to negotiate peace. Mrs. Apfel was certain those idiots would come to their senses. He would see, she said; there wouldn't be a war after all.

Andras hadn't heard. He ran to Forestier's and spent the next two days with his ear sewn to the wireless. And on the thirtieth of September it was announced that Hitler had reached an accord with France, Britain, and Italy: Germany would have the Sudetenland in ten days' time. There would, after all, be a military occupation. The Sudeten Czechs would be required to leave their homes and shops and farms without taking a stick of furniture, a single bolt of cloth or ear of corn, and there was to be no program of compensation for the lost goods. In the regions occupied by Polish and Hungarian minorities, popular votes would determine new frontiers; Poland and Hungary would almost certainly reclaim those lost territories. The radio announcer read the agreement in quick grainy French, and Andras struggled to make sense of it. How was it possible that Britain and France had accepted a plan almost identical to the one they'd rejected out of hand a few days earlier? The radio station broadcast the noise of celebration from London; Andras could hear the local jubilation well enough just outside Forestier's studio, where hundreds of Parisians cheered the peace, celebrating Daladier, praising Chamberlain. The men who had been called up could now come home. That was an unarguable good—so many written into the Book of Life for another year. Why, then, did he feel more as Forestier seemed to feel— Forestier, who sat in the corner with his elbows on his knees, his forehead hammocked in his hands? The recent series of events seemed clothed in disgrace. Andras felt the way he might have if, after the attack on Polaner, Professor Perret had preserved peace at the École Spéciale by expelling the victim.

On the eve of Yom Kippur, Andras and Polaner went to hear Kol Nidre at the Synagogue de la Victoire. With solemn ceremony, with forehead-scraping genuflections, the cantor and the rabbi prayed for *rachmones* upon the congregation and the House of Israel. They declared that the congregants were released from the vows they'd made that year, to God and to each other. They thanked the Almighty that Europe had avoided war. Andras gave his thanks with a lingering sense of dread, and as the service progressed, his unhappiness flowed into another channel. That week, the threat of war had once again proved an effective distraction from the situation with Klara. For a time he had fooled himself, had let himself believe that her month of silence might contain a tacit promise, a suggestion that she was still wrestling with the problem that had sent them home early from Nice. But he couldn't deceive himself any longer. She didn't want to see him. They were finished; that was clear. Her silence could not be read otherwise.

That night he went home and put her things into a wooden crate: her comb and brush, two chemises, a stray earring in the shape of a daffodil, a green glass pillbox, a book of Hungarian short stories, a book of sixteenth-century French verse from which she liked to read aloud to him. He lingered for a moment over the book; he'd bought it for her because it contained the Marot poem about the fire that dwelt secretly in snow. He turned to the poem now. Carefully, with his pocketknife, he cut the page from the book and put it into the envelope that contained her letters. Those he kept, because he couldn't bear to part with them. He wrote her a note on a postcard he'd bought as a keepsake months earlier: a photograph of the Square Barye, the tiny park at the eastern tip of the Île Saint-Louis, where he'd spoken the Marot poem into her ear on New Year's Day. *Dear Klara*, he wrote, *here are a few things you left with me. My feelings for you are unchanged, but I cannot continue to wait without knowing the reason for your silence, or whether it will be broken. So I must make the break myself. I release you from your promises to me. You need not be faithful to me any longer, nor conduct yourself as if you might someday be my wife. I have released you, but I cannot release myself from what I vowed to you; you must do that, Klara, if that is what you want. In the meantime, should you choose to come to me again, you will find that I am still, as ever, your ANDRAS.*

He nailed the top onto the crate and hefted it. It weighed almost nothing, those last vestiges of Klara in his life. In the dark he went to her house one last time and set the box on the doorstep, where she would find it in the morning.

The next day he prayed and fasted. During the early service he felt certain he had made a terrible mistake. If he'd waited another week, he thought, she might have come back to him; now he had secured his own unhappiness. He wanted to run from the synagogue to the rue de Sévigné and retrieve the box before anyone found it. But as the fast scoured him from the inside, he began to believe that he'd done the right thing, that he'd done what he had to do to save himself. He pulled his tallis around his shoulders and leaned into the repetition of the eighteen benedictions. The familiar progression of the prayer brought him greater certainty. Nature had its cycles; there was a time for all things, and all things passed away.

By the evening service he was scraped out and numb and dizzy from fasting. He knew he was sliding toward some abyss, and that he was powerless to stop himself. At last the service concluded with the piercing spiral of the shofar blast. He and Polaner were supposed to go to dinner on the rue Saint-Jacques; József had invited them to break the fast with his friends from the Beaux-Arts. They walked across the river in silence, sunk into the last stages of their hunger. At József's there was music and a vast table of liquor and food. József wished them a happy new year and put glasses of wine into their hands. Then, with a confidential crook of his finger, he drew Andras aside and bent his head toward him.

"I heard the most remarkable thing about you," he said. "My friend Paul told me you're involved with the mother of that tall girl, his obstreperous Elisabet."

Andras shook his head. "Not anymore," he said. And he took a bottle of whiskey from the table and locked himself in József's bedroom, where he got blind drunk, shouted curses at himself in the mirror, terrified pedestrians by leaning out over the balcony edge, vomited into the fireplace, and finally passed into unconsciousness on the floor.

CHAPTER EIGHTEEN

Café Bédouin

JUDAISM OFFERED no shivah for lost love. There was no Kaddish to say, no candle to burn, no injunction against shaving or listening to music or going to work. He couldn't live in his torn clothes, couldn't spend his days sitting in ashes. Nor could he turn to more secular modes of comfort; he couldn't afford to drink himself into oblivion every night or suffer a nervous collapse. After he had scraped himself off József's parquet floor and crawled back to his own apartment, he concluded that he had reached the nadir of his grief. The thought itself was medicinal. If this was the lowest point, then things would have to improve. He had made the break with Klara. Now he had to go on without her. Classes would soon begin again at the École Spéciale; he couldn't fail his second year of school on her account. Nor could he justify hanging himself or leaping from a bridge or otherwise indulging in Greek tragedy. He had to go about the business of his life. He thought these things as he stood at the window of his garret, looking down into the rue des Écoles, still nursing a wild and irrepressible hope that she'd come around the corner in her red hat, half running to see him, the skirt of her fall coat flying behind her.

But when her silence stretched into a seventh week, even his most fantastical hopes began to dull. Life, oblivious to his grief, continued. Rosen and Ben Yakov returned to Paris with the rest of the students of the École Spéciale, Rosen in a state of chronic rage over what had happened and was still happening in Czechoslovakia, Ben Yakov pale with love for a girl he'd met in Italy that summer, the daughter of an Orthodox rabbi in Florence. He had vowed to bring the girl to Paris as his bride; he'd taken a job reshelving books at the Bibliothèque Nationale to save money for that purpose. Rosen had a new passion, too: He had joined the Ligue Internationale Contre l'Antisemitisme, and was consumed with rallies and meetings. Andras himself had less time than ever to consider his situation with Klara. With the help of Vago's recommendation, he had been offered the architecture internship for which he'd applied in the spring. He'd had to cut back his hours at Forestier's, but there was a small stipend to make up for the loss of income. Now, three afternoons a week, he found himself at the elbow of an architect named Georges Lemain, playing the junior intern's role of plan-filer, pencil-line-eraser, black-coffee-fetcher, calculation-maker. Lemain was a ruler-narrow man with a sleek head of clipped gray hair. He spoke rapid metallic French and drew with machinelike precision. Often he infuriated his colleagues by singing operatic airs as he worked. As a result he'd been sequestered in a far corner of the office, walled off by bookshelves filled with back issues of *L'Architecture d'Aujourd'hui*. As Andras worked at his own lowly desk beside Lemain's great drawing table, he learned the airs and could soon sing them on his own. In return for his tolerance and diligence, Lemain began to help Andras with his school assignments. His fleet-looking angles of glass and polished planes of stone began to find their way into Andras's designs. He encouraged Andras to keep a portfolio of private sketches, work that had nothing to do with his École Spéciale projects; he urged Andras to show him ideas that he'd been developing. And so, one afternoon in late October, Andras ventured to bring in the plans for the summer house in Nice. Lemain spread the plans on his own worktable and bent over the elevations.

"A wall like this won't last five years in Nice," he said, framing a segment of Andras's drawing with his thumbs. "Consider the salt. These crevices will give it a foothold." He laid a piece of tracing paper over Andras's drawing and sketched in a smooth wall. "But you've found a clever way to use the grade of the hill. The oblique orientation of the patio and terrace works well with the topography." He placed another sheet of tracing paper over the rear elevation and joined two levels of the terrace into a single curving slope. "Not too much terrace, though. Keep the shape of the hill intact. You can plant rosemary to hold the soil in place."

Andras watched, making further changes in his mind. In the hard light of the office, the plans seemed less like a blueprint for a life he desired and more like the blank shape of a client's house. That room need not be called a ballet studio; it was simply a light-filled *salon*. And those two small bedrooms on the main level might not be children's rooms; they could be *chambres 2* and *3*, to be filled according to the client's whims. The kitchen did not have to contain the imagined remnants of an abandoned meal; the *chambre principal* didn't have to accommodate two Hungarian émigrés, or anyone in particular. All afternoon he erased and redrew until he believed he had chased the ghosts from the design.

With the rolled-up plans and Lemain's sheets of tracing paper under his arm, he made his way toward the rue des Écoles through a confetti of dry leaves. The sound of their scrape and crunch against the sidewalk made him think of a thousand autumn afternoons in Konyár and Debrecen and Budapest, the burnt smell of nuts roasting in the street vendor's cast-iron kettle, the stiff gray wool of school uniforms, the flower-sellers' jars suddenly full of wheat sheaves and velvet-faced sunflowers. He paused at the window of a photographer's studio on the rue des Écoles, where a new series of portraits had just been displayed: somber Parisian children in peasant clothing posed against a painted harvest backdrop. The children all wore shoes, and the shoes were brilliant with polish. He had to laugh aloud, imagining Tibor and Mátyás and himself arrayed in front of a real hay wagon in the clothes they'd worn when they were children: not these impeccable smocks and trousers, but brown workshirts sewn by their mother, hand-me-down dungarees, rope belts, caps made from the cloth of their father's disintegrated overcoats. On their feet they would have worn the fine brown dust of Konyár. Their pockets would have been packed with small hard apples, their arms sore from baling hay for the neighboring farmers. From the house would come the rich red smell of chicken paprikás; their father would have sold so much wood for new hay wagons and sheds that they would eat chicken every Friday until winter. It was a good time, that stretch of warm days in October after the hay came in. The air was still soft and fragrant, the pond that would soon be frozen still a bright liquid oval reflecting mill and sky.

In the photographer's window glass, a faint shape passed across the portraits of the children: the flash of a green woolen coat, the gold sheaf of a braid. The reflection crossed the street in his direction. As it approached, its anonymous features knit themselves into a form he knew: Elisabet Morgenstern. She gave him a hard tap on the shoulder and he turned.

"Elisabet," he said. "What are you doing in the Latin Quarter on a Thursday afternoon? Going to meet Paul?"

"No," she said, and gave him her hard stare. "I came to find you." She pulled a tin of pastilles from her bag and shook one into her palm. "I'd offer you one, but I'm almost out."

"What's wrong?" he said, his insides clenching. "Has something happened to your mother?"

Elisabet rolled the pastille around in her mouth. When she spoke, Andras caught a whiff of anise. "I don't want to talk here on the sidewalk," she said. "Can't we go somewhere?"

The Blue Dove was close by, but Andras didn't want to meet his friends. Instead he led her around the corner and up the hill to the Café Bédouin, where he and Klara had met for a drink what seemed a lifetime ago. He hadn't been back since that night. The same toothy row of liquor bottles stood behind the bar, and the same faded lilac curtains hung at the windows. They sat down at a table along the banquette and ordered tea.

"What's this about?" he said, once the waiter had left them.

"Whatever you're doing to my mother, you'd better stop," Elisabet said.

"I don't know what you mean. I haven't seen her in weeks."

"That's exactly my point! To put it bluntly, Andras, you're acting like a cad. My mother's been miserable. She hardly eats. She won't listen to music. She sleeps all the time. And she's at me for every little thing. My marks in school aren't high enough, or I'm not doing my chores properly, or I've taken the wrong tone with her."

"And this is somehow my doing?"

"Who else's? You've dropped her entirely. You don't come to the house anymore. You sent back all her things."

In an instant his grief rushed back as if it had never left him. "What was I supposed to do?" he said. "I stood it as long as I could. She wouldn't write to me or see me. And I did go to her. I went after Rosh Hashanah, when everyone was talking about an evacuation. Mrs. Apfel said your mother wasn't receiving anyone, least of all me. Even after that, she didn't send word. I had to give it up. I had to respect her wishes. And I had to keep myself from losing my mind, too."

"So you walked away because it was easier for you."

"I didn't walk away, Elisabet. I wrote to her when I sent her things. I told her my feelings were unchanged. She didn't write back. It's clear she doesn't want to see me."

"If that's true, then why is she so unhappy? It's not as though she's seeing someone else. She never goes out. At night she's always home. On Sunday afternoons she lies in bed." The waiter delivered their tea, and Elisabet stirred milk into her cup. "She never gives me a moment alone with Paul. I have to sneak out in the middle of the night to see him."

"Is that what this is about? You can't get a moment alone with Paul?"

She glared at him, her mouth tight with disgust. "You're an ass, do you know that? A real ass. Despite what you think, I do care how my mother feels. More than you do, apparently."

"I care!" he cried, leaning across the table. "I've been going mad over this. But I can't change her mind for her, Elisabet. I can't make her feel for me what she doesn't feel. If we're going to speak, she'll have to be the one to contact me."

"But she won't, don't you see? She'll stay miserable. She can keep it up, you know. She's made a project of it all her life. And she'll make me miserable, too." She glanced down at her hand, where Andras noticed for the first time a ring on her fourth finger: a diamond with two leaf-shaped emeralds. As he studied it, she gave the band a contemplative twist.

"Paul and I are engaged," she said. "He wants to take me to New York when I'm finished with school next June."

He raised an eyebrow. "Does your mother know about this?"

"Of course not! You know what she'd say. She wants me to wait until I'm thirty before I look at a man. But I'd think she wouldn't want me to end up like her, alone and old."

"She *doesn't* want you to end up like her. That's the point! She was too young when she had you. She doesn't want you to have to struggle like she did."

"Let me tell you something," Elisabet said, and gave him her granite-hard look. "I would never end up like her. If I got pregnant by some man who didn't love me, I know what I'd do. I know girls who've done it. I'd do what she should have done."

"How can you speak that way?" he said. "She gave up her whole life to raise you."

"That's not my fault," Elisabet said. "And it doesn't mean she can decide what I do once I turn eighteen. I'll marry whomever I want to. I'll go to New York with Paul."

"You're a selfish child, Elisabet."

"Who are you calling selfish?" She narrowed her eyes and pointed a finger at him across the café table. "You're the one who dropped her when she got depressed. A person in that state doesn't invite people to lunch or send love notes. But you probably never cared for her at all, did you? You wanted to be her lover, but you didn't really want to know her."

"Of course I did!" he said. "She was the one who pushed

me away." But as he said it, he experienced a kind of pressure change, a quiet shock that thrummed in his ears. She *had* pushed him away, had done it more than once. But he had pushed her away, too. At Nice, at the Hotel Taureau d'Or, when she'd seemed on the verge of speaking to him about her past, he'd left her alone at the table rather than hear what she might say. And later that night at the cottage, when he'd demanded she tell him everything, he had done it so roughly he'd frightened her. Then he'd packed her things and driven her back to Paris. He had tried to see her exactly once since then. He'd written a single postcard and returned her things, then set about erasing her from his mind, his life. Their love would have a neat, sad ending: a box of things dispatched, a note unanswered. He would never have to hear the revelations that might hurt him or change the way he thought of her. Instead he'd chosen to preserve his idea of her—his memory of her small strong body, of the way she listened and spoke to him, of their nights together in his room. As much as he'd told himself he wanted to know everything about her, part of him had retreated in fear. He thought he'd loved her, but what he had loved wasn't all of her—no more than the silvery images on those long-ago cards had been, or her name on an ivory envelope.

"Do you think she'll see me?" he asked Elisabet.

She looked at him for a long moment, a faint wash of relief warming the cold blue pools of her eyes. "Ask her yourself," she said.

CHAPTER NINETEEN

An Alley

IN THE NINE WEEKS since he'd seen her, time had not lain dormant. The earth had continued its transit around the sun, Germany had marched into the Sudetenland, and change had worked its way into the smaller orbit of his life. There was the raw feeling of wind at the back of his neck; he had cut the hair he'd grown long at her request. His morning tutorials with Vago had ended, and last year's graduates were gone; the new first-year students paid mute attention when he and his classmates gave their critiques in studio. He had mastered the French language, which had crossed the boundary of his unconscious mind and established itself in the territory of his dreams. He had begun his internship at the architecture firm, his first job in his chosen field. And there were new set designs at Forestier's (for *Lysistrata*, a foreshortened Parthenon and a forest of column-like phalluses; for *The Cherry Orchard*, a drawing room whose walls, made of sheer scrim fabric and lined with hidden lights, became increasingly transparent throughout the play until they disappeared to reveal the rows of trees beyond).

Then there was his room on the rue des Écoles. He had pulled the table into the sloping cave of the eaves, where he could pin plans against the ceiling. He'd gotten a green-shaded lamp to illuminate his work, and had tacked drawings of buildings to the walls—not the ocean liners and icebergs his professors designed, nor the monumental architecture of Paris, but the neat ovoids of Ghanaian huts and the nestlike clusters of American Indian cliff-dwellings and the gold stone walls of Palestine. He'd copied the images from magazines and books, had water-colored them with paints bought cheaply at Nice. On the floor was a thick red rug that smelled of woodsmoke; on the bed, a butter-colored bedspread made from a torn theater curtain. And beside the hearth was a deep low armchair of faded vermilion plush, a reject he'd found one morning on the sidewalk in front of the building. It had been lying facedown in a posture of abject indignity, as though it had tried and failed to stagger home after a night of hard drinking. The chair had a droll companion, a fringed and tufted footstool that resembled a shaggy little dog.

It was in this armchair that Klara sat now. He had written to her, had told her he wanted to see her, had asked for nothing more than her company for an evening. Though he'd told himself not to expect an answer, he hoped Elisabet might prevail upon her to write back. Then tonight he had come home from Forestier's to find her sitting in the chair, her black shoes lined up beside it like a pair of quarter notes. He stood in the doorway and stared, afraid she might be an apparition; she got up and took the bag from his shoulder, slid her arms underneath his coat, held him against her chest. There was her smell of lavender and honey, the bready scent of her skin. The familiarity of it nearly brought him to tears. He put a thumb to the hollow of her throat, touched the amber button of her blouse.

"You've cut your hair," she said.

He nodded, unable to speak.

"And you look thin," she continued. "You look as if you haven't been eating."

"Have *you*?" he said, and studied her face. The hollows beneath her eyes were shaded violet; the beach gold of her skin had faded to ivory. She looked almost transparent, as if a wind had blown her empty from the inside. She held her body as if every part of it hurt.

"I'm going to make you some tea," he said.

"Don't trouble."

"Believe me, Klara, it's no trouble." He put water on to boil and made tea for both of them. Then he built up the fire and sat down on the fringed footstool. He pushed her skirt up above the knee, unhooked the metal loops of her garters from their rubber nubs, removed her stockings. He didn't caress her legs, though he wanted to; he didn't bury his face in her thighs. Instead he took her feet in his hands and followed their arches with his thumbs.

She let out a cry, a sigh. "Why do you persist with me?" she said. "What is it you want?"

He shook his head. "I don't know, Klara. Maybe just this."

"I've been so unhappy since we came back from Nice," she said. "I could hardly drag myself from bed. I couldn't eat. I couldn't write a letter or mend a dress. When it looked like France might go to war, I had the terrible thought that you might volunteer to fight." She paused and shook her head. "I spent two sleepless nights trying to work up the nerve to come to you, and gave myself such a terrible headache that I couldn't get out of bed. I couldn't teach. I've never been too sick to teach, not in fifteen years. Mrs. Apfel had to post a note saying I was ill."

"You told her to send me away if I came to see you."

"I didn't think you'd come except to tell me you were going off to war. I didn't think I could survive that piece of news. And then you sent back my things. God, Andras! I read your note a hundred times. I made a hundred drafts of a reply and threw them away. Everything I wrote seemed wrong or cowardly."

"And then France didn't go to war after all."

"No. And I was selfishly happy, believe me, even though I knew what it meant for Czechoslovakia."

He smiled sadly. "I didn't really send back all your things, after all. I kept the poem about *Anne qui luy jecta de la Neige.*"

"The Marot."

"Yes. I cut it out of your book."

"You vandalized my book!"

"I'm afraid so."

She shook her head and rested her forehead in her palm, her elbow pillowed on the arm of the chair. "When your letter came this week, my daughter told me she'd lose all respect for me if I didn't go to see you at once." She paused to give him a wry half smile. "At first I was just astonished to learn that she had any respect for me at all. Then I decided I had better come."

"Klara," he said, moving closer and taking her hands in his own. "I'm afraid I'm going to have to ask you the difficult questions now. I have to know what you were thinking when we came back from Nice. You have to tell me about—I don't even know the man's name. Elisabet's father. You have to tell me why you came here to France."

She sighed and looked into the fire, where the heat ran like a volatile liquid through the coals. Her eyes seemed to drink the red light of it. "Elisabet's father," she said, and ran a hand along the velvet arm of the chair. "That man."

And then, though it was already past midnight, she told him her story.

In the second decade of that century, the best ballet students in Budapest had studied under Viktor Vasilievich Romankov, the willful and eccentric third son of a family of penniless Russian aristocrats. In St. Petersburg, when it had still been St. Petersburg, Romankov had studied at the Imperial School of Ballet and danced in the famous ballet company at the Mariinsky Theater; at thirty-five he left to open his own school, where he taught hundreds of dancers, among them the great Olga Spessivtzeva and Alexandra Danilova. As a young man, he himself had struggled to distill the tincture of precision into his ballet technique; his efforts to demystify the physiology of dance, and the patience he had developed in his own training, had made him an unusually effective teacher. His renown spread west and crossed the Atlantic. When his family lost the last of its once-great fortune in the early rumblings of the revolution, he fled St. Petersburg, intending to emigrate to Paris along the path traced by his hero Diaghilev, founder of the Ballets Russes. But by the time Romankov reached Budapest he was exhausted and broke.

He found himself unexpectedly in love with that city of bridges and parks, of ornately tiled buildings and tree-lined boulevards. Not more than a few days passed before he made inquiries into the Hungarian Royal Ballet; it turned out that its academy had a hopelessly antiquated system of training, and had long been in need of a change. The artistic director of the school knew of Romankov. He was precisely the sort of person the school had wanted to recruit; she was more than happy to have him join the faculty. So there in Budapest he'd stayed.

Klara had been one of his earliest pupils. She had started with him when she was eleven. He had picked her out of a class he'd glimpsed through a window as he walked through the Jewish Quarter; he went straight into the studio, took her by the hand from among her classmates, told the instructress that he was a friend of the family and that there was an urgent matter at home. Outside, he explained to Klara that he was a ballet teacher from St. Petersburg, that he had taken note of her talent and wanted to see her dance. Then he walked her to the Royal Ballet School on Andrássy út, a third-floor honeycomb of practice studios much shabbier than the school Klara had just left behind. The floors were gray with age, the pianos scarred, the walls devoid of even a single Degas print, the air redolent of feet and shoe satin and rosin. No classes were meeting that day; the studios stood empty of everything but the strange humming resonance that hovered in rooms whose natural state was to be filled with music and dancers. Romankov took Klara to one of the smaller studios and sat down at the piano. As he pounded out a minuet she danced her butterfly piece from the previous year's recital. The music was wrong but the tempo was right; as she danced, she had the sense that something fateful was taking place. When she'd finished, Romankov clapped his hands and made her take a bow. She was splendid for her age, he said, and not too old for him to correct what was wrong with her technique. She must begin her training immediately; this was the school where she would become a ballerina. He must speak to her parents that very day.

Eleven-year-old Klara, flattered by his vision of her future, took him home to her parents' villa on Benczúr utca. In the sitting room with its salmon-colored sofas, Romankov announced to Klara's startled mother that her daughter was wasting her time at the studio on Wesselényi utca and must enroll at the Royal Ballet School at once. It was possible that Klara had a brilliant future in ballet, but he must undo the damage that her current teacher had done. He showed Mrs. Hász the mannered curl of Klara's hand, the exaggerated flatness of her fifth position, the jerky exactitude of her port de bras; then he smoothed her hands into a more childlike curl, made her stand in a looser fifth, took her arms by the wrists and floated them through the positions as though through water. *This* was how a dancer should look, how she should move. He could train her to do this, and if she excelled she would have a place in the Royal Ballet.

Klara's mother, who, through an accident of fate and love, had found herself extracted from rural oblivion in Kaba and placed at the center of the most exalted Jewish social circle of Budapest, had never imagined that Klara might someday become a professional dancer; she had imagined lives of ease and comfort for her children. Of course Klara studied ballet, grace being a necessary attribute for young ladies of her social position. But a career as a ballerina was out of the question. She thanked Romankov for his interest and wished him well with his new position at the Royal Ballet School; she would speak to Klara's father that evening. Once she had sent him away she took Klara upstairs to the nursery and explained to her why she could not study ballet with the nice Russian man. Dancing was a pleasant pastime for a child, not something one did in front of audiences for money. Professional dancers led lives of poverty, deprivation, and exploitation. They rarely married, and when they did, their marriages ended unhappily. When Klara was grown she would be a wife and mother. If she wanted to dance she could give balls for her friends, as her anya and apa did.

Klara nodded and agreed, because she loved her mother. But

at eleven years old she already knew she would be a dancer. She'd known it since her brother had taken her to see *La Cendrillon* at the Operaház when she was five. The next time her governess dropped her off for a dancing lesson at the school on Wesselényi utca, she ran the seven blocks to the Royal Ballet School on Andrássy út and asked one of the dancers there where she might find the tall red-bearded gentleman. The girl took her to a studio at the end of a hallway, where Romankov was just preparing to teach an intermediate lesson. He didn't seem at all surprised to see Klara; he made a place for her at the practice barre between two other children, and, in his Russian-accented baritone, led them through a series of difficult exercises. At the end of class Klara returned to the other ballet school in time to meet her governess, to whom she mentioned nothing of her adventure. It was three weeks before Klara's parents discovered her defection from the studio on Wesselényi utca. By then it was too late: Klara had become a devotee of Romankov and the Royal Ballet School. Klara's indulgent father convinced her mother that there could be no real danger of their daughter's ending up on the stage; the school was merely a more rigorous version of the one she'd attended before. He'd inquired into Romankov's professional history, and there could be no denying that the man was an exceptionally gifted teacher. To have his daughter studying under that famous ballet master was an honor that touched Tamás Hász's sense of bourgeois pride and confirmed his paternal prejudices.

Of the twenty children that comprised the Royal Ballet School's beginning class, seventeen were girls and three were boys. One of the boys was a tall dark-haired child named Sándor Goldstein. He was the son of a carpenter and had a perpetual smell of fresh-cut wood about him. Romankov had discovered Sándor Goldstein not in a dance class but at the pool at Palatinus Strand, where Goldstein had been practicing acrobatic dives with a group of friends. At twelve years old he could do a handstand on the edge of the board and push himself off, then flip backward to enter the water headfirst. At his school he'd won the gymnastics medal three years in a row. When Romankov proposed taking him on as a student, Goldstein had denounced ballet as a pursuit for girls. Romankov had responded by engaging one of the male dancers of the Hungarian Royal Ballet to meet Goldstein on his way home from school, lift him overhead like a barbell, and run through the streets with him until Goldstein begged to be put down. The next day Goldstein enrolled in Romankov's beginning class, and by the time he was thirteen and Klara twelve, they were both performing children's roles with the Royal Ballet.

To Klara, Sándor was brother, friend, co-conspirator. He taught her to send Romankov into a fury by dancing half a beat behind the music. He introduced her to delicacies she'd never tried: the savory dry end of a Debrecen sausage; the crystalline scrapings of the sugared-nuts kettle, which could be bought for half a fillér at the end of the day; the tiny sour apples that were meant for jelly but that made for fine eating if you didn't eat too many. And at the great market on Vámház körut he taught her how to steal. While Klara showed off pirouettes for the candy vendor, Sándor nicked a handful of peach-pit candy for both of them. He tipped tiny Russian dolls into his cap, looped embroidered kerchiefs onto his smallest finger, plucked pastries from the market baskets of women haggling over fruit and vegetables. Klara invited him to lunch at her parents' house, where he soon became a favorite. Her father talked to him as though he were a full-grown gentleman, her mother fed him pink-iced chocolates, and her brother dressed him in a military jacket and taught him to shoot imaginary Serbs.

When they had both attained the necessary strength, Romankov made Klara and Sándor dancing partners. He taught Sándor to lift Klara with no sign of effort, to make her seem light as a reed. He taught them to become a single dancer in two bodies, to listen to the rhythm of each other's breath, the flow of blood in each other's veins. He made them study anatomy textbooks together and tested them on musculature and bone structure. He took them to see dissections at the medical school. Five times a week they performed with the Royal Ballet. By the time she was thirteen, Klara had been a moth, a sylph, a sugarplum, a member of a swan court, a lady-in-waiting, a mountain stream, a moonbeam, a doe. Her parents had resigned themselves to her appearing on the stage; her growing fame had earned them a certain prestige among their friends. When she turned fourteen and Sándor fifteen they began dancing principal roles, edging out dancers who were four and five years older. Great ballet masters from Paris and Petrograd and London came to see them. They danced for the dispossessed royalty of Europe and for the heirs of French and American fortunes. And amid the confusion of auditions and practices and costume fittings and performances, the inevitable happened: They fell in love.

A year later, in the spring of 1921, it came to the attention of Admiral Miklós Horthy that the star dancers of his kingless kingdom were two Jewish children who had been taught to dance by a White Russian émigré. Of course, no law forbade Jews from becoming dancers; no quota existed in the Royal Ballet Company to mirror the numerus clausus that kept Jews in universities and public positions to a reasonable six percent. But the matter offended Horthy's sense of nationalism. Hungarian Jews might be Magyarized, but they were not really Hungarian. They might participate in the economic and civic life of the country, but they ought not stand as shining examples of Magyar achievement on the stages of the world. And that was what these children had been asked to do; that was why the minister of culture had brought the matter to Horthy's attention. They'd been invited to perform in seventeen cities that spring, and had applied for the necessary visas.

Horthy couldn't be troubled with the matter beyond forming the opinion that something ought to be done. He told the minister of culture to handle it as he saw fit. The minister of culture assigned the problem to an undersecretary who was known for his ambition and his unambiguous feelings toward Jews. This man, Madarász, lost no time in carrying out his assignment. First he forbade the visa office to grant exit passes to the two dancers. Then he assigned two police officers, known members of the right-wing Arrow Cross Party, to carry out a regular watch over the dancers' comings and goings. Klara and Sándor never guessed that the policemen they saw every night in the alley had anything to do with the troubles they were having at the visa office; the men scarcely seemed to notice them. Usually the policemen were arguing. Invariably they were drunk: They had an army canteen they passed back and forth between them. No matter how late Klara and Sándor stayed at the Operaház—and sometimes they stayed until twelve thirty or one o'clock, because the theater was the only place where they could be alone—the men were always there. After a week or so of listening to their arguments, Sándor learned their names: Lajos was the tall block-jawed one; Gáspár was the one who looked like a bulldog. Sándor got into the habit of waving to them in greeting. The policemen never waved back, of course; they would give stony stares as Klara and Sándor passed.

A month went by and the men were still there, their presence as much a mystery as ever. But by that time they'd come to seem part of the neighborhood furniture, the fabric of Sándor and Klara's everyday lives. The situation might have gone on indefinitely, or at least until the Ministry of Culture had lost interest, had not the policemen themselves tired of their endless watch. Boredom and drink made their silence oppressive. They started calling out to Klara and Sándor: Hey, lovers. Hey, darlings. How does she taste? Can we have some? Do dancer boys have anything down there? Does he know what to do with it, sugar? Sándor would take Klara's arm and hurry her along, but she could feel him shaking with anger as the men's taunts followed them down the street.

One night the man called Gáspár approached them, stinking of cigarettes and liquor. Klara remembered thinking that the leather strap across his chest looked like the kind of strap teachers used to beat unruly children at school. He drew his baton from its holster and tapped it against his leg.

"What are you waiting for?" the man called Lajos goaded him.

Gáspár took the baton and slipped it under the hem of Klara's dress; in one swift motion he raised the hem as high as her head, exposing her to the waist for an instant.

"There you go," called Gáspár to Lajos. "Now you've seen it."

Before Klara knew what was happening, Sándor had stepped forward and grabbed the free end of the baton; as he tried to twist it away, the officer held fast to the other end. Sándor kicked the man in the knee, making him howl in pain. The officer wrenched the baton away and struck Sándor in the head. Sándor fell to his knees. He raised his arms, and the officer began to kick him in the stomach. For a moment Klara was caught in a paralysis of horror; she couldn't understand what was happening or why. She screamed for the man to stop, she tried to pull him off Sándor. But the other officer, Lajos, caught her by the arm and wrenched her away. He dragged her into a recess of the alley, where he forced her down onto the paving stones and pushed her skirt up around her waist. He stuffed his handkerchief into her mouth, put a gun under her chin, and did what he did to her.

The pain of it had a kind of clarifying power. She scuttled her fingers across the pavement, looking for what she knew was there: the baton, cold and smooth against the cobblestones. He'd dropped it when he'd bent to unbutton his pants. Now she closed her hand around it and struck him in the temple. When he yelped and put a hand to his head, she kicked him in the chest as hard as she could. He reeled back against the opposite wall of the alcove, hit his head against the base of the wall, and went still. At that moment, from the alley where Sándor and the officer had been struggling, there came a sharp percussive crack. The sound seemed to fly into Klara's brain and explode outward.

Then a terrible silence.

She got to her knees and crawled out of the alcove, toward the place where one male form crouched over another. Sándor lay on his back with his eyes open toward the sky. The bulldog-faced officer knelt beside him, one hand on Sándor's chest. The officer was crying, telling the boy to get up, damn him, get up. He called the boy a rotten piece of filth. His hand came away from Sándor's chest covered in blood. From the pavement he retrieved the gun he'd dropped and turned it upon Klara; its barrel caught the light and quavered in the dim cave of the alley. Klara edged back into the alcove where the first officer lay. She went to her knees, searching for the man's revolver; she'd heard it clatter to the pavement when she'd knocked him away. There it was, cold and heavy on the ground. She picked it up in one hand and tried to hold it still against her leg. The officer who had shot Sándor advanced toward her, weeping. If she hadn't seen him holding the gun a moment earlier, he might have seemed to be approaching her in supplication. Now she looked at Sándor on the ground and felt the weight of the weapon in her own hand, the same gun that the officer called Lajos had pushed against the hollow of her throat. She raised it and held it steady.

A second explosion. The man stumbled back and fell; afterward, a deep stillness.

It was the ache of the recoil in her shoulder that made her know that it had happened: She had fired the gun, had shot a man. From Andrássy út came a woman's shout. Farther away, a siren sent up its two-note howl. She came out of the alcove with the gun in her hand and approached the officer she had shot. He had fallen backward onto the pavement, one arm flung over his head. From the alcove came a groan and a word she couldn't understand. The other officer had gotten to his hands and knees. He saw the revolver in her hand and the man dead on the street.

In three days he himself would be dead of his head injury, but not before he'd revealed the identity of his partner's killer and his own. The distant sirens grew closer; Klara dropped the gun and ran.

She had killed one officer and fatally wounded another. Those were the facts. That she had been raped by one of those officers could never be proved in court. All the witnesses were dead, and within days Klara's bruises and abrasions had disappeared. By that time, at the urging of her father's lawyer, she'd been spirited over the border into Austria, and from there into Germany, and from Germany into France. The city of Paris would be her refuge, the famed ballet teacher Olga Nevitskaya, a cousin of Romankov's, her protector. The arrangement was meant to be temporary. She would live at Nevitskaya's only as long as it took her parents to determine who might be bribed, or how her safety might otherwise be guaranteed. But before two weeks had passed, the peril of Klara's situation became clear. She had been accused of murder. The gravity of the crime assured that she would be tried as an adult. Her father's lawyer believed there could be no guarantee of success in an argument of self-defense; the police had determined that the man she'd killed had been unarmed when she'd shot him. Of course he'd *had* a gun; he'd shot Sándor with it a few moments earlier. But the other officer, the one who had witnessed the shooting, had testified that his partner had dropped the gun before he had approached Klara. The testimony had been confirmed by material evidence: the gun had been found beside Sándor's body, ten feet away from the fallen officer.

To make matters worse, it turned out that the man Klara had shot had been a war hero. He had saved fifteen members of his company in the battle of Kovel, had received an official commendation from the Emperor. And if that were not enough to turn any judge's favor against Klara, it emerged—or the police claimed—that the right-wing members of their department had recently received threatening messages from Gesher Zahav, a Zionist organization to which Klara and Sándor had been linked. Three times in the past month the dancers had been seen coming and going from the organization's headquarters on Dohány utca; never mind that what they'd been doing was attending Sunday night dances, not plotting the murder of police operatives. The fact that Klara had disappeared was considered to be a confirmation of her guilt, of her position as an instrument of Gesher Zahav's plot. News of it was all over town; every paper in Budapest had run a front-page article about the young Jewish dancer who had murdered a war hero. And that was the end of Klara's parents' hopes to bring her home. It was a lucky thing, her father's lawyer wrote, that they'd managed to get her out of the country when they had. If she'd stayed, there would have been another bloodbath.

For the first two months of her time at Madame Nevitskaya's, Klara lay in a tiny dark room that looked out onto an airshaft. Every piece of bad news from Budapest seemed to push her farther toward the bottom of a well. She couldn't sleep, couldn't eat, couldn't stand to have anyone touch her. Sándor was dead. She would never see her parents or her brother again. Would never go home to Budapest. Would never again live in a place where everyone she passed on the street spoke Hungarian. Would never skate in the Városliget or dance on the stage of the Operaház, would never see any of her friends from school or eat a cone of chestnut paste as she walked the Danube strand on Margaret Island. Would never see any of the pretty things in her room, her leather-bound diaries and Herend vases and embroidered pillows, her Russian nesting dolls, her little menagerie of glass animals. She had even lost her name, would never again be Klara Hász; she would forever be Claire Morgenstern, a name chosen for her by a lawyer. Every morning she woke to face the knowledge that it had all really happened, that she was a fugitive here at Madame Nevitskaya's in France. It seemed to have made her physically ill. She spent the first hours of each day hunched over a basin, vomiting and dry-heaving. Every time she stood she thought she would faint. One morning Madame Nevitskaya came into Klara's room and asked a series of mysterious-seeming questions. Did her breasts hurt? Did the smell of food make her sick? When was the last time she had bled? Later that day a doctor came and performed a painful and humiliating examination, after which he confirmed what Madame Nevitskaya had suspected: Klara was pregnant.

For three days all she could do was stare at the dart of sky she could see from her bed. Clouds passed across it; a vee of brown birds flew through it; in the evening it darkened to indigo and then filled with the gold-shot black of Paris night. She watched it as Nevitskaya's maid, Masha, fed her chicken broth and bathed her forehead. She watched it as Nevitskaya explained that there was no need for Klara to endure the torture of carrying that man's child. The doctor could perform a simple operation after which Klara would no longer be pregnant. After Nevitskaya left her alone to contemplate her fate, she stared and stared at that changeable dart of sky, scarcely able to comprehend what she had learned. Pregnant. A simple operation. But Madame Nevitskaya didn't know the whole story; she and Sándor had been lovers for six months before he'd been killed. They had made love the very night of the attack. They had taken precautions, but she knew those precautions didn't always work. If she was pregnant, it was just as likely that the child was his.

The thought was enough to get her out of bed. She told Madame Nevitskaya that she wouldn't have an operation, and why. Madame Nevitskaya, a stern, glossy-haired woman of fifty, took Klara in her arms and began to weep; she understood, she said, and would not try to dissuade her. Klara's parents, informed of her pregnancy and her plans, felt otherwise. They couldn't abide the idea that she might find herself raising that other person's child. In fact, her father was so strongly opposed to the idea that he threatened to cut Klara off altogether if she kept the child. What would she do, alone in Paris? She couldn't dance, not when she was pregnant, and not with an infant to care for; how would she support herself? Wasn't her situation difficult enough already?

But Klara had made up her mind. She would not have that operation, nor would she give up the baby after she'd carried it. Once it had occurred to her that the child might be Sándor's, the idea began to take on the weight of a certainty. Let her father cut her off. She would work; she knew what she could do. She went to Madame Nevitskaya and begged to be allowed to teach a few classes of beginning students. She could do it until her pregnancy showed, and she could do it once she'd recovered from the birth. If Nevitskaya would have her as an instructor, it would save her life and the child's.

Nevitskaya would. She gave Klara a class of seven-year-olds and bought her the black practice dress worn by all the teachers at the school. And soon Klara began to live again. Her appetite came back and she gained weight. Her dizziness disappeared. She found she could sleep at night. Sándor's child, she thought; not that other's. She went to a barber shop and got her hair cut short. She bought a sack dress of the kind that was fashionable then, a dress she could wear until late in the pregnancy. She bought a new leather-bound diary. Every day she went to the ballet school and taught her class of twenty little girls. When she couldn't teach anymore, she begged Masha to let her help with the work around the house. Masha showed her how to clean, how to cook, how to wash; she taught her to navigate the market and the shops. When, in her sixth month, Klara noticed the vendors glancing at her belly and at her bare left hand, she bought a brass band she wore on her third finger like a wedding ring. She bought it as a convenience, but after a time it came to seem as though it really were a wedding ring; she began to feel as if she were married to Sándor Goldstein.

As her ninth month approached, she began to have vivid dreams about Sándor. Not the nightmares she'd had in her first weeks in Paris—Sándor lying in the alley, his eyes open to the sky—but dreams in which they were doing ordinary things together, working on a difficult lift or arguing over the answer to some arithmetic problem or wrestling in the cloakroom of the Operaház. In one dream he was thirteen, stealing sweets with her at the market. In another he was younger still, a thin-armed boy teaching her to dive at Palatinus Strand. She thought of him when the first contractions came on; she thought of him when the water rushed out of her. It was Sándor she cried for when the pain grew long and deep inside her, a white-hot stream of fire threatening to cleave her. When she woke after the cesarean she put out her arms to receive his child.

But it wasn't his child at all, of course. It was Elisabet.

When she'd finished her story they sat silent by the fire, Andras on the footstool and Klara in the vermilion chair, her feet tucked under her skirt. The tea had grown cold in their cups. Outside, a hard wind had begun to rattle the trees. Andras got up and went to the window, looked down at the entrance of the Collège de France, at its ragged lace collar of clochards.

"Zoltán Novak knows about this," Andras said.

"He knows the basic facts. He's the only one in France who does. Madame Nevitskaya died some time ago."

"You told him so he'd understand why you couldn't love him."

"We were very close, Zoltán and I. I wanted him to know."

"Not even Elisabet knows," Andras said, smoothing the rim of his cup with his thumb. "She believes she's the child of someone you loved."

"Yes," Klara said. "It couldn't have helped her to know the truth."

"And now you've told me. You've told me so I'd understand what happened at Nice. You fell in love once, with Sándor Goldstein, and you can't love anyone else. Madame Gérard guessed as much—she told me a long time ago that you were in love with a man who'd died."

Klara gave a quiet sigh. "I did love Sándor," she said. "I adored him. But it's romantic nonsense to suggest that what I felt for him would keep me from falling in love again."

"What happened at Nice, then?" Andras said. "What made you turn away?"

She shook her head and put her cheek into her hand. "I was frightened, I suppose. I saw what it might be like to have a life with you. For the first time that seemed possible. But there were all the terrible things I hadn't told you. You didn't know I had shot and killed a man, or that I was a fugitive from justice. You didn't know I'd been raped. You didn't know how damaged I was."

"How could it have done anything but make me feel closer to you?"

She came to stand beside him at the window, her face flushed and damp, raw-looking in the dim light. "You're a young man," she said. "You can love someone whose life is simple. You don't need any of this. I was certain you'd see the situation that way as soon as I told you. I was certain I'd seem a ruin of a person."

Last December she'd stood in just the same place with a cup of tea shivering in her hands. *You have some too*, she'd said, offering the cup. *Te.*

"Klara," he said. "You're mistaken. I wouldn't trade your complication for anyone else's simplicity. Do you understand?"

She raised her eyes to him. "It's difficult to believe."

"Try," he said, and drew her close so he could breathe the warm scent of her scalp, the darkness of her hair. Here in his arms was the girl who had lived in the house near the Városliget, the young dancer who had loved Sándor Goldstein, the woman who loved him now. He could almost see inside her that unnameable thing that had remained the same through all of it: her *I*, her very life. It seemed so small, a mustard seed with one rootlet shot deep into the earth, strong and fragile at once. But it was all there needed to be. It was everything. She had given it to him, and now he held it in his hands.

They spent that night together on the rue des Écoles. In the morning they washed and dressed in the blue chill of Andras's room, and then walked together to the rue de Sévigné. It was the seventh of November, a cold gray morning feathered with frost. Andras went inside with her to light the coal stove in the studio. He hadn't entered that place, her own place, for two months. It was quiet in the expectant way of classrooms; it smelled of ballet shoes and rosin, like the Budapest studio she'd described. In a corner stood the drawing table she had given him for his birthday, draped to keep out the dust. She went to it and pulled the sheet free.

"I've kept it, just as you asked," she said.

Andras took the sheet from her and wrapped it around them both. He drew her so close he could feel her hipbones hard against his own, her ribcage pressing against his ribcage as they breathed. He draped the end of the sheet over their heads so they stood shrouded together in a corner of the studio. In the white privacy of that tent he lifted her chin with one finger and kissed her. She drew the sheet tighter around them.

"Let's never come out," he said. "Let's stay here always."

He bent to kiss her again, full of the certainty that nothing could make him move from that place—not hunger, nor exhaustion, nor pain, nor fear, nor war.

CHAPTER TWENTY

A Dead Man

THE NEWS CAME to Andras at studio. Though he was half blind with exhaustion after his night with Klara, he had to go to school; he had a critique that day. It was an emulation project: he'd had to design a single-use space in the style of a contemporary architect. He had designed an architecture studio after Pierre Charreau, modeling it upon the doctor's house on the rue Saint-Guillaume: a three-level building composed of glass block and steel, flooded with diffuse light all day and glowing from inside at night. Everyone had arrived early to pin their designs to the walls; once Andras had found a place for his drawings, he took a stool from his worktable and sat with the older students around a paint-spattered radio. They were listening to the news, expecting nothing but the usual panchromium of worries.

It was Rosen who caught it first; he turned up the volume so everyone could hear. The German ambassador had just been shot. No, not the ambassador, an embassy official. A secretary of legation, whatever that was. Ernst Eduard vom Rath. Twenty-nine years old. He'd been shot by a child. A child? That couldn't be right. A youngster. A boy of seventeen. A Jewish boy. A German-Jewish boy of Polish extraction. He had shot the official to avenge the deportation of twelve thousand Jews from Germany.

"Oh, God," Ben Yakov said, pulling his hands through his pomaded hair. "He's a dead man."

Everyone crowded closer. Had the embassy official been killed, or was he still alive? The answer came a moment later: He had been shot four times in the abdomen; he was undergoing surgery at the Alma Clinic on rue de l'Université, not ten minutes from the École Spéciale. It was rumored that Hitler was sending his personal physician from Berlin, along with the director of the Surgical Clinic of the University of Munich. The assailant, Gruenspan or Grinspun, was being held at an undisclosed location.

"Sending his personal physician!" Rosen said. "I'm sure he is. Sending him with a nice big capsule of arsenic for their man."

"What do you mean?" someone demanded.

"Vom Rath has to die for Germany," Rosen said. "Once he does, they can do whatever they want to the Jews."

"They'd never kill their own man."

"Of course they would."

"They won't have to," another student said. "The man's been shot four times."

Polaner had stepped away from the crowd near the radio and had gone to smoke a cigarette by the window. Andras went over and looked down into the courtyard, where two fifth-year students were hanging a complicated wooden mobile from a tree. Polaner cracked the window open and blew a line of smoke out into the chilly air.

"I knew him," he said. "Not the Jewish boy. The other."

"Vom Rath?" Andras said. "How?"

Polaner glanced up at Andras and then looked away. He tapped his ash onto the windowsill outside, where it circled for a moment and then scattered. "There's a certain bar I used to go to," Polaner said. "He used to go, too."

Andras nodded in silence.

"Shot," Polaner said. "By a seventeen-year-old Jewish kid. Vom Rath, of all people."

Vago came in at that moment and turned off the radio, and everyone began to take their seats for the brief lecture he'd give before the critique. Andras sat on his wooden stool only half listening, scratching a box into the surface of the studio desk with the metal clip of his pencil. It was all too much, what Klara had told him the night before and what had happened at the German Embassy. In his mind they became one: Klara and the Polish-German teenager, both violated, both holding guns in trembling hands, both firing, both condemned. Nazi doctors hastened toward Paris to save or kill a man. And the Polish-German boy was in jail somewhere, waiting to learn if he was a murderer or not. Andras's drawing had slipped one of its pins and hung askew from the wall. He looked at it and thought, *That's right.* At that moment, everything seemed to hang at an angle by a single pin: not just houses, but whole cities, countries, peoples. He wished he could quiet the din in his mind. He wanted to be in the smooth white bed at Klara's house, in her white bedroom, in the sheets that smelled like her body. But there was Vago now, taking Andras's drawing by its corner and repinning it to the wall. There was the class gathering around. It was time for his critique. He made himself get up from the table and stand beside his drawing while they discussed it. It was only afterward, when everyone was patting him on the shoulder and shaking his hand, that he realized it had been a success.

"Vom Rath didn't hate the Jews," Polaner said. "He was a Party member, of course, but he loathed what was going on in Germany. That's why he came to France: He wanted to get away. At least that was what he told me."

Two days had passed; Ernst vom Rath had died that afternoon at the Alma Clinic. Hitler's doctors had come, but they had deferred to the French doctors. According to the evening news broadcast, vom Rath had died of complications from damage to his spleen. A ceremony would be held at the German Lutheran Church that Saturday.

Andras and Polaner had gone to the Blue Dove for a glass of whiskey, but they'd discovered they were short on cash. It was the end of the month; not even the pooled contents of their pockets would buy a single drink. So they told the waiter they would order in a few minutes, and then they sat talking, hoping they could pass half an hour in that warm room before they'd be asked to leave. After a while the waiter brought their usual whiskey and water. When they protested that they couldn't pay, the waiter twisted one end of his moustache and said, "Next time I'll charge you double."

"How did you meet him?" Andras asked Polaner.

Polaner shrugged. "Someone introduced us. He bought me a drink. We talked. He was intelligent and well read. I liked him."

"But when you learned who he was—"

"What would you have had me do?" Polaner said. "Walk away? Would you have wanted him to do the same to me?"

"But how could you sit there and speak to a Nazi? Especially after what happened last winter?"

"*He* didn't do that to me. He wouldn't have done it. I told you."

"That's what he said, at least. But he may have had other motives."

"For God's sake," Polaner said. "Can't you leave it alone? A man I knew just died. I'm trying to take it in. Isn't that enough for now?"

"I'm sorry," Andras said.

Polaner laid his folded hands on the table and rested his chin upon them. "Ben Yakov was right," he said. "They'll make an example of that boy. Grynszpan. They'll have him extradited and then kill him in some spectacular way."

"They can't. The world is watching them."

"All the better, as far as they're concerned."

Klara stood at the window with the newspaper in her hand, looking down into the rue de Sévigné. She had just read aloud a brief article about the actions the German government would take against the Jewish people *in recompense for the catastrophic destruction of German property that resulted from the violence of 9 November.* The newspapers were calling it the Night of Broken Glass. Andras walked up and down the length of the room, his hands shoved deep into his pockets. At the writing desk Elisabet opened a school notebook and scratched a series of figures with a pencil.

"A billion reichsmarks," she said. "That's the amount of the fine against the Jews. And there are half a million Jews in Germany. That means each person has to pay two thousand reichsmarks, including children."

The logic was astounding. He had tried and failed to grasp it. Grynszpan had shot vom Rath; vom Rath had died; November 9, the Night of Broken Glass, was supposed to have been the German people's natural reaction to the killing. Therefore the responsibility for the destruction of Jewish shops, and the burning of synagogues, and the ransacking of homes—to say nothing of the killing of ninety-one Jews and the arrest of thirty thousand more—lay with the Jews themselves, and so the Jews had to pay. In addition to the fines, all insurance payments for damaged property would go directly to the government. And now it was illegal for Jews to operate businesses in Germany. In Paris and New York and London there had been protests against the pogrom and its aftermath, but the French government had been strangely silent. Rosen said it was because von Ribbentrop, Hitler's foreign minister, was supposed to visit Paris in December to sign a declaration of friendship between Germany and France. It all seemed a great ugly sham.

From downstairs came the flutter and clang of the afternoon mail arriving through the slot. Elisabet got to her feet so quickly she overturned the chair, sending it backward into the fire screen, then ran downstairs to get the letters.

"I used to have to bribe her with gingerbread to get the mail," Klara said as she righted the desk chair. "Now she won't let it sit for half a minute."

Elisabet was a long time coming up again. When she reappeared, breathless and flushed, it was only to throw a few envelopes onto the writing desk before she ran off down the hall to her room. Klara sat at the desk and thumbed through the mail. One piece, a thin cream-colored envelope, seemed to catch her attention. She took her letter knife and opened it.

"It's from Zoltán," she said, and scanned the single page. Her eyebrows drew together and she read more closely. "He and Edith are leaving in three weeks. He's writing to say goodbye."

"Leaving for where?"

"Budapest," she said. "This isn't the first I've heard of it. Marcelle said she'd heard a rumor that they were leaving—she told me last week when I met her at the Tuileries. Zoltán's been asked to manage the Royal Hungarian Opera. And Madame Novak wants to raise their child near her family." She rolled her lips inward and pressed a hand against her mouth.

"Are you so unhappy to see him go, Klara?"

She shook her head. "Not for the reason you're thinking. You know how I feel about Zoltán. He's a dear friend to me, an old friend. And a good man. He employed you, after all, when the Bernhardt could scarcely afford it." She went to sit beside Andras on the sofa and took his hand in her own. "But I'm not unhappy to see him go. I'm glad for him."

"What's the matter, then?"

"I'm envious," she said. "Terribly so. He and Edith can get on a train and go home. They can take the baby home to Edith's mother, to raise it with its cousins." She smoothed her gray skirt over her knees. "That pogrom in Germany," she said. "What if such a thing were to happen in Hungary? What if they were to arrest my brother? What would become of my mother?"

"If anything were to happen in Hungary, I could go to Budapest and see about your mother."

"But I couldn't go with you."

"Perhaps we could find a way to bring your mother to France."

"Even if we could, it would only be a temporary solution," she said. "To our larger problem, I mean."

"What larger problem?"

"You know the one. The problem of where we might live together. In the longer term, I mean. You know I can't go home to Hungary, and you can't stay here."

"Why can't I?"

"Your family," she said. "What if there's a war? You'd want to go home to them. I've thought about it a hundred times. You must know I thought about it a great deal in September. It was one of the reasons I couldn't bring myself to write to you. I couldn't see a way around it. I knew that if we decided to be together, I'd be keeping you from your family."

"If I stay here it'll be my own decision," Andras said. "But if I have to go, I'll find a way to bring you with me. We'll see a lawyer. Isn't there some statute of limitations?"

She shook her head. "I can still be arrested and tried for what I did. And even if I could go home, I couldn't leave Elisabet."

"Of course not," Andras said. "But Elisabet has plans of her own."

"Yes, that's just what I fear. She's still a child, Andras. She wears that engagement ring, but she doesn't really understand what it means."

"Her fiancé seems utterly sincere. I know he has the best intentions."

"If that were the case, he might have consulted his parents before he started filling her head with ideas about marriage and America! He still hasn't told them he's engaged. Apparently they've got a girl in mind for him already, some beer heiress from Wisconsin. He's got no attachment to her, he says, but I'm not certain his parents will see it that way. At the very least, he might have thought to ask *my* permission before he gave Elisabet that ring."

Andras smiled. "Is that how it's done? Do young men still ask permission?"

She surrendered a smile in return. "Good young men," she said.

And then he drew closer and bent to her ear. "I'd like to ask someone's permission, Klara," he said. "I'd like to write a letter to your mother."

"And what if she says no?" she whispered back.

"Then we'd have to elope."

"But to where, darling?"

"I don't care," he said, looking deep into the gray landscape of her eyes. "I want to be with you. That's all. I know it's impractical."

"It's entirely impractical," she said. But she put her arms around his neck and raised her face to him, and he kissed her closed eyes, tasting a trace of salt. At that moment they heard Elisabet's step in the hallway; she appeared in the doorway of the sitting room in her green wool hat and coat. Andras and Klara drew away from each other and got to their feet.

"Pardon me, disgusting adults," Elisabet said. "I'm going to the movies."

"Listen, Elisabet," Andras said. "What if I were to marry your mother?"

"Please," Klara said, raising a hand in caution. "This isn't the way we should talk about it."

Elisabet tilted her head at Andras. "What did you say?"

"Marry her," Andras said. "Make her my wife."

"Do you mean that?" Elisabet said. "You want to marry her?"

"I do."

"And she'll have you?"

A long moment passed during which Andras experienced terrible suspense. But then Klara took his hand in her own and pressed it, almost as though she were in pain. "He knows what I want," she said. "We want the same thing."

Andras let out a breath. A flash flood of relief washed over Elisabet's features; her perpetually knotted forehead went smooth. She crossed the room and put her arms around Andras, then kissed her mother. "It's splendid," she said, with plain sincerity. Without another word she flung her purse over her shoulder and clattered down the stairs.

"Splendid?" Klara said, in the reverberating silence that always followed Elisabet's departures. "I'm not certain what I was expecting, but that wasn't it."

"She thinks it'll make things easier for her and Paul."

Klara sighed. "I know. If I marry you, she won't have to feel guilty about leaving me."

"We'll wait, then, if you think it'll make a difference. We'll wait until she's finished with school."

"That's another seven months."

"Seven months," he said. "But then we'll have the rest of our lives."

She nodded and took his hand. "Seven months."

"Klara," he said. "Klara Morgenstern. Have you just agreed to marry me?"

"Yes," she said. "Yes. When Elisabet's done with school. But that doesn't mean I'm letting her run off to America with that smooth-talking young man."

"Seven months," he said.

"And perhaps by then we'll solve our geographic problem."

He held her by the shoulders and kissed her mouth, her cheekbones, her eyelids. "Let's not worry about that now," he said. "Promise me you won't think about it."

"I can't promise that, Andras. We'll have to think about it if we're to solve it."

"We'll think about it later. Now I want to kiss you. May I?"

In answer she put her arms around him, and he kissed her, wishing he had nothing else to do all day, all year, all his life. Then he pulled away and said, "I'm unprepared for this. I don't have anything for you. I don't have a ring."

"A ring!" she said. "I don't want a ring."

"You'll have one, though. I'll see to it. And I wasn't speaking lightly when I said I wanted to write to your mother."

"That's a tricky business, as you know."

"I wish we could speak to József," Andras said. "He could write to her, or enclose a letter from me inside one of his own."

Klara pulled her lips together. "From what you've told me about his life, it hasn't come to seem any wiser to involve him in our situation."

"If we're to be married, he'll have to know sometime. The Latin Quarter is a small place."

She sighed. "I know. It's rather complicated." She went back to the sofa and opened the folded newspaper. "At least we've got some time to think about it. Seven months," she said. "Who knows what will happen by then? Shouldn't we all just get married at once? Shouldn't I be glad that my child might go across the ocean to America? If there's a war, she'll be safer there."

That elusive ghost, safety. It had fled Hungary, had fled the halls of the École Spéciale, had fled Germany long before November 9. But as he sat down beside her and looked at the newspaper on her lap, he tasted the shock of it all over again. He followed the line of her hand to the front-page photograph: a man and woman in their nightclothes, standing in the street; a little boy between them, clutching what looked to be a Punch doll with a cone-shaped hat; and before them, shedding its violent light on them, a house on fire from its doorstep to its rafters. In the places where the fire had burned away carpets and flooring, wallpaper and plaster, he could see the structure of the house illuminated like the stripped bones of an animal. And he saw what an architect might see, what the man and woman and boy could not have seen as they stood in the street at that moment: that the main supports had already burned through, and in another moment the structure would fall in upon itself like a poorly built model, its beams crumbling to ash.

PART THREE

Departures and Arrivals

CHAPTER TWENTY-ONE

A Dinner Party

IN EARLY DECEMBER, Madame Gérard threw a party for her own birthday. Klara received an invitation on a heavy ivory-colored card printed with gold ink; Andras was invited as her guest. The night of the party he put on an immaculate white shirt and a black silk tie, sprinkled and brushed his best dinner jacket, and polished the shoes Tibor had brought him the year before from Budapest. He told himself that there was nothing extraordinary about the fact that Marcelle had invited him; in fact, though, this was to be the first time he had seen her since her departure from the Théâtre Sarah-Bernhardt, and the first time he would appear in public as Klara's future husband, among people who might consider him her inferior. What he feared was not just what her friends might think of him but what *she* might think, seeing him for the first time among the members of her circle. Those choreographers, those dancers, those composers who sometimes made her gifts of their music: How could he appear in comparison to them except as a novice, an aspirant, a perhaps-someday-but-not-yet? He wondered if that was the effect Marcelle had intended. But Klara herself distracted him from his concerns; when he arrived at the rue de Sévigné that night her manner was light and intimate. They walked the chilly boulevards toward Marcelle's new apartment in the Eleventh, through streets that smelled of woodsmoke and approaching cold. It was difficult to believe it was nearly January, a year since they'd first met. Soon the skating ponds in the Bois de Vincennes and the Bois de Boulogne would be frozen solid once again.

At Madame Gérard's they were received by a girl in a crisp white apron who took their coats and ushered them into a parquet-floored drawing room. The building belonged to the Belle

Époque, but Madame Gérard had decorated her new apartment in the modern style: in the drawing room there were low black leather sofas and African masks and vases of veined malachite on glass shelves. Grass-green draperies hung at the windows, and two steel tables stood at attention beside the sofas like slim-legged greyhounds. On the tables were a pair of Brancusis, two tense flames of black marble. All of it was the fruit of her recent success; she had conquered Paris in every role she'd played since *The Mother*, and had just received a series of enthusiastic reviews for her Antigone at the Théâtre des Ambassadeurs, where Andras and Forestier had installed an elaborate surrealist set. Now Madame Gérard herself, dressed in a chartreuse silk gown, crossed the drawing room to welcome Andras and Klara. She kissed them both, and after they'd exchanged their greetings she led Andras to a black lacquered console table where drinks were being served.

"Look how you've turned out," she said, and touched his lapel. "A gentleman after all. Evening dress suits you. I may have a terrible fit of jealousy before the night is over."

"It was kind of you to invite me," Andras said. He heard the forced calm in his own voice, and he thought he saw the hint of a smile at the corner of Madame Gérard's mouth.

"It was kind of you to indulge me on my birthday," she said. And then, more pointedly: "You'll enjoy the company, I believe. Our friend Monsieur Novak is here with his wife. Have you heard they're to return to Hungary?" She tilted her head toward a corner of the room, where Novak and his wife stood talking to a silver-haired man in a cravat. "I must say, he reacted with some surprise when I told him you and Klara would be here. I imagine you must know all about . . . ?"

"Yes, I know *all about*," he said. "Though I'm sure you'd rather I hadn't. It would have entertained you, wouldn't it, to have been able to tell me yourself."

"I've only ever looked out for your well-being," Madame Gérard said. "I warned you about getting involved with Klara. I must say I was astonished to hear that things had become so serious between you. I was certain she viewed you as a kind of entertainment."

Andras felt the heat rising beneath his skin. "And is this *your* idea of an entertainment?" he said. "To invite people to your house and then insult them?"

"Lower your voice, darling," Madame Gérard said. "You attribute too much cleverness to me. How is one to keep straight everyone else's romantic intrigues? If I'd invited only those of my friends whose connections were uncomplicated, I couldn't have invited anyone at all!"

"I know you better than that," Andras said. "I don't think you do anything by mistake."

"Well, I can see you've got me thoroughly romanticized," she said, obviously pleased. "What a charming young man you are."

"And when exactly does Monsieur Novak depart for Hungary?" he asked.

She gave her low dissonant laugh. "January," she said. "I can't imagine you'll be sad to see him go. Though I'm not certain how Klara will take it. They were very close, you understand." She handed him a glass of whiskey with ice, and turned her head toward Klara, who had taken a seat beside Novak on a low black sofa. "You mustn't worry what people will say about the two of you, by the way—about your engagement, I mean. Everyone loves Klara's eccentricities. I find the situation irresistible myself. It's like a fairy tale! Look at you. She's turned you from a frog into a prince."

"If that's all," he said, "I'll bring Klara a drink."

"You'd better," Madame Gérard said. "In another moment *he'll* be obliged to get one for her." She turned her gaze again to the low black sofa, where Novak was explaining something to Klara in urgent tones. Klara shook her head, smiling sadly; Novak seemed to press his point, and Klara lowered her eyes.

Andras got her a glass of wine and made his way through a cluster of dinner guests in evening dress; he brushed past

Novak's wife, Edith, a tall, dark-haired woman in a velvet gown, redolent of jasmine perfume. The last time he'd seen her, almost a year earlier at the Sarah-Bernhardt, she'd handed him her bag while she searched her pockets for a handkerchief. She'd given him no more regard than if he'd been a hook on the wall. Now she held her back rigid while another woman leaned close to her ear; it was clear that the other woman was narrating the progression of Novak's tête-à-tête with Klara. When Andras reached the sofa, Monsieur Novak got to his feet and held out a damp red hand for Andras to shake. His eyes were raw, his breathing labored. After his first words of greeting he seemed unable to introduce a subject of conversation.

"I understand you're going home to Budapest," Andras said.

Novak smiled with obvious effort. "Yes, indeed," he said. "And what will I do this time for a lunchtime companion? Madame Novak prefers the dining car."

"You'll probably cheer up some young fool on his way from Paris to Budapest."

"Fool indeed, if he's young and heading back to Budapest."

"Budapest is a fine place for a young man," Andras said.

"Perhaps you ought to have stayed there, then," Novak said, leaning a shade too close to Andras; in an instant Andras knew he was drunk. By now Klara knew, too, of course; she stood and placed a hand on Novak's sleeve. A flash of resentment kindled in Andras's chest. If Novak was going to undo himself, Klara shouldn't feel under an obligation to protect him. But she gave Andras a look that begged forbearance, and he had to relent. He couldn't fault Novak. It had been only three months, after all, since his own bout of drunken howling at József Hász's flat.

"Monsieur Novak was telling me about his new position with the Royal Hungarian Opera," Klara said.

"Ah, yes. They're lucky to have you," Andras said.

"Well, Paris won't miss me," Novak said, looking pointedly at Klara. "That much is evident."

Madame Gérard had crossed the room to join their group,

and she took Novak's hands in her own. "We shall all miss you terribly," she said. "It's a great loss to us. A great loss to *me*. What will I do without you? Who will preside at my dinner parties?"

"*You* will preside, as always," Novak said.

"Not 'as always,' " she said. "I used to be morbidly shy. You used to do all the talking for me. But perhaps you don't remember that. Perhaps you don't remember how you were forced to ply me with wine in your office, just to convince me to take Madame Villareal-Bloch's role."

"Ah, yes, poor Claudine," Novak said, his voice rising in volume as he spoke. "She was brilliant, and she threw it all away for that boy. That press attaché from Brazil. She followed him to São Paolo, and then he dropped her for a young tart." He turned a glare upon Andras. "And she was so certain he loved her. But he made a fool of her." He drained his glass, then went toward the window and stared down into the street.

A wave of silence spread from Novak to the rest of the guests; conversation faltered in one small group after another. It seemed they'd all been watching the exchange between Andras and Klara and Novak; it was almost as though they'd been notified of the situation in advance, and advised to pay particular attention. At last an elderly woman in a black Mainbocher gown cleared her throat delicately, fortified herself with a sip of gin, and declared that she had just heard that the forty thousand railroad workers fired by Monsieur Reynaud *would* stage a protest, and that the only good that might come of it would be that Monsieur and Madame Novak's departure might be delayed.

"Oh, but that would be terrible," said Madame Novak. "Mother is giving a party to welcome us, and the invitations have already been sent."

Madame Gérard laughed. "No one could ever accuse you of being a populist, Edith," she said, and the conversation soon resumed its former pace.

At dinner, Andras found himself seated between Madame Novak and the elderly woman in the Mainbocher gown. Andras found Madame Novak's jasmine perfume so overpowering that it seemed to lace the flavor of every dish set before him; he ate jasmine terrapin soup, jasmine sorbet, jasmine pheasant. Klara was seated beside Novak down the table to Andras's right, where it was impossible for him to see her face. The talk at the table was at first of Madame Gérard: her career and her new apartment and her enduring beauty. Marcelle listened with poorly acted modesty, her mouth slipping into a self-satisfied smile. When she'd grown bored of basking in flattery she turned the conversation to Budapest, its charms and difficulties and how it had changed since the Hungarians among them had lived there in their youth. She kept beginning her sentences by saying, "When we were Monsieur Lévi's age." A Captain Something-von-Other seated across from Andras declared that Europe would be at war before long, and that Hungary must be involved, and that Budapest would undergo profound changes before the decade closed. Madame Novak voiced the hope that the park where she'd played as a child would not be altered, at least; that was where she intended for her own child to play.

"Isn't that right?" she asked her husband across the table. "I'll have János's nurse take him there as soon as we get to town."

"Where, my dear?"

"The park on Pozsonyi út, at the river's edge."

"Of course," said Novak absently, turning again to Klara.

The dinner concluded with cheeses and port, and the guests retired to a buff-walled room that held velvet settees and a Victrola. Madame Gérard demanded that they have dancing. The settees were moved aside, a record placed upon the Victrola, and the guests began swaying to a new American song, "They Can't Take That Away from Me." Monsieur Novak took Klara by the waist and led her to the center of the room. They danced awkwardly, Klara with her hands braced against Novak's arms, Novak trying to lower his head onto her shoulder. Madame Novak, willfully oblivious, danced a jerky jazz step with Captain Something-von-Other, and Andras found himself partnered with the elderly woman in black. *The way you wear your hat,* she sang into Andras's ear. *The way you sip your tea. The memory of all that—no, they can't take that away from me.*

"It's about lost love!" she said, when he protested that his English was terrible. She seemed to think she had to shout into his ear in order to be heard above the music and conversation. "The man is parted from the woman, but he'll never forget her! She haunts his dreams! She's changed his life!"

No one could get enough of the song. Madame Gérard declared it her new favorite. They played it four times before they tired of it. Andras danced with Madame Gérard, and with Edith Novak, and with the elderly woman again; but Zoltán Novak would not release Klara. In a short time he would leave Paris forever; nothing could prevent that—not a rail strike, nor the threat of war, nor the force of his own love. Klara tried to extricate herself from his arms, but each time she pulled away he protested so loudly she had to stay with him to avoid a scene. Finally, too drunk to stand, he stumbled back onto a settee and wiped his forehead with a large white handkerchief. Madame Gérard took the record from the turntable and announced that the birthday cake would now be served, and Klara motioned Andras into a hallway.

"Let's go," she whispered. "We should never have come. I should have known Marcelle would arrange some horrible drama."

He was only too eager to leave. They retrieved their coats from a red bedroom and slipped out into the hall. But Novak must have missed Klara, and then heard the lift descending; or perhaps he had just decided he couldn't bear the heat of the room any longer. When they emerged onto the sidewalk he was there on the balcony, calling out to Klara as she and Andras walked arm in arm down the street. Andras, far from feeling any triumph, was sick with empathy. It seemed just as likely that he himself might have been the one she was leaving behind forever, the one who'd been sent back to Hungary without her, and the

feeling was so strong he had to sit down on a bench and put his
head between his knees. It was a fresh shock to feel her close
beside him, her gloved hand on his shoulder. They sat there on
the bench in the cold for what seemed a long time, neither of
them speaking a word.

CHAPTER TWENTY-TWO

Signorina di Sabato

ON A DAY of knifelike December wind, the Ligue Internationale Contre l'Antisemitisme staged a protest against the German foreign minister's visit to Paris. Andras and Polaner and Rosen and Ben Yakov stood in a tight group of demonstrators outside the Élysée Palace, shouting slogans of protest against the French and German governments, waving signs—NO FRIENDSHIP WITH FASCISTS; VON RIBBENTROP GO HOME—and singing the Zionist songs they'd learned at earlier meetings of the Ligue, which Rosen had insisted they all join after the pogrom in Germany. That morning he had woken them at dawn to paint placards. There could be no excuse for passivity, he said as he dragged them from their beds, no excuse for lying around while Joachim von Ribbentrop prepared to sign a nonaggression treaty with France; Bonnet, the French foreign minister who had been so accommodating about Hitler's annexation of the Sudetenland, had arranged it all. At Rosen's they drank a pot of Turkish coffee and made a dozen signs, Rosen stirring the paint with a ruler and insisting they all breathe the fumes of revolution. Andras knew Rosen's performance was largely for the benefit of his new *copine*, a Zionist nursing student whom he'd met that summer. The girl, Shalhevet, had joined them that morning to make the signs. She was tall and fierce-eyed, with a heartbreaking lock of white in her black hair; her occasional winks at Andras and Polaner and Ben Yakov suggested she knew how absurd Rosen could be, but she watched him with an admiration that betrayed her deeper feelings.

Though Andras had complained at being dragged from bed, he was glad to be called upon to do something more substantial than read the newspaper and lament its contents. As he stood outside the Élysée Palace holding his sign aloft, he thought of the young Grynszpan in Fresnes prison—what he must have been feeling at that moment, and whether or not he knew France was welcoming the German foreign minister that day. At noon, von Ribbentrop's black limousine pulled up to the gates of the palace and was quickly ushered through. While the police watched warily and guarded the barricades around the palace, the Friendship Declaration was signed. There was nothing the protesters could have done to stop it from happening, but they'd made their feelings known. After the foreign minister had departed again, the Ligue marched all the way to the river, shouting and singing. And at the quai des Tuileries Andras and his friends broke away to end their afternoon at the Blue Dove, where the talk was not of politics but of their other favorite subject. Ben Yakov, it seemed, faced a terrible problem: Despite all his efforts, he'd only managed to save two thirds of the money he needed to bring his Florentine bride back to Paris—to steal her away, as Rosen said. And time was of the essence; they couldn't wait any longer. In another month she would be married to the old goat to whom her parents had promised her.

Rosen knocked a fist against the table. "To arms, men," he said. "At all costs, we must save girls from goats."

Shalhevet agreed. "Yes, please," she said. "Save girls from goats."

"You people insist upon making a joke out of everything," Ben Yakov said.

"It's your own medicine, I'm afraid," Polaner said.

"This is the most critical moment of my life," Ben Yakov said. "I can't lose Ilana. For four months I've been working like a dog to bring her here. Day and night, at school and at the library, trying to save every centime. I've thought about nothing but her. I've written her nearly every day. I've been as celibate as a monk."

"Excuse me," Rosen said. "What about the Carousel Dance Club last weekend? What were you doing there with Lucia if you've been celibate as a monk?"

"One lapse!" Ben Yakov said, raising his hands heavenward. "A farewell to bachelorhood."

Andras shook his head. "You must know you'll make a terrible husband," he said. "You ought to wait a few years until your blood cools down."

Ben Yakov frowned at his empty glass. "I'm in love with Ilana," he said. "We can't wait any longer. But I'm still missing a thousand francs. I can afford to get there and back, but I can't afford *her* ticket."

"What about your brother?" Polaner asked, turning to Andras. "Can he help?"

Tibor was coming to visit in three weeks; he would spend his winter holiday in Paris. He and Andras had been saving the money for months. Even Klara had contributed to Tibor's ticket; she'd insisted that as Andras's fiancée she had a right to do so. "I won't let him give up his ticket," Andras said. "Not even for Ben Yakov's fiancée."

"He wouldn't have to give it up," Rosen said. "Ben Yakov can afford to buy her ticket if he doesn't have to get one of his own. And then Tibor could escort her. He would just have to get to Florence, that's all."

Ben Yakov rose from his chair. He put his hands to his head. "That's brilliant," he said. "My God. We could do it. It can't cost much to get from Modena to Florence."

"Wait a minute," Andras said. "Tibor hasn't agreed, and neither have I. How is this meant to work? He goes to Florence, and elopes with her in your place?"

"He'll meet her at the train station and they'll leave together," Rosen said. "Isn't that right, Ben Yakov? He would have to do nothing but show up in Florence."

"But what about when she gets here?" Andras said. "She can't just step off a train and marry you at once. Where will she stay before the wedding?"

Ben Yakov stared. "She'll stay at my apartment, of course."

"She's an Orthodox girl, remember."

"I'll give her my room. I'll come stay with one of you."

"Not with me," Rosen said, glancing sideways at Shalhevet.

"If Shalhevet is staying with you," Ben Yakov said, "let Ilana stay at her place."

"You can't leave her all alone in a dormitory," Shalhevet said. "She'll be miserable."

"Well, what am I supposed to do?" Ben Yakov said.

"What about Klara?" Polaner asked. "Could Ilana stay with her?"

Andras set his chin on his hand. "I don't know," he said. "She's preparing her students for their winter recital. It's the busiest time of year." And, though he didn't say it aloud, there were aspects of the situation he knew Klara wouldn't like. What business did they have importing a bride for Ben Yakov, their notorious scoundrel? The girl was running away from home to come to Paris; she had grown up in a close-knit Sephardic community in Florence, and was only nineteen years old. It was one thing to involve Tibor, but quite another to ask Klara to be an accomplice.

Polaner looked at Andras with concern. "What's the matter?" he said.

"I'm not sure. Suddenly I find I've got doubts about all of this."

"Please," Ben Yakov said, putting a hand on Andras's shoulder. "I'm begging you. Of all people, you have to understand my situation. You've struggled for the past year, and you're happy now. Can't you help me? I know I haven't always acted like a gentleman, but you know how hard I've worked since I came back from Florence. I've done everything in my power to get that girl here."

Andras gave a sigh and put a hand on Ben Yakov's hand. "All right," he said. "I'll write to Tibor. And I'll talk to Klara."

. . .

12 December 1938
Modena, Italy

Andráska,
I consider it an honor to be asked to conduct the future Madame
Ben Yakov to Paris. I'm glad to be of help to any friend of yours.
I do feel for the girl's parents, though. What will they think when
they learn she's gone? I hope Ben Yakov will reconcile with them
as soon as he can. He may be just charming enough to pull it off.
Please have him wire me Signorina di Sabato's train information
and I will meet her at the station in Firenze.
    As for me, I'm more than ready to spend a few indolent weeks
with you in your self-loving city. I'm exhausted. No one warns
medical students that the course of study itself may produce any
number of the diseases studied. I hope I may cure myself with
sleep, wine, and your company.
    Madame Morgenstern's book of anatomy continues to serve
me well. I'll always be in debt to her for that gift. But please tell
her not to make me any more such presents in the future! When
my friends see that I own such a fine book, they overestimate my
wealth and expect me to buy them dinner. At this rate I will soon
be ruined entirely. In the meantime, I remain
your merely impoverished brother, TIBOR

Andras brought the letter to Klara and asked for her help.
Accompanying him was François Ben Yakov; it was the first time
he had made Klara's acquaintance. He had dressed for the occasion in a jacket of fine black wool and a red tie figured with bar-
ley-sized fleurs-de-lis. As Ben Yakov held Klara's hands in his
own and begged her understanding, meeting her gaze with his
dark film-star eyes, Andras half-wondered if Klara might fall
under the spell Ben Yakov seemed to cast upon every woman he
met. She was enchanted enough to agree to help, at least; she
allowed Ben Yakov to kiss her hand and to call her an angel. Once
Ben Yakov had gone, leaving Andras and Klara alone, she laughed

and said she could see why he caused such trouble among the young ladies of his acquaintance.

"I hope you won't elope with him before the bride arrives," Andras said. He pulled a chair close to the fire for her and they sat down to watch the coals burn low.

"Not a chance," Klara said, and smiled. But then her expression grew serious, and she crossed her arms over her chest. "I share your brother's reservation, though. I wish the girl didn't have to run away. Would it really have been impossible for Ben Yakov to approach her father?"

"Would you allow your daughter to marry François Ben Yakov? Particularly if you'd raised her as an observant Jew? I'm afraid Ben Yakov was right when he came to the conclusion that they had to do it in secret."

Klara sighed. "What will my own daughter think?"

"She'll think she has a compassionate and understanding mother."

"I understand too well," Klara said. "So will Elisabet. This Florentine girl is restless, most likely. She wants a way out of the fate her parents have chosen for her. So she imagines herself to be in love with your friend. She must be very strong-willed if she's ready to leave her family behind for his sake."

"Strong-willed, indeed," Andras said. "And in love. To hear him tell it, she wants to come more than anything. And he wants it too."

"Do you think he can make her happy?"

Andras looked into the fire, at the heat swimming up through the coals. "He'll do his best. He's a good man."

"I hope he does," she said. "I hope he is."

On the night of Tibor and Ilana's arrival they all went to the station to meet the train. They stood in a group on the platform, Andras and Klara and Polaner, Rosen and Shalhevet, while Ben Yakov paced the platform a little distance away; in one clenched hand he held a nosegay of pansies for Signorina di Sabato. Pansies were a terrible extravagance in winter, but he'd insisted upon buying them. They were the flowers he'd given her when they first met.

It was Shalhevet who spotted the train, the speck of light far off down the line. They heard the throaty alto notes of the whistle; their group pressed forward with the rest of the Parisians who'd come to meet their holiday visitors. The train pulled in, letting off a skirt of steam, and the waiting crowd surged closer still as it came to a stop. After a maddeningly long time, the doors opened with their metallic clack and the gold-epauletted conductors jumped down onto the platform. Everyone took half a step back and waited.

Tibor was among the first to appear. Andras saw him at the door of one of the third-class cars, his expression anxious and weary; he held a pale green bandbox and a lady's fancy umbrella. He moved aside to make way for a young girl with a long dark braid, who paused on the top step to cast a searching look over the crowd.

"It's her," Ben Yakov shouted over his shoulder to them. "It's Ilana!" He called her name and waved the pansies. And the girl broke into an anxious smile so beautiful that Andras nearly fell in love with her himself. She came down the steps and crossed the platform to meet Ben Yakov, stopping just short of running into his arms, and let forth a stream of quick and insistent Italian as she gestured toward the train. Andras wondered how Ben Yakov could keep from embracing her; it gave him a moment's worry before he remembered it was forbidden by her observance. Ben Yakov would not touch her until he placed the ring on her finger at the wedding. But she raised her eyes to him with a look more intimate than an embrace, and he offered her the pansies, and she gave him that smile again.

Tibor had crossed the platform behind Signorina di Sabato; he set the bandbox at her feet and propped the umbrella against it. She spoke a few words in a tone of gratitude and he made a quiet reply, not meeting her gaze. Then he put an arm around Andras, bent to his ear, and said, "Congratulations, little brother."

"Congratulate Ben Yakov!" Andras said. "He's the groom."

"He is now," Tibor said. "But you'll be next. Where's your bride?" He went to Klara, kissed her on both cheeks and embraced her. "I've never had a sister," he told her. "You'll have to teach me how to be a proper brother to you."

"You've got a fine start," Klara said. "Here you are, all the way from Modena."

"I'm afraid I won't be very good company tonight," Tibor said. He put a hand on Andras's sleeve. "I've got a rather bad headache. I don't think I'm fit for a celebration at the moment." In fact he seemed overcome with exhaustion; he took off his glasses and rubbed his eyes with two fingers before he greeted the others. He shook Ben Yakov's hand, gave Polaner an appreciative clap on the shoulder, told Rosen what a pleasure it was to see him with such a lovely companion. And then he drew Andras aside.

"Get me to bed," he said. "I'm whipped. I think I may be ill."

"Of course," Andras said. "We'll get your bags and go." He had planned to accompany Signorina di Sabato to Klara's house, to see her comfortably settled there, but Klara insisted she could manage on her own. There wasn't much to transport: Signorina di Sabato had a small trunk and a wooden crate in addition to the bandbox, and those pieces, along with the fancy umbrella, made up the sum of her possessions. They got everything to the curb and Ben Yakov hailed a cab. He held the door for Signorina di Sabato and ushered her inside; to preserve her modesty he allowed Klara to slide in next. Finally, with a salute to the rest of them, he ducked into the cab and pulled the door closed.

Rosen and Shalhevet remained on the sidewalk with Andras and his brother. "Won't you come have a drink?" Rosen asked.

Tibor made his apologies in his confident but skeletal

French, and Shalhevet and Rosen assured him that they understood. Andras called another cab. He had thought they might walk home, but Tibor looked as if he might fall to his knees at any moment. He was quiet on the way to the rue des Écoles; all he would say about the journey was that it had been long and that he was relieved it was over.

They climbed out of the cab and took Tibor's things inside. By the time they got to the top, Tibor was taking rapid shallow breaths and bracing himself against the wall. Andras hastily unlocked the door. Tibor went in and lay down on the bed, not bothering to remove his shoes or overcoat, and put an arm over his eyes.

"Tibi," Andras said. "What can I do? Shall I go to the pharmacist's? Do you want something to drink?"

Tibor kicked his shoes loose and let them drop to the floor. He rolled onto his side and curled his knees to his chest. Andras went to the bed and leaned over him. He touched Tibor's forehead: dry and hot. Tibor pulled the quilt over himself and began to shiver.

"You're sick," Andras said, one hand on his brother's shoulder.

"Common virus. I felt it coming on all week. I just need to sleep."

In another instant Tibor had drifted off. He slept as Andras took his coat off, as Andras undressed him and laid a cool cloth over his forehead. Around midnight the fever broke and Tibor threw the covers off, but it wasn't long before he was shivering again. He woke and told Andras to get a box of aspirin from his suitcase. Andras gave him the medicine and covered Tibor with every blanket and coat he had. Finally Tibor turned over onto his side and slept. Andras unrolled the mattress he'd borrowed from the concierge and lay down on the floor beside the fire, but found himself unable to sleep. He paced the room, checking on Tibor every half hour until his forehead grew cooler and his breathing deepened. Andras lay down in his clothes on the borrowed mattress; he didn't want to take the covers from his brother.

In the morning it was Tibor who woke first. By the time Andras opened his eyes his brother had made tea and toasted a few pieces of bread. Sometime in the night he must have spread a blanket over Andras. Now he sat in the orange velvet chair, clean and close-shaven, wearing Andras's robe and eating toast with jam. At intervals he blew his nose loudly into a handkerchief.

"Well," Andras said, from his mattress on the floor. "You're alive."

"You'd better not get near me, though. I've still got a fever."

"Too late. I took care of you all night." He sat up and ran his hands through his hair to stand it on end.

Tibor smiled. "That style suits you, brother."

"Thank you, brother. And how are you feeling this morning? Any better?"

"Better than I felt on the train." He looked down into his teacup. "I'm sure Signorina di Sabato must have thought me a fine companion."

"She seemed in good enough spirits when you arrived."

"She had a few bad moments when we left Florence, but on the whole she was rather brave."

"Made bold by love," Andras said.

Tibor gave a nod and turned the cup in its saucer. "Tell me," he said. "What kind of person is this Ben Yakov?"

"You've met him," Andras said, and shrugged. "He's a good enough man."

"Is that the best you can say for him?"

It wasn't, after all. Andras remembered the talk they'd had at Polaner's bedside after the attack. It was Ben Yakov who had shamed them both into realizing how little they knew of their friend, and how unlikely it was that he would have chosen to confide in either of them. "He's a good friend," Andras said.

"He's a good student. Women like him. He hasn't always been honest with them, but he's been nothing but sincere about Ilana."

"She told me how they met," Tibor said. "It was at the marketplace. She was there with a friend. She had just bought two live chickens, but they broke their cage and got away. They went down an alley and ran into someone's courtyard. Ben Yakov caught them. He got them back into their cage and fixed it with wire. Then he insisted on carrying them home for her."

"Escaped chickens," Andras said. "A romantic beginning."

"And then he started visiting her in secret," Tibor said.

"Yes, of course. He's always had a flair for the dramatic."

"And there was the problem of her family's plans for her. But it all seems rather dishonorable on his part, doesn't it? He might have declared himself to her father and made an argument for himself."

Andras gave a short laugh. "That's just what Klara said, almost to the letter."

Tibor frowned and put his cup on the table. He laced his fingers over his chest, looking out at the gray sky and the ostrich plumes of chimney smoke fading into its heights. "The girl is nineteen," he said. "I saw her passport. Her birthday was last week. Do you know what else? She has a birthmark on her neck in the shape of a flying bird."

"What sort of bird?" Andras said. "A chicken?"

Tibor gave a great helpless laugh, which led him into a cough. He leaned forward in the chair, covering his mouth with the handkerchief. When he sat back, he had to wipe his eyes with his sleeve and drink the rest of his tea before he could speak.

"Why do I bother talking to you?" he said.

"I suppose you got into the habit years ago and never quit."

"Anyway, we've got more important things to discuss. Your engagement to Madame Morgenstern, for one."

"Ah, yes. By some miracle, Klara Morgenstern has agreed to be my wife."

"So you'll be the first of the three of us to marry, too."

"Unless the world ends before next summer."

"A distinct possibility, the way things stand at the moment," Tibor said.

"But if not, she'll be Madame Lévi."

"And what about this secret history of hers?"

Andras had refused to write him about it, saying instead that they would talk once Tibor came to visit; he had remembered the elder Mrs. Hász's caution and decided it might be unwise to send the story via post. Now he joined Tibor at the little table and related Klara's history from beginning to end, a revelation Klara herself had given him permission to make. When he'd finished, Tibor regarded him in stunned silence for a long moment.

"What a horror," he said finally. "All of it. And now she's an exile."

"And there's our problem," Andras said. "Apparently insoluble."

"You haven't written to Anya and Apa about this, have you? Haven't told them you're engaged, or any of it?"

"I haven't had the heart. I suppose I'm hoping Klara's situation will change."

"But how, if there's no statute of limitations?"

"I don't know how, I confess. Until it does, I'll share her exile."

"Ah, Andráska," Tibor said. "Little brother."

"You did warn me," Andras said.

"And you ignored me, of course." He bent to cough into his fist. "I shouldn't be sitting up so long. I should be in bed. And I shouldn't be giving anyone advice about love, of all things. Here's what I know of the heart: It's a four-chambered organ whose purpose is to pump blood. Left ventricle, right ventricle, left atrium, right atrium, and all the valves, tricuspid, mitral, pulmonary, and aortic." He coughed again. "Ah, get me back to bed and let me sleep. And don't give me any more bad news when I wake."

* * *

The next day, when he was well enough to venture out, Tibor suggested they pay a visit to Signorina di Sabato—to make sure she was comfortably settled, he said, and to return a book he'd borrowed from her on the train: a beautiful old edition of the *Divina Commedia*, bound in tooled leather. When Andras expressed surprise that Signorina di Sabato would be reading Dante, Tibor insisted that she was better read than any girl he'd ever met. From the age of twelve she'd been a secret borrower from the library near her home in the Jewish Quarter. The *Divina Commedia* belonged to that library; Tibor showed Andras the stamp on the spine. She hadn't meant to steal it, but as she was packing she realized that if she left it behind, her parents would find out that she'd been borrowing from the library in secret. She had told Tibor about it on the train, laughing sadly at herself as she did: There she'd been, running off to Paris to get married, and what had worried her was the idea that her parents might be scandalized by her having borrowed secular library books.

At Klara's they found Signorina di Sabato engaged in hemming the ivory silk dress that was to be her wedding gown. Klara sat beside her on the sofa, sewing a fine band of scalloped lace along the edge of a veil. Elisabet, not usually one to take an interest in what everyone else was doing, pored over a book of fancy cakes; she gave Tibor a look of mild curiosity and waved to him from her chair. But Ilana di Sabato was on her feet the moment she saw him, the ivory dress falling from her lap to the floor.

"Ah, Tibor!" she said, and followed with a few quick words in Italian. She made a gesture toward the library book and offered a smile of gratitude.

"You brought the book," Klara said. "She told me you'd borrowed it. I understood that much. We've been getting by, between my bit of Italian and her bit of French."

"And what does Signorina di Sabato think of Paris?" Andras asked.

"She likes it very well indeed," Klara said. "We had a walk in the Tuileries this morning."

"I'm sure she despises it," Elisabet answered, not raising her eyes from the book of cakes. "So cold and dismal. I'm sure she wants to go back to Florence."

Signorina di Sabato gave Elisabet a questioning look. Tibor translated, and Signorina di Sabato shook her head and made an insistent reply.

"She doesn't hate it at all," Tibor said.

"She will, soon enough," Elisabet said. "It's depressing in December."

Klara set down the wedding veil and declared that she would like some tea. "Won't you help me with the tray?" she asked Andras. He followed her into the kitchen, where a raft of recipe books lay open on the table.

Andras touched a page on which there was a drawing of a whole fish dressed in thin slices of lemon. "And when will the wedding be?" he asked.

"Next Sunday," Klara said. "Ben Yakov has arranged it with the rabbi. His parents are taking the train from Rouen. We'll have the luncheon here afterward."

"Klárika," Andras said, taking her by the waist and turning her toward him. "No one meant for you to host a wedding luncheon."

She put his arms around his neck. "They have to have some sort of party."

"But it's too much. You've got the recital to think about."

"I want to do it," she said. "I may have been too quick to judge the situation when we talked before. Your friend seems to have some serious notions of love, after all. And I think I expected Signorina di Sabato to be a different sort of girl."

"Different in what way?"

"Less confident, perhaps. Less mature. Maybe even less intelligent, which should indicate to you how small-minded I've become. I consider myself a Jew, with my occasional observances, but I think of truly observant Jews as old-fashioned and myopic. Evidence of my ignorance, I suppose."

"And Ben Yakov? Has he been here?"

"He spent most of Shabbos with us," Klara said. "He's been terribly kind and respectful, if a bit anxious. This morning he brought the rabbi to meet her, and they made all the plans for the wedding. Afterward, privately, he begged me to tell him if she seemed at all unhappy."

"And what did you say?"

Klara arranged the teacups and saucers on a blue tray. "I told him she seemed fine, given the circumstances. I know she misses her parents. She showed me their photograph and wept. But I don't think she regrets what she's done." She measured the tea into a strainer and lowered it into the pot. "Of course, Elisabet has been difficult. She's suffering from jealousy. I'm terrified she'll run off at any moment to marry her American. But this morning she told me she wanted to make the cake, which is something." She shook her head and gave him a wry half smile. "And what about your brother? Is he well? I worried when you didn't come yesterday."

Andras paused before he spoke, running his hand along the edge of the tea tray. "He's exhausted from overwork. And he's been ill, but not dangerously so. He's been sleeping almost constantly, and when he's awake he burns through my handkerchiefs like wildfire." He raised his eyes to Klara. "He's concerned about our situation. I told him everything yesterday."

She lowered her eyes. "Is he sorry we're engaged?"

"Oh, no. He's sorry about what happened to you. And he's sorry you can't go home to your family." He touched the handle of one of the fragile cups and noticed for the first time that the pattern of her china was almost identical to her mother's. "Of course, he's worried about how our parents will take the news. But he doesn't oppose our engagement. He knows what I feel for you."

She put her arms around him and sighed. "I didn't want to bring you this unhappiness."

"Stop that at once," he said, and kissed her bruise-colored eyelids.

When they returned to the sitting room they found Elisabet making a list of cake ingredients at her mother's desk while Tibor sat on the sofa beside Signorina di Sabato, speaking to her in rapid Italian. He leaned toward her, his eyes steady upon hers, his hands trembling on his knees as he spoke. Signorina di Sabato shook her head, then shook it again more emphatically as she bent over her sewing. Finally she fixed her needle in the ivory silk and looked up at Tibor with something like dismay.

"Mi dispiace," she said. *"Mi dispiace molto."*

Tibor sat back and scrubbed his face with both hands. He glanced at the tea tray, at the clock on the mantel, and finally at Andras. "What time are you expected at studio?" he asked.

Andras wasn't expected at any particular time, and Tibor knew it; this was Sunday, and he was going in simply because he needed to work. But Tibor was looking at him with such fixed concentration that Andras knew he had to respond with some concrete projection of their remaining time at Klara's.

"Half an hour from now," he said. "Polaner will be waiting."

"Half an hour!" Klara said. "You should have told me. There's no time for tea."

"Yes, we should be off, I'm afraid," Tibor said. He thanked Klara for her kindness and voiced the hope that he would see her again soon. As they put on their coats in the hallway, Andras wondered if Signorina di Sabato would let them leave without offering a word of farewell. But just before they went down, she appeared in the hallway with a hand on her chest as though she were trying to mute her heartbeat. She paused before Tibor and spoke a few sentences in such warm insistent Italian that Andras thought she might burst into tears. Tibor made an unintelligible reply and went down the stairs.

"What was that about?" Andras asked once they were out on the street. "What did she say?"

"She thanked me for the book," Tibor said, and refused to speak another word all the way to the École Spéciale.

Ben Yakov married his Florentine bride on the coldest day of the year. A fine frozen mist was falling outside the Synagogue de la Victoire; Signorina di Sabato, in her white silk gown and icy veil, seemed dressed in a coalescence of winter air. But inside the synagogue it was hot and close, and Andras could feel the warmth emanating from the bride's body as she entered the wedding canopy. Her features were hidden beneath the layers of the veil, but he could see her hands trembling as she circled Ben Yakov seven times. Andras exchanged a look with Rosen, who held another of the wedding canopy poles, and with Polaner, who held a third; the fourth canopy-bearer was Tibor himself. Ben Yakov was resplendent in his groom's cloak; like the tallis, the kittel was pure white to serve as a reminder of death. The cloak was meant to be used someday as his shroud. After the rabbi had said a blessing over the wine, Ben Yakov placed a ring on Ilana's finger and declared that she was consecrated to him according to the laws of Moses and Israel. In accordance with the custom, she remained silent beneath her veil and would not give Ben Yakov a ring of his own until after the ceremony. Ben Yakov's uncles and grandfathers were called to the wedding canopy to recite the Seven Blessings. Andras could feel tension gathering in the sanctuary as they spoke, could sense it like a rise in barometric pressure; beneath the solemnity of the Hebrew words he felt the congregation's awareness that this was an elopement, an act of rebellion on the part of the bride. And there was another sensation, too, a darker sense of anticipation: Before them stood a virgin who would not be a virgin for long.

When the uncles and *grands-pères* had taken their turns, and the wine had been blessed again, Ben Yakov broke the wedding cup beneath his heel. The bride lifted her veil at last as if she'd been startled by the sound, and the small party of guests sang *siman tov u'mazal tov*. And then everyone went to the rue de Sévigné for the bridal luncheon.

In the dining room there was a filet of roasted salmon, a wedding challah, steaming dishes of red potatoes and sweet golden noodles; there was costly white asparagus from Morocco, a bowl of oranges from Spain, and, on its own side table, the astonishing cake Elisabet had baked: a splendid three-tiered confection decorated with sugar beads and silver candy leaves. In the bedroom just on the other side of the dining-room wall, Madame and Monsieur Ben Yakov were spending their half hour of ritual seclusion. A violinist and a clarinet player entertained some of the guests in the sitting room, and others stood drinking white wine and admiring the luncheon dishes.

In the kitchen, Tibor had concerned himself with the care of a child who had slipped on a patch of ice outside. Andras helped him bandage the girl's cut knee and clean the abrasions on her palms. She was a small cousin of Ben Yakov's, dark-eyed and somber in a blue velvet dress; she seemed to relish the close attention of two such finely dressed young men, and when they had finished applying the bandages she instructed them to stay with her until she was better. She began a game with Tibor in which she would point to an object in the kitchen and call out the French word, to which Tibor would respond with the corresponding word in Hungarian; she seemed to find every Hungarian word hilarious. Andras was grateful for the distraction. He had begun to suspect that something momentous and unspeakable had passed between Tibor and Signorina di Sabato on the train from Florence. Andras and Tibor had spent the past week in what should have been enjoyable pursuits—they'd gone to the cinema and to a jazz show in Montmartre; they'd had a night of drinking with Rosen and Polaner and Ben Yakov to mark the end of the groom's bachelorhood; they had accompanied Ben Yakov to the tailor to pick up his wedding suit, and had helped to lay in supplies at the couple's apartment—but Tibor had been distant and abstracted through all of it, often receding into silence when Ilana's name arose in conversation. Today he had been in a black mood, cursing his shoelace when it broke, railing at the chill of the water in the basin, nearly shouting at Andras when Andras had hurried him along toward Klara's after the ceremony. But his attendence upon the little girl had calmed him; he seemed more like himself now, playing the game she'd invented.

"*Passoire,*" said the girl, pointing to a colander.

"*Szűrő edény,*" Tibor said in Hungarian.

"Ha! And what about *spatule*?"

"*Spachtli.*"

"*Spachtli!* And what about *couteau*?" The little girl grabbed a fierce-looking carving knife from the table and held it out for Tibor's pronouncement.

"*Kés,*" he said. "But you'd better give that to me." He took it from her and turned to put it away; just at that moment the new Madame Ben Yakov appeared in the doorway, her cheeks wildly flushed, a haze of black curls escaping from her coiled braids. The knife hovered in Tibor's hand just centimeters from the ivory buttons of her dress. If she had come rushing into the room, he would have run her through.

"Ah!" she exclaimed, and took a small step back.

Their eyes met, and they both laughed.

"Don't kill the bride, brother," Andras said.

Tibor set the knife on the counter, slowly, as if it couldn't be trusted.

The little girl, feeling the strangeness of the moment, looked up at all of them with frank curiosity. When no one spoke, she took it upon herself to begin a conversation.

"I hurt my knee," she explained to the bride, showing her the bandage. "This man fixed it."

Madame Ben Yakov nodded her understanding and bent to inspect the bandage. The little girl turned her knee this way and that. When the inspection was complete she got down from her chair and arranged her velvet skirts. She made a show of limping delicately out of the room.

Madame Ben Yakov gave Tibor a fleeting smile. "*Ché buon medico siete,*" she said. She edged past him and turned on the faucet at the porcelain sink, where she performed the ritual of hand-washing. Tibor watched every movement: the filling of the cup, the removal of her new wedding ring, the passing of water three times over the right hand, three times over the left.

After the luncheon there was dancing downstairs in the studio. In observance of Orthodox tradition, the men danced on one side of the room and the women on the other, shielded from each other's view by a folding screen. Every now and then the men glimpsed the flying hem of a dress or the flash of a hair ribbon; every now and then a woman's satin shoe came sliding out toward the wall, where the men could witness its suggestion of a woman's bare foot. The women laughed behind their screen, their feet beating quick rhythmic couplets on the studio floor. But the men were awkward with each other on their side of the screen. No one wanted to dance. It wasn't until Rosen produced a flask of whiskey from his pocket, and passed its fire around the circle twice, that they began to shuffle in time with the music. Ben Yakov and Rosen linked arms and jostled each other to the right and left. They took each other's hands and began to spin until they both stumbled. Rosen grabbed Andras's shoulder, Andras grabbed Polaner's, Polaner grabbed Ben Yakov's, Ben Yakov grabbed his father's, and soon all the men were following each other in a clumsy circle. Ben Yakov and his father broke off into the center of the ring, taking each other by the shoulders; they kicked their heels skyward until their shirttails flew free and their pomaded hair swung loose in waves. Only Tibor stood with his back against the practice barre, watching.

Finally the moment arrived when Madame and Monsieur

Ben Yakov would be lifted in chairs and carried around the room. The women emerged from behind their screen to watch; the sight of Klara with her hair fallen from its knot, her dress faintly damp against her breastbone, made Andras lose his breath. For a moment it seemed unfair that this was anyone else's wedding but their own. Then she caught his eye and smiled, seeming to understand what he was thinking, and there was so much certainty and promise in her look that he couldn't begrudge Ben Yakov his happiness.

After the wedding, only three days remained of Tibor's visit. His mood seemed to lighten somewhat; he followed Andras to school and work and earned everyone's admiration wherever he went. Monsieur Forestier gave him tickets to the shows whose sets he had designed, including Madame Gérard's *Antigone*, which Tibor found admirable in every regard with the exception of the lead actress's performance. Georges Lemain, at the architecture firm, was enthralled by Tibor's ability to identify any opera by nothing more than a few hummed bars; he treated them to a matinee of *La Traviata*, and afterward they toured a *maison particulier* under construction in the Seventeenth, a house Lemain had designed for a Nobel laureate chemist and his family. He showed Tibor the northern-lit laboratory, the library with its ebony bookshelves, the high-ceilinged bedrooms that overlooked a landscaped courtyard. Tibor praised everything in his earnest French, and Lemain promised to design a similar house for him when he was a famous doctor. All through those three days, as Tibor and Andras went from one place to another, one commitment to another, Andras looked for a chance to ask Tibor about Signorina di Sabato, but never found the right moment to introduce the subject. At night, when they might have stayed up late to drink and talk, Tibor claimed exhaustion. Andras lay awake on the mattress on the floor, wondering how to break the fragile cell wall that seemed to separate him from his brother; he had a sense of Tibor hiding behind that translucent membrane as if he were afraid to be seen in sharp focus.

Tibor's train departed on the night of Klara's students' Spectacle d'Hiver. Andras was to take him to the station and then meet Klara afterward at the Théâtre Deux Anges. The prospect of parting made them both quiet on the Métro; as they rode beneath the city, Andras found himself considering the long list of things they hadn't talked about during the days that had just passed. Now, once again, they would part without knowing when they would see each other next. They hauled Tibor's things out of the Métro and took them into the station. Once they'd checked the suitcases, they sat down together on a high-backed bench and shared a thermos of coffee. Across the platform stood the locomotive that would pull Tibor's train to Italy: a giant insect of glossy black steel, its wheel pistons bent like the legs of a grasshopper.

"Listen, brother," Tibor said, his dark eyes fixed upon the train. "I hope you'll forgive my behavior at the wedding. It was abominable. I acted dishonorably."

So here it was, half an hour before his train departed. "What was abominable?"

"You know what I mean. Don't make me say it."

"I didn't see you do anything dishonorable."

"I couldn't be happy for them," he said. "I couldn't eat that gorgeous cake. I couldn't bring myself to dance." He took another breath. "I did an abominable thing, Andras. Not at the wedding. Before."

"What are you talking about?"

"I did something unforgivable on the train." He crossed his arms over his chest and lowered his eyes. "I'm ashamed to tell you. It was ungentlemanly. Worse. It was a scoundrel's move."

And then he admitted that he'd fallen in love with Ilana di Sabato from the beginning, from the moment he saw her coming across the platform in Florence with her umbrella and her pale green bandbox. There was a little boy with her—her brother, who had come along to help with the suitcases. He had a look of importance about him, Tibor said—importance and great secrecy. But Tibor saw the realization dawning upon him that this wasn't a game, that his sister was really going to climb aboard a train and go to Paris. The little boy's face had crumpled. He'd put the suitcase down and sat on it and cried. And Ilana di Sabato sat down with him and explained that it would be all right, that she'd get him to come visit her, that she'd bring her fine new husband home to meet him and the rest of the family. But he mustn't tell anyone, not for a while yet. You had to see it, Tibor said, how she'd made him understand that.

"I told myself it was natural to feel a certain tenderness for her," he went on. "She'd been entrusted to my care, and she was entirely without defenses, and she was out in the world for the first time. Everything was new to her. Or not entirely new, because she'd read about it all in books—it was all *coming true* for her, a world she'd imagined but had never seen. I watched it happen. I was the one she turned to when we crossed the Italian border. It was like watching a person being born. The pain of it, too. I saw her understand she'd left her parents, her family, behind. When she cried after the crossing, I put my arms around her. I did it almost without thinking." He paused and took off his glasses, rubbed his eyes with thumb and forefinger. "And she looked up at me, Andras, and by now you've guessed it. I kissed her. Not an innocent kiss, I'm afraid. Not a brief one. So you see, I did transgress against your friend. And I transgressed against Ilana. And not just then." He paused again. "I want to tell you this, because it's been weighing on me since it happened. I said something to her, here in this station, just before we got off the train."

"What did you say?"

"I reminded her she still had a choice," Tibor said. "I told her I'd be happy to take her back to Italy if she changed her mind."

He shook his head and put on his glasses again. "And I confessed myself to her, Andras. Later. I did it the morning we went to see her at Klara's. When we went to give her that library book."

Andras remembered the whispered conversation, Tibor's trembling hands, Ilana's dismay. "Oh, Tibor," he said. "So that's what was happening when I came in from the kitchen."

"That's right," Tibor said. "And for a moment I thought I saw her hesitate. I deluded myself that she might feel something for me, too." He shook his head. "If I'd gone to see her again, I might have ruined your friend's happiness."

"But you didn't," Andras said. "Everything went as planned. And they both seemed perfectly happy at the wedding." He believed it as he said it, but a moment later he found himself wondering whether it had been true. Hadn't Ilana seemed distressed that morning with Tibor? Hadn't there been some strange exchange of energy between them in the kitchen on her wedding day? Was she sitting in Ben Yakov's apartment and thinking of Tibor at that very moment?

"They're married," Tibor said. "It's done. Now my feelings for her are their own punishment."

Andras understood. He put an arm around his brother's shoulders and looked at the insect form of the locomotive.

"I've been terribly lonely in Modena," Tibor said. "It must have been the same for you, coming here. But you met Klara."

"Yes," he said. "And that was terrible, too, at times."

"I see how it is between you now," Tibor said. "So many times this week I was sick with envy." He pressed his hands between his knees. At the window of the locomotive an argument was taking place between the engineer and an official-looking conductor, as though they were debating whether to make the trip to Italy after all.

"Don't go back," Andras said. "Come live with me, if you want."

Tibor shook his head. "I have to go to school. I want to finish my studies. And in any case, I don't know if I could stand to be so close to *her*."

Andras turned to his brother. "She's beautiful," he said. "It's true."

There was an almost imperceptible shift in Tibor's features, a softening of the lines around his mouth. "She is," he said. "I can see her in that gown and veil. God, Andras, do you think she'll be happy?"

"I hope so."

Tibor nudged the corner of his leather satchel with the toe of his polished shoe. "I think you'd better write to Anya and Apa," he said. "Let them know what's happened between you and Klara. Tell them as much as you can about her situation. I'll write them too. I'll tell them I've gotten to know her, and that I don't consider you mad for wanting to marry her."

"I *am* mad, though."

"No more so than any man in love," Tibor said.

The conductor blew the boarding whistle. Tibor got to his feet and drew Andras close in a quick embrace. "Be a good man, little brother," he said.

"Bon voyage," Andras said. "Have a good spring. Study hard. Cure the sick."

Tibor crossed the platform and boarded the train, his bag slung over his shoulder. Moments after he'd climbed aboard, the train gave a vast metallic groan; with a series of grunts and screeches it began to roll from the station. The grasshopper legs of the engine bent and flexed. Andras hoped Tibor had found a window seat, where he would have the comfort of watching the city fade into the darkness of the wintry fields. He hoped Tibor would be able to sleep. He hoped he'd get home swiftly, and that once he was there he would forget there had ever been a girl called Ilana di Sabato.

* * *

That year's Spectacle d'Hiver was a quiet and humble affair. The Théâtre Deux Anges was small and shabby and ill-heated, its blue velvet seats faded to gray; the dark upper tiers seemed full of ghosts. Girls chased each other across the stage in costumes of blue and white satin, and a silver snow drifted down from some cold cloud in the flyspace. A group of twelve-year-olds in icy pink tulle put Andras in mind of dawn on New Year's Day. He thought of Klara at the Square Barye: the flush of her forehead beneath her red wool hat, the crystalline dew on her eyebrows, the fog of her breath in the cold air. He could scarcely believe she would be waiting for him backstage after the recital—the same woman who had kissed him in that frozen park nearly a year ago. It seemed a miracle that any man who loved a woman might be loved by her in return. He rubbed his hands together in the chill and waited for the violet lights to fade.

CHAPTER TWENTY-THREE

Sportsclub Saint-Germain

EVERY SPRING the students of the École Spéciale competed for the Prix du Amphithéâtre, which brought its winner a gold medal worth a hundred francs, the admiration of the other students, and a measure of prestige for the winner's curriculum vitae. Last year's prize had gone to the beautiful Lucia for her design of a reinforced-concrete apartment building. This year's subject was an urban gymnasium for Olympic sports: swimming, diving, gymnastics, weightlifting, running, fencing. It seemed to Andras a ridiculous notion to design a gymnasium while Europe edged toward war. Refugees poured into France from fractured Spain; the Marais had become a swamp of asylum-seekers. Hundreds of thousands more had been detained at the border and sent to internment camps in the foothills of the Pyrenees. Every day brought bad news, and the worst always seemed to come from Czechoslovakia. Hitler had told the Czech foreign minister that the nation must take a more aggressive approach to its Jewish problem; a week later the Czech government threw Jewish men and women out of their university professorships and civil-service jobs and public-health positions. In Hungary, Horthy followed suit by calling for a new cabinet that would support a stronger alliance with the Axis powers. It wouldn't be long, newspaper columnists speculated, before the Hungarian parliament passed new anti-Jewish laws, too.

In the face of such news, how was Andras supposed to design a swimming pool, a locker room, a yard for fencing practice? Late one night he sat in the studio with an open letter on the table before him, his drawing tools still in their box. The letter had come earlier that day from his brother Mátyás:

12 February 1939
Budapest

Andráska,
*Anya and Apa have just told me your great news. Mazel tov! I
must meet the lucky girl as soon as possible. Since it seems you'll
be in France for the foreseeable future, I will have to join you
there. I'm saving money already. By now you've heard from our
parents that I have left school. I am living in Budapest and
working as a window trimmer. It's a good trade. I make
20 pengő a week. My best client is the haberdasher on Molnár
utca. I heard from a friend that their old window trimmer had
quit, so I went there the next day and offered my services. They
told me to trim the window as a trial. I made a hunting display:
two riding suits, one cloak, four neckties, a hunting blanket, a
hat, a horn. I finished in an hour, and in another hour they had
sold everything in the window. Even the horn.*

*Budapest is grand. I have many new friends here and per-
haps one girlfriend. Also a fabulous dance teacher, an American
Negro who calls himself Kid Sneeks. A month ago I saw him at
the Gold Hat with his tap-dance team, the Five Hot Shots. After
the show I stayed to meet the star. With the help of my girlfriend,
who speaks a few words of English, I told him I was a dancer
and asked him to take me on as a pupil. He said, Let's see what
you can do. I showed him everything. On the spot he gave me the
English nickname of Lightning and agreed to teach me as long as
he's in Budapest. And his show is so popular it's been held over
another month.*

*I know you will scold me for quitting gimnázium, but
believe me I am happier now. I hated school. The masters punished me for my bad attitude. The other boys were idiots. And
Debrecen! What a place. Not the country nor the city, not modern
nor quaint, not home nor a place I would want to make my home.
In Budapest there is a better Jewish gimnázium. If I can, I will
transfer my records and finish my studies there. Then I will come*

to you in Paris and go onto the stage. If you're kind to me I will teach you to tap-dance.

Do not worry about me, brother. I am fine. I'm glad you are also fine. Don't marry before I get there. I want to kiss the bride on your wedding day.

Love, Your MÁTYÁS

He read and reread the letter. *I will finish my studies. Come to you in Paris. Go onto the stage.* How did Mátyás expect any of those things to happen if Europe went to war? Did he read the newspapers? Did he expect that the world's problems might be solved through tap-dancing? What was Andras supposed to write in return?

He heard footsteps approaching in the hall; it was the middle of the night, and he hadn't arranged to meet anyone. Without thinking, he opened his pencil box and reached for his sharpening knife. But then the footsteps resolved into a familiar tread, and there was Professor Vago in his evening clothes, leaning against the doorjamb.

"It's three o'clock in the morning," Vago said. "If you wanted to read your mail, couldn't you have done it at home?"

Andras shrugged and smiled. "It's warmer here," he said. Then, raising an eyebrow at Vago's suit: "Nice tuxedo."

Vago tugged at his lapels. "This is the last suit of clothing I own without an ink or charcoal stain."

"So you've come here to spill ink on yourself."

"Something like that."

"Where were you, the opera?"

He plucked the rose out of his buttonhole and gave it a slow reflective twirl. "I was out dancing with Madame Vago, if you want to know. She likes that sort of thing. But she gets tired around halfway to dawn, whereas I find I can't sleep after dancing." He came toward the worktable and bent over Andras's drawings. "Are these for the contest?"

"Yes. Polaner started them. I'm supposed to finish."

"You were wise to partner with him. He's one of our best."

"He was unwise," Andras said. "He chose me."

"May I?" Vago said. He took Andras's notebook and looked through the sketches, pausing over the drawings of the pool with its retractable roof. He flipped the page to the drawing of the natatorium with the roof open, and then back to the drawing of the same room with its roof closed.

"It's all done with hydraulics," Andras said, pointing out the closet that would house the machinery. "And the panels are curved and overlapped at the meeting point here, so the weather won't come through." He paused and bit the end of his drafting pencil, anxious to know what Vago thought. It was a design inspired as much by Forestier's chameleonic stage sets as by Lemain's sleek public buildings.

"It's fine work," Vago said. "You do your mentors credit. But why are you mooning around here in the middle of the night? If you're going to come to school at three in the morning, at the very least you ought to be working."

"I can't concentrate," Andras said. "Everything's falling apart. Look at this." He took a newspaper from his schoolbag and pushed it across the desk toward Vago. On the front page, a photograph showed Jewish students crowded at the gates of a university in Prague; they had been summarily disenrolled and were not allowed to enter. Vago picked up the paper and studied the photograph, then dropped it onto the worktable.

"*You're* still in school," he said. "Are you going to do your work?"

"I want to," Andras said.

"Then do."

"But I feel like I have to do something more than draw buildings. I want to go to Prague and march in the streets."

Vago pulled up a stool and sat down. He took off his long silk scarf and folded it over his knees. "Listen," he said. "Those bastards in Berlin can go to hell. They can't kick anyone out of school here in Paris. You're an artist and you have to practice."

"But a gymnasium," Andras said. "At a time like this."

"At a time like this, everything's political," Vago said. "Our Magyar countrymen didn't let Jewish athletes swim for them in '36, though their time trials were better than the medalists'. But here you are, a Jewish architecture student, designing an athletic club to be built in a country where Jews can still qualify for the Olympics."

"For now, anyway."

"Why 'for now'?"

"It hasn't escaped my notice that Daladier brought von Ribbentrop here to sign a friendship pact. And do you know that only the quote-unquote Aryan cabinet ministers were invited to Bonnet's banquet afterward? Can you guess who wasn't invited? Jean Zay. Georges Mandel. Jews, both."

"I heard about that dinner, and who was and wasn't there. It's not as simple as you make it out to be. More than a few who were asked declined in protest."

"But Zay and Mandel *weren't* asked. That's my point." He opened his box and took out a pencil and the sharpening knife. "With due respect," he said, "it's easy for you to talk about this in the abstract. Those aren't your people at the school gate."

"They're people," Vago said. "That's enough. It's a stain upon humanity, this Jew-hating dressed up as nationalism. It's a sickness. I've thought about it every day since those little fascists attacked Polaner."

"And this is what you've concluded?" Andras said. "That we should put our heads down and keep working?"

"Polaner did," Vago said. "So should you."

. . .

18 March 1939
Konyár

My dear Andras,
You can imagine how your mother and I feel about the fate of
Czechoslovakia. The rape of the Sudetenland was injury
enough. But to see Hitler strip away Slovakia, and then march
into Prague unchecked! Those streets where I spent my student
days, now filled with Nazi soldiers! Perhaps I was naïve to
expect otherwise. Once Slovakia was gone, the country Britain
and France agreed to protect had ceased to exist. But one feels as
though this string of outrages cannot go on indefinitely. It has to
stop, or must be stopped.

There has been much right-wing rejoicing here, of course,
about the return of Ruthenia to Hungary. What was stolen from
us is ours again, and so on. You know I am a veteran of the
Great War and have some sense of national pride. But we know
by now what is beneath the flag-wavers' desire for vindication.

All this bad news notwithstanding, your mother and I agree
with Professor Vago. You must not allow recent events to distract
you from your studies. You must stay in school. If you're to be
married you must have a trade. You've done well so far and will
make a fine architect. And perhaps France will be a safer place
for you than Hungary. In any case, I will be angry indeed if you
throw away what's been given to you. A chance like that comes
only once.

How stern I sound. You know I send my love. I've enclosed a
letter from your mother.

APA

Dear Andráska,
Listen to your apa! And keep warm. You've always been prone to

fevers in March. And send me the photograph of your Klara. You made a promise. I will hold you to it.

Love,
ANYA

Each letter with its payload of news and love, each with its reminder of his parents' mortality. The fact that they had survived two more winters in Konyár without illness or injury hardly helped to assuage his worry; every winter would carry greater danger. He thought about them constantly as the bad news poured in, a deluge of it all spring. In late March the bloody horror of the Spanish Civil War drew to a close; the Republican army surrendered on the morning of the twenty-ninth, and Franco's troops entered the capital. It was the beginning of the dictatorship foreseen by Hitler and Mussolini, he knew—the very reason they had poured their armaments and troops into the blast furnace of that war. He wondered if those two victories—the splintering of Czechoslovakia and the triumph of Franco in Spain—were what gave Hitler the courage to defy the American president in April. All the papers carried the story: On the fifteenth, Roosevelt had sent Hitler a telegram demanding assurance that Germany would not attack or invade any of a list of thirty-one independent states for at least ten years—including Poland, across which Hitler had proposed a highway and rail corridor to link Germany with East Prussia. After two weeks' stalling, Hitler responded. In a speech at the Reichstag he denounced Germany's naval accord with England, tore up the German-Polish Non-Aggression Pact, and ridiculed Roosevelt's telegram in every detail. He finished by accusing Roosevelt of meddling in international affairs while he, Hitler, concerned himself only with the fate of his own small nation, which he had already rescued from the ignominy and ruin of 1919.

Debate raged in the halls of the École Spéciale. Rosen wasn't the only one who believed that Europe was certain to go to war. Ben Yakov wasn't the only one who argued that war might still be averted. Everyone had an opinion. Andras held with Rosen—he couldn't see any other way out of the web into which Europe had fallen. As he and Polaner bent over their plans, he found himself thinking of his father's stories of the Great War—the stench and the bloodshed of combat, the nightmare of planes that rained bullets and fire upon the foot soldiers, the confusion and hunger and filth of the trenches, the surprise of escaping with one's own life. If there were a war, he would fight. Not for his own country; Hungary would fight alongside Germany, its ally, who had given it not only Ruthenia but also the Upper Province, which it had lost at Trianon. No: If there were a war, Andras would join the Foreign Legion and fight for France. He imagined appearing before Klara in the full glory of a dress uniform, a sword at his waist, the buttons of his coat polished to a painful sheen. She would beg him not to go to war, and he would insist that he must go—that he must protect the ideals of France, the city of Paris, and Klara herself within it.

But in May, two unexpected events served to blot out his awareness of the approaching conflict. The first was a tragedy: Ben Yakov's bride lost the baby she'd been carrying for five months. It was Klara who went to tend her at Ben Yakov's apartment, Klara who sent for the doctor when she found Ilana bleeding and wild with fever. At the hospital, in a long linoleum-tiled corridor decorated with lithographs of French doctors, Klara and Andras waited with Ben Yakov while a surgeon emptied Ilana's womb. Ben Yakov sat in stunned silence, still wearing his pajama shirt. Andras knew he believed this to be his fault. He hadn't wanted the child. He'd confessed it just a week earlier, late at night in the studio, as they sat working on a problem set for their statics class. "I'm not equal to it," he'd said, laying his six-sided pencil on the lip of the desk. "I can't be a father. I can't support a child. There's no money. And the world's falling apart. What if I have to go off and fight a war?"

Andras had thought then of Klara's womb, that sacred inward space they'd taken pains to keep empty. He'd had to force himself to make an empathetic reply. What he'd wanted to ask was why Ben Yakov had married Ilana di Sabato if he hadn't wanted a child. Now the subject seemed to hover in the antiseptic air of the corridor: Ben Yakov had wished the child gone, and it was gone.

Outside the hospital windows, the eastern margin of the sky had turned blue with the coming morning. Klara was exhausted, Andras knew: Her spine, usually held so straight, had begun to droop with fatigue. He told her to go home, promised he'd come to see her after they talked to the doctor. He insisted: She had a class to teach that morning at nine. She protested, saying she was willing to stay as long as it took, but in the end he persuaded her to go home and sleep. She said goodbye to Ben Yakov, and he thanked her for having known what to do. They both watched her walk off down the hall, her shoes ticking out their quiet rhythm against the linoleum.

"She knows," Ben Yakov said, once Klara had disappeared around the corner.

"Knows what?"

"She knows how I felt about the baby."

"What makes you say that?"

"She would hardly look at me."

"You're imagining things," Andras said. "I know she thinks well of you."

"Well, she shouldn't." He pressed his fingers against his temples.

"It's not your fault," Andras said. "No one thinks it is."

"What if I think it is?"

"It's still not."

"What if *she* thinks it is? Ilana, I mean?"

"It's still not. And anyway, she won't think so."

After the doctor had finished, a pair of orderlies wheeled Ilana out on a gurney and brought her to a ward, where they transferred her to a hospital bed. Andras and Ben Yakov stood beside the bed and watched her sleep. Her skin was wax-white from the loss of blood, her dark hair pushed back from her forehead.

"I think I'm going to faint," Ben Yakov said.

"You'd better sit down," Andras said. "Do you want some water?"

"I don't want to sit down. I've been sitting for hours."

"Take a walk, then. Get some air."

"I'm hardly dressed for it."

"Go ahead. It'll do you good."

"All right. You'll stay here with her?"

He promised he wouldn't move.

"I'll just be a minute," Ben Yakov said. He tucked his pajama shirt into his trousers, then went off down the long avenue of beds. Just as he disappeared through the door of the ward, Ilana gave a rising cry of pain and shifted her hips beneath the sheet.

Andras glanced around for a nurse. Three beds away, a silver-haired woman in a crisp cap ministered to another deathly pale girl. *"S'il vous plaît,"* Andras called.

The nurse came to examine Ilana. She took her pulse and glanced at the chart at the end of the bed. "One moment," she said, and ran down the ward; she returned a minute later with a syringe and a vial. Ilana opened her eyes and looked around in a daze of pain. She seemed to be searching for something. When her gaze fell upon Andras, her focus sharpened and her forehead relaxed. A faint flush came to her lips.

"It's you," she said in Italian. "You came all the way from Modena."

"It's Andras," he told her. "You're going to be all right."

The nurse uncovered Ilana's shoulder and swabbed it with alcohol. "I'm giving her morphine for the pain," she said. "She'll feel better in a moment."

Ilana drew a sharp breath as the needle went in. "Tibor," she said, turning her eyes again toward Andras. Then the morphine found its mark, and her eyelids fluttered and closed.

"Go home, now," the nurse said. "We'll take care of your wife. She needs to rest. You can visit her this afternoon."

"She's not my wife," Andras said. "She's a friend. I told her husband I'd stay with her until he got back."

The nurse raised an eyebrow, as if something weren't quite right about Andras's story, and went back to her patient down the ward.

Through the windows the sky continued its slow bleed toward blue. The quiet of the ward seemed to deepen as he looked at Ilana, her chest rising and falling beneath the sheet. The drug had enclosed her within a transparent capsule of sleep, like the princess in the fairy tale, Hófehérke—in French it must be Blanche-Neige—the exiled princess sleeping in her glass coffin on a hill, while those little men, the *törpék*, watched over her. He thought again of the Marot poem he'd cut from Klara's book. *If fire dwells secretly in snow, how can I escape burning?* He was glad Ben Yakov hadn't been there when Ilana had spoken, glad he hadn't seen her lips flush with color when she'd thought it was Tibor watching over the bed.

Ben Yakov returned forty minutes later, redolent of new-mown grass; the back of his pajama shirt was damp with dew. He took off his cap and smoothed his hair.

"How is she?"

"Fine," Andras said. "The nurse gave her a shot of morphine."

"Go on home, now," Ben Yakov said. "I'll stay with her until she wakes up."

"We're both supposed to leave. The nurse says she has to rest. We can come back this afternoon."

Ben Yakov didn't protest. He touched Ilana's pale forehead and let Andras lead him from the ward. All the way back to the Latin Quarter they walked in silence, their hands stuffed into their pockets. It seemed a particularly cruel morning to have lost a child, Andras thought: A loamy damp scent arose from the window boxes, from the new flowerbeds in the park; the branches of the chestnuts were crowded with small wet leaves. He walked Ben Yakov to the door of his apartment building and they faced each other on the sidewalk.

"You're a good friend," Ben Yakov said.

Andras shrugged and looked at the pavement. "I didn't do anything."

"Of course you did. You and Klara, both."

"You would have done the same for us."

"I'm not much good as a friend," Ben Yakov said. "Still worse as a husband."

"Don't say that."

"People like me shouldn't be allowed to marry." Even after a night at the hospital and an hour's sleep on a bench, he was elegant in his angular, cinematic way. But he twisted his mouth into a grimace of self-disgust. "I'm neglectful," he said. "And, to be honest, unfaithful."

Andras kicked at the boot scraper beside the entryway. He didn't want to hear anything more about it. He wanted to turn and walk home to the rue des Écoles, climb into bed and sleep. But he couldn't pretend he hadn't heard what Ben Yakov had just said.

"Unfaithful," he said. "When?"

"Always. Whenever she'll see me. It's Lucia, of course. From school." Ben Yakov's voice had fallen to a half whisper. "I've never been able to break it off. Even this morning she came out and sat in the park with me while you watched over my wife. I'm in love, I think, or something horrible like that. I have been ever since I met her."

Andras felt a surge of indignation on behalf of the girl in the hospital bed. "If you were in love with her, why did you bring Ilana here?"

"I thought she might cure me," Ben Yakov said. "When I met

her in Florence, she made me forget Lucia. She delighted me. And, though it's shameful to say, her innocence was arousing. She made me think I could be a different person, and for a time I was." He lowered his eyes. "I was excited about the prospect of marrying her. I knew I couldn't have married Lucia. She doesn't want to marry, for one thing. She wants to be an architect and travel the world. For another thing, she's—*une negresse*. My parents, you know. I couldn't."

Andras thought of the classmate who'd been attacked in the graveyard, the man from Côte d'Ivoire. That style of bigotry was supposed to belong to the other side. But it didn't, of course. Hadn't he himself been terrified to speak to Lucia because of her race, and, at the same time, inexplicably excited by her? What if he had fallen in love with her? Could he have married her? Could he have brought her to his parents? He took Ben Yakov's shoulder in his hand. "I'm sorry," he said. "Truly."

"It's my own fault," Ben Yakov said. "I should never have married Ilana."

"You ought to get some sleep now," Andras said. "You'll need to go back to see her this afternoon."

A flint spark of fear burned for an instant in Ben Yakov's eyes. Andras recognized the expression; he'd seen it countless times on his younger brother's face at bedtime, just before Andras snuffed the candle. It was the panic of a child afraid to be left alone in the dark. Countless times, Andras had lain down beside Mátyás and listened to him breathing until he fell asleep. But they were adults, he and Ben Yakov; the comfort they could ask of each other was finite. Ben Yakov repeated his thanks and turned away to unlock the door.

The second thing that happened that month—the second thing important enough to turn Andras's attention away from the increasingly grim headlines—was that the architecture contest came to a close. After a week of sleepless nights during which he experienced nausea, hallucinations, and the vertiginous thrill of last-minute inspiration, he and Polaner found themselves in the crowded amphitheater, waiting to defend their project before the judging panel. Professor Vago had invited Monsieur Lemain to lead the trio of judges. The other two, whose identities had been kept secret until the day of the prize critique, turned out to be none other than Le Corbusier and Georges-Henri Pingusson. Le Corbusier was dressed as if he had come directly from a construction site; his plaster-whitened trousers and sweat-stained workshirt seemed a silent reproach to Lemain in his impeccable black suit, and to Pingusson in his pearl-gray pin-striped jacket. Perret, presiding over the contest, had waxed his moustache to crisp points and put on his most dramatic military cape. The judges walked a slow circuit of the room, examining the models on their display tables and the plans posted on cork-boards around the periphery of the amphitheater, and the students followed in a respectful cluster.

Before long, it became clear that a profound difference of opinion existed between Le Corbusier and Pingusson. Everything one said, the other denounced as pure foolishness. At one point Le Corbusier went so far as to poke Pingusson in the chest with his pencil; Pingusson responded by shouting directly into Le Corbusier's reddened face. The issue at hand was a pair of Dianalike caryatids, the entryway ornamentation of a sports club for women designed by a pair of fourth-year women. Le Corbusier declared the caryatids neoclassicist kitsch. Pingusson said he found them perfectly elegant.

"Elegant!" Le Corbusier spat. "Perhaps you would have said the same of Speer's monstrosity at the International Exposition! Plenty of hack neoclassicism in evidence there."

"I beg your pardon," Pingusson said. "Are you suggesting we forget the Greeks and Romans entirely, simply because the Nazis have appropriated them? Bastardized them, I might say?"

"Everything must be taken in context," Le Corbusier said.

"At the present political moment, this choice seems indefensible. Though perhaps we're to give the young women a pass because, after all, they're *just women*." Those were the words he punctuated with a pair of jabs to Pingusson's chest.

"Rubbish!" Pingusson shouted. "How dare you accuse me of chauvinism? When you dismiss this choice as kitsch, are you not entirely disregarding the tradition of feminine power in classical mythology?"

"A fine point," Lemain said. "And since you're both so enlightened, gentlemen, why not let the women defend the choice themselves?"

The taller of the student architects—Marie-Laure was her name—began to explain in a neat, clipped French that these were no ordinary caryatids; they were modeled after Suzanne Lenglen, the recently deceased French tennis champion. She went on to defend other features of the design, but Andras lost the thread of the argument. He and Polaner would be critiqued next, and he was too nervous to concentrate on anything but that. Polaner stood beside him, crushing his handkerchief into a dense ball; on his other side was Rosen, who wore a look of vaguely interested detachment. *He* didn't have to worry; he hadn't entered the contest. He'd been too busy with meetings of the Ligue Contre l'Antisemitisme, of which he had recently been elected secretary.

Far too soon for Andras's comfort, the critique of the women's sports club concluded and the judges moved on. The students collected behind them around the table where Andras's and Polaner's model was displayed.

"Introduce your project, gentlemen," Perret said, with a wave of his hand.

Polaner was the first to speak. He tugged at the hem of his jacket, and, in his Polish-tinged French, began to explain the need for an inclusive sports club, one that would stand as a symbol of the founding principles of the Republic. The design would be oriented toward the future; the building's predominant materials would be reinforced concrete, glass, and steel, with panels of dark wood crowning the doors and windows.

He paused and looked at Andras, who was to speak next. Andras opened his mouth and found that his French had fled entirely. In its place there was an astounding blankness, a book washed clean of text.

"What's the matter, young man?" Le Corbusier said. "Can't you speak?"

Andras, who hadn't slept in three days, was afflicted with a temporal hallucination. Time slowed to a chelonian crawl. He watched the cycle of Le Corbusier's blink, taking place over what seemed an eternity, behind the plaster-flecked lenses of his glasses. From the back of the amphitheater someone launched an oceanic cough.

He might never have found his voice had not Pierre Vago, Master of Ceremonies, come swiftly to his rescue. Vago was the one who had taught Andras the language he was supposed to speak now; he knew the words that might put Andras at ease. "Why don't you begin with the *piste*," he said. *Piste:* the running track, French for *pálya*. They'd had the conversation two days ago in studio: how one said *sports track* in French, and how that word differed from the ones that meant *road, trail, rail,* and *trace*. Andras could talk about the *piste*; it was the most unusual element of their design, a stroke of recent late-night inspiration. *"La piste,"* he began, *"est construit d'acier galvanisée,"* and would be suspended from the roof of the building, halolike, on steel cables attached to reinforced I-beams. The words had come back to him; he spoke them, and Le Corbusier and Lemain and Pingusson listened, making notes on their yellow pads. The suspension design allowed for a longer track than would be possible if the *piste* were housed inside the building. The sports club would be constructed higher than the surrounding buildings, and the track could hang over their uppermost stories. The roof of the building itself was also the ceiling of the natatorium;

Andras bent over the model and demonstrated how it might be retracted in fine weather. Both design elements, the exposed track and the retractable roof, reflected the sports club's principles of inclusivity and freedom.

When he'd finished, there was a hush in the room. He sent a look of gratitude in the direction of Professor Vago, who refused to acknowledge that he had helped Andras. Then the judges' questions began: How would a suspended track be kept from bouncing under the runners' impact? What would happen in a wind? How quickly could the retracted roof be closed again in case of thunderstorms? How did they propose to deal with the problem of housing a hydraulic system in the open space of the natatorium?

Now the words came faster. These were problems Andras and Polaner had discussed and argued about for hours in the studio at night. The supporting cables would be wrapped in thin bands of steel to make them rigid without entirely eliminating their elasticity; a certain degree of spring would cushion the runners' tread. The track would be braced against the building with support struts to prevent sway. And the hydraulic system would be housed within this closetlike enclosure. After they'd answered all the questions, it seemed to take hours for Pingusson and Lemain and Le Corbusier to inspect the materials and make their notes; even Perret himself insisted upon taking a closer look, muttering to himself as he examined the cross-section of an external wall.

"And who are you, Monsieur Lévi?" Le Corbusier asked finally, lodging his pencil behind his ear.

"I'm a Hungarian, from Konyár, sir," Andras said.

"Ah. You're the young man they discovered at the art exhibition. They admitted you to the school based on some linoleum cuts, I understand."

"Yes," Andras said, and cleared his throat self-consciously.

"And you, Monsieur Polaner?" Pingusson asked. "From Kraków? They tell me you've got a taste for engineering."

"I do, sir," Polaner said.

"Well, I'd call the design superb but impractical," Le Corbusier said. "The zoning is the problem. You'll never get Parisians to hang a track off a building. It looks a bit like what ladies used to wear under their dresses in the eighteenth century. Those whatever-you-call-them. Martingale. Frimple."

"More like some sort of outlandish hat," said Pingusson. "But it's an awfully good use of urban space."

"Rather fantastical," Lemain said. "The building itself is well designed, though. And the wood ornamentation is a fine element. Echoes of gymnasium parquet."

And then the judges moved on to the next set of designs. It was over. Andras and Polaner exhanged a look of exhausted satisfaction: Their design, if imperfect, had at least been worthy of praise. As the other students surged past them, Rosen clapped them on the shoulders and kissed them on both cheeks.

"Congratulations, boys," he said. "You've created the first ever architectural frimple. If I weren't entirely broke, I'd treat you both to a drink."

The next morning, when Andras came in through the blue courtyard doors—the same threshold he'd crossed nearly two years earlier as a novice student—he was greeted by cheers all around. The students in the courtyard clapped and began to chant his name. On a chipped wooden chair in the corner of the yard, Polaner sat in state: Students crowded around him, and a gold medal hung from his neck. Someone had draped the tricolor over his shoulders. A photographer bent to a camera and shot pictures. When Rosen heard the new round of cheers, he rushed over to Andras and took him by the arm.

"Where have you been?" he said. "Everyone's been waiting for you! You won, idiot. You and your adorable partner. You won the Grand Prix. Your medal's hanging on display in the amphitheater."

Andras ran to the amphitheater, where he saw that it was true: Their Sportsclub Saint-Germain was crowned with a gold-stamped certificate and flanked by a medal on a tricolor ribbon. There were the judges' signatures on the certificate, Le Corbusier's and Lemain's and Pingusson's. He stood alone for a long moment, trying to believe it; he took the medal and turned it over in his hand. It was heavy and burnished, with a portrait of Emile Trélat sculpted in low relief upon its surface. *Grand Prix du Amphithéâtre*, it read; on the back it was inscribed with Andras's and Polaner's names, and the year, 1939. He put the medal on, the weight of it pulling the tricolor ribbon against his neck. He had to see Polaner, and then Professor Vago.

"Lévi," someone said, and he turned.

It was a pair of students who'd entered the contest, two third-year men. Andras had seen them around the École Spéciale but didn't know them; neither of them had been among his studio group or his third-year mentors. The tall fellow with ink-black hair was a Frédéric something; the one with the broad chest and horn-rimmed glasses went by the nickname of Noirlac. The tall one reached for Andras's medal and gave it a yank.

"Nice trinket," he said. "It's a shame you had to cheat to get it."

"Pardon?" Andras said. He didn't trust his comprehension of the man's French.

"I said it's a shame you had to cheat to get it."

Andras narrowed his eyes at Frédéric. "What's this about?"

"Everyone knows they gave it to you out of pity," said the one called Noirlac. "They felt bad for your little friend, the one who got buggered and beat up. It wasn't enough that Lemarque had to hang himself over it. They had to make a public statement."

"We all know you work for Lemain," said the other. "And don't think we don't know about Pingusson and your scholarship. We know it was fixed. You'd better admit it to yourself. You'd never win for a monstrosity like that, not unless you were someone's little pet."

A muted cheer reached them from the courtyard. Andras could just make out Rosen's voice as he delivered a laudatory speech. "If you touch Polaner, I'll kill you," he said. "Both of you."

The taller man laughed. "Defending your lover?"

"What's going on, gentlemen?" It was Vago, striding across the amphitheater with a sheaf of plans under his arm. "Congratulating the winner, are we?"

"That's right, sir," said Frédéric, and grabbed Andras's hand as if to shake it. Andras pulled away.

Vago seemed to take in Andras's expression and the mocking smiles of the third-year students. "I'd like a word with Monsieur Lévi," he said.

"Of course, Professor," said Noirlac, and made a half bow to Vago. He took his friend's arm and crossed the amphitheater, turning to give Andras a salute at the courtyard door.

"Bastards," Andras said.

Vago put his hands on his hips and sighed. "I know those two," he said. "I'd kill them myself if it wouldn't get me fired."

"Just tell me. Is it true? Did you give us the prize to make a point?"

"What point?"

"About Polaner."

"Of course," said Vago. "To make the point that he's an excellent designer and draftsman. As are you. The entry isn't perfect, of course, but it was by far the most innovative and well-realized in the contest. The decision was unanimous. All the judges agreed, for once. But it was Pingusson who was your biggest champion. He said it was worth every cent to keep you here. In fact, he promised to increase the amount of your fellowship. He's keen to get you more studio time."

"But this design," Andras said, tweaking the hanging track with one finger. "It's absurd, isn't it? Le Corbusier was right when he said a thing like this could never be built."

"Maybe not in Paris," Vago said. "Maybe not this decade. But Le Corbusier's been making notes and sketches for a project in India, and he says he'd like to exchange some ideas with you and Polaner."

Andras squinted at him in disbelief. "He wants to exchange ideas with us?"

"Why shouldn't he? The best ideas often come out of the classroom. After all, you haven't spent years dealing with planning commissions and zoning boards and neighborhood associations. You're more likely to imagine something impossible, which is how the most interesting buildings come into being."

Andras turned the medal over in his hands. The third-years' insults were still fresh in his mind, his temples still beating with adrenaline.

"Jealous men will always try to take you down," Vago said. "It's the way of humankind."

"A fine species we are," Andras said.

"Oh, indeed. There's no saving us. Eventually we'll destroy ourselves. But in the meantime we've got to have shelter, so the architect's work goes on."

At that moment Rosen appeared at the entrance to the amphitheater. "What's keeping you?" he called. "The photographer's waiting."

Vago put a hand on Andras's shoulder and led him to the courtyard, where a group had gathered in a grassy corner. The judges had emerged to be photographed with the winners; Polaner stood between Le Corbusier and Pingusson, a look of deep solemnity on his pale boyish face, and Lemain stood beside them, proud and grave. The photographer placed Andras next to Le Corbusier, and Vago on his other side. Andras adjusted the medal around his neck and drew his shoulders back. As he looked toward the lens of the camera, still trying to shake off his anger, he saw Noirlac and Frédéric watching him, their arms crossed over their chests, reminding him of what seemed to be one of the central truths of his life: that in any moment of happiness there was a reminder of bitterness or tragedy, like the ten plague drops spilled from the Passover cup, or the taste of wormwood in absinthe that no amount of sugar could disguise. And that was why, even though it was the only photograph he'd ever have of himself at the École Spéciale, he would never hang that picture on his wall. When he looked at it he could see nothing but his own anger, and the source of it staring at him from the crowd.

That summer, the constant subject of discussion was the fate of the Free City of Danzig. The papers reported that Germany was smuggling armaments and troops across the border; officers of the Reich were reported to be training the local Nazis in war maneuvers. While Britain and France stalled over a military-assistance agreement with Russia, the radio carried rumors of deeper cooperation between Berlin and Moscow. In early July, Chamberlain pledged Britain's help to Poland if Danzig were threatened, and on Bastille Day the Champs-Élysées bristled with French and British tanks, armored cars, artillery. Two days later the Polish flag mysteriously appeared above the offices of the Reich in Breslau. How that act of defiance had been accomplished, no one could guess; the building must have been crawling with guards. Polaner, who'd had a string of anxious letters from his parents all summer, was sick with the need for good news. Having received that piece, however small, he proposed that they all go to the Blue Dove and let him buy them drinks. It was a hot July afternoon, the streets still littered with Bastille Day trash, the sidewalks awash in greasy bags and empty beer bottles and tiny French and British flags. When they arrived at the Blue Dove they found Ben Yakov already installed at a table with a bottle of whiskey before him. A look of drink-eased resignation had settled over his features.

"Good afternoon, darlings," he said. "Have a drink on me."

"The drinks are on me today," Polaner said. "Did you hear about the Polish flag?"

"I heard it's scheduled to be replaced," Ben Yakov said. "I hear they've come up with something in black and white on a red ground. Rather ugly, if you ask me." He drained his glass and filled it again. "Congratulate me, boys, I'm going to see the rabbi."

They'd never seen Ben Yakov drunk in public. His handsome mouth looked blurred around the edges, as if someone had been trying to erase it.

"Going to see the rabbi?" Rosen said. "Why should we congratulate you for that?"

"Because it'll make me a free man. I'm going to get a divorce."

"What?"

"An old-fashioned Jewish divorce. I can do it, you see, because we've got a note from the doctor saying Ilana's barren. That means we qualify. How's that for chivalry? She can't bear children, so I can cast her off." He bent over his glass and rubbed his eyes. "Have a drink, will you?"

None of it was news to Andras. For the past month, Ilana had been living under Klara's roof again, occupying the other half of Klara's bed. Klara had offered to take care of her while she recovered; Ilana had gone to the rue de Sévigné when she'd left the hospital, and hadn't gone home since. She was miserable, she told Klara; she'd come to understand that Ben Yakov didn't love her, at least not as he once had. She understood that he felt caged by their marriage. She'd long suspected that he was seeing someone else. When Ben Yakov went to visit her at Klara's, they would sit together in the front room, scarcely saying a word; what was there to say? She was often inconsolable with grief over the baby, a grief Ben Yakov was surprised to find he shared; he grieved, too, Klara said, for the loss of a certain idea of himself. And then there was the unanswerable question of what might be next for Ilana. On the other side of her recovery was a blank page. There was nothing to keep her in Paris now, but she didn't know how her parents would receive her if she went home. Her letters to them had gone unanswered.

Andras hadn't mentioned Ilana's situation in his own letters to Tibor. He hadn't wanted to worry his brother, nor, on the other hand, to raise Tibor's hopes. But a week earlier, Ben Yakov and Ilana had met at Klara's to discuss how they might extract themselves from their marriage. Ilana told Ben Yakov they might be granted a divorce if the doctor would attest that she could no longer bear children. It was uncertain whether that was really true, but the doctor might be persuaded to say so. Ben Yakov had agreed to pursue that avenue. Once they'd made the decision they both seemed to feel some relief. Ilana's health began to improve, and Ben Yakov went back to the studio to make up the work he'd missed that spring. But now that the first meeting with the rabbi was approaching, Ben Yakov had broken down. The possibility of divorce would soon become reality, evidence of what a disaster he'd made of Ilana's life, and his own.

As the four of them drank together, Ben Yakov laid himself bare without shame. Not only had his marriage with Ilana fallen apart; the beautiful Lucia, tired of waiting, had left him too. She was spending the summer under the tutelage of a master architect in New York, and there were rumors that the architect had fallen in love with her and that she might be leaving the École Spéciale for a design school in Rhode Island. The rumors had arrived through a string of mutual friends. Lucia herself hadn't written to Ben Yakov since she'd left Paris.

At the end of the evening, after they'd spilled onto the sidewalk outside the Blue Dove, Andras volunteered to take Ben Yakov home. Rosen and Polaner clapped Ben Yakov on the back and expressed the hope that he'd feel better in the morning.

"Oh, I'll feel grand," Ben Yakov said, and the next moment he bent over beside a lamppost and sent a stream of vomit into the gutter.

Andras gave him a handkerchief and helped him clean himself; then he put an arm around Ben Yakov's shoulders and led him home. At the door there was some fumbling for a key, and as Ben Yakov searched he came dangerously close to crying. At last he located the key in his shirt pocket, and Andras helped him upstairs. The place looked exactly as Andras had imagined: as though the person responsible for making it habitable had departed weeks before. Dirty plates choked the sink, the geraniums on the windowsill had died, newspapers and books lay everywhere, and on the unmade bed there were croissant flakes and piles of discarded clothes. Andras made Ben Yakov sit in the chair beside the bed while he stripped the linens and replaced them with fresh ones. He made Ben Yakov take off his soiled shirt. That was as much as he could manage; the rest of the place saddened and daunted him. Worst of all was the little table with its empty teacups and its crust of bread: Andras recognized a tablecloth edged with forget-me-nots, Klara's wedding gift to the bride.

Ben Yakov crawled into bed and turned off the light, and Andras picked his way to the door. The ancient lock confounded him. He bent to it and fiddled with a rusted latch.

"Lévi," Ben Yakov said. "Are you still there?"

"I'm here," Andras said.

"Listen," he said. "Write to your brother."

Andras paused with his hand on the doorknob.

"I'm not an idiot," Ben Yakov said. "I know what happened between the two of them. I know what happened on the train."

"What do you mean?" Andras said.

"Please, don't—don't try to *shield* me, or whatever it is you're doing. It's insulting."

"How do you know what happened on the train?"

"I *know*. I could tell something was wrong when they got here. And she confessed, one night when I'd said some cruel things to her. But it was already obvious. She tried—to fight it, I mean. She's a good girl. But she fell in love with him. That's all. I'm not the sort of man he is, Andras, you ought to know that."

He stopped and said, "Oh, God—," and then pulled the chamber pot from beneath the bed and threw up into it. He stumbled to the bathroom in the hallway and returned, wiping his face with a towel. "Write him," he said. "Tell him to come see her. But don't tell me what happens, all right? I don't want to know. And I can't see you for a while. I'm sorry, really. I know it's not your fault." He got into bed, turned over to face the wall. "Go home now, Lévi." His voice was muffled against the pillow. "Good of you to look after me. I'd have done the same for you."

"I know you would have," Andras said. He tried the stubborn latch again; this time the door opened. He went home to the rue des Écoles, took out a notebook, and began to draft a letter to his brother.

CHAPTER TWENTY-FOUR

The S.S. *Île de France*

ELISABET'S ELOPEMENT was not really an elopement in the true sense of the word; by the time it happened, Klara had known of her impending departure for months. Paul Camden came to lunch nearly every Sunday afternoon in his quest to earn her trust and favor. In his slow French with its flattened vowels, he told Klara about his family home in Connecticut, where his mother raised and trained show horses; about his father's position as the vice president of an energy conglomerate in New York; about his sisters, who were both in school at Radcliffe and who would love Elisabet. But the problem remained of what Camden père and mère would think of their son's returning home with a moneyless Jewish girl of obscure parentage. The best solution, Paul thought, was for the wedding to take place before they left for New York. It would be simpler to travel as husband and wife; once they reached America, the fait accompli of their marriage would make everything clear to his parents, whatever their objections. Paul believed they would welcome Elisabet once they'd gotten to know her. But Klara begged that they wait to get married until after they'd arrived, until Paul had revealed everything and had a chance to bring them around to the idea. If he married Elisabet without consulting them first, Klara was certain they'd react by cutting off their son. In any case, as a safeguard against that eventuality, Paul had begun saving half of the astonishing sum his father's accountant sent him each month. He had moved to a smaller apartment and begun to take his meals at a student dining club, rather than having them sent in by restaurants; he had stopped adding to his wardrobe and had bought used books for his classes. He had learned these economies from Andras, who had found him to be profoundly ignorant of the most basic principles of frugality. He had never heard of buying day-old bread, for example, and had never polished his own shoes nor washed his own shirts; he was amazed that a man might have his hat reblocked rather than buy a new one.

"But everyone will see it's your old hat," he protested, and then repeated the last words in English: "*Old hat*. In the States, it's a pejorative. It's what you call something predictable or trite or *démodé*."

"All you have to do is change the hatband," Andras said. "No one will know it's your *ohld het*. If you think anyone looks that closely at what you're wearing, you're mistaken."

Paul laughed. "I suppose you're right, old man," he said, and let Andras show him where a hat could be taken to be reblocked.

Often, on those Sundays when Paul came to lunch, Andras would see Klara retreat into watchful silence. He knew she was observing her daughter's intended, sizing him up, taking note of how he treated Elisabet, how he responded to Andras's queries about his work, how he spoke to Mrs. Apfel as she served the *káposzta*. But she was also watching Elisabet. There seemed to be a kind of urgency in her watching, as if she had to record every nuance of Elisabet's existence. She seemed acutely aware that these were the last days her daughter would live under her roof. There was nothing Klara could do to stop it; Elisabet had been on her way out for years, slowly but unmistakably, and now she would be gone for good, across the ocean, into a fledgling marriage with a non-Jewish man whose parents might not accept her. To make matters worse, there at the same table sat Ilana di Sabato, newly divorced: evidence of how a marriage between two very young people might go wrong. Ilana sat in lonely despair, hardly touching her food; she'd cut her gorgeous dark braid at the nape of her neck when she'd married Ben Yakov, and her hair clung forlornly to her head like the kind of close-fitting cap that had been fashionable a decade earlier. *Old hat*, Andras thought. It was painful to look at her. He had not yet received a reply to his letter, and didn't want to speak to her about Tibor until he did.

Elisabet would sail at the beginning of August, and many things had to be prepared for the voyage. Her clothes were a schoolgirl's clothes; she had to assemble the wardrobe of a married woman. Paul insisted on contributing to the preparations, at first presenting Elisabet with the kind of extravagances he had only ever thought of as necessities: a linen tennis costume with a pair of rubber-soled canvas shoes; a pearl necklace with a platinum clasp; a set of traveling cases made of fawn-colored leather, her initials stamped upon them in gold. Each purchase devastated the savings he'd accumulated by practicing the small economies Andras had taught him. At last Klara suggested, as gently as one could, that Paul might ask her how the money might best be spent. Elisabet needed things like cambric slips, nightgowns, walking shoes. One of the fillings in her teeth had to be replaced. She wanted her long hair cut into a short style. All of these things cost money and took time. When Andras left in the evenings, Klara would always have her sewing basket out; he imagined her as a kind of Penelope by proxy, each night tearing out the work she'd done so that Elisabet would never have to marry. It terrified her, she'd told him, to think of Elisabet setting out across the ocean while Europe stood on the brink of war. It was not uncommon for civilian ships to be torpedoed. Couldn't Elisabet wait another few months at least, until the situation in Poland had quieted down and the problems with the Anglo-French Mutual Assistance Agreement with Russia had been resolved? Did Paul and Elisabet really have to sail in August, that month when wars traditionally began? But Elisabet had insisted that if she waited, France might indeed go to war; then the journey would be impossible. The subject had sparked arguments that had brought Klara and Elisabet close to emotional collapse. Andras had the sense that this was their last great opportunity to demonstrate their love in the way they'd practiced most, through a struggle in which neither party would yield and neither could win, a conflict whose subject was not the matter at hand but the complicated nature of mother-and-daughterhood itself.

On the rare nights when Klara came to him at his garret during those weeks, she made love to him with an insistence that seemed to have nothing to do with him at all. He had never imagined he might be so lonely in her arms; he wanted her unfocused eyes to settle upon him. When he stopped her once and said, "Look at me," she rolled away from him and broke into tears. Then she apologized, and he held her, unable to suppress the selfish wish that this would all be over soon. On the other side of Elisabet's departure was the fulfillment of the promise they'd made last fall: They, too, would be married, and would live together at last. In her grief over the loss of her child, Klara had ceased to talk about what would happen once Elisabet was gone.

. . .

21 July 1939
Modena

Dear Andras,
I am sorry, truly sorry, to hear that the marriage between Ilana and Ben Yakov has ended so sadly. It grieves me to consider the role I may have played in their unhappiness. If regret could mend that error, it would have been undone long ago.
When I first received your letter I thought I couldn't possibly come to Paris. How could I face Ilana, I asked myself, knowing how I had wronged her? Love insists upon its own expression; it tells us it is right simply by virtue of being love. But we are human beings and must decide what is right. My feelings for Ilana were so acute that I failed to govern them. I hardly deserve

a second chance to prove myself her friend; still less to plead my case as a lover.

But, Andráska—and perhaps you'll consider me a scoundrel for saying so—I find that my feelings for her are unchanged. How my pulse raced when I read that she'd asked after me! How it moved me to hear that she'd spoken of me with tenderness! You know me too well to have mentioned these things lightly; you must have known what they would mean to me.

And so, finally, I am coming. I am ashamed, but I am coming. At least you'll never have reason to doubt my constancy; neither, I hope, shall Ilana. By the time you receive this letter I will have reached Paris. I will take a room at the Hôtel St. Jacques, where you can find me on Friday.

With love, Your TIBOR

It was Saturday morning by the time Andras got his brother's letter. He had been at the architecture firm all night, helping Lemain complete a set of drawings for a client. The letter was sitting on the front table, along with a handwritten note from Tibor: *Andras: Came to see you this morning. Waited until 9. Can't wait longer! I must try to see her. Meet me at Klara's. T.*

He knocked on the concierge's door. There was a long silence; then came an unintelligible French curse and approaching footsteps. The concierge came out in a grime-stained apron and sooty work gloves, a stripe of grease across her brow.

"Tsk!" she said. "A visitor arrives with great commotion at an inconvenient hour. What a surprise: He's a relative of yours."

"When did my brother leave?"

"Not three minutes ago. I was cleaning the oven, as you can see."

"Three minutes ago!"

"There's no need to shout, young man."

"Excuse me," Andras said. He stuffed the note into his pocket and charged out into the street. The door slammed behind him; the concierge's muffled curse followed him down the block. He took off at a run toward the Marais. It was a bright, hot morning; the streets were already crowded with tourists and their cameras, families out for Saturday strolls, lovers walking arm in arm. At the Pont Louis-Philippe, Andras glimpsed a familiar hat in the crush of the crowd. He called his brother's name, and the man turned.

They met at the center of the bridge. Tibor seemed to have grown thinner since Andras had last seen him; the angles of his cheekbones were sharper now, the shadows beneath his eyes darker. When they embraced, he seemed made of a substance lighter than flesh.

"Are you all right?" Andras asked, studying his features.

"I haven't slept since I got your letter," Tibor said.

"When did you arrive?"

"Last night. I came to your building, but you weren't there."

"I was at work all night. I just got your note."

"So you haven't spoken to her? She doesn't know I'm in Paris?"

"No. She doesn't even know I wrote to you."

"How is she, Andras?"

"Just as before. Very sad. But I think that will change shortly."

Tibor gave his brother a bemused smile. "If you're so sure she'll be glad to see me, why did you chase me all the way here?"

"I suppose I wanted to see you first!" Andras said, and laughed.

"Well?" Tibor spread his arms.

"Hideous as ever. And me?"

"Shoes untied. Ink spots on your shirt. And you haven't shaved."

"Perfect. On our way, then." He took Tibor's arm and turned him toward the rue de Sévigné. But Tibor didn't move. He put a hand on the bridge rail and looked down into the Seine.

"I'm not sure I can do this," he said. "I'm petrified."

"Of course you are," Andras said. "But now that you're here, you have to do it." He cocked his head toward the Marais. "Come on."

They walked together, both of them lightheaded from lack of sleep. On their way, Tibor bought a bouquet of peonies from a corner florist. By the time they reached Klara's corner, Andras had absorbed his brother's misgivings; he worried that they should have sent word that they were coming. He looked through the windowpanes into the tranquil light of the studio, still empty before the first class, and regretted their intrusion upon the quiet of Saturday morning at the Morgensterns'.

But all was already in chaos there. The front door opened at Andras's touch; from upstairs came the sounds of some disaster—Klara's voice raised in panic, Mrs. Apfel shouting. For an instant Andras thought they were too late: in her despair, Ilana di Sabato had taken her own life, and Klara had just now discovered her body. He grabbed the banister and raced up the stairs, and Tibor followed.

But Ilana was nowhere to be seen. It was Mrs. Apfel who met them at the top of the stairs. "She's gone!" she said. "The little vixen ran away!"

"Who?" Andras said. "What happened?"

"She's gone off to America with her Monsieur Camden. Left her mother a note. I could strangle that child! I could wring her neck."

From down the hall came a great clattering of something bulky and rigid. Andras went to Klara's room to find that she had just pulled a suitcase down from the top of the wardrobe. She threw it onto the unmade bed, flung it open, and pulled her driving coat out of its brown paper.

"What are you doing?" Andras said.

She looked at him, her lovely features raked raw by grief. "Going after her," she said, and thrust a note into his hands. In her round childish script, Elisabet explained that she must go, that she couldn't wait any longer, that she was afraid the situation in Poland might push France toward war before they could sail. They had left Paris by train that morning; they would depart for New York the next day on the S.S. *Île de France*, and would be married by the captain on board. She apologized—and here the letters were blurred—and the next thing he could read was *might be easier for everyone if I*, and then another illegible line. *Will write when I arrive*, the note concluded. *Thanks for trousseau and everything else. Love, &c.*

"When did you get this?"

"This morning. All her things are gone."

"And you're going to try to catch her?"

"I can follow her to Le Havre. If we drive, we can get there by this afternoon."

Andras sighed. The bond between Klara and Elisabet would be a difficult one to break; he could see why Elisabet might want to get a running start. But it made him furious to think of Elisabet moving her things out quietly in the night, those carefully packed crates of clothing and linen Klara had assembled for her. "Did you hire a car?" he asked.

"I had Mrs. Apfel call. It should arrive in a moment."

"Klara—"

"Yes, I know." She sat down on the bed, holding the driving coat on her lap. "She's a grown girl. She's going to leave anyway. I ought to allow her to go off and do what she wants to do."

"Are you going to try to stop her? Do you think you can convince her not to sail?"

"No," she said, and sighed. "But since she's determined to go, I'd like to see her off. I'd like to say goodbye to my daughter."

He understood, of course. Elisabet's war of independence was over; what Klara wanted now was to negotiate the peace in person, rather than from opposite sides of the Atlantic. If there was a remnant of struggle in her capitulation, he understood that, too. She had been fighting this battle for years, and couldn't so easily give up the habit.

"I'll come with you," he said. "Or I won't, if you'd prefer that."

"I want you to come. Please come."

"But Klara, there's something else I have to tell you," he said. "Tibor's here."

"Tibor? Your brother is here?"

"Yes. He's here right now, in the apartment."

"You didn't tell me he'd written back!"

"I didn't get the letter until this morning."

"Ilana," she said, and they went down the hall to deliver the news.

But Ilana and Tibor had already found each other. They were sitting together on the sofa in the front room. On her face was a look of disbelieving joy; on his, relief and exhaustion. They were not unhappy to learn that Andras and Klara were going to Le Havre, and that they would have to spend the day in each other's company.

"But you'll call us when you get to Le Havre," Tibor said. "Let us know if you've found her."

From downstairs came the double blast of a klaxon; the rental agency had delivered the car, and it was time to go. Mrs. Apfel handed over a basket of things she'd packed for the journey. Minutes later they were off, weaving their way through the streets of Paris, Andras white-knuckled in the passenger seat, Klara resolute and grim behind the wheel. By the time they hit the countryside, Klara's forehead had relaxed. Morning sun flooded the rippling sunflower fields ahead of them. They didn't talk above the wind and engine noise, but when they reached a stretch of open road she took his hand.

There was no secrecy to Paul and Elisabet's plans; they were staying at the very hotel they'd settled upon a month earlier when it was decided they would leave from Le Havre. Andras and Klara went into the high white lobby and inquired at the desk. They were told to wait, and then were told to follow the bellman. The couple themselves were seated on a veranda overlooking the port, where the S.S. *Île de France* could be seen in her strict nautical uniform, her crimson smokestacks circumscribed in black. Klara rushed across the veranda, calling Elisabet's name, and Elisabet rose from her chair with an expression of surprise and relief. Andras had never before seen her look so happy to see her mother. And then she did a remarkable thing: She threw her arms around Klara's neck and burst into tears.

"Forgive me!" Elisabet cried. "I shouldn't have left the way I did. I didn't know what else to do!" And she wept on her mother's shoulder.

Paul watched the scene with evident embarrassment; he gave Andras a sheepish nod of greeting and then ordered a round of drinks for everyone.

"What were you thinking?" Klara said when they'd sat down together. She touched Elisabet's face. "Couldn't you have allowed me the comfort of an ordinary goodbye? Did you think I'd lock you in your room and keep you there?"

"I don't know," Elisabet said, still crying. "I'm sorry." She twisted the shorn ends of her hair self-consciously; without the long yellow braid, her head looked oddly small and bereft. The bob drew attention to her pale naked mouth. "I was frightened, too. I didn't know if I could bear to say goodbye."

"And you," Klara said, turning to Paul. "Was this how you left your mother when you came to France?"

"Ah—no, Madame."

"Ah—no, indeed! In the future you'll treat me with the respect you'd give your own mother, if you please."

"I apologize, Madame." He looked genuinely chastened. Andras wondered if his own mother had ever spoken to him in such a tone. He tried to conjure up an image of Paul's mother, but all he could muster was a jodhpur-clad version of the Baroness Kaczynska, a sixteenth-century aristocrat whose complicated history and lineage he'd had to study at school in Debrecen.

"Do you really mean to be married by a sea captain?" Klara asked her daughter. "Is that what you'd like?"

"It's what we've decided," Elisabet said. "I think it's exciting."

"So I'm not to see you married, then."

"You'll see me after I'm married. When we come back to visit."

"And when do you imagine that will be?" Klara said. "When do you think you'll be able to buy passage back across an ocean? Particularly if your husband's parents don't accept your union?"

"We thought maybe you'd want to come live in the States," Paul said. "To be close to the children and all, when we have children."

"And what about my own children?" Klara said. "It might not be an easy thing for me to dash across an ocean."

"What children?"

She looked at Andras and took his hand. "Our children."

"Maman!" Elisabet said. "You can't mean you plan to have children with—!" She cocked a thumb at Andras.

"We may. We've discussed it."

"But you're *un femme d'un certain age*!"

Klara laughed. "We're all of a certain age, aren't we? You, for example, are of an age at which it's impossible to understand how thirty-two might seem like the beginning of a life, rather than the end of one."

"But *I'm* your child," Elisabet said, looking as though she might cry again.

"Of course you are," Klara said, and tucked one of Elisabet's short blond locks behind her ear. "That's why I came here to you. I couldn't let you go across the ocean without saying a proper goodbye."

"Mesdames," Andras said. "Pardon me. I think Mr. Camden and I will take a walk now and leave you alone."

"That's right," Paul said. "We'll go down to see the ship."

It had all become rather overwhelming; there had been too much crying already for Paul's taste, and Andras had become lightheaded at the mention of his future children. It was a relief to them both to take leave of Klara and Elisabet and strike out on their own.

They walked through a street market on their way to the

docks, past men selling mackerel and sole and langoustines, boxes of *myrtilles*, net sacks of summer squashes, tiny yellow plums by the dozen. Families on holiday thronged the streets, so many children in sailor suits they might have formed a child navy. Self-consciously, as if the outpouring of emotion they'd just witnessed had threatened their masculinity, Andras and Paul talked of ships and of sports, and then, as they passed an English navy ship docked in one of the enormous berths, of the prospect of war. Everyone had hoped that Chamberlain's declaration of support for Poland might lead to a few weeks of calm over the Danzig question, and perhaps even a peaceable settlement in the end, but Hitler had just concluded a meeting at Berchtesgaden with the leader of Danzig's Nazi Party and had sent a warship into the Free City's port. If Germany claimed Danzig, then England and France would go to war. That week, French aircraft had staged a mock attack on London to test the readiness of England's air-defense system. Some Londoners had thought war had already broken out, and three people had been killed in a rush to the air-raid shelters.

"What do you think America will do?" Andras asked.

Paul shrugged. "Roosevelt will issue an ultimatum, I guess."

"Hitler doesn't fear Roosevelt. Look what happened last April."

"Well, I don't claim to know much about it," Paul said, raising his hands in a pantomime of self-defense. "I'm just a painter. Most days I don't even read the news."

"Your fiancée is Jewish," Andras said. "Her family is here. The war will affect her, whether America gets involved or not."

They stood in silence for a long moment, looking at the ship with its spiny encrustation of guns. "What kind of service would you choose, if you had to fight?" Paul asked.

"Not the navy, that's for certain," Andras said. "The first time I saw the sea was a year ago. And nothing in a ditch. No trenches. I could learn to fly a plane, though. That's what I'd like to do."

Paul broke into a grin. "Me too," he said. "I've always thought it would be fantastic to fly planes."

"But I wouldn't want to have to kill anyone," Andras said.

"Right," Paul said. "That's the problem. I wouldn't mind being a hero, though. I'd like to win medals."

"Me too," Andras said. It felt good, if slightly shameful, to admit it.

"See you in the air, then," Paul said, and laughed, but there was something forced about it, as if the possibility of a war and his involvement in it had suddenly become real to him.

They'd reached the S.S. *Île de France*, its bulk towering above them like the leading edge of a glacier. Its hull was glossy with new paint; each letter of its name was as tall and as broad as a man. The sea sloshed around it in its berth, sending up a rich stink of dead fish and oil and dock weed, and something briny and calciferous that must have been the smell of seawater itself. The ship rose fifteen stories from the waterline; they could count five terraces from where they stood. The decks teemed with stevedores, sailors, chambermaids with their arms full of linen. Hundreds were making the final preparations for the departure of a small town's worth of people on a seventeen-day voyage. There would be fifteen hundred passengers on board, Paul told him; there were five ballrooms, a cinema, a shooting gallery, a vast gymnasium, an indoor swimming pool, a hundred lifeboats. The ship was nearly eight hundred feet long and would travel at twenty-four knots. And on board was a surprise for Elisabet, one final extravagance: They had a stateroom with a private balcony, and he'd arranged for the delivery of three dozen white roses and a case of champagne.

"At least you got your hat reblocked," Andras said. "Think what it would have cost to buy a new one."

That evening they all dined together on the terrace of a restaurant overlooking the water. They ate fresh clams in tomato broth and whole fish roasted with lemons and olives, drank two bottles of wine, talked about their childhood fancies and the exotic places they wanted to see before they died: India, Japan, Morocco. It was almost like a holiday. Klara was in high spirits for the first time in weeks, as if by having found Elisabet she might still avert the long-dreaded separation. But the new arrangements remained in place: Elisabet and Paul would sail in the morning. And as the evening went on, Andras became aware of a familiar tautness inside him, a coil that had been winding itself tighter by the day: It was the fear that once Elisabet had gone, Klara would somehow vanish too, as if the tension between them were what anchored them both to the earth.

At the hotel after dinner, he and Klara parted ways for the night. She would sleep in Elisabet's suite while Paul and Andras shared a simple room under the eaves. As Klara said *bonne nuit* she pressed a hand to his cheek like a promise; that night he fell asleep with the hope that the life they made together might be a balm for her grief. But when he went downstairs at dawn he found her standing alone on the veranda, her driving coat draped around her shoulders, watching as the pink light climbed the smokestacks of the *Île de France*. He stood at the French doors for a long moment without approaching her. A tide was turning. Her daughter was leaving. There was nothing he could ever do to replace what would be taken away.

At eight o'clock they went to the docks to say goodbye to Paul and Elisabet. The ship would sail at noon; the passengers were to board by nine. They had bought Elisabet a bouquet of violets to take on board with her, and a dozen fancy pastries, and a cylinder of yellow streamers for her to set free when the ship pulled away. She wore a straw hat with a red ribbon, and her blue eyes were feverish with the prospect of the voyage.

Paul was anxious to get on board, anxious to show Elisabet

what he'd planned for her. But he insisted on having the ship's photographer take a picture of the four of them together on the dock, the *Île de France* looming in the background. Then there was a flurry about the trunks, some article of clothing that had to be removed at the last moment. Finally, at the appointed hour, a volcanic horn-blast sounded from somewhere near the summit of the ship, and the passengers who had not yet embarked began to crowd toward the gangway.

The moment had come. Klara drew Paul aside to speak a few final words to him, and Andras and Elisabet were left looking at each other on the dock. He hadn't considered what he might say to her at this moment. He was surprised to feel as sorry as he did that she was leaving; at dinner the night before, he'd begun to see what she might be like as an adult, and he'd found her to have more of her mother in her than he had imagined.

"I don't suppose you're sad to see me go," she said. But she was looking at him with a hint of humor at the corners of her eyes, and she'd spoken in Hungarian.

"Yes," Andras said, and took her hand. "Get lost already, will you?"

She smiled. "Make my mother visit us, all right?"

"I will," Andras said. "I want to see New York."

"I'll send you a postcard."

"Good."

"I haven't gotten used to the idea that you're marrying her," Elisabet said. "That'll make you my—"

"Please don't say it."

"All right. But listen: If I ever hear you've hurt her, I'll come kill you myself."

"And if I hear that you've hurt that strapping husband of yours," Andras began, but Elisabet cuffed him on the shoulder, and then it was time for her to say goodbye to Klara. They stood close together, Elisabet bending her head to touch her mother's. Andras turned away and shook Paul's hand.

"See you in the funny papers," Paul said in English. "That's what they say in the States." He translated for Andras: *"Je te verrai dans les bandes dessinées."*

"Sounds better in French," Andras said, and Paul had to agree.

The ship's horn blasted again. Klara kissed Elisabet one last time, and Paul and Elisabet climbed the gangway and disappeared into the crowd of passengers. Klara held Andras's arm, silent and dry-eyed, until Elisabet appeared at the rail of the ship. Already, hours before the ship would leave the dock, Elisabet was so far away that she was recognizable only by the red ribbon fluttering from the brim of her hat, and by the pinprick of deep purple that was the cone of violets in her hand. The navy blur beside her was Paul in his nautical-looking jacket. Klara took Andras's hand and gripped it. Her slender face was pale beneath the dark sweep of her hair; in her haste to get to Le Havre she'd neglected to bring a hat. She waved her handkerchief at Elisabet, who waved hers in return.

Three hours later they watched the *Île de France* slip out toward the flat blue distance of the open sea and sky. How astounding, Andras thought, that a ship that size could shrink to the size of a house, and then to the size of a car; the size of a desk, a book, a shoe, a walnut, a grain of rice, a grain of sand. How astounding that the largest thing he'd ever seen was still no match for the diminishing effect of distance. It made him aware of his own smallness in the world, his insignificance in the face of what might come, and for a moment his chest felt light with panic.

"Are you ill?" Klara said, putting a hand to his cheek. "What's wrong?"

But he found it impossible to put the feeling into words. In a moment it had passed, and then it was time for them to go to the car and start for home.

CHAPTER TWENTY-FIVE

The Hungarian Consulate

ALL THE TIME Andras and Klara had been at Le Havre, Tibor and Ilana had been together at the apartment on the rue de Sévigné. Tibor related the story the following day as he and Andras walked along the bank of the Seine, watching the long flat barges pass beneath the bridges. Now and then they would catch a strain of Gypsy music that made Andras feel as if they were back in Budapest, as if he might look up and see the gold-traced dome of the Parliament on the right bank, Castle Hill on the left. The afternoon was humid and smelled of damp pavement and river water; in the oblique light Tibor looked haggard with joy. He told Andras that Ilana had known on the train that she was making a mistake, but had felt powerless to stop what had already been set in motion. There was guilt all around, an endless carousel of guilt: her own, Ben Yakov's, Tibor's. Each had wronged the others, each had been wronged by the others. It was a miracle that any of them had emerged from the harrowing whirl of it with faculties intact. But Tibor had been protected by his physical distance from Paris, and Ilana had been tended by Klara as if she were her own daughter, and Ben Yakov had talked to Andras in his room at night.

"She'll come back to Italy with me," Tibor said. "I'll take her home to Florence and spend the rest of the summer there. I'd ask her to marry me today if I could, but I'd rather not have her parents consider me the enemy. I'd like to have their permission."

"That's brave of you. And what if they refuse?"

"I'll take my chances. You never know, after all. Maybe they'll like me."

They'd crossed the Île de la Cité and the Petit Pont into the Quartier Latin, where they found themselves walking down the rue Saint-Jacques. József's building lay just ahead; the last time Andras had been there was the night after the Yom Kippur fast. He had seen József a few times since then in passing, but hadn't crossed the threshhold of his building for months. The time was fast approaching when he and Klara would have to revisit the idea of taking him into their confidence. Now, as he reached the building, he saw that the street door had been propped open with two polished and bestickered leather traveling cases, József's name and address clearly marked on their sides. A moment later József himself appeared in a summer traveling suit.

"Lévi!" he said. He let his gaze rove over Andras, who felt himself appraised in a bemused, brotherly fashion. "I must say, old boy, you're looking well. And here's the other Lévi, the future doctor, if I'm not mistaken. What a shame you've caught me just as I'm rushing off. We could have all had a drink. On the other hand, how convenient for me. You can help me get a cab."

"Off on holiday?" Tibor asked.

"I was supposed to be," József said, and an unaccustomed expression passed across his features—a look Andras could only have described as chagrin. "I was supposed to meet some friends at Saint-Tropez. Instead I'm off to lovely Budapest."

"Why?" Andras said. "What's happened?"

József raised an arm at a passing taxi. It pulled to the curb and the driver climbed out to get József's bags. "Listen," József said. "Why don't the two of you ride to the station with me? I'm going all the way to the Gare du Nord, and it'll take half an hour in this traffic. Unless you've got something better to do."

"Better than a long hot ride in traffic?" Andras said. "I can't imagine."

They climbed into the cab and set off down the rue Saint-Jacques in the direction from which they'd come. József settled a long arm across the back of the seat and turned toward Andras.

"Well, Lévi," he said. "It's the damnedest thing, but I think I ought to tell you."

"What is it?" Andras asked.

"Have you gotten your student visa renewed?"

"Not yet. Why?"

"Don't be surprised if you run into trouble at the Hungarian Consulate."

Andras squinted at József; the slanting five o'clock light poured through the windows of the cab and illuminated what he hadn't seen before: the shadow of worry beneath József's eyes, the aftertraces of lost sleep. "What kind of trouble?" he said.

"I went to get my visa renewed. I thought I still had a few weeks left. I didn't think there'd be any difficulty. But then they said they couldn't do it, not here in France."

"But that doesn't make sense," Tibor said. "That's what the consulate does."

"Not anymore, apparently."

"If they won't renew your visa in France, where are they supposed to do it?"

"Back home," József said. "That's why I'm going."

"Couldn't you get your father to work it out for you?" Andras said. "Couldn't he use his influence to make someone do something? Or else, if you'll excuse the vulgarity, couldn't he just bribe someone?"

"One would think," József said. "But apparently not. My father's influence isn't what it once was. He's not the president of the bank anymore. He goes to the same office, but he's got a different title now. Advisory secretary, or some such nonsense."

"Is it to do with his being Jewish?"

"Of course. What else would it be?"

"And I suppose it's only Jews who have to go back to Hungary to renew their visas."

"Does that surprise you, old man?"

Andras pulled his papers from his jacket pocket. "My visa's still good for another three weeks."

"That's what I thought, too. But it's no good unless you're taking summer classes. Next term doesn't count anymore, apparently. You'd better go to the consulate before someone asks for your papers. As far as the authorities are concerned, you're here illegally now."

"But that's impossible. It doesn't make sense."

József shrugged. "I wish I could tell you otherwise."

"I can't go to Budapest now," Andras said.

"Truth to tell, I'm almost looking forward to it," József said. "I'll have a soak at the Szécsenyi baths, take a coffee at the Gerbeaud, see a few of the boys from gimnázium. Maybe go to the house at Lake Balaton for a while. Then I'll do what I have to do at the passport office, and I'll be back by the start of fall term—if there is a fall term, of course, which depends in part on the whims of Herr Hitler."

Andras collapsed against the cab seat, trying to take in what he'd just heard. Ordinarily he might have welcomed the excuse to go home for a few weeks; after all, he hadn't seen his parents or Mátyás in two years. But he was supposed to get married; it was supposed to happen while Tibor was still in Paris. He was supposed to move his things to the rue de Sévigné. And then there was the problem of Hitler and Danzig. This was no time to get on a train to Budapest, no time to cross the continent, no time for his visa to be in question. In any case, how could he afford to travel? The cost of a two-way ticket would consume what he'd managed to set aside for Klara's ring and for tuition in the fall. He didn't have the savings Tibor had; he hadn't worked for six years before going to school. He felt suddenly ill, and had to roll down the cab window and turn his face toward the breeze.

"I should have spoken to you sooner," József said. "We might have traveled together."

"It's my fault," Andras said. "I haven't been eager to see you since I got blind drunk in your bedroom."

"Never feel ashamed," József said. "Not with me. Not for that reason." And then he turned to Tibor. "What about you?" he said. "How's medical school? Was it Switzerland?"

"Italy."

"Of course. So you're nearly a doctor now."

"Not quite nearly."

"And what brings you to town?"

"That's a long story," Tibor said. "The short version is something like this: I'm courting someone who was recently married to a friend of Andras's. I'm glad you're leaving town before you can make me say more about it."

József laughed. "That's grand," he said. "I wish I had time for the long version."

They had reached the station, and the driver got out to untie the bags from the roof. József opened his wallet and counted out money. Andras and Tibor slid out after him and helped him carry the bags inside.

"I suppose you'd better go," Andras said, once they'd consigned the luggage to a porter. "You'll miss your train."

"Listen," József said. "If you do make it to Budapest, look me up. We'll have a drink. I'll introduce you to some girls I know."

"Monsieur Hász, the playboy," Tibor said.

"Don't forget it," József said, and winked. Then he slung his chestnut-colored satchel over his shoulder and loped off into the crowded station.

Before a week had passed, Andras would be obliged to return to the Gare du Nord with his own suitcases, his own satchel. But all he knew, as he and Tibor began the long walk to the rue de Sévigné that evening, was that he had to go to the consulate and explain that he must be granted legal visitor status. Only until the end of the month—only as long as it would take to get a marriage license and wed his bride. Once they were married, wouldn't he have a claim to French citizenship? Couldn't he come and go, then, as he wished?

At Klara's, all the lights were burning and the women were cloistered in the bedroom. Ilana came out to tell Andras he was not to go in; the dressmaker was there, and behind Klara's door there were secret preparations regarding her wedding gown.

Andras made a noise of dismay. He and Tibor went to the front room and sat down on either side of the sofa, where Tibor pulled his own papers from his trouser pocket and scrutinized the visa.

"Mine's good until next January," he said. "And I've been enrolled in summer study, though I'm afraid I won't pass the course I've just abandoned."

"But you're enrolled. You ought to be all right."

"But what about you? What will you do?"

"I'll go to the consulate," Andras said. "Then I'll go to the Mairie. I'll do whatever I have to do. I've got to have valid papers before we can get a marriage license."

From the bedroom came a trio of exclamations, a crescendo of laughter. Tibor folded his papers again and set them on the table. "What'll you tell her?"

"Nothing yet," he said. "I don't want her to worry."

"We'll go to the consulate tomorrow," Tibor said. "If you explain the problem, maybe they'll grant you an extension. And if they give you trouble, watch out." He held up his fists in a threatening manner. But his hands were as elegant as a pianist's, long and lean; his knuckles had the polished look of river stones, and his tendons fanned like the delicate bones of a bird's wing.

"God help us all," Andras said, and managed a smile.

The Hungarian Consulate was located not far from the German Embassy, where Ernst vom Rath had met his assassin. At first glance the building might have made an expatriate long for home; its façade was inlaid with mosaics depicting scenes from Budapest and the countryside. But the artist had an uncanny knack for ugliness: his humans seemed to suffer from anemia and bloating, his landscapes from a failure of perspective just noticeable enough to evoke vague nausea in the viewer. Andras had had no appetite for breakfast, in any case; he'd hardly slept the night before. Somehow he'd made it through the previous

evening without mentioning the situation to Klara, but she suspected something was wrong. After dinner, as Andras and Tibor
were preparing to leave for the Latin Quarter, she'd stopped him
in the passageway and asked if he were having misgivings about
the wedding.

"Not at all," he said. "Just the opposite. I'm anxious for it to
happen."

"So am I," she said, and put her arms around him in the shadowy hall. He'd kissed her, but his mind hadn't been present. He
was thinking about what had troubled him most since the cab
ride that afternoon: not the prospect of resistance at the consulate, nor the problem of how he might afford a ticket home,
but the fact that the young man rushing to the station had been
József Hász, who had always seemed miraculously exempt from
the difficulties of ordinary life—József Hász, packed off to
Budapest for the sake of a stamp on a document.

The next day at the consulate, a red-haired matron with a
Hajdú accent told Andras that his visa had expired when his
classes had ended at the beginning of the summer, and that he'd
been staying in France illegally for a month and a half; he must
leave the country at once if he didn't want to be arrested. He was
given a copy of a form letter stating that he would be permitted
to reenter Hungary. That seemed like an unnecessary measure;
he was a Hungarian citizen, after all. But he was too upset to
consider it for long. He needed to know what to do once he got
to Budapest, how to return to Paris as soon as possible. Tibor,
who had come along as promised, kept his hands in his pockets
and asked polite questions when Andras might have demanded
and shouted and raised arguments. Through Tibor's gentle
inquiries, they learned that if Andras carried a letter from the
school stating that he was a registered student, and that his
scholarship would be renewed in the fall, he ought to be able to
get another two-year visa once he was back in Budapest. Any
faculty member at the school could write the letter; it was valid
as long as it appeared on the school's letterhead and carried the

school's official seal. Tibor was effusive in his thanks, and the red-haired woman went so far as to say she regretted the inconvenience. But her small watery eyes were impassive as she stamped a red *ÉRVÉNYTELEN* across Andras's visa. Expired. Invalid. He had to leave at once. There was no use going to the Mairie to apply for a marriage license; he could be arrested if he showed his expired documents there. The train ticket would exhaust his savings, but he had no choice. He could begin to save again when he returned.

He and Tibor went to the École Spéciale to get the official letter, but when they tried the front doors they found them locked. Of course: The school was closed for the remainder of August. Everyone, even the office attendants, were on vacation; they wouldn't return until the beginning of September. Andras threw a Hungarian profanity into the hot milky sky.

"How can we get letterhead?" Tibor said. "How can we get an official seal?"

Andras cursed again, but then he had an idea. If there was one thing he knew, it was the architecture of the École Spéciale. It was one of the first designs they'd studied in studio; they had made an exhaustive survey of every aspect of the building, from the stone foundation of the neoclassical entry hall to the pyramidal glass roof of the amphitheater. He knew every door, every window, even the coal-delivery chutes and the network of pneumatic tubes that allowed the central office to send messages to the professors' studies. He knew, for example, that if you approached the school's back wall through the Cimetière du Montparnasse, you would find a door behind a cataract of ivy— a door so well hidden it was never locked. It communicated with the courtyard, which allowed access to the office through windows that swung wide on loose hinges. By the aid of those passages Andras and Tibor found themselves inside the vacation-deadened sanctum of the school. A stationer's box in the office yielded a supply of letterhead and envelopes, and Tibor located the official seal in a secretary's desk drawer. Neither he nor Andras were adept with a typewriter; it took eight tries to come up with a fair copy of a letter declaring that Andras was indeed a registered student at the École Spéciale, and that he would continue to receive his scholarship in the fall term. They listed Pierre Vago as the author of the letter, and Tibor forged Vago's signature with a flourish so grand Vago himself might have envied it. Then they embossed the letter with the school's official stamp.

Before they left, Andras showed Tibor the plaque stating that he'd won the Prix du Amphithéâtre. Tibor stood for a long time looking at the plaque, his arms crossed over his chest. Finally he went back to the office, where he got two blank sheets of letterhead and a pencil. He laid the paper over the plaque and made two rubbings.

"One for our parents," he said. "One for me."

They had to go to the telegraph office to wire Mátyás that he was coming. He wouldn't notify his parents until he got to Budapest; a telegram would only alarm them, and a letter from France might not reach them until he was back in Paris. At the office, worried-looking men and women bent over cards at the writing counters, composing accidentally elegant haiku which took as their subjects birth and love, money and death. Half-written messages littered the floor: MAMAN I RECEIVED—, MATHILDE: REGRET TO INFORM—. While Tibor consulted the train timetable, of which the telegraph office kept a copy, Andras went to the window to get his message card and pencil. The green-visored attendant pointed him toward one of the counters. He went to the appointed place and waited for his brother, who told him that the Danube Express would leave the next morning at seven thirty-three and arrive in Budapest seventy-two hours later.

"What do we write?" Andras asked. "There's too much to say."

"How about this," Tibor suggested, and licked the end of the pencil. "Mátyás: Arrive Budapest Thursday AM. Please bathe. Love Andras."

"Please bathe?"

"You'll likely have to share a bed with him."

"Good point. It's lucky you're here to help."

They paid, and the telegram went into the queue. Now Andras had only to go to the rue de Sévigné to tell Klara of his plans. He dreaded the coversation, the news he would have to deliver: their wedding plans disrupted, his visa expired. The confirmation that she'd been right when she guessed something was the matter. With Europe's fate so uncertain, how could he convince her that their own would be less so? But when they got to the apartment, they found that Klara and Ilana had gone off on a mysterious mission together—to where, Mrs. Apfel wouldn't say. It was four o'clock; on an ordinary day, Klara would have been teaching. But her establishment had an August hiatus too. Had it not been for Ilana's divorce and Elisabet's departure, they might have gone somewhere themselves, perhaps back to the stone cottage at Nice. Now they were here together in the city, the shops and restaurants closed all around them, the city drowsing in a gold haze. Andras wondered where Klara and Ilana might have gone in secret. They came home a quarter of an hour later with wet hair, their skin pink and luminous, a glow about them; they had been to the Turkish baths in the Sixth Arrondissement. He couldn't keep from following Klara into her bedroom to watch her dress for dinner. She smiled over her shoulder as she let her summer dress fall to the floor. Her body was cool and pale, her skin velvety as a sage leaf. It was impossible to think of getting on a train that would take him away from her, even for a day.

"Klárika," he said, and she turned to face him. Her hair had dried in soft tendrils around her neck and forehead; he had such a strong desire for her that he wanted almost to bite her.

"What is it?" She put a hand on the bare skin of his arm.

"Something's happened," he said. "I have to go to Budapest."

She blinked at him in surprise. "But Andras—my God, did someone die?"

"No, no. My visa's expired."

"Can't you just go to the consulate?"

"They've changed the rules. József was the one who told me. He had to leave too—he was on his way to the Gare du Nord when I saw him. I'm here illegally now, according to the government. I have to leave at once. There's a train tomorrow morning."

She took a white silk robe and wrapped it around herself, then sat down on the low chair beside the vanity table, her face drained of color.

"Budapest," she said.

"It's only for a few days."

"But what if you run into trouble? What if they won't renew your visa? What if a war begins while you're away?" Slowly, pensively, she untied the green ribbon that bound her hair at the nape of her neck, and for a long time she sat holding that bit of silk. When she spoke again, her voice had lost its careful balance. "We were supposed to be married next week. And now you're going to Hungary, the one place I can't go with you."

"I'll be gone just long enough to get there, see my parents, and come back."

"I couldn't stand it if something happened."

"Do you think I want to go without you?" he said, and pulled her to her feet. "Do you think I can stand the thought of it? Two weeks without you, while Europe's on the brink of war? Do you think I want that?"

"What if I came with you?"

He shook his head. "We know that's impossible. We've talked about it. It's too dangerous, particularly now."

"I never would have considered it while Elisabet was here, but now I don't need to protect myself for her sake. And Andras—now I know something of what my mother must have suffered when I had to go away. She's getting older. Who knows when I'll have a chance to see her? It's been more than eighteen years. Perhaps I can arrange to meet her in secret, and no one will be the wiser. If we stay a short time, we won't be in danger—I've been Claire Morgenstern for nearly two decades now. I have a French passport. Why would anyone question it? Please, Andras. Let me come."

"I can't," he said. "I couldn't forgive myself if you were discovered and arrested."

"Would that be worse than being kept from you?"

"But it's only two weeks, Klara."

"Two weeks during which anything might happen!"

"If Europe goes to war, you'll be far safer here."

"My safety!" she said. "What does that mean to me?"

"Think of what it means to me," he said. He kissed her pale forehead, her cheekbones, her mouth. "I can't let you come," he said. "There's no use discussing it. I can't. And very soon I've got to go home and get my things together. My train leaves at half past seven tomorrow. So you've got to think now. You've got to sit down and think about what you'd like to send to Budapest. I can carry letters for you."

"What small consolation!"

"Imagine what comfort a letter will be to your mother." With trembling hands he touched her hair, her shoulders. "And I can speak to her, Klara. I can ask her if she'll allow me to have you for my wife."

She nodded and took his hand, but she was no longer looking at him; it seemed she'd retreated to some small and remote place of self-protection. As they went to the sitting room so she could write, he stood by the open window and watched the sapling chestnuts show the pale undersides of their leaves. The breeze outside smelled of thunderstorm. He knew he was acting for her safety, acting as a husband should. He knew he was doing what was right. Soon she would finish her letters, and then he would kiss her goodbye.

* * *

How could he have known it would be his last night as a resident of Paris? What might he have done, how might he have spent those hours, if he'd known? Would he have walked the streets all night to fix in his mind their unpredictable angles, their smells, their variances of light? Would he have gone to Rosen's flat and shaken him from sleep, bid him luck with his political struggles and with Shalhevet? Would he have gone to see Ben Yakov at his bereft apartment one last time? Would he have gone to Polaner's, crouched at his friend's side and told him what was true: that he loved him as much as he had ever loved a friend, that he owed his life and happiness to him, that he had never felt such exhilaration as when they'd worked together in the studio at night, making something they believed to be daring and good? Would he have taken a last stroll by the Sarah-Bernhardt, that sleeping grande dame, its red velvet seats flocked with dust, its corridors empty and quiet, its dressing rooms still redolent of stage makeup? Would he have crept into Forestier's studio to memorize his catalogue of disappearance and illusion? Would he have gone back through the secret door he knew about in the Cimetière du Montparnasse, back to his studio at school, to run his hands across the familiar smooth surface of his drawing table, the groove of the pencil rail, the mechanical pencils themselves, with their crosshatched finger rests, their hard smooth lead, the satisfying click that signified the end of one unit of work, the beginning of another? Would he have gone back to the rue de Sévigné, his heart's first and last home in Paris, the place where he had first glimpsed Klara Morgenstern with a blue vase in her hands? The place where they had first made love, first argued, first spoken of their children?

But he didn't know. He knew only that he was right to keep Klara from going with him. He would go, and then he would come back to her. No war could keep him from her, no law or regulation. He rolled himself into the blankets they'd shared and thought about her all night. Beside him, on the floor, Tibor slept on a borrowed mattress. There was an unspeakable comfort in the familiar rhythm of his breathing. They might almost have been back in the house in Konyár, both of them home from gimnázium on a weekend, their parents asleep on the other side of the wall, and Mátyás dreaming in his little cot.

All he had was his cardboard suitcase and his leather satchel. It wasn't enough luggage to require a cab. Instead he and Tibor walked to the station, just as they had when Andras had left Budapest two years earlier. When they crossed the Pont au Change he considered turning once more toward Klara's house, but there wasn't time; the train would leave in an hour. He stopped only at a boulangerie to buy bread for the trip. In the windows of the tabac next door, the newspapers proclaimed that Count Csaky, the Hungarian foreign minister, had gone on a secret diplomatic mission to Rome; he'd been sent by the German government, and had gone directly from the airport to a meeting with Mussolini. The Hungarian government had refused to comment on the purpose of the visit, saying only that Hungary was happy to facilitate communication between its allies.

The station was crowded with August travelers, its floor a maze of rucksacks and trunks, boxes and valises. Soon Tibor would get on a train and go back to Italy with Ilana; in the ticket line Andras touched Tibor's sleeve and said, "I wish I could be there to see you married."

Tibor smiled and said, "Me too."

"I couldn't have guessed it would turn out this way for you."

"I didn't dare to hope it would," Tibor said.

"Lucky bastard," Andras said.

"Let's hope it runs in the family," Tibor said. His gaze had drifted toward the front of the line, where a slight, dark-haired woman had opened a wallet to count out notes. Andras felt a pang: She wore her hair the way Klara did, in a loose knot at the nape of her neck. Her summer coat was cut like Klara's, her posture elegant and erect. How cruel of fate, he thought, to place a vision of her before him at that moment.

And then, as she turned to replace the wallet in her valise, it seemed his heart would stop: It was her. She met his eyes with her gray eyes and raised a hand to show him a ticket: She was going with him. Nothing he could say would keep her from it.

PART FOUR

The Invisible Bridge

CHAPTER TWENTY-SIX

Subcarpathia

In January of 1940, Labor Service Company 112/30 of the Hungarian Army was stationed in Carpatho-Ruthenia, somewhere between the towns of Jalová and Stakčin, not far from the Cirocha River. This was the territory Hungary had annexed from Czechoslovakia after Germany had taken back the Sudetenland. It was a craggy wild landscape of scrub-covered peaks and wooded hillsides, snow-filled valleys, frozen rock-choked streams. When Andras had read about the annexation of Ruthenia in the Paris newspapers or seen newsreel footage of its forested hills, the land had been nothing more than an abstraction to him, a pawn in a game of Hitlerian chess. Now he was living under the canopy of a Carpatho-Ruthenian forest, working as a member of a Hungarian Labor Service road-construction crew. After his return to Budapest, all hope of having his visa renewed had quickly evaporated. The clerk at the visa office, his breath reeking of onions and peppers, had met Andras's request with laughter, pointing out that Andras was both a Jew and of military age; his chances of being granted a second two-year visa were comparable to the chances that *he*, Márkus Kovács, would spend his next holiday in Corfu with Lily Pons, ha ha ha. The man's superior, a more sober-minded but equally malodorous man—cigars, sausages, sweat—scrutinized the letter from the École Spéciale and declared, with a patriotic side-glance at the Hungarian flag, that he did not speak French. When Andras translated the letter for him, the superior proclaimed that if the school was so fond of him now, it would still want him after he'd finished his two years of military service. Andras had persisted, going to the office day after day with increasing frustration and urgency. August was coming to an end. They had to get back to Paris. Klara's situation was perilous and could only become more so the longer they stayed. Then, in the first week of September, Europe went to war.

On the flimsiest of pretexts—SS men dressed as Polish soldiers had faked an attack on a German radio station in the border town of Gleiwitz—Hitler sent a million and a half troops and two thousand tanks across the Polish border. The Budapest daily carried photographs of Polish horsemen riding with swords and lances against German panzer divisions. The next day's paper showed a battlefield littered with dismembered horses and the remnants of ancient armor; grinning panzer troops clutched the greaves and breastplates to their chests. The paper reported that the armor would be displayed in a new Museum of Conquest that was under construction in Berlin. A few weeks later, as Germany and Russia negotiated the division of the conquered territory, Andras received his labor-service call-up. It would be another eighteen months before Hungary entered the war, but the draft of Jewish men had begun in July. Andras reported to the battalion offices on Soroksári út, where he learned that his company, the 112/30th, would be deployed to Ruthenia. He was to depart in three weeks' time.

He brought the news to Mátyás at the lingerie shop on Váci utca where he was arranging a new display window. A group of correctly dressed middle-aged ladies watched from the sidewalk as Mátyás draped a line of dress forms with a series of progressively smaller underthings, a chaste burlesque captured in time. When Andras rapped on the glass, Mátyás raised a finger to signal his brother to wait; he finished pinning the back of a lilac slip, then disappeared through an elf-sized door in the display window. A moment later he appeared at the human-sized door of the shop, a tape measure slung over his shoulders, his lapel laddered with pins. Over the past two years he had changed from a rawboned boy into a slim, compact youth; he moved through the mundane ballet of his day with a dancer's unselfconscious grace. At his jawline a perpetual shadow of stubble had emerged, and at his throat the neat small box of an Adam's apple. He had their mother's heavy dark hair and high sharp cheekbones.

"I've got a couple more wire girls to dress," he said. "Why don't you join me? You can give me the news while I'm pinning."

They went into the shop and entered the display window through the elf-sized door. "What do you think?" Mátyás said, turning to a narrow-waisted dress form. "The pink chemise or the blue?" It was his practice to trim his windows during business hours; he found it drew a steady stream of customers demanding to buy the very things he was installing.

"The blue," Andras said, and then, "Can you guess where I'll be in three weeks?"

"Not Paris, I'd imagine."

"Ruthenia, with my labor company."

Mátyás shook his head. "If I were you, I'd run right now. Hop a train back to Paris and beg political asylum. Say you refuse to go into service for a country that takes gifts of land from the Nazis." He sank a pin into the strap of the blue chemise.

"I can't become a fugitive. I'm engaged to be married. And the French borders are closed now, anyway."

"Then go somewhere else. Belgium. Switzerland. You said yourself that Klara's not safe here. Take her with you."

"Ride the rails like vagrants, both of us?"

"Why not? It's a lot better than being shipped off to Ruthenia." But then he straightened from his work and regarded Andras for a long moment, his expression darkening. "You've really got to go, don't you."

"I can't see any way around it. The first deployment's only six months."

"And then you'll have a stingy furlough, and then you'll be sent back for another six months. And then you'll have to do that twice more." Mátyás crossed his arms. "I still think you should run."

"I wish I could, believe me."

"Klara's not going to be too happy about any of this."

"I know. I'm on my way to see her now. She's expecting me at her mother's."

Mátyás cuffed him on the shoulder for luck and held the little door open so he could slip through. He stepped down into the shop and went out through the bigger doors, waving to Mátyás through the glass as he made his way past the women who had gathered to watch. He could scarcely believe it was nearing October and he wasn't on his way back to school; in recent days he'd found himself combing the *Pesti Napló* obsessively for news of Paris. Today's papers had shown a crush at the railway stations as sixteen thousand children were evacuated to the countryside. If he and Klara had remained in France, perhaps they would have left the city too; or perhaps they would have chosen to stay, bracing themselves for whatever was to come. Instead here he was in Budapest, walking along Andrássy út toward the Városliget, toward the tree-shadowed avenues of Klara's childhood. It had come to seem almost ordinary now to spend an afternoon at the house on Benczúr utca, though only a month had passed since they had first arrived in Budapest. At that time they'd been so uncertain about Klara's situation that they'd been afraid even to go to the house; they'd taken a room under Andras's name at a tiny out-of-the-way hotel on Cukor utca, and decided that the best course of action would be to warn Klara's mother of her fugitive daughter's presence in Budapest before Klara herself appeared at the house. The next afternoon he'd gone to Benczúr utca and presented himself to the housemaid as a friend of József's. She had shown him into the same pink-and-gold-upholstered sitting room where he'd passed an uncomfortable hour on the day of his departure for Paris. The younger and elder Mrs. Hász were engaged in a card game at a gilt table by the window, and József was draped over a salmon-colored chair with a book in his lap. When he saw Andras in the doorway, József peeled himself from the chair and delivered the expected jovial greetings, the expected expressions of regret that Andras, too, had been forced to return to Budapest. The younger Mrs. Hász offered a polite nod, the elder a smile of welcome and recognition. But something about Andras's look must have caught Klara's mother's attention, because a moment later she laid her fan of cards on the table and got to her feet.

"Mr. Lévi," she said. "Are you well? You look a bit pale." She crossed the room to take his hand, her expression stoic, as if she were bracing for bad news.

"I'm well," he said. "And so is Klara."

She regarded him with frank surprise, and József's mother rose too. "Mr. Lévi," she began, and paused, apparently unsure of how she might caution him without revealing too much to her son.

"Who is Klara?" József said. "Surely you don't mean Klara Hász?"

"I do," Andras said. And he explained how he'd carried a letter to Klara from her mother two years earlier, and then how he'd been introduced to her. "She lives under the name of Morgenstern now. You know her daughter. Elisabet."

József sat down slowly on the damask chair, looking as though Andras had struck him with a fist. "Elisabet?" he said. "Do you mean to say that Elisabet Morgenstern is Klara's daugher? Klara, my lost aunt?" And then he must have remembered the rumors of what had existed between Andras and the mother of Elisabet Morgenstern, because he seemed to focus more sharply on Andras, staring at him as if he'd never seen him before.

"Why have you come?" the younger Mrs. Hász asked. "What is it you want to tell us?"

And finally Andras broke the news he had come to deliver: that Klara was not only well, but here in Budapest, staying at a hotel in the Ferencváros. As soon as he'd spoken, Klara's mother's eyes filled with tears; then her expression became overshadowed with terror. Why, she asked, had Klara had undertaken such a terrible risk?

"I'm afraid I'm partly to blame," Andras said. "I had to return to Budapest myself. And Klara and I are engaged to be married."

At those words, a kind of pandemonium broke upon the sitting room. József's mother lost her composure entirely; in a panic-laced soprano she demanded to know how such a thing could have come to pass, and then she declared that she didn't want to know, that it was absurd and unthinkable. She called the housemaid and asked for her heart medication, and then told József to fetch his father from the bank immediately. A moment later she retracted the command on the basis that György's hasty exit in the middle of the day might raise unnecessary suspicion. Meanwhile, the elder Mrs. Hász implored Andras to tell her where Klara might be found, whether she was safe, and how she might be visited. Andras, at the center of this maelstrom, began to wonder whether he would emerge on the other side of it still engaged to Klara, or if her brother and his wife could exercise some esoteric power that would nullify any attachment between a member of Klara's class and one of his own. Already József Hász was looking at Andras with an unfamiliar, perhaps even a hostile expression—of confusion, betrayal, and, most disturbingly to Andras, distrust.

Soon it became clear that the elder Mrs. Hász could not be prevented from going to Klara at once. She had already called for the car; she wanted Andras to accompany her. The chauffeur would drive them halfway to the tiny hotel on Cukor utca, and they would walk the remaining blocks. József, without a parting word to Andras, took his mother upstairs to tend to her nerves. Klara's mother gave Andras a single look that seemed to indicate how ridiculous she considered her daughter-in-law's behavior to be. She threw a coat over her dress and they ran outside to the waiting car. As they drove through the streets she begged him to tell her if Klara were well, and what she looked like now, and, finally, whether she wanted to see her mother.

"More than anything," Andras said. "You must know that."

"Eighteen years!" she said in a half whisper, and then fell silent, overcome.

A few moments later the car let them out at the base of Andrássy út, and Andras put a hand on Mrs. Hász's elbow as they hurried through the streets. Her hair loosened from its knot as she went, and her hastily tied scarf fell from her neck; Andras caught the square of violet silk in his fingertips as they entered the narrow lobby of the hotel. At the foot of the cast-iron stair a wordless trepidation seemed to take Klara's mother. She climbed the steps with a slow and deliberate tread, as though she needed time to rehearse in her mind a few of her thousand imaginings of this moment. When Andras indicated that they'd reached the correct floor, she followed him down the hall without a word and watched gravely as he took the key from his pocket. He unlocked the door and pushed it open. There was Klara at the window in her fawn-colored dress, midmorning light falling across her face, a handkerchief crushed in her hand. Her mother approached like a somnambulist; she went to the window, took Klara's hands, touched her face, pronounced her name. Klara, trembling, laid her head on her mother's shoulder and wept. And there they stood in shuddering silence as Andras watched. Here was the reverse of what he'd witnessed a few weeks earlier at Elisabet's embarkation: a vanished child returned, the intangible made real. He knew the reunion was taking place on the shabby top floor of a cramped hotel room on an unlovely street in Budapest, but he felt he was witnessing a kind of unearthly reconnection, a conjunction so stunning he had to turn away. Here was the closing of the distance between Klara's past life and her present; it seemed not unthinkable that he and she might enter a new life together now. At that time his difficulties at the Budapest visa office had not yet begun. The French border was still open. All seemed possible.

Now, four weeks later, what he had learned for certain was that he wouldn't return to Paris as they'd hoped. Worse than that: He'd soon be sent far away from Klara, into a distant and unknown forest. When he arrived at Benczúr utca that afternoon with the news he'd just delivered to his brother—that he was to be deployed to Carpatho-Ruthenia in three weeks' time—he found to his relief that no one was awaiting him besides Klara herself. She'd asked to have tea served in her favorite upstairs room, a pretty boudoir with a window seat that faced the garden. When she was a child, she told Andras, this was where she had come when she wanted to be alone. She called it the Rabbit Room because of the beautiful Dürer engraving that hung above the mantel: a young hare posed in half profile, its soft-furred haunches bunched, its ears rotated back. She'd lit a fire in the grate and requested pastries for their tea. But once he told her what he'd learned at the battalion office, they could only sit in silence and stare at the plate of walnut and poppyseed strudel.

"You've got to get home as soon as the French border opens again," he said, finally. "It terrifies me to think of the danger you're in."

"Paris won't be safer," she said. "It could be bombed at any time."

"You could go to the countryside with Mrs. Apfel. You could go to Nice."

She shook her head. "I won't leave you here. We're going to be married."

"But it's madness to stay," he said. "Sooner or later they'll learn who you are."

"There's nothing for me in Paris now. Elisabet's gone. You're here. And my mother, and György. I can't go back, Andras."

"What about your friends, your students, the rest of your life?"

She shook her head. "France is at war. My students are gone to the countryside. I'd have to close the school in any case, at least for a time. Perhaps the war will be a short one. With any luck it'll be over before you finish your military service. Then you'll get another visa and we'll go home together."

"And all that time you'll stay here, in peril?"

"I'll live quietly under your surname. No one will have reason to come looking for me. I'll rent the apartment and studio in Paris and take a little place in the Jewish Quarter here. Maybe I'll teach a few private students."

He sighed and rubbed his face with both hands. "This will be the death of me," he said. "Thinking of you living in Budapest, outside the law."

"I was living outside the law in Paris."

"But the law was so much farther away!"

"I won't leave you here in Hungary," she said. "That's all."

He had never dared to imagine that he and Klara might be married at the Dohány Street Synagogue, nor that his parents and Mátyás might be there to witness it; he had certainly never dreamed that Klara's family might be there, too—her mother, who had shed her widow's garb for a column of rose-colored silk, weeping with joy; the younger Mrs. Hász tight-lipped and erect in a drooping Vionnet gown; Klara's brother, György, his affection for Klara having overcome whatever reservations he might have had about Andras, striding about with as much bluster and anxiety as if he were the bride's father; and József Hász, watching the proceedings with silent detachment. Their wedding canopy was Lucky Béla's prayer shawl, and Klara's wedding ring the simple gold band that had belonged to Béla's mother. They were married on an October afternoon in the synagogue courtyard. A grand ceremony in the sanctuary was out of the question. There could be nothing public about their union except the paperwork that would place the bride's name at a still-farther remove from the Klara Hász she had once been. She couldn't become a citizen, thanks to a new anti-Jewish law that had been passed in

May, but she could still legally change her surname to Andras's, and apply for a residence permit under that veil. Andras's father himself read the marriage contract aloud, his rabbinical-school training in Aramaic having prepared him for the role. And Andras's mother, shy before the few assembled guests, presented the glass to be broken under Andras's foot.

What no one mentioned—not during the wedding itself, nor during the luncheon at Benczúr utca that followed—was Andras's imminent departure for Carpatho-Ruthenia. But the awareness of it ran underneath every event of the day like an elegy. József, it turned out, had been saved from a similar fate; the Hász family had managed to secure his exemption from labor service by bribing a government official. The exemption had come at a price proportionate to the Hászes' wealth: They had been forced to give the government official their chalet on Lake Balaton, where Klara had spent her childhood summers. József's student visa had been renewed and he would return to France as soon as the borders opened, though no one knew when that might be, nor whether France would admit citizens of countries allied with Germany. Andras's parents were in no position to buy him an exemption. The lumberyard barely supplied their existence. Klara had suggested that her brother might help, but Andras refused to discuss the possibility. There was the danger, first of all, of alerting the government authorities to the link between Andras and the Hász family; nor did Andras want to be a financial burden to György. In desperation, Klara suggested selling her apartment and studio in Paris, but Andras wouldn't let her consider that either. The apartment on the rue de Sévigné was her home. If her situation in Hungary became more precarious, she would have to return there at once by whatever means possible. And there was a less practical element to the decision too: As long as Klara owned the apartment and studio, they could imagine themselves back in Paris someday. Andras would endure his two years in the work service; by then, as Klara had said, the war might be over, and they could return to France.

For a few sweet hours, during the wedding festivities on Benczúr utca, Andras found it possible almost to forget about his impending departure. In a large gallery that had been cleared of furniture, he was lifted on a chair beside his new bride while a pair of musicians played Gypsy music. Afterward, he and Mátyás and their father danced together, holding each other by the arms and spinning until they stumbled. József Hász, who could not resist the role of host even at a wedding of which he seemed to disapprove, kept everyone's champagne glasses full. And Mátyás, in the tradition of making the bride and groom laugh, performed a Chaplinesque tap dance that involved a collapsing cane and a top hat that kept leaping away. Klara cried with laughter. Her pale forehead had flushed pink, and dark curls sprang from her chignon. But it was impossible for Andras to forget entirely that all of this was fleeting, that soon he would have to kiss his new bride goodbye and board a train for Carpatho-Ruthenia. Nor would his joy have been uncomplicated in any case. He couldn't ignore the younger Mrs. Hász's coldness, nor the reminders on all sides of how different Klara's early life had been from his own. His mother, elegant as she was in her gray gown, seemed afraid to handle the delicate Hász champagne flutes; his father had little to say to Klara's brother, and even less to say to József. If Tibor had been there, Andras thought, he might have found a way to bridge the divide. But Tibor was absent, of course, as were three others, the lack of whom made the day's events seem somehow unreal: Polaner and Rosen, who had nonetheless sent telegrams of congratulations, and Ben Yakov, from whom there had been continued silence. He knew Klara was experiencing her own private pain in the midst of her happiness: She must have been thinking of her father, and of Elisabet, thousands of miles away.

The war was discussed, and Hungary's possible role in it. Now that Poland had fallen, György Hász said, England and France might pressure Germany into a cease-fire before Hungary could be forced to come to the aid of its ally. It seemed to

Andras a far-fetched idea, but the day demanded an optimistic view. It was mid-October, one of the last warm afternoons of the year. The plane trees were filled with slanting light, and a gold haze pooled in the garden like a flood of honey. As the sun slipped toward the edge of the garden wall, Klara took Andras's hand and led him outside. She brought him to a corner of the garden behind a privet hedge, where a marble bench stood beneath a fall of ivy. He sat down and took her onto his lap. The skin of her neck was warm and damp, the scent of roses mingled with the faint mineral tang of her sweat. She inclined her face to his, and when he kissed her she tasted of wedding cake.

That was the moment that came back to him again and again, those nights in the foothills of the Carpathian Mountains. That moment, and the ones that came afterward in their suite at the Gellért Hotel. Their honeymoon had been a brief one: three days, that was all. Now it sustained him like bread: the moment they'd registered at the hotel as husband and wife; the look of relief she'd given him when they were alone in the room together at last; her surprising shyness in their bridal bed; the curve of her naked back in the tangled sheets when they woke in the morning; the wedding ring a surprising new weight on his hand. It seemed an incongruous luxury to wear the ring now as he worked, not just because of the contrast of the gold with the dirt and grayness of everything around him, but because it seemed part of their intimacy, sweetly private. *Ani l'dodi v'dodi li*, she had said in Hebrew when she'd given it to him, a line from the Song of Songs: *I am my beloved's and my beloved is mine.* He was hers and she was his, even here in Carpatho-Ruthenia.

He and his workmates lived on an abandoned farm in an abandoned hamlet near a stone quarry that had long since given up all the granite anyone cared to take from it. He didn't know how long ago the farm had been deserted by its inhabitants; the barn held only the faintest ghost odor of animals. Fifty men slept in the barn, twenty in a converted chicken house, thirty in the stables, and fifty more in a newly constructed barracks. The platoon captains and the company commander and the doctor and the work foremen slept in the farmhouse, where they had real beds and indoor plumbing. In the barn, each man had a metal cot and a bare mattress stuffed with hay. At the foot of each cot was a wooden kit box stamped with its owner's identification number. The food was meager but steady: coffee and bread in the morning, potato soup or beans at noon, more soup and more bread at night. They had clothing enough to keep them warm: overcoats and winter uniforms, woolen underthings, woolen socks, stiff black boots. Their overcoats, shirts, and trousers were nearly identical to the uniforms worn by the rest of the Hungarian Army. The only difference was the green *M* sewn onto their lapels, for Munkaszolgálat, the labor service. No one ever said *Munkaszolgálat*, though; they called it *Musz*, a single resentful syllable. In the Musz, his company-mates told him, you were just like any other member of the military; the difference was that your life was worth even *less* than shit. In the Musz, they said, you got paid the same as any other enlisted man: just enough for your family to starve on. The Musz wasn't bent on killing you, just on using you until you wanted to kill yourself. And of course there was the other difference: Everyone in his labor-service company was Jewish. The Hungarian Ministry of Defense considered it dangerous to let Jews bear arms. The military classified them as unreliable, and sent them to cut trees, to build roads and bridges, to erect army barracks for the troops who would be stationed in Ruthenia.

There were privileges Andras hadn't foreseen. Because he was married, he received extra pay and a housing-assistance stipend. He had a pay book stamped with the Hungarian royal seal; he was paid twice a month in government checks. He could send and receive letters and packages, though everything was subject to inspection. And because he had his baccalaureate, he was given the status of labor-service officer. He was the leader of his squad of twenty men. He had an officer's cap and a double-chevron badge on his pocket, and the other members of the squad had to salute and call him sir. He had to take roll and organize the night watch. His twenty men had to address their special requests or problems to him; he would adjudicate in cases of disagreement. Twice a week he had to report to the company commander on the status of his squad.

The 112/30th had been sent to clear a swath of forest where a road would be built in the spring. In the morning they rose in the dark and washed in snowmelt water; they dressed and shoved their feet into cold-hardened boots. In the dim red glow of the woodstove they drank bitter coffee and ate their ration of bread. There were morning calisthenics: push-ups, side bends, squat jumps. Then, at the sergeant's command, they formed a marching block in the courtyard, their axes slung over their shoulders like rifles, and struck out through the dark toward the work site.

The one miracle afforded to Andras in that place was the identity of his work partner. It was none other than Mendel Horovitz, who had spent six years at school with Andras in Debrecen, and who had broken the Hungarian record in the hundred-meter dash and the long jump in the 1936 Olympic trials. For all of ten minutes, Mendel had been a member of the Hungarian Olympic Team—after his final jump, someone had draped an official jacket around his shoulders and had led him to a registration table, where the team secretary was recording the personal information of all the athletes who had qualified. But the third question, after *name* and *city of origin*, had been *religion*, and that was where Mendel had failed. He had known in advance, of course, that Jews weren't allowed to participate; he'd gone to the trials as a form of protest, and in the wild hope that they might make an exception for him. They hadn't, of course, a decision the team officials later came to regret: Mendel's hundred-meter record was a tenth of a second shy of Jesse Owens's gold-medal time.

When Mendel and Andras first saw each other at the Labor Service rail yard in Budapest, there was so much back-slapping and exclamation that they had each begun their time in the

Munkaszolgálat with a comportment demerit. Mendel had a craggy face and a wry *V* of a mouth and eyebrows like the feathery antennae of moths. He'd been born in Zalaszabar and educated at the Debrecen Gimnázium at the expense of a maternal uncle who insisted that his protégé train for a future as a mathematician. But Mendel had no inclination toward mathematic abstraction; nor did he aspire to a career in athletics, despite his talents. What he wanted was to be a journalist. After the Olympic team disappointment, he'd gotten a copyediting job at the evening paper, the *Budapest Esti Kurír*. Soon he'd started penning his own columns, satirical journalistic petits-fours which he slipped into the editor's mailbox under a pen name and which occasionally saw print. He'd been working at the *Esti Kurír* for a year before he was conscripted, having survived a round of firings that followed the new six percent quota on Jewish members of the press. Andras found him remarkably sanguine about having been shipped off to Subcarpathia. He liked being in the mountains, he said, liked being outside and working with his hands. He didn't even mind the relentless labor of woodcutting.

Andras might not have minded it himself had the tools been sharp and the food more plentiful, the season warm and the job a matter of choice. For every tree they cut at the vast work site in the forest, there was a kind of satisfying ritual. Mendel would make the first notch with the axe, and Andras would fit the crosscut saw into the groove. Then they would both take their handles and lean into the work. There was a sweet-smelling spray of sawdust as they breached the outer rings, and more friction as the blade of the saw sank into the bole. They had to shove thin steel wedges into the gap to keep it open; near the center, where the wood grew denser, the blade would start to shriek. Sometimes it took half an hour to get through thirty centimeters of core. Then there was the double-time march to the other side, the completion of the struggle. When they had a few centimeters to go, they inserted more wedges and withdrew the saw. Mendel would shout *All clear!* and give the tree a shove. Next came a series of creaking groans, momentum traveling the length of the trunk, the upper branches shouldering past their neighbors. That was the true death of the tree, Andras thought, the instant it ceased to be an upward-reaching thing, the moment it became what they were making it: *timber.* The falling tree would push a great rush of wind before it; the branches cut the air with a hundred-toned whistle as the tree arced to the ground. When the trunk hit, the forest floor thrummed with the incredible weight of it, a shock that traveled through the soles of Andras's boots and up through his bones to the top of his head, where it ricocheted in his skull like a gunshot. A reverberant moment followed, the silent Kaddish of the tree. And into that emptiness would rush the foreman's shouted commands: *All right, men! Go! Keep moving!* The branches had to be chopped for firewood, the bare trunks dragged to massive flatbed trucks for transportation to a railway station, from which they would be sent to mainland Hungary.

He and Mendel made a good team. They were among the fastest of their workmates, and had earned the foreman's praise. But there could be little satisfaction in any of it under the circumstances. He had been lifted out of his life, separated not just from Klara but from everything else that had mattered to him for the past two years. In October, while he was supposed to have been consulting with Le Corbusier over plans for a sports club in India, he was felling trees. In November, when he should have been constructing projects for the third-year exhibition, he was felling trees. And in December, when he would have been taking his midyear exams, he was felling trees. The war, he knew, would have disrupted the academic year temporarily, but it would likely have resumed by now; Polaner and Rosen and Ben Yakov—and worse, those sneering men who had taunted him after the Prix du Amphithéâtre—would be sailing on toward their degrees, translating imagined buildings into sharp black lines on drafting paper. His friends would still be meeting nightly at the Blue Dove for drinks, living in the Quartier Latin, carrying on their lives.

Or so he imagined, until Klara sent a packet of letters that contained missives from Paris. Polaner, Andras learned, had joined the Foreign Legion. *If only you could have enlisted with me,* he wrote. *I'm training at the École Militaire now. This week I learned to shoot a rifle. For the first time in my life I have a burning desire to operate firearms. The newspapers carry frequent reports of horrors: SS Einsatzgruppen rounding up professors, artists, boy scouts, executing them in town squares. Polish Jews being loaded onto trains and relocated to miserable swamplands around Lublin. My parents are still in Kraków for now, though Father has lost his factory. I'll fight the Reich and die if I have to.*

Rosen, it had turned out, was planning to emigrate to Palestine with Shalhevet. *The city's dead boring without you,* he'd scrawled in his loose script. *Also, I find I've no patience for my studies. With Europe at war, school seems futile. But I won't throw myself in front of tanks like Polaner. I'd rather stay alive and work. Shalhevet thinks we can set up a charitable foundation to get Jews out of Europe. Find wealthy Americans to fund it. She's a bright girl. Perhaps she'll make it happen. If all goes well, we leave in May. From now on I'm going to write to you only in Hebrew.*

Ben Yakov, mentally exhausted by the events of the previous year, had taken a leave of absence from school and decamped to his parents' home in Rouen. The news came not from him but from Rosen, who predicted that Ben Yakov would soon try to contact Andras himself. Sure enough, enclosed in the same packet of letters was a telegram sent to Klara's address in Budapest: ANDRAS: NO HARD FEELINGS BETWEEN US. DESPITE ALL, EVER YOUR FRIEND. GOD KEEP YOU SAFE. BEN YAKOV.

Klara herself wrote weekly. Her official residence permit had arrived without event; as far as the government was concerned she was Claire Lévi, the French-born wife of a Hungarian labor serviceman. She had rented her apartment on the rue de Sévigné to a Polish composer who had fled to Paris; the composer knew a ballet teacher who would be glad to have a new studio, so the practice space was rented too. Klara was living now in an apartment on Király utca and had found a studio, as she'd hoped. She had taken on a few private students, and might soon begin to teach small classes. She was living a life of quiet seclusion, seeing her mother daily, walking in the park with her brother on Sunday afternoons; they had gone together to visit the grave of her teacher Viktor Romankov, who had died of a stroke after twenty years of teaching at the Royal Ballet School. Budapest was cobwebbed with memories, she wrote. Sometimes she forgot entirely that she was a grown woman; she would find herself wandering toward the house on Benczúr utca, expecting to find her father still alive, her brother a tall young gimnázium student, her girlhood room intact. At times she was melancholy, and most of all she missed Andras. But he must not fear for her. She was well. All seemed safe.

He worried still, of course, but it was a comfort to hear from her—to hear at least that she felt safe, or safe enough to tell him so. He always kept her most recent letter in his overcoat pocket. When a new one came, he would move the old one to his kit box and add it to the sheaf he kept tied with her green hair-ribbon. He had their wedding photograph in a marbled folder from Pomeranz and Sons. He counted the days before his furlough, counted and counted, through what seemed the longest winter of his life.

In spring the forest filled with the scent of black earth and the dawn-to-dusk cacophony of birdsong. Overnight, new curtains appeared in the windows of the empty houses along the way to the work site. There were children in the fields, bicyclists on the roads, the smell of grilled sausage from the roadside inns. The promised furlough had been postponed until the end of summer; there was too much work, their commander told them, to allow any of their company a break. *Thank God the winter's over,* his mother wrote. *Every day I worried. My Andráska in those mountains, in that terrible cold. I know you are strong, but a mother imagines the worst. Now I can imagine something better: You are warm, your work is easier, and before long you will be home.* In the same circlet of foothills where Andras and his workmates had suffered endless months of labor, Hungarians now gathered to take the air and eat berries with fresh cream and swim in the freezing lakes. But for the labor servicemen, the work went on. Now that the ground had thawed and softened, now that the trees in the path of the road had been cleared, Labor Company 112/30 had to uproot the giant stumps so the roadbed might be leveled, the gravel spread for the road. The summer months appeared on the horizon with their promise of hot days amid asphalt and tar. The solstice came and went. It seemed nothing would ever change. Then, in early July, another packet of letters came from Klara, and with it news of Tibor and of France.

Tibor and Ilana had been married in May, after a long engagement and a period of reconciliation with her parents. A certain Rabbi di Samuele had interceded on behalf of the couple. He had proved such a good intermediary that Ilana's mother and father had at last invited Tibor to Shabbos dinner. *Even so,* Tibor wrote, *I thought her father would punch me in the eye. I was the villain, you see, not Ben Yakov; I was the man who had accompanied their daughter on the train. Every time I ventured a comment on a point of biblical interpretation, her father laughed as if my ignorance delighted him. Ilana's mother deliberately neglected to pass me food. Halfway through the meal, the Holy One made a risky intervention: Ilana's father fell out of his chair, half dead of a heart attack. I kept him alive with chest compressions until a real doctor was called in. In the end he survived; I was the hero of the evening; Signor and Signora di Sabato changed their views. Ilana and I were married within the month. We returned to Hungary when my visa expired and have been living here in Budapest, not far from your own lovely bride, doing what we can to keep her company and to get my papers in order for a return to Italy. I have brought my Ilana to meet Anya and Apa. They loved her, she loved them, and our father became tipsy and encouraged us at the end of the evening to go make grandchildren. As for our younger brother, he continues to run wild. This month he makes his debut at the Pineapple Club, where people will pay good money to see him tap-dance atop a white piano. Somehow he has also managed to pass his baccalaureate exams. He is still arranging shop windows and has more clients than he can serve. His girlfriend, however, has deserted him for a scoundrel. He sends his regards and the enclosed photo.* The photo showed Mátyás in top hat, white tie, and tails, a cane in his hand, one foot cocked over the other to flash a glint of tap metal at the sole.

My thoughts are with you always, Tibor wrote. *I hope you will never have use for the medical supplies I'm sending with this letter, but just in case, I have made an attempt to assemble a field hospital in miniature. Meanwhile I remain, in continual fear for your safety and belief in your fortitude, your loving brother,* TIBOR.

The next letter was from Mátyás, dated May 29 and written in an angry scrawl. *I've been called up,* he informed Andras. *The stinking bastards. They'll never make me work for them. Horthy says he will protect the Jews. Liar! My gimnázium friend Gyula Kohn died in the labor service last month. He had a pain in his side and a fever but they sent him to work anyway. It was appendicitis. He died three days later. He was my age, nineteen.*

The final letter was from Klara herself, with a newspaper clipping that showed the German Eighteenth Army marching through the streets of Paris, and an enormous Nazi flag hanging from the Hotel de Ville. Andras sat on his cot and stared at the photographs. He thought of his first brief passage through Germany what seemed a geologic age ago—his stopover in Stuttgart, when he'd tried to buy bread at a bakery that did not serve Jews. That was where he'd seen the red flag hanging from the façade of the train station, a blast of National Socialist fervor five stories high. He refused to believe what the attached article told him: that the same flag now flew from every official building in

Paris; that Paul Reynaud, successor to Daladier, had resigned; that the new premier, Philippe Pétain, had declared that France would collaborate with Hitler in the formation of a New Europe. Even *Liberté, Egalité, Fraternité* had been replaced with a new slogan: *Travail, Famille, Patrie.* There was a rumor that all Jews who had volunteered for the French Army would be removed from their battalions and imprisoned in concentration camps, from which they would be deported to the East.

Polaner. He said it aloud into the damp hay-smelling air of the bunk. His eyes burned. Here he was, thousands of miles away, and helpless; there was nothing he could do, nothing anyone could do. Already Hitler had what he wanted of Poland. He had Luxembourg and Belgium and the Netherlands, he had Czechoslovakia and Yugoslavia, he had Italy as a member of the Tripartite Pact; he had Hungary as an ally, and now he had France. He would win the war, and what would happen to the Jews of the conquered nations? Would he force them to emigrate, deport them to marshlands at the center of ravaged Poland? It was impossible to conceive of what might happen.

He went out into the moonlit yard to read Klara's letter. It was a humid night; a mist hovered in the assembly field, where the grass had grown shaggy with the June rains. The soldier stationed beside the barn door tipped his hat at Andras. They were all familiar with each other by now, and no one really thought anyone would try to desert. There was nowhere to go, here in Carpatho-Ruthenia. They would all be granted their first furlough soon, in any case—free transport to Budapest. Andras chose one of the large stones at the edge of the assembly field, where the moonlight came in strong and white through a few crumpled handkerchiefs of cloud.

My dear Andráska,
France has fallen. I can scarcely believe the words as I write
them. It is a tragedy, a horror. The world has lost its mind. Mrs.

Apfel writes that all of Paris has fled to the south. I am fortunate indeed to be here in Hungary now, rather than in France under the Nazi flag.

I was grateful for your letter of May 15. What a vast relief to know you're well and have gotten through the winter. Now it is only a few months before you'll be here. In the meantime, know that I am well—or as well as I can be without you. I have twenty-five students now. All of them talented children, all Jewish. What will become of them, Andras? I do not speak of my fears, of course; we practice and they improve.

Mother is well. György and Elza are well. József is well. Your brothers are well. We are all well! That is what one must write in letters. But you know how we are, my love. We are full of apprehension. Our lives are shadowed by uncertainty. You are always in my thoughts: That, at least, is certain. The days cannot pass fast enough until I see you.

With love, Your K.

CHAPTER TWENTY-SEVEN

The Snow Goose

ALL SUMMER he sustained himself with the thought that he'd soon be with her—close enough to touch and smell and taste her, at liberty to lie in bed with her all day if he wanted, to tell her everything that had happened during the long months of his absence, and to hear what had been in her mind while he'd been away. He thought of seeing his mother and father, of taking her to their house in Konyár for the first time, of strolling with his parents and his wife through the apple orchards and into the flat grasslands. He thought, too, of seeing Tibor, who hadn't managed to get his student visa renewed after all, and was now stranded in Hungary with Ilana. But in August, when Andras's postponed furlough was due, Germany gave Hungary the gift of Northern Transylvania. The Carpathians, that white ridge of granite between the civilized West and the wild East, Europe's natural barrier against its vast Communist neighbor: Horthy wanted it, even at the price of a deeper friendship with Germany; Hitler delivered it, and soon afterward the friendship was formalized by Hungary's entry into the Tripartite Pact. The 112/30th, having completed its road-building assignment in Subcarpathia ahead of schedule, was shipped off by railway car to Transylvania. There, in the virgin forest between Mármaros-Sziget and Borsa, the company embarked on a tree-clearing and ditch-digging project that was supposed to last through the rest of fall and winter.

When the weather began to grow cold again, it occurred to him that it had been a year, *a year*, since he'd seen Klara. Of their married life they'd spent a week together. Every night in the barracks, men lay weeping or cursing over the loss of their girlfriends, their fiancées, their wives, women who had loved them but who'd grown tired of waiting. What assurance did he have that Klara wouldn't tire of her solitude? She had always surrounded herself with people; her social circle in Paris had consisted of actors and dancers, writers and composers, people who offered her unstinting stimulation. What would keep her from making ties like that in Budapest? And once she did, what would prevent her from turning toward one of her new friends for more tangible comfort? The specter of Zoltán Novak appeared to Andras one night in a dream, walking barefoot through Wesselényi utca in his smoking jacket, toward the Dohány Street Synagogue, where a woman who might have been Klara was waiting for him in the gloomy courtyard. Surely, Novak would have heard that she'd returned; surely he would try to see her. Perhaps he already had. Perhaps she was with him that moment, in some room he'd taken for their assignations.

At times Andras felt as though the work service were causing his mind to float away, piece by piece, like ashes from a fire. What would be left of him, he wondered, once he returned to Budapest? For months he'd struggled to keep his mind sharp as he worked, tried to design buildings and bridges on the slate of his brain when he couldn't draw them on paper, tried to sing himself the French names of architectural features to keep himself awake as he slung mud with his shovel or hacked branches with his axe. *Porte, fenêtre, corniche, balcon*, a magic spell against mental deterioration. Now, as the prospect of a furlough slipped farther into the distance, his thoughts became a source of torment. He imagined Klara with Novak or with her memories of Sándor Goldstein; he thought about the grim progress of the war, which had gone on now for more than a year. In a series of newspaper clippings that his father sent, he read about the brutal bombardment of London, the attack by Luftwaffe planes every night for fifty-seven nights. And as the war burned on in England, he and his workmates fought a smaller war against the ravages of the Munkaszolgálat. Gradually, man by man, the 112/30th was crumbling: One man broke a leg and had to be sent home, another had a diabetic seizure and died, a third shot himself with an officer's gun after learning that his fiancée had given birth to another man's child. Mátyás was in the labor service now, and Tibor had just been called. Andras had heard stories of labor-service companies being sent to clear minefields in Ukraine. He imagined Mátyás in a field at dawn, making his way through a fog; in his hand a stick, a broken branch, with which to prod the ground in search of mines.

In December, when a string of blizzards scoured the mountains and the workers were often confined to the bunkhouse, Andras fell into a paralyzing depression. Instead of reading or writing letters or drawing in his damp-swollen sketchbook, he lay in bed and nursed the mysterious bruises that had begun to appear beneath his skin. He was supposed to be a leader; nominally he was still squad captain, and he still had to march the men to the assembly field and supervise the cleaning of the barracks and the maintenance of the woodstove and all the small details of their straitened lives; but more and more often he felt as if they were leading him while he trailed behind, his boots filling with snow. He hardly took notice when, one Sunday afternoon during a grinding blizzard, Mendel Horovitz conceived the idea of a Munkaszolgálat newspaper. Mendel scratched away at a series of ideas in a notebook, then borrowed a sheaf of paper and a typewriter from one of the officers so he could make the thing look official. He was not a swift typist; it took him three nights to finish two pages of articles. He typed at all hours. The men threw boots at him to stop the racket, but his desire to finish the paper exceeded his fear of flying objects. He worked every day for a week, every chance he had.

When at last he'd finished typing, he brought his pages to Andras and sat down on the edge of his cot. Outside, the wind set up a noise like the wailing of foxes. It was the third consecutive day of the worst-yet storm of the season, and the snow had reached the high windows of the bunkhouse. Work had been cancelled that day. While the other men mended their uniforms or smoked damp cigarettes or talked by the stove, Andras lay in bed, staring at the ceiling and pushing at his teeth with his tongue. His back teeth felt frighteningly loose, his gums spongy. Earlier that day he'd had a slow nosebleed that had lasted for hours. He wasn't in the mood to talk. He didn't care what was typed on the pages Mendel held in his hand. He pulled the coarse blanket over his head and turned away.

"All right, Parisi," Mendel said, and pulled the blanket down. "Enough sulking." Parisi: It was Mendel's nickname for him; he was envious of Andras's time in France, and had wanted to hear about it in detail—particularly about evenings at József's, and the backstage drama of the Sarah-Bernhardt, and the romantic exploits of Andras's friends.

"Leave me alone," Andras said.

"I can't. I need your help."

Andras sat up in bed. "Look at me," he said, holding out his arms. Clusters of blood-violets bloomed beneath the skin. "I'm sick. I don't know what's wrong with me. Do I look like a person who can be of help to anyone?"

"You're the squad captain," Mendel said. "It's your duty."

"I don't want to be squad captain anymore."

"I'm afraid that's not up to you, Parisi."

Andras sighed. "What is it, exactly, that you want me to do?"

"I want you to illustrate the newspaper." He dropped his typed pages onto Andras's lap. "Nothing fancy. None of your art-school nonsense. Just some crude drawings. I've left space for you around the articles." He deposited a modest cache of pencils into Andras's hand, some of them colored.

Andras couldn't remember the last time he'd seen colored pencils. These were sharp and clean and unbroken, a small revelation in the smoky dark of the bunkhouse.

"Where did you get these?" he asked.

"Stole them from the office."

Andras pushed himself up onto his elbows. "What do you call that rag of yours?"

"The Snow Goose."

"All right. I'll take a look. Now leave me alone."

In addition to news of the war, *The Snow Goose* had weather reports *(Monday: Snow. Tuesday: Snow. Wednesday: Snow.)*; a fashion column *(Report from a Fashion Show at Dawn: The dreaming labor workers lined up in handsome suits of coarse blanket, this winter's most stylish fabric. Mangold Béla Kolos, Budapest's premier fashion dictator, predicts that this picturesque style will spread throughout Hungary in no time)*; a sports page *(The Golden Youth of Transylvania love the sporting life. Yesterday at 5:00 a.m., the woods were full of youth disporting themselves at today's most popular amusements: wheelbarrow-pushing, snow-shoveling, and tree-felling)*; an advice column *(Dear Miss Coco: I'm a twenty-year-old woman. Will it hurt my reputation if I spend the night in the officers' quarters? Love, Virgin. Dear Virgin: Your question is too general. Please describe your plans in detail so I can give an appropriate reply. Love, Miss Coco)*; travel ads *(Bored? Want a change of scene? Try our deluxe tour of rural Ukraine!)*; and in honor of Andras, an article about a feat of architecture *(Engineering Marvel! Paris-trained architect-engineer Andras Lévi has designed an invisible bridge. The materials are remarkably lightweight and it can be constructed in almost no time. It is undetectable by enemy forces. Tests suggest that the design of the bridge may still need some refinement; a battalion of the Hungarian Army mysteriously plunged into a chasm while crossing. Some argue, however, that the bridge has already attained its perfect form)*. And then there was the pièce de résistance, the Ten Commandments à la Munkaszolgálat:

1. IF THOU MAKEST A GRAVE MISTAKE, THOU SHALT NOT TELL. THOU SHALT LET OTHERS TAKE THE BLAME FOR THEE.

2. THOU SHALT NOT SHARPEN THINE OWN SAW. LEAVE THE SHARPENING TO WHOMSOEVER MAY USE IT NEXT.

3. THOU SHALT NOT BOTHER TO WASH THYSELF. THY WORKMATES STINKETH ANYWAY.

4. WHEN THOU STANDEST IN LINE FOR LUNCH, THOU SHALT ELBOW TO THE FRONT. OTHERWISE THOU GETTEST NOT THE SINGLE POTATO IN THE SOUP.

5. ON THE WAY TO WORK, THOU SHALT DISAPPEAR. LET THE FOREMAN FIND SOMEONE ELSE TO REPLACE THEE.

6. IF THOU COVETEST THY NEIGHBOR'S THINGS, KEEPEST THINE OWN COUNSEL. IF THOU DOST NOT, THY NEIGHBOR'S THINGS MAY DISAPPEAR BEFORE THOU CANST STEAL THEM.

7. IF THY WORKMATE IS NAÏVE, THOU SHALT BORROW EVERYTHING FROM HIM AND NEGLECT TO RETURN IT.

8. WHEN THOU COMEST IN FROM THE NIGHT WATCH, THOU SHALT MAKE A GREAT NOISE. WHY SHOULDST THOU LET OTHERS SLEEP WHILST THOU WAKEST?

9. IF THOU FALLEST ILL, THOU SHALT LIE ABED AS LONG AS THOU CANST. IF THY MATES SUFFER FROM OVERWORK THEREFORE, THEY MAY GAIN THE PRIVILEGE OF ILLNESS TOO.

10. FOLLOW THESE RULES THAT THOU MAYST HAVE TIME TO PREACH CONSIDERATION.

Grudgingly at first, and then with growing enjoyment, Andras illustrated *The Snow Goose*. For the weather report he drew a series of boxes, each more thickly swarmed with snowflakes. For the fashion column he drew a likeness of Mendel himself, his hair raked upright, his torso swathed toga-style in a ragged gray blanket. On the sports page, three perspiring labor servicemen dragged gravel wagons up a steep hill. The advice column sported a sketch of the saucy, bespectacled Coco, her legs long and bare, a pencil held to her lips. The travel ad for Ukraine showed a beach umbrella planted in the blowing snow. The architecture piece called for an image of the architect pointing proudly at an empty gorge. And the Ten Commandments required only the background sketch of two stone tablets. When he'd finished, he held the work at arm's length and squinted at the drawings. They were the lowest grade of caricature, rendered in haste while the artist lay in bed. But Mendel was right: They suited *The Snow Goose* perfectly.

That single copy of the newspaper made its way through the hands of two hundred men, who could soon be heard quoting the Fourth Commandment in the soup line or speculating wistfully about vacations to Ukraine. Andras couldn't keep from feeling a certain proprietary satisfaction, a sensation he hadn't experienced in months. Once it was determined that the illustrator who signed himself *Parisi* was actually Squad Captain Lévi, men began to approach him to ask for drawings. The most frequent request was for a nude version of Coco. He drew her on the lid of a man's wooden footlocker, and then in the lining of someone else's cap, and then on a letter to someone's younger brother, holding a sign that said *Hi, Sugar!* The drawing of Mendel spawned another fad, this one for likenesses; men would line up to have Andras draw their portraits. He wasn't a very good portraitist, but the men didn't seem to care. The roughness of the lines, the charcoal haze around a subject's eyes or chin, captured the essential uncertainty of their lives in the Munkaszolgálat. Mendel Horovitz, too, began receiving requests: He became a kind of professional letter-writer, penning expressions of love and regret and longing that would slip into the turbulent stream of the military mail service, and might or might not reach the wives and brothers and children for whom they were intended.

When the first issue of *The Snow Goose* finally disintegrated, Mendel wrote a new one and Andras illustrated it again. Emboldened by the popularity of the earlier edition, they brought their newspaper directly to the office, where there was a mimeograph machine. They offered the company secretary fifteen pengő as a bribe. At the risk of punishment and loss of position the company secretary printed ten copies, which were quickly subsumed into the ranks of the 112/30th. A third issue of thirty copies followed. As the men read and laughed over the paper, Andras began to feel as if he had awakened from a long, drugged sleep. He was surprised he'd been so weak, so willing to allow his mind to be overtaken by miserable thoughts and then hollowed to nothingness. Now he was drawing every day. They were absurd little sketches, to be sure, but they oxygenated him, made the effort of breathing seem worthwhile.

Then, on a raw, wet day in March, Andras and Mendel were summoned to the office of the company commander. The summons came from Major Kálozi's first lieutenant, a scowling, boarlike man by the unfortunate name of Grimasz. At dinnertime he approached Andras and Mendel in the assembly ground and knocked their mess tins from their hands. He held a crumpled copy of the most recent *Snow Goose*, which contained a love poem from a certain Lieutenant G to a certain Major K, and made other insinuations as to the nature of the relationship between them. Lieutenant Grimasz's face burned red; his neck seemed to have swollen to twice its normal size. He crushed the paper in his blocky fist. The other men took a step back from Andras and Mendel, who were left to absorb the full force of Grimasz's glare.

"Kálozi wants you in the office," he growled.

"Right away, Lieutenant, sir," Mendel said, and dared to wink at Andras.

Grimasz caught the tone, the wink. He raised his hand to cuff Mendel, but Mendel ducked the blow. The men gave a muffled cheer. Grimasz grabbed Mendel by the collar and half shoved, half dragged him to the office, while Andras followed at a run.

Major János Kálozi wasn't a cruel man, but he was ambitious.

The son of a Gypsy woman and an itinerant knife-grinder, he'd been promoted through the Munkaszolgálat himself, hoping for a transfer to the gun-carrying branch of the military. He'd been given his present assignment because he had actual knowledge of forestry; he had worked the forests of Transylvania before he'd emigrated to Hungary in the twenties. Andras had never before been called to his office, which was located in the only barracks building that had a porch and its own outhouse. Kálozi had, of course, appropriated the room with the largest window. This had proved to be a mistake. The window, a many-paned affair gleaned from the south-facing wall of a burned farmhouse, smelled of carbon and welcomed the cold. Kálozi had been obliged to cover it with army blankets of the same kind touted in the Fashion Column, rendering the office dark as a cellar. Beneath the smell of carbon was a distinct odor of horse; before the blankets had been put to their current use, they had been stored in a stable. Kálozi sat in the midst of this pungent gloom behind a massive metal desk. A coal brazier kept the place just warm enough to suggest that warm rooms existed and that this was not one of them.

Andras and Mendel stood at attention while Kálozi glanced through a near-complete set of *The Snow Goose*, beginning in December 1940 and ending with this week's edition, dated March 7, 1941. Only the disintegrated inaugural issue was lacking. The major had grown visibly older in the time he'd directed the 112/30th. The hair at his temples had gone gray and his broad nose had become cobwebbed with tiny red veins. He looked up at Andras and Mendel with the air of a weary school principal.

"Fun and games," he said, removing his glasses. "Please explain, Squad Captain Lévi. Or shall I call you Parisi?"

"It was my doing, sir," Mendel said. He held his Munkaszolgálat cap in his hands, his thumb working over the brass button at its forward-tilted peak. "I wrote the first issue and asked the squad captain to illustrate it. And we went on from there."

"You did indeed," Kálozi said. "You gained access to the mimeograph machine and printed dozens of copies."

"As squad captain I accept full responsibility," Andras said.

"I'm afraid I can't give you all the credit, Parisi. Our man Horovitz is so very talented, we can't let his efforts go unrecognized." Kálozi turned to an article he'd bookmarked with a bitten pencil. "Change of Leadership at Erdei Camp," he read aloud. "The veteran potentate Commander Jánika Kálozi the Cross-Eyed, at the behest of Regent Miklós Horthy himself, was deposed from his military appointment this week due to gross ineptitude and disgraceful behavior. In a ceremony at the parade ground he was replaced by a leader deemed more worthy, a male baboon by the name of Rosy Buttocks. The commander was escorted from the parade ground amid a deafening chorus of flatulence and applause." He turned the newspaper around to reveal Andras's drawing of the major, cross-eyed, in full uniform on top and ladies' underdrawers beneath, mincing on high heels beside his first lieutenant, an unmistakably boar-headed man, while in the background a florid-assed monkey saluted the assembled work servicemen.

Andras fought to suppress a grin. He was particularly fond of that drawing.

"What are you laughing at, Squad Captain?"

"Nothing, sir," Andras said. He'd known Kálozi for a year and a half now, and understood that he was soft at heart; in fact, he seemed to take a certain pride in his own reluctance to mete out harsh punishment. Andras had hoped Kálozi wouldn't come across that particular issue of *The Snow Goose*, but he hadn't felt any particular trepidation when he'd drawn the picture.

"I don't mind a laugh now and then," Kálozi said, "but I can't have the men ridiculing me. This company will fall into chaos."

"I understand, sir," Andras said. "We meant no harm."

"What do you know of harm?" Kálozi said, rising from his chair. A vein had begun to pump at his temple; for the first time since they'd entered the office, Andras felt a stirring of fear.

"When I served in the Great War, an officer might have flayed a man who drew something like this."

"You've always been kind to us," Andras said.

"That's right. I've coddled you flea-bitten Jews. I've kept you clothed and fed and I've let you loll in bed on cold days and driven you half as hard as I should have. And in return you produce this filth and spread it through the company."

"Just for laughs, sir," Mendel said.

"Not any longer. Not at my expense."

Andras pressed his unsteady teeth with his tongue. The pain radiated deep into his gums, and he fought an urge to turn and flee. But he drew himself up to his full height and met Kálozi's eye "I offer my sincere apologies," he said.

"Why apologize?" Kálozi said. "In one sense you've done the Munkaszolgálat a great favor. It seems some people have been spreading lies about the gross mistreatment of work servicemen in our national armed forces. A rag like this will be a powerful piece of counterevidence." He rolled a copy of *The Snow Goose* into a stiff tube. "The work service encourages fellowship and humor, et cetera. Conditions are so humane that you men are free to joke and laugh and make light of your situation. You've even had typewriters, drawing supplies, and mimeograph machines at your disposal. Free speech. It's practically French." He grinned, because they all knew what had become of free speech in France.

"But there *is* something I want from you," Kálozi went on. "I think you'll consider it fair, given the situation. Since you've humiliated me publicly, I think it's fitting that you be punished publicly in return."

Andras swallowed. At his side, Mendel had gone pale. They had both heard rumors of what went on in other labor-service companies, and neither was so naïve as to think those things couldn't happen in the 112/30th. Most horrifying was the case of the brother of one of their own workmates, who had been a member of the Debrecen labor battalion. As a punishment for stealing a loaf of bread from the officers' pantry, the man had been stripped naked and buried to his knees in mud; he'd been made to stand there for three days as the weather got progressively colder, until, on the third night, he'd died of exposure.

"I'm speaking to you, Squad Captain Lévi," Kálozi said. "Look at me. Don't hang your head like a dog."

Andras raised his eyes to Kálozi's. The major didn't blink. "I've thought long and hard about an appropriate punishment," he said. "As it happens, I'm rather fond of you boys. You've both been good workers. But you've shamed me. You've shamed me in front of my men. And so, Lévi and Horovitz"—here Kálozi paused for effect, tapping his rolled-up copy of *The Snow Goose* against the desk—"I'm afraid you will have to eat your words."

That was how Andras and Mendel came to find themselves stripped to their underclothes, their hands manacled behind their backs, kneeling before the assembled 112/30th at six o'clock on a cold March morning. Ten issues of *The Snow Goose* lay on a bench before them. While the labor servicemen watched, Lieutenant Grimasz tore off strips of the newspaper, crumpled them up, dunked them in water, and stuffed them into the mouths of co-publishers Lévi and Horovitz. Over a period of two hours they were each forced to eat twenty pages of *The Snow Goose*. As Andras clenched his teeth against Grimasz's prodding hands, he began to understand for the first time what a comfortable and protected life he had led, relatively speaking, in the Munkaszolgálat. He had never before had his hands bound behind his back, or been forced to kneel coatless and pantless in the snow for hours on end; he had, in fact, been fed and clothed and housed, his miseries eased by the knowledge that all the men of Company 112/30 were suffering similar miseries. Now he became aware of a new kind of hell, one he could scarcely allow himself to imagine. He knew that what was happening here, on the grand continuum of punishment, might still be classed as relatively humane; far off down that tunnel existed punishments that could make a man long for death. He forced himself to chew and swallow, chew and swallow, telling himself it was the only way to get through the hideous thing that was happening to him. Somewhere after the fifteenth page he tasted blood in his mouth and spat out a molar. His gums, spongy with scurvy, had finally begun to give up their teeth. He screwed his eyes shut and ate paper and ate paper and ate paper until finally he lost consciousness, and then he collapsed into the cold wet shock of the snow.

He was dragged to the infirmary and placed in the care of the company's only doctor, a man named Báruch Imber, whose sole purpose in life had become to save labor servicemen from the ravages of the labor service. Imber nursed Andras and Mendel for five days in the infirmary, and when they had recovered from hypothermia and forced paper consumption, he diagnosed them both with advanced scurvy and anemia and sent them home to Budapest for treatment in the military hospital, to be followed by a two-week furlough.

CHAPTER TWENTY-EIGHT

Furlough

AFTER A WEEK-LONG train journey, during which their hair became infested with lice and their skin began to flake and bleed, they were transferred to an ambulance van that held sick and dying work servicemen. The floor of the van was lined with hay, but the men shivered in their coarse wool blankets. There were eight men in the van, most of whom were far worse off than Andras and Mendel. A man with tuberculosis had a massive tumor at his hip, another man had been blinded when a stove exploded, a third had a mouth full of abscesses. Andras put his head out the open back windows of the van as they entered Budapest. The sight of ordinary city life—of streetcars and pastry shops, boys and girls out for an evening, movie marquees with their clean black letters—filled him with unreasonable fury, as if it were all a mockery of his time in the Munkaszolgálat.

The van pulled up at the military hospital and the patients walked or were carried to a registration hall, where Andras and Mendel waited all night on a cold bench while hundreds of workers and soldiers had their names and numbers recorded in an official ledger. Sometime in the early morning, Mendel was inscribed in the hospital book and taken away to be bathed and treated. It was another two hours before they came to Andras, but at last, dazed with exhaustion, he found himself following a male nurse to a shower room, where the man stripped him of his filthy clothes, shaved his head, sprayed him with a burning disinfectant, and stood him in a torrent of hot water. The nurse washed his bruised skin all over with a kind of impersonal tenderness, a knowing forbearance for the failings of the human body. The man dried him and led him to a long ward heated by radiators that ran its entire length. Andras was shown to a narrow metal bed, and for the first time in a year and a half he slept on a real mattress, between real sheets. When he awoke after what seemed only a few moments, Klara was there at his bedside, her eyes red and raw. He pushed himself upright, took her hands, demanded the terrible news: Who had died? What new tragedy had befallen them?

"Andráska," she said, in a voice fractured with pity; and he understood that *he* was the tragedy, that she was weeping over what remained of him. He didn't know how much weight he'd lost in the work service, on that diet of coffee and soup and hard bread—only that he'd had to keep cinching the belt of his trousers tighter, and that his bones had become more prominent beneath the skin. His arms and legs were roped with the wiry muscles he'd built from the constant labor; even through the previous winter's depression he'd never actually felt weak. But he saw how little his body disturbed the blanket that was pulled over him. He could only imagine how bony and strange he must look in his hospital pajamas, with his blood-blotched arms and his shaved head. He almost wished Klara had stayed away until he looked like a man again. He lowered his eyes and held his own elbows in what felt like self-protection. He watched her fold her hands in her lap; there was the gold glint of her wedding band. The ring was still smooth and reflective, her hands as white as they'd been when he'd last seen her. His own ring was scratched to dullness, his hands brown and cracked with work.

"The doctor's been here," Klara said. "He says you'll be all right. But you've got to take vitamin C and iron and have a long rest."

"I don't need rest," Andras said, determined that she should see him on his feet. He wasn't wounded or crippled, after all. He swung his legs off the bed and planted his feet on the cool linoleum. But then a wave of dizziness hit him, and he put a hand to his head.

"You have to eat," she said. "You've been asleep for twenty hours."

"I have?"

"I'm to give you some vitamin tablets and some broth, and later some bread."

"Oh, Klara," he said, and lowered his head into his hands. "Just leave me alone here. I'm a horror."

She sat down on the bed next to him and put her arms around him. Her smell was vaguely different—he detected a hint of lilac soap or hairdressing, something that reminded him of the long-ago Éva Kereny, his first love in Debrecen. She kissed his dry lips and put her head on his shoulder. He let her hold him, too exhausted to resist.

"Have some respect, Squad Captain," came a voice from across the ward. It was Mendel, lying in his own clean bed. He, too, had had his head shaved bare.

Andras raised his hand and waved. "My apologies, Serviceman," he said. It gave him a feeling of vertigo to be here in a military hospital with Mendel Horovitz, and to have Klara beside him at the same time. His head ached. He lay back against his pillow and let Klara give him his vitamins and broth. His wife. Klara Lévi. He opened his eyes to look at her, at the familiar sweep of her hair across her brow, the lean strength of her arms, the way she pressed her lips inward as she concentrated, her deep gray eyes resting on him, on him, at last.

It didn't take him long to understand that the furlough was another form of torture, a lesson that had to be learned in preparation for a more difficult test. Before, when he'd gotten his call-up notice, he'd had only the vaguest idea of what it might mean to be separated from Klara. Now he knew. In the face of that misery, two weeks seemed an impossibly short time.

His furlough began officially when he was released from the military hospital, three days after he had entered it. Klara had had his uniform laundered and mended, and on the day of his release she brought him the miraculous gift of a new pair of boots. He had new underclothes, new socks, a new peaked cap with a shining brass button at the front. He felt more than a little ashamed to appear in front of Mendel Horovitz in those fine clean clothes. Mendel had no one to take care of him. He was unmarried, and his mother had died when he was a boy; his father was still in Zalaszabar. As he stood with Andras and Klara near the hospital gate, waiting for the streetcar, Andras asked him how he planned to spend the furlough.

Mendel shrugged. "An old roommate of mine still lives in Budapest. I can stay with him."

Klara touched Andras's arm, and they exchanged a glance. It was a difficult thing to decide without discussion; it had been so long since they'd been alone together. But Mendel was an old friend, and during their time in the 112/30th he'd become Andras's family. They both knew Andras had to make the offer.

"We're going to my parents' house in the country," he said. "There's room, if you'd like to come. Nothing fancy. But I'm certain my mother would take good care of you."

The shadows around Mendel's eyes deepened into an expression of gratitude. "It's good of you, Parisi," he said.

So that morning it was the three of them together on the train to Konyár. They rode past Maglód, past Tápiogyörgy, past Újszász, into the Hajdú flatlands, sharing a thermos of coffee among them and eating cherry strudel. The tart sweetness of the fruit nearly brought tears to Andras's eyes. He took Klara's hand and pressed it between his own; she met his gaze and he felt she understood him. She was a person who knew something about shock, about returning from a state of desperation. He wondered how she had tolerated his own ignorance for so long.

It was the first week of April. The fields were still barren and cold, but a haze of green had begun to appear on the shrubs that clustered near the farmhouses; the bare branches of the creek willows had turned a brilliant yellow. He knew that the loveliness of the farm would still be hidden, its yard a disaster of mud, its stunted apple trees bare, its garden empty. He regretted that he couldn't show it to Klara in the summertime. But when they

finally arrived, when they disembarked at the familiar train station and saw the low whitewashed house with its dark thatched
roof, the barn and the mill and the millpond where he and
Mátyás and Tibor used to sail wooden boats, he thought he had
never seen any place more beautiful. Smoke rose from the stone
chimney; from the barn came the steady whine of the electric
saw. Stacks of fresh-cut lumber had been piled around the yard. In
the orchard, the bare apple trees held their branches toward the
April sky. He dropped his army duffel in the yard, and, taking
Klara's hand, ran to the front door. He rapped on the window-
pane and waited for his mother to come.

A young blond woman opened the door. On her hip was a
red-faced infant with a macerated zwieback in its hand. When
the woman saw Andras and Mendel in their military coats, her
eyebrows lifted in fear.

"Jenő!" she cried. "Come quick!"

A stocky man in overalls came running from the barn.
"What's the matter?" he called. And when he'd reached them,
"What's your business here?"

Andras blinked. The sun had just come out from behind a
cloud; it was difficult to focus on the man's features. "I'm Captain Lévi," he said. "This is my parents' house."

"*Was* their house," the man said, with an edge of pride. He
narrowed his eyes at Andras. "You don't look like a military officer."

"Squad Captain Lévi of Company 112/30," Andras said, but
the man wasn't looking at Andras anymore. He glanced at
Mendel, whose coat was devoid of officers' bars. Then he turned
his eyes upon Klara and raked her with a slow appreciative gaze.

"And you don't look like a country girl," he said.

Andras felt the blood rush to his face. "Where are my parents?" he said.

"How should I know?" the man said. "You people wander
here and there."

"Don't be an ass, Jenő," the woman said, and then to Andras, "They're in Debrecen. They sold this place to us a month ago. Didn't they write you?"

A month. It would have taken that long for a letter to reach Andras at the border. It was probably there now, moldering in the mail room, if they hadn't burned it for tinder. He tried to look past the woman and into the kitchen; the old kitchen table, the one whose every knot and groove he knew by heart, was still there. The baby turned its head to see what had interested Andras, then began to chew the zwieback again.

"Listen," the woman said. "Don't you have family in Debrecen? Can't someone tell you where your parents are staying?"

"I haven't been there in years," Andras said. "I don't know."

"Well, I've got work to do," the man said. "I think you're finished talking to my wife."

"And I think you're finished looking at mine," Andras said.

But the man reached out at that moment and pinched Klara's waist, and Klara gasped. Without thinking, Andras put a fist into the man's gut. The man blew out a breath and stumbled back. His heel hit a rock and he fell backwards into the dense rich mud of the yard. When he tried to get to his feet, he slid forward and fell onto his hands. By that time Andras and Klara and Mendel were running toward the station, their bags flying behind them. Until that moment Andras had never appreciated the advantage of living so close to the train; now he did something he'd seen Mátyás do countless times. He charged toward an open boxcar and swung his bag inside, and he gave Klara a leg up. Then he and Mendel jumped into the car, just as the train began to creak out of the station toward Debrecen. There was just enough time for them to witness the new owner of the lumberyard charging from the house with his shotgun in his hand, calling for his wife to find his goddamned shells.

In the chill of that April afternoon they rode toward Debrecen in the open boxcar, trying to catch their breath. Andras was certain Klara would be horrified, but she was laughing. Her shoes and the hem of her dress were black with mud.

"I'll never forget the look on his face," she said. "He didn't see it coming."

"Neither did I," Andras said.

"He deserved worse," Mendel said. "I would have liked to get a few licks in."

"I wouldn't advise you to go back for another try," Klara said.

Andras sat back against the wall of the boxcar and put an arm around her, and Mendel took a cigarette from the pocket of his overcoat and lay on his side, smoking and laughing to himself. The breeze was so thrilling, the noontime sun so bright, that Andras felt something like triumph. It wasn't until he looked at Klara again—her eyes serious now, as though to convey a private understanding of what had taken place in that mud-choked yard—that he realized he had just seen the last of his childhood home.

It didn't take them long to find his parents' apartment in Debrecen. They stopped at a kosher bakery near the synagogue, and Andras learned from the baker that his mother had just been there to buy matzoh; Passover began on Friday.

Passover. Last year the holiday had come and gone so quickly: a few Orthodox men had staged a seder in the bunkhouse, said the blessings just as if they'd had wine and greens and charoset and matzoh and bitter herbs before them, though all they had was potato soup. He vaguely remembered refusing the bread at dinner a few times, then becoming so weak that he had to start eating it again. He hadn't bothered to hope that he might be with his parents for Passover this year. But now he led Klara and Mendel down the avenue that led to Simonffy utca, where the baker had said his parents lived. There, in an ancient apartment building with two white goats in the courtyard and a still-leafless vine strung from balcony to balcony, they found his mother scrubbing the tiles of the second-floor veranda. A bucket of hot water steamed beside her; she wore a printed blue kerchief, and her arms were bright pink to the elbow. When she saw Andras and Klara and Mendel, she got to her feet and ran downstairs.

His little mother. She crossed the courtyard in an instant, still nimble, and took Andras in her arms. Her quick dark eyes moved over him; she pressed him to her chest and held him there. After a long while she released him and embraced Klara, calling her *kislányom, my daughter.* Finally she put her arms around Mendel, who tolerated this with a good-natured side glance at Andras; she knew Mendel from Andras's school days, and had always treated him as though he were another of her sons.

"You poor boys," she said. "Look how they've used you."

"We'll be all right, Anya. We've got a two-week furlough."

"Two weeks!" She shook her head. "After a year and a half, two weeks. But at least you'll be here for Pesach."

"And who's that garden slug living in our house in Konyár?"

His mother put a hand to her mouth. "I hope you didn't quarrel with him."

"Quarrel with him?" Andras said. "No! He was delightful. I kissed his hand. We're friends for life."

"Oh, dear."

"He chased us with a shotgun," Mendel said.

"God, what a terrible man! It pains me to think of him living in that house."

"I hope you got a good price for the place, at least," Andras said.

"Your father arranged it all," his mother said, and sighed. "He said we were lucky to get what we did. We're comfortable here. There aren't so many chores. And I still have Kicsi and Noni." She nodded at the two little dairy goats who stood in their fenced enclosure in the yard.

"You ought to have telephoned me," Klara said. "I would have come to help you move."

His mother lowered her eyes. "We didn't want to disturb you. We knew you were busy with your students."

"You're my family."

"That's kind of you," Andras's mother said, but there was a note of reserve in her voice, almost a hint of deference. The next moment Andras wondered if he'd only imagined it, because his mother had taken Klara's arm and begun to lead her across the courtyard.

The apartment was small and bright, a three-room corner unit with French doors leading out onto the veranda. His mother had planted winter kale in terra-cotta pots; she boiled some of it for their lunch and served it to them with potatoes and eggs and red peppers, and Andras and Mendel took their vitamin pills and ate a few apples Klara had brought for them, each in its own square of green paper. As they ate, his mother told them the news of Mátyás and Tibor: Mátyás was stationed near Abaszéplak, where his labor company was building a bridge over the Torysa River. But that wasn't all; before his conscription he'd created such a sensation at the Pineapple Club, dancing atop that piano in his white tie and tails, that the manager had offered him a two-year contract. In his letters he wrote that he was practicing, always practicing—working out steps in his mind while he and his mates built the Torysa Bridge, then keeping the poor fellows up at night while he danced the steps he'd worked out that day. By the time he got home, he said, he'd be tapping so fast they'd have to invent a new kind of music just to keep up with him.

Tibor, Andras's mother told them, had joined a detachment of his labor-service battalion in Transylvania last November; his training in Modena had won him the job of company medic. His letters didn't carry much news about his work—Andras's mother suspected he didn't want to horrify her—but he always told her what he was reading. At the moment it was Miklós Radnóti, a young Jewish poet from Budapest who'd been conscripted into the labor service last fall. Like Andras, Radnóti had lived in Paris for a time. Some of his poems—one about sitting with a Japanese doctor on the terrace of the Rotonde, another about indolent afternoons in the Jardin du Luxembourg—put Tibor in mind of the time he'd spent there. It was rumored that Radnóti's battalion was serving not far from Tibor's own; the thought had helped Tibor endure the winter.

To Andras it seemed a terrible and surreal luxury to sit in the kitchen of this clean sunny apartment while his mother delivered news of Mátyás and Tibor and their time in the labor service. How could he relax into this familiar chair, how could he eat apples with Klara and Mendel and listen to the bleating of white goats in the courtyard, while his brothers built bridges and treated sick men in Ruthenia and Transylvania? It was terrible to feel this sweet drowsiness, terrible to find himself anticipating an afternoon nap in his own childhood bed, if indeed his childhood bed had been brought here from Konyár. Even the table before him—the small yellow one from the outdoor summer kitchen—gave him a pang of displaced longing, as though he'd become the conduit of his brothers' homesickness. This little table his father had built before Andras was born: He remembered sitting underneath it on a hot afternoon as his mother shelled peas for their dinner. He was eating a handful of peas as he watched an inchworm scale one of the table legs. He could see the inchworm in his mind even now, that snip of green elastic with its tiny blunt legs, coiling and stretching its way toward the tabletop, on a mission whose nature was a mystery. Survival, he understood now—that was all. That contracting and straining, that frantic rearing-up to look around: It was nothing less than the urgent business of staying alive.

"What are you thinking of?" his mother asked, and pressed his hand.

"The summer kitchen."

She laughed. "You recognized this table."

"Of course."

"Andras used to keep me company while I baked," his mother told Klara. "He used to draw in the dirt with a stick. I used to sweep the rest of the kitchen every day, but I would sweep around his drawings."

There was a soft hoarse intake of breath from Mendel; he hadn't waited to find a comfortable place for a nap. He'd fallen asleep at the kitchen table, his head pillowed on his arms. Andras led Mendel to the sofa and covered him with a quilt. Mendel didn't wake, not through the walk across the room, nor through the arrangement of his limbs upon the sofa. It was a talent he had. Sometimes he'd sleep all the way through the morning march to the work site.

"Will you sleep too?" Klara asked Andras. "I'll help your mother."

But the bright sharp taste of the apples had woken him; now he didn't feel like sleeping. What he wanted, what he couldn't wait another moment to do, was to find his father.

It was a piece of raw Hungarian irony that his father was employed in the milling of timber—some of it, perhaps, the very same timber that Andras had cut in the forests of Transylvania and Subcarpathia. Debrecen Consolidated Lumber bore no resemblance to the lumberyard Lucky Béla had sold to the hateful young man in Konyár. This was a large-scale government-funded operation that processed hundreds of trees daily, and turned out thousands of cords of lumber for use in the building of army barracks and storage facilities and railroad stations. For months now Hungary had been girding itself for war, anticipating that it might be forced to enter the conflict alongside Germany. If that were to happen, vast quantities of timber would be needed to support the army's advance. Of course, if he'd had a choice, Lucky Béla would have preferred to work for a smaller company whose products were to be sold for peaceful purposes. But he knew how fortunate he was to have a job at all when so many Jews were out of work. And if Hungary went to war, even the smaller lumber companies would be drafted into government service. So he'd taken the job of second assistant foreman when the previous second assistant foreman had died of pneumonia that past winter. The first assistant foreman, a school friend of Béla's, had offered him the job as a temporary measure, a way to see Béla through the lean winter months. For two months Béla had lived in Debrecen and gone home on weekends, leaving the care of his own mill to his foreman. When the school friend had offered the job on a permanent basis, Béla and Flóra had decided that the time had come to sell their tiny operation. They were getting older. The chores had become more difficult, their debt deeper. With the money from the sale, they could pay their creditors and rent a small apartment in Debrecen.

It was their bad luck that the only interested buyer had been a member of Hungary's National Socialist Party, the Arrow Cross, and that the man's offer was half of what the lumberyard was worth. Béla had no choice but to sell. It had been a hard winter. They'd had barely enough to eat, and for an entire month the trains had failed to come to Konyár. There had been a track failure that no one seemed inclined to fix. Certain normal processes—the delivery of mail, the restocking of provisions, the hauling away of milled lumber—had shut down altogether. But in Debrecen there was no food shortage, no slowdown at the mill. He would be paid twice what he could pay himself at his own lumberyard. It was a terrible shame to have had to sell at such a price, but the move had already done them good—Flóra had regained the weight she had lost during that long starved winter, and Béla's cough and rheumatism had abated. His voice and gait were strong as he walked through the lumberyard with Andras, telling the story.

"What we need, you and I," he concluded, as he hung his

hard hat in the foremen's locker room, "is a nice cold glass of lager."

"I'd be a fool to argue," Andras said, and they set off together toward his father's favorite beer hall, a cavelike establishment not far from Rózsa utca, with taxidermied wolves' heads and deer antlers hanging on the walls and a giant old-fashioned barrel of beer on a wooden stand. At the tables, men smoked Fox cigarettes and argued about the fate of Europe. The bartender was an enormous mustachioed man who looked as though he subsisted on fried doughnuts and beer.

"How's the lager today, Rudolf?" his father asked.

Rudolf gave him a small-toothed smile. "Gets you drunk," he said.

It seemed to be a routine of theirs. The bartender filled two glasses and poured himself a shot of whiskey, and they toasted each other's health.

"Who's this skinny lad?" Rudolf asked.

"My middle boy, the architect."

"Architect, eh?" Rudolf raised an eyebrow. "Build anything around here?"

"Not yet," Andras said.

"Army service?"

"Munkaszolgálat."

"That who's starving you?"

"Yes, sir."

"I was a *huszár* in the Great War, like your father. On the Serbian front. Nearly lost a leg at Varaždin. But the labor service, now, that's a different story. Digging around in the muck all day, no excitement, no chance for glory, and a starvation diet on top of it." He shook his head. "That's no job for a smart boy like you. How much longer have you got?"

"Six months," Andras said.

"Six months! That's not so long. And good weather all the way. You'll do fine. But have another round on me, just in case. Bottoms up. May we all cheat death a thousand times!"

They drank. Then Andras and his father retreated to their own table in a dark corner of the room, beneath a wolf head frozen in a howl. The head gave Andras a chill to the base of his spine. That winter in Transylvania he'd heard wolves howling at night, and had imagined their yellow teeth and silvered fur. There had been times when he'd felt so desperate he'd wanted to give himself up to them. As if to remind himself that he was home on furlough, he reached into his pocket and touched his father's watch; he'd left it with Klara when he'd gone to the Munkaszolgálat. Now he took it out to show his father.

"It's a good watch," Béla said, turning it over in his fingers. "A great watch."

"In Paris," Andras said, "whenever I was in a bad spot, I used to take it out and think about what you might do."

His father gave him a rueful smile. "I'll bet you didn't always do what I would have done."

"Not always," Andras said.

"You're a good boy," his father said. "A thoughtful boy. You're always putting on a brave face in your letters from the Musz, to keep your mother's spirits up. But I know it's much worse than you let on. Look at you. They've half killed you."

"It's not so bad," Andras said, feeling as he said it that it was true. It was just work, after all; he'd worked all his life. "We've been fed," he said. "They give us clothes and boots. We have a roof over our heads."

"But you've had to leave school. I think about that every day."

"I'll go back," he said.

"To where? France doesn't exist anymore, not as a place for Jews. And this country . . ." He shook his head in dismay and disgust. "But you'll find a way to finish. You've got to. I don't want to see you abandoning your studies."

Andras understood what he was thinking. "You didn't abandon your studies," he said. "You left Prague because you had to."

"But I didn't go back, did I?"

"You didn't have much of a choice." He couldn't see any

point in continuing the line of conversation; he was powerless to do anything about school now, and his father knew it as well as he did. The thought that it had been almost two years since he'd been at the École Spéciale made him feel pressed under a great and immovable weight. He looked up at a cluster of men who were going over the sports page in the *Pesti Hírlap*, arguing over which wrestler would win a tournament at the National Sports Club that night. He had never heard any of the wrestlers' names before.

"It's good to see Klara, I'm sure," his father said. "It's hard to be away from your wife for so long. She's a nice girl, your Klara." But there was an echo of the look Andras had seen on his mother's face earlier, a shadow of hesitation, of reserve.

"I wish you'd written to tell her you were moving," Andras said. "She would have come out to help you."

"Your mother's kitchen girl helped. She was glad to have the extra work."

"Klara's our family, Apa."

His father pushed his lips out and shrugged. "Why should we trouble her with our problems?"

Andras wasn't going to say what had occurred to him as his father had narrated their story: that he wished Klara might have been the one to negotiate the sale of the lumberyard, that he was certain she would have insisted on a better price and gotten it. But such a negotiation, which might have taken place in Paris without raising the slightest notice, would have been unthinkable in Konyár; here on the Hajdú plains, women did not haggle over real estate with men. "Klara's no stranger to hard work," Andras said. "She's had to support herself since she was sixteen. And in any case, she thinks of you and Anya as her own parents."

"Now that's a quaint notion," Béla said, and shook his head. "Don't forget, my boy, that we celebrated your wedding at her mother's house. I've met Mrs. Hász. I've met Klara's brother. I don't think Klara could ever mistake us for her own family."

"That's not what I mean. You're pretending not to understand me."

"In Paris, maybe you and Klara were just two Hungarians keeping each other company," Béla said. "Here at home, things are different. Look around you. The rich don't sit down with the poor."

"She's not *the rich*, Apa. She's my wife."

"Her family bought out that nephew of hers. *He* didn't have to break his back in the work service. But they didn't do the same for you."

"I told her brother I wouldn't consider it."

"And he didn't argue, did he?"

Andras felt the back of his neck grow warm; a flash of anger moved through him. "It's not fair of you to hold that against Klara," he said.

"What's unfair is that some should have to work while others don't."

"I didn't come here to argue with you."

"Let's not argue, then."

But it was too late. Andras was furious. He didn't want to be in his father's presence a moment longer. He put money on the table for the beer, but his father pushed it away.

"I'm going for a walk," Andras said, getting to his feet. "I need some air."

"Well, let your old father walk with you."

He couldn't conceive of a way to say no. His father followed him out of the bar and they walked together in the blue light of evening. All along the avenue, yellow streetlamps had come on to illuminate the buildings with their flaking plaster and faded paint. He didn't think about where he was walking; he wished he could walk faster, lose his father in the dusk, but the fact was that he was exhausted, anemic, and in need of sleep. He pressed onward past the Aranybika Hotel, an aging dowager in white wooden lace; he walked past the double towers of the Lutheran church with its stolid spires. He kept walking, head down, all the way to the park across the street from the Déri Museum, a squat Baroque-style building clad in yellow stucco. The April evening, soft at the edges, reminded him of a thousand evenings he'd spent here as a schoolboy, with friends or alone, worrying the edges of his adolescent problems like the pages of favorite books. In those days he could always console himself with thoughts of home, of that patch of land in Konyár with its orchard and barn and lumberyard and millpond. Now his home in Konyár would never be his home again. His past, his earliest childhood, had been stolen from him. And his future, the life he had imagined when he was a student here, had been stolen too. He sat on a bench and bent over his knees, his head in his hands; the hurt and dislocation he'd suffered for eighteen months seemed to come over him all at once, and he found himself choking out hoarse sobs into the night.

Lucky Béla stared at this son of his, this boy whose troubles had always been closest to his own heart. He himself had never been subject to fits of weeping, nor had he encouraged them in his sons. He'd taught them to turn their hurt into work. That was what had saved his own life, after all. He hadn't raised his sons with much physical affection; that had been their mother's domain, not his. But as he watched his boy, this sick and beaten-down young man, sobbing jaggedly into his knees, he knew what he had to do: He sat down beside Andras on the bench and put his arms around him. His love had always seemed to mean something particular to this boy. He hoped it would mean something still.

They stayed in Debrecen for a week. His mother fed him and tended his ravaged feet and made hot baths for him in the kitchen; she laughed at Mendel's stories about their mates in the work service, and cleaned the house for Passover with Klara. The new kitchen maid, an aging spinster named Márika, developed a fierce attachment to Mendel, whom she claimed was the spitting image of her brother who'd been killed in the Great War. She left him surreptitious gifts of woolen socks and underclothes, which must have cost a good portion of her wages. When he protested that the gifts were too fine, she pretended to know nothing about them. To Andras the dull familiarity of Debrecen was a kind of relief. He was glad to walk with his friend and his wife through the old neighborhoods, to buy them conical doughnuts at the same doughnut shop where he'd spent his pennies as a child, to show Klara the Jewish Gimnázium and the outdoor skating rink on Piac utca. His body grew stronger, his spongy gums firm again. The patches of old blood beneath his skin began to fade.

He'd been painfully shy with Klara those first few days. He couldn't stand to have her see his body in its weakened state, and he doubted he would be equal to the demands of lovemaking. But he was a twenty-five-year-old man, and she was the woman he loved; it wasn't long before he moved toward her in the night, on the thin mattress they shared in the tiny extra room his mother used for sewing. All around them were garments his mother was mending or making to give to Andras or to send to his brothers in their work-service companies. The room was redolent of laundered cotton and the scorched sweetness of ironing. In that bower, in their second marriage bed, he reached for her and she came into his arms. He could scarcely believe that her physical being still existed, that he was allowed to revisit the parts of her he'd carried in his mind like talismans those eighteen months: her small high breasts, the silvery-white scar on her belly, the twin peaks of her hips. As they made love she kept her eyes open and steady on his. He couldn't read their color in the faint light that filtered through the covered window, but he could see the sharp intensity he recognized and loved. At times they seemed to struggle like old foes; part of him wanted almost to punish her for the longing she had made him feel. She seemed to understand, and met his anger with her own. When he collapsed against her at last, his heart beating against her chest, he knew they would find their way back across the distance that their long separation had opened between them.

By the end of their week in Debrecen, a subtle change had occurred between Andras's mother and Klara. Knowing looks passed between them during meals; his mother insisted upon having Klara along when she went to the market, and she had asked her to make the matzo balls for their Passover seder. The matzo balls were the glory of the meal, more highly anticipated even than the fried cutlets of chicken or the potato kugel or the gefilte fish she always made from a live carp, which in Konyár had lived in a large tin tub of water in the summer kitchen, but which in Debrecen was forced to reside in the courtyard, on public display. (Two children, a girl and her brother, had befriended the fish, feeding it bits of bread when they got home from school; when it disappeared to become the second course of the seder, Andras told them he'd taken it to the city park and set it free, which earned him their enmity forever—though he insisted that it was what the carp had wanted, its instructions whispered to him in Carpathian, a language he claimed to have learned in the Munkaszolgálat.) His mother's matzoh-ball recipe was written in a spidery lace of black ink upon a holy-looking piece of what could only have been parchment. It had been the property of Flóra's great-grandmother Rifka, and it had been given to Flóra on her wedding day in a small silver box tooled with the Yiddish word *Knaidlach*.

One afternoon, when he came in from a walk with Mendel, he found his mother and Klara in the kitchen together, the silver box open on the table, the precious recipe in Klara's hands. Her hair was tied back in a kerchief, and she wore an apron embroidered with strawberries; her skin was bright with the heat of the kitchen. She squinted at the spidery script and then at the ingredients Andras's mother had laid out on the table.

"But how much of everything?" she asked Flóra. "Where are the measures?"

"Don't worry about that," Andras' mother said. "Just do it by feel."

Klara gave Andras a panicked smile.

"Can I help?" Andras asked.

"Yes, darling boy," Flóra said. "Get your father from work. If I know him, he'll have forgotten he's supposed to come home early."

"All right," Andras said. "But first I'd like a word with my wife." He took the recipe from her and laid it with care in the silver box; then he grabbed Klara's hand and pulled her into the little sewing room. He closed the door. Klara put her hands over her face and laughed.

"Oh, God!" she said. "I can't make these matzo balls."

"You could just surrender, you know."

"What a recipe, that recipe! It might as well be written in secret code!"

"Maybe it's magic. Maybe the quantities don't matter."

"If only Mrs. Apfel were here. Or Elisabet." A wash of grief darkened her features, as it did every time she'd mentioned Elisabet's name that week. Her expectations had come to pass: The parents who lived on an estate in Connecticut had wanted nothing to do with Elisabet, and had cut off their son entirely. Undaunted, Paul and Elisabet had taken an apartment in Manhattan and had gone to work—Paul as a graphic artist, Elisabet as a baker's apprentice. Elisabet had excelled at the job, and had been promoted to assistant pastry chef; the fact that she was French gave her a certain cachet, and she had written a few months ago to say that a cake she'd decorated had served as the centerpiece for a grand wedding in the ballroom of the Waldorf-Astoria Hotel. The mothers of wealthy young ladies had begun to come to her with requests. But now there was a child on the way. That piece of news had arrived in the most recent letter, just a few weeks earlier.

"Klara," he said, and touched her hand. "Elisabet will be all right, you know."

She sighed. "It's been a comfort to be here," she said. "To be with you. And to spend time with your mother. She loves her children like I love that girl."

"You have to tell me what you did," he said. "You've bewitched her."

"What are you talking about?"

"My mother's fallen in love with you, that's what."

Klara leaned against the wall and crossed her slender ankles. "I took her into my confidence," she said.

"What do you mean?"

"I told her the truth. Everything. I wanted her to know what happened when I was a girl, and how I've lived since then. I was sure it would make a difference."

"And it has."

"Yes."

"But now you've got to make matzo balls."

"I think it's a kind of final test," Klara said, and smiled.

"I hope you pass," he said.

"You don't seem confident."

"Of course I'm confident."

"Go get your father," she said, and pushed him toward the door.

By the time he and Mendel returned with Lucky Béla, there were matzo balls boiling in a pot on the stove. The gefilte fish was finished, the table laid with a white cloth, the plates and silverware gleaming in the light of two white tapers. At the center of the table was a silver seder plate, the one they'd used every year since Andras could remember, with greens and bitter herbs, salt water and charoset, egg and shank bone laid out in its six silver cups.

Lucky Béla stood beside his chair at the head of the table, silent with the news he'd received just before the boys had met him at work. In the foremen's office he'd heard it come in on the radio: Horthy had decided to let Hitler invade Yugoslavia from Hungarian soil—Yugoslavia, with whom Hungary had signed an agreement of peace and friendship a year before. Nazi troops had gathered at Barcs and swarmed across the Drava River while Luftwaffe bombers decimated Belgrade. Béla knew what it was all about: Hitler was punishing the country for the military coup and the popular uprising that had followed Yugoslavia's entry into the Tripartite Pact. Not a week earlier, Germany had pledged to guarantee the borders of Yugoslavia for a thousand years; now Hitler had set his armies against it. The invasion had begun that afternoon. Hungarian troops would be sent to Belgrade later that week to support the German Army. It would be Hungary's first military action in the European conflict. It seemed clear to Béla that this was only the beginning, that Hungary could not avoid being drawn further into the war. Thousands of boys would lose their lives. His children would be sent to work on the front lines. He had listened to the news and let it sink into his bones, but when Andras and Mendel had arrived he'd kept it from them. Nor would he say anything now, in the presence of this sacred-looking table. He couldn't bear the thought that the news might ruin what his wife and his son's wife had created. He led the seder as usual, feeling the absence of his youngest and eldest sons as a sharp constriction in his chest. He retold the story of the exodus and let Mendel recite the Four Questions. He managed to eat the familiar meal, with the boiled egg on greens and the fresh gefilte fish and the matzo balls in their gold broth. He sang the blessings afterward as he always did, and was grateful for the fourth ceremonial glass of wine. When he opened the door at the end of the seder to give the prophet Elijah his welcome, he saw open doors all around the courtyard. It was a comfort to know he was surrounded by other Jews. But he couldn't keep the news at bay forever. From the courtyard came the gritty sound of the national news station; someone downstairs had put a radio in the window so others could hear. A man was making a speech in a grave aristocratic voice: It was Miklós Horthy, their regent, mobilizing the country toward its glorious destiny within the new Europe. Béla could see the understanding come over his wife's face, then his son's. Hungary was involved now, irrevocably so. As they crowded out onto the balcony to listen to the broadcast, Béla pushed the door open a few more centimeters. *Eliahu ha Navi*, he sang, under his breath. *Eliahu ha Tishbi*. He stood with one hand on the doorframe, intoning the holy man's name; he had not yet given up hope for a different kind of prophecy.

CHAPTER TWENTY-NINE

Bánhida Camp

WHEN ANDRAS AND MENDEL reported to the battalion office at the end of their furlough, they learned that they would not rejoin the 112/30th in Transylvania. Major Kálozi, they were told by the battalion secretary, had had enough of them. Instead they would be deployed at Bánhida, fifty kilometers northwest of Budapest, where they would join Company 101/18 at a coal mine and power plant.

Fifty kilometers from Budapest! It was conceivable that he might be able to see Klara on a weekend furlough. And the mail might not take a month to travel between them. He and Mendel were sent to wait for the returning members of their new company at the rail yard, where they were divided into work groups and assigned to a passenger carriage. The men returning to Bánhida seemed to have passed an easier winter than Andras and Mendel had. Their clothes were intact, their bodies solid-looking. Between them there was a casual jocularity, as though they were schoolmates returning to gimnázium after a holiday. As the train moved west through the rolling hills of Buda, then into the wooded and cultivated country beyond, the passenger car filled with the earthy smell of spring. But the workers' conversation grew quieter the closer they got to Bánhida. Their eyes seemed to take on a sober cast, their shoulders an invisible weight. The greenery began to fall away outside the window, replaced at first by the low, desperate-looking habitations that always seemed to precede a train's arrival into a town, and then by the town itself with its twisting veinery of streets and its red-roofed houses, and then, as they passed through the railway station and moved toward the power plant, by an increasingly unlovely prospect of hard-packed dirt roads and warehouses and machine shops. Finally they came into view of the plant itself, a battleship with three smokestacks sending plumes of auburn smoke into the blue spring sky. The train shrieked to a halt in a rail yard choked with hundreds of rusted boxcars. Across a barren field were rows of cinderblock barracks behind a chain-link fence. Farther off still, men pushed small coal trolleys toward the power plant. Not a single tree or shrub interrupted the view of trampled mud. In the distance, like a sweet-voiced taunt, rose the cool green hills of the Gerecse and Vertes ranges.

Guards threw open the doors of the railcars and shouted the men off the train. In the barren field the new arrivals were separated from the returnees; the returnees were sent off to work at once. The rest of the men were ordered to deposit their knapsacks at their assigned barracks and then to report to the assembly ground at the center of the compound. The cinderblock barracks at Bánhida looked to have been built without any consideration besides economy; the materials were cheap, the windows high and small and few. As he entered, Andras had the sensation of being buried underground. He and Mendel claimed bunks at the end of one of the rows, a spot that afforded the privacy of a wall. Then they followed their mates out to the assembly ground, a vast quadrangle carpeted in mud.

Two sergeants lined the men up in rows of ten; that day there were fifty new arrivals at Bánhida Camp. They were ordered to stand at attention and wait for Major Barna, the company commander, who would inspect them. Then they would be divided into work groups and their new service would begin. They stood in the mud for nearly an hour, silent, listening to the far-off commands of work foremen and the electric throb of the power plant and the sound of metal wheels on rails. At last the new commander emerged from an administrative building, his cap trimmed with gold braid, a pair of high glossy boots on his feet. He walked the rows briskly, scanning the men's faces. Andras thought he resembled a schoolbook illustration of Napoleon; he was dark-haired, compact, with an erect bearing and an imperious look. On his second pass through Andras's line, he paused in front of Andras and asked him to state his position.

Andras saluted. "Squad captain, sir."

"What was that?"

"Squad captain," Andras said again, this time at a higher volume. Sometimes the commanders wanted the men to shout their responses, as if this were the real military and not just the work service. Andras found these episodes particularly depressing. Now Major Barna ordered him to step out of the ranks and march to the front.

He hated being told to march. He hated all of it. A few weeks at home had refreshed in him the dangerous awareness that he was a human being. When he reached the front of the lineup he stood at a tense and quivering attention while Major Barna looked him over. The man seemed to regard him with a kind of disgusted fascination, as if Andras were a freak in a traveling show. Then he pulled out a pearl-handled pocketknife and held it beneath Andras's nose. Andras sniffed. He thought he might sneeze. He could smell the metal of the blade. He didn't know what Barna meant to do. The mayor's small dark eyes held a glint of mischief, as if he and Andras were meant to be co-conspirators in whatever was about to happen. With a wink he moved the knife away from Andras's face and wedged its tip under the officer's insignia on Andras's overcoat, and with a few quick strokes he tore the patch from Andras's chest. The patch fell into the mud; Barna pressed it down with his foot until it disappeared. Then he put a hand on Andras's head, on the new cap Klara had given him. Another few strokes of the knife and he'd removed the officer's insignia from the cap as well.

"What's your rank now, Serviceman?" Major Barna shouted, loud enough for the men at the back to hear.

Andras had never heard of such a thing happening. He hadn't known it was possible to be stripped of rank if you hadn't been convicted of a crime. With a surge of daring, he pulled himself up to his full height—a good six inches taller than Barna—and shouted, "Squad captain, sir!"

There was a flash of movement from Barna, and an explosion of pain at the back of Andras's skull. He fell to his hands and knees in the mud.

"Not at Bánhida," Major Barna shouted. In his quivering hand he held a white beech walking-stick hazed with Andras's blood. Despite the pain, Andras almost let out a laugh. It all seemed so absurd. Hadn't he just been eating apples in his mother's kitchen? Hadn't he just been making love to his wife? He put a hand to the back of his head: warm blood, a painful lump.

"Get to your feet, Labor Serviceman," the major shouted. "Rejoin ranks."

He had no choice. Without another word, he complied.

His welcome to Bánhida was a taste of what was to come. Something had changed in the brief time Andras had been away from the Munkaszolgálat, or perhaps things were different in the 101/18th. There were no Jewish officers at any level; there were no Jewish medics or engineers or work foremen. The guards were crueler and shorter-tempered, the officers quicker to deliver punishment. Bánhida was an unabashedly ugly place. Everything about it seemed designed for the discomfort or the unhappiness of its inhabitants. Day and night the power plant let forth its three great billows of brown coal smoke; the air reeked of sulfur, and everything was filmed with a fine orange-brown dust that turned to a chalky paste in the rain. The barracks smelled of mildew, the windows let in heat but little light or air, and the roofs leaked onto the bunks. The paths and roads, it seemed, had been laid out to run through the wettest parts of camp. There was a downpour every afternoon promptly at three, turning the place into a treacherous mud-slick swamp. A hot wet breeze swept the smell of the latrines across the camp, and the men choked on the stench as they worked. Mosquitoes bred in the puddles and attacked the men, clustering on their foreheads and necks and arms. The flies were worse, though; their bites left tender red welts that were slow to heal.

Andras and Mendel had been assigned to shovel brown coal into mine carts and then to push the carts along rusted tracks to the power plant. The tracks were laid upon the ground but not fixed in place, and the reason for this soon became clear: as the rains increased, the tracks had to be taken up and redirected around puddles the size of small ponds. When there was no way to avoid the puddles, timbers had to be laid across them and the rails on top of those. The carts weighed hundreds of kilograms with their full loads. The men pulled and pushed and winched them, and when they still wouldn't move, the men cursed and struck them with their shovels. Each truck was emblazoned with the white letters KMOF, for Közérdekű Munkaszolgálat Országos Felügyelője, the National Administration of the Labor-Service System; but Mendel insisted that the letters stood for Királyi Marhák Ostobasági Földbirtoka, the Royal Idiots' Stupidity Farm.

There were things to be grateful for. It would have been worse if they'd had to work in the power plant, where the coal dust and chemical fumes turned the air into a thick unbreatheable stew. It would have been worse if they'd been sent down into the mines. It would have been worse to be there without each other. And it would have been worse to be hundreds of kilometers from Budapest, as they'd been in Ruthenia and Transylvania. At Bánhida the mail moved quickly. His parents' letters took two weeks to arrive, and Klara's came in a week. Once she enclosed a missive from Rosen, five pages of large loose script sent all the way from Palestine. He and Shalhevet had slipped out of France just before its borders were closed to emigrating Jews, and had been married in Jerusalem, where they were both working for the Palestine Jewish Community: Rosen in the department of settlement planning, and Shalhevet in the immigration advocacy office. They had a child on the way, due in November. There were even letters from Andras's brothers: Tibor, home to spend his furlough with Ilana, had taken her to the top of Castle Hill for the first time; a photograph showed the two of them before a parapet, Ilana's smile radiant, her hand enclosed in Tibor's. Mátyás, still stuck in his labor-service company but struck with spring fever, had made a secret foray to a nearby town, where he had drunk beer, waltzed with girls at the local tavern, tap-danced on the zinc bar in his boots, and made it back to his battalion without getting caught.

In the face of the misery of Bánhida, Mendel conceived a new publication called *The Biting Fly*. Though at first it seemed to Andras an act of audacity verging on foolhardiness to revive the idea of a newspaper after what had happened in the 112/30th, Mendel argued that they had to do something to keep from going mad. The new publication, he said, would maintain a tone of protest while avoiding direct ridicule of the camp authorities. If they were caught, there would be nothing for their commander to take personally. There would be a certain degree of risk involved, of course, but the alternative was to allow themselves to be silenced by the Munkaszolgálat. After the humiliation Andras had suffered on the assembly ground, how could he refuse to raise his voice in protest?

In the end, Andras agreed to join Mendel again as co-publisher. His decision was driven in part by vanity, he suspected, and in part by desire to maintain his dignity; a greater part was the idea that he and Mendel were conspiring on behalf of free speech and their workmates' morale. In the 112/30th he had seen how *The Snow Goose* had become an emblem of the men's struggle. It had given them a certain relief to see their daily miseries recorded—to see them recognized as outrages that demanded the publication of an underground paper, even one as absurd as *The Snow Goose*. Here at Bánhida, at least, it would be easier to get drawing materials; there was a black market for all sorts of things. In addition to Debrecen sausages, Fox cigarettes, pinups of Hedy Lamarr and Rita Hayworth, cans of peas, woolen socks, tooth powder, and vodka, one could buy paper and drawing pencils. And there was plenty to illustrate. The first issue of *The Biting Fly* contained a lexicon that defined such terms as Morning Lineup *(a popular parlor game involving alternating rounds of boredom, calisthenics, and humiliation)*, Water Carrier *(a laborman with an empty bucket and a full mouth)*, and Sleep *(a rare natural phenomenon about which little is known)*. There was a horoscope promising woe for every sign of the Zodiac. There was an advertisement for the services of a private detective who would let you know if your wife or girlfriend had been unfaithful, with a disclaimer releasing the detective from blame if a relationship should inadvertently develop between himself and the subject of his investigation. There were classified ads *(Wanted: Arsenic. Will pay in installments)* and a serialized adventure novel about a North Pole expedition, increasingly popular as the weather grew hotter. With the aid of a Jewish clerk in the supply office, the paper was printed in weekly editions of fifty copies. Before long Andras and Mendel began to enjoy a quiet journalistic fame among the camp inhabitants.

But what *The Biting Fly* failed to provide was the one thing they all wanted most from a paper: real news of Budapest and the world. For that they had to rely on the few tattered copies of newspapers that had been sent by relatives or thrown out by the guards. Those papers would be passed around until they were unreadable and the news they contained had long ago gone stale. But there were some events of such great importance that they became known to the men not long after they occurred. In the third week of June, scarcely a year after France had fallen, Hitler's troops invaded the Soviet Union along a twelve-hundred-kilometer front that ran from the Baltic to the Black Sea. The Kremlin seemed just as shocked by that turn of events as the men of Bánhida Camp. It appeared that Moscow had believed Germany to be committed to its nonaggression pact with the Soviet Union. But Hitler, Mendel pointed out, must have been planning the attack for months. How else would he have mustered so many hundreds of thousands of troops, so many planes, so many panzer divisions? Not a week later, Andras and Mendel learned from the camp postmaster that Soviet planes—or what had appeared at first to be Soviet planes, but might have been German planes in disguise—had bombed the Magyar border town of Kassa. The message was clear: Hungary had no choice but to send its armies into Russia. If Prime Minister Bárdossy refused, Hungary would lose all the territories Germany had returned to it. In fact, Bárdossy, who had long opposed Hungary's entry into the war, now seemed to view it as inevitable. Soon the headlines trumpeted a declaration of war against the Soviet Union, and Hungarian Army units were on their way to join the Axis invasion. The men of the 101/18th knew what that meant: For every Hungarian unit sent to the front, a unit of labor servicemen would be sent to support it.

No one knew how long the war might go on, or what the labor servicemen might be called upon to do. In the barracks there were rumors that they would be used as human shields, or sent first across the lines to draw enemy fire. But at Bánhida there was no immediate change; the coal came out of the ground, the men loaded it into the carts, the power plant burned it, the sulfurous dust rose into the air. In July, when the mud dried up and the spring insects died of thirst, the pace of work seemed to grow more urgent, as if more power were needed to fuel the engines of war. The heat was so intense that the men stripped down to their underwear each day by noon. There were no trees to provide shelter from the sun, no swimming hole to cool their sunburned skin. Andras knew that cold raspberry-flavored seltzer existed not far off, in the town they'd passed en route to the camp, and on the hottest days he thought he might abandon his cart—damn the consequences—and walk until he reached the cool umbrella forest of a sidewalk café. He began to see shimmering mirages of water beside the tracks; at times the whole expanse of the camp floated atop a glittering silver-black sea. How long had it been since he'd seen the real sea, with its aquamarine swells and its icy-looking whitecaps? He could see it just beyond the chain-link fence as he pushed the carts of coal: the Mediterranean, a hammered copper-blue, stretching away toward the unimaginable shores of Africa. There was Klara in her black swimsuit, her white bathing cap with racing stripes, stepping into the foam at the water's edge; Klara submerged to her thighs, her legs zigzagging into watery distortion. Klara on the wooden diving tower; Klara executing an Odettelike swan dive.

And then the foreman was at Andras's side, shouting his orders. The coal had to be shoveled, the carts had to be moved, because somewhere to the east a war had to be fought.

The most stunning news of Andras's life reached him on a still, hot evening in July, a month after Hungary had entered the war, in the dead hour between work and dinner, on the front steps of Barracks 21. He and two of his barracks-mates, a pair of lanky red-haired twins from Sopron, had gone to the office after work to get their letters and parcels. The men were blistered with sunburn, their eyes dazed from the brightness of the day; their sweat had turned the dust into a fine paste, which had dried into a thin crackling film on their skin. As ever, there was an interminable line at the post office. The mail was subject to inspection by the postmaster and his staff, which meant that every parcel had to be opened, inspected, and robbed of any food or cigarettes or money it might contain before its recipient could take away what was left. The Sopron twins chuckled over a recent copy of *The Biting Fly* as they waited. Andras's mind was muffled with heat; he could scarcely remember illustrating that issue. He uncorked his canteen and drank the last few drops of water. If they had to wait in this line much longer, there wouldn't be time to wash before dinner. Had he asked Klara to send him shaving soap? He envisioned a clean cake of it, wrapped in waxy white paper and printed with the image of a girl in an old-fashioned bathing costume. Or perhaps there would be something else, something less necessary but just as good: a box of violet pastilles, say, or a new photograph of Klara.

When they reached the window at last, the mail clerk put two identical packages into the twins' hands. Each had been opened and inspected as usual, and the wrappers of four chocolate bars lay nested inside the packages like a taunt. But there must have been a surplus of baked goods in the mail that day: the parcels still contained identical tins of cinnamon rugelach. Miku and Samu were generous boys, and they admired Andras for his role in the creation of *The Biting Fly*; they waited for him while he retrieved a single thin envelope from Klara, and on the way back to the barracks they shared their bounty with him. Despite the comforts of cinnamon and sugar, Andras couldn't help but feel disappointed with his own lean envelope. He was out of shaving soap and vitamins and a hundred other things. His wife might have thought about his needs. She might have sent him even a small package. While the twins went inside with their own parcels, he sat down on the steps and tore open the letter with his pocketknife.

From across the quadrangle, Mendel Horovitz saw Andras sitting on the barracks steps with a letter in his hands. He hurried across the yard, hoping to catch his friend before he went to the sinks to wash for dinner. Mendel had just come from the supply office, where the clerk had allowed him to use the typewriter; in a mere forty-five minutes he'd managed to type all six pages of the new *Biting Fly*. He thought there might still be time for Andras to begin the illustrations that evening. He whistled a tune from *Tin Pan Alley*, the movie he'd seen while in Budapest on furlough. But when he reached the barracks steps he stopped and fell silent. Andras had raised his eyes to Mendel, the letter trembling in his hand.

"What is it, Parisi?" Mendel said.

Andras couldn't speak; he thought he might never speak

again. Perhaps he had failed to understand. But he looked at the letter again, and there were the words in Klara's neat slanted script.

She was pregnant. He, Andras Lévi, was going to be a father.

What did it matter now how many tons of coal he had to shovel? Who cared how many times the cart tipped from its unstable rails, how many times his blisters broke and bled, how brutally the guards abused him? What did it matter how hungry or thirsty he was, or how little sleep he got, or how long he had to stand in the quadrangle for lineup? What did he care for his own body? Fifty kilometers away in Budapest, Klara was pregnant with his child. All that mattered was that he survive the months between now and the date she'd projected in her letter—the twenty-ninth of December. By then he would have fulfilled his two years of military service. The war might even be finished, depending upon the outcome of Hitler's campaign in Russia. Who knew what life might be like for Jews in Hungary then, but if Horthy was still regent it might not be an impossible place to live. Or maybe they would emigrate to America, to the dirty and glamorous city of New York. The day he got Klara's letter he drew a calendar on the back of a copy of *The Biting Fly*. At the end of each workday he crossed off a square, and gradually the days began to queue up into a long succession of Xs. Letters flew between Budapest and Bánhida: Klara was still teaching private students, would continue to teach as long as she could demonstrate the steps. She was putting money away so they might rent a larger apartment when Andras came home. A friend of her mother's owned a building on Nefelejcs utca; the neighborhood wasn't fashionable, but the building was close to the house on Benczúr utca and only a few blocks from the city park. *Nefelejcs* was the name of the tiny blue flower that grew in the woods, the one with the infinitesimal yellow ring at its center: forget-me-not. He couldn't, of course, not for a moment; his life seemed balanced on the edge of an unimaginable change.

In September a miracle occurred: Andras received a three-day furlough. There was no particular reason for that piece of luck, as far as he could determine; at Bánhida it seemed furloughs were granted at random except in the case of a death in the family. He learned of the furlough on a Thursday, received his papers on Friday, boarded a train to Budapest on Saturday morning. It was a luminous day, the air soft with the last radiant warmth of summer. The sky overhead burned a clear pale blue, and as they moved away from Bánhida the smell of sulfur faded into the sweet green smell of cut grass. Along the dirt roads that ran beside the tracks, farmers drove wagons heavy with hay and corn. The markets in Budapest would be full of squashes and apples and red cabbages, bell peppers and pears, late grapes, potatoes. It was astonishing to remember that such things still existed in the world—that they'd existed all along while he'd survived on a daily diet of coffee and thin soup and a couple hundred grams of sandy bread.

Klara was waiting for him at Keleti Station. He had never seen a woman so beautiful in all his life: She wore a dress of rose-colored jersey that grazed the swell of her belly, and a neat close-fitting hat of cinnamon wool. In continued defiance of the prevailing fashion, her hair was uncut and uncurled; she had looped it into a low chignon at the base of her neck. He folded her into his arms, breathing in the dusky smell of her skin. He was afraid to crush her against him as fiercely as he wanted to. He held her at arm's length and looked at her.

"Is it true?" he said.

"As you can see."

"But is it *really*?"

"I suppose we'll find out in a few months." She took his arm and led him from the station toward the Városliget. He could hardly believe it was possible to stroll through the September afternoon with Klara at his side, his work tools far away in Bánhida, nothing ahead of him but the prospect of pleasure and rest. Then, as they turned at István út and it became apparent that they were heading for her family's house, he braced himself for the necessity of an interaction with her brother and sister-in-law and possibly even with József, who had rented an atelier in Buda so he could paint again. The absence of Andras's officer's insignia would have to be explained, his gauntness remarked over and regretted, and all that time he would have to look into the complacent and well-fed countenances of Klara's relatives and feel the painful difference between their situation and his own. But when they reached the corner of István and Nefelejcs, Klara paused at the door of a gray stone building and took a key ring from her pocket. She held up an ornate key for Andras to admire. Then she fitted the key into the lock of the entry door, and the door swung inward to admit them.

"Where are we?" Andras asked.

"You'll see."

The courtyard was filled with courtyard things: bicycles and potted ferns and rows of tomato plants in wooden boxes. At the center there was a mossy fountain with lily pads and goldfish; a dark-haired girl sat at its edge, trailing her hand in the water. She looked up at Andras and Klara with serious eyes, then dried her hand on her skirt and ran to one of the ground-floor apartments. Klara led Andras to an open stairway with a vine-patterned railing, and they climbed three flights of shallow stairs. With a different key she opened a set of double doors and let him into an apartment overlooking the street. The place smelled of roasted chicken and fried potatoes. There were four brass coat hooks beside the door; an old homburg hat of Andras's hung on one of them, and Klara's gray coat on the other.

"This can't be our apartment," Andras said.

"Who else's?"

"Impossible. It's too fine."

"You haven't even seen it yet. Don't judge it so quickly. You might find it not at all to your taste."

But of course it was exactly to his taste. She knew perfectly well what he liked. There was a red-tiled kitchen, a bedroom for Andras and Klara, a tiny second bedroom that might be used as a nursery, a private bath with its own enameled tub. The sitting room was lined with bookshelves, which Klara had begun to fill with new books on ballet and music and architecture. There was a wooden drafting table in one corner, a distant Hungarian cousin of the one Klara had given Andras in Paris. A phonograph stood on a thin-legged taboret in another corner. At the far end of the room, a low sofa faced an inlaid wooden table. Two ivory-striped armchairs flanked the high windows with their view of the neo-Baroque apartment building across the street.

"It's a home," he said. "You made us a home." And he took her into his arms.

What he wanted most during the short span of his furlough, he told Klara, was to be at liberty to see to his pregnant wife's needs. She resisted at first, pointing out that he had no one to care for him at Bánhida. But he argued that to care for her would be a far greater luxury than to be cared for himself. And so, that first night home, after they'd eaten the roasted chicken and potatoes, she allowed him to make her coffee and read to her from the newspaper, and then to run a bath for her and bathe her with the large yellow sponge. Her pregnant body was a miraculous thing to him. A pink bloom had come out beneath the surface of her pale skin, and her hair seemed thicker and more lustrous. He washed it himself and pulled it forward to drape over her breasts. Her areolae had grown larger and darker, and a faint tawny line had emerged between her navel and her pubic triangle, transected by the silvery scar of her earlier pregnancy. Her bones no longer showed so starkly beneath the skin. Most notably, a complicated inward look had appeared in her eyes—such a deep commingling of sadness and expectancy that it was almost a relief when she closed them. As she lay back in the bathtub, cooling her arms against the enamel, he was struck by the fact that at Bánhida his life had been reduced to the simplest needs and emotions: the hope for a piece of carrot in his soup, the fear of the foreman's anger, the desire for another fifteen minutes of sleep. For Klara, who had lived in greater security here in Budapest, there remained the opportunity for more complicated reflection. It was happening as he watched, as he bathed her with the yellow sponge.

"Tell me what you're thinking," he said. "I can't guess."

She opened her gray eyes and turned to him. "How strange it is," she said. "To be pregnant while we're at war. If Hitler controls all of Europe, and perhaps Russia, too, who knows what may happen to this child? There's no use pretending Horthy can keep us from harm."

"Do you think we should try to emigrate?"

She sighed. "I've thought about it. I've even written to Elisabet. But the situation is as I expected. It's almost impossible to get an entry visa now. Even if we could, I'm not certain I'd want to. Our families are here. I can't imagine leaving my mother again, particularly now. And it's hard to imagine starting another life in a strange country."

"The travel, too," he said, stroking her wet shoulders. "It's hardly safe to cross an ocean during a war."

Encircling her knees with her arms, she said, "It's not just the war I've been thinking about. I've had all kinds of doubts."

"What doubts?"

"About what sort of mother I'll be to this child. About the hundred thousand ways I failed Elisabet."

"You didn't fail Elisabet. She turned out a strong and beautiful woman. And your situation was different then. You were alone, and you were just a child yourself."

"And now I'm practically an old woman."

"That's nonsense, Klara."

"Not really." She frowned at her knees. "I'm thirty-four, you know. The birth was a near disaster last time. The obstetrician says my womb may have been damaged. My mother came to my last appointment, and I wish now that she hadn't. She's been driving herself mad with worry."

"Why, Klara? Is there a danger to the baby?" He took her chin and made her raise her eyes to him. "Are you in danger yourself?"

"Women give birth every day," she said, and tried to smile.

"What did the doctor say?"

"He says there's a risk of complication. He wants me to have the child at the hospital."

"Of course you'll have it at the hospital," Andras said. "I don't care what it costs. We'll find a way to pay."

"My brother will help," she said.

"I'll get work," Andras said. "We'll make the money some-how."

"György wouldn't begrudge us anything," Klara said. "No more than your own brothers would."

Andras didn't want to argue, not during the brief time they had together. "I know he'd help if we needed it," he said. "Let's hope we don't have to ask him."

"My mother wants me to move home to Benczúr utca," Klara said, twisting her wet hair into a rope. "She doesn't understand why I insist that you and I must have our own apartment. She thinks it's a needless expense. And she doesn't like me to be alone. What if something were to happen? she says. As if I hadn't spent all those years alone in Paris."

"She wants to protect you all the more, because of that," he said. "It must have tortured her not to be with you when you were pregnant with Elisabet."

"I understand, of course. But I'm not a child of fifteen any-more."

"Perhaps she's right, though. If there's a danger, wouldn't it be better for you to be at home?"

"Not you, too, Andráska!"

"I hate to think of you being alone."

"I'm not alone. Ilana is here with me almost every day. And I can walk to my mother's house in six minutes. But I can't live there again, and not just because I'm accustomed to being on my own. What if the authorities were to discover who I am? If I were living in my family's house, they'd be directly implicated."

"Ah, Klara! How I wish you didn't have to think about any of this."

"And how I wish you didn't either," she said. And then she stood from the bath, and the water fell from her skin in a glittering curtain, and he followed the new curves of her body with his hands.

Later that night, when he found he couldn't sleep, he got out of bed and went into the sitting room, to the drafting table Klara had bought for him; he ran his hands over that smooth hard surface devoid of paper or tools. There was a time when he might have comforted himself with work, even if it were just a project he had set himself; the pure concentration required to draw a series of fine unbroken black lines could turn his mind aside, even if just for a few moments, from the gravest of problems. But the fact was that he'd never before had to worry about the fate of his pregnant wife and his unborn child and the entire Western world. In any case, there was no project he could imagine taking up now; when it came to the study and practice of architecture, his mind was as blank and planless as the drafting table before him. The work he'd done those past two years when he wasn't cutting trees or building roads or shoveling coal—scratching in notebooks, doodling in the margins of Mendel's newspapers— might have kept his hands from lying idle; it might even have kept him from going mad. But it had also been a distraction from the fact that his life as a student of architecture was slipping farther and farther away, his hands losing their memory of how to make a perfect line, his mind losing its ability to solve problems of form and function. How far away he felt now from that atelier at the École Spéciale where he and Polaner had suspended a running track from the roof of a sports club. How astounding that such an idea had occurred to them. It seemed an eternity since he'd looked at a building with any thought in his mind beside the hope that its roof wouldn't leak and that it would keep out the wind. He'd hardly even taken note of what the façade of this building looked like.

He wished he could talk to Tibor. He would know what Andras should do, how he might protect Klara and begin to reclaim his life. But Tibor was three hundred kilometers away in the Carpathians. Andras couldn't imagine when they might next sit down together to make sense of who they were now, or at least to take some comfort in their shared uncertainty.

As it happened, it was his younger brother—the one whose function had always been to cause trouble, rather than to alleviate it—who materialized in Budapest during Andras's furlough. Mátyás rolled into Nyugati Station with the rest of his company, which had been posted nearby while it awaited a transfer, and jumped off the train to enjoy a furlough of his own making. His company was directed by a lax young officer who allowed his men to buy an occasional exemption from work. Mátyás, who had hoarded money during his window-trimming days, had bought a few days off to see a shopgirl he'd met on one of his jobs. He had no idea that Andras was home on furlough, too, and so it was purely by accident that, on Monday afternoon, Mátyás jumped onto the back of a streetcar and found himself face-to-face with his brother. He was so surprised that he would have fallen off again if Andras hadn't grabbed his arm and held him.

"What are you doing here?" Mátyás cried. "You're supposed to be slaving at a mine."

"And you're supposed to be—doing what?"

"Building bridges. But not today! Today I'm going to see a girl named Serafina."

An elderly woman in a kerchief gave them a disapproving look, as if they ought to know better than to engage in such loud and animated conversation on a streetcar. But Andras pulled Mátyás's face close to his own and said to the woman, "It's my brother, do you see? My brother!"

"You must have had donkeys for parents," the woman said.

"Pardon us, your ladyship," Mátyás said. He tipped his hat and executed a perfect backflip from the side rail of the streetcar to the pavement, so swiftly that the woman gave a little scream. As the passengers watched in astonishment, he tapped out a soft-shoe rhythm against the cobblestones and then fleetfooted his way up onto the curb, scattering the pedestrians there; he turned a double spin, whipped off his hat, and bowed to a young woman in a blue twill coat. Everyone who'd seen him gave a cheer. Andras jumped down from the streetcar and waited until his brother had finished taking his curtain calls.

"Needless foolishness," Andras said, once the applause had died down.

"I must emblazon that on a flag and carry it everywhere."

"You might well. Then everyone would have some warning."

"Where are you going with a market bag full of potatoes?" Mátyás asked.

"Home to my apartment, where my wife is waiting for me."

"*Your* apartment? What apartment?"

"Thirty-five Nefelejcs utca, third floor, apartment B."

"Since when do you live there? And for how long?"

"Since last night. And for another day and a half, until I have to go back to Bánhida."

Mátyás laughed. "Then I suppose I caught you by your shirt-tails."

"Or I caught you. Why don't you come for dinner?"

"I might be otherwise engaged."

"And what if this Serafina sees you for the glib young fool you are?"

"In that case I'll come over at once." Mátyás kissed Andras on both cheeks and hopped aboard the next streetcar, which by that time had pulled up beside them.

For a few blocks, as Andras walked toward home, he felt inclined to tap-dance himself. Chance favored him at times; it had delivered the unexpected furlough, and now it had delivered Mátyás. But not even that welcome surprise could divert his mind from its new channel of worry. The newspaper he'd bought that afternoon had delivered a sobering view of events in the east: Kiev had fallen to the Germans, and Hitler's armies lay within a hundred miles of Leningrad and Moscow. In a radio address earlier that week, the Führer had proclaimed the imminent capitulation of the Soviet Union. Andras feared that the British, who had held out fiercely in the Mediterranean, would lose hope now; if their defenses crumbled, Hitler would rule all of Europe. He thought of Rosen at the Blue Dove three years earlier, declaring that Hitler wanted to make a Germany of the world. Not even Rosen could have predicted the degree to which that speculation would prove true. German territory had spread across the map of Europe like spilled ink. And the people of the conquered countries had been turned from their homes, deported to wastelands or clapped into ghettoes or sent to labor camps. He wanted to believe that Hungary might remain a refuge at the center of the firestorm; it was easier to believe such a thing here in Budapest, far from the heat and stink of Bánhida Camp. But if Russia were to fall, no country in Europe would be safe, particularly not for Jews—certainly not Hungary, where the Arrow Cross had gained strength in every recent election. Into this baffling uncertainty, Andras and Klara's child would be born. He began to understand how his own parents must have felt when his mother had become pregnant with him during the Great War, though the situation had been different then: His father had been a Hungarian soldier, not a forced laborer, and there had been no crazed Führer dreaming of a Jew-free Europe.

At home he found Klara and Ilana sitting at the kitchen table and laughing over some intimacy, Ilana's hands clasped in Klara's own. It was clear to him, even at first glance, that the connection between them had deepened in his absence; in her letters Klara had often mentioned how grateful she was for Ilana's companionship, and he'd been relieved to know that they lived just a few blocks from each other and crossed the distance often. If Klara had been Ilana's confidante and protector in Paris, now she seemed to have become something like an older sister. Soon after Ilana had arrived in Budapest, Klara had told him, they'd begun a ritual of going to the market together every Monday and Thursday morning. When Tibor had gone to the Munka-szolgálat, Klara had seen to it that Ilana wasn't lonely; they cooked together, spent evenings with Klara's records or Ilana's books, strolled the boulevards and parks on Sunday afternoons. That particular night, just before Andras had arrived, Ilana had delivered a piece of sweet and complicated news: She was pregnant. She repeated the news now in her tentative Hungarian. It had happened while Tibor was home on his last furlough. If all went well, the babies would be born two months apart. She'd written to Tibor and received a letter assuring her that he was well, that his labor company was far from the dangerous action farther east, that the summer weather had made everything more bearable, that her news had made him happier than he'd believed he could be.

But there was no happiness that fall of 1941 that wasn't complicated by worry. Andras could see it in the narrow lines that had gathered on Ilana's brow. He knew what this pregnancy must mean to her after her miscarriage, and how terrified she would be for the baby's safety even if they weren't in the midst of a war. He would have embraced her if her observance hadn't forbidden it. As it was, he had to be content to congratulate her and express his fervent wish that all would go well. Then he told the two of them how he had run into Mátyás on the streetcar.

"Well," Klara said. "It's a good thing I bought extra pastries for dessert. That young goat would eat us into starvation otherwise."

Mátyás arrived just as Klara was setting out the pastries in the sitting room after dinner. He gave her a kiss on the cheek and plucked a cream-filled mille-feuille from the silver tray. For Ilana he had a deep bow and a flourish of his hat.

"Your romancing must have gone well," Andras said. "Your cheeks are on fire with lipstick."

"It's not lipstick," Mátyás said. "It's the stain of breached innocence. Serafina is far too worldly for me. I'm still blushing from what she said when we parted."

"We won't ask what it was," Klara said.

"I wouldn't tell anyway," he said, and winked. He looked around him at the furnishings of the sitting room. "What a place," he said. "All of this just for the two of you!"

"For the three of us, soon," Klara said.

"Of course. I nearly forgot. Andras is going to be a papa."

"And so is Tibor," Ilana said.

"Good God!" Mátyás said. "Is it true? Both of you?"

"It's true," Ilana said, and then pointed a teasing finger at him. "Now your anya and apa will want you to be married, too, just to complete the picture."

"Not a chance," Mátyás said, with another wink. He laid down a quick combination of syncopated steps across the parquet floor of the sitting room, then mock-fell over the back of the sofa and landed upright beside the low table. "Tell me I haven't got talent," he demanded, and knelt before Klara with his arms outstretched. "You should know, dancing mistress."

"We don't call that dancing where I come from," Klara said, and smiled.

"How about this, then?" Mátyás got to his feet and executed a double-pirouette with his arms above his head. But at the end he lost his balance and had to catch himself on the mantel. He stood for a moment breathing hard, shaking his head as if to clear it of a gyrational ghost, and for the first time Andras noticed how exhausted and ravenous he looked. He took Mátyás by the shoulder and led him to one of the striped ivory chairs.

"Sit here for a while," Andras said. "You'll feel better when you get up."

"Don't you like my dancing?"

"Not at the moment, brother."

Klara made a plate of pastries for Mátyás, and Andras poured him a glass of slivovitz. For a while they all sat together and talked as though there were no such thing as war or worry or the work service. Andras kept the dessert plates and coffee cups filled. Ilana blushed at the attention, protesting that it wasn't right to allow herself to be waited upon by her husband's brother. Andras thought he had never seen her look so beautiful. Her skin, like Klara's, seemed lit from within. Her hair was hidden under the kerchief worn by observant married women, but the scarf she'd chosen was made of lilac-colored silk shot through with silver. When she laughed at Mátyás's jokes, the black-brown depths of her eyes seemed to flare with intelligent light. It was astonishing to think that this was the same girl who had lain pale and terrified in a hospital bed in Paris, her lips whitening with pain as she woke from the anesthesia.

After they finished their coffee, Andras and Mátyás went out for a walk together in the mild September night. From Nefelejcs utca it was only a few blocks to the city park, where gold floodlights illuminated the Vajdahunyad Castle. The paths were full of pedestrians even at that hour; in the shadowy recesses of the castle walls they could see men and women moving against each other in imperfect privacy. Mátyás's high spirits had quieted now that the two of them were alone. He crossed his arms over his chest as if he were cold in the warm breeze. His time in the Munkaszolgálat seemed to have sharpened him somehow; the planes of his face had become harder and more distinct. His high forehead and prominent cheekbones, so much like their mother's, had begun to lend him a gravity that seemed at odds with his prankster wit.

"My brothers have beautiful wives," he said. "I'd be lying if I said I wasn't jealous."

"Well, I'd be rather disappointed if you weren't."

"You're truly going to be a father?"

"So it seems."

He let out a low whistle. "Excited?"

"Terrified."

"Nonsense. You'll be wonderful. And Klara's been through it once before."

"Her child wasn't born during a war," Andras said.

"No, but she didn't have a husband then, either."

"She didn't seem so much the worse for it. She got work. She raised her daughter. Elisabet might have been a more pleasant girl if she'd had a different sort of family—a brother or sister to play with, and a father to stop her from being so unkind to her mother. But she turned out all right, after all. I'm not much use as a husband. So far I've been nothing but a weight around Klara's neck."

"You were drafted," Mátyás said. "You had to serve. It's not as though you had any choice."

"I haven't finished my studies. I can't come home and start working as an architect."

"Then you'll go back to school."

"If I can get into school. And then there's the time and expense."

"What you need," Mátyás said, "is some well-paid work that doesn't take all your time. Why not go into business with me?"

"What, as a tap dancer? Do you imagine us as a performing team? The Amazing Lévi Brothers?"

"No, you dolt. We'll be a team of window-trimmers. The work will go twice as fast with two of us doing it. I'll be the stylist. You'll be my slave. We'll get double the clients."

"I don't know if I could take orders from you," Andras said. "You'd break my back."

"What'll you do for money, then? Sit on a street corner and make caricatures?"

"I've been thinking," Andras said. "My old friend Mendel Horovitz worked at the *Budapest Evening Courier* before he went into the labor service. He says they're always looking for layout artists and illustrators. And the pay's not bad."

"Akh. But then you'd just be someone else's slave."

"If I've got to be someone's slave, I might as well do it in a field where I've got experience."

"What experience?"

"Well, there was my old job at *Past and Future*. And then there are the newspapers Mendel and I have been making, the ones I wrote you about. I would have brought you a copy if I'd known I was going to see you."

"I understand," Mátyás said. "Window-trimming isn't fancy enough work for you. Not after your Paris education." He was teasing, but his expression betrayed a flicker of pique. Andras remembered the fierce letters Mátyás had written from Debrecen while Andras was in Paris—the ones in which Mátyás had claimed his own share of an education. Then the war had begun, and Mátyás had been stuck in Hungary, working first at window-trimming and then in the Munkaszolgálat. Andras was ashamed to realize that he did feel as if he should have moved beyond a job like window-trimming, which carried a flavor of commercial servitude. It was the wild luck of his last months in Paris that had made him feel that way, the kindness of his professors and his mentors that had led him to expect something different. But that was behind him now. He needed to earn money. In a few months he would be a father.

"Forgive me," Andras said. "I didn't mean to suggest your work wasn't an art. It's a higher art than newspaper illustration, that's for certain."

Mátyás's look seemed to soften, and he put a hand on his

brother's arm. "That's all right," he said. "I might think myself too fine for window-trimming, too, if Le Corbusier and Auguste Perret had been my drinking companions."

"We were never drinking companions," Andras said.

"Don't try to go in for humility now."

"Oh, all right. We were great friends. We drank together constantly." He fell silent, thinking of his real friends, the ones who were scattered across the Western Hemisphere now. Those men were his brothers too. But there hadn't been word from Ben Yakov after that conciliatory telegram, nor from Polaner since he'd joined the Foreign Legion. Andras wondered what had happened to the photograph that had been taken when he and Polaner had won the Prix du Amphithéâtre. It seemed strange to think it might still exist somewhere, a record of a vanished life.

"You look grim, brother," Mátyás said. "Do we need to get some wine into you?"

"It couldn't hurt," Andras said.

So they went to a café overlooking the artificial lake, the one that became a skating rink in winter, and they sat at a table outside and ordered Tokaji. The war had made wine expensive, but Mátyás insisted upon the indulgence and further insisted upon paying, since he didn't have a wife or future child to support. He promised to let Andras pay the next time, once he'd landed a job at a newspaper, though of course neither of them knew when that might happen, or even when they might next be home together.

"Now, who's this Serafina?" Andras asked, looking at his brother through the amber lens of his glass of Tokaji. "And when will we meet her?"

"She's a seamstress at a dress shop on Váci utca."

"And?"

"*And*, I met her when I was working on a window. She was wearing a white dress embroidered with cherries. I made her take it off so I could put it in the window display."

"You made her take her dress off?"

"Do you see why it might be an attractive job?"

"Did she go back to her sewing machine naked?"

"No. Sadly, the dressmaker had something else for her to put on."

"Now, that's a shame."

"Yes. I've felt the sting of it ever since. That's why I decided to pursue her. I wanted to see what I missed when she stepped behind the changing-room curtain."

"You must have seen enough to make it seem worth the pursuit."

"Plenty. She's what I like. Just a shade taller than me. Black hair cut into a neat little cap. And a mole on her cheek like a spot of brown ink."

"Well, I can't wait to make her acquaintance."

Again, the glint of mirth faded out of Mátyás's eyes; the faint shadows beneath them seemed to deepen as he looked down into his glass of wine. "I'm going to follow my company tomorrow," he said. "We're off to the big party."

"What big party?"

"Belgorod, in Russia. The front lines."

A terrible clang in Andras's chest, as though the bell of his ribcage had been struck with an iron hammer. "Oh, Mátyás. No."

"Yes," Mátyás said. He looked up and grinned, but his expression was one of fear. "So you see, it's a good thing we ran into each other."

"Can't you get a transfer? Have you tried?"

"Money's the only way, and I've only got enough for small bribes."

"How much would it cost?"

"Oh, I don't know. At this point, hundreds. Maybe thousands."

Andras thought again of György Hász in his villa on Benczúr utca, where he was most likely sitting by the fire in a cashmere robe and reading one of the financial papers. He wanted to take

Hász and turn him upside down, shake him until gold coins rained out of him as if from a broken bank. He could think of no reason why that man's son should have a painting studio and a stretch of leisure-filled months ahead, while Mátyás Lévi, son of Lucky Béla of Konyár, had to go to the Eastern Front and take his chances in the minefields. He, Andras, would be a fool, worse than a fool, if he allowed his pride to keep him from applying to György for help. This wasn't a matter of whether or not Andras could support Klara and their child; Mátyás's life was at stake.

"I'll pay a visit to Hász," Andras said. "They've got to have a chest of kroner hidden somewhere, or something they can sell."

Mátyás nodded. "I don't suppose József Hász has to go to the front lines."

"No, indeed. József Hász has got himself a nice atelier in Buda."

"How timely," Mátyás said. "The destruction of the Western world should make an interesting subject."

"Yes. Although, strange to say, I haven't felt the urge to visit him and check the progress of his work."

"That *is* strange."

"In seriousness, though, I'm not sure Hász the Elder has ready cash. I think it's all they can do to keep that house on Benczúr utca and maintain Madame's furs and their opera box. They had to sell their car to get József exempted from his second call-up."

"At least they still have the opera box," Mátyás said. "Music can be such a comfort when other people are dying." He winked at Andras, then raised his glass and drained it.

The next day, after Andras had seen his brother off at Nyugati Station, he went to call on György Hász at home. He knew Hász came home every day to have lunch with his wife and mother, and that afterward he liked to spend half an hour with the newspaper before he went back to his office. Even in uncertain times he was a man of regular habits. In defiance of the change in his professional circumstances, he had retained the gentlemanly schedule of his days as the bank's director; his services were too valuable for the new bank president to prevent him from taking that liberty. As Andras had expected, he found his brother-in-law in the library of the house on Benczúr utca, his reading glasses on, the newspaper butterflied in his hands. When the manservant announced Andras's arrival, Hász dropped the paper and got to his feet.

"Is everything well with Klara?" he said.

"Everything's fine," Andras said. "We're both fine."

Hász's brow relaxed and he gave a sharp sigh. "Forgive me," he said. "I wasn't expecting to see you. I didn't know you were home."

"I've had a few days' furlough. I'm going back tomorrow."

"Please sit down," Hász said. To the man who had conducted Andras in, he said, "Tell Kati to bring us tea." The man went out silently, and György Hász gave Andras a slow, careful perusal. Andras had chosen to wear his Munkaszolgálat uniform that day, with its green M on the breast pocket and its mended places where Major Barna had torn off his marks of rank. Hász glanced at Andras's uniform, then put a hand to his own tie, blue silk with a narrow ivory stripe. "Well," he said. "You've got only three more months of service, by my calculation."

"That's right," Andras said. "And then the baby will be born."

"And you're well? You seem well."

"As well as can be expected."

Hász nodded and sat back in his chair, crossing his fingers over his vest. In addition to the blue silk tie he was wearing an Italian poplin shirt and a suit of dark gray wool. His hands were the soft hands of a man who had always worked indoors, his fingernails pink and smooth. But he looked at Andras with such genuine and unguarded concern that it was impossible to resent him entirely. When the tea arrived, he prepared Andras's cup himself and handed it across the table.

"How can I help you?" he said. "What brought you here?"

"My brother Mátyás has been deployed to the Eastern Front," Andras said. "His company left this afternoon to meet the rest of their battalion in Debrecen, and from there they'll go to Belgorod."

Hász put down his cup and looked at Andras. "Belgorod," he said. "The minefields."

"Yes. They'll be clearing the way for the Hungarian Army."

"But what can I do?" Hász said. "How can I help him?"

"I know you've done a great deal for us already," Andras said. "You've looked out for Klara while I've been away. That's the best service you could have rendered me. Believe me, I would never ask for anything more if I didn't believe it was a matter of life and death. But I wonder if it might be possible to do for Mátyás something like what you've done for József. If not exempt him entirely, at least get him transferred to another company. One that's not likely to be so close to the action. He's got eleven months left."

György Hász raised an eyebrow, then sat back in his chair. "You'd like me to buy his freedom," he said.

"At least his freedom from working on the front lines."

"I understand." He steepled his hands and looked at Andras across the desk.

"I know the price isn't the same for everyone," Andras said. He set his cup in the saucer and gave it a careful turn. "I imagine it would be a great deal less for my brother than it was for your son. I have the name of Mátyás's battalion commander. If we could arrange for a certain sum to be transferred to him through an independent agent—a lawyer of your acquaintance, say—we might accomplish it all without revealing to the authorities the connection between your family and mine. That is to say, without compromising Klara's security. I'm certain we could buy my brother's freedom at what would seem to you a negligible sum."

Hász pressed his lips together and brought his steepled hands against them, then tapped his fingers as he looked toward the fire. Andras waited for his answer as if György were a magistrate and Mátyás in the seat of judgment before him. But Mátyás was not, of course, before him; he was already on a train headed toward the Eastern Front. All at once it seemed a folly to have imagined that György Hász might have the power to stop what had already been set in motion.

"Does Klara know you came to me?" Hász asked.

"No," Andras said. "Though she wouldn't have discouraged me. She's confident of your help in all matters. I'm the one whose pride generally prevents the asking."

György Hász pushed himself up from the leather chair and went to tend the fire. The previous day's soft heat had blown away overnight; a sharp wind rattled the casement windows. He moved the logs with the poker and a flight of sparks soared up into the heights of the fireplace. Then he replaced the tool and turned to face Andras.

"I have to apologize before I speak further," he said. "I hope you'll understand the decisions I've made."

"Apologize for what?" Andras said. "What decisions?"

"For some time I've been operating under a rather heavy financial and emotional burden," he said. "It's entirely independent of my son's situation, and I'm afraid it's going to continue for some time. I can't imagine what the end of it will be, in fact. I haven't spoken to you about it because I knew it would be a source of worry at a time when your greatest concern was to stay alive. But I'm going to tell you now. It's a grave thing you've come to ask of me, and I find it impossible to give an answer without making you understand my situation. Our situation, I should say." He took his seat across from Andras once again and pulled his chair closer to the table. "It concerns someone dear to us both," he said. "It's about Klara, of course. Her troubles. What happened to her when she was a girl."

Andras's skin went cold all at once. "What do you mean?"

"Not long after you went into the Munkaszolgálat, a woman came forward and informed the authorities that the Claire Morgenstern who had recently entered the country was the same Klara Hász who had fled eighteen years earlier."

His ears rang with the shock of it. "Who?" he demanded. "What woman?"

"A certain Madame Novak, who had returned from Paris herself not long before."

"Madame Novak," Andras repeated. In his mind she appeared as she had that night at Marcelle Gérard's party, quietly triumphant in her velvet gown and jasmine perfume—on the verge of effecting a twelve-hundred-kilometer separation between her husband and the woman he loved, the woman who had been his mistress for eleven years.

"So you know the situation, and why she might have done such a thing."

"I know what happened in Paris," Andras said. "I know why she has reason to hate Klara—or why she *had* reason to, in any case."

"It seems to have been a persistent hate," György said.

"You're telling me that the authorities know. They know she's here, and who she is. You're telling me they've known for months."

"I'm afraid so. They've compiled a great dossier on her case. They know everything about her flight from Budapest and what she's done since then. They know she's married to you, and they know all about your family—where your parents live, where your father works, what your brothers did before they entered the military, where they're stationed now. There's no chance, I'm afraid, that we could arrange an exemption for your brother at the common rate. Our families are connected, and the connection is known by those who have power in these matters. But even if we could convince your brother's battalion commander to name a price—and that in itself is not at all certain, considering how many of those men are terrible anti-Semites—it might be impossible to produce the money. You see, I've had to make a financial arrangement to preserve Klara's freedom, too. The chief magistrate in charge of her case happens to be an old acquaintance of mine—and happens, as well, to be intimate with my financial affairs, due to my removal from the bank presidency and my efforts to protest it. When the information about Klara emerged, he was the one to offer a kind of solution—or what one might call a solution, in the absence of any other source of hope. A sort of trade, as he put it to me. I would pay a certain percentage of my assets every month in perpetuity, and the Ministry of Justice would leave Klara alone. They would also see to it that the Central Alien Control Office renews her official residence permit each year. They don't want her deported, of course, now that they've got her back in the country and can use her to their advantage."

Andras drew a breath into the constricted passages of his lungs. "So that's what you've done," he said. "That's where the money's going."

"I'm afraid so."

"And she knows nothing about it?"

"Nothing. I want her to have the illusion of safety, at least. I think it's best to say nothing to her unless the situation changes significantly for the better or the worse. If she knew, I'm certain she would try to stop me. I don't know what form her attempt might take or what its consequences might be. I've informed my wife about the arrangement, of course—I've had to explain to her why it's been necessary to dissolve so many of our assets— and she agrees it's best to keep the whole thing from Klara for now. My mother disagrees, but thus far I've managed to make her see my perspective."

"But how long can it go on?" Andras said. "They'll bleed you dry."

"That seems to be their plan. I've already had to place this house under a second mortgage, and recently I've had to ask my wife to part with some of her jewelry. We've sold the car and the piano and some valuable paintings. There are other things that can be sold, but not an endless supply. And as my assets diminish, the percentage inches up—it's a way to keep the arrangement lucrative for this magistrate and his cronies in the Ministry of Justice. I believe we'll have to sell the house soon and take a flat closer to the center of town. I dread that—it'll become increasingly difficult to explain to Klara why we have to do these things. It's not possible to claim József's exemption as a continual drain of that magnitude. But Klara's freedom may be infinitely dear. Now that the government has found a way to siphon away our assets, I'm sure they won't stop until there's nothing left."

"But the government is the guilty party! Sándor Goldstein was killed. Klara was raped. Her daughter is the evidence. The government was responsible. They're the ones who should be paying *her*."

"In a just world, it might be possible to prove their guilt," said Hász. "But my lawyers assure me that Klara's accusations of rape would mean nothing now, particularly considering the fact that Klara fled justice herself. Not that they would have meant much at the time, mind you. Her situation was desperate from the beginning. If she'd stayed, the authorities would have pulled every dirty trick to demonstrate her guilt and hide their own. That was why my father and his lawyer decided she had to leave the country, and why they couldn't bring her back. My father never stopped trying, though—until his dying day he hoped it might still be done."

Andras rose and went to the fire, where the logs had burned down to glowing coals. The heat of them seemed to reach inside him and send a bright wave of anger through his chest. He turned to look into his brother-in-law's eyes. "Klara has been in danger for months, and you didn't tell me," he said. "You didn't think I could bear to know. Maybe you thought I didn't know what existed between Klara and Novak in Paris. Maybe you're afraid yourself that something's happened between them here in Budapest. Did you plan to keep making these payments until the problem went away? Were you going to leave me in the dark forever?"

The furrows of Hász's brow deepened again. "You have a right to be angry," he said. "I did keep you in the dark. I didn't feel I could trust you not to tell her. You have an uncommon relationship with your wife. The two of you seem to confide everything to each other. But perhaps you can understand my position, too. I wanted to protect her, and I didn't see how the knowledge could help either of you. I imagined it could only bring you pain."

"I'd rather have worried," Andras said. "I'd rather have had the pain than been kept ignorant of any problem that concerns my wife."

"I know how Klara loves you," György said. "I wish you and I had gotten to know each other better before you were conscripted. Maybe if we had, you'd understand why I felt it was right to act as I did."

Andras could only nod in silence.

"But as to the question of Klara's fidelity, I can assure you I've never felt the slightest uncertainty in that quarter. As far as I can divine, my sister adores you and you alone. She's never given me reason to believe otherwise, not in all the time you've been away." He took the poker in his hand and looked toward the fire again, and his shoulders rose and fell in a sigh. "If I had anything like my former property or influence, I might be more certain of being able to do something for your brother. The military has become increasingly greedy regarding bribes and favors. But I'll see if I can speak to someone I know."

"And what about Klara?" Andras said. "How can we be certain she's safe?"

"For now, apparently, the payments protect her. We can hope that the authorities will lose interest before my assets are exhausted. If the war goes on, they'll have more pressing worries. As for taking the course we took before—in 1920, I mean—Klara's leaving the country is an impossibility, particularly in her current state. Her comings and goings are too closely watched. In any case, it's impossible to get entry visas now to the countries where she might be safe. We'll have to persevere, that's all."

"Klara is an intelligent woman," Andras said. "Perhaps she could help us see a way through this."

"I have the most profound admiration for my sister's intelligence," Hász said. "She's managed brilliantly in adverse circumstances. But I don't want these concerns to weigh upon her. I want her to feel safe as long as she can."

"So do I," Andras said. "But, as you observed, I'm not in the habit of keeping secrets from my wife."

"You've got to promise me you won't speak to her about it. I don't like to place you in a position of incomplete honesty, but in this situation I find I have no choice."

"You mean to say that *I* have no choice."

"Understand me, Andras. We've invested a great deal in Klara's safety already. If you were to tell her now, it might all have been in vain."

"What if it were my wife's wish not to bring her family to ruin?"

"What else can we do? Would you prefer that she turn herself in? Or that she risk her own life and your child's in an escape attempt?" He got to his feet and paced before the fireplace. "I assure you I've considered the problem from every angle. I see no other course. I beg you to respect my judgment, Andras. You must believe that I have some insight into Klara's character too."

Though it still seemed a betrayal, Andras agreed to keep his silence. In fact he had no other choice; he had no money of his own, no high connections, no way to step between Klara and the law. And he was to leave again for Bánhida in the morning. At least the current arrangement would keep Klara protected while he was away. He thanked Hász for his pledge to see what might be done for Mátyás, and they parted with handshakes and serious looks that suggested they would move through this difficulty with the stoicism of Hungarian men. But as Andras left the house on Benczúr utca the news struck him again with all its original force. He felt as if he were walking through a different city, one that had lain all this time just behind the city he had known; the feeling brought to mind Monsieur Forestier's stage sets, those palimpsestic architectures in which the familiar concealed the strange and terrifying. In this inside-out reality, the secret of Klara's identity had become a secret kept from her, rather than one held by her; now Andras, no longer deceived, had agreed to become his wife's deceiver.

He thought it might calm his nerves to go down to the river and stand on the Széchenyi Bridge. He needed some time to arrange the situation in his mind before he went home to Klara. How long after he'd entered the work service, he wondered, had Madame Novak gone to the authorities? Was it merely the memory of past wrongs that had sent her there, or had there been a more recent wound? What did he really know of the present situation between Klara and Novak? Was it possible that, despite György's reassurances, Andras had been betrayed? A jolt of nausea went through him, and he had to stop at the curb and sit down. A stray mutt sniffed around his ankles; when he extended a hand toward the dog it drew back and ran away. He got up and pulled his coat closer, tightened his muffler around his throat. From Benczúr utca he walked to Bajza utca, and from Bajza to the tree-lined stretch of Andrássy út, where pedestrians huddled against the chilly wind and the streetcar sounded its familiar bell. But as he walked down Andrássy he found himself becoming increasingly anxious, and he realized that it was because he was approaching the Opera House, where, as far as he knew, Zoltán Novak was still director. It had been more than two years since he'd seen Novak; the party at Marcelle's had been the last time. He wondered if the wounds Novak had suffered that night could have moved him to a cruel and subtle act—if he might have brought Klara's peril to his wife's attention, might have betrayed Klara through his knowledge that Edith would want to be rid of her. Andras stopped on the street

before the Operaház and considered what he might say to
Novak that very moment if he could walk into the man's office
and confront him. What accusations might he make, what would
Novak admit? The knot of connection among the three of them,
himself and Novak and Klara, was so convoluted that to pull at
any one of its strands was to draw the whole mess tighter. It was
possible that if Andras walked into that building he might
emerge with the knowledge that Klara had betrayed him, had
been unfaithful to him for months—even that the child she was
carrying was not his own. But wasn't it worse to stand outside in
ignorance, worse to return to Bánhida and not know? The doors
of the Operaház were open to the brisk afternoon; he could see
men and women inside, waiting in line at the box-office window.
He drew a breath and went in.

How many months had passed, he wondered, since he'd been
inside a theater? It had been since his last summer in Paris—
he and Klara had gone to see a dress rehearsal of *La Fille Mal
Gardée*. Now he walked in through one of the Romanesque
doorways of the performance space and made his way down the
carpeted aisle. Onstage, the curtains had been drawn aside to
reveal an Italian village square with a white marble fountain at its
center. The buildings surrounding it were made of fake stone cut
from yellow-painted pasteboard, with awnings of green-and-
white-striped canvas. A carpenter bent over a set of steps leading
into one of the buildings; the sound of his hammer in the open
space of the auditorium gave Andras a pang of nostalgia. How he
wished he were arriving here to install a set, or even to set up a
coffee table for the actors and deliver their messages and fetch
them when it was time to go onstage. How he wished he had a
deskful of half-finished drawings waiting for him at home, a studio deadline looming in the near distance.

He ran to the front of the auditorium and climbed the steps
at the side of the stage. The carpenter didn't look up from his
work. In the wings, a man who must have been the properties
master was arranging props on their shelves; the whine of an

electric saw rose from the set-building shop, and the smell of fresh-cut wood came to Andras with its layered suggestions of his father's lumberyard and the Sarah-Bernhardt and Monsieur Forestier's workshop and the labor camp in Subcarpathia. He wandered farther into the back hallways of the theater, up a set of stairs to the dressing rooms; the whitewashed doors, with their copperplate-lettered names in brass cardholders, chastely hid the disasters of makeup boxes and stained dressing gowns and plumed hats and torn stockings and dog-eared scripts and moldering armchairs and cracked mirrors and wilted bouquets that he knew must lie on the other side. When Klara had been a girl, he realized, she must have dressed for her performances in one of these rooms. He remembered a photograph from those days, Klara in a skirt of tattered leaves, her hair interwoven with twigs like a woodland fairy's. He could almost see her sylphid shadow slipping across the hall from one room to another.

He walked down the hallway and climbed a flight of stairs; at the top, a hallway held another row of dressing rooms. The hall ended at a wooden door with a white enameled nameplate, the same one Novak had used at the Sarah-Bernhardt in Paris. There were the familiar words etched in black paint, their gold highlights and curlicues dimmed by the travel between Paris and Budapest: *Zoltán Novak, Directeur.* From behind the door came a deep cough. Andras raised a hand to knock, then let it drop. Now that he had arrived at this threshold, his courage had fled. He had no idea what he would say to Zoltán Novak. From within came another deep cough, and then a third, closer. The door opened, and Andras found himself face-to-face with Novak himself. He was pale, wasted, his eyes bright with what appeared to be fever; his moustache drooped, and his suit hung loose on his frame. When he saw Andras before him his shoulders went slack.

"Lévi," he said. "What are you doing here?"

"I don't know," Andras said. "I suppose I wanted a word with you."

Novak stood for a long moment before Andras, taking in the Munkaszolgálat uniform and the other changes that accompanied it. He let out a long and labored exhalation, then lifted his eyes to Andras's.

"I must say you're the last person I would have expected to find outside my door," he said. "And, to be perfectly honest, among the last I might have wanted to see. But since you're here, you might as well come in."

Andras found himself following Novak into the dim sanctum of the office and standing before the large leather-topped desk. Novak waved a hand toward a chair, and Andras took off his cap and sat down. He glanced around at the shelves of libretti, the ledger books, the photographs of opera stars in costume. It was the Sarah-Bernhardt office refigured in a smaller, darker form.

"Well," Novak said. "You might as well tell me what brings you here, Lévi."

Andras folded and unfolded his Munkaszolgálat cap. "I had some news this afternoon," he said. "I've just learned that your wife revealed Klara's identity to the Hungarian police."

"You learned that just this afternoon?" Novak said. "But it happened nearly two years ago."

Andras's face flamed, but he kept his eyes steady on Novak's. "György Hász saw to it that I knew nothing. I went to him today to see if he could help exempt my brother from front-line duty, and he told me that his funds were engaged in keeping my wife out of jail."

Novak got up to pour himself a drink from the decanter that stood on a table in the corner. He glanced back over his shoulder. Andras shook his head.

"It's just tea," Novak said. "I can't take spirits anymore."

"No, thank you," Andras said.

Novak returned to the desk with his glass of tea. He was pale and haggard, but his eyes burned with a terrible fierce light, the source of which Andras was afraid to guess. "The government is a clever extortionist," Novak said.

"Thanks to Edith, Klara's life is in danger," Andras said. "And my brother is on a train to Belgorod as we speak. I'm to rejoin my company in Bánhida tomorrow morning and can do nothing about any of it."

"We all have our tragedies," Novak said. "Those are yours. I've got mine."

"How can you speak that way?" Andras said. "It's your own wife who did this. And it wouldn't surprise me if you'd had a hand in it."

"Edith did what she got it into her mind to do," Novak said curtly. "She heard a rumor from a friend that Klara had come back to town. Heard she'd married you, and that you'd gone to the work service. I suppose she thought I might go looking for Klara, or that Klara might look for me." He spoke the last words in a tone of bitter irony. "Edith wanted to give her what she thought she deserved. She thought it would be a simple matter, but she didn't count on the Ministry of Justice to be so willing to be bought off. When she heard about the arrangement they'd made with your brother-in-law, she was furious."

"And now? How do I know she won't do something more, or worse?"

"Edith died of ovarian cancer last spring," Novak said. He gave Andras a challenging look, as if daring him to show pity.

"I'm sorry," Andras said.

"Spare me your condolences. If you're sorry, it's only because you've lost the chance to hold her accountable for what she did. But she was punished enough while she lived. Her death was a terrible one. My son and I had to watch her go through it. Carry that back with you to the work service, if you want something to ease your anger."

Andras twisted his hat in silence. There was no way to reply. Novak, seeing he'd rendered Andras mute, seemed to relent a little. "I miss her," he said. "I was never as good to her as she deserved. I suspect it's my own guilt that makes me cruel to you."

"I shouldn't have come here," Andras said.

"I'm glad you did. I'm glad to know Klara's still safe, at least. I've tried not to hear of her at all, but I'm glad to know that much." He began to cough deeply, and had to wipe his eyes and take a drink of his tea. "I won't know more of her for a long time, if ever. I'm leaving here in a month. I've been called too."

"Called where?"

"To the labor service."

"But that's impossible," Andras said. "You're not of military age. You have your position here at the Opera. You're not even Jewish."

"I'm Jewish enough for them," Novak said. "My mother was a Jew. I converted as a young man, but no one cares much about that now. I shouldn't have been allowed to keep this job after the race laws changed, but some friends of mine in the Ministry of Culture chose to look the other way. They've all lost *their* jobs by now. As for my position in the community, that's part of the problem. They mean to remove me from it. Apparently there's a new secret quota for the labor battalions. A certain percentage of conscripts must be so-called prominent Jews. I'll be in illustrious company. My colleague at the symphony was called to the same battalion, and we've just learned that the former president of the engineering college will be joining us too. Age isn't a factor. Nor, unfortunately, is fitness for service. I've never quite shaken the consumption that brought me back here in '37. You've been through the service yourself; you know as well as I do that I'm not likely to return."

"Surely they won't make you do hard labor," Andras said. "Surely they'll give you a job in an office, at least."

"Now, Andras," Novak said, with a note of reproach. "We both know that's not true. What will happen will happen."

"What about your son?" Andras said.

"Yes, what about my son?" Novak said. "What about him?" His voice trailed into silence, and they sat together without saying a word. Into Andras's mind came the image of his own child, that boy or girl sitting cross-legged in Klara's womb—that child who might never be born, and who, if born, might never live past babyhood, and who might then live only to see the world consumed by flames. Novak, watching Andras, seemed to apprehend a new grief of his own.

"So," he said, finally. "You understand. You're a father too."

"Soon," Andras said. "In a few months."

"And you'll be finished with the labor service by then?"

"Who knows? Anything might happen."

"It'll be all right," he said. "You'll make it home. You'll be with Klara and the child. György will maintain his arrangement with the authorities. It's not her they want, you know; it's his money. If they prosecute her it will only bring their own guilt to light."

Andras nodded, wanting to believe it. He was surprised to feel reassured, and then ashamed that it was Novak who had reassured him—Novak, who had lost everything but his young son. "Who will look after your boy?" he asked again.

"Edith's parents. And my sister. It's fortunate we came back when we did," Novak said. "If we'd stayed in France, we might be in an internment camp by now. The boy too. They're not sparing the children."

"God," Andras said, and put his head into his hands. "What'll become of us? All of us?"

Novak looked up at him from beneath his graying brows; the last trace of anger had gone out of his eyes. "In the end, only one thing," he said. "Some by fire, some by water. Some by the sword, some by wild beasts. Some by hunger, some by thirst. You know how the prayer goes, Andras."

"Forgive me," Andras said. "Forgive me for saying you weren't a Jew." For it was the verse from the Rosh Hashanah liturgy, the prayer that prefigured all ends. Soon he would say that prayer himself, in the camp at Bánhida among his workmates.

"I am a Jew," Novak said. "That was why I hired you in Paris. You were my brother."

"I'm sorry, Novak-úr," Andras said. "I'm sorry. I never meant you any harm. You were always kind to me."

"It's not your fault," Novak said. "I'm glad you came here. At least this way we can take leave of each other."

Andras rose and put on his military cap. Novak extended his hand across the desk, and Andras took it. There was nothing more to do except bid each other farewell. They did it in few words, and then Andras left the office and pulled the door closed behind him.

CHAPTER THIRTY

Barna and the General

THAT EVENING, when he returned home to the apartment on Nefelejcs utca, he told Klara nothing of what had passed between him and her brother; nor did he mention that he had seen Novak. He said only that he'd been on a long walk around the city, that he had been thinking about what he might do when he returned from the service. He knew she'd taken note of his anxious distraction, but she didn't ask him to explain his mood. The fact that he was going back to Bánhida the next day must have seemed explanation enough. They ate a quiet dinner in the kitchen, their chairs close together at the little table. Afterward, in the sitting room, they listened to Sibelius on the phonograph and watched the fire burning in the grate. Andras wore a flannel robe Klara had bought for him, and a pair of lambswool slippers. He couldn't have imagined a setting more replete with comfort, but soon he'd be gone and Klara would be alone again to face whatever might come. The more comfortable he felt, the more contented and drowsy Klara looked as she lay back against the sofa cushions, the more painful it was to imagine what lay on the other side. György was right, he thought, to have protected Klara from the knowledge of what had happened. Her tranquility seemed worth his own dishonesty. She was utterly serene as she spoke of the changes pregnancy had brought about in her body, and of the comfort of being able to talk to her mother about them. She was tender with Andras, physically affectionate; she wanted to make love, and he was happy for the distraction. But when they were in bed, her body surprising in its new balance, he had to turn his face away. He was afraid she would sense he was keeping something from her, and would demand to know what it was.

Once he was back at Bánhida he was spared that danger, at

least. He had never been so glad to have to do heavy work. He could numb his mind with the endless loading of brown coal into dusty carts, the endless pulling and pushing of the carts along the tracks. He could stun his limbs with calisthenics in the evening lineup, could submit to the drudgery of chores—the cleaning of barracks, the cutting of firewood, the hauling away of kitchen garbage—in the hope that the exhaustion would allow him to fall asleep at once, before his mind opened its kit bag of worries and began to display them in graphic detail, one after the next. Even if he managed to avoid that grim parade, he was at the mercy of his dreams. In the one that recurred most frequently, he would come upon Ilana lying in the hospital in a place that wasn't quite Paris but wasn't Budapest either, on the brink of death; then it wasn't Ilana but Klara, and he knew he had to give his blood to her, but he couldn't figure out how to transfer it from his own veins into hers. He stood at her bedside with a scalpel in his hand, and she lay in bed pale and terrified, and he thought he must first press the scalpel to his wrist and then think of a solution. Night after night he woke in the dark among the coughs and snores of his squad-mates, certain that Klara had died and that he had done nothing to save her. His sole consolation was that his term of service would end on December fifteenth, two weeks before she was due. He knew that it was foolish to pin all his hopes on that release date when the Munkaszolgálat showed so little respect for the promises it had made to its conscripts; he tried to remember the hard lessons of disappointment he'd learned in his first year of service. But the date was all he had, and he held on to it like a talisman. December fifteenth, December fifteenth: He said it under his breath as he worked, as if the repetition might hasten its arrival.

One morning when he was feeling particularly desperate, he went to the prayer service before work. A group of men met in an empty storage building every day at dawn; some of them had tiny dog-eared prayer books, and there was a miniature Torah from which they read on Mondays, Thursdays, and Shabbos.

Inside his tallis, Andras found himself thinking not of the prayers, but, as often happened when he performed any religious observance, of his parents. When he'd written to tell them Klara was pregnant, his father had written back to say they'd make a trip to Budapest at once. Andras had been skeptical. His parents hated to travel. They hated the noise and expense and crowds, and they hated the crush of Budapest. But a few weeks later they had gone to visit Klara and had stayed for three days. Andras's mother had promised to come back before the baby was born and to stay as long as Klara needed her.

She must have known it would be a comfort to Andras. She was expert at comforting him, at making him feel safe; she had done it unfailingly all through his childhood. During the silent Amidah, what came to him was a memory from Konyár: For his sixth birthday he'd been given a wind-up tin circus train with little tin animals rattling behind the bars of their carriages. You could open the carriages to take out the elephants and lions and bears, who could then be made to perform in a circus ring you'd drawn in the dust. The toy had come from Budapest in a red cardboard box. It so exceeded any Konyár child's imagining of a toy that it made Andras the subject of jealous rage among his classmates—most notably the two blond boys who chased him home from school one afternoon, trying to catch him and take the train away. He ran with the red cardboard box clutched against his chest, ran toward the figure of his mother, whom he could see up ahead in the yard: She was beating rugs on wooden racks at the edge of the orchard. She turned at the sound of the boys' approaching footsteps. By that time Andras couldn't have been three meters away. But before he could reach her, his foot caught on an apple-tree root and he flew forward, the red box leaving his hands in a rising arc as he threw out his hands to catch himself. In one graceful motion his mother dropped her rug-beating baton and caught the box. The footsteps of Andras's pursuers came to a halt. Andras raised his head to see his mother tuck the train box under one arm and pick up her rug-beater in the other hand. She didn't make a move, just stood there with the tool upraised. It was a stout branch with a sort of flat round basket fixed to one end. She took a single step toward the two blond boys. Though Andras knew his mother to be a gentle person—she had never struck any of her sons—her posture seemed to suggest that she was ready to beat Andras's attackers with just as much fervor as she had employed in beating her rugs. Andras got up in time to see the blond boys fleeing up the road, their bare feet raising clouds of dust. His mother handed him the red box and suggested that he keep the train at home for a while. Andras had entered the house with the sense that his mother was a superhuman creature, ready to fly to his aid in moments of peril. The feeling had faded soon enough; not long afterward he'd left for school in Debrecen, where his mother couldn't protect him. But the incident had left a deep imprint upon him. He could feel his mother's power now as if it were all happening again: The red cardboard box of his life was flying through the air, and his mother had stretched out her hands to catch it.

When he wasn't consumed with thoughts of Klara, he was thinking about his brothers. The mail distribution center had become a source of constant dread. Every time he passed it he imagined receiving a telegram that brought terrible news about Mátyás's fate. There had been no word since his deployment to the east, and György's efforts to help him had met with frustration. György had sent a series of letters to high Munkaszolgálat officials, but had been told that no one could bother with a problem of this scale when there was a war to be fought. If he wanted to arrange Mátyás's exemption from service he would have to contact the boy's battalion commander in Belgorod. Further inquiry revealed that Mátyás's battalion had finished its service in Belgorod and had been sent farther east; now the battalion command headquarters was situated somewhere near Rostov-on-Don. György sent a barrage of telegrams to the commander but heard nothing for weeks. Then he received a brief handwritten note from a battalion secretary, who informed him that Mátyás's company had slipped into the whiteout of the Russian winter. They had registered their location via wireless a few weeks earlier, but their communication lines had since been broken and their whereabouts could not be determined now with any certainty.

So this was what he had to picture: his brother Mátyás somewhere far away in the snow, the tether to his battalion command center severed, his company drifting with its army group toward deeper cold and danger. What was he eating? What was he wearing? Where was he sleeping? How could Andras lie in a bunk at night and eat bread every morning when his brother was lost in Ukraine? Did Mátyás imagine that Andras hadn't tried to help him, or that György Hász had refused? Who was responsible for Mátyás's current peril? Was it Edith Novak, who had spilled Klara's secret? Was it Klara's long-ago attackers? Was it Andras himself, whose connection to Klara had made the price of his brother's freedom so high? Was it Miklós Horthy, whose desire to restore Hungary's territories had drawn him into the war, or Hitler, whose madness had driven him into Russia? How many other men besides Mátyás found themselves in extremis that winter, and how many more would die before the war was over?

It was some comfort to know that Tibor, at least, remained far from the front lines. His letters continued to drift in from Transylvania according to the whims of the military postal service. Three weeks would go by without a word, then a clutch of five letters would come, then a single postcard the next day, and then nothing for two weeks. During his time in the Carpathians, the tone of Tibor's writing had devolved from its casual banter to a stricken monotone: *Dear Andras, another day of bridge-building. I miss Ilana terribly. Worry about her every minute. Plenty of disaster here: Today my workmate Roszenzweig broke his arm. A complex open fracture. I have no splints or casting materials or antibiotics, of course. Had to set the fracture with strip of planking from the barracks floor.* Or, *Eight servicemen down with pneumonia last week. Three died.*

How it grieves me to think of it! I know I could have kept them hydrated if I hadn't been sent out with the road crew. And another letter, in its entirety: *Dear Andráska, I can't sleep. Ilana is in her 21st week now. Last time the miscarriage occurred in the 22nd.* Andras wished he could write to Tibor about what he'd learned in Budapest, but he didn't want to compound Tibor's fears with his own. He wasn't alone in his anxiety, though; every week a pair of ivory-colored envelopes arrived from Benczúr utca with words of reassurance. One would be from György—*No news, no new threats. All goes on as before*—and the other would carry Klara's mother's seal—*Dear Andras, know that we are all thinking of you and wishing you a speedy return. How Klara misses you, dear boy! And how happy it will make her when you come home. The doctor believes her to be getting on quite well.* Once she sent Andras a small package, the contents of which had evidently been so attractive that nothing remained in the box except her note: *Andráska, here are a few sweets for you. If you like them, I'll send more.* Andras had brought the box back to the barracks to show it to Mendel, who had roared with laughter and suggested they display it on a shelf as an icon of life at Bánhida. It was a comfort, too, to have Mendel there; they would finish their terms of service together and would travel back to Budapest on the same train. At least that was what they planned, marking off the boxes on their hand-drawn calendar as the days grew colder and the distant hills faded to winter brown.

But on the twenty-fifth of November, a day whose gray blankness yielded in the evening to a confetti storm of snow, there was a telegram from György waiting for Andras at the central office. He tore it open with shaking hands and read that Klara had given birth the previous night, five weeks before her due date. They had a son, but he was very ill. Andras must come home at once.

It was a long time before he could move or speak. Other work servicemen tried to shuffle him aside to get to the counter; was he going to stand there all day? He made his way to the door of the office and staggered out into the snow. The lights of the camp had been lit early that evening. They formed a brilliant halo around the quadrangle, broken only by a brace of brighter, taller lights on either side of the administrative offices. Andras moved toward that bracket of lights as if toward a portal through which he might be conducted to Budapest. He had a son, but he was very ill. A son. A boy. His boy, and Klara's. Fifty kilometers away. Two hours by train.

The guards who usually flanked the door had gone to supper. Andras went in unhindered. He passed by offices with electric heaters, telephones, mimeograph machines. He didn't know where Major Barna's office was, but he felt his way into the heart of the building, following the architectural lines of force. There, where he would have placed the major's office if he had designed this building, was the major's office. But its door was locked. Barna, too, had gone to supper. Andras went back outside into the blowing snow.

Everyone knew where the officers' mess hall was. It was the only place at Bánhida from which the smell of real food issued. No thin broth, no hard bread there; instead they ate chicken and potatoes and mushroom soup, veal paprikás, stuffed cabbage, all of it with white bread. Servicemen who had been assigned to deliver coal or remove garbage from the officers' mess hall had to suffer the aromas of those dishes. No serviceman, except those who waited on the officers, could enter the mess hall; it was guarded by soldiers with guns. But Andras approached the building without fear. He had a son. The first flush of his joy had mingled with the physical need to protect this child, to interpose his own body between him and whatever might do him harm. And Klara: If their child was dangerously ill, she needed him too. Guards with guns were of no consequence. The only thing that mattered was that he get out of Bánhida.

The guards at the door were not ones he recognized; they must have been fresh from Budapest. That was to Andras's advantage. He approached the door and addressed himself to the shorter and stockier guard, a fellow who looked as though the smells of meat and roasted peppers were a torment to him.

"Telegram for Major Barna," Andras said, raising the blue envelope in one hand.

The guard squinted at him in the glow of the electric lights. Snow swirled between them. "Where's the adjutant?" he asked.

"He's at dinner, too, sir," Andras said. "Kovács at the communications center ordered me to bring it myself."

"Leave it with me," the guard said. "I'll see he gets it."

"I was ordered to deliver it in person and wait for a reply."

The short stocky guard glanced at his counterpart, a bullish young soldier half asleep at his post. Then he beckoned Andras closer and bent his head to him. "What do you really want?" he asked. "Work servicemen don't deliver telegrams to camp commanders. I may be new here, but I'm not an idiot." He held Andras's gaze steady with his own, and Andras's instinct was to answer truthfully.

"My wife just gave birth five weeks early," he said. "The baby's sick. I have to get home. I want to ask for a special leave."

The guard laughed. "In the middle of dinner? You must be crazy."

"It can't wait," Andras said. "I've got to get home now."

The guard seemed to consider what might be done. He looked over his shoulder into the mess hall, and then at the bullish young soldier again. "Hey, Mohács," he said. "Cover guard duty for a minute, will you? I have to take this fellow inside."

The bullish man shrugged, made a grunt of assent, and sank back almost immediately into his half-conscious state.

"All right," said the first soldier. "Come in. I'll have to pat you down."

Andras, speechless with gratitude, followed the soldier into the vestibule and submitted to a search. When the guard had determined that Andras was not carrying a weapon, he put a hand on his arm and said, "Come with me. And don't speak to anyone, understand?"

Andras nodded, and they stepped into the clamor of the officers' dining room. The long tables were arranged in rows, the officers seated according to rank. Barna dined with his lieutenants at a raised table overlooking the others. At his side was a high-ranked officer Andras had never seen before, a compact silver-haired man in a coat bright with braid, his shoulders bristling with decorations. He had a fine steely beard in an antiquated style, and a gold-rimmed monocle. He looked like an old general from the Great War.

"Who is that?" Andras asked the guard.

"No idea," the guard said. "They don't tell us anything. But it looks like you've picked a good night to make your début in dinner theater." He led Andras to another soldier who stood at attention near the head table, and he bent his head to that soldier's ear and said a few words. The soldier nodded and went to an adjutant who was sitting at one of the tables close to the front. He bent to the adjutant and spoke, and the adjutant raised his head from his dinner and regarded Andras with an expression of wonderment and pity. Slowly he got up from his bench and went to the head table, where he saluted Major Barna and repeated the message, glancing back over his shoulder at Andras. Barna's brows drew together and his mouth hardened into a white line. He put down his fork and knife and got to his feet. The men fell silent. The splendid elderly officer glanced up in inquiry.

Barna drew himself to his full height. "Where is this Lévi?" he said.

Andras had never heard his name sound so much like a curse. He struggled to keep his shoulders straight as he answered, "Here I am, sir."

"Step forward, Lévi," said the major.

It was the second time Barna had given him that command. He remembered well what had happened the first time. He took a few steps forward and dropped his gaze to the floor.

"You see, sir," Barna said, addressing the decorated gentleman beside him. "This is why we can't be too careful about the liberties we give our laborers. Do you see this cockroach?" He indicated Andras with his hand. "I've disciplined him before. He dared to be insolent to me on an earlier occasion. And here he is again."

"What was the earlier occasion?" the general said—with, Andras thought, a hint of mockery, almost as though it might please him to hear of someone's insolence to Barna.

But Barna didn't seem to catch the note. "It was when he first arrived," he said, and narrowed his eyes at Andras. "Did you think I'd forgotten, Lévi? I had to strip him of his rank." Barna smiled at the elder officer. "He tried to cling to it, so I punished him."

"Why was he stripped of rank?"

"Because he'd misplaced his foreskin," Barna said.

The room broke out in laugher, but the general frowned at his dinner plate. Barna didn't seem to notice that either. "Now he's come to us with an important request," he went on. "Why don't you step forward and state your business, Lévi?"

Andras took a step forward. He refused to be cowed by Barna, though his pulse pounded deafeningly in his temples. He held the telegram in his clenched hand. "Request permission for special family leave, sir," he said.

"What's so urgent?" Barna said. "Does your wife need a fuck?"

More laughter from the men.

"You can be sure that problem will take care of itself," Barna said. "It always does."

"With your permission, sir," Andras began again, his voice tight with rage.

"What's that in your hand, Lévi? Adjutant, bring me that piece of paper."

The adjutant approached Andras and took the telegram from his hand. Andras had never felt such profound humiliation or fury. He stood no more than eight feet from Barna; in another moment he might have his hands around the major's throat. The thought was some consolation as he watched Barna scan the telegram. Barna raised his eyebrows in bemused surprise.

"What do you know?" he said to the assembled men. "Mrs. Lévi just had a kid. Lévi is a father."

Applause from the men, along with whistles and cheers.

"But the baby's very sick. *Come home at once.* That sounds bad."

Andras fought the impulse to run at Barna. He bit his lip and fixed his eyes again on the floor. What he did not want was to be shot.

"Well, there's no use giving you a special leave now, is there?" Barna said. "If the boy's really that sick, you can just go home when he's dead."

A dense silence filled Andras's ears like the rushing of a train. Barna looked around the room, his hands on the table; the men seemed to understand that he wanted them to laugh again, and there was a swell of uncomfortable laughter.

"You're dismissed, Lévi," Barna said. "I'd like to enjoy my coffee now."

Before anyone could move, the elderly general brought his hand down against the table. "This is a disgrace," he said, getting to his feet, his voice graveled with anger. He turned a thick-browed scowl on Barna. "*You* are a disgrace."

Barna gave a crooked smile, as if this were all part of the joke.

"Don't you smirk at me, Major," the general said. "Apologize to this serviceman at once."

Barna hesitated a moment, then nodded at the guard who'd brought Andras in. "Remove that clod of dirt from my sight."

"Did you mishear me?" the general said. "I ordered you to apologize."

Barna's eyes darted from Andras to the general to the officers at their tables. "We're done with this, sir," he said, in an undertone that Andras was close enough to hear.

"You're not done, Major," the general said. "Get down off this platform and apologize to that man."

"I beg your pardon?"

"You heard what I said."

The men sat in silence, watching. Barna stood still for a long time, seeming to wage an inner battle; his color changed from red to purple to white. The general stood beside him with his arms crossed over his chest. There was no way for him to disobey. The elder man held unquestionable military superiority. Barna stepped down off the dais and marched toward Andras. He paused in front of him, and, with a medicine-swallowing grimace, extended a hand. Andras sent the general a look of gratitude and took Barna's hand. But no sooner had his own hand touched Barna's than Barna spat in his face and slapped him with the hand Andras had touched. Without another word, the major made his way through the rows of tables and went out into the night. Andras drew a sleeve across his face, numb with pain.

The general remained at the center of the dais, looking down upon the officers on their benches. Everything had come to a standstill: The servicemen who waited on the officers had paused at the edges of the room with dirty plates in their hands; the cook had ceased to bang the pots in the kitchen; the officers were silent, their tin forks and spoons laid beside their plates.

"The Royal Hungarian Army is dishonored by what has happened here," the general said. "When I entered the army, my first commanding officer was a Jew. He was a brave man who lost his life at Lemberg in the service of his country. Whatever Hungary is now, it's not the country he died to defend." He picked up the crumpled telegram form and handed it down to Andras. Then he threw his napkin onto the table and commanded the young guard to bring Andras to his quarters at once.

General Martón was quartered in the largest and most comfortable set of rooms at Bánhida, which meant that he had a bedroom and a sitting room, if the cold and uninviting cubicle in which Andras found himself could have been called a sitting room; it contained nothing but a table with an ashtray and a pair of rough wooden chairs so narrow and straight-backed as to discourage all but the briefest sitting. Electric lights blazed. The fireplace was dark. An assistant was packing the general's things in the adjacent room. As Andras stood near the door, waiting to hear what the general would say, the general gave orders for his car to be brought around.

"I won't stay at this place another night," he told a frightened-looking secretary who hovered near his side. "My inspection of this camp is complete, as far as I'm concerned. Send word to Major Barna to tell him I've gone."

"Yes, sir," the secretary said.

"And go to the office and get this man's dossier," he said. "Be quick about it."

"Yes, sir," the secretary said, and hurried out.

The general turned to Andras. "Tell me, now," he said. "How much time is left in your army service?"

"Two weeks, sir," Andras said.

"Two weeks. And in relation to the time you've already spent in the service, do you consider two weeks to be a long time?"

"Under the circumstances, sir, it's an eternity."

"What would you say, then, to getting out of this hellhole altogether?"

"I'm not sure I understand you, sir."

"I'm going to arrange for your discharge from Bánhida," the general said. "You've served here long enough. I can't guarantee you won't be called up again, particularly not with matters as uncertain as they are. But I can get you to Budapest tonight. You can ride in my car. I'm going there at once. I was sent to conduct a detailed inspection of Barna's establishment here, as he's being considered for promotion, but I've already seen as much as I care to see." He took a box of cigarettes from his breast pocket and tapped one out, then put it away again as if he didn't have the heart to smoke it. "The gall of that man," he said. "He's unfit to lead a donkey, let alone a labor battalion. It's not the Jews that are the problem, it's men like him. Who do you think got us into this mess? At war with Russia and Britain at once! What do you think will come of that?"

Andras couldn't bring himself to consider the question. There was another issue that seemed, at that moment, to be of even greater magnitude. "Do I understand you, sir?" he asked. "Am I to leave for Budapest tonight?"

The general gave a brisk nod. "You'd better pack your things. We'll leave in half an hour."

At the barracks there was general incredulity, and then, when Andras had related the story, raucous cheering. Mendel kissed Andras on both cheeks, promising to come to the apartment on Nefelejcs utca as soon as he returned to Budapest. When the half hour had passed, everyone came out to see the black car pull up and the driver help Andras lift his duffel bag into the sloping trunk. When was the last time anyone had helped one of them, the workers, lift a heavy object? When was the last time any of them had ridden in a car? The men clustered near the barracks steps, the wind lifting the lapels of their shabby coats, and Andras felt a stab of guilt to think of leaving them. He stood before Mendel and placed a hand on his arm.

"I wish you were coming," he said.

"It's only two more weeks," Mendel said.

"What will you do about *The Biting Fly*?"

Mendel smiled. "Maybe it's time to shut down the operation. The flies are all dead anyway."

"Two weeks, then," Andras said, and squeezed Mendel's shoulder.

"Good luck, Parisi."

"Let's go," the driver called. "The general's waiting."

Andras climbed into the front seat and shut the door. The motor roared, and they drove off to the officers' quarters. When they arrived, it became clear that there had been some further argument between Barna and the general; Barna could be seen pacing furiously inside the general's quarters as the general emerged with his traveling bag. The driver threw the general's bag into the trunk and the general slid into the backseat without a word.

Before Andras could grasp the idea that he was truly leaving, that he would never have to return to the sulfurous coal pits of Bánhida again, the car had pulled through the gate and onto the road. All through that long dark drive, the only sounds were the purring of the engine and the susurrus of tires on snow. As the headlights cut through endless flocks of snowflakes, Andras thought again of that New Year's Day when he and Klara had gone to the Square Barye to watch the sun rise over the chilly Seine. That long-ago January morning, he would never have believed that he would someday be the father of Klara's child, that he would someday be flying through the night in a Hungarian Army limousine to see their newborn son. He remembered the Schubert piece Klara had played for him one winter evening, *Der Erlkönig*, about a father carrying his sick child on horseback through the night while the elf-king followed them, trying to get his hands on the child. He remembered the father's desperation, the son's inexorable slide toward death. He had always envisioned the chase taking place on a night like this. His hands grew cold in the heat of the car. He turned around to see what lay behind them. All he could see was the general snoring softly in the backseat, and, through the small oval of rear-window glass, a swarm of snowflakes lit up red in the taillights.

It took them an hour and a half to get to Gróf Apponyi Albert Hospital. When the car pulled to a stop, the general awoke and cleared his throat. He settled his hat onto his head and straightened his decorated jacket.

"All right, now," he said. "Let's go."

"You don't mean to come inside with me, sir," Andras said.

"I mean to finish what I started. Give the driver your address and he'll leave your things with the caretaker there."

Andras gave the driver the address on Nefelejcs utca. The driver jumped out to open the door for the general, and the general waited until Andras had joined him on the curb. He turned and marched into the hospital with Andras at his side.

At the night attendant's desk, a narrow-shouldered man with an eye patch sat with his feet propped on a metal garbage can, reading a Hungarian translation of *Mein Kampf.* When he looked up to see the general approaching, he dropped the book and got to his feet. His good eye shifted between Andras and the general; he seemed baffled by the sight of this decorated leader of the Hungarian Army in the company of a gaunt, shabby work serviceman. He stammered an inquiry as to how he might serve the general.

"This man needs to see his wife and son," the general said.

The attendant glanced away down the hall, as if it might yield some form of help or enlightenment. The hall remained empty. The attendant twisted his hands. "Visiting hours are between four and six, sir," he said.

"This man is visiting now," the general said. "His surname is Lévi."

The attendant paged through a logbook on his desk. "Mrs. Lévi is on the third floor," he said. "Maternity ward. But sir, I'm not supposed to let anyone upstairs. I'll be fired."

The general took a name card from a leather case. "If anyone gives you trouble, tell them to discuss the situation with me."

"Yes, sir," the attendant said, and sank back down into his chair.

The general turned to Andras with another name card. "If there's anything else I can do, send word to me."

"I don't know how to thank you," Andras said.

"Be a good father to your son," the general said, and put a hand on Andras's shoulder. "May he live to see a more enlightened age than our own." He held Andras's gaze a moment longer, then turned and made his way out into the snow. The door closed behind him with a breath of cold air.

The attendant stared after the general in amazement. "How'd you make a friend like that?" he asked Andras.

"Luck, I suppose," Andras said. "It runs in my family."

"Well, go on," said the attendant, cocking a thumb toward the stairway. "If anyone asks who let you in, it wasn't me."

Andras raced up the staircase to the third floor, then followed signs to Klara's ward. There, in the semidark of the hospital night, new mothers lay in a double row of beds with bassinets at their feet. Some of the bassinets held swaddled babies; other babies nursed, or drowsed in their mothers' arms. But where was Klara? Where was her bed, and which of these children was his son? He ran the row twice before he saw her: Klara Lévi, his wife, pale and damp-haired, her mouth swollen, her eyes ringed in dark shadow, lying in a dead sleep in the glow of a green-shaded light. He crept closer, his heart hammering, to see what she held in her arms. But when he reached the bedside he saw that it was an empty blanket, nothing more. The bassinet at the foot of her bed was empty too.

The ground seemed to fall away beneath him. So he had come too late despite everything. The world held no possibility for happiness; his life and Klara's were a ruin of grief. He covered his mouth, afraid he'd cry aloud. Someone laid a cool hand on his arm; he turned to see a nurse in a white apron.

"How did you get in?" she asked, more perplexed than angry. "Is this your wife?"

"The child," he said, in a whisper. "Where is he?"

The nurse drew her eyebrows together. "Are you the father?"

Andras nodded mutely.

The nurse beckoned him into the hall, toward a bright-lit room filled with padded tables, infant scales, cloth diapers, feeding bottles and nipples. Two nurses stood at the tables, changing babies' diapers.

"Krisztina," said the nurse. "Show Mr. Lévi his son."

The nurse at the changing table held up a tiny pink froglet, naked except for a blue cotton hat and white socks, a bandage covering its umbilicus. As Andras watched, the baby raised a fist to its open mouth and extended its petal of a tongue.

"Great God," Andras said. "My son."

"Two kilos," the nurse said. "Not bad for a baby born so early. He has a bit of a lung infection, poor thing, but he's doing better than he was at first."

"Oh, my God. Let me look at him."

"You can hold him if you like," the one called Krisztina said. She pinned the baby's diaper, wrapped him in a blanket, and set him in Andras's arms. Andras didn't dare breathe. The baby seemed to weigh almost nothing. Its eyes were closed, its skin translucent, its hair a dark whorl on its head. Here was his son, his son. He was this person's father. He put his cheek to the curve of the baby's head.

"You can take him back to your wife," Krisztina said. "As long as you're here in the middle of the night, you might as well be of use."

Andras nodded, unable to move or speak. In his arms he held what seemed the sum of his existence. The baby wrestled its blankets, opened its mouth, and pronounced a strong one-note cry.

"He's hungry," the nurse said. "You'd better take him to her."

And so, for the first time, he answered his son's need: He brought him down the ward to Klara's bed. At the sound of the baby's next cry, Klara opened her eyes and pushed herself up onto her elbows. Andras bent over her and put their son into her arms.

"Andráska," she said, her eyes filling with tears. "Am I dreaming?"

He bent to kiss her. He was shaking so hard he had to sit down on the bed. He embraced them both at once, Klara and the baby, holding them as close as he dared.

"How can it be?" she said. "How did you get here?"

He pulled back just far enough to look at her. "A general gave me a ride in his car."

"Don't tease me, darling! I've just had a cesarean."

"I'm perfectly serious. I'll tell you the story sometime."

"I had a terrible fear that something had happened to you," she said.

"There's nothing to fear now," he said, and stroked her damp hair.

"Look at this boy," she said. "Our little son." She pulled the blanket lower so he could see the baby's face, his curled hands, his delicate wrists.

"Our son." He shook his head, still unable to believe it. "I've seen him. He was au naturel when I came in."

The baby turned his face toward Klara's breast and opened his mouth against her nightgown. She unbuttoned the gown and settled him in to nurse, stroking his featherlike hair. "He looks just like you," she said, and her eyes filled again.

"*Életem.*" *My life.* "Five weeks early! You must have been terrified."

"My mother was with me. She brought me to the hospital herself. And now to have you here, too, even if just for a short time!"

"I'm finished with Bánhida," he said. "My service is over." He could hardly believe it himself, but it had happened. Nothing could make him go back. "I'm home with you now," he told her. And slowly that truth came to seem real to him as he and Klara sat on her bed at Gróf Apponyi Albert Hospital, laughing and crying over the sleek downy head of their little son.

CHAPTER THIRTY-ONE

Tamás Lévi

THEY NAMED THE BABY after Klara's father. The first weeks of his life were a blue haze to Andras: There were ten days in the hospital, during which the baby lost weight, fought his lung infection, nearly died, and recovered again; there was the home-coming to their apartment on Nefelejcs utca, which seemed not really to be their home at all, stuffed as it was with flowers and gifts and guests who had come to see the baby; there was Klara's mother, unfailingly solicitous but incapable of doing anything practical to help, as her own babies had been tended entirely by nurses; there was Andras's mother, who knew how to tend to the baby's needs, but who also felt it important to show Klara the *correct* way to pin a diaper or elicit a baby's eructation; there was Ilana, now seven months pregnant, cooking endless Italian meals for Andras and Klara and their well-wishers; there was Mendel Horovitz, liberated from the Munkaszolgálat, sitting in the kitchen until the middle of the night, sipping vodka and inviting Andras to describe in detail the vicissitudes of new parenthood; and then there was the plain relentless work of caring for a new-born child: the feedings every two hours, the diaper changes, the brief and broken sleep, the moments of incredulous joy and bottomless fear. Every time the baby cried it seemed to Andras he might never stop, that his crying would exhaust him and make him sick again. But Klara, who had already raised a child, understood that the baby was crying because he had a simple need, and she knew she could determine the need and meet it. Soon the baby would stop crying; the house would fall into a state of delicate peace. Andras and Klara would sit together and look at the baby, their Tamás, admiring the eyebrows that were like hers, the mouth that was like his, the chin with its dimple like Elisabet's.

Through those dreamlike days he was aware of little else beside the ebb and flow of Tamás Lévi's needs. The war seemed far away and irrelevant, the Munkaszolgálat a bad dream. But on the night of the seventh of December, the eve of Tamás's bris, Andras's father brought the news that the Japanese had bombed an American naval base in Hawaii. Pearl Harbor: The name conjured a tranquil image, pale gray sky above an expanse of nacreous water. But the attack had been a bloodbath. The Japanese had badly damaged or destroyed four U.S. battleships and nearly two hundred planes, and had killed more than twenty-four hundred men and wounded twelve hundred others. Andras knew that the States would declare war on Japan now, closing the ring of the war around the earth. And in fact the declaration came the next morning as Tamás Lévi entered the covenant of circumcision. Three days later Germany and Italy declared war on the United States, and then Hungary declared war on the Western Allies.

As Andras stood at the bedroom window that night, listening to a volley of voices from Bethlen Gábor tér, he found himself considering what the new declaration of war might mean for his little family, and for his brothers and his parents and Mendel Horovitz. The city might be bombed. What had become scarce would get scarcer. More troops would be called, more labor servicemen deployed. He had just told Klara that he was home for good, but how long would this spell of freedom last? The KMOF wouldn't care that he was just now beginning to recover the health and strength he'd lost during his months in the Munkaszolgálat. They would use him as they'd used him all along, as a simple tool in a war whose aim was to destroy him. But they didn't have him yet, he thought: Not yet. For the moment he was here at home, in this quiet bedroom with his sleeping wife and child. He could look for work, could begin to support Klara and the baby. And he could give something to György Hász, some small part of the vast sum he was paying each month to keep Klara out of the hands of the authorities. He had hoped he might approach Mendel Horovitz's editor at the *Evening Courier* and speak to him about a position in layout or illustration, but Mendel had left the *Courier* when he'd been conscripted; his old job had long since been filled, and the editor himself had been fired and called into the Munkaszolgálat. Since his return, Mendel had been pounding the pavement every day with his portfolio of clips. In the afternoons he could be found at the Café Europa at Hunyadi tér, a cup of black coffee before him, a notebook open on the table. Well, Andras would go to Hunyadi tér the next day and approach Mendel with a proposition: the two of them might present themselves at the office of Frigyes Eppler, Andras's former editor at *Past and Future*, and ask to be hired jointly as writer and illustrator. Frigyes Eppler now worked at the *Magyar Jewish Journal*. The paper's offices were located on Wesselényi utca, a few blocks from the Café Europa.

At three o'clock the next afternoon, Andras walked through the gilt-scrolled doors of the café to find Mendel at the usual table with the usual notebook before him. He sat down across from his friend, ordered a cup of black coffee, and stated the proposition.

Mendel pulled the *V* of his mouth into a narrow point. "It *would* have to be the *Magyar Jewish Journal*," he said.

"What's wrong with the *Journal*?"

"Have you read it lately?"

"I've been the full-time servant of Tamás and Klara Lévi lately."

"It's been dishing up a steady diet of assimilationist drivel. Apparently, we've just got to put our faith in the Christian aristocrats in the government and all will be well. We're supposed to keep saluting the flag and singing the anthem, just as though the anti-Jewish laws didn't exist. Be Magyar first and Jewish second."

"Well, we're safer if the government considers us Magyar first."

"But the government doesn't consider us Magyar! I don't have to tell you that. You've just done your time in the Munka-szolgálat. The government considers us Jews, plain and simple."

"At least they consider us necessary."

"For how much longer?" Mendel said. "We can't work for that paper, Parisi. We should look for work at one of the left-wing rags."

"I don't have connections at any of those places. And I don't have time to spare. I've got to start supporting this son of mine before I'm conscripted again."

"What makes you think Eppler would consider taking us both?"

"He knows good work when he sees it. Once he reads you, he'll want to hire you."

Mendel gave a half laugh. "The *Jewish Journal*!" he said. "You're going to drag me down there and get me a job, aren't you."

"Frigyes Eppler's no conservative, or at least he wasn't when I knew him. *Past and Future* was a Zionist operation if ever there was one. Every issue carried some romantic piece about Palestine and the adventures of emigration. And you might remember their lead story from May of '36. It concerned a certain record-breaking sprinter who wasn't to be allowed on the Hungarian Olympic team because he was a Jew. Eppler was the one who pushed that story. If he's at the *Jewish Journal* now, it must be because he means to stir things up."

"Oh, for God's sake," Mendel said. "All right. We'll talk to the man." He closed his notebook and paid his bill, and they went off together toward Wesselényi utca.

On the editorial floor of the *Journal* they found Frigyes Eppler embroiled in a shouting match with the managing editor inside the managing editor's glassed-in office; through the windows that looked upon the newsroom, the two men could be seen carving a series of emphases into the air as they argued. Since Andras had last seen his former editor, Eppler had gone entirely bald and had adopted a pair of horn-rimmed glasses. He was round-shouldered and heavyset; his shirttails were apt to fly free of his trousers, and his tie often showed the mark of a hasty lunch. He never seemed to be able to find his hat or his keys or his cigarette case. But in his editorial work he missed no detail. *Past and Future* had won international awards every year Frigyes Eppler had edited it. His greatest triumph had been his placement of the young men and women who had worked for him; his efforts on Andras's behalf were among the many generous acts he undertook to promote the careers of his writers and copy editors and graphic artists. He had shown no surprise when Andras had been offered a place at the École Spéciale. As he had told Andras then, his aim had always been to hire people who would quit for better work before he had a chance to fire them.

Andras couldn't make out the content of the argument with the managing editor, but it was clear that Eppler was losing. His gestures increased in size, his shouts in volume, as the altercation went on; the managing editor, though wearing a look of triumph, backed toward the door of his own office as if he meant to flee as soon as his victory was complete. At last the door flew open and the managing editor stepped onto the newsroom floor. He called an order to his secretary, trundled off down the length of the room, and escaped into the stairwell as if he were afraid Eppler might chase him. The fuming and defeated Eppler stood alone in the empty office, polishing his scalp with both hands. Andras waved in greeting.

"What is it now?" Eppler said, not looking at Andras; then, recognizing him, he gave a cry and clapped his hands to his chest as if to keep his heart from falling out. "Lévi!" he shouted. "Andras Lévi! What in God's name are you doing here?"

"I'm here to see you, Eppler-úr."

"How long has it been now? A hundred years? A thousand? But I'd have recognized that face anywhere. What are you wasting your time at these days?"

"Not enough," Andras said. "That's the problem."

"Well, I hope you haven't come here looking for a job. I sent you off into the world long ago. Aren't you an architect by now?"

Andras shook his head. "I've just finished a two-year spell in the Munkaszolgálat. This tall fellow is a childhood friend and company-mate of mine, Mendel Horovitz."

Mendel gave a slight bow and touched his hat in greeting, and Frigyes Eppler looked him up and down. "Horovitz," he said. "I've seen your picture somewhere."

"Mendel holds the Hungarian record in the hundred-meter dash," Andras said.

"That's right! Wasn't there some scandal about you a number of years back?"

"Scandal?" Mendel showed his wry grin. "Don't I wish."

"They wouldn't allow him on the Hungarian Olympic team in '36," Andras said. "There was a piece about it in *Past and Future*. You edited it yourself."

"Of course! What a fool I am. You're that Horovitz. Whatever have you done with yourself since then?"

"Gotten into journalism, I'm afraid."

"Well, of all ridiculous things! So you're here as a supplicant too?"

"Parisi and I come as a team."

"You mean Lévi, here? Ah, you call him Parisi because of that stint of his at the École Spéciale. I was responsible for that, you know. Not that he'd ever give me credit. He'd claim it was all due to his own talent."

"Well, he's not such a bad draughtsman. I hired him for the paper I was editing."

"And what paper was that?"

From his satchel, Mendel produced a few dog-eared copies of *The Biting Fly*. "This is the one we made in the camp at Bán-hida. It's not as funny as the one we wrote when we were posted in Subcarpathia and Transylvania, but that one got us kicked out of our company. We were made to eat our words, in fact. Twenty pages of them apiece."

For the first time, Frigyes Eppler's expression grew serious; he looked carefully at Andras and Mendel, and then sat down at his managing editor's desk to page through *The Biting Fly*. After reading for a while in silence, he glanced up at Mendel and gave a low chuckle. "I recognize your work," he said. "You were the one writing that man-about-town column for the *Evening Courier*. A smart political instrument dressed up as a young good-for-nothing's good-for-nothing ravings. But you were pretty sharp, weren't you?"

Mendel smiled. "At my worst."

"Tell me something," Eppler said in a lowered tone. "Just what are you doing here? This paper doesn't represent the leading edge of modern thought, you know."

"With all respect, sir, we might ask you the same question," Mendel said.

Eppler massaged the sallow dome of his head with one hand. "A man doesn't always find himself where he wants to be," he said. "I was at the *Pesti Napló* for a while, but they let some of us go. By which you understand what I mean." He let out an unhappy laugh that was half wheeze; he was an inveterate smoker. "At least I stayed out of the Munkaszolgálat. I'm lucky they didn't send me to the Eastern Front, just to make an example of me. In any case, to put it simply, I had to keep body and soul together—an old habit, you might say—so when a position opened here, I took it. Better than singing in the street for my bread."

"Which is what we'll be doing soon," Mendel said. "Unless we find some work."

"Well, I can't say I recommend this place," Eppler said. "As you may have gathered, I don't always see eye to eye with the rest of the editorial staff. I'm supposed to be the chief, but, as you witnessed, my managing editor often ends up managing me."

"Perhaps you could use someone to take your side," Andras said.

"If I were to hire you, Lévi, it wouldn't be to take sides. It would be to get a job done, just as when you were fresh from gimnázium."

"I've learned a thing or two since then."

"I'm sure you have. And your friend here seems an interesting fellow. I can't say, Horovitz, that I would have hired you on the basis of your *Biting Fly*, but I did follow your column for a time."

"I'm flattered."

"Don't be. I read every rag in this town. I consider it my job."

"Do you think you can find something for us?" Mendel asked. "I hate to be blunt, but someone's got to be. Lévi here has a son to look out for."

"A son! Good God. If you've got a son, Lévi, then I'm an old man." He sighed and hitched up his trousers. "What the hell, boys. Come to work here if you want to work so badly. I'll dig something up for you."

That night Andras found himself at the kitchen table at home, sitting with his mother and the baby while Klara lay asleep on the sofa in the front room. His mother removed a pin from the nightshirt she was sewing and sank it into her gray velveteen pincushion, the same one she'd used for as long as Andras could remember. She had brought her old sewing box with her to Budapest, and Andras had been surprised to find that his mind contained a comprehensive record of its contents: the frayed tape measure, the round blue tin that held a minestrone of buttons, the black-handled scissors with their bright blades, the mysterious prickle-edged marking wheel, the spools and spools of colored silk and cotton. Her tiny whipstitches were as tight and precise as the ones that had edged Andras's collars when he was a boy. When she finished her row of hemming, she tied off the thread and cut it with her teeth.

"You used to like to watch me sew when you were little," she said.

"I remember. It seemed like magic."

She raised an eyebrow. "If it were magic, it would go faster."

"Speed is the enemy of precision," Andras said. "That's what my drawing master in Paris used to tell us."

His mother knotted the end of the thread and raised her eyes to him again. "It's a long time since you left school, isn't it?" she said.

"Forever."

"You'll go back to your studies when this is all over."

"Yes, that's what Apa says, too. But I don't know what will happen. I have a wife and son now."

"Well, it's good news about the job," his mother said. "You were wise to think of Eppler."

"Yes, it's good news," Andras said, but it felt less like good news than he'd imagined it would. Though he was relieved to know he had a way to earn money, the idea of going back to work for Eppler seemed to erase his time in Paris entirely. He knew it made no sense; he'd met Klara in Paris, after all, and here on the table before him, asleep in a wicker basket, was Tamás Lévi, the miraculous evidence of their life together. But to arrive at work the next morning and receive the day's assignments from Eppler—it was what he had been doing at nineteen, at twenty. It seemed to negate the possibility that he would ever complete his training, that he would ever get to do the work he craved. Everything in the world stood against his going back to school. The France in which he'd been a student had disappeared. His friends were dispersed. His teachers had fled. No school in Hungary would open its doors to him. No free country would open its borders to him. The war worsened daily. Their lives were in danger now. He suspected it wouldn't be long before Budapest was bombed.

"Don't give me such a dark look," his mother said. "I'm not responsible for the situation. I'm just your mother."

The baby began to stir in his basket. He shifted his head back and forth against the blankets, scrunched his face into a pink asterisk, and let out a cry. Andras bent over the basket and lifted the baby to his chest.

"I'll walk him around the courtyard," he said.

"You can't take him outside," his mother said. "He'll catch his death of cold."

"I won't have him wake Klara. She's been up every night for weeks."

"Well, for pity's sake, put a blanket over him. And put a coat over your shoulders. Here, hold him like this, and let me put his hat on. Keep his blanket over his head so he'll stay warm."

He let his mother swaddle them both against the cold. "Don't stay out long," she said, patting the baby's back. "He'll fall asleep after you walk him for a minute or two."

It was a relief to get out of the close heat of the apartment. The night was clear and cold, with a frozen slice of moon suspended in the sky by an invisible filament. Beyond the haze of city lights he could make out the faint ice crystals of stars. The baby was cocooned against him, quiet. He could feel the rapid rise and fall of his son's chest against his own. He walked around the courtyard and hummed a lullaby, circling the fountain where he and Klara had seen the little dark-haired girl trailing a hand through the water. The stone basin was crusted with ice now. The courtyard security light illuminated its depths, and as he leaned over it he could make out the fiery glints of goldfish beneath the surface. There, beneath the cover of the ice, their flickering lives went on. He wanted to know how they did it, how they withstood the slowing of their hearts, the chilling of their blood, through the long darkness of winter.

* * *

There was something otherworldly, it seemed to Andras, about the advertisements published in the *Magyar Jewish Journal*. As assistant layout editor it was his job to arrange those neatly illustrated boxes in the margins that flanked the articles; inside the bordered rectangles depicting clothes and shoes and soap, ladies' perfume and hats, the war seemed not to exist. It was impossible to reconcile this ad for cordovan leather evening shoes with the idea of Mátyás spending a winter outdoors in Ukraine, perhaps without a good pair of boots or an adequate set of foot rags. It was impossible to read this druggist's advertisement listing the merits of its Patented Knee Brace, and then to think of Tibor having to set a serviceman's compound fracture with a length of wood torn from a barracks floor. The signs of war—the absence of silk stockings, the scarcity of metal goods, the disappearance of American and English products—were negations rather than additions; the blank spaces where the advertisements for those items would have appeared had been filled with other images, other distractions. The sporting-goods store on Szerb utca was the only one whose ad made reference to the war, however obliquely; it proclaimed the merits of a product called the Outdoorsman's Equipage, a knapsack containing everything you would need for a sojourn in the Munkaszolgálat: a collapsible cup, a set of interlocking cutlery, a mess tin, an insulated canteen, a thick woolen blanket, stout boots, a camping knife, a waterproof slicker, a gas lantern, a first-aid kit. It wasn't advertised for use in the Munkaszolgálat, but what else would Budapest residents be doing outdoors in the middle of January?

As for the articles that occupied the space between the ads, Andras could only gape at the rigid and shortsighted optimism he saw reflected there. This paper was supposed to be the mouthpiece of the Jewish community; how could it proclaim, on its editorial page, that the Hungarian Jew was *at one with the Magyar nation in language, spirit, culture, and feeling*, when the

Hungarian Jew was, in fact, being sent into the mouth of battle to remove mines, so that the Hungarian army might pass through to support its Nazi allies? Mendel had been right about the paper's content. To the extent that it reported the news, it did so with the sole apparent aim of keeping Hungarian Jews from falling into a panic. His second week at the paper, it was reported with great relish that Admiral Horthy had fired the most staunchly pro-German members of his staff; here was concrete evidence of the solidarity of the Hungarian leadership with the Jewish people.

But the *Journal* wasn't the only paper in town, and the smaller left-leaning independents carried news that reflected the world Andras had glimpsed in the labor service. There were reports of a massacre carried out in Kamenets-Podolsk not long after Hungary entered the war against the Soviet Union; one paper printed an anonymous interview with a member of a Hungarian sapper platoon, a man who'd been present at the mass killing and had been consumed by guilt since his return. After the Hungarian Central Alien Control Office had rounded up Jews of dubious citizenship, this man reported, the detainees had been handed over to the German authorities in Galicia, trucked to Kolomyya, and marched ten kilometers to a string of bomb craters near Kamenets-Podolsk, under the guard of SS units and the source's Hungarian sapper platoon. There, every one of them was shot to death, along with the original Jewish population of Kamenets-Podolsk—twenty-three thousand Jews in all. The idea had been to clear Hungary of Jewish aliens, but many of the Jews who were killed were Hungarians who hadn't been able to produce their citizenship papers quickly enough. This, it seemed, was what had troubled the Hungarian who'd given the interview: He had killed his own countrymen in cold blood. So it seemed that the Hungarians did feel a certain solidarity with their Jewish brethren after all, though in the source's case the solidarity hadn't run deep enough to keep him from pulling the trigger.

Then, in the last week of February, there was a report published in the *People's Voice* about another massacre of Jews, this one in the Délvidék, the strip of Yugoslavia that Hitler had returned to Hungary ten months earlier. A certain General Feketehalmy-Czeydner, the paper reported, had ordered the execution of thousands of Jews under the guise of routing Tito partisans. Refugees from the region had begun to drift back to Budapest with horrifying stories of the killings—people had been dragged to the Danube beach, made to strip in the freezing cold, lined up in rows of four on the diving board over a hole that had been cannon-blasted into the ice of the river, and machine-gunned into the water. Andras arrived early one morning at the *Magyar Jewish Journal* to find his employer sitting in the middle of the newsroom in a mute paroxysm of horror, a copy of the *Voice* open on the desk before him. He handed the paper to Andras and retreated into his office without a word. When the managing editor arrived, another glass-enclosed argument ensued, but no word about the massacre appeared in the *Jewish Journal*.

Later that same week, Ilana Lévi went to Gróf Apponyi Albert Hospital and gave birth to a baby boy. There had been a letter from Tibor only three days before: He hoped to be released from his labor company by Wednesday evening, and so hadn't despaired of being home in time for the birth. But the event had come and gone without any sign of him. On Ilana's first night home from the hospital, Andras and Klara brought her Shabbos dinner. Though she was still exhausted from the loss of blood, she had insisted upon setting the table herself; there were the candlesticks she'd received as a wedding present from Béla and Flóra, and the Florentine plates her mother had given her to take back to Hungary. She and Klara lit the candles, Andras blessed the wine, and they sat down to eat while the babies slept in their arms. The room held a deep and pervasive quiet that seemed to emanate from the architecture itself. The apartment was on the ground floor, three narrow rooms made smaller by the heavy wooden beams that supported them. The French doors of the dining room looked out onto the courtyard of the building, where a bicycle mechanic had cultivated a bone-yard of rusted frames and handlebars, clusters of spokes, mounds of petrified chains. The collection, dusted with snow, looked to Andras like a battlefield littered with bodies. He found himself staring out into it as the light grew blue and dim, his eyes moving between the shadows. He was the one who saw the figure through the frosty glass: a dark narrow form picking its way through the bicycles, like a ghost come back to look for his fallen comrades. At first he thought the form was nothing more than the congelation of his own fear; then, as the figure assumed a familiar shape, a manifestation of his desire. He hesitated to call Ilana's attention to it because he thought at first that he might be imagining it. But the figure approached the windows and stared at the scene within—Andras at the head of the table with Klara at his side, a baby at Klara's breast; Ilana with her back to the window, her arm crooked around something in a blanket—and the ghost's hand flew to his mouth, and his legs folded beneath him. It was Tibor, home from his labor company. Andras shoved his chair away from the table and ran for the door. In an instant he was in the courtyard with his brother, both of them sitting in the snow amid the litter of dismembered bicycles, and then the women were beside them, and in another minute Tibor held his son and his wife in his arms.

Tibor. Tibor.

They shouted his name in a frenzy of insistence, as if trying to convince themselves he was real, and they brought him into the house. Tibor was deathly pale in the dim light of the sitting room. His small silver-rimmed glasses were gone, the bones of his face a sharp scaffolding beneath the skin. His coat was in rags, his trousers stiff with ice and dried blood, his boots a disaster of shredded leather. His military cap was gone. In its place he wore a fleece-lined motorcyclist's cap from which one ear-covering had been torn away. The exposed ear was crimson with cold. Tibor tugged the cap from his head and let it fall to the floor. His hair looked as though it had been hacked to the scalp with dull scissors some weeks earlier. He had the smell of the Munkaszolgálat about him, the reek of men living together without adequate water or soap or tooth powder. That smell was mingled with the sulfurous odor of brown-coal smoke and the shit-and-sawdust stink of boxcars.

"Let me see my boy," he said, his voice scarcely louder than a whisper, as if he hadn't used it in days.

Ilana handed him the baby in its white swaddling of blankets. Tibor laid the baby on the sofa and knelt beside him. He took off the blanket, the cap covering the baby's fine dark hair, the long-sleeved cotton shirt, the little pants, the socks, the diaper; through it all, the baby was silent and wide-eyed, its hands curled into fists. Tibor touched the dried remnant of the baby's umbilical cord. He held the baby's feet, the baby's hands. He put his face against the crease of the baby's neck. The baby's name was Ádám. It was what Tibor and Ilana had decided in the letters they'd exchanged. He said the name now, as if trying to bring together the idea of this baby and the actual naked child lying on the sofa. Then he glanced up at Ilana.

"Ilanka," he said. "I'm so sorry. I wanted to be home in time."

"No," she said, bending to him. "Please don't cry."

But he was crying. There was nothing anyone could do to stop it. He cried, and they sat down on the floor with him as though they were all in mourning. But they were not in mourning, not then; they were together, the six of them, in what was still a city unghettoized, unburned, unbombed. They sat together on the floor until Tibor stopped crying, until he could draw a full breath. He drew one deep throaty breath after another, and finally took a slow inhale through his nose.

"Oh, God," he said, with a horrified look at Andras. "I stink. Get me out of these clothes." He began pulling at the collar of his shredded coat. "I shouldn't have touched the baby before I washed. I'm filthy!" He got up off the floor and went to the kitchen, leaving a trail of stiff clothing behind him. They heard the clang of a tin washtub being dropped onto the kitchen tiles, and the roar of water in the sink.

"I'll help him," Ilana said. "Will you take the baby?"

"Give him to me," Klara said, and handed Tamás to Andras. They sat together on the sofa, Andras and Klara and the two babies, while Ilana heated water for Tibor's bath. In the meantime, Tibor ate dinner in his ragged undershirt and Munkaszolgálat trousers. Then Ilana undressed him and washed him from head to toe with a new cake of soap. The smell of almonds drifted in from the kitchen. When that was finished she dressed him in a pair of flannel-lined pajamas, and he moved toward the bedroom as though he were walking in a dream. Andras followed him to the bed and sat down beside him with Tamás in his arms. Klara was close behind, holding Tibor's son. Ilana put a pair of hot towel-wrapped bricks into the bed at Tibor's feet and pulled the eiderdown up to his chin. They all sat with him on the bed, still trying to believe he was there.

But Tibor, or part of Tibor, had not yet returned; as he drifted to the edge of sleep he made a frightened noise, as if a stone had fallen onto his chest and knocked the wind out of him. He looked at them all, eyes wide, and said, "I'm sorry." His eyes closed again, and he drifted again, and made that frightened noise—*Hunh!*—and jerked awake. "I'm sorry," he said again, and drifted, and woke. He was sorry. His eyelids closed; he breathed; he made his noise and jerked awake, haunted by something that waited on the other side of consciousness. They stayed with him through a full hour of it until he fell into a deeper sleep at last.

Tibor's favorite coffeehouse, the Jókai, had been replaced by a barbershop with six gleaming new chairs and a brace of mustachioed barbers. That morning the barbers were practicing their art upon the heads of two boys in military uniform. The boys looked as though they could scarcely be out of high school.

They had identical jutting chins and identical peaked eyebrows; their feet, on the barber-chair footrests, were identically pigeon-toed. They must have been brothers, if not twins. Andras glanced at Tibor, whose look seemed to ask what these two brothers meant, patronizing the barbers who had neatly razored away the Jókai Káveház and replaced it with this sterile black-and-white-tiled shop. There was no question of Andras and Tibor's stopping in for a shave. The Jókai Barbershop was a trai-tor.

Instead they went back down Andrássy út to the Artists' Café, a Belle Époque establishment with wrought-iron tables, amber-shaded lamps, and a glass case full of cakes. Andras insisted upon ordering a slice of Sachertorte, against Tibor's objections—it was too expensive, too rich, he couldn't eat more than a bite.

"You need something rich," Andras said. "Something made with butter."

Tibor mustered a wan smile. "You sound like our mother."

"If I do, you should listen."

That smile again—a pale, preserved-looking version of Tibor's old smile, like something kept in a jar in a museum. When the torte arrived, he cut a piece with his fork and let it sit at the edge of the plate.

"You've heard the news from the Délvidék by now," Tibor said.

Andras stirred his coffee and extracted the spoon. "I've read an article and heard some awful rumors."

Tibor gave a barely perceptible nod. "I was there," he said.

Andras raised his eyes to his brother's. It was disconcerting to see Tibor without his glasses, which had refracted his unusually large eyes into balance with the rest of his features. Without them he looked raw and vulnerable. The diet of cabbage soup and brown bread and coffee had whittled him down to this ele-mental state; he was essence of Tibor, reduction of Tibor, the necessary ingredient that might be recombined with ordinary life to produce the Tibor that Andras knew. He wasn't sure he wanted to hear what had happened to Tibor in the Délvidék. He bent to his coffee rather than meet those eyes.

"I was there a month and a half ago," Tibor began, and told the story. It had been late January. His Munkaszolgálat company had been attached to the Fifth Army Corps; they'd been slaving for an infantry company in Szeged, building pontoon bridges on the Tisza so the company could move its materiel across. One morning their sergeant had called them away from that work and told them they were needed for a ditch-digging project. They were trucked to a town called Mošorin, marched to a field, and commanded to dig a trench. "I remember the dimensions," Tibor said. "Twenty meters long, two and a half meters wide, two meters deep. We had to do it by nightfall."

At the table beside them, a young woman sitting with her two little girls gave Tibor a long look and then glanced away. He touched the scroll embellishment at the end of his fork and continued in a lowered voice.

"We dug the trench," he said. "We thought it was for a battle. But it wasn't for a battle. After dark, they marched a group of people to the field. Men and women. A hundred and twenty-three of them. We were sitting on one side of the ditch eating our soup."

The young woman had turned slightly in her chair. She was perhaps thirty years old; they saw now that she wore a silver Star of David on a narrow chain at her neck. She raised her eyes toward her children, who were sharing a cup of chocolate and finishing the last crumbs of a slice of poppyseed strudel.

When Tibor spoke again, his voice was scarcely louder than a whisper. "There were children there, too," he said. "Teenagers. Some of them couldn't have been older than twelve or thirteen."

"Zsuzsi, Anni," the woman said. "Why don't you go choose some little cakes to take to your grandmother?"

"I'm not done with my chocolate," the smaller girl said.

"Tibor," Andras said, laying a hand on his brother's arm. "Tell me later."

"No," the woman said quietly, meeting Andras's eye. "It's all right." To the girls she said, "Go ahead, I'll come in a moment." The older girl put on her coat and helped the younger one get her sleeves turned right side out. Then they went to the pastry counter and stared at the display of cakes, their fingers pressed against the glass. The woman folded her hands in her lap and looked down at her empty teacup.

"They lined up these people in front of the ditch," Tibor said. "Hungarians. Jews, all of them. They made them strip naked and stand there in the freezing cold for half an hour. And they shot them," he said. "Even the children. Then we had to bury them. Some of them weren't dead yet. The soldiers turned their guns on us while we did it."

Andras glanced at the woman beside them, who had covered her mouth with her hand. At the pastry counter beyond, her two little girls argued the merits of the cakes.

"What's to stop them from doing it to us?" Tibor said. "We're not safe here. Do you understand me?"

"I understand," Andras said. Of course they weren't safe. There wasn't a minute that passed without his thinking about it. And the danger was deeper than Tibor knew: Andras still hadn't told him about the situation with Klara and the Ministry of Justice.

"The threat is here inside the country," Tibor said. "We're lying to ourselves if we think we'll be fine as long as Horthy holds off a German occupation. What about the Arrow Cross? What about plain old Hungarian bigotry?"

"What do you propose we do?" Andras said.

"Let me tell you something," Tibor said. "I want to get off this continent. I want to get my wife and son out. If we stay in Europe we're going to die."

"How are we supposed to get out? The border's closed. It's impossible to get travel documents. No one will let us in. And there are the babies. It's bad enough to imagine doing it by ourselves." He looked over his shoulder; even to speak of these things in public seemed dangerous. "We can't leave now," he said. "It's impossible."

The woman at the next table sent a glance in Andras and Tibor's direction, her dark eyes moving between the two of them. At the counter, her little girls had made their selections; the older one turned and called for her to come. She stood and put on her hat and coat. As she slipped through the narrow space between the tables, she gave Andras and Tibor a curt nod. It wasn't until after she and her girls had disappeared through the beveled glass doors of the café that Andras noticed she'd dropped her handkerchief on the table. It was a fine linen hand-kerchief with a lace edge, embroidered with the letter *B*. Andras lifted it to reveal a folded scrap of paper, the stub of a streetcar ticket, onto which something had been scratched in pencil: *K might be able to help you.* And an address in Angyalföld, near the end of the streetcar line.

"Look at this," Andras said, and handed the ticket stub to his brother.

Glassesless, Tibor squinted at the woman's tiny writing. "*K might be able to help you*," he said. "Who's K?"

They rode out past the apartment blocks of central Pest, out into an industrial suburb where textile factories and machine works exhaled gray smoke into a mackerel sky. Military supply trucks rumbled down the streets, their beds stacked with steel tubes and I-beams, concrete flume sections and cinderblocks and giant parabolas of iron like leviathan ribs. They got off the streetcar at the end of the line and walked out past an ancient madhouse and a wool-washing plant, past three blocks of crumbling tenements, to a small side street called Frangepán köz, where a cluster of cottages seemed to have survived from the days when Angyalföld had been pastureland and vineyard; from behind the houses came the chatter and musk of goats. Number 18 was a plaster-and-timber cottage with a steep wood-shingled roof and flaking shutters. The window frames were peeling, the door scuffed and toothy along its edge. Winter remnants of ivy traced an unreadable map across the façade. As Andras and Tibor crossed the garden, a high gate at the side of the house opened to let forth a little green cart pulled by two strong white wethers with curving horns. The cart was packed with milk cans and crates of cheese. At the gate stood a tiny woman with a hazel switch in her hand. She wore an embroidered skirt and peasant boots, and her deep-set eyes were hard and bright as polished stones. She gave Andras a look so penetrating it seemed to touch the back of his skull.

"Does someone with the initial K live here?" he asked her.

"The initial K?" She must have been eighty, but she stood straight-backed against the wind. "Why do you want to know?"

Andras glanced at the ticket scrap on which the woman at the café had written the address. "This is 18 Frangepán köz, isn't it?"

"What do you want with K?"

"A friend sent us here."

"What friend?"

"A woman with two little girls."

"You're Jewish," the old woman said; it was an observation, not a question. And something changed in her features as she said it, a certain softening of the lines around her eyes, an almost imperceptible relaxation of the shoulders.

"That's right," Andras said. "We're Jewish."

"And brothers. He's the elder." She pointed her hazel stick at Tibor.

They both nodded.

The woman lowered her stick and scrutinized Tibor as if she were trying to see beneath his skin. "You're just back from the Munkaszolgálat," she said.

"Yes."

She reached into a basket for a paper-wrapped round of cheese and pressed it into his hand. When he protested, she gave him another.

"K is my grandson," she said. "Miklós Klein. He's a good boy, but he's not a magician. I can't promise he can help you. Talk to him if you like, though. Go to the door. My husband will let you in." She closed and locked the gates of the yard behind her; then she touched the wethers on their backs with the hazel wand, and they tossed their white heads and pulled the cart into the street.

As soon as she had gone, a clutch of goats came up to the gate and bleated at Andras and Tibor. The goats seemed to expect some kind of gift. Andras showed them his empty pockets, but they wouldn't back away. They wanted to butt their heads against Andras's and Tibor's hands. The kids wanted a sniff at their shoes. At the far end of the yard a stable had been converted into a goat house, sheltered from the wind and piled with new hay. Four does stood feeding at a tin trough, their coats glossy and thick.

"Not a bad place to be a goat," Andras said. "Even in the middle of winter."

"A better place to be a goat than a man," Tibor said, glancing toward the factory chimneys in the near distance.

But Andras thought he wouldn't mind living farther from the city center someday. Not, preferably, in the shadow of a textile factory, but maybe in a place where they could have a house, a yard big enough for goats and chickens and a few fruit trees. He wanted to come back with his notebook and drawing tools and study the construction of this cottage, the layout of these grounds. It was the first time in months he'd had the desire to do an architectural drawing. As he followed his brother up the walk he experienced a strange sensation in his chest, a feeling of rising, as if his lungs were filled with yeast.

When Tibor knocked on the door, a dust of yellow paint drifted down like pollen. There were shuffling footsteps from inside; the door opened to reveal a tiny dried man with two uplifted wings of gray hair. He wore a white undershirt and a dressing gown of faded crimson wool. From behind him came a strain of scratchy Bartók and the smell of pancakes.

"Mr. Klein?" Tibor said.

"The same."

"Does Miklós Klein live here?"

"Who wants to know?"

"Tibor and Andras Lévi. We were told to come see him. Your wife said he was at home."

The man opened the door and beckoned them into a small bright room with a red-painted concrete floor. On a table near the window, the remains of breakfast lay beside a crisply folded newspaper. "Wait here," the elder Klein said. He went to the end of a brief hallway decorated with portraits of men and women in antique-looking costumes, the men in military uniform, the women in the cinch-waisted gowns of the previous century. A door opened and closed at the end of the hall. On the wall, a cuckoo clock struck the hour and the cuckoo sang eleven times. A collection of photographs on a side table showed a bright-eyed boy of six or seven holding the hands of a beautiful dark-haired young woman and a melancholy, intelligent-looking man; there were photographs of the three of them at the beach, on bicycles, in a park, on the steps of a synagogue. The collection conveyed the sense of a shrine or a memorial.

After a few minutes the door opened at the end of the hall, and the elder Klein shuffled toward them and beckoned with one hand. "Please," he said. "This way."

Andras followed his brother down the hall, past the portraits of the military men and tight-laced women. At the door, the old man stepped aside to let them in, then retreated to the sitting room.

The doorway was a portal to another world still. On one side was the universe they had just left, where breakfast things lay on a wooden table in a shaft of sun, and the bleating of goats floated in from the yard, and a dozen photographs suggested what had vanished; on the other side, in this room, were what looked like the accoutrements of a spy operation. The walls were plastered with pin-studded maps of Europe and the Mediterranean, with intricate flowcharts and newspaper clippings and photographs of men and women working the dry soil in desert settlements. On the desk, wedged between towering stacks of official-looking documents, stood a brace of typewriters, one with a Hungarian keyboard and the other with a Hebrew one. An Orion radio whined and crackled on a low table, and a quartet of clocks beside it showed the time in Constanţa, Istanbul, Cairo, and Jerusalem. Papers and dossiers rose in waist-high columns all around the room, crowding the desk, the bed, every centimeter of windowsill and table. At the center of it all stood a pale young person in a moth-eaten sweater, his short black hair like a ragged crown, his eyes raw and red as if from drink or grief. He looked to be about Andras's age, and was unmistakably the little boy from the photographs, grown into this haggard young man. He pulled out the desk chair, moved a stack of dossiers onto the floor, and sat down to face the brothers.

"It's all over," he said by way of greeting. "I'm not doing it anymore."

"We were told you could help us," Tibor said.

"Who told you that?"

"A woman with two little girls. Initial B. She heard me talking to my brother at a café."

"Talking to your brother about what?"

"About getting out of Hungary," Tibor said. "One way or another."

"First of all," Klein said, pointing a narrow finger at Tibor, "you shouldn't have been talking to your brother about a thing like that at a café, where anyone could hear you. Secondly, I should strangle that woman, whoever she is, for giving you my address! Initial B? Two little girls?" He put his fingers to his forehead and seemed to think. "Bruner," he said. "Magdolna. It's got to be. I got her brother out. But that was two years ago."

"Is that what you do?" Andras said. "Arrange emigrations?"

"Used to," Klein said. "Not anymore."

"Then what's all this stuff?"

"Ongoing projects," Klein said. "But I'm not accepting new work."

"We've got to leave the country," Tibor said. "I've just been in the Délvidék. They're killing Hungarian Jews there. It won't be long before they come for us. We understand you can help us get out."

"You *don't* understand," Klein said. "It's impossible now. Look at this." He produced a clipping from a Romanian newspaper. "This happened just a few weeks ago. This ship left Constanţa in December. The *Struma*. Seven hundred and sixty-nine passengers, all Romanian Jews. They were told they'd get Palestinian entry visas once the ship reached Turkey. But the ship was a wreck. Literally. Its engine was salvaged from the bottom of the Danube. And there were no entry visas. It was all a scam. Maybe at one time they'd've gotten in without visas—the British used to allow some paperless immigrations. Not anymore! Britain wouldn't take the boat. They wouldn't take anyone, not even the children. A Turkish coast guard ship towed it into the Black Sea. No fuel, no water, no food for the passengers. Left it there. What do you think happened? It was torpedoed. Boom. End of story. They think it was the Soviets who did it."

Andras and Tibor sat silent, taking it in. Seven hundred and sixty-nine lives—a ship full of Jewish men, women, and children. An explosion in the night—how it must have sounded, how it must have felt from a berth deep inside the ship: the shock and quake of it, the sudden panic. And then the inrush of dark water.

"But what about Magdolna Bruner's brother?" Tibor asked. "How did you get him out?"

"Things were different then," Klein said. "I got people out along the Danube. Smuggled them out on cargo barges and riverboats. We had contacts in Palestine. We had help from the Palestine Office here. I got a lot of people out, a hundred and sixty-eight of them. If I were smart, I'd have gone, too. But my grandparents were all alone. They couldn't make a trip like that, and I couldn't leave them. I thought I might be of more use here. But I won't do it anymore, so you might as well go home."

"But this is a disaster for Palestine, this *Struma*," Andras said. "They'll have to loosen the immigration restrictions now."

"I don't know what'll happen," Klein said. "They have a new colonial secretary now, a man called Cranborne. He's supposed to be more liberal-minded. But I don't know if he can convince the Foreign Office to relax its quotas. Even if he could, it's far too dangerous now."

"If it's a matter of money, we'll come up with it," Tibor said.

Andras gave his brother a sharp glance. Where did Tibor expect them to get the money? But Tibor wouldn't look at him. He kept his eyes fixed on Klein, who ran his hands through his electrified hair and leaned forward toward them.

"It's not the money," Klein said. "It's just that it's a mad thing to try."

"It might be madder to stay," Tibor said.

"Budapest is still one of the safest places for Jews in Europe," Klein said.

"Budapest lives in the shadow of Berlin."

Klein pushed back his chair and got up to pace his square of floor. "The horrible thing is that I know you're right. We're mad to feel any sense of security here. If you've been in the labor service, you know that well enough. But I can't take the lives of two young men into my hands. Not now."

"It's not just us," Tibor said. "It's our wives, too. And a couple of babies. And our younger brother, once he returns from Ukraine. And our parents in Debrecen. We all need to get out."

"You're crazy!" Klein said. "Plain crazy. I can't smuggle babies down the Danube while the country's at war. I can't be responsible for elderly parents. I refuse to discuss this. I'm sorry. You both seem like good men. Maybe we'll meet in happier times and have a drink together." He went to the door and opened it onto the hallway.

Tibor didn't move. He scanned the stacks of papers, the type-writers, the radio, the dossier-smothered furniture, as if they might offer a different answer. But it was Andras who spoke.

"Shalhevet Rosen," he said. "Have you heard that name?"

"No."

"She's in Palestine, working to get Jews out of Europe. She's the wife of a friend of mine from school."

"Well, maybe she can help you. I wish you luck."

"Maybe you've had some correspondence with her."

"Not that I recall."

"Maybe she can help get us visas."

"A visa means nothing," Klein said. "You've still got to get there."

Tibor glanced around the room again. He gave Klein a pene-trating look. "This is what you do," he said. "Do you mean to say you're finished now?"

"I won't send people to another *Struma*," Klein said. "You can understand that. And I have to look out for my grandpar-ents. If I get caught and thrown in jail, they'll be all alone."

Tibor paused at the door, his hat in his hands. "You'll change your mind," he said.

"I hope not."

"Let us leave our address, at least."

"I'm telling you, it's no use. Goodbye, gentlemen. Farewell. Adieu." He ushered them into the dim hallway and retreated into his room, latching the door behind him.

In the main room Andras and Tibor found the breakfast things cleared away and the elder Klein installed on the sofa, newspaper in hand. When he became aware of them standing before him, he lowered the paper and said, "Well?"

"Well," Tibor said. "We'll be going now. Please tell your wife we appreciate her kindness." He raised one of the paper-wrapped rounds of goat cheese.

"One of her best," Klein-the-elder said. "She must have taken a shine to you. She doesn't give those away lightly."

"She gave me two," Tibor said, and smiled.

"Ah! Now you're making me jealous."

"Maybe she can prevail upon your grandson to help us. I'm afraid he turned us away without much hope."

"Miklós is a moody boy," the elder Klein said. "His work is difficult. He changes his mind about it daily. Does he know how to reach you?"

Tibor took a small blunt pencil from his breast pocket and asked Klein's grandfather for a piece of paper, apologizing for the fact that he didn't have a name card. He wrote his address on the scrap and left it on the breakfast table.

"There it is," Tibor said. "In case he changes his mind."

Klein's grandfather made a noise of assent. From the yard, the raised voices of goats made a pessimistic counterpoint. The wind clattered the shutters against the house, a sound directly from Andras's deepest childhood. He had the feeling of having stepped out of the flow of time—as if he and Tibor, when they passed through the doorway of this house, would reenter a different Budapest altogether, one in which the cars had been replaced by carriages, the electric streetlights by gaslights, the women's knee-length skirts by ankle-length ones, the metro system erased, the news of war expunged from the pages of the *Pesti Napló*. The twentieth century cut clean away from the tissue of time like an act of divine surgery.

But when they opened the outer door it was all still there: the trucks rumbling along the broad cross-street at the end of the block, the towering smokestacks of the textile plant, the film advertisements plastered along a plywood construction wall. He and his brother walked in silence back toward the streetcar line and caught a near-empty train back toward the city center. It took them down Kárpát utca, with its machine-repair shops, then over the bridge behind Nyugati Station, and finally to Andrássy út, where they got off and headed toward home. But when they reached the corner of Hársfa utca, Tibor turned. Hands in his pockets, he walked the block to the gray stone building where they'd lived before Andras had gone to Paris. On the third floor were their windows, now uncurtained and dark. A row of broken flowerpots stood on the balcony; an empty bird feeder hung from the rail. Tibor looked up at the balcony, the wind lifting his collar.

"Can you blame me?" he said. "Do you understand why I want to get out?"

"I understand," Andras said.

"Think about what I told you at the café. That happened here in Hungary. Now think what must be happening in Germany and Poland. You wouldn't believe the things I've heard. People are being starved and crowded to death in ghettoes. People are being shot by the thousands. Horthy can't hold it off forever. And the Allies don't care about the Jews, not enough to make a difference on the ground. We have to take care of ourselves."

"But what's the use, if we die doing it?"

"If we have visas, we'll have some measure of protection. Write to Shalhevet. See if there's anything her organization can do."

"It'll take a long time. Months, maybe, just to exchange a few letters."

"Then you'd better start now," Tibor said.

CHAPTER THIRTY-TWO

Szentendre Yard

THAT AFTERNOON he told Klara about the cottage in Frangepán köz, and about Klein in his bedroom surrounded by the manila files of a thousand would-be emigrants. They were in the sitting room, the baby at Klara's breast, its hand clenching and unclenching in her hair.

"What do you think?" she said quietly. "Do you think we should try to get out?"

"It seems insane, doesn't it? But I haven't seen the things Tibor's seen."

"What about your parents? And my mother?"

"I know," he said. "It's a desperate thing to think about. Maybe it's not the right time. If we wait, things might get better. But maybe I should write to Shalhevet anyway. Just in case there's something she can do."

"You can write," she said. "But if there were something she could do, wouldn't she have told us about it already?" The baby moved his head and released his grip on Klara's hair. She shifted him to the other side, draping herself with his blanket.

"I wrote to Rosen from the labor service," Andras said. "He knew I couldn't have left then, even if I'd wanted to."

"And now we have the baby," Klara said.

Andras tried to envision her feeding their son in the cargo hold of a Danube riverboat, under the cover of a tarpaulin. Did people make escape attempts with infants, he wondered? Did they drug their children with laudanum and pray they wouldn't cry? The baby pulled the blanket away from Klara's breast and she arranged it again.

"There's no need to do that," Andras said. "Let me see you."

Klara smiled. "I suppose I got into the habit of covering up at my mother's house. Elza can't abide the sight of it. She considers it unsanitary. She'd be scandalized to know I do it in your presence."

"It's perfectly natural. And look at *him*. Doesn't he look happy?"

The baby's toes curled and uncurled. He waved a dark hank of Klara's hair in his fist. His eyes moved to her eyes, and he blinked, and blinked again more slowly, and his eyelids drifted closed. Intoxicated with milk, he released Klara's hair and let his legs fall limp against her arm. His hands opened into starfish. His mouth fell away from her breast.

Klara raised her eyes to Andras and held his gaze. "What if *you* were to go?" she said. "You and Tibor? Get there safely and send for us when you can? At least it would keep you out of the Munkaszolgálat."

"Never," he said. "I'd sooner die than leave without the two of you."

"What a dramatic thing to say, darling."

"I don't care if it's dramatic. That's how I feel."

"Here, take your little son. My leg's asleep." She lifted the child and handed him to Andras, then fastened the buttons of her blouse. With a grimace of pain she got to her feet and walked the length of the room. "Write to Shalhevet," she said. "Just to see. At least then we'll know if there's another course of action to consider. Otherwise we're only speculating."

"I'm not going anywhere without you."

"I hope not," she said. "But it seems the wrong time for broad resolutions."

"Won't you let me preserve the illusion that I have a choice?"

"It's a dangerous time for illusions, too," she said, and came back to sit beside him on the sofa, laying her head on his shoulder. As they sat together and watched their son sleep, Andras felt a renewed pang of guilt: He was, in fact, allowing her to live inside an illusion—that she was safe, that the past was securely lodged in the past, that her fears of endangering her family by her return to Hungary had been unfounded.

* * *

The illusion continued all that spring. A reorganization in the Ministry of Justice slowed the mechanisms of extortion, and the need to give up the house on Benczúr utca was temporarily relieved. Andras continued to work as a layout artist and illustrator, with Mendel penning articles nearby in the newsroom. If it seemed surreal at first to have as their legitimate employment what had until a few months earlier been a covert and guilty extracurricular, the feeling was soon replaced by the ordinary rhythms and pressures of work. Tibor, once he had recovered his health and strength, found employment too. He became a surgical assistant at a Jewish hospital in the Erzsébetváros. In March there was news from Elisabet: Paul had joined the navy and would ship out to the South Pacific in late April. His parents, in a fit of remorse occasioned by their son's enlistment and by the birth of their first grandchild the previous summer, had by now relented entirely and had insisted that Elisabet and little Alvie come to live with them in Connecticut. Elisabet had enclosed a photograph of the family in sledding gear, herself in a dark hooded coat, the muffled-up Alvie in her arms, Paul standing beside them holding the ropes of a long toboggan. Another photograph showed Alvie by himself, propped in a chair with pillows all around him, wearing a velvet jacket and short pants. The high round forehead and wry mouth were all Paul, but the ice-hard penetration of his baby gaze could only have been Elisabet's. She promised that Paul's father would speak to his contacts in the government to see if anything could be done to secure entry visas for Andras, Klara, and the baby.

Andras wrote to Shalhevet, and a reply came four weeks later. She promised to speak to the people she knew in the Immigration Office. Though she couldn't foresee how long the process might take or whether she would succeed, she thought she could make a strong case for Andras and Tibor's being granted visas. As Andras must know, the department's main concern at the moment was to extract Jews from German-occupied territories. But future doctors and architects would be of great value to the Jewish community of Palestine. She might even be able to do something for Andras's friend, the political journalist and record-breaking athlete; he, too, was the kind of exceptional young man the Immigration Office liked to help. And if Andras and Tibor came, of course their families must come with them. What a shame that they hadn't all emigrated together before the war! Rosen missed his Paris friends desperately. Had Andras heard from Polaner or Ben Yakov? Rosen had made dozens of inquiries, to no avail.

Andras sat on the edge of the courtyard fountain and reread the letter. He hadn't heard from Polaner or Ben Yakov, not since the missives he'd received during his first Munkaszolgálat posting. If Ben Yakov was still with his parents in Rouen, he would be living in occupied France under the Nazi flag. And Polaner, who had been so eager to fight for his adopted country—where would he have been sent after his discharge from the French military? Where would he be now? What hardships, what humiliations, would he have had to face since the last time Andras had seen him? How would Andras ever learn what had become of him? He trailed his hand through the cold water of the fountain, released now from its winter ice. Beneath the surface, the shapes of the fish moved like slender ghosts. There had been coins at the bottom of the fountain last fall, five- and ten-fillér coins glinting against the blue tiles. Someone must have removed them when the ice thawed. Now, no one would throw coins into a fountain. No one could spare ten fillér for a wish.

In the darkness of the barracks in Subcarpathia and Transylvania and Bánhida, Andras had forced himself to consider the possibility that Polaner might be dead, that he might have been beaten or starved or infected or shot; but he had never allowed himself to think that he would not someday *know* what had happened—not know for certain whether to search or hope or mourn. He could not mourn by default. It ran against his nature. But it had been twenty-three months since there had been any word of Polaner—soft-voiced Eli Polaner, hidden somewhere within the dark explosive tangle of Europe. He dared not follow the thought around to its other side, where the image of his brother Mátyás waited, a white shape glimpsed through the veil of a blizzard. Mátyás, still lost. No word from his Munkaszolgálat company since last November. Now it was April. In Ukraine the steady cold would have just begun to relent. Soon it would become possible to bury the winter's dead.

He had left Klara with the baby, the rest of the mail in a jumble on his desk. He would go and see if he could help her; it would only make him feel worse to sit at the edge of the fountain and consider all the things he could not know. He climbed the stairs and opened the apartment door, listening for the baby's lifted voice. But a film of silence had settled over the rooms. The kettle had ceased to bubble on the stove. The baby's bathwater stood cold in its little tin tub, still awaiting the addition of the hot. The baby's towel lay folded on the kitchen table, his jacket and pants beside it.

Andras heard the baby make a noise, a brief two-note plaint; the sound came from the sitting room. He entered to find Klara on the sofa with the baby in her arms. An opened letter lay on the low table before her. She raised her eyes to Andras.

"What is it?" he said. "What's happened?"

"You've been called again," she said. "You've been called back to work duty."

He scrutinized the letter, an abbreviated rectangle of thin white paper stamped with the insignia of the KMOF. He was to report to the Budapest Munkaszolgálat Office two mornings hence; he would be assigned to a new battalion and company, and given orders for six months of labor service.

"This can't be," he said. "I can't leave you again, not with the baby."

"But what can we do?"

"I still have General Martón's card. I'll go to his office. Maybe he can help us."

The baby twisted in Klara's arms and made another sound of protest. "Look at him," she said. "Naked as a newborn. I forgot all about his bath. He must be freezing." She got up and brought him into the kitchen, holding him against her. She emptied the kettle into his little tub and stirred the water with her hand.

"I'll go tomorrow morning," Andras said. "I'll see what can be done."

"Yes," she said, and lowered the baby into the tub. She laid him back against her arm and rubbed soap into the fine brown fluff of his hair. "And if he can't help, I'll write to my solicitor in Paris. Maybe it's time to sell the building."

"No," Andras said. "I won't have you do it."

"I won't have you go back to the service," she said. She wouldn't look at him, but her voice was low and determined. "You know what goes on there now. They're sending men to clean up minefields on the front. They're starving them to death."

"I survived it for two years. I can survive it for six more months."

"Things were different before."

"I won't let you sell the building."

"What do I care for the building?" she cried. The baby looked at her, startled.

"I'll speak to Martón," Andras said, putting a hand on her shoulder.

"And Shalhevet?" she said. "What did she write?"

"She knows some people in the Ministry of Immigration. She'll try to make a case for our being granted visas."

The baby kicked an arc of water into Klara's hair, and she let out a sad laugh. "Maybe we should pray," she said, and covered her eyes with one hand as if she were reciting the Shema. He wanted to believe that someone could be watching in pity and horror, someone who could change things if he chose. He wanted to believe that men were not in charge. But at the center of his sternum he felt a cold certainty that told him otherwise. He believed in God, yes, the God of his fathers, the one to whom he'd prayed in Konyár and Debrecen and Paris and in the work service, but that God, the One, was not One who intervened in the way they needed someone to intervene just then. He had designed the cosmos and thrown its doors open to man, and man had moved in and begun a life there. But God could no more step inside and rearrange that life than an architect could rearrange the lives of a building's inhabitants. The world was their place now. They would use it in their fashion, live or die by their own actions. He touched Klara's hand and she opened her eyes.

General Martón's powers, though considerable, could not exempt Andras from work service. They could not even get his service postponed. But they prevented his being posted to the Eastern Front, and they won the same reprieve for Mendel Horovitz, who had been called at the same time. Andras and Mendel were assigned to Company 79/6 of the Budapest Labor Service Battalion. The company had been put to work in a rail yard so close to Budapest that the men who lived in the city could sleep at home rather than in barracks at the work site. Every morning Andras rose at four o'clock and drank his coffee in the dark kitchen, by the light of the stove; he slung his pack over his shoulder, took the tin pail of food Klara had prepared for him the night before, and slipped out into the predawn chill to meet Mendel. Now, instead of reporting to the offices of the *Magyar Jewish Journal*, they walked all the way to the river and crossed the Széchenyi Bridge, where the stone lions lay on their pedestals and the Romany women in black head scarves and cloaks slept with their arms around their thin-limbed children. In that blue hour a mist hovered above the surface of the

Danube, rolling up from the braided currents of the water. Sometimes a barge would slide past, its low flat hull parting the vapor, and they might glimpse the bargeman's wife standing at a glowing brazier and tending a pot of coffee. On the other side of the river they would take the tram to Óbuda, where they could get the bus that would take them to Szentendre. The bus ran along the river, and they liked to sit on the Danube side and watch the boats glide south. Often they would pass the time in silence; the subject most on their minds could not be discussed in public. Andras had received the news from Shalhevet that the Immigration Office had responded favorably to her first inquiries, and that the process was moving along more quickly than expected. There was reason to hope that they might have papers in hand by midsummer. But what then? He didn't know whether or not he should dare to hope Klein might help them, or how much it would cost to make the journey, or how many visas Shalhevet could muster. And though spring had arrived in full force now, there was still no word from Mátyás. György's most recent inquiries had proved fruitless. It seemed impossible to think of leaving Hungary while his brother was lost in Ukraine, perhaps dead, perhaps taken prisoner by the Soviets. But now that spring had come, Mátyás could materialize any day. It wasn't beyond reason to hope that in three or six months they might all emigrate together. A year from now, Andras and his brothers might be going off to work in an orange grove in Palestine, perhaps at one of the kibbutzim Rosen had described, Degania or Ein Harod. Or they might be fighting for the British—Mendel had heard that there was a battalion of soldiers that had been formed from members of the Yishuv, the Jewish community of Palestine.

When the bus reached Szentendre, they climbed down with the other men—their workmates who had boarded at Óbuda or Rómaifürdő or Csillaghegy—and walked the half kilometer to the train-loading yard. The first trucks pulled in at seven o'clock. The drivers would roll up the tarps to reveal corded cubes of blankets, crates of potatoes, bolts of military canvas, cases of ammunition, or whatever else it was that they happened to be shipping to the front that day. Andras and Mendel and their workmates had to move the goods from the trucks to the boxcars that waited on the tracks, doors yawning wide in the growing light. When they had finished loading one car, they would move on to another and another. But the operation wasn't as simple as it looked. The cars, once filled, were not sealed; they were left open to roll into a shed where they would be inspected. At least that was what Andras and Mendel had been told when the foreman had set them to work: After the cars were loaded, they would be inspected by a corps of specially trained soldiers. If anything was missing, the work servicemen would be held responsible and punished. Only when every item had been tallied would the trains be sealed and sent to the front.

The inspectors came and went in covered trucks. Soldiers drove the trucks directly into the inspection shed and parked them beside the train. Through the broad rectangular doors, Andras could see the soldiers moving quickly between the train and the trucks. The inspectors didn't bother to conceal what was going on; they oversaw the operation with the confidence of their privileged place in the chain of command. Overcoats, blankets, potatoes, cans of beans, guns: Every day, a tithe of it drifted from the boxcars to the trucks. When the soldiers had finished with one boxcar, the inspectors would seal it and the train would roll forward so the soldiers could get to work on the next. They had to work fast for the trains to run on time; the railway schedule made no allowance for black-market siphoning. Once the soldiers had done their work, the inspectors would declare the trainload complete and sign the paperwork. Then they would send the train off to the front. The covered trucks would roll out, the siphoned goods would slide into the black market, and the inspectors would share the proceeds among themselves. It was a tidy and profitable business. In their shed, the inspectors smoked expensive cigars and compared gold pocket watches and played cards for piles of pengő. The guards must have been getting their share of the profits, too—at lunchtime, instead of standing in line at the mess tent, they drank beer and grilled strings of Debrecen sausages, smoked Mirjam cigarettes, and paid the work servicemen to polish their new-looking boots.

Andras knew what the skimming would mean to the soldiers and laborers on the front. There would be too few blankets to go around, too few potatoes in the soup. Someone might not get new boots when his old boots fell apart. The work servicemen would be the hardest hit: They'd be forced to write promissory notes for hundreds of pengő to buy the most basic supplies. Later, when the guards and officers went home on furlough, they would present the notes to the servicemen's families, threatening that the men would be killed if their wives or mothers didn't produce the money. But the labor servicemen at Szentendre Yard seemed to regard the practice as a matter of course. What could any of them have done to stop it? Day after day they loaded the trains and the soldiers unloaded them.

As if to remind them of their powerlessness, all the Jewish workers now had to wear distinguishing armbands, ugly canary-yellow tubes of fabric that slid over their sleeves. Klara had had to sew these for Andras before he reported for duty. Even Jews who had long ago converted to Christianity had to wear armbands, though theirs were white. The bands were mandatory at all times. Even when the weather turned unseasonably hot, the sun reflecting off the crushed rock of the rail yard as though from a million mirrors, and the laborers stripped off their shirts—even then, they had to wear the armbands over their bare arms. The first time Andras had been told to retrieve his band from his discarded shirt, he had stared at the guard in disbelief.

"You're just as much a Jew with your shirt off as you are with it on," the man had said, and he waited for Andras to put on the armband before he turned away.

The commander at Szentendre was a man called Varsádi, a

tall paunchy flatlander with an even temper and a taste for leisure. Varsádi's chief vices were mild ones: his pipe, his flask, his sweet tooth. He was a constant smoker and a happy drunk. He left the matter of discipline to his men, who were less forgiving, less easily distracted by a fine tin of Egyptian tobacco or a smoky Scotch. Varsádi himself liked to sit in the shade of the administrative office, which stood on a low artificial hill overlooking the river, and watch the proceedings of his rail yard while he entertained visiting commanders from other companies or enjoyed his share of the goods that had been intended for the front. Andras knew to be grateful that he was not a Barna nor even a Kálozi, but the sight of Varsádi with his heels on a wooden crate, his arms crossed over his chest in contentment, a lemniscate of smoke drifting from his pipe, was its own special brand of torture.

By the end of their first week, Andras and Mendel had begun to discuss the newspaper they might publish at Szentendre Yard— *The Crooked Rail*, it would be called. "À la Mode at Szentendre," Mendel had extemporized to Andras one morning on the bus, indicating the band on his arm. "The color yellow, ever popular for spring, has surged to the leading edge of fashion." Andras laughed, and Mendel took out his little notebook and began to write. *The trendsetting young men of the 79/6th have made a bold statement in buttercup*, he read aloud a few minutes later: *Accessorize! The* au courant *favor a trim band of ten centimeters worn about the bicep, in an Egyptian twill suitable for all occasions. Next week: Our fashion correspondent investigates a new rage for nakedness among soldiers on the Eastern Front.*

"Not bad," Andras said.

"The Yard's an easy target. I'm surprised they don't have a paper already."

"I'm not," Andras said. "The other men seem half asleep."

"That's just it. Every day they're watching these army stooges steal bread from the men on the front, and they take it all as a matter of course!"

"Only because *they're* not being starved to death themselves."

"Well, let's wake them up," Mendel said. "Let's get them a little angry about what's going on. First we'll make them laugh in the usual manner. Then, later, we'll slide in a piece or two about what it's like in a real camp. Especially if you're short on food or missing an overcoat. Maybe we'll inspire them to slow down the operation a little. If we all drag our feet in the loading, the soldiers won't have as much time to unload. The trains still have to roll out on time, you know."

"But how to do it without risking our necks?"

"Maybe we don't have to hide the paper from Varsádi and the guards. If the coating's sweet enough, they'll never taste what's in the pill. We'll praise Szentendre to the skies in comparison to the other hellholes we've been in, and both sides will hear what we want them to hear."

Andras agreed, and that was where it began. *The Crooked Rail* would be a more elaborate operation than the previous two papers; their residence in Budapest would give them access to a typewriter, a drafting table, an array of supplies. The journey to and from Szentendre would provide time for two daily editorial meetings. They would begin slowly, filling the first issues with nothing but jokes. There would be the usual fabricated news, the usual sports, fashion, and weather; there would be a special arts section complete with event reviews. *This week the Szentendre Ballet debuted "Boxcar,"* Mendel wrote for the first issue, *a brilliant ensemble piece choreographed by Varsádi Varsádius, Budapest's enfant terrible of dance. A certain element of repetition was offset by a delightful variability in the ages and physiques of the dancers.* And then there would be a new feature called "Ask Hitler." On their second Monday at Szentendre, Mendel presented Andras with a typescript:

DEAR HITLER: Please explain your plan for the progress of the war in the East. With affection, SOLDIER

DEAR SOLDIER: I'm so pleased you asked! My plan is to build a large meat-grinder in the vicinity of Leningrad, fill it with young men, and crank the handle as fast as I can. With double affection, HITLER

DEAR HITLER: How do you propose to fight the British fleet in the Mediterranean? Yours most sincerely, POPEYE

DEAR POPEYE: First of all, I'm a fan! I forgive you for being American. I hope you'll pay us a visit in the Reich when this nasty business is all over. Secondly, here is my plan: Fire my admirals until I find one who'll take orders from a Führer who's never been to sea. With admiration, HITLER

DEAR HITLER: What is your position on Hungary? Yours, M. HORTHY

DEAR HORTHY: Missionary, though at times I favor the croupade, just for variation. Love, HITLER

"Maybe we should speak to Frigyes Eppler," Andras said, once he'd read the piece. "Maybe he'd let us print this paper on the *Journal*'s press. I'd hate to subject a piece of work as fine as this to the mimeograph."

"You flatter me, Parisi," Mendel said. "But do you think he'd go for it?"

"We can ask," Andras said. "I don't think he'd begrudge us a little ink and paper."

"Make your illustrations," Mendel said. "That can only help our case."

Andras did, spending a sleepless night at the drafting table. He made an elaborate heading for the paper, two empty boxcars flanking a title stencilled in Gothic script. The fashion section carried a drawing of a young dandy in full Munkaszolgálat uniform, his armband radiating light. The dance review showed a line of laborers, fat and slender, young and old, struggling to hold crates of ammunition aloft. For the Hitler section, austerity and gravity seemed the best approach; Andras made a detailed pencil drawing of the Führer from an old edition of the *Pesti Napló*. At two in the morning Klara woke to feed Tamás, who had not yet learned to sleep through the night. After she'd put him to bed again, she came out to the sitting room and went to Andras, pressing her body against his back.

"What are you doing up so late?" she said. "Won't you come to bed?"

"I'm almost finished. I'll be in soon."

She leaned over the drafting table to look at what he'd taped to its tilted plane. *"The Crooked Rail,"* she read. "What is that? Another newspaper?"

"The best one we've made so far."

"You can't be serious, Andras! Think of what happened in Transylvania."

"I have," he said. "This isn't Transylvania. Varsádi's not Kálozi."

"Varsádi, Kálozi. It's all the same. Those men have your life in their hands. Isn't it bad enough you had to be called again? 'Ask Hitler'?"

"The situation's different at Szentendre," he said. "The command structure hardly deserves the name. We're not even going to publish underground."

"How will you not publish underground? Do you plan to offer Varsádi a subscription?"

"As soon as we've got the first issue printed."

She shook her head. "You can't do this," she said. "It's too dangerous."

"I know the risks," he said. "Perhaps even better than you do. This paper's not just fun and games, Klara. We want to make the men think about what's going on at Szentendre. We're shorting our brothers on the front every day. In my case, perhaps literally."

"And what makes you think Varsádi won't object?"

"He's a sybarite and a fond old fool. The paper will praise his leadership. He won't see anything past that. He's got no loyalty to anything but his own pleasures. I'd be surprised if he had any politics at all."

"And what if you're mistaken?"

"Then we'll stop publishing." He stood and put his arms around her, but she kept her back erect, her eyes on his own.

"I can't stand the thought of anything happening to you," she said.

"I'm a husband and a father," he said, following the ridge of her spine with his palm. "I'll stop immediately if I think there's any real danger."

At that moment Tamás began to cry again, and Klara drew herself away and went to soothe him. Andras stayed up all night to finish the work. Klara would come to understand his reasons, Andras felt, even those he hadn't voiced aloud—those that were more personal, and concerned the difference between feeling at the mercy of one's fate and, to some small degree, the master of it.

That evening, Saturday night, he knew Eppler would be at the offices of the *Journal*, wrangling with the final edits of Sunday's edition. After dinner he and Mendel took their pages to the newspaper's offices and made their plea. They wanted permission to typeset and print a hundred copies of the paper each week. They would come in after hours and use the outdated handpress that the *Journal* retained strictly for emergencies.

"You want me to make you a gift of the paper and ink?" Eppler said.

"Think of it as the *Magyar Jewish Journal*'s contribution to the welfare of forced laborers," Mendel said.

"What about my welfare?" Eppler said. "My managing editor does nothing but grouse about finances as it is. What will he say when supplies begin to disappear?"

"Just tell him you're suffering from war shortages."

"We're already suffering from war shortages!"

"Do it for Parisi," Mendel said. "The mimeograph blurs his drawings terribly."

Eppler regarded Andras's illustrations through the shallow refraction of his horn-rimmed glasses. "That's not a bad Hitler," he said. "I should have made better use of you when you were working for me."

"You'll make good use of me when I work for you again," Andras said.

"If you let us print *The Crooked Rail*, Parisi will swear to work for you when he's done with the Munkaszolgálat," Mendel said.

"I hope he'll get himself back to school once he's done with the Munkaszolgálat."

"I'll need to have some way to pay tuition," Andras said.

Eppler blew a stuttering breath, took out a large pocket handkerchief and wiped his brow, then glanced at the clock on the wall. "I've got to get back to work," he said. "You can print fifty copies of your rag, and no more. Monday nights. Don't let anyone catch you at it."

"We kiss your hand, Eppler-úr," Mendel said. "You're a good man."

"I'm a bitter and disillusioned man," Eppler said. "But I like the idea that one of our presses might print a true word about the state we're in."

When Andras and Mendel presented Major Varsádi with the inaugural copy of *The Crooked Rail*, he gratified them by laughing so hard he was forced to remove his pocket handkerchief and wipe his eyes. He praised them for knowing how to make light of their situation, and opined that the other men might have something to learn from their attitude. The right state of mind, he said, pointing the burning tip of his cigar at them to make his point, could lighten any load. That night Andras brought home to Klara the news that they'd gotten permission to publish *The Crooked Rail*, and she gave him her reluctant blessing. The next day he and Mendel distributed fifty copies of the first issue, which spread as quickly and were consumed with as much relish as the first issues of *The Snow Goose* and *The Biting Fly*. Before long Varsádi began the practice of reading the paper aloud to the Munkaszolgálat officers who paid lunchtime visits to Szentendre Yard; Andras and Mendel could hear their laughter drifting down from the artificial hill where they took their long lunches.

Everyone at Szentendre wanted to make an appearance in the paper, even the foremen and guards who had seemed so stern in comparison to Varsádi. Their own squad foreman, Faragó, a mercurial man who liked to whistle American show tunes but had a habit of kicking his men from behind when his temper ran short, began to wink at Andras and Mendel in a companionate manner as they worked. To gratify him and avert his kicks, they wrote a piece entitled "Songbird of Szentendre," a music review in which they praised his ability to reproduce any Broadway melody down to the thirty-second note. Their third week at the camp provided another fortuitous subject: The rail yard received a vast and mysterious shipment of ladies' underthings, and the men had gotten them half loaded onto a train before anyone thought to wonder why the soldiers at the front might need a hundred and forty gross of reinforced German brassieres. The inspectors, giddy with the prospect of the black-market demand for those garments, appropriated three squads of labor service-men to get the German brassieres off the train and into the covered trucks; at midday, the lunch break devolved into a fashion show of the latest support garments from the Reich. Labor servicemen and guards alike paraded in the stiff-cupped brassieres, pausing in front of Andras so he might capture their likenesses. Though the rest of the afternoon was consumed with a harder variant of labor—a half-dozen truckloads of small munitions arrived and had to be transferred to the trains—Andras scarcely felt the strain in his back or the shipping-crate splinters in his hands. He was considering the set of fashion drawings he might make—*Berlin Chic Angles into Budapest!*—and calculating how long it might be before he and Mendel began to shift the paper toward their aim. As it turned out, the following week's shipments provided the ideal material. For three days the supply trucks contained nothing but medical supplies, as if to stanch a great flow of blood in the east. As the soldiers transferred crates of morphine and suture to the black-market trucks, Andras thought of Tibor's letters from his last company posting—*No splints or casting materials or antibiotics, of course*—and began to roll out a new section in his mind. "Complaints from the Front" it would be called, a series of letters from Munkaszolgálat conscripts in various states of illness and hunger and exposure, to which a representative of the KMOF would reply with admonitions to buck up and accept the hardships of war: Who did these whimpering fairies think they were? They should act like men, goddamn it, and consider that their suffering served the Magyar cause. Andras introduced the idea to Mendel that evening on the bus, and they mounted the series the following week, in a small box that ran on the back page.

By the end of the month an almost imperceptible shift had taken place among the ranks of the 79/6th. A few of the men seemed to be paying a different kind of attention to what went on each day in the inspection shed. In small huddled groups they watched the soldiers rushing to unload crates of food and clothing stamped with the KMOF logo. They followed the movement of the boxes from the train to the covered trucks, then watched the trucks depart through the rail-yard gates. Andras and Mendel, who had attained a certain status thanks to their role as publishers of *The Crooked Rail*, began to approach the groups and speak to a few of the men. In lowered voices they pointed out how little time the soldiers had to move the goods; a few small adjustments on the part of the laborers might delay the siphoning just long enough to get a few more bandages, a few more crates of overcoats, sent to the men at the front.

By the next week, almost unnoticeably, the 79/6th had begun to drag its feet as it loaded goods onto the boxcars. The change happened slowly enough and subtly enough that the foremen failed to notice a general trend. But Andras and Mendel could see it. They watched with a kind of quiet triumph, and compared their impressions in whispered conferences on the bus. All indications suggested that the small shift they'd hoped for had come to pass. Their conversations with the other men confirmed it. There was no way to know, of course, whether the change would make a difference to the men at the front, but it was something, at least: a tiny act of protest, a sole unit of drag inside the vast machine that was the Labor Service. The following week, when they brought the news to Frigyes Eppler at the *Journal*, he clapped them on the shoulders, offered them shots of rye from the bottle in his office, and took credit for the whole thing.

On Sundays, when Andras was free from Szentendre Yard, he and Klara went to lunch at the house on Benczúr utca, which had been stripped by now of all but its most essential furnishings. As they dined in the garden at a long table spread with white linen, Andras had the sense that he had fallen into a different life altogether. He didn't understand how it was possible that he could have spent Saturday loading sacks of flour and crates of weapons into boxcars, and was now spending Sunday drinking sweet Tokaji wine and eating filets of Balatoni fogas in lemon sauce. József Hász would sometimes show up at these Sunday family dinners, often with his girlfriend, the lank-limbed daughter of a real-estate magnate. Zsófia was her name. They had been childhood friends, playmates at Lake Balaton, where their families had owned neighboring summer houses. The two of them would sit on a bench in a corner of the garden and smoke thin dark cigarettes, their heads bent close together as they talked. György Hász detested smoking. He would have sent József to smoke in the street if the girl hadn't been with him. As it was, he pretended not to see them with their cigarettes. It was one of many pretenses that complicated the afternoons they spent at Benczúr utca. Sometimes it was difficult to keep track, so numerous were they. There was the pretense that Andras hadn't spent the rest of the week loading freight cars at Szentendre while József painted at his atelier in Buda; the pretense that Klara's long exile in France had never occurred; the pretense that she was safe now, and that the purpose of the gradual but steady disappearance of the family's paintings and rugs and ornaments, of the younger Mrs. Hász's jewelry and all but the most necessary servants, of the car and its driver, the piano and its gilded stool, the priceless old books and the inlaid furniture, was not to keep Klara out of the hands of the authorities but to keep József out of the Munkaszolgálat.

It was a testament to József's egotism that he considered himself worth his family's sacrifices. His own luxuries were undiminished. In his large bright flat in Buda, he lived among gleanings from the family home: antique rugs and furniture and crystal he'd removed before the slow, steady drain had begun. Andras had seen the flat once, a few months after the baby had been born, when they'd gone for an evening visit. József had provided them with a dinner ordered from Gundel, the famous old restaurant in the city park; he'd held the baby on his knee while Andras and Klara ate roasted game hens and white asparagus salad and a mushroom galette. He praised the shape of his baby cousin's head and hands and declared that he looked exactly like his mother. József's manner toward Andras was breezy and careless, though it had never quite lost the edge of resentment it had acquired when Andras had delivered the news of his relationship with Klara. It was József's habit to mask any social discomfort with humor; Andras was Uncle Andras now, as often as József could find occasion to say his name. After dinner he took

Andras and Klara into the north-facing room he used as his studio, where large canvases were propped against the walls. Four of his previous works had been sold recently, he said; through a family connection he'd begun working with Móric Papp, the Váci utca dealer who supplied Hungary's elite with contemporary art. Andras noted with chagrin that József's work had improved considerably since his student days in Paris. His collage paintings—nets of dark color thrown against backgrounds of fine-ground black gravel and scraps of old road signs and pieces of railroad track—might be called good, might even be seen as evocative of the uncertainty and terror into which Europe had plunged. When Andras praised the work, József responded as though accepting what was due to him. It had taken all of Andras's effort to remain civil through the evening.

On Sunday afternoons at Benczúr utca, when József and his Zsófia joined the group at the table, what he generally had to talk about was how dull it was in Budapest during the warmer months—how much nicer it would have been at Lake Balaton, and what they'd be doing that very moment if they were there. He and Zsófia would start in on some memory from when they were children—how her brother had sailed them far out into the lake in a leaking boat, how they'd gotten sick from eating unripe melons, how József had tried to ride Zsófia's pony and had been thrown off into a blackberry bramble—and Zsófia would laugh, and the elder Mrs. Hász would smile and nod, remembering it all, and György and his wife would exchange a look, because it was the summer house that had kept József out of the labor service, after all.

One Sunday in early June, they arrived to find József's usual bench unoccupied. For Andras, the prospect of an afternoon without him was a relief. Tibor and Ilana had arrived some time earlier, and Ilana played in the grass with young Ádám while Tibor sat beside them on a wicker chaise longue, fixing the bent brim of Ilana's sun hat. Andras fell into a chair beside his brother. It was a hot and cloudless day, one of a series; the new grass had gone limp for want of rain. The week at Szentendre had been an unusually grueling one, bearable only because Andras knew that on Sunday he'd be sitting in this shady garden, drinking cold soda water flavored with raspberry syrup. Klara sat down on the grass with Ilana, holding Tamás on her lap. The babies stared at each other in their usual manner, as if astonished at the revelation that another baby existed in the world. The younger Mrs. Hász emerged from the house with a bottle of seltzer, a miniature pitcher of ruby-colored syrup, and half a dozen glasses. Andras sighed and closed his eyes, waiting for a glass of raspberry soda to materialize on the low table beside him.

"Where's your son today?" Tibor asked Elza Hász.

"In the study with his father."

Andras caught a note of tension in her voice, and he emerged from his torpor to watch her closely as she handed the glasses of soda around. The past five years had aged her. Her dark hair, still cut fashionably short, was shot with silver now; the faint lines beside her eyes had grown deeper. She had lost weight since he'd last seen her—whether from worry or from undereating, he didn't know. He wondered with some anxiety what György and József might be discussing in the study. He could hear their voices coming through the open windows—György's low, grave tones, József's higher notes of indignation. A few minutes later József burst through the French doors and crossed the terracotta paving stones of the patio, then strode over the lawn toward his mother, who had seated herself in a low garden chair. When he reached her, he gave her a look so charged with fury that she got to her feet.

"Say you haven't agreed to this," he demanded.

"We're not going to discuss this now," Elza Hász said, laying a hand on his arm.

"Why not? We're all here."

Elza sent a panicked glance in the direction of her husband, who had come out onto the patio and was hurrying toward the lawn. "György!" she said. "Tell him he's not to discuss it."

"József, you will drop this subject at once," his father said as he reached them.

"I won't have you sell this house. This is *my* house. It's meant to be part of my property. I mean to bring my wife to live here someday."

"Sell the house?" Klara said. "What do you mean?"

"Tell her about it, Father," József said.

György Hász fixed his son in his cool, stern gaze. "Come inside," he said.

"No." It was the elder Mrs. Hász who had spoken, her hands firm on the armrests of her wicker chair. "Klara deserves to know what's happening. It's time we told her."

Klara looked from József to her mother to György, trying to understand what this meant. "The house belongs to you, György," Klara said. "If you're thinking of selling it, I'm certain you must have a good reason. But is it true? Are you really?"

"You mustn't worry, Klara," György said. "Nothing's certain yet. We can discuss the matter after dinner, if you'd like."

"No," said the elder Mrs. Hász again. "We ought to discuss it now. Klara should be part of the decision."

"But there *is* no decision," the younger Mrs. Hász said. "We have no choice. There's nothing to discuss."

"It's Lévi's fault," József said, turning to Andras. "If it hadn't been for him, this wouldn't have happened. He's the one who convinced her to come back to Hungary."

Andras met Klara's questioning glance, and then József's angry one, his heart galloping in his chest. He got to his feet and stood before József. "Listen to your father," he said. "Take it back inside."

József's mouth curled with spite. "Don't tell me what to do, Uncle."

Now Tibor was standing beside Andras, glaring at József. "Watch your tone," he said.

"Why not call him Uncle? That's what he is. He married my aunt." He spat at Andras's feet.

If Klara hadn't taken Andras's arm at that moment, he might have hit József. He hovered on the balls of his feet, his hands clenched. He hated József Hász. He had never known it before that moment. He hated everything he was, everything he represented. He could feel the fragile twig-structure of his own life losing its center, beginning to slip. It was József who had done this. Andras wanted to tear the man's hair out, tear the fine cotton shirt from his back.

"Sit down, both of you," the elder Mrs. Hász said. "It's too hot. You're overexcited."

"Who's overexcited?" József shouted. "It's the loss of my family home, that's all. Mother's right: There's no decision. It's finished already, and no one consulted me. You all kept me in the dark. Even worse, you made me feel like it was for *my* sake that we had to give up the furniture, the paintings, the car, and God knows how much money! And all this time we were paying for *her* mistakes, and her husband's."

"What are you talking about?" Klara said. "How does this concern Andras and me?"

"*He* brought you back here. *You* came back. The authorities have known about it for nearly three years. Did you think you could hide behind your French name and your married name forever? Didn't you know you'd be endangering the family?"

"Tell me what he means, György," Klara said, turning to her brother. She held the baby on her hip and moved closer to Andras.

There was no way to avoid a disclosure now. As briefly and clearly as he could, György laid out the situation: how Madame Novak had brought Klara's identity to light; how György had been approached, and when; how he'd arranged a solution; how he'd hoped that the authorities would have satisfied their greed, or grown tired of the whole affair, before he was forced to give up the house; and how they'd persisted, bringing the family to its current pass.

Klara grew pale as her brother spoke. She covered her mouth with her hand, looking from György to her husband. "Andras," she said, when György had finished. "How long have you known?"

"Since last fall," he said, forcing himself to look at her.

She took a step back and sat down in one of the wicker chairs. "Oh, God," she said. "You knew, and you didn't tell me. All this time."

"Andras wanted to tell you," György said. "I made him promise not to. I didn't think it would be wise to worry you, in your condition."

"And you agreed?" she asked Andras. "You thought it wouldn't be wise to worry me, in my condition?"

"We argued about it," György said. "He thought you would rather know. Mother, too, has always believed you should know. But Elza and I disagreed."

Klara was crying with frustration now. She got to her feet and began to walk up and down the lawn with the baby in her arms. "This is a disaster," she said. "I might have done something. We might have come to some solution. But no one said a word to me! Not a word! Not my husband. Not even my own mother!" She turned and went into the house, and Andras went after her; before he could catch her, she'd grabbed her cotton jacket and gone out through the heavy front door, carrying Tamás with her. Andras opened the door and followed her out onto the sidewalk. She half ran down Benczúr in the direction of Bajza utca, her melon-colored jacket fluttering behind her like a flag. The baby's dark hair shone in the afternoon sunlight, his hand on her back just the shape and size of the starfish pin she'd worn in the south of France. Andras chased her now as he'd chased her then. He would have chased her all the way across the continent if he'd had to. But the traffic at the corner of Bajza utca and the Városliget fasor brought her to a stop, and she stood looking at the passing cars, refusing to acknowledge him. He caught up to her and took up her jacket, which had slipped from her shoulders to trail a sleeve on the sidewalk. As he draped it around her again he could feel her trembling with anger.

"Can't you understand?" he said. "György was right. You would have risked yourself and the baby."

The light changed, and she crossed the street toward Nefelejcs utca at the same brisk pace. He followed close behind.

"I was afraid you'd try to leave," he said. "I had to go back to the work service. I couldn't have gone with you."

"Leave me alone," she said. "I don't want to speak to you."

He matched her pace as she sped on toward home. "I respect György," he said. "He took me into his confidence. I couldn't betray him."

"I don't want to hear about it."

"You've got to listen, Klara. You can't just run away."

She turned to face him now. The baby whimpered against her shoulder. "You let me beggar my family," she said. "You made the decision for me."

"György made the decision," Andras said. "And be careful how you choose your words. Your brother's not a beggar. If he has to move to an eight-room parlor-level flat in the Erzsébetváros, he'll survive."

"It's my *home*," she said, starting to cry again. "It's my childhood home."

"I lost mine, too, if you'll recall," Andras said.

She turned again and walked toward their building. At the entryway she fumbled in her pocketbook for the key. He extracted it for her and opened the outer door. From inside came the splash of the fountain and the sound of children playing hopscotch. She crossed the courtyard at a run and began to climb the staircase; the children stopped their game, holding their broken pot shards in their hands. Her quick steps rang on the stairs above, sounding in a spiral as she climbed. She had disappeared into the apartment by the time he reached the top. The front door stood open; the air of the hallway vibrated with silence. She had locked herself in the bedroom. The baby had begun to cry, and Andras could hear her trying to soothe him, their Tamás—talking to him, wondering aloud if he was hungry or wet, walking him up and down the room. Andras went into the kitchen and put his head against the cool flank of the icebox. His instinct had told him to tell her the truth at once. Why hadn't he done it?

He sat in the kitchen and waited for her to come out. He waited as the shadows of the furniture lengthened across the kitchen floor and climbed the eastern wall. He made coffee and drank it. He tried to look at a newspaper but couldn't concentrate. He waited, his hands folded in his lap, and when he got tired of waiting he went down the hallway and stood outside the door. He put a hand on the doorknob. It turned in his fingers, and there was Klara on the other side. The baby was asleep on the bed, his arms flung over his head as if in surrender. Klara's eyes were pink, her hair loose around her shoulders. She looked exactly as Elisabet had looked when Andras had gone to see if he could coax her from her room on the rue de Sévigné. She held one arm across her chest, cupping her shoulder as if it were sore. Her footsteps had sounded on the bedroom floor for hours; all that time she must have been pacing with the baby.

"Come sit with me," Andras said, taking her hand. He led her to the front room and brought her to the sofa, then sat down with her, keeping her hand in his own.

"I'm sorry," he said. "I should have told you."

She looked down at his hand, closed around her own, and pushed the back of her other hand across her eyes. "I let myself think it was over," she said. "We came back here and made a different life. I wasn't afraid anymore. Or at least I didn't fear the things I'd feared when I left here the first time."

"That was what I wanted," Andras said. "I didn't want you to be afraid."

"You should have trusted me to do what was right," she said. "I wouldn't have endangered our child. I wouldn't have tried to leave the country while you were away in the Munkaszolgálat."

"But what would you have done? What are we going to do now?"

"We're going to go," she said. "We're all going to go, before György loses what's left. Even if he can't keep the house, he's not destitute yet. There's a great deal that might still be saved. We're going to go talk to that Klein, you and I, and we're going to ask him to arrange the trip. We have to try to get to Palestine. From there it might be easier to get to the United States."

"You're going to give up the building in Paris."

"Of course," she said. "Think of how much my brother's already lost."

"But how will we get them to stop dunning him? If you flee, won't they go after him to tell them where you are?

"He's got to come too. He's got to sell whatever's left and get out as soon as he can."

"And your mother? And my parents? And Mátyás? We can't leave without knowing what's happened to him. We've talked about this, Klara. We can't do it."

"We'll take our parents. We'll arrange for Mátyás to have passage too, if he returns in time."

"And if he doesn't?"

"Then we'll speak to Klein and arrange for him to join us when he does return."

"Listen to me. Hundreds of people have died trying to get to Palestine."

"I understand. But we have to try. If we stay, they'll bleed the family of everything. And in the end they might not be satisfied with the money."

Andras sat silent for a long moment. "You know how Tibor feels about this," he said. "He wanted us to go a long time ago."

"And what do you think?"

"I don't know. I don't know."

Her chest rose and fell beneath the drape of her blouse. "You have to understand," she said. "I can't stay here and allow us, or my family, to be *done to* this way. I didn't then. And I won't now."

He did understand. Of course he'd known this about her: It was her nature. This was why György hadn't told her. They were going to have to leave Hungary. They would sell the property in Paris; they would go to Klein and beg him to arrange one last trip. That night they would begin to plan how it might be done. But for the moment there was nothing more to say. He took her hand again and she held his gaze, and he knew, too, that she understood why he'd kept the truth from her for so many months.

CHAPTER THIRTY-THREE

Passage to the East

IN THE WEEKS that followed, he tried not to think about the *Struma*. He tried not to think about the deceived passengers who found themselves aboard a wreck of a ship, ill-provisioned and ill-equipped for the journey. He tried not to think about the prospect of their own passage down the Danube, the constant fear of discovery, his wife and son suffering for lack of food and water; he tried not to think about leaving his brother and his parents behind in Europe. He tried to think only of the necessity of getting out, and the means for arranging the trip. He wired Rosen to tell him of the change in their situation, the new urgency that had come upon them. Two weeks later, a reply came via air mail with the news that Shalhevet had secured six emergency visas—six!—enough for Andras and Klara, Tibor and Ilana, and the children. Once they arrived in Palestine, he wrote, it would be easier to arrange visas for the others—for Mendel Horovitz, who would be so valuable to the Yishuv; and for György and Elza and Andras's parents and the rest of the family. There was no time to celebrate the news; there was too much to be done. Klara had to write to her solicitor in Paris to hasten the sale of the property. Andras had to write to his parents to explain what was happening, and why. And they had to see Klein.

It was Klara's idea that they should go together, all six of them. She believed he might be more inclined to help if he met the people he'd be saving. They arranged to go on a Sunday afternoon; they dressed in visiting clothes and pushed the babies in their perambulators. Klara and Ilana walked ahead, their summer hats dipping toward each other like two bellflowers. Andras and Tibor followed. They might have been any Hungarian family out for a Sunday stroll. No one would have guessed that they were missing a seventh, a brother who was lost in Ukraine. No one would have guessed that they were trying to arrange an illegal flight from Europe. In her pocketbook Klara carried a telegram from her solicitor, stating that her property on the rue de Sévigné would be listed for ninety thousand francs, and that the transfer of the money from the sale, though difficult, might be accomplished through his contacts in Vienna, who had contacts in Budapest. Nothing would be done in Klara's name; ownership of the building had already been officially transferred to the non-Jewish solicitor himself, because it had become illegal for Jews to own real estate in occupied France. Everyone would have to be paid along the way, of course, but if the sale went well, there would still be some seventy thousand francs left over. No one would have known, looking at Klara as she walked along Váci út that Sunday afternoon—her fine-boned back held straight, her features composed under the pale blue shadow of her hat—how unhappy she'd been two nights earlier as she'd drafted a telegram to her solicitor, instructing him to make the sale. It had been a long time since she and Andras had imagined they might go back someday to reclaim their Paris lives. But the apartment and the studio were real things that still belonged to her, things that marked out a territory for her in the city that had been her home for seventeen years. The property had made the impossible seem possible; it made them believe that everything might change, that they might return someday. The decision to sell the building carried a sense of finality. They were giving up that source of hope in order to fund a desperate journey that might fail, to a place that was utterly foreign to them—an embattled desert territory ruled by the British. But they had made their decision. They would try. And so Klara had written to her solicitor, directing him to forward the proceeds of the sale to his agents in Vienna and Budapest.

At the house in Frangepán köz, where time stood still and the very sunlight filtering down through the high clouds seemed antique, they found the milk goats bleating in their yard and pulling at a stack of sweet hay. Seven-month-old Tamás stared in fascination. He looked at Klara as though to ask if he should be alarmed. When he saw she was smiling, he turned again to the goats and pointed a finger.

"Our sons are city boys," Tibor said. "By the time I was his age, I'd seen a thousand goats."

"Perhaps they won't be city boys for long," Klara said.

They turned away from the goats and walked the stone path to the door. Tibor knocked, and Klein's grandmother answered, her white hair hidden under a kerchief, her dress covered with a red-embroidered apron. From the kitchen came the smell of stuffed cabbage. Andras, exhausted from the week's work, became suddenly and ravenously hungry. Klein's grandmother beckoned them into the bright sitting room, where the elder Mr. Klein sat in an armchair with his feet soaking in a tin basin. He wore the same faded crimson robe he'd worn when Andras and Tibor had last visited; his hair stood up in the same winged style, as if his head meant to take flight. A haze of tea-scented steam wreathed his legs. He raised a hand in greeting.

"My husband's bunions are bothering him," his wife said. "Otherwise he would get up to welcome you."

"I welcome you," the old man said, and made a polite half bow. "Please sit."

Mrs. Klein went off down the portrait-lined hall to get her grandson. None of them sat, despite the elder Klein's invitation. Instead they waited in a close-shouldered group, glancing around at the room's ancient furniture and its profusion of photographs. Andras saw Klara's eyes move over the images of the little family—the boy that must have been the child Klein, the beautiful and mysterious woman, the sad-eyed man—and he felt again as though the house contained the ghost of some long-ago loss. Klara must have sensed it too; she drew Tamás closer and passed her thumb across his mouth, as if removing an invisible film of milk.

Klein followed his grandmother back down the hall and into the sitting room. She ducked into the kitchen; he came forward, blinking in the afternoon light. Andras had to wonder how long it had been since he'd last emerged from his den of dossiers and maps and radios. His eyes were dark-shadowed, his hair stiff for want of washing. He wore a cotton undershirt and a pair of ink-stained trousers. His feet were bare. He needed a shave. He scrutinized the group of them and shook his head.

"No," he said. "No, I tell you. Not a chance."

"Let me make some tea while you're talking," Klein's grandmother called.

"No tea," he called back to her. "We're not talking. They're leaving. Do you understand?" But they could hear a kitchen cabinet open and close, and water rolling into the metallic hollow of a teapot.

Klein raised his hands toward the ceiling.

"Be civil," the elder Klein said to his grandson. "They've come all this way."

"What you're asking is impossible," Klein said, speaking to Andras and Tibor. "Impossible, and illegal. You could all end up in jail, or dead."

"We've considered that," Klara said, her tone demanding that he look at her. "We still want to go."

"Impossible!" he repeated.

"But this is what you do," Andras said. "You've done it before. We can pay you. We've got the money, or we'll have it soon."

"Lower your voice," Klein said. "The windows are open. You don't know who might be listening."

Andras lowered his voice. "Our situation has become urgent," he said. "We want you to arrange our transport, and then we want to get the rest of our family out."

Klein sat down on the sofa and put his head in his hands. "Get someone else to help you," he said.

"Why should they get someone else?" his grandfather said. "You're the best."

Klein made a sound of frustration in his throat. His grandmother, having finished her preparations in the kitchen, wheeled a little tea cart into the room, parked it beside the sofa, and began to fill ancient-looking Herend cups.

"If you don't help them, they *will* try someone else," she said, with a note of quiet reproach. She cocked her head, pausing in her tea-pouring to scrutinize Klara, as if the future were written upon the dotted swiss of her dress. "They'll go to Pál Behrenbohm, and he'll turn them away. They'll go to Szászon. They'll go to Blum. And if *that* fails, they'll go to János Speitzer. And you know what will happen then." She handed the cups around, offering sugar and cream, and poured a final cup for herself.

Klein looked from his grandmother to Andras and Klara, Tibor and Ilana and the babies. He wiped his palms against his undershirt. He was one man against all of them. He raised his hands in defeat. "It's your funeral," he said.

"Please sit and drink your tea," Klein's grandmother said. "And Miklós, you need not use that morbid language."

They took their places around the table and drank the strange smoky tea she'd prepared for them. It tasted like wood fires burning, and it made Andras think of fall. In lowered voices they talked about the details: how Klein would arrange transport down the Danube with a friend who owned a barge, and how the families would be secreted away in two ingeniously built compartments in the cargo area, and how drugged milk must be prepared for the babies so they wouldn't cry, and how they would need to bring emergency food enough for two weeks' travel, because a trip that ordinarily took a few days might take much longer in wartime. Klein would have to make inquiries about ships leaving from Romania, and where and how they might gain passage aboard one of them. It might take a month or two to arrange the journey, if all went well. He, Klein, was not a swindler, not like János Speitzer. He would not book passage for them upon an unsound boat, nor tell them to bring less food than was needed so they would have to buy more from his friends at cruel prices. He would not place them in care of a crew that would steal their luggage or prevent them from going ashore to a doctor if they needed one. Nor would he make false promises about the safety or success of the trip. It might fail at any point. They had to understand that.

When Klein had finished, he sat back against the sofa and scratched his chest through his undershirt. "That's how it works," he concluded. "A hard, risky trip. No guarantees."

Klara moved forward in her chair and placed her cup on the little table. "No guarantees," she repeated. "But at least we'll have a chance."

"I'm not going to speculate about your chances," Klein said. "But if you still want to engage my services, I'm willing to do the work."

They exchanged a look—Andras and Klara, Tibor and Ilana. They were ready. This was what they'd hoped for. "By all means," Tibor said. "We'll take whatever risks we have to take."

The men shook hands and arranged to meet again in a week. Klein bowed to the women and retreated back down the hallway, where they heard the door of his room open and close. Andras imagined him taking a new manila folder from a box and inscribing their family name upon its tab. The thought filled him with sudden panic. So many files. Stacks and stacks of them, all over the bed and desk and bureau. What had happened to those people? How many of them had made it to Palestine?

The next evening Klara went to her brother to ask his forgiveness. She and Andras walked together to the house on Benczúr utca, pushing the baby in his carriage. In György's study, Klara took her brother's hands in her own and asked that he excuse her, that he understand how surprised she'd been and how incapable, at that moment, of appreciating what he'd done. She hated the thought that he'd already lost so much of his estate.

She had authorized the sale of her property in Paris, she told him, and would begin to repay her debt to him as soon as she had access to the money.

"You're in no debt to me," György said. "What's mine is yours. Most of what I had came from our father's estate, in any case. And it'll do little good for you to put money into my hands now. Our extortionists will only find a way to take it."

"But what can I do?" she said, on the verge of tears. "How can I repay you?"

"You can forgive me for operating on your behalf without your knowledge. And perhaps you can convince your husband to forgive me for requiring that he keep the secret from you."

"I do, of course," Klara said; and Andras said he did as well. Everyone agreed that György had acted in Klara's best interest, and György expressed the hope that his son would seek Klara and Andras's forgiveness too. But as he said it, his voice faltered and broke.

"What is it?" Klara said. "What's happened?"

"He's received another call-up notice," György said. "This time he'll have to go. There's nothing more we can do about it. We've offered a percentage of the proceeds from the sale of the house, but it's not the money they want. They want to make an example of young men like József."

"Oh, György," Klara said.

Andras found himself speechless. He could no more imagine József Hász in the Munkaszolgálat than he could imagine Miklós Horthy himself showing up one morning on the bus from Óbuda to Szentendre, a tattered coat on his back, a lunch pail in his hand. His first sensation was one of satisfaction. Why shouldn't József have to serve, when he, Andras, had already served for two years and was serving still? But György's pained expression brought him back to himself. Whatever else József was, he was György's child.

"I haven't done a very good job of raising my son," György said, turning his gaze toward the window. "I gave him everything he wanted, and tried to keep him from anything that would hurt him. But I gave him too much. I protected him too much. He's come to believe that the world should present itself at his feet. He's been living in comfort in Buda while other men serve in his place. Now he'll have to get by on his strength and his wits, like everyone else. I hope he's got enough of both."

"Perhaps he can be assigned to one of the companies close to home," Andras said.

"That won't be up to him," György said. "They'll put him where they want to."

"I can write to General Márton."

"You don't owe József anything," György said.

"He helped me in Paris. More than once."

György nodded slowly. "He can be generous when he wants to be."

"Andras will write to the general," Klara said. "And then maybe József will come to Palestine, with the rest of us."

"To Palestine?" György said. "You're not going to Palestine."

"Yes," Klara said. "We have no other choice."

"But, darling, there's no way to get to Palestine."

Klara explained about Klein. György's eyes grew stern as she spoke.

"Don't you understand?" he said. "This is why I paid the Ministry of Justice. This is why I sold the paintings and the rugs and the furniture. This is why I'm selling the house! To keep you from taking a foolish risk like this."

"It would be foolish to throw away what we have left," Klara said.

György turned to Andras. "Please tell me you haven't agreed to this wild scheme."

"My brother witnessed the massacre in the Délvidék. He thinks it could happen here, and worse."

György sank back in his chair, his face drained of blood. From outside came the drumbeat and brass of a military band; they must have been marching up Andrássy út to Heroes' Square.

"What about us?" he said, faintly. "What's going to happen once they discover you're gone? Who do you think they'll question? Who'll get the blame for spiriting you away?"

"You must join us in Palestine," Klara said.

He shook his head. "Impossible. I'm too old to begin a new life."

"What choice do you have?" she said. "They've taken away your position, your fortune, your home. Now they're taking your son."

"You're dreaming," he said.

"I wish you'd talk to Elza about it. By the end of the year they'll call you to the labor service too. Elza and Mother will be left all alone."

He touched the edge of his blotter with his thumbs. A stack of documents lay before him, thick sheaves of ivory legal paper. "Do you see this?" he said, pushing at the papers. "These are the documents assigning possession of the house to the new owner."

"Who is it?" Klara asked.

"The son of the minister of justice. His wife has just given birth to their sixth child, I understand."

"God help us," Klara said. "The house will be a shambles."

"Where will you live?" Andras said.

"I've found lodgings for us in a building at the head of Andrássy út—it's really quite grand, or it was at one time. According to these papers, we're allowed to take whatever furniture remains." He swept an arm around the denuded room.

"Please speak to Elza," Klara said.

"Six children in this house," he said, and sighed. "What a disaster."

General Martón's reaction was quick and sympathetic, but he lacked range: His solution was to secure József a place in the 79/6th. When the news arrived, Andras felt as though he were being punished personally. Here was retribution for the moment of satisfaction he'd experienced when he'd first heard that József had been called. Now, every morning, József was there at the Óbuda bus stop, looking like an officer in his too-clean uniform and his unbroken military cap. He was assigned to Andras and Mendel's work group and made to load boxcars like the rest of the conscripts. Through the first week of it he glared at Andras every chance he got, as if this were all his fault, as if Andras himself were responsible for the blisters on József's feet and hands, the ache in his back, the peeling sunburn. He was roundly abused by the work foreman for his softness, his sloth; when he protested, Faragó kicked him to the ground and spat in his face. After that, he did his work without a word.

June turned into July and a dry spell ended. Every afternoon the sky broke open to drop sweet-tasting rain onto the tedium of Szentendre Yard. The yellow bricks of the rail yard buildings darkened to dun. On the hills across the river, the trees that had stood immobile in the dust now shook out their leaves and tossed their limbs in the wind. Weeds and wildflowers crowded between the railroad ties, and one morning a plague of tiny frogs descended upon Szentendre. They were everywhere underfoot, having arrived from no one knew where, coin-sized, the color of celery, sprinting madly toward the river. They made the work servicemen curse and dance for two days, then disappeared as mysteriously as they'd come. It was a time of year Andras had loved as a boy, the time to swim in the millpond, to eat sun-hottened strawberries directly from the vine, to hide in the shadow of the long cool grass and watch ants conduct their quick-footed business. Now there was only the slow toil of the rail yard and the prospect of escape. At night, during his few hours at home, he held his sleeping son while Klara read him passages from Bialik or Brenner or Herzl, descriptions of Palestine and of the miraculous transformation the settlers were enacting there. In his mind he had begun to see his family replanted among orange trees and honeybees, the bronze shield of the sea glittering far below, his boy growing tall in the salt-flavored air. He tried not to dwell upon the inevitable difficulties of the journey. He was no stranger to hardship, nor was Klara. Even his parents, whose recent move to Debrecen represented the most significant geographic displacement of their married lives, had agreed to undertake the trip if it was possible, if entry visas could be obtained for them; they refused to be separated from their children and grandchildren by a continent, a sea.

After the drought broke, the journey began to take shape. Klein had identified a barge captain named Szabó who would take them as far as the Romanian border, and another, Ivanescu, who would conduct them to Constanţa; he booked them passage under the family name of Gedalya aboard the *Trasnet*, a former fishing boat that had been converted into a refugee-smuggling vessel. They must be prepared to be crowded and hungry, over-heated, dehydrated, seasick, delayed for days in Turkish ports where they could not take the risk of disembarking; they must bring with them only what was necessary. They should be glad they were undertaking the trip in summer, when the seas were calm. They would travel through the Bosporus past Istanbul, through the Marmara Denizi and into the Aegean Sea; from there they would move into the Mediterranean, and if they evaded the patrol boats and submarines they would dock three days later at Haifa. From start to finish the journey would take two weeks, if all went well. They would leave on August second.

Klara had an old-fashioned wooden wall calendar painted with the image of a bluebird on a cherry branch. Three diminutive windows showed day, date, and month; each morning Andras rolled the little wheels forward before he left for Szentendre Yard. He rolled July through its thunderstorm-drenched days, from single digits into teens, as plans for the trip went forward. They assembled clothing, boots, hats; they packed and repacked suitcases, trying to determine the densest possible arrangement of their belongings. On Sunday afternoons they walked the city together, packing their minds with the things they wanted to remember: the green haze of river-cooled air

around Margaret Island; the thrumming vibration of cars crossing the Széchenyi Bridge; the smells of cut grass and hot-spring
sulfur in the Városliget; the dry concrete pan of the skating
pond; the long gray Danube embankment where Andras had
walked with his brother a lifetime ago, when they were recent
gimnázium graduates living in a room on Hársfa utca. There was
the synagogue where he and Klara had been married, the hospital where their son had been born, the small bright studio where
Klara taught her private students. There was their own apartment on Nefelejcs utca, the first place they'd ever lived together.
And then there were the haunted places they would not visit in
farewell: the house on Benczúr utca, which now stood empty in
preparation for the arrival of the son of the minister of justice;
the Opera House, with its echoing corridors; the patch of pavement in an alley where what had happened long ago had happened.

One Sunday, two weeks before the second of August, Andras
went alone to see Klein. The packet of entry visas had arrived
from Palestine. That was the last thing they needed to complete
their dossier, that set of crisp white documents imprinted with
the seal of the British Home Office and the Star of David stamp
of the Yishuv. Klein would make facsimile copies, which he
would keep in case anything happened to the originals. When
Andras arrived, Klein's grandfather was in the yard, feeding the
goats. He put a hand to his hat.

"You'll be off soon," he said.

"Fourteen more days."

"I knew the boy would take care of things."

"He seems to have a talent for it."

"That's our boy. He's like his father was, always planning,
planning, working with his gadgets, making things happen. His
father was an inventor, a man whose name everyone would have
known, if he'd lived." He told Andras that Klein's parents had
died of influenza when Klein was still in short pants; they were
the man and woman depicted in the photograph, as Andras had

guessed. Another child might have been destroyed by the loss, the elder Klein said, but not Miklós. He'd gotten top marks in school, particularly in the social sciences, and had grown up to become a kind of inventor in his own right—a creator of possibilities where none existed.

"What a stroke of luck it was that we found him," Andras said.

"May your luck continue," the grandfather said. He spat thrice and knocked on the wooden lintel of the goat house. "May your journey to Palestine be exceptional only for its tedium."

Andras tipped his cap to the elder Klein and walked the stone path to the door. Klein's grandmother was there in the front room, sitting in the armchair with an embroidery hoop in her lap. The design, embroidered in tiny gold Xs, showed a braided challah and the word *Shabbos* in Hebrew letters.

"It's for your table in the holy land," she said.

"Oh, no," Andras said. "It's too fine." He thought of their packed and repacked suitcases, into which not a single thing more could possibly fit.

But nothing could be hidden from Klein's grandmother. "Your wife can sew it into the lining of her summer coat," she said. "It's got a good luck charm in it."

"Where?"

She showed him two minuscule Hebrew letters cross-stitched into the end of the challah. "It's the number eighteen. *Chai.* Life."

Andras nodded his thanks. "It's very kind of you," he said. "You've been a help to us all along."

"The boy's waiting for you in his room. Go on."

In his file-crowded den, Klein sat on the bed with his hair in wild disorder, shirtless, a radio disemboweled on the blanket before him. If he had been disheveled and ripe-smelling the first time Andras had met him, now, after a month of planning their escape, he seemed on his way to a prehistoric state of existence. His beard had grown in scraggly and black. Andras couldn't remember the last time he'd seen him wear a shirt. His smell was reminiscent of the barracks in Subcarpathia. Had it not been for the open window and the breeze that riffled the topmost papers on the stacks, no one could have remained in that room for long. And yet, there on the desk was a cleared-away space in which a crisp folder lay open, a coded travel itinerary stapled to one side, a fat sheaf of instructions on the other. Gedalya, their code name, on the tab. And in Andras's hand the final piece, the packet of documents that would complete the puzzle, the legal element of their illegal flight. Never before the planning of this trip had he imagined what a byzantine maze might lie between emigration and immigration. Klein tucked a tiny screwdriver into his belt and raised his eyebrows at Andras. Andras put the documents into his lap.

"Genuine," Klein said, touching the raised letters of the British seal. His dark-circled eyes met Andras's own. "Well, that's it. You're ready."

"We haven't talked about money."

"Yes, we have." Klein reached for the folder and extracted a page torn from an accountant's notebook, a list of figures penned in his thin left-sloping script. The cost of false papers, in case they were discovered. The fees for the barge captains and the fishing-boat captains and their part of the petrol for the journey and the cost of food and water and the extra money set aside for bribes, and the harbor fees and taxes and the cost of extra insurance, because so many boats had accidentally been torpedoed in the Mediterranean in recent months. Everything to be paid in person, incrementally, along the way. "We've been through it all," he said.

"I mean your fee," Andras said. "We haven't talked about that."

Klein scowled. "Don't insult me."

"I'm not insulting you."

"Do I look like I need anything?"

"A shirt," Andras said. "A bath. Maybe a new radio."

"I won't take money from you."

"That's absurd."

"That's the way it is."

"Maybe you won't take it for yourself. But take it for your grandparents."

"They've got all they need."

"Don't be an idiot," Andras said. "We can give you two thousand pengő. Think what that could mean."

"Two thousand, five thousand, a hundred thousand, I don't care! This is not paid work, do you understand? If you wanted to pay, you should have gone to Behrenbohm or Speitzer. My services aren't for sale."

"If you don't want money, what do you want?"

Klein shrugged. "I want this to work. And then I want to do it again for someone else, and for someone else after that, until they stop me."

"That's not what you said when we first met you."

"I was scared after the *Struma*," Klein said. "I'm not scared anymore."

"Why not?"

He shrugged. "Things got worse. Paralyzing fear came to seem like a luxury."

"What if *you* wanted to leave? My friend could help you get a visa."

"I know. That's good. I'll keep it in mind."

"You'll keep it in mind? That's all?"

He nodded at Andras and took the screwdriver from his belt again. "If you'll excuse me, I've got more work to do today. We're done, unless you hear from me. You leave in two weeks." He bent to the radio and began to loosen a screw that secured a copper wire to its base.

"So?" Andras said. "That's it?"

"That's it," Klein said. "I'm not a sentimental person. If you want a long goodbye, talk to my grandmother."

But Klein's grandmother had fallen asleep in her chair. She'd finished embroidering the challah cover and had wrapped it in a piece of tissue paper, written Andras's and Klara's names on a little card, and affixed the card to the paper with a pin. Andras bent to her ear and whispered his thanks, but she didn't wake. The goats made their remarks in the yard. From Klein's room came a low curse and the clatter of a thrown tool. Andras tucked the parcel under his arm and let himself out without a sound.

And then it was the week before their journey. Andras and Mendel produced the last illustrated issue of *The Crooked Rail*, though Andras made Mendel promise that he would continue to publish until his own visa came through. The issue featured a faux interview with a star of Hungarian pornography, a crossword puzzle whose circled letters spelled the name of their own Major Károly Varsádi, and an optimistic economic column entitled "Black Market Review," in which all indicators pointed to an unending series of lucrative shipments. "Ask Hitler," which had become a permanent fixture of the newspaper, carried only one letter that week:

> DEAR HITLER: When will this hot weather end? Sincerely, SUNSTRUCK.
> DEAR SUNSTRUCK: It'll end when I goddamn say it will, and not a moment sooner! Heil me, HITLER.

In midweek, Andras's parents came to Budapest to see their children and grandchildren once more before they left. They went to dinner at the new residence of the Hász family, a high-ceilinged apartment with crumbling plaster moldings and a parquet floor in the herringbone pattern called *points de Hongrie*. It had been nearly five years now, Andras realized, since he'd studied parquetry at the École Spéciale; five years since he'd learned what kind of wood suited each design, and replicated the patterns in his sketchbook. Now here he was in this apartment with his stricken parents, his fierce and lovely wife, his baby son, preparing to say goodbye to Europe altogether. The architecture of this apartment mattered only insofar as it reminded him of what he would leave behind.

His brother and Ilana arrived, their boy asleep in Ilana's arms. They sat close together on the sofa while József perched beside them on a gold chair and smoked one of his mother's cigarettes. Andras's father perused a tiny book of psalms, marking a few for his sons to repeat along the journey. The elder Mrs. Hász made conversation with Andras's mother, who had learned that her own sister knew the remnant of Mrs. Hász's family that remained in Kaba, not far from Konyár. György arrived from work, his shirtfront damp with perspiration, and kissed Andras's mother and shook hands with Béla. Elza Hász ushered them all into the dining room and begged them to take their places at the table.

The room was decorated as if for a party. There were tapers in silver candelabra, clusters of roses in blue glass bowls, decanters of tawny wine, the gold-rimmed plates with their design of birds. Andras's father made the blessing over the bread, and the usual grim serving man stepped forward to fill their plates. At first the conversation was about trivial things: the fluctuating prices of lumber, the almanac's predictions of an early fall, the scandalous relationship between a certain member of parliament and a former star of the silent screen. But inevitably the conversation turned to the war. The morning papers had reported that German U-boats had sunk a million tons of British-American shipping that summer, seven hundred thousand tons in July alone. And the news from Russia was no better: The Hungarian Second Army, after a bloody battle at Voronezh in early July, was now pushing onward in the wake of the German Sixth toward Stalingrad. The Hungarian Second Army had already paid a heavy toll to support its ally. It had lost, György had read, more than nine hundred officers and twenty thousand soldiers. No one mentioned what they were all thinking: that there were fifty thousand labor servicemen attached to the Hungarian Second Army, nearly all of them Jewish, and that if the Hungarian Second had fared badly, the labor battalions were certain to have fared worse. From the street below, like a note of punctuation, came the familiar gold-toned clang of the streetcar bell. It was a sound peculiar to Budapest, a sound amplified and made resonant by the walls of the buildings that lined the streets. Andras couldn't help but think of that other departure five years earlier, the one that had brought him from Budapest to Paris and to Klara. The journey that lay ahead now was more desperate but strangely less frightening; between himself and the terror of the unknown lay the comfort of Klara's presence, and Tibor's. And at the other end of the journey would be Rosen and Shalhevet, and the prospect of hard work he wanted to do, and the promise of an unfamiliar variety of freedom. Mendel Horovitz might join them in a few months; Andras's parents might follow soon after. In Palestine his son would never have to wear a yellow armband or live in fear of his neighbors. He himself might finish his architecture training. He couldn't help feeling a kind of pity for József Hász, who would remain here in Budapest and struggle on alone in Company 79/6 of the Munkaszolgálat.

"You ought to be coming to Palestine, Hász," he said. The journey to the Middle East would make Andras better traveled than József, a fact he had apprehended with a certain satisfaction.

"You wouldn't want me," József said flatly. "I'd be a terrible traveling companion. I'd get seasick. I'd complain constantly. And that would just be the beginning. I'd be useless in Palestine. I can't plant trees or build houses. In any case, my mother can't spare me, can you, Mother?"

Mrs. Hász looked first at Andras's mother and then at her own dinner plate. "Maybe you'll change your mind," she said. "Maybe you'll come with us when we go."

"Please, Mother," József said. "How long will you keep up that pretense? *You're* not going to Palestine. You won't even get into a boat at Lake Balaton."

"No one's pretending," his mother said. "Your father and I mean to go as soon as our visas arrive. We certainly can't stay here."

"Grandmother," József said. "Tell my mother she's out of her mind."

"I certainly will not," said the elder Mrs. Hász. "I intend to go myself. I've always wanted to see the Holy Land."

"See it, then. But don't live there. We're Hungarians, not desert Bedouins."

"We were a tribal people before we were Hungarians," Tibor said. "Don't forget that."

"Pardon me, Doctor," József said. He liked to call Tibor "Doctor" as much as he liked to call Andras "Uncle." "And before that we were hunters and gatherers in Africa. So perhaps we should bypass the Holy Land altogether and proceed directly to the darkest Congo."

"József," György said.

"A thousand pardons, Father. I'm sure you'd rather I kept quiet. But it's hard, you know, to be the only sane person in the asylum."

Béla shifted in his delicate chair, feeling the pull of his city suit against his shoulders. He was thinking that he would have liked to take the younger Hász by the shoulders and shake him. He wondered how the boy could dare speak so flippantly about what was about to befall Andras and Tibor and their wives and sons. If one of his own sons had spoken that way, Béla would have risen from his chair and given him a good tongue-lashing, even before guests. But he would never have raised a child who spoke that way. Not he, nor Flóra. She put a hand on his wrist now as if she could see what was in his mind; he wasn't surprised she understood. Everyone could see that the boy was intolerable. At least Klara's mother had spoken to him sternly. Béla looked across the table at her, that grave gray-eyed woman who had lost and regained her child once already and now seemed stoic at the prospect of losing her again. They had raised fine children, this woman and Béla and Flóra. He didn't wonder anymore at the connection between Andras and Klara; he knew now that they were made of the same stuff, whatever luxuries the girl had had as a child. There she was, sitting calm as grass with the baby in her arms, looking as though she were about to take a trip to the countryside rather than down a dangerous river and across a torpedo-salted sea. He told himself to take note of that tranquil look of hers, that radiant calm; in the days and weeks ahead he would want to remember it.

That week, their last in Budapest, was the hottest yet of the summer. On Thursday the bus to Szentendre was stifling even at six in the morning; this was the kind of day Andras's mother called *gombás-idő*—mushroom-growing weather. A damp wind blew through the channel of the Danube. Birds hustled through the wet turbulence of air, and the trees across the water flashed the white undersides of their leaves. All that week, it seemed, the command ranks at Szentendre had been out of sorts. The same foremen who'd failed to take note of the subtle slackening of work now began to drive the laborers relentlessly. Ill temper seemed to have spread through the camp like a fever. There had been a series of arguments in the officers' headquarters between Major Varsádi and the black-market inspectors, with the result that Varsádi had unleashed a rare storm of anger upon his lieutenants; the lieutenants had behaved vilely to the guards and work foremen, and the foremen, in turn, swore at the labor servicemen, kicked them, and sliced at their backs and legs with doubled lengths of packing rope.

That morning there was to be an inspection lineup before work began. The men had been instructed in advance that their uniforms and equipment were to be in top shape. Beginning at seven o'clock, the men were made to stand at attention beside the tracks for what seemed an interminable length of time. Rain began to fall, a barrage of fat hard drops that penetrated the fabric of the men's clothing. The waiting went on and on; the guards paced the rows of men, as bored as their charges.

"What a waste of time," József said. "Why don't they just send us home?"

"Hear hear," Mendel said. "Cut us loose."

"Quiet there, both of you," a guard called to them.

Andras kept an eye on the low brick building that housed Varsádi's headquarters. Through a steam-hazed window he could make out the commander holding a phone receiver to his ear. Andras rocked back and forth from his heels to the balls of his feet; he studied the stippling of rain on the back of the man in front of him. In his mind he reviewed the tasks that lay ahead in the next few days: the final packing, the rechecking of their lists of clothing and supplies, the tying up and locking of the suitcases, the departure from their apartment on Nefelejcs utca, the midnight meeting at Tibor's, the walk to the point just north of the Erzsébet Bridge where a barge would be waiting, their consignment to the damp dark hiding place where they would huddle together as the barge slipped into the current. He was there in his mind, so thoroughly hidden in the hold of that Danube barge, that at first he didn't notice the rumble of trucks on the road. He felt a low vibration in his sternum and thought, *More thunder.* But the rumble continued and increased, and when he looked up at last he saw a six-truck convoy bearing Hungarian soldiers. The trucks roared through the gates of Szentendre Yard, their tires turning up dry dust beneath the rain-damp surface of the road. They parked on the bare stretch of earth that lay between the tracks and the officers' building. The soldiers in back carried rifles fixed with bayonets; Andras could see the blades glinting in the olive-colored gloom of the canvas enclosures. When the trucks stopped, the soldiers jumped out onto the muddy gravel and held their weapons loosely at their sides. The officers in the first truck went into the low brick building, and the door closed behind them.

The work servicemen eyed the soldiers. There must have been fifty of them at least. With their officers occupied inside headquarters, the soldiers leaned their rifles against the trucks and began to smoke. One of them pulled out a deck of cards and dealt poker. Another group of men clustered around a newspaper while one of the soldiers read the headlines aloud.

"What's going on?" whispered the man beside Andras, a tall hairless man who had been dubbed the Ivory Tower. He had been a history professor at the university; like Zoltán Novak he had been recruited to the Munkaszolgálat to fill a quota of Jewish luminaries. He was new to the work service, and had not yet learned to accept its mysteries and contradictions without protest.

"I don't know," Andras said. "We'll find out."

"Silence in the lines!" shouted a guard.

The wait continued. Some of the guards drifted toward the soldiers to trade cigarettes and news. A few of them seemed to know each other. They slapped each other on the back and shook hands. Another half hour passed, and still no one emerged from the headquarters. Finally the guards' captain gave the command for the labor servicemen to be at ease. They could eat or smoke if they wanted. Andras and Mendel sat down on a damp railroad tie and opened their tin lunch pails, and József drew a slim leather case from his breast pocket and extracted a cigarette.

A moment later, the door of the squat brick building opened and the officers emerged—first the army officers in their crisp brass-buttoned uniforms, then the familiar Munkaszolgálat officers who had commanded them since the beginning of their time at Szentendre. Varsádi's first lieutenant blew a whistle and ordered the servicemen to stand at attention. There was a moment of rustling confusion as the men put away their lunches.

Then the sergeant shouted his orders: The men were to form ranks at the supply trucks and move the goods to the boxcars as quickly as possible.

If it hadn't been for the presence of the soldiers, their bayonets needling skyward as if to pierce the underbellies of the low-hanging clouds, it would have seemed like any other afternoon at Szentendre Yard. The 79/6th carried crates of ammunition across the same expanse of gravel they'd crossed and recrossed a thousand times. If the guards kept a tighter rein on the men, if the officers were more strident as they shouted their orders, it seemed only an extension of the animus that had permeated the command ranks all week. Faragó, their foreman, failed to whistle a single show tune; instead he shouted *Siessetek!* in his thin tenor and wondered aloud how he'd been cursed with the command of such slugs, such turtles.

Halfway through the unloading, when there were still five supply trucks' worth of goods to be transferred to the train, an adjutant of Varsádi's approached Andras's work group and drew Faragó aside. A moment later, Faragó was calling Andras and Mendel from their duties. The company commander, it seemed, wanted a word with them in his office.

Mendel and Andras exchanged a look: *It's nothing. Don't panic.*

"Did the fellow say what it was about, sir?" Mendel asked, though there was only one thing it could be about, only one reason for the commander to call the two of them to his office.

"You'll find out soon enough," Faragó said. And then, to the adjutant, "See they get back here as soon as Varsádi's finished with them. I can't spare them for long."

The major's young adjutant led them across the rail yard toward the low brick building. A clutch of armed soldiers stood at attention in the anteroom, rifles angled against their shoulders. Their eyes moved toward Andras and Mendel as they entered, but otherwise they remained still as sculptures. An orderly ushered Andras and Mendel into Varsádi's office and

closed the door behind them, and they found themselves standing unaccompanied before their commander. Varsádi's uniform
shirt was crisp despite the heat, his eyes narrow behind a pair of
demilune glasses. On his desk, as Andras knew it would be, was a
complete set of *The Crooked Rail*.

"Well, then," Varsádi said, straightening the pages before
him. "I'll be brief. You know I like you boys and your newspaper.
It's given the men a good laugh. But I'm afraid it's not—er—
opportune to have it circulating at the moment."

Andras experienced a moment of confusion. He had believed
this meeting was to be about the resistance he and Mendel had
stirred up. The quickened pace of work, the shift in the foremen's attitude, had pointed in that direction. But Varsádi wasn't
accusing them of agitating. He seemed only to be asking them to
stop publishing.

"The paper's not really circulating, sir," Mendel said. "Not
beyond the 79/6th."

"You've made fifty copies of each issue," Varsádi said. "The
men take them home. Some of those copies might find their way
out into the city. And then there's the matter of printing, the
matter of your plates and originals. This is a sharp-looking
paper. I know you're not hand-cranking copies at home."

Andras and Mendel exchanged the briefest of looks, and
Mendel said, "We destroy the printing plates each week, sir. The
circulation copies are all there are."

"I understand you were both recently employed at the
Budapest Jewish Journal. If we were to inquire there, or take a
look around, we wouldn't happen to find. . . ?"

"You can look wherever you like, sir," Mendel said. "There's
nothing to find."

Andras watched with a kind of dreamlike detachment as the
commander opened his desk drawer, removed a small revolver,
and held it loosely in his hand. The body of the gun was velvet
black, the muzzle snub-nosed. "There can't be any mistake
about this," Varsádi said. "Fifty copies of each paper. That's

enough uncertainty in this equation. I need your originals and your printing plates. I need to know where those things are kept."

"We've destroyed—" Mendel began again, but his eyes flicked toward the gun.

"You're lying," Varsádi said, matter-of-factly. "I don't like that, after the leniency I've shown you." He turned the gun over and ran a thumb along the safety. "I need the truth, and then you'll be on your way. You printed this paper at the *Budapest Jewish Journal*. Can we find your originals there? I ask, gentlemen, because the only other place I can think to search is your homes. And I would prefer not to disturb your families." The words hung in the air between them as he polished the revolver with his thumb.

Andras saw it all: The apartment on Nefelejcs ransacked, every paper and book thrown onto the floor, every cabinet emptied, the sofa disemboweled, the walls and floorboards torn open. All the preparations for their trip to Palestine laid bare to official scrutiny. And Klara, huddled in a corner, or held by the wrists—How? By whom?—as the baby wailed. He met Mendel's eyes again and understood that Mendel had seen it, too, and had made his decision. If Andras himself didn't tell the truth, Mendel would. And in fact, a moment later, Mendel spoke.

"The originals are at the *Journal*," he said. "One copy of each issue, in a filing cabinet in the chief editor's office. No need to disturb anyone's family. We don't keep anything at home."

"Very good," said Varsádi. He replaced the gun in the desk drawer. "That's all I need from you now. Dismissed," he said, and waved a hand toward the door.

They moved as if through some viscous liquid, not looking at each other. They had compromised Frigyes Eppler, his person, his position; they both knew it. There was no telling what the consequences might be, or what price Eppler would be made to pay. Outside, they found that the entire company had been moved to the assembly ground, where they stood now at uncomfortable attention. As Andras took his place in line, József threw him a look of frank curiosity. But there was no time to enlighten him; it seemed that the promised inspection was now to occur. The soldiers who had arrived that morning had dispersed themselves along the edge of the assembly ground, and the officers who had conferred with Varsádi stood at the head of the formation. When Andras looked across the expanse of gravel to the far edge of the field, he found that soldiers had lined up there as well. In front of Varsádi's headquarters, soldiers. Along the tracks behind them, more soldiers. All at once he understood: The 79/6th had been corralled, surrounded. The soldiers who had been smoking and laughing with the guards now stood at attention with their hands on their rifles, their eyes fixed at that dangerous military middle distance, the place from which it was impossible to recognize another human being.

Varsádi emerged from the low brick building, his back erect, his medals flashing in the afternoon sun. "Into your lines," he shouted. "Marching formation."

Andras told himself to keep calm. They were half an hour from Budapest. This wasn't the Délvidék. It was likely Varsádi meant to do nothing more than to scare them, make a show of control, correct for the laxity of his command. At his order the 79/6th marched out of the assembly ground and along the tracks, toward the south gate of the rail yard. The soldiers kept their lines tight around the block of work servicemen. They all stopped when they reached the end of the row of boxcars.

Three empty cars had been coupled to the end of the train, their sides emblazoned with the Munkaszolgálat acronym. Over the small, high windows of the boxcars, iron bars had been installed. The doors stood open as if in expectation. Far ahead, beyond the cars that had just been loaded with supplies, an engine exhaled brown smoke.

"At attention, men," Varsádi shouted. "Your orders have

been changed. Your services are needed elsewhere. You will leave immediately. Your duties have become classified. We cannot give you further information."

There was a burst of incredulous protest from the men, a sudden din of shouting.

"Silence," the commander cried. "Silence! Silence at once!" He raised his pistol and fired it into the air. The men fell silent.

"Pardon me, sir," József said. He stood just a few feet from Andras, close enough for Andras to see a narrow vein pumping at his temple. "As I recall, the KMOF Rules of Duty Handbook says we've got to have a week's notice before any change of posting. And if you don't mind my mentioning it, we've hardly got the supplies."

Major Varsádi strode toward József, pistol in hand. He took the gun by its short muzzle and delivered two swift blows with the butt-end across József's face. A bright stuttering dart of blood appeared on the shoulder of Andras's uniform.

"Take my advice and shut your mouth," Varsádi said. "Where you're going, you'd be shot for less."

The major gave another order; the soldiers tightened their lines around the labor servicemen and squeezed them toward the train cars. Andras found himself jammed between Mendel and József. Behind them was a crush of men. They had no choice but to climb into the open mouth of the boxcar. Through the single high window Andras could see the soldiers in a line around the cars, the dull glint of their bayonets against the marbled sky. More and more servicemen were pushed into the cars until the air seemed to be made of them. Andras inhaled wet canvas and hair oil and sweat, the smell of the morning's work cut with the tang of panic. His heart drummed in his ribcage, and his throat closed with terror. Klara would be home now, packing the last of their things. In an hour she would begin to look at the clock. He had to get off the train. He would plead illness; he would offer a bribe. He shoved and elbowed his way toward the door again, but before he could reach that rectangle of light there was an all-clear cry. Then the rattle of the door sliding closed, the descent of darkness, the sound of a chain against metal, the unmistakable click of a padlock.

A moment later the train whistle let out an indifferent screech. Through the wooden floorboards, through the soles of his summer boots and the bones of his legs, came a deep mechanical shudder, the first grinding jolt of motion. The men fell against each other, against Andras; the weight of them seemed heavy enough to squeeze his heart to stillness in his chest. And then the train lurched into its rhythm and carried them forward through the north gates of Szentendre Yard, toward a destination none of them could name.

PART FIVE

By Fire

CHAPTER THIRTY-FOUR

Turka

IN THE DAYS and nights he spent on the train, after he'd shouted himself hoarse with protest and exhausted all hope of escape, a kind of numbness seemed to overtake him. He stood with Mendel for hours at the small high window, watching the world pass by outside like a catalogue of the impossible: That motorbike, with its suggestion of a quick escape. That road, and the freedom to follow it home to Klara. That mail truck, which might carry a letter to her. He knew from the direction of the light that they were headed northeast. He would have known it anyway because the train was climbing. They ascended into the northern uplands through Gyöngyös and Füzesabony; at times the train crawled, and at other times it stopped for hours. Each time it stopped, Andras thought they might be led off to their new work site. On the second night they were actually ordered to leave the train, and herded into an empty warehouse that must have once been used to store the red wine of the region, Egri Bikavér, bull's blood. The air had the sweet oaky tang of wine barrels; the dirt floor was stained with faded purple rings. Two army cooks fed them a thin cabbage soup and hunks of hard dark bread, the familiar Munkaszolgálat food. They stood in line to wash at a spigot in a corner of the warehouse. They weren't allowed to speak to each other, or to venture outside, not even for a piss; they had to use a barrel for that. The warehouse door was locked, the building guarded by soldiers. In the morning they were put back on the train and sent east again.

That was the third day of travel. He was supposed to have embarked for Palestine the next morning. What would Klara be doing now? He knew it was futile to hope she would have gone on without him. What would she have thought two nights before, when the hour grew later and later and he hadn't come home? He imagined her bending over the valises, packing the baby's things, checking the clock on the dresser; he imagined her mild worry when the usual hour of his return had passed—had he stopped to have a last drink in Budapest with Mendel, or a last stroll through the familiar streets? The dinner she'd made would have grown cold in the kitchen. She would have put Tamás to bed, her worry shading into fear as eight o'clock became nine, and nine became ten.

What did she imagine had happened to him? Did she think he'd been thrown in jail or killed? Had the work-service administration told her anything, even now? In all probability she still didn't know. And what about Varsádi's threat? Would he be content when his men found the originals of *The Crooked Rail* at Eppler's offices, or would he insist that the apartment be searched, too?

There was constant speculation on the train about where they were going and what awaited them at the end of the journey. The prevailing opinion was that there had been some mistake about the company's transfer. They were supposed to have been sent northwest to Esztergom at the end of the month, to work at another rail yard. The orders must have gotten confused. The mix-up would soon be discovered, and they would be put on a westbound train. But that didn't explain why soldiers had been sent to Szentendre Yard to load the men onto the trains, nor why they'd been shipped off with such haste. The Ivory Tower, the former professor of history, offered another theory: He believed they were being sent east because they had all been witness to a crime, the slow and systematic diversion of millions of pengős' worth of goods into the black market. The government had begun a campaign to rout out military embezzlement, the Ivory Tower said. The stealing of goods intended for use on the battlefront was considered an act of treason punishable by death. A panic had spread among the labor service company commanders, who were the worst offenders of all. The Jewish labor servicemen could not be trusted to vouch for the innocence of officers who had abused them daily; instead they had to be shunted away out of sight, perhaps even to the Eastern Front.

József was terrified. Andras could see it. He hardly spoke. He kept to himself, gingerly touching his face where Varsádi had struck him. He never slept, not that Andras saw; he sat up all night sorting and rearranging the few items in his pack. He wouldn't crack a joke. He wouldn't eat the Munkaszolgálat food, preferring instead to pick at a crust of challah left over from the last lunch he'd brought to Szentendre. He refused at first to use the communal toilet can in the corner of the train; when necessity forced him to use it at last, he returned looking as though he'd been beaten.

Day became night again and the train went on. There was no stop for food or water. There was no respite from the heat. The men couldn't lie down; there wasn't room. They could take turns sitting on the floor of the boxcar or raising their faces to the window. There was some relief in those moments when they could breathe fresh air. But by the fourth day there was no way to ignore the deepening stink nor the clawing thirst that had come upon them, and Andras began to wonder if the true purpose of the trip was to keep them on the train until they died of thirst. In the haze of his dehydration, he came to understand that it was all his fault that they were imprisoned on this eastbound train. *The Crooked Rail*, however tongue-in-cheek, had in fact documented Szentendre's involvement in the black market; it had made the situation known to any labor serviceman too blind or naïve to see it on his own, and might well have spread word of the operation beyond Szentendre. Klara had been right; he'd taken an absurd and unnecessary risk. The paper might have been a slender tree in a forest of incriminating evidence, but there it was nonetheless. Varsádi considered it important enough to have called a private conference with Andras and Mendel, important enough to have threatened them with a gun. If fifty copies of the paper hadn't made their way among the men each week, and perhaps out into the city, would Varsádi have been transformed from a tippling laxard into a man willing to send an entire company to the front just to save his own skin?

That afternoon, Andras stood at the window as they climbed through a rainstorm into a region of rock-strewn hills. A massive black shape emerged from behind a curtain of fog: the ruin of a medieval fortress, a jagged-toothed castle thrusting its black donjon into the sky. Andras prodded Mendel's shoulder and made him look. His own chest constricted with the sensation that he had dreamed this moment long ago. Everything about it seemed familiar: the sound of the wheels on the tracks, the filtered darkness of the boxcar, the stink of men packed close together, the chewed-off black shape of the fortress. A metallic taste came into his mouth, and his skin prickled with a feeling akin to shame. How had he let himself believe that he and Klara and Tamás, Tibor and Ilana and Ádám, would be hidden in the hold of a Danube barge by now, making their way toward Romania, where they would board a boat that would take them to Palestine? How had he let himself believe they would safely cross a submarine-laced sea, that they would reach Haifa unscathed and start a new life in one of the settlements, that they would bring their parents over, that he himself would help to assemble the bones of a Jewish homeland? He had even let himself believe that Mátyás would return from the work service alive and unhurt and join them in Palestine. But the castle on the hilltop, the fog, this train: Somehow he'd known it was coming all along. Somehow he'd known they would never leave Budapest together, that they would never make it out of Hungary and across the Mediterranean. He wondered if Klara had known too. If she had, how had they allowed each other to persist in their mutual delusion?

For years now, he understood at last, he'd had to cultivate the habit of blind hope. It had become as natural to him as breathing. It had taken him from Konyár to Budapest to Paris, from the lonely chill of his room on the rue des Écoles to the close heat of the rue de Sévigné, from the despair of Carpathian winter to Forget-Me-Not Street in the Erzsébetváros. It was the inevitable by-product of love, the clear and potent distillate of fatherhood. It had prevented him from thinking too long or too hard about what might have happened to Polaner, to Ben Yakov, to his own younger brother. It had kept him from dwelling upon the possible consequences of publishing a paper like *The Crooked Rail*. It had stopped him from imagining himself shipped east into the mouth of the battle. But here he was, and here was Mendel Horovitz, watching the castle disappear into the fog.

The train went on and on, always climbing, moving slowly into thinner, drier air. The brutal heat began to fall away, and a scent of fir trees edged through the small high window. The men were silent, parched, faint with hunger and lack of sleep. They took turns sitting and standing. They drifted between sleep and wakefulness, their legs swaying with the motion of the train, their feet numb with the vibration of the wheels on the endless tracks. When the train stopped at a station on the fifth day, Andras could think only of how good it would feel to stretch himself out on the ground and sleep. From outside came the rattle of the door being unchained and drawn aside; a wave of fresh air moved through the stinking car, and the men pushed out onto the platform. Through the fog of his exhaustion, Andras read the station sign. Тұрка. A click at the front of the palate, a pursing of the lips around *ka*, the Hungarian diminutive. A shock of relief went through him: They weren't on the Eastern Front after all. They were still within their own borders.

Тұрка. He didn't realize he'd said it aloud until the Ivory Tower, standing next to him, shook his head and corrected him. "Turka," he said. "It's written in Cyrillic."

And so it was, because they had reached Ukraine.

The camp where they were supposed to stay had been bombed a week earlier. A hundred and seventy men had been killed, the

barracks leveled. The remaining men had had to dig vast graves
to bury their comrades; the turned dirt had slumped into the pits
with that week's rain. That labor company had left nothing
behind but the bones of their dead—no sign or tool or scrap of
comfort for the men of the 79/6th. Andras and the others
camped in the mud of the assembly ground, and the next day
they were installed in the main house and outbuildings of an
empty Jewish orphanage half a kilometer away.

The place was built of Soviet cinderblock, its whitewash
greened with mildew. Everything inside the main house had
been intended for the use of children. The bunks were absurdly
short. The only way to lie on them was to curl one's knees to
one's chest. The sinks had running water, which was nothing less
than a miracle, but they were built so low that it was necessary
almost to kneel in order to wash one's face. The mess hall was
furnished with tiny benches and low tables; the hallways were
still marked with the children's heel-scuffs and muddy footprints. There was no other sign of them in the place. Every
shred of clothing, every shoe and book and spoon, had been
removed as though the children had never existed.

Their new commander was a beefy-looking black-haired
Magyar whose face was bisected by a spectacular keloid scar.
The scar ran in an arc from the middle of his forehead to the tip
of his chin, obliterating his right eyelid, skirting his nose by a
millimeter, splitting his lips into four unequal parts. The lidless
right eye gave his features a cast of perpetual surprise and horror, as if the initial shock of the wound had never left him. His
name was Kozma. He came from Győr. He had a gray wolfhound whom he alternately kicked and petted, and a lieutenant
named Horvath whom he treated in the same manner. On their
first morning at the orphanage, Kozma assembled the company
in the yard and marched them five kilometers down the road,
double-time, to a wet field where grass had grown unevenly over
a long filled-in trench. This was where the children of the

orphanage had been lined up and shot, their new commander told them, and this was where they, too, would be shot when their usefulness to the Hungarian Army had been exhausted. Their dog tags might return home, but *they* never would; they were filthier than pigs, lower than worms, already as good as dead. For now, though, their company would join the five hundred work servicemen who were rebuilding the road between Turka and Stryj. The old road flooded every time the Stryj River topped its banks. The new road would be laid on higher ground. Minefields posed a minor obstacle to the operation; on occasion, servicemen must clear the fields in order to allow the road to pass through. They were to finish the road by the time the snows came. Then they would be responsible for keeping it clear. The records-master, Orbán, would see to their pay books. Tolnay, the medical officer, would treat them if they fell ill. But shirkers would not be tolerated. Tolnay was under strict orders to do everything in his power to keep the men from missing work. They were to obey the guards and officers in all matters; troublemakers would be punished, deserters shot.

When he'd concluded his speech, Kozma clicked his heels, swiveled the mass of his body with surprising speed, and stepped aside to let his lieutenant address the company. Lieutenant Horvath seemed a kind of collapsible model, his frame and features accordioned into a slimmer version of an ordinary man. He balanced a pair of spectacles on his nose and drew a memo from his breast pocket. There would be no electric light after dark, he told them in his thin monotone, no letter-writing, no canteen shop where they might replenish their supplies, no replacement uniforms if their uniforms got worn out or torn, no forming of groups, no fraternizing with guards, no pocketknives, no smoking, no hoarding of valuables, no shopping at stores in town or trading with the local peasantry. Their families would soon be informed of their transfer, but there was to be no postal communication between the 79/6th and the outside world—no packages, no letters, no telegrams. For safety's sake they must wear their armbands at all times. Without the proper identification, a person might be mistaken for the enemy and shot.

Horvath shouted them into five columns and marched them into the road again; they were to depart for their work site at once. The road was wet with deep sucking mud. As the light began to rise, Andras saw that they were in a broad river valley that stretched between foothills dense with evergreens. In the distance rose the jagged gray peaks of the Carpathians. Clouds lay on the hillsides, bleeding fog into the valley. The rain-swollen Stryj rushed past between steep brown banks. Before long, Andras could feel the upward slope of the road in his back and thighs. The list of prohibitions kept spooling itself through his head: no electric light after dark, no letter-writing, no postal communication. No way to get word to Klara. No way to learn what had happened to her, or to Tibor and Ilana and Ádám, or to Mátyás, if news of Mátyás ever came. During his other periods of service, it had been Klara's letters that had kept him from despairing; the need to write *I am well* that had kept him, relatively speaking, well. How could he bear not to communicate, particularly after what had happened? He would have to find a way to send word to her, whatever the consequences. He'd bribe someone, sign promissory notes if he had to. He would write letters and his letters would find her. In the midst of the vast uncertainty that surrounded him, he knew that much.

It was ten kilometers to the work site; there, they were issued picks and shovels and divided into twenty teams of six. Each team had two wheelbarrow men and four shovelers. They could see hundreds of these teams shoveling dirt and carting it away, leveling the roadbed for the laying of gravel and asphalt. A line of leveled road stretched back toward Turka; a trail of red surveyors' markers pricked the green infinity between the work site and Skhidnytsya. Overseers snaked among the groups, slicing at the labor servicemen's backs and legs with narrow wooden rods.

They worked for five hours without pause. At noon they

were given ten decagrams of a bread so gritty it must have been baked with sawdust, and a ladleful of watery turnip soup. Then they worked until nightfall and marched home in the dark. At the orphanage the company cook gave them each a cupful of onion broth. They were lined up in the courtyard and made to stand at attention for three hours before Kozma sent them to bed in their child-sized bunks. And that was to be the structure of their new lives.

Andras had a top bunk near a window, and Mendel had the bunk beside him, above the Ivory Tower. József occupied the bunk below Andras. Their first week at the orphanage Andras could hear József turning and shifting for hours on the hard wooden slats. Every time he turned, he shook Andras from the edge of sleep. By the fifth night Andras felt inclined to strangle him. All he wanted was to sleep so he wouldn't have to think about where he was, and why. But József wouldn't allow it. He rolled and shifted, rolled and shifted, for hours and hours.

"Stop it!" Andras hissed. "Go to sleep."

"Go to hell," József whispered.

"You go to hell."

"I'm in hell already," József said. "I'm going to die here. I know it."

"Something will kill us all, eventually," Mendel offered from the neighboring bunk.

"I've got a weak constitution and a short temper," József said. "I make bad decisions. I'm liable to talk back to someone with a gun."

"You've been in the work service for two months now," Andras said. "You haven't died yet."

"This isn't Szentendre," József said.

"Think of it as Szentendre with worse food and an uglier commander."

"For God's sake, Lévi, aren't you listening? I need help."

"Keep it down!" someone said.

Andras climbed down from his bunk and sat at the edge of József's. He found József's eyes in the dark. "What is it?" he whispered. "What do you want?"

"I don't want to die before I'm thirty," József whispered back, his voice breaking like a boy's. He ran a hand under his nose. "I'm unprepared for this. I've done nothing these past five years but eat and drink and fuck and make paintings. I can't survive work camp."

"Yes, you can. You're young and healthy. You'll get through it."

They sat silent for a long moment, listening to the breathing of the men around them. The sound of fifty men breathing in their sleep: It was like the string section of an orchestra playing on stringless violins and violas and cellos, an endless shushing of horsehair on wood. Every now and then a woodwind sneeze or a brassy cough would break the stream of breathing, but the stringless music continued, a constant sighing in the dark.

"Is that all, then?" József said, finally. "That's what you've got for me?"

"Here's the truth," Andras said. "I don't have much heart to give you a pep talk."

"I don't want a pep talk," József whispered. "I want to know how to survive. You've been doing this for almost three years. Don't you have any advice?"

"Well, don't publish a subversive newspaper, for one thing," Andras said. "You might find your commanding officer pointing a gun at you across his desk."

"Is that what happened?" József said. "What did he want?"

"Our printing plates and originals. He threatened to search our houses if we didn't produce them."

"Oh, God. What did you tell him?"

"The truth. The originals are in our editor's office at the *Jewish News*. Or were. Varsádi's got them by now, I'm sure."

József let out a long breath. "That'll have been a bad day at work for your editor."

"I know. I've been sick about it. But what were we going to do? We couldn't send Varsádi's men to Nefelejcs utca."

"All right," József whispered. "I'll be certain not to publish a subversive newspaper. What else?"

Andras told József what he knew: Keep quiet. Become invisible. Don't make enemies of the other work servicemen. Don't talk back to the guards. Eat what they give you, no matter how bad it is, and always save something for later. Keep as clean as you can. Keep your feet dry. Take care of your clothes so they don't fall apart. Know which guards are sympathetic. Follow all the rules you can stand to follow; when you break the rules, don't get caught. Don't let yourself forget the life back home. Don't forget that your term of service is finite.

He went silent, remembering the other list he and Mendel had made long ago, the ten commandments of the Munkaszolgálat. Had it only been three years since he'd been sent to Carpatho-Ruthenia? By whose reckoning could the term of service be called finite? Suddenly he couldn't stand to think or talk about it a moment longer. "I've got to get to sleep," he said.

"All right," József said. "Listen, though. Thanks."

"Shut up, you idiots," Mendel whispered from the neighboring bunk.

"You're welcome," Andras said. "Now go to sleep."

Andras climbed up into his own bunk and wrapped himself in his blanket. József didn't make another sound; his tossing and shifting had stilled. But Andras lay awake and listened to the other men's breathing. He remembered quiet nights like this from the beginning of his first conscription. Before long there would be no easy sleep for any of them; someone would always be coughing or groaning or running for the latrine, and there would be the torment of lice, and the dull nauseating pain of hunger. Midnight lineups, too, if Kozma was inclined. The

Munkaszolgálat was like a chronic disease, he thought—its symptoms abated at times, but always returned. When he'd begun his service in Transylvania he'd felt precisely what József was feeling now, the deep injustice of it all. This couldn't possibly be happening to him, not to him and Klara, not to his mind, not to his body, that sturdy and faithful machine. He couldn't believe that all the great urgencies of his time in Paris—everything that had seemed important, all his studies, every project, every moment with Klara, every secret, every worry about money or school or work or food—had been boxed away, stripped of context, made nonsensical, made small, consigned to impossibility, crammed into a space too narrow to admit life. But today as he'd marched to work and shoveled dirt and eaten the miserable food and slogged home through the mud, he hadn't felt indignant; he'd hardly felt anything at all. He was just an animal on the earth, one of billions. The fact that he'd had a happy childhood in Konyár, had gone to school, learned to draw, gone to Paris, fallen in love, studied, worked, had a son—none of it was predictive of what might happen in the future; it was largely a matter of luck. None of it was a reward, no more than the Munkaszolgálat was a punishment; none of it entitled him to future happiness or comfort. Men and women suffered all over the world. Hundreds of thousands had already died in this war, and he himself might die here in Turka. He suspected the chances were heavily in favor of it. The things he could control were few and small; he was a particle of life, a speck of human dust, lost on the eastern edge of Europe. He knew there would come a time, perhaps not far off, when he would find it hard to follow the rules he'd just set out for József.

He had to think of Klara, he told himself. He had to think of Tamás. And his parents, and Tibor, and Mátyás. He had to pretend it wasn't hopeless; he had to allow himself to be fooled into staying alive. He had to make himself a willing party to the insidious trick of love.

* * *

At the end of Andras's second week in Turka, the road surveyor's assistant was killed by a land mine. It happened at the cusp of the new road, a few kilometers from Andras's work site, but word traveled quickly through the line of work teams. The surveyor's assistant had been one of them, a labor serviceman. He'd been helping the surveyor map the road through a Soviet minefield. The field was supposed to have been cleared months earlier by another labor company, but that group must have been anxious to call the job finished. The assistant had tripped the mine as he'd been setting up the tripod. The explosion had killed him instantly.

The surveyor was a work serviceman too, an engineer from Szeged. Andras had seen him pass by on his way to the surveying site. He was short and pallid, with rimless spectacles and a brushy gray moustache; his uniform jacket was just as threadbare as anyone else's, his boots wrapped with rags to keep them from falling apart. But because his function was so important to the army, he had an official-looking hat and an insignia on the pocket of his overcoat. He was allowed to buy things in town and to smoke cigarettes. And he was always being called upon to interpret for someone: He knew Polish, Russian, even some Ukrainian, and could speak to any Galician peasant in his native tongue. His assistant, a slim dark-eyed boy who couldn't have been more than twenty, had been a silent shadow at his heels. After the boy died, the surveyor tore his sleeve in mourning and rubbed his face with ashes. He dragged his equipment to and from the surveying site with an expression of abstracted despair. The boy had been like a son to him, everyone said; in fact, Andras learned later, he had been the son of the surveyor's closest friend in Szeged.

As August rolled forward, it became clear that the surveyor would have to choose a new assistant soon. He was too old to drag the equipment around by himself; someone would have to help him if the road were to be marked out to Skhidnytsya by the time the German inspectors arrived in November. The surveyor began asking around as he made his way past the groups of work servicemen: Did anyone know mathematics? Had anyone studied engineering? Was there a draftsman among them, an architect? At the noon meal they saw him studying lists of the work servicemen's names and former occupations, looking for someone who could be of use.

One morning, as Andras and Mendel and the rest of their group worked to clear a mass of broken asphalt, the surveyor came shuffling up the road behind Major Kozma. When they reached Andras's group, the major stopped and cocked a thumb at Andras.

"That's the one," he said. "Lévi, Andras. He doesn't look like much, but apparently he's had some training."

The surveyor scrutinized his list. "You were a student of architecture," he said.

Andras shrugged. It hardly seemed true anymore.

"How long did you study?"

"Two years. One course in engineering."

"Well," the surveyor said, and sighed. "That'll do."

Mendel, who had been listening, moved closer to Andras now; he fixed his eyes on the surveyor and said, "He doesn't want the job."

In an instant, Major Kozma's hand had moved to the riding crop tucked into his belt. He turned to Mendel and squinted his good eye. "Did anyone speak to you, cockroach?"

For a moment Mendel hesitated, but then he continued as though the major were not to be feared. "The job is dangerous, sir. Lévi is a husband and a father. Take someone who's got less to lose."

The major's scar flushed red. He pulled the crop from his belt and struck Mendel across the face. "Don't tell me how to manage my company, cockroach," he said. And then to Andras: "Present your work papers, Lévi."

Andras did as he was told.

Kozma withdrew a grease pencil from his uniform pocket and made a notation on the papers, indicating that Andras was now under the surveyor's immediate command. While he wrote, Andras extracted a crumpled handkerchief from his pocket and offered it to Mendel, whose cheek showed a line of blood; Mendel pressed the handkerchief to his cheek. The surveyor watched them, seeming to understand the relationship between them. He cleared his throat and signaled to Kozma.

"Just a thought," the surveyor said. "If you please, Major."

"What is it now?"

"Why don't you give me that one, too?" He cocked a thumb at Mendel. "He's tall and strong. He can carry the equipment. And if there's dangerous work to be done, I can make *him* do it. I wouldn't want to lose another good assistant."

Kozma pursed his ruined lips. "You want both of them?"

"It's an idea, sir."

"You're a greedy little Jew, Szolomon."

"The road has to be mapped. It'll go faster with two of them."

By that time, another officer had made his way over to their work group. This man was the general work foreman, a reserve colonel from the Royal Hungarian Corps of Engineers. He wanted to know the reason for the delay.

"Szolomon wants these two men to assist with the surveying."

"Well, sign them up and send them off. We can't have men standing around."

And so Andras and Mendel became the surveyor's new assistants, heirs to the position of the boy who had been killed.

* * *

By day they mapped the course of the road between Turka and Yavora, between Yavora and Novyi Kropyvnyk, between Novyi Kropyvnyk and Skhidnytsya. They learned the mysteries of the surveyor's glass, the theodolite; the surveyor taught them how to mount it on the tripod and how to calibrate it with plumb and spirit level. He taught them how to orient it toward true north and how to line up the sight axis and the horizontal axis. He taught them to think of the landscape in the language of geometric forms: planes bisected by other planes lying at oblique or acute angles, all of it comprehensible, quantifiable, sane. The jagged hills were nothing more than complex polyhedrons, the Stryj a twisting half cylinder extending from the border of Lvivska Province to the deeper, longer trench of the Dniester. But they found it impossible to see only the geometry of the land; evidence of the war lay in plain view everywhere, demanding to be acknowledged. Farms had been burned, some of them by the Germans in their advance, others by the Russians in retreat. Untended crops had rotted in the fields. In the towns, Jewish businesses had been vandalized and looted and now stood empty. There was not a Jewish man or woman or child to be seen. The Poles were gone too. The Ukrainians who remained were opaque-eyed, as if the horrors they'd witnessed had led them to curtain their souls. Though the summer grasses still grew tall, and tart blackberries had come out on the shrubs along the roadside, the country itself seemed dead, an animal killed and gutted on the forest floor. Now the Germans were trying to stuff it full of new organs and make it crawl forward again. A new heart, new blood, a new liver, new entrails—and a new nerve center, Hitler's headquarters at Vinnitsa. The road itself was a vein. Soldiers, forced laborers, ammunition, and supplies would run through it toward the front.

The surveyor was a clever man, and knew that his theodolite might be useful beyond its role in mapping the road. He had realized, not long into his sojourn in Ukraine, that it might work as a powerful tool of persuasion. When they came upon a prosperous-looking farmhouse or inn, he would set up the theodolite within view of the owners; someone would come out of the farmhouse or inn to ask what the surveyor was doing, and he would tell them that the road was to pass through their land, and possibly through their very house. Bargaining would follow: Could the surveyor be persuaded to move the road just a little to the east, just a little farther off? The surveyor could, for a modest price. In that manner he collected bread and cheese, fresh eggs, late summer fruit, old overcoats, blankets, candles. Andras and Mendel brought food and supplies home to the orphanage nearly every night and distributed them among the men.

The surveyor also had valuable connections, among them a friend at the Royal Hungarian Officers' Training School in Turka—an officer there who had once been a well-known actor back in Szeged. This man, Pál Erdő, had been charged with staging a production of Károly Kisfaludy's famous martial drama, *The Tatars in Hungary*. When he and the surveyor met in town, Erdő complained of the difficulty and the absurdity of producing a play in the midst of preparing young men to go to war. The surveyor began lobbying him to use the play as an excuse to do some good—to request, for example, the help of the labor servicemen, who might benefit from spending a few of their evening hours in the relative calm and safety of the school's assembly hall. In particular he mentioned Andras's background in set design and Mendel's literary ability. Captain Erdő, an old-guard liberal, was eager to do what he could to ease the labor servicemen's situation; in addition to Andras and Mendel he requested the aid of six others from the 79/6th, among them József Hász, with his talent for painting, as well as a tailor, a carpenter, and an electrician. Three evenings a week this group marched directly from the work site to the officers' training school, where they assisted in the staging of a smaller military drama within the larger one. For payment they received an extra measure of soup from the kitchen of the officers' training school.

On the days when the surveyor didn't need them—days when

he had to sit in an office and make calculations, correct topo-graphical maps, and write his reports—Andras and Mendel worked with the others on the road. Those days, Kozma made them pay for their time with the surveyor and their evenings at the officers' training school. Without fail he gave them the hard-est work. If the work required tools, he took the tools away and made them do it with their rag-wrapped hands. When their work group had to transport wooden pilings to shore up the embankments on either side of the road, he made a guard sit in the middle of Andras's and Mendel's pilings while they carried them. When they had to cart barrowfuls of sand, he removed the wheels from their wheelbarrows and made them drag the carts through the mud. They paid the price without a word. They knew that their position with the surveyor and their work at the officers' training school might keep them alive once the cold weather set in.

There was no discussion between Andras and Mendel of writing a newspaper for the 79/6th, of course; even if they'd had the time, there was no way to convince themselves that it would be safe. Only once did the subject of *The Crooked Rail* come up again between them. It was on a rainy Tuesday in early Septem-ber, when they were out with the surveyor at the far end of the road, mapping a course toward a bridge that had to be rebuilt. Szolomon had left them in an abandoned dairy barn while he went to speak to a farmer whose pigsties were situated too close to the roadbed-to-be. Outside the barn, a steady drizzle fell. Inside, Andras and Mendel sat on overturned milk pails and ate the brown bread and soft-curd cheese the surveyor had gleaned for them that morning.

"Not bad for a Munkaszolgálat lunch," Mendel said.

"We've had worse."

"It's no milk and honey, though." Mendel's usual wry expres-sion had fallen away. "I think about it every day," he said. "You might have been in Palestine by now. Instead, thanks to me, we're touring beautiful rural Ukraine." Their old joke from *The Snow Goose.*

"Thanks to you?" Andras said. "That's ridiculous, you know."

"Not really," Mendel said, his moth-antenna eyebrows drawing close together. "*The Snow Goose* was my doing. So was *The Biting Fly. The Crooked Rail* came naturally, of course. I was the one who wrote the first piece. And I was the one who suggested we use the paper to get the men angry and make them slow down the operation."

"What does that have to do with it?"

"I keep thinking about it, Andras. Maybe Varsádi's operation fell under suspicion because we were making the trains run late. Maybe we slowed things down just enough to raise a red flag."

"If the trains ran late, it's because the men in charge of the operation were too greedy to send them out on time. You can't take the blame for that."

"You can't ignore the connection," Mendel said.

"It's not your fault we're here. There's a war on, in case you haven't heard."

"I can't help thinking we might have pushed things over the edge. It's been keeping me up at night, to tell you the truth. I can't help but feel like we're the ones to blame."

The same thought had occurred to him, on the train and many times since. But when he heard Mendel speak the words aloud, they seemed to reflect a novel kind of desperation, a brand of desire Andras had never considered before. Here was Mendel Horovitz insisting, even at the price of terrible burning guilt, that he'd had some control over his own fate and Andras's, some agency in the events that had swept them up and deposited them on the Eastern Front. Of course, Andras thought. Of course. Why would a man not argue his own shameful culpability, why would he not crave responsibility for disaster, when the alternative was to feel himself to be nothing more than a speck of human dust?

* * *

Every Munkaszolgálat commander, as Andras had learned by now, possessed his own special array of neuroses, his own set of axes to grind. One way to survive in a labor camp was to determine what might elicit the commander's anger and to shape one's own behavior to avoid it. But Kozma's triggers were delicate and mysterious, his moods volatile, the roots of his neuroses hidden in darkness. What made him so cruel to Lieutenant Horvath? What made him kick his gray wolfhound? Where and how had he gotten the scar that bisected his face? No one knew, not even the guards. Kozma's anger, once evoked, could not be turned aside. Nor was it reserved for men like Andras and Mendel who received special privileges. Any form of weakness drew his attention. A man who showed signs of fatigue might be beaten, or tortured: made to stand at attention with full buckets of water in his outstretched arms, or perform calisthenics after the workday was finished, or sleep outside in the rain. By mid-September the men began to die, despite the still-mild weather and the attentions of Tolnay, the company medic. One of the older men contracted a lung infection that devolved into fatal pneumonia; another succumbed to heart failure at work. Bouts of dysentery came and went, sometimes taking a man with them. Injuries often went untreated; even a shallow cut might lead to blood poisoning or result in the loss of a limb. Tolnay made frequent and alarming reports to Kozma, but a man had to be near death before Kozma would send him to the Munkaszolgálat infirmary in the village.

Nights at the orphanage held unpredictable terrors. At two o'clock in the morning Kozma might wake all the men and command them to stand at attention until dawn; the guards would beat them if they fell asleep or dropped to their knees. Other nights, when Kozma and Horvath drank with their fellow officers in their quarters, four of the labor servicemen might be called to come before them and play a horrible game: two of the men would have to sit on the others' shoulders and try to wrestle each other to the ground. Kozma would beat them with his riding crop if the fighting wasn't fierce enough. The game ended only when one of the men had been knocked unconscious.

But Kozma's cruelest form of torture, and the one he exercised most frequently, was the withholding of rations. He seemed to love knowing that his men were hungry, that he alone controlled their food supply; he seemed to enjoy the fact that they were at his mercy and desperate to have what he alone could give them. If it hadn't been for the extra food Andras and Mendel brought back secretly from their surveying trips, the 79/6th might have starved outright. As it was, the younger men among them were always ravenous. Even the full ration wouldn't have been enough to replace the energy they lost at work. They didn't understand how the other labor companies in Turka could have withstood the hunger for months on end; what was keeping them alive? They began to ask, up and down the lines of servicemen who worked along the road, what one did to keep from starving. Soon the news came back that there was a thriving black market in the village, and that all kinds of provisions were available if the men had something to trade. It seemed a bitter irony that a company of men who'd been sent away because of their officers' black-market dealings would now be forced to buy from the black market themselves, but the fact was that no other alternative existed.

One night in the bunk room, the men of the 79/6th pooled a few valuables—two watches, some paper money, a silver cigarette lighter, a pocketknife with an inlaid ebony handle—and held a hushed conference to decide who would risk the trip to the village. The perils were well known. How many times had Horvath reminded them that unaccompanied labor servicemen would be shot? The Ivory Tower, acting as moderator, began by laying out a set of parameters for their decision: No one who was sick would be allowed to go, and no one older than forty or younger than twenty. No one who had had to play Kozma's hor-

rible game that week, and no one who had recently been subjected to exposure in the courtyard. No one who had children at
home. No one who was married. The men looked around at
each other, trying to determine who was left.

"I'm still eligible," Mendel said, "Anyone else?"

"I'm up," said a man called Goldfarb, a sturdy shock-haired
redhead whose nose looked to have been broken in a series of
fights dating back to early boyhood. He was a pastry chef from
the Sixth District of Budapest, a favorite among them.

"Is that all?" asked the Ivory Tower.

Andras knew who else had survived the elimination: József
Hász. But József was edging toward the door of the bunk room
as if he meant to slip away. Just before he could duck through,
the Ivory Tower called him.

"How about you, Hász?"

"I believe I'm getting a fever," József said.

The men of the 79/6th, who had been subjected to József's
complaints ever since his conscription three months earlier, had
little patience for his excuses now. A few of them pulled him back
into the room and stood him at the middle of their circle. A
tense silence ensued, and József must have grasped his situation
quickly: No one would mind seeing him risk his skin for the benefit of the group. Too often it was his shirking that brought
Kozma's anger down upon the rest of them. He seemed to shrink
into himself, his shoulders curling.

"I'm no good at sneaking around in the woods," he said. "I'm
as obvious as day."

"It's time you started pulling your weight," said Zilber, the
electrician who worked with them at the officers' training
school. "You don't hear Horovitz complaining, and he's been
scrounging extra food for the rest of us for weeks now."

"Why would he complain?" József said. "He's been walking
the countryside with Szolomon while the rest of us shovel
asphalt."

"You'll remember what happened to Szolomon's last assistant," the electrician said. "I wouldn't take that job if it came with a private room and a pair of melon-titted farm girls."

A number of men voiced their willingness to take Mendel's job under those circumstances. Mendel assured them that the job carried no such benefits. But József Hász wasn't laughing; he was scanning the circle, his expression shading toward panic as he failed to find an ally. Andras watched with a pang of sympathy—and, he had to admit, a certain guilty satisfaction. Here was Hász learning once again that he was not exempt from the forces that shaped the lives of mortal men. In this orphanage in Ukraine, no one cared whose heir he was or what he owned, nor were they impressed by his dark good looks or his side-leaning smile. They were hungry; they needed someone to go to town for food; he fit their parameters. In another moment he would have to capitulate.

But József Hász disliked being cornered, above all else. In a cool and reasonable tone that masked his panic, he said, "You can't possibly choose me over Horovitz."

"And why is that?" the electrician said.

"If it weren't for him, you wouldn't be here."

Zilber laughed, and others joined in. "I suppose he put us on the train himself!" Zilber said. "I suppose he started the war."

"No, but he did publish that newspaper full of articles about the black market. He let Varsádi know that we all knew what was going on."

Andras couldn't believe what was happening, what he was hearing. Among the men there was a moment of vibrating silence, then a rumble of discussion. The Ivory Tower called for order. "Quiet, all of you," he whispered. "If the guards overhear us, this project is through."

"You understand me," József said, looking around at the men in the dim light. "If it weren't for the paper, Varsádi might not have lost his head." He glanced at Andras, but didn't call attention to his role as illustrator; he must have been offering that omission as a form of thanks for Andras's advice.

"That's pure idiocy," the electrician said. "No one shipped us off because of *The Crooked Rail.* We were all slowing down the operation, for the sake of the poor buggers in postings like the one we're in now. Maybe *that's* why Varsádi got scared of being found out." But a few of the men had begun to whisper to each other and look at Mendel, then at Andras. Mendel lowered his eyes in shame; József Hász had only given voice to what he already felt.

József, sensing a shift in the sentiment of the group, grasped his advantage. "The day we were sent off," he said. "Do you know what happened? Varsádi called Horovitz to his office for a conference. What do you think he wanted? It wasn't to congratulate our colleague on his talents as a writer, I'm afraid."

"That's enough, Hász," Andras said, stepping toward him.

"What's the matter, Uncle?" József said, staring a threat back at Andras. "I'm just telling them what you told me."

"What *did* he want?" one of the men asked.

"According to Lévi here, he wanted all the originals and printing plates of *The Crooked Rail.* He was desperate enough to turn a gun on our co-editors. I'm sure we can all understand, given the circumstances, why Horovitz betrayed the editor at the *Jewish Journal* who'd been helping him print the paper. In any case, half an hour later we were all being loaded onto the train."

The men stared at Mendel, who would not refute a word József had said. Andras wanted nothing more than to fly at József and knock him to the barracks floor; all that stopped him was the knowledge that a fight would bring the guards.

"Listen, men," the Ivory Tower said. "This isn't about *The Crooked Rail,* and it's not a trial. We didn't come here to decide who's responsible for our being sent off. We're hungry and there's food to be got if someone's willing to get it. Perhaps we'd have been better off drawing straws."

A rumbling from the men, a shaking of heads: They weren't going to leave the matter to chance now.

"Let me go to the village on my own," Mendel said, his eyes

set on the Ivory Tower's. "I'm fast, you know. If I go alone I'll be there and back in no time."

The Ivory Tower protested. There were fifty men in their squad, all of them hungry; the hope was that the load of black-market goods would be too much for one person to carry.

The rest of the men looked at Goldfarb, at József Hász, and finally at Andras. Andras and Mendel were understood to be a team; what they did, they did together. A sense of expectation seemed to collect in the dim light of the bunkroom. Andras met Mendel's eyes, ready to volunteer, but Mendel gave an almost imperceptible shake of his head. *Hold out.*

Another long silent moment passed before anyone spoke. József stood with his arms crossed over his chest, confident that his argument would have the desired result. And finally it was Goldfarb who stepped forward. "I'll go," he said. "It won't be the last time we have to do this. Next time we'll send Lévi and Hász, or whoever else we're in the mood to blame."

The 79/6th let out its breath. A decision had been reached: Horovitz and Goldfarb would make the trip. Much time had been wasted already; the night was slipping away, and the men had to depart at once. Mendel and his partner loaded the pooled valuables into their trouser pockets, wrapped themselves against the cold, and crept out into the dark. And the 79/6th climbed into its bunks to wait—all except Andras Lévi and József Hász, who could be heard conducting a hushed argument in the latrine. Before József could climb into his bunk, Andras had caught him by the collar and dragged him into the washroom with its tiny commodes, its line of child-sized sinks. He pushed József against the wall and twisted his collar until he was struggling for breath.

"Stop it," József gasped. "Let me go."

"I'll stop when I'm ready to stop, you self-serving little worm!"

"I didn't say anything that wasn't true," József said, and wrenched Andras's hand from his collar. "You published that rag with Horovitz. You're just as much to blame as he is. I could have made a point of that, but I didn't."

"What do you want me to do? Say thanks? Kiss your filthy hand?"

"I don't care what you do. You can go to hell, Uncle."

"You were right the other night," Andras said. "You're not cut out for labor camp. It's going to kill you, and I hope it won't take long."

"I'm not so sure about that," József said, cutting Andras his tilted smile. "After all, I'm in here now instead of out in the woods."

And finally Andras did what he'd been longing to do for months: He pulled back his fist and hit József square across the face, hard enough to send him to the floor. József knelt on the concrete, holding his jaw with one hand, and spat blood into a metal drain. Andras rubbed his bruised knuckles. He expected to feel the familiar shock of remorse that always tempered his hatred for József, but the shock failed to arrive. All he felt now was hunger and exhaustion and the desire to hit József again, just as hard as the first time. With some effort he left József on the bathroom floor and went back to his bunk to wait for Mendel.

It was three kilometers to the village through the woods in the dark; Andras figured it might take them an hour to get there. Once they arrived they'd have to find their contact and negotiate the trade—all the while avoiding the night patrols who would shoot them on sight. If they did find their contact, and if the contact was willing to trade, and if he had anything worth trading for, it might be another hour before they could return; they might not be back until just before reveille. He lay awake picturing the two men making their way through the woods, Mendel's long legs covering ground quickly, Goldfarb half running to keep up. It was a clear night, cold enough to make the men's breath visible before them. The moon and stars were out; there would be light even in the forest. A wind would rile the fallen leaves and hide their trail. Mendel and Goldfarb would see the glow of the village from far off, would navigate through the trees toward that amber wash in the sky. They might be halfway there by now.

But then Andras began to hear a frenzied barking from the woods behind the orphanage. He knew the sound; they all did. It was Major Kozma's ill-tempered dog, the gray wolfhound they hated and who hated them. A din of shouting rose from the woods. The men half fell out of their beds and rushed to the windows. The woods were full of the swinging beams of flashlights, the sound of branches snapping; unintelligible shouts drew closer and resolved into a stream of abusive Hungarian. Dark shadows struggled toward the light, flashed into momentary view, and disappeared before anyone could identify them. Men's forms approached the orphanage wall and pushed through its gates. Five minutes later, Kozma himself was shouting all the men out of the bunk room and commanding them to file into the courtyard.

They stumbled outside bareheaded and coatless in the cold. The moon was bright enough to make midnight seem like day; the men's shadows fell sharp against the brick wall of the yard. In the northwest corner there was a commotion of guards, the growl of a dog, a struggle, shouts of pain. Kozma commanded the men to stand at attention and keep their eyes on him. He climbed onto a little schoolroom chair so he could see them all. Andras and József stood close to the front. It was cold in the courtyard, the wind a skate blade across the back of Andras's neck. Kozma barked a command; two guards marched László Goldfarb and Mendel Horovitz out of their corner. They were both covered in bleeding scratches, as though they had stumbled through a tangle of briars. The left leg of Goldfarb's pants was torn away below the knee. In the hard moonlight they could see the marks of the dog's teeth on his shin. Mendel held an arm against his chest. His blood-streaked face was contracted in pain, and on his right foot he dragged a small animal trap. The steel teeth had gone through his boot.

"Look what Erzsi turned up in the woods tonight," Kozma said, petting the dog so roughly it whimpered. "Lieutenant Horvath was kind enough to go out and see what all the commotion was about, and he came across these two fine specimens in a culvert. Not what we thought we'd catch in our trap, was it, Erzsi?" He scoured the dog's back with his gloved hand. Then he commanded Mendel and Goldfarb to strip to their skins.

When Goldfarb made a noise of protest, Lieutenant Horvath silenced him with a blow from the butt of his pistol. The two men struggled out of their clothes, Horvath shouting at them all the while; Mendel couldn't remove his right pant leg around his boot and the trap, so he stood with his trousers at his feet until Horvath cut the pants off with his knife. Once they were naked, the men huddled against the wall and shivered violently, their hands crossed over their groins. Goldfarb looked out toward the rest of his comrades in a kind of stupefied daze, as if the lines of men were part of an incomprehensible show he'd been commanded to watch. Mendel met Andras's eye for a single agonizing moment and gave a wink. The gesture was meant to reassure, Andras knew, but it clenched his insides in pain: That naked and bleeding man was *Mendel Horovitz*, his childhood friend and co-editor, not some clever simulacrum devised as another Munkaszolgálat torture. Kozma ordered one of the guards to blindfold the two men with their own shirts. The guard was someone who had become familiar to Andras, a former plumber's assistant named Lukás, who escorted them to the officers' school every evening and slipped them cigarettes whenever he could. His expression, too, was incredulous and fearful. But he covered the men's eyes as he had been commanded. Goldfarb put a hand under the blindfold to loosen it a bit. Andras couldn't bear to look at Mendel's lowered head, his shaking arms. He dropped his gaze to Mendel's feet, but then there was the trap, its teeth penetrating Mendel's boot. Goldfarb was shoeless; he had crossed his feet to keep them warm. The quiet of the courtyard hummed with the men's breathing.

For a long time nothing happened—long enough to make Andras believe that this cold naked humiliation was to be the sum of the punishment. Soon, Mendel and Goldfarb would be allowed to dress and report to Tolnay, the medical officer, who would see to their wounds. But then something happened that Andras could not at once understand: A line of five guards marched into the space that separated the ranks of the 79/6th from the shivering men against the wall. The guards filled that space as if in protection, as if their function were to shield Mendel and Goldfarb's nakedness from the eyes of their comrades. Kozma gave a command, and the guards braced rifles against their shoulders and leveled them at the blindfolded men. A murmur of disbelief from the lines; a wild rage of protest in Andras's chest. Then the sound of rifles being cocked.

From Kozma, a single word: *Fire.*

An explosion of gunpowder rocketed through the yard, reverberated against the stone walls and poured up into the sky. Beyond a haze of smoke, Mendel Horovitz and László Goldfarb had slumped against the wall.

Andras pressed his fists against his eyes. The noise of the explosions seemed to go on and on inside his head. The two men who had been standing a moment before now sat on the ground, their knees folded against their chests. They sat still and white, no longer shivering; they sat without the slightest movement, their heads bent close together as though in secret conference.

"Deserters," Kozma said, once the smoke had cleared. "Thieves. Their pockets were full of pretty things. Now you've been warned against following their example. Desertion is treason. The penalty is death." He got down from his little chair, turned, and marched into the orphanage with his dog at his heels and Lieutenant Horvath close behind.

As soon as the door had closed, Andras ran to Mendel at the wall, knelt beside him, put a hand to his neck, his chest. No drumbeat of life; nothing. In the courtyard, silence. Not even the guards made a move. The Ivory Tower stepped forward and bent to László Goldfarb; no one stopped him. Then he got up and spoke quietly to the guard called Lukás. When he'd finished speaking, Lukás gave a nod and went to the corner of the yard. He removed a key ring from his belt and unlocked the wooden shed that held the shovels. The Ivory Tower took out a shovel and began to dig a hole near the courtyard wall. Andras watched through the haze of a nightmare, saw other men join the Ivory Tower at that incomprehensible task. József stood in open-mouthed silence until someone prodded him in the back; then he, too, took up a shovel and began to dig. Someone else must have helped Andras to his feet. He found himself stumbling toward the shed, taking the shovel Lukás handed him, bending beside József. As if in a dream, he angled the shovel toward the earth and jammed it in with all his strength. The earth was hard, compacted; the jolt of the blade radiated up the handle and into his bones. Under his breath he began to murmur a series of words in Hebrew: *You deliver us from the snare of the fowler and the pestilence of destruction, cover us with your pinions, protect us from the plague that stalks in darkness and the disease that wastes at noon. You are our protection. No evil will befall us. The angels guard us on our way, carrying us in their hands.* He knew the words came from the Ninety-first Psalm, the one recited at funerals. He knew he was digging a grave. But he could not make himself believe that the body beside the wall belonged to Mendel Horovitz, could not believe that this man he'd loved since boyhood had been killed. He could not grasp that stunning absolute. He could not breathe, could not think. In his head, the Ninety-first Psalm, the flash and crack of gunshots, the sound of shovels against cold earth.

CHAPTER THIRTY-FIVE

The Tatars in Hungary

THE MEN WERE BURIED at daybreak. There was no time for shivah, no time even to wash the bodies. Kozma considered it a kindness that he had let the 79/6th bury its fallen comrades. In compensation for that kindness, he withheld their soup rations for the rest of the week. The days passed in a kind of shocked silence, a vibrating disbelief. It was terrible enough to see older men worked to death, or dying of illness; it was another thing altogether to see young men shot. József Hász seemed to react with the deepest shock of all, as though it were new information that any action of his, any exercise of his will, might have disastrous consequences for another human being. After that first week, during which he ate little and slept less, he stunned the company by volunteering for Mendel's position as the surveyor's second assistant. By now the position was believed to be cursed; no one else would touch it. But József seemed to consider it a kind of penance. On the surveying runs he made himself Andras's servant. If there was heavy equipment to carry, he carried it. He gathered wood, built the cooking fires, surrendered his share of any food the surveyor gleaned. The surveyor, who had heard the story of what had happened to Mendel Horovitz and László Goldfarb, accepted József's servitude with quiet gravity. What had taken place was yet another of the Munkaszolgálat atrocities, playing out its second act now in the emotional torture of this inexperienced young man. But Andras, two decades younger than the surveyor and still capable of being stunned by human selfishness and cruelty, refused to forgive József, refused even to look at him. Every time he passed through Andras's field of vision, the same ribbon of thoughts would unspool in Andras's mind. Why had it been Mendel and not József? Why not József in the woods that night, József's foot in a trap? Why could they not trade places still? Why not József, now, irrevocably gone? Andras had thought he'd tasted frustration and futility; he thought he'd been an intimate of grief. But what he felt now was sharper than any frustration, any grief, he'd ever known before. It seemed to refer not only to Mendel but to Andras, too; it was not only the horror of Mendel's death, the undeniable fact of Mendel's being gone, but also the knowledge that Andras himself and all the 79/6th had entered another level of hell, that their lives were worthless to their commanding officers, that it was likely Andras would never see his wife and son again. József had done this, too, had brought Andras to this dangerous state of hopelessness. He found he could inhabit that place and still feel a burning anger at József for bringing him there. When a surveying assignment led Andras and József near a stretch of mined earth, he found himself wishing to see József subsumed in a deafening blast of fire. It seemed no worse than he deserved. Twice that year—once in Budapest, once in Ukraine— József had betrayed Andras at excruciating cost. The fact that József was connected by blood to Klara, the person Andras loved most in the world, was another agony; if he could have erased József from Klara's memory, erased him from the Hász family altogether, he would have done it in an instant. But József stubbornly refused to be erased. He refused to trip a land mine. He hovered at the edge of Andras's vision, a reminder that what had happened was not an illusion and would not change.

Evenings at the officers' training school brought no relief. Andras and József were meant to be partners there too, Andras the set designer and József the artistic director. The play, Kisfaludy's *The Tatars in Hungary*, was more than familiar to Andras; he'd studied it ad nauseam at his village school in Konyár. A strict schoolmaster had lodged the history soundly in his brain: Before Kisfaludy was a playwright, he'd been a soldier in the Napoleonic wars. When he came home from battle he wanted to bring his experience to the stage, but the recent wars seemed too fresh; instead he fixed his gaze on Hungary's distant past. Andras had written a long essay on Kisfaludy for his graduation from primary school. Now here he was, designing sets for *The Tatars in Hungary* at an officers' training school in Ukraine in the midst of a world war, and his design partner was a man responsible, in some measure, for Mendel Horovitz's death. But there was no time to dwell on that slice of irreality. Captain Erdő, the director of the project, was operating under a great urgency. The new minister of defense was soon to pay a visit to the officers' training school; the play would make its debut in his honor.

On a Thursday evening early in October, Andras and József found themselves standing at attention in the cavernous meeting hall of the officers' training school while Erdő reviewed their plans. The captain was a tall barrel-chested man with a corona of whitening hair cut close to the scalp. He cultivated a goatee and affected a monocle, but his air of self-mockery suggested it was all a farce, a costume: He considered himself ridiculous and wanted everyone else to be in on the joke. As he critiqued the plans, he spoke as if he were three or four people instead of just one. Instead of these painted trees, he said, might not a few real trees be brought in to suggest woods? Was that impractical? Terribly impractical! Real trees? Who had the time or inclination to dig up trees? But wasn't it important to achieve an air of realism? Of course. Real trees, then; real trees. Real tents, too, might be used for the encampment. That was a fine idea. There were plenty of tents around, they wouldn't cost a thing. This large-as-life cave meant to be constructed from chicken wire and papier-mâché, could it be built in two pieces to make it easier to move? Of course it could, if it were designed properly, and that was why he'd engaged József and Andras, wasn't it? Everything had to be designed and carried out with the utmost professionalism. He didn't have an enormous budget, but the school wanted to make a good impression upon the new minister of defense. He told

Andras and József to make a list of building materials: wood, chicken wire, newspaper, canvas, whatever it was they needed. Then, leaning closer, he began to speak in a different tone.

"Listen, boys," he said. "Szolomon tells me what goes on in that company of yours. Kozma's a beast of a man. It's abominable. Let me know what I can do for you. Anything. Do you need food? Clothes? Do you have enough blankets?"

Andras could hardly begin to answer. What did the 79/6th need? Everything. Morphine, penicillin, bandages, food, blankets, overcoats, boots and woolen underthings and trousers and a week's worth of sleep. "Medical supplies," he managed to say. "Any kind. And vitamin tablets. And blankets. We're grateful for anything."

But József had another thought. "You can send letters, can't you?" he said. "You can let our families know we're safe."

Erdő nodded slowly.

"And you can get mail for us, too, if they send it to your attention."

"I can, yes. But it's a dangerous matter. What you're suggesting goes against regulations, of course, and everything's censored. You'll have to be sure your family understands that. The wrong kind of letter might compromise us all."

"We'll make them understand," József said. And then, "Can you get us pens and ink? And some kind of writing paper?"

"Of course. That's easy enough."

"If we bring the letters tomorrow, can you send them by the next day's post?"

Erdő gave another stern and somber nod. "I can, boys," he said. "I will."

That night, as the guard named Lukás marched Andras and József back to the orphanage along with the others who'd been requisitioned to work on *The Tatars in Hungary*, Andras found himself forced to admit that József's idea had been a good one. It made him dizzy to imagine what he might write to Klara that night. *By now you know why I didn't return home the day before our journey: I was kidnapped along with the rest of my company and sent to Ukraine. Since we've been here we've been starved, beaten, made sick with work, allowed to die of illness, killed outright. Mendel Horovitz is dead. He died blindfolded and naked before a firing squad, in part thanks to your nephew. As for myself, I can scarcely tell if I'm dead or alive.* None of that could be written, of course; the truth would never pass the censors. But he could beg Klara to go to Palestine—he could find a way to get that into the letter, however coded the message might be. He even dared to hope she might be in Palestine already—that a reply from Elza Hász might bring the news that Klara and Tamás had gone down the Danube with Tibor and Ilana and Ádám, had crossed the Black Sea and passed through the Bosporus just as they'd planned, had taken up a life in Palestine where she and Tamás were safe from the war, relatively speaking. If he had known he would be posted to Ukraine, he would have begged her to go. He would have asked her to weigh her life and Tamás's against his own, and would have made her see what she had to do. But he hadn't been there to persuade her. Instead he had been deported, and the uncertainty of his situation would have argued for her to stay— her love for him a snare, a trap, but not the kind likely to keep her alive.

Dear K, he wrote that night. *Your nephew and I send greetings from the town of T. I write with the hope that this letter will not reach you in Budapest, that you will have already departed for the country. If you have postponed that trip, I beg you not to delay longer for my sake. You must go at once if the opportunity arises. I am well, but would be better if I knew you were proceeding with our plans.* And then the terrible news: *Our friend M.H., I must tell you, was forced to depart a month ago for Lachaise.* A reference to the cemetery in Paris. Would she understand? *I feel as you might imagine. I miss you and Tamás terribly and think of you day and night. Will write again as soon as possible. With love, your A.*

He folded the letter and hid it in the inner pocket of his jacket, and the next day he put it into Erdő's hands. There was no way to know when or whether or how it might find its way to Klara, but the thought that it might do so eventually was the first consolation he'd had in recent memory.

If Andras was surprised when the young officers-in-training, his set-building crew, accepted his direction with respectful deference, the surprise faded quickly. After a few weeks of evening duty at the officers' training school, it came to seem ordinary to walk among them as a kind of foreman, checking their adherence to his plans. Between them there was little consciousness of difference and little formality. The officers-in-training and the work servicemen called each other by their first names, then by diminutives—Sanyi, Józska, Bandi. They weren't allowed to eat together in the officers' mess hall, but often the crew went to the back door of the kitchen at dinnertime and brought back food for all of them. They ate on the stage, cross-legged amid the construction projects and half-painted backdrops. Andras and József, locked in a wordless struggle, nonetheless gained weight and got the sets built. They waited for answers to their letters, hoping each time Erdő entered the officers' meeting hall that he would call them into his office and pull a smudged envelope from his breast pocket. But the weeks dragged on and no response came. Erdő told them to be patient; the mail service was notoriously slow, and even slower when the correspondence had to cross borders.

As the performance of *The Tatars in Hungary* drew nearer and still no response arrived, Andras grew half mad with worry. He was sure that Klara and György and Elza had been arrested and thrown in jail, that Tamás had been left in the care of strangers. Klara would be tried and convicted and killed. And he was trapped here in Ukraine, where he could do nothing, nothing; and once the play was finished he would lose his connection to

Erdő, and with it the possibility of sending or receiving word from home.

On the twenty-ninth of October, the new Hungarian minister of defense arrived in Turka. There was to be an official procession through the village. All the companies in the vicinity were to be present. That morning, Major Kozma marched the men of the 79/6th to the central square of the village and commanded them to stand at attention along its western side. They had been ordered to wash and mend their torn uniforms in preparation for General Vilmos Nagy's visit; thread and patches had been provided. They had done what they could, but still they looked like scarecrows. Roadwork had destroyed their jackets and trousers. They had managed to cadge a few pieces of civilian clothing from the Ukrainian black-market ragmen, but they couldn't replace their torn uniforms with new ones; the army no longer supplied clothing for labor servicemen. Andras had observed the degeneration of his own uniform during his time at the officers' training school. His jacket and trousers had come to look more and more like a vagrant's costume alongside the young officers' starched khakis.

At the head of a company of scrubbed-looking officer-trainees on the opposite side of the square, Andras could make out Erdő's erect posture and winking monocle. His buttons flashed gold fire in the morning light. This was high drama for him, all of it. He was satisfied with the work Andras and József had done. When they'd displayed the finished sets and backdrops just before the dress rehearsal, he'd been so enthusiastic in his praise that he had burst a capillary in his left eye. The dress rehearsal itself had been perfect except for a few forgotten lines, but all had been rectified now, all had been polished to a military sheen. The sets, the costumes, even a grand curtain of red-and-gold-painted canvas, waited in readiness for the general's arrival. The play would make its debut that night.

The general's motorcade was preceded by the officer-trainees' marching band: a few desperately earnest trumpeters, a phlegmatic trombonist, a fat flautist, a red-faced drummer. Behind them came a pair of armored trucks flying the Hungarian flag, then a string of military policemen on motorcycles, and finally General Vilmos Nagybaczoni Nagy in an open car, a glossy black Lada with white-rimmed tires. The general was younger than Andras had expected, not yet gray, still inhabiting a vigorous middle age. His uniform bristled with decorations of every shape and color, including the turquoise-and-gold cross that represented the Honvédség's highest award for bravery in combat. Riding beside him was a younger man in a less resplendent uniform, apparently an adjutant or secretary. Every few moments the general would look away from the ranks of men to whisper something in the young officer's ear, and the young officer would scribble furiously on a stenographer's pad. The general's gaze seemed to linger over the companies of work servicemen in particular. Andras didn't dare look at him directly, but felt Nagy's eyes passing over him as the motorcade rolled by. The general bent his head and spoke to the adjutant, and the young man took notes. After the motorcade had made its turn around the square, the band stepped out of its way and the cars roared off in the direction of the officers' training school.

When Andras and József arrived at the meeting hall to make the last preparations for the show, they found that all had fallen into confusion. The stage sets had been shoved aside so the chief officer of the academy might give the official welcome speech, and in the process, two of the backdrops had been torn and one side of the papier-mâché cave had been crushed. Erdő paced from one end of the stage to the other in panicked dismay, declaring at full volume that the repairs would never be finished in time, while Andras and József and the others rushed to make things right. Andras patched the cave with a bucket of paste and some brown paper; József mended a Roman ruin with a roll of canvas tape. The other men realigned and rehung the second torn backdrop. By the time the dinner hour was over, all was in order. The actors arrived to don their Tatar and Magyar costumes and practice their vocal exercises. They preened and buzzed and mumbled their lines backstage with as much gravity and self-importance as the actors at the Sarah-Bernhardt.

At half past eight the meeting hall filled with officers-in-training. There was a tense festivity in their clamor, a rising thrum of anticipation. Andras found a dim corner of the wings from which he could watch the speeches and the show. He caught a glimpse of the martial glitter of the general's jacket as he strode up the center aisle and took his seat in the front row of benches. The school's chief officer mounted the stage and made his address, a rhetorical pas de deux of deference and pomposity, punctuated with gestures that Andras recognized from newsreels of Hitler: the hammerlike fist on the podium, the uptwisting index finger, the conductorial palm. The chief officer's bluster earned him six seconds of dutiful applause from the officers-in-training. But when General Nagy rose to take the stage, the men got to their feet and roared. He had chosen them, had graced them with the first stop of his eastern tour; when he left them he would go directly to Hitler's headquarters at Vinnitsa. He raised a hand to thank them, and they sat down again and fell silent with anticipation.

"Soldiers," he began. "Young men. I won't make a long speech. I don't have to tell you that war is a terrible thing. You're far from home and family, and you'll go farther still before you return. You're brave boys, all of you." Vilmos Nagy had none of the swagger or dramatic fire of the school's commanding officer; he spoke with the rounded vowels of a Hajdú peasant, gripping the podium with his large red hands. "I'll speak frankly," he said. "The Soviets are stronger than we thought. You're here because we didn't take Russia in the spring. Many of your comrades have died already. You're being trained to lead more men into battle. But you are Magyars, boys. You've survived a thousand years of battle. No enemy can match you. No foe can defeat you. You slew the Tatars at Pest. You routed eighty thousand Turks at Eger Castle. You were better warriors and better leaders."

A round of wild cheers broke forth from the officers-in-training; the general waited until the noise had subsided. "Remember," he said, "you're fighting for Hungary. For Hungary, and no one else. The Germans may be our allies, but they're not our masters. Their way is not our way. The Magyars are not an Aryan people. The Germans see us as a benighted nation. We've got barbarian blood, wild ideas. We refuse to embrace totalitarianism. We won't deport our Jews or our Gypsies. We cling to our strange language. We fight to win, not to die."

Another cheer from the men, this one more tentative. The young officers-in-training had been taught to revere German authority absolutely; they had been taught to speak of Hungary's all-important and all-powerful ally with unconditional respect.

"Remember what happened this summer on the banks of the Don," Nagy said. "Our General Jány's ten divisions were spread over a hundred kilometers between Voronezh and Pavlovsk. With just those ten light divisions, Generalfeldmarschall von Weichs expected us to keep the Russians on the east bank. But you know the story: Our tanks were defenseless against the Soviets' T-34s. Our arms were outmatched. Our supply chain failed. Our men were dying. So Jány pulled his divisions back and made them take defensive positions. He saw where he stood and made a decision that saved the lives of thousands of men. For this, von Weichs and General Halder accused us of cowardice! Perhaps they would have admired us more if we'd let forty or sixty thousand of our men die, instead of only twenty thousand. Perhaps they would have liked to see us spill every last drop of our barbarian blood." He paused and looked out across the rows of silent men, seeming to meet their eyes in the dark. "Germany is our ally. Her victory will strengthen us. But never believe that Germany has any other aim besides the survival of the Reich. *Our* aim is Hungary's survival—and by that I mean not just the preservation of our sovereignty and our territories, but of our young men's lives."

The men had fallen into a rapt silence. No one applauded now; they were all waiting for Nagy to go on. So seldom had they been told the truth, Andras thought, that it had struck them dumb.

"You men have been trained to fight intelligently and minimize our losses," Nagy continued. "We want to bring you home alive. We won't need you any less once the war is over." He paused and gave a deep sigh; his hands were trembling now, as if the effort of delivering the speech had exhausted him. He glanced into the wings of the stage, into the darkness where Andras stood watching. His eyes settled on Andras for a long moment, and then he looked out at the young officers-in-training again. "And one more thing," he said. "Respect the labor servicemen. They're getting their hands dirty for you. They're your brothers in this war. Some officers have chosen to treat them like dogs, but that's going to change. Be good men, is what I'm saying. Give respect where it's due." He bowed his head as if in thought, and then shrugged. "That's all," he said. "You're fine brave soldiers, all of you. I thank you for your work."

He stepped down from the podium to an accompaniment of somber, bewildered applause. No one seemed to know quite what to think of this new minister of defense; some of the things he'd just said sounded as though they shouldn't have been uttered in public, and certainly not at an officers' training school. But there was little opportunity to react. It was time for the play to begin. The Magyars assembled onstage for the first scene, and the work servicemen dragged the Roman ruin into place and lowered a backdrop that depicted a wash of blue sky above the moss-colored hills of Buda. When they hoisted the curtain a flood of light filled the stage, illuminating the martial-looking Hungarians in their painted armor. The Magyar chieftain drew his sword and raised it aloft. Then, just before he could speak his opening line, the air itself seemed to break into a deep keening. The assembly hall reverberated with a rising and falling plaint of grief. Andras knew the sound: It was an air-raid siren. They had all practiced the drill, both here and at the orphanage. But there was no drill planned for this evening, nor was this part of the play. This was the real thing. They were going to be bombed.

All at once the audience got to its feet and began pushing toward the exits. A cluster of officers surrounded General Nagy, who lost his hat in the crush. He clutched at his bare head and glanced around him as his staff hustled him to a side door. The actors fled the stage, dropping their pasteboard weapons, and began to crowd toward a stairway at the back of the hall. Andras and József and the other work servicemen followed the actors down a flight of stairs that led to a shelter beneath the building. The shelter was a honeycomb of concrete rooms linked by low-ceilinged hallways. The men pushed into a dark enclosure at a turn of one of the hallways; more officers-in-training poured into the room after them. Far above, the air-raid sirens wailed.

When the first bombs hit, the shelter shook as if the moon itself had fallen from its orbit and crashed to earth just overhead. Concrete dust rained from the ceiling, and the lightbulbs flickered in their wire cages. A few men cursed. Others closed their eyes as if in prayer. József asked an officer-in-training for a cigarette and began to smoke it.

"Put that out," Andras whispered. "If there's a gas leak down here, we'll all be killed."

"If I'm about to die, I'm going to smoke," József said.

Andras shook his head. Beside him, József released a complex luxuriant cloud through his nostrils, as if he meant to take his time. But another concussive blast threw him against Andras, and he dropped the cigarette. A series of shuddering jolts rocketed through the foundation of the building like small earthquakes; this was anti-aircraft fire, the kick of the artillery installation housed not far from the assembly hall. Glass exploded above, and faint cries reached the men through the walls of the shelter.

"At attention, men!" one of the officers commanded. They stood at attention. It took some concentration, there in the flickering dark; they stood that way until the next bombs hit. As the foundation shuddered, Andras thought of the weight of building materials arranged above him: the heavy beams, the flooring, the walls, the tons of cinderblock and brickwork, the roof struts and frame, the thousands and thousands of slate tiles. He thought of all those materials raining down upon the architecture of his own body. Fragile skin, fragile muscle, fragile bone, the clever structures of the organs, the intricate arrangement of his cells— all the things Tibor had pointed out in Klara's anatomy book a lifetime ago in Paris. Suddenly he couldn't breathe. Another detonation knocked the room sideways, and a crack appeared in the ceiling.

Then there was a lull. The men stood silent, waiting. The anti-aircraft artillery must have been hit, or the gunners must have been waiting for the next wave of planes. That was worse— not to know when the next barrage was going to come. József's lips moved with some whispered incantation. Andras leaned in, wondering what psalm or prayer might have brought such a look of tranquility to József's features; when the words resolved into an intelligible line, he almost laughed aloud. It was a Cole Porter tune József had often played on his phonograph at parties. *I'm with you once more under the stars / And down by the shore an orchestra's playing / And even the palms seem to be swaying / When they begin the beguine.* The quiet ended with the renewed staccato of anti-aircraft fire, then a percussive chord of blasts, as if a trio of bombs had struck all at once. The men fell to their knees and the lights went out. József made an animal noise of panic. So this was how it would happen, Andras thought: József would receive his retribution here in this tomb under the officers' meeting hall. How like a fairy tale, where selfish wishes often carried a cruel price: József would die, but Andras would have to die with him. As the bombs continued to fall, József lowered his forehead to

Andras's collarbone and said, "I'm sorry, I'm sorry." The cigarette smoke in his hair was the smell of evenings in Paris. For one unthinking moment, Andras put a hand on József's head.

Then, all at once, the lights flickered on again. The men got to their feet. They dusted off their uniforms and pretended they hadn't just been clutching each other's arms, crushing their faces against each other's chests, praying and crying and apologizing. They glanced around as if to confirm that none of them had really been afraid. The earth had gone still now; the bombing had stopped. Above, all was silent.

"All right, men," said the officer who had commanded them to stand at attention. "Wait for the all clear."

It was a long time before the signal sounded. When it came at last there was a push toward the hallways, a crush of men talking in shock-dulled voices. No one knew what they would find when they emerged. Andras thought of the labor camp where they were supposed to stay when they had first arrived in Turka—its mass grave, the wet dirt slumped into the ground like a sodden blanket. He and József shouldered into a stream of men making their way back toward the staircase. The air in the bunker seemed overbreathed, devoid of oxygen.

There was a bottleneck at the foot of the stairway. As Andras shuffled toward the stairs, someone bumped against him and pushed something into his hand. It was Erdő, his face red and wet, his monocle fallen. "I didn't think of it earlier," he said into Andras's ear. "I was preoccupied with the play. I might have died and never given it to you, or you might have died and never gotten it."

Andras looked down to see what he held in his hand. It was a piece of folded paper wrapped in a handkerchief.

He couldn't wait. He had to see. He unwrapped the corner of the handkerchief, and there was Klara's handwriting on a thin blue envelope. His heart lurched in his chest.

"Hide that," Erdő said, and Andras did.

* * *

Back at the orphanage he wanted only to be alone—to get to some private place where he could read Klara's letter. But the men of Company 79/6 met him and the others with a storm of questions. What had happened? Had they seen the planes? Had anyone been killed? Had they themselves been injured? What was the meaning of an air raid so far from the front lines? The guards had been listening to the radio in Kozma's private quarters, but had told the men nothing, of course; the bombing had gone on for so long that the men thought everyone at the school must be dead.

Men had died. That much was true. When they'd come out of the meeting hall—the three walls that remained of it, in any case—they'd been swept into a stream of men running for one of the shelters, which had caved in upon the officers-in-training who had been huddled there. For three hours the labor servicemen and soldiers worked with shovels and pickaxes, ropes and jeeps, to move the mass of wood and concrete that had trapped the men. Seventeen of them had been killed outright by the cave-in. Dozens of others were injured. There were other casualties elsewhere: The mess hall had been flattened before the cooks and dishwashers could get to a shelter, and eleven men had died. It was deduced that General Vilmos Nagy had been the reason for the raid; intelligence of his visit must have reached the NKVD, and Soviet Air Force troops commissioned to attempt an assassination via bombing. But General Nagy had survived. He had personally supervised the attempt to rescue the men from the collapsed shelter, to the dismay of his young adjutant, who stood nearby surveying the firelit cloud cover as if another rain of Soviet YAK-1s might drop out of it at any moment.

All that time, Andras had carried Klara's letter in his pocket, not daring to read it. Now, finally, he was at liberty to climb into his bunk and try to decipher her lines in the dark. József seemed nearly as anxious as Andras; he sat cross-legged on the bunk below, awaiting news. Andras slit the envelope carefully with his razor, then maneuvered into a position that would allow him to use the moonlight as a torch. He pulled the letter out and unfolded it with trembling hands.

15 October 1942
Budapest

Dear A,
Imagine my relief, and your brother's, when we received your letter! We have all decided to postpone our trip to the country until you return. Tamás is well, and I am as well as might be expected. Your parents are in good health. Please send greetings to my nephew. His parents are well, too. As for what you wrote about M.H.'s departure for Lachaise, I must hope I have misunderstood you. Please write again soon.
As ever, Your K.

We have all decided to postpone. It was just as he had feared, only worse. Not just Klara, but Tibor and Ilana too. He would have done the same, of course—would never have left Ilana and Ádám alone in Budapest three days after Tibor had disappeared—but it was sad and infuriating nonetheless. In one stroke the Hungarian Army had grounded the entire Lévi clan. For the sake of an underground business in army boots and tinned meat, ammunition and jeep tires, they had all been tied to a continent intent upon erasing its Jews from the earth. That horrible truth lodged beneath his diaphragm and made it impossible for him to draw a full breath. He put his hand over the side of the bed and slipped the letter to József, who reacted with a low note of distress— József, who had long argued the foolishness of the trip to Palestine. Now, after three months in Ukraine, and after what they had just experienced and seen at the officers' training school, József knew what it meant to feel one's own vulnerability, to taste the salt of one's own mortality. He understood what it meant for Klara and Tamás, Tibor and Ilana and Ádám, to be stranded in Hungary while the war drew closer on all sides. He must have known what his own deportation would have meant to his parents; beneath the *well* in Klara's single line about them, he must have sensed the truth.

But at least he and Andras had this letter, this evidence that life continued at home. Andras could hear Klara's voice reading the coded lines of the letter aloud; for a moment it was as though she were with him, curled small against him in his impossibly short bunk. Her skin hot beneath her close-wrapped dress. The warm black scent of her hair. Her mouth forming a string of spy words, dropping them into his ear like cool glass beads. *We have decided to postpone our trip to the country.* In another moment he would reply, would tell her all that had happened. Then the illusion vanished, and he was alone in his bunk again. He rolled over and stared into the cold muddy square of the courtyard, where the footprints of his comrades had long ago obscured the child-sized prints that had been there when they'd first arrived. In the moonlight he could make out the twin mounds of earth that were Mendel's and Goldfarb's graves, and beyond them the high brick wall, and above it the tops of the trees, and, farther still, a mesh of stars against the blue-black void of the sky.

CHAPTER THIRTY-SIX

A Fire in the Snow

THE DAY AFTER the air raid, work on the Turka–Skhidnytsya highway came to a temporary halt. All the Hungarian labor companies in the area were sent to the officers' training school to repair the damage. The bombed buildings had to be rebuilt, the torn-up roads repaired. General Vilmos Nagy was still in residence; he couldn't go on to Hitler's headquarters in Vinnitsa until it could be determined that the way was safe. Major Kozma, energized by Nagy's presence but not yet appraised of his unconventional political views, took the opportunity to arrange a work circus for his entertainment. The broken bricks and splintered timbers of the officers' dining hall were supposed to be hauled away by horse cart, but there were more carts than there were horses to fill the traces; the stables, too, had suffered in the raid. So Kozma put his men into the traces instead. Eight forced laborers, Andras and József among them, were lashed in with leather harness straps and made to pull cartloads of detritus from the ruined mess hall to the assembly ground, which had become a salvage yard for building materials. The distance could not have been more than three hundred meters, but the cart was always loaded to overflowing. The men moved as if through a lake of hardening cement. When they fell to their knees in exhaustion, the guards climbed down from the driver's bench and laid into them with whips. A group of officer trainees had stopped their own work to watch the spectacle. They booed when the men fell to their knees, and applauded when Andras and József and the others struggled to their feet again and dragged the cart a few meters farther toward the unloading area.

By midmorning the spectacle had generated enough talk to come to the attention of Nagy himself. Against the protests of his young adjutant he emerged from the bunker where he'd taken shelter and marched across the assembly ground to the ruin of the mess hall. With his thumbs hooked into his belt, he paused to watch the work servicemen toss debris into the bed of the cart and draw it forward. The general walked from cart bed to harness line, running his hand along the leather straps that connected the men to the traces. Kozma hustled across the mess-hall ruin and positioned himself close to the general. He pulled himself up to his full height and snapped a hand to his forehead.

The general didn't return the salute. "Why are these men harnessed to the wagon?" he asked Kozma.

"They're the best horses we've got," Kozma said, and winked his good eye.

The general removed his glasses. He was a long time cleaning them with his handkerchief, and then he put them on and gave Kozma a cool stare. "Cut your men loose," he said. "All of them."

Kozma looked disappointed, but he raised a hand to signal one of the guards.

"Not him," the general said. "You do it."

The words sent a shock of energy through the line of harnessed men, a frisson Andras felt through the leather straps at his chest and shoulders.

"At once, Major," Nagy said. "I don't like to repeat an order."

And Kozma had to go to each man and cut the leather straps with his pocketknife, which required him to get closer to them than he'd gotten since they had first come under his command— close enough to smell them, Andras thought, close enough to put himself in danger of catching their chronic cough, their body lice. The major's hands trembled as he fumbled with the interlaced straps. It took him a quarter of an hour to free the eight of them. The officer-trainees who had stopped to watch had disappeared now.

"Have your guards bring a truckload of wheelbarrows from the supply warehouse," the general ordered Kozma. To the men he said, "You will rest here until the wheelbarrows arrive. Then you will remove the debris by the barrow-load." He watched as the work foremen broke the men into their groups as they waited for the carts. Kozma stood silent at the general's side, twisting and twisting his hands as if he meant to shuck them of their skins. The general seemed to have forgotten that his life was in danger, that the NKVD was aware of his presence at the camp. He paid no attention to his adjutant's urgent request that he return to the bunker. At lunchtime, Nagy and the adjutant escorted the men to the new mess tent and saw that they received an extra twenty decagrams of bread and ten grams of margarine. The general had his adjutant drag a bench over to the patch of bare earth where the work servicemen were eating; he took his lunch with them, asking questions about their lives before the war and what they planned to do when it was over. The men responded tentatively at first, uncertain whether or not to trust this exalted person in his decorated jacket, but before long they began to speak more freely. Andras didn't speak; he hovered at the edge of the group, aware that he was witnessing something extraordinary.

After lunch, the general ordered that the men of the 79/6th be deloused and bathed and given clean uniforms from the storehouses of the officers' training school. They were to be examined by the medics at the school infirmary, their wounds and illnesses treated. Then they were to be reassigned to jobs that would allow them to recover their health. It was clear that they were too weak and sick to perform hard labor. For the rest of the day he sent them to work in the damp heat of the mess tent, where the cook set them to peeling potatoes and cutting onions for the officers' dinner.

At dinnertime the men received another supplemental ration: twenty decagrams of bread again, and ten more grams of margarine. An unfamiliar officer, a tall ursine man who introduced himself to them as Major Bálint, announced that the supplement was to be permanent; the general had ordered that the men's diet be altered. For the time being they would continue to serve in the mess tent rather than return to their work on the road. And there was to be another change: Bálint himself would be their new commander. Major Kozma would no longer have anything to do with the 79/6th, nor, if General Nagy had anything to say about it, with any other Munkaszolgálat company, except perhaps the one in which he would be forced to serve.

Not once since their arrival at Turka had there been a night at the orphanage that might have been called festive. Even when they'd observed the High Holidays they had done so with a sense of mournful duty, and an awareness of how far they were from everything and everyone they loved. That night at the barracks, at an hour when Kozma might ordinarily have lined them up outside and made them stand at attention until they fell to their knees, the men gathered in one of the downstairs classrooms to play cards and sing nonsense songs and read the news aloud from scraps of newspaper gleaned from the officers' training school. The Soviets, the Ivory Tower read, continued to hold off the Nazi offensive at Stalingrad as the battle entered its eleventh week; bitter fighting continued on the streets of the city and in the northern suburbs, raising speculation that the Nazis might find themselves still entrenched in that fight when the Russian winter arrived. "Let them freeze!" the Ivory Tower cried, and crowned himself with a nautical hat Andras had folded from a page of advertisements. He grabbed Andras by the arms and made him dance a peasant dance. "We're free, my darlings, free," he sang, whirling him around the room. It wasn't true, of course; Lukás and the other guards still kept watch at the door, and any member of the 79/6th could have been shot for walking down the road unaccompanied. But they had indeed been freed from Major Kozma. And as if that weren't enough, they were clean and free of lice. General Nagy had gone so far as to order that their mattresses and blankets be dragged outside, burned, and replaced immediately with new bedding.

That night, from the fragrant comfort of a mattress stuffed

with sweet hay, Andras wrote to Klara. *Dear K, There has been a surprising turn of events. Our circumstances in T. have changed for the better. We are well, and have just received new uniforms and a good work assignment. You must not worry on our account. If an opportunity arises for you to go to the country again, you must go. I'll follow as soon as I can. Unfortunately, I must confirm what you seem to have guessed about M.H. Please send love to my brother and Ilana. Kiss Tamás for me. As ever, your devoted A.*

The next day, as he served lunch to the officer-trainees and their superiors, he waited impatiently for Erdő to come through the serving line. When Erdő came at last—grim-faced and devoid of his monocle, still mourning the loss of *The Tatars in Hungary* amid the camp's other losses—Andras passed the letter to him underneath his tin plate. Without a sign or a wink or any other acknowledgment, Erdő moved down the serving line; Andras saw a flash of white as he transferred the note from his hand to his trouser pocket. As long as the mail kept moving between Ukraine and Hungary, Klara would know that Andras was well and that he wanted her to go to Palestine if she could.

General Nagy's plan for the rehabilitation of the 79/6th continued through the middle of November. The sick men were treated at the infirmary, and those who could still work gained weight on the extra rations. It helped that they had been assigned to kitchen duty. Though the cooks kept the food supply under careful watch, it was often possible to glean a stray carrot or potato or an extra measure of soup. If Andras missed his long walks to the end of the road with the surveyor, he had the pleasure of Szolomon's weekly visits to the officers' training school. The surveyor brought news of the war, and, when he could, slipped Andras and József some Ukrainian delicacy or a piece of warm clothing. One chilly afternoon Andras watched József tear open a paper-wrapped package of the rolled dumplings called *holushky*—little ears—and felt he was watching his own ravenous self in Paris, unwrapping a poppyseed roll sent by the elder Mrs. Hász. What were they now, he and József, but a pair of hungry men on the ragged edge of a country at war, at the mercy of forces beyond their control? All the barriers between them, or at least all the markers of class that had seemed to separate them when they had lived in Paris, were arbitrary to the point of absurdity now. When József offered him the package of *holushky*, he took it and said *köszönöm*. József sent him a look of surprised relief, a reaction that confused Andras until it occurred to him that this was the first time he'd spoken a kind word to József since Mendel's death. Strange, Andras thought, that war could lead you involuntarily to forgive a person who didn't deserve forgiveness, just as it might make you kill a man you didn't hate. It must have been the amnesiac effect of extremity, he thought, that bitter potion they ingested every day in Ukraine with their ration of soup and sandy bread.

One morning later that week, the men woke to find the court-yard of the orphanage blurred in a gray-white nimbus of snow. The clouds seemed intent upon giving up their contents all at once, the flakes speeding to earth in acorn-sized clusters. Here was the winter they'd dreaded, making its unambiguous entrance; the temperature had dropped twenty degrees over-night. At lineup, snow swarmed into their ears and mouths and noses. It found its way into the crevices between their overcoats and neck wraps, worked itself in through the grommets of their boots. Major Bálint took his place at the front of the assembly yard and announced with regret that the men had been removed from their duties at the officers' training school and assigned to snow removal. The guards unlocked the shed and handed the men their tools—the same pointed spades they'd used for road-building, not the curved rectangular blades that would have suited the job—and marched them out toward the village to begin their winter work.

That afternoon, when Szolomon found Andras and József among the snow-removal teams, he delivered the news that he'd been posted to a mapping office in Voronezh, and would depart on a military train that afternoon. He wished them a safe passage through the winter, said a blessing over their heads, and stuffed their pockets with long-unseen varieties of food—tins of meat and sardines, jars of pickled herring, bags of walnuts, dense rye biscuits. Then, without a word of goodbye, their reticent patron and protector hurried down the road and disappeared behind a veil of snow.

All week the temperature fell and fell, far below zero. Andras's back burned with the work; his hands wept with new blisters. Nothing he had done in the Munkaszolgálat was as hard as clearing that snow, day after day, as the cold deepened. But it was impossible to give up hope when there was always a chance that a letter might arrive from Budapest. Every time they went to clear snow from the roads at the officers' training school, Andras and József looked for Captain Erdő; whenever he had mail for them he found a way to slip it into their pockets. At the beginning of December a letter came from György Hász: The family fortunes had dwindled further still, and György, Elza, and the elder Mrs. Hász had been obliged to abandon the high-ceilinged flat on Andrássy út and move in with Klara. But they must not worry. K was safe. Everyone was fine. They must concern themselves only with their own survival.

Klara's next missive brought the news that Tibor had been called back to the Munkaszolgálat and sent to the Eastern Front. Ilana and Ádám had come to live on Nefelejcs utca along with everyone else. Now the seven of them were getting by on the money that had been intended for the trip to Palestine, which Klara's lawyer forwarded in small increments each month. Andras tried to imagine it: the bright rooms of the apartment filled with all the things the Hász family had brought from Andrássy út, the remaining rugs and armoires and bric-a-brac of their princely estate; Elza Hász, a mourning dove in a morning dress, her wings folded at her sides; Klara and Ilana trying to keep the babies clean and calm and fed in the midst of a crowd; Klara's mother stoic and silent in her corner; the constant smell of potatoes and paprika; the flat blond light of Budapest in winter, falling indifferently through the tall windows. Absent from the letter was any mention of Mátyás, of whom Andras thought constantly as blizzards abraded the hills and fields of Ukraine.

In mid-December a note came from József's mother: György had been admitted to the hospital with a burning pain in his chest and a high fever. The diagnosis was an infection of the pericardium, the membrane that surrounded the heart. His doctor wanted him to be treated with colchicine, pericardiocentesis, and three weeks of rest on a cardiac ward. The cost of this medical disaster, nearly five thousand pengő, threatened to unhouse them all; Klara was trying to arrange to have her lawyer send the money.

József was downcast and silent all day after he'd received the letter. That night at the orphanage he didn't get into bed at the ordinary hour. Instead he stood at the window and stared down into the snowy depths of the courtyard, a coarse blanket wrapped around him like a dressing gown.

Andras rolled over on his bunk and propped himself up on an elbow. "What is it?" he said. "Your father?"

József gave a nod. "He hates to be sick," he said. "Hates to be a burden to anyone. He's miserable if he has to miss a day of work." He pulled the blanket closer and looked down into the courtyard. "Meanwhile I've done nothing at all with my life. Nothing of use to anyone, certainly not my parents. Never had a job. Never even been in love, or been loved by anyone. Not by any of those girls in Paris. No one in Budapest, either. Not even Zsófia, who was pregnant with my child."

"Zsófia's pregnant?" Andras said.

"Not anymore. Last spring. She got rid of it somehow. She didn't want it any more than I did, that was how little she cared for me." He released a long breath. "I can't imagine you'd have any sympathy for me, Andras. But it's a hard thing to have to see oneself clearly all of a sudden. You must understand what I mean."

Andras said he believed he did.

"I know you don't think much of my paintings," József said. "I could see it when you came by last year, the time you and Klara brought the baby to my flat."

"On the contrary, I thought the new work was good. I told Klara as much."

"What if I were to try to contact my art dealer in Budapest?" József said, turning to Andras. "Have him sell something? I never considered the new pieces to be finished, but a collector might think otherwise. I might ask Papp to see what he can get for those nine big pieces."

"You'd sell your unfinished work?"

"I can't imagine what else I can do," József said, turning from the window. For a moment the curve of his forehead and the dark wing of his hair were like Klara's, and Andras experienced an unwelcome jolt of affection for him. He lay back in bed and stared at the dark plane of the ceiling.

"The pieces I saw were good," he told József. "They didn't seem unfinished. They might fetch a high price. But it might not be necessary to sell them. Klara may be able to get the money sent from Vienna."

"And what if she can?" József said. "Do you think they won't need more money for something else next month? What if one of the children gets sick, or my grandmother? What if it's something that can't wait for Klara to contact her lawyer?" The question hovered in the air for a long moment while they both considered that frightening possibility.

"What can I tell you?" Andras said. "I think it's a fine idea. If I had work to sell right now, I'd sell it."

"Give me your pen," József said. "I'll write my mother. Then I'll write to Papp."

Andras felt around in his knapsack for his pen and the last

precious bottle of India ink left over from their set-design supplies. Using the windowsill as a desk and the moonlight as a
lamp, József began to write. But a moment later he spoke again
into the dark.

"I've never given my father a single thing," he said. "Not one
thing."

"He'll know what it means for you to sell those paintings."

"What if he dies before my mother gets this letter?"

"Then at least your mother will know what you meant to do,"
Andras said. "And Klara will know too."

The next morning they woke and cleared snow, and the day
after that they cleared snow, and the following day they encountered Captain Erdő as he was marching his trainees along the
road, and József managed to slip the letters into his hand. Every
day after that they cleared snow, and cleared snow, until, on the
twentieth of December, Major Bálint announced that they were
to pack their things and clean the orphanage from top to bottom; their unit was to move east the following day.

As much as they hated the orphanage, as much as every man had
loathed his too-short bunk and cursed when he had to stoop to
the child-sized sinks in the chill of a winter morning, as much as
they had lived in terrified awareness of the killings that had taken
place on the grounds, the murder of the children that had preceded their arrival, and the execution of Mendel Horovitz and
László Goldfarb, as much as they had yearned to leave those
rooms where they had been starved, beaten, and humiliated,
they felt a strange resistance to the thought of turning the place
over to another company, a group of unknown men. The 79/6th
had become the caretakers of the graves of all their dead, the
mounds marked with stones carried from the roadbed. They had
kept the ground swept, the stones clean; they had placed smaller
stones upon the larger ones in tribute to the men who had been
shot or died of illness or overwork. They had become the care-

takers, too, of the ghosts of the Jewish orphans of Turka; the 79/6th were the only ones who had seen those undersized footprints left behind in the hallways and the courtyard. They had eaten at the children's abandoned tables, memorized the shapes of the Cyrillic letters scratched into the tops of the schoolroom desks, been bitten at night by the same bedbugs that had bitten the children, stubbed their toes on the bed frames where the children had stubbed their toes. Now they would have to abandon them, too, those children who had already been abandoned three times: once by their own parents, once by the state, and finally by life itself. But the men of the 79/6th—those who survived the winter—would say Kaddish for the Jewish orphans of Turka every August for as long as they lived.

They moved east, on foot, in the direction of danger. The land all around looked just as it did in Turka: snow-laden hills, heavy pines, the papery remains of cornstalks stubbling the white fields, stands of cows chuffing cumuli into the freezing air. The towns were nothing more than scatterings of farmhouses in the shadowy folds of the hills. The wind came through the men's overcoats and settled into their bones. They had to quarter in stables with the workhorses or sleep on the floors of the peasants' houses, where they lay open-eyed all night in fear of the peasants, who lay open-eyed all night in fear of them. At times there was no stable or village at all, and they had to bivouac in the freezing cold under the aurora-lit sky. The temperature dropped at night to −20°C. The men always had a fire, but the fire itself was dangerous; it could mesmerize you, it could cause you to stop moving, it could distract you from the difficult work of staying alive. If you fell asleep beside it during the night watch, tricked by its warmth into letting your blanket drop from your shoulders, it might burn itself to ash and leave you exposed to the cold. One morning Andras found the Ivory Tower that way, his arms around his knees, his large head bent forward in what appeared to be sleep. In front of him was the dead black ring where the fire had burned out in the snow, and on his shoulders lay a dusting of ice and frost. Andras put a hand to the Ivory Tower's neck, but the skin was as cold and unyielding as the ground itself. They had to carry his body with them for three days before they came across a patch of earth soft enough to receive him. It was beside a stable, where the horses' warmth had kept the ground from being frozen solid. They buried the Ivory Tower in the middle of the night and scratched his name and the date of his death into the side of the barn. They said the Ninety-first Psalm again. By that time they could all recite it from memory.

The cold was with them day and night. Even inside the stables or the peasants' houses it was impossible to get warm. They stitched clumsy mittens from the linings of their overcoats, but the mittens were thin and leaked cold at the seams. Their feet froze inside their cracked boots. The men tore horse blankets into foot rags and bound their feet like the Ukrainian peasants did. Their diet contained little to keep them warm, though Major Bálint tried to maintain the rations prescribed by General Nagy. Every now and then the peasants took pity on them and gave them something extra: a tablespoon of goose fat for their bread, a marrow bone, a bit of jam. Andras thought of the surveyor and hoped he was eating too—hoped the army was feeding him in Voronezh.

By day they shoveled snow from the roads, often not as fast as it fell. Their backs became hunched with the work, their hands crabbed from gripping the shovels. Along the half-cleared roads came trucks, jeeps, artillery, men, tanks, airplane parts, ammunition. Sometimes a German inspector would come to shout them into their lines and abuse them in his language of guttural consonants and air-starved vowels. News floated in like ash from a fire: The battle crawled onward in Stalingrad, killing tens of thousands every week; a strand of the Hungarian Second Army fought for its life at Voronezh, battered by superior Soviet forces. The men of the 79/6th shoveled their way toward that battle, though it seemed as distant as everything else. Sometimes they shoveled all night while the northern sky shouted a stream of bright curses. The men thought of their wives and girlfriends lying in warm beds in Budapest, their legs bare and smooth, their breasts asleep in the midwinter dark, their hands folded and fragrant like love letters. They repeated the names of those distant women in their minds, the twist of longing never abating, even when the names became abstractions and the men had to wonder whether the women really still existed, if they could be said to exist when their existence was taking place somewhere so far distant, beyond the granite grin of the Carpathians, across the flat cold plains of Hungarian winter. *Klara* was the sound of a shovel hitting frozen snow, the scrape of a blade against frozen ground. Andras told himself that if he could only clear this road, if he could only open the way for the trucks to speed toward the Eastern Front, then the war would flow in that direction and pool there, far away from Hungary and Klara and Tamás.

But in mid-January something went wrong. The traffic, which until that point had largely flowed in the direction of Russia, began to run the other way. At first it was just a trickle: a few truckloads of provisions, a few companies of foot soldiers in jeeps. After a while it became a steady stream of men and vehicles and weaponry. Then, in late January, it became a deluge, and the river of it turned red with blood. There were Red Cross ambulances full of dead and horribly injured men, casualties of the battle that had raged in Stalingrad for five months, since August of 1942. One night the news came that the Hungarian Second Army, along with the thousands of work servicemen who had been attached to it, had suffered a final and brutal defeat at Voronezh. It came just as Andras received his ration of bread with its smear of margarine. As hungry as he was, he gave his ration to József and sat down in a corner of the barn where they were quartered that night. They were sharing the barn with two dozen black-faced sheep whose wool had been allowed to grow long for the winter. The sheep nosed into the stall where Andras had sequestered himself; they lay their dusty bodies down in the hay, made their shuddering cries, snuffled at each other with their black velvet noses. It wasn't just the surveyor, Szolomon, that Andras was thinking of; it was Mátyás, who had at one time been attached to the Hungarian Second Army. If he had lived through the last year's winter, he might have been one of the fifty thousand posted at Voronezh. Andras imagined his parents getting the dreaded news at last, his mother standing in the kitchen of their Debrecen apartment with a telegram in her hand, his father crumpled in his chair like an empty glove. Andras had been a father for only fourteen months, but he knew what it would mean to lose a son. He thought of Tamás, of the familiar whorl of his hair, the speed of his heartbeat, the folded landscape of his body. Then he put his face into his knees and saw Mátyás standing on the rail of a Budapest streetcar, his blue shirt fluttering.

He swallowed the knot of coarse rope that had lodged itself in his throat, and drew an arm across his eyes. He would not mourn, he told himself. Not until he knew.

The river of blood continued, and before long it swept up Andras and József and the rest of the 79/6th and carried them west, back toward Hungary. Fragments of labor-service companies drifted through, men who had reached nightmarish states of emaciation. The 79/6th, whose rations had been steady, carried food each night to forced laborers who were nearly dead, whose commanders had abandoned them, who had no work now but to flee in the direction of home. They received more news of what had happened at Stalingrad—the bombing that had turned every block of the city to rubble, its buildings to a forest of broken brick and concrete; the surrounding of the German Sixth Army at the center of the city, its commander, General Paulus, hidden in a basement while the battle raged around him; the downing of the few Luftwaffe supply flights; then the Soviet Army pounding through to retake control of the Don bend, and to prevent the German Fourth from advancing to rescue the surrounded Sixth. No one knew how many had been killed—two hundred thousand? Five hundred thousand? A million?—or how many were dying still, of cold and starvation and untreated wounds, there at the dead center of winter, on the dark and barren steppes. The Soviets were said to be chasing the remnants of the Hungarian Army back across the plains. In the midst of his own fear, his own flight, Andras felt a fierce satisfaction. The German Sixth had failed to take the oil fields around Grozny; they had failed to take the city that carried Stalin's name. Those defeats might beget others. What had failed might continue to fail. It was a terrible thing to take pleasure in, Andras knew—the fate of Hungarian companies and labor servicemen were tied to the fate of the Wehrmacht, and in any case these were human beings who were dying, whatever their nationality. But Germany had to be defeated. And if it could be defeated while Hungary remained a sovereign state, then the Jews of Hungary might never have to live under Nazi rule.

The confusion of the retreat toward Hungary begat strange convergences, foldings of fate that arose from the mingling of dozens of labor-service companies. Again and again they came across men they knew from the far-off life before the war. One night they quartered with a group of men from Debrecen, among whom were several old schoolmates of Tibor's. Another night they encountered a group from Konyár itself, including the baker's son, the elder brother of Orsolya Korcsolya. A third night, stranded in a March blizzard, Andras found himself sharing a corner of a granary-turned-infirmary with the managing editor of the *Magyar Jewish Journal*, the man who had been Frigyes Eppler's colleague and adversary. The man was scarcely recognizable, so stripped down by cold and hunger as to seem only the wire armature upon which his former self had been built; no one could have imagined that this ravenous thin-armed man, his eyes glittering with fever, had once been a bellicose editor in an Irish tweed jacket.

The managing editor had news of Frigyes Eppler, who had lost his job after the military police had found a file of incriminating documents in his office, a set of papers rumored to have connected him to a black-market operation at Szentendre, of all places. Not long afterward, Eppler had been conscripted into the Munkaszolgálat; no one had heard from him since, or at least not as far as the managing editor knew. He himself had been called up into a different company a few weeks later. Now the managing editor was part of a group of sick and wounded men whose commander had left them in the granary to starve or to succumb to fever. Major Bálint had ordered the 79/6th to tend to the sick men—to bring them food and water and change the dirty makeshift dressings on their wounds. As Andras performed these duties for the managing editor, he learned the fate of another member of their company, a man whose story was so grim that he had earned the nickname of Uncle Job. This man, the editor told him, had once been married to a beautiful woman, a former actress, with whom he'd had a child; it was rumored that he had lived in Paris, where he had run a grand theater at the center of town. Before the war he had been forced to return to Budapest, where, for a brief time, he had taken over the directorship of the Opera. It was in Budapest that his wife had become ill and died. Soon afterward, the man, already suffering from tuberculosis, had been conscripted into the labor service—made an example of, to be certain—and had been placed into service with the labor company that the editor would join sometime later. Last fall they had been sent through the waystation of the Royal Hungarian Field Gendarmerie at Staryy Oskol, where they had been interrogated and beaten and robbed of everything they had brought with them. The Hungarian Field Gendarmerie knew who this great man was, this former luminary of the theater; they stood him up in front of the others and beat him with their rifles, and then they produced a telegram in which it was reported that the man's son had died of measles. The telegram had been sent by the boy's aunt to a relative in Szeged; it had been intercepted in Budapest and forwarded all the way to Staryy Oskol apparently for the express torment of this gentleman. The man begged them to kill him, too, but they left him alone with the rest of the battalion, and the next day they were all sent east again.

"But what happened to him?" Andras asked, his hands on his knees, looking into the hollowed-out eyes of the managing editor. "Did he die at Voronezh?"

"That's the pity of it," the editor said. "He never did die, though he kept trying. He volunteered to clear land mines. Ran into the line of fire every chance he got. Survived it all. Even the consumption couldn't kill him."

"How did you leave him? Where did you last see him?"

"He's there in the corner, where your friend is sitting now."

Andras looked over his shoulder. József had knelt to give water to a man who lay propped on a pile of folded grain sacks; the man turned his head away, and through the veil of illness and emaciation Andras recognized Zoltán Novak.

"I know him," Andras told the editor.

"Of course. Who didn't? He was well known."

"Personally, I mean."

"Go pay your regards, then." He put a hand to Andras's chest and gave him a push in the man's direction, the gesture like a dim ghost of his old energy, his old vehemence.

Andras approached József and the man supported on the grain sacks. He caught József's eye and beckoned him into a corner.

"That's Zoltán Novak," Andras whispered.

József wrinkled his forehead and glanced back toward the man. "Novak?" he said. "Are you certain?"

Andras nodded.

"God help us," József said. "He's nearly dead."

But the man raised his head from the grain sacks and looked at Andras and József.

"I'll be right back," József said.

"Give me water," said Novak, his voice a raw whisper in his throat.

"I'll go to him," Andras said.

"Why?"

"He knows me."

"Somehow I don't think that'll be a comfort," József said.

But Andras went to kneel on the floor beside Novak, who raised himself an inch or two on the folded sacks, his eyes closed, his breath rattling like the stroked edge of a comb.

"Give me water, there," he said again.

Andras raised his canteen and Novak drank. When he was done, he cleared his throat and looked at Andras. A slow heat came to his expression, a faint flushing of the skin around the eyelids. He pushed himself up onto his elbows.

"Lévi," he said, and shook his head. He made three burrs of noise that might have been consternation or laughter. The exertion seemed to have drained him. He lay back again and closed his eyes. It was a long time before he spoke again, and when he did, the words came slowly and with effort. "Lévi," he said. "I must have died, thank God. I've died and gone down to Gehenna. And here you are with me, also dead, I hope."

"No," Andras said. "Still alive and here in Ukraine, both of us."

Novak opened his eyes again. There was a softness in his gaze, a complicated pity that did not exclude himself but was not focused upon himself alone; it seemed to take in all of them, Andras and József and the editor and the other sick and dying men and the laborers who were bringing them water and tending their wounds.

"You see how it stands with me," Novak said. "Maybe it gives you some satisfaction to see me like this."

"Of course not, Novak-úr. Tell me what I can do for you."

"There's only one thing I want," Novak said. "But I can't ask for it without making a murderer of you." He gave a half smile, pausing again to catch his breath. Then he coughed painfully and turned onto his side. "I've wished to die for months. But I'm quite strong, as it turns out. Isn't that a lovely thing? And I'm too much of a coward to take my own life."

"Are you hungry?" Andras asked. "I've got some bread in my knapsack."

"Do you think I want bread?"

Andras glanced away.

"That other man's her nephew, isn't he," Novak said. "He resembles her."

"I'd like to think she's a good deal better looking than that," Andras said.

Novak coughed out a laugh. "You're right, there," he said, and then shook his head. "Andras Lévi. I hoped I wouldn't see you again after that day at the Opera."

"I'll go away if you want."

Novak shook his head again, and Andras waited for him to say something more. But he had exhausted himself with speaking; he fell into a shallow open-mouthed sleep. Andras sat with him as he struggled for breath. Outside, the wind was shrill with the force of the blizzard. Andras put his head on his arm and fell asleep, and when he woke it had grown dark inside the granary. No one had a candle; those who still had flashlights hadn't had batteries for months. The sound and smell of sick men closed in around him like a close-woven veil. Novak was wide awake now and looking intently at him, his breathing more labored than before. Each intake of breath sounded as though he were building a complicated structure from inappropriate materials with broken tools; each exhalation was the defeated collapse of that ugly and imbalanced structure. He spoke again, so quietly that Andras had to lean close to hear.

"It's all right now," he was saying. "Everything's all right."

It was unclear whether he meant to reassure Andras or himself or both of them at once; he seemed almost to be addressing someone who wasn't present, though his eyes were fixed on Andras in the darkness. Soon he went quiet and fell asleep again. Andras stayed beside him all night as he wandered in and out of sleep, and the next day he gave Novak his ration of bread. Novak couldn't eat it dry, but Andras mashed it into crumbs and mixed it with melted snow. They spent three days that way, Novak drifting awake and sleeping, Andras giving him small measures of food and water, until the weather had cleared and the snow had melted enough for the 79/6th to go on again toward the border. When Bálint announced that the men would move out the following morning, Andras's relief was cut with dismay. He begged a moment's conference with the major; they couldn't leave the other men there to die.

"How do you propose to move them, Serviceman?" Bálint asked, his tone stern, though not unkind. "We don't have ambulances. We don't have materials for litters. And we can't possibly stay here."

"We can improvise something, sir."

Bálint shook his shaggy head. "These men are better off inside. The medical corps will be along in a few days. Those who can be moved will be moved then."

"Some of them will be dead by then," Andras said.

"In that case, Lévi, dragging them into the cold and snow won't save them."

"One of those men saved my life when I was a student in Paris. I can't abandon him."

"Listen to me," Bálint said, his large earth-colored eyes steady on Andras's. "I have a son and daughter at home. The others are husbands and fathers, too, many of them. We're young men. We've got to get home alive. That's the principle by which I've commanded this company since we turned back.

We're still a hundred kilometers from the border, five days' walk at least. If we carry sick men with us we'll slow the entire company. We could lose our lives."

"Let me stay, then, sir."

"That's not in my orders."

"Let me."

"No!" Bálint said, angry now. "I'll march you out at gunpoint if I have to."

But in the end there was no need for a show of force. Zoltán Novak, former husband and father, former director of the Théâtre Sarah-Bernhardt and the Budapest Operaház, the man Klara Morgenstern had loved for eleven years and in some measure must have loved still, fell asleep that night and did not wake again.

CHAPTER THIRTY-SEVEN

An Escape

BY THE TIME his train reached Budapest, the forsythia had come into bloom. All else was gray or vaguely yellow-green; a few of the trees along the outer ring road showed the swelling of buds, though the city retained the wet rawness of recent snow-melt. Nineteen forty-three still felt unreal to him. He had lost his sense of time entirely through the last phase of the journey home. But he knew today's date: It was the twenty-fifth of March, seven months and three weeks since he'd been sent to Ukraine. Klara had come to meet his train at Keleti Station. He'd nearly gone faint at the sight of her on the platform with a child standing beside her—standing! His son, Tamás, in a knee-length coat and sturdy little boy's shoes. Tamás, almost a year and a half old now; Tamás who had been a baby in Klara's arms the last time Andras had seen him. Klara's brow showed a narrow pleat of worry, but she was otherwise unchanged; her dark hair was caught in its loose knot at her nape, the beloved planes of her clavicles exposed by the neckline of her gray dress. She made no attempt to hide her dismay at Andras's physical state. She put a hand over her mouth, and her eyes filled. He knew what he looked like, knew he looked like a man who'd been threshed almost free of his body. His head had been shaved for delousing; his clothes, or what was left of them, hung loosely on his frame. His hands were crabbed and bent, his cheek scarred with three white rays where the glass from a shot-out barn window had cut him. When Klara took him into her arms he felt how careful she was with him, as though she might hurt him with an embrace. József was not there to witness their reunion; he was still in Debrecen, recovering at a military hospital. His knee had been wounded during the border crossing, and he was receiving treatment for an infection of the soft tissues. He would return in another week or two. From a post office near the hospital, Andras had been able to wire Klara the news of his own return.

Darling. Darling. They would have stood there saying it to each other all night, looking at each other and kissing each other's hands, touching each other's faces, had not Tamás made his protest and begged to be picked up. Andras held him and looked into the round face with its inquisitive eyebrows and its large expressive eyes.

"Apa," Klara instructed the boy, and pointed to Andras's chest. But Tamás turned and put his arms out to Klara, afraid of this unfamiliar man.

Andras bent to his knapsack and opened the flap. Inside he found the red India-rubber ball he'd bought for three fillér from a street vendor in Debrecen. The ball had a white star at each of its poles and was bisected by a band of green paint. Tamás put out his hands for it. But Andras tossed it high into the air and caught it on his back, between his shoulder blades. He'd learned the trick from one of his schoolmates in Konyár. Now he plucked the ball from his back and bowed to Tamás, who opened his mouth and crowed with laughter.

"More," Tamás said.

It was the first word Andras had heard him speak. The trick proved equally funny a second and third time. At last Andras gave Tamás the ball, and he held it raptly as Klara carried him through the Erzsébetváros toward home. Andras walked beside them with his hand at Klara's waist. No longer with him was the feeling he'd had when he'd returned home from the Munkaszolgálat before: that the continuation of ordinary life in Budapest was impossible after what he'd come from, that his mental and physical torment must necessarily have changed the rest of the world. There was a certain numbness where he had once experienced incredulity. It almost frightened him, that stillness. It was inarguable evidence of his having grown older.

As they walked, Klara told him the news of the family:

how the money from the sale of József's paintings had allowed György to regain his health in the hospital; how Klara's mother, who'd had pneumonia over the winter, was now hale enough to go to the market every morning for the day's vegetables and bread; how Ilana had mastered Hungarian and had proved to be a genius at economizing on their rations; how Elza Hász, who before that past December had never even known how to boil an egg, had learned to make potato paprikás and chicken soup. There had even been news from Elisabet: She'd had another child, a girl. She was still living on the family estate in Connecticut while Paul served in the navy, but they planned to move to a larger apartment in New York when he returned. Of the possibility of emigrating to the States there had been no word. Other possibilities of escape had evaporated. Klein, Klara revealed in a whisper as they paused at a street corner, had been arrested for arranging illegal emigrations. He'd been in jail since the previous November, awaiting trial. She had gone a few times to visit his grandparents, who demonstrated no sign of need. They persisted with their little flock of goats in the ancient cottage in Frangepán köz; perhaps the authorities considered them too old to be worth pursuing. The names of Klein's clients—former, current, and would-be emigrants—were concealed in his labyrinth of codes, but there was no telling how long it might be before the police found their way through the maze.

"And your parents?" she asked. "Are they well?"

"They're fine," Andras said. "Still sick with worry about Mátyás, though. They haven't had a word of news. They weren't pleased to see me looking like this, either. I didn't tell them the half of what happened."

"Tibor's anxious to see you," she said. "Ilana had to resort to threats to keep him from coming to the station. But his doctor says he's got to rest."

"How is he? How does he look?"

Klara sighed. "Thin and exhausted. Quiet. Sometimes he

seems to see terrible things in the air between himself and us. Every minute since he's been back he's had Ádám in his arms. The boy is so attached to him now, Ilana can hardly feed him."

"And you?" He put a hand to her hair, her cheek. "Klárika."

She raised her chin to him and kissed him, there on the street with their child in her arms.

"Your letters," she said. "If I hadn't had them, I don't know."

"They can't always have been a comfort."

Tears came to her eyes again. "I wanted to think I'd misunderstood about Mendel. I read and reread that letter, hoping I was wrong. But it's true, isn't it."

"Yes, darling, it's true."

"Sometime soon you'll tell me everything," she said, and took his hand.

They walked on together until they reached the door of the apartment building. He looked up toward the window he knew to belong to their bedroom; she'd installed a window box full of early crocuses.

"There's one more piece of news," she said, so gravely that at first he was certain it was news of a death. "There's someone else staying with us now. Someone who traveled a long way to get here."

"*Who?*"

"Come upstairs," she said. "You'll see."

He followed her into the courtyard, his heartbeat quickening. He wasn't certain he could face a surprise guest. He wanted to sit down on the edge of the fountain at the center of the courtyard, stay there and gather himself for a few days. As they climbed the open stairway he could see the flicker of goldfish in the fountain's green depths.

They were at the door, and the door opened. There was Tibor, drawn and pale, his eyes full of tears behind his silver-framed glasses. He put his arms around his brother and they held each other in the hallway. Andras inhaled Tibor's faint smell of soap and sebum and clean cotton, not wanting to move or speak. But Tibor led him into the sitting room, where the family was waiting. There was his nephew, Ádám, standing beside his mother; Ilana, her hair covered beneath an embroidered kerchief; György Hász, grayer and older; Elza Hász austere in a cotton work dress; Klara's mother, smaller than ever, her eyes deep and bright. And beyond them, rising from the couch, a pale oval-faced man in a dark jersey that had belonged to Andras, a crumpled handkerchief in his hand.

Andras experienced a tilt of vertigo. He put a hand on the back of the sofa as the feeling passed through him like a pressure wave.

Eli Polaner.

"Not possible," Andras said. He looked from Klara to his brother to Ilana, and then again at Polaner himself. "Is it true?" he asked in French.

"True," Polaner said, in his familiar and long-lost voice.

It was a nightmare version of a fairy tale, a story grim enough to teach Andras new horrors after what he'd seen in Ukraine. He wished almost that he'd never had to know what had happened to Polaner at the concentration camp in Compiègne where he'd been sent after his removal from the Foreign Legion in 1940— how he'd been beaten and starved and deported half dead to Buchenwald, where he'd spent two years in forced labor and sexual slavery, his arm tattooed with his number, his chest bearing an inverted pink triangle superimposed over an upright yellow one. Polaner's homosexuality had remained a secret until one of his workmates had given up a list of names in exchange for a position as a kapo; afterward, Polaner had found himself at the lowest level of the camp hierarchy, marked with a symbol that made him a target for the guards and kept the other prisoners from getting too close to him. He'd been assigned to the stone quarry, where he hauled bags of crushed rock for fourteen hours a day. When his shift at the quarry was finished, he had to clean

the latrines of his barracks block—a reminder, the block sergeant told him, that at this camp he was lower than shit, a servant to shit. Sometimes, late at night, he and a few of the others
would be led to a back door of the officers' quarters, where they
would be tied and raped, first by one of the officers and then by
his secretaries and his orderly.

One night they had been presented as a secret gift to a
visiting dignitary from the SS Economic-Administrative Main
Office, a high-ranking concentration-camp inspector who was
known to enjoy the company of young men. But the exalted official's preferences were not what had been assumed; he was a
lover of young men, not a rapist. He had the prisoners untied
and washed and shaved and dressed in civilian clothes. What he
wanted was to engage them in conversation, as though they were
all at a party. He had them sit on sofas in his private quarters and
share delicacies with him—tea and cakes, when what they'd lived
on for the past three years was thin soup and beweeviled bread.
The inspector was charmed by Polaner's French and his knowledge of contemporary art and architecture. It turned out that the
man had known the late vom Rath, to whom he had been a kind
of political mentor. By the end of the evening he had decided to
have Polaner transferred to his personal service at once. He
brought Polaner to his private apartments at another camp a
hundred kilometers away, and registered him as a kind of under-
servant, a hauler of coal and blacker of boots; in actuality
Polaner was treated as a patient, kept in bed and nursed by the
camp inspector's domestic staff.

At the end of two months, when Polaner had recovered his
health, the inspector performed a kind of alchemy of identity:
He had false records drawn up to show that Eli Polaner, the
young Jewish man who had been transferred to his service, had
contracted meningitis and died; then he procured for Polaner a
set of forged papers declaring him to be a young Nazi Party
member by the name of Teobald Kreizel, a junior secretary
with the Economic-Administrative Main Office. With Polaner

dressed as a member of the inspector's staff they traveled to Berlin, where the inspector installed Polaner in a small bright flat on the Behrenstrasse. He left Polaner with fifty thousand reichsmarks in cash and a promise that he would return as soon as possible, bringing with him books and magazines and drawing supplies, phonograph records, black-market delicacies, whatever Polaner might want. Polaner asked only for news of his family; he hadn't heard from his parents or his sisters since he'd entered the Foreign Legion.

The high-ranking inspector returned as often as he could, bringing the promised drawing supplies and records and delicacies, but he was slow to produce news of Polaner's family. Polaner waited, rarely venturing out of the apartment, thinking of little else but the fact that he might soon learn his parents' and sisters' fate. He nursed a hope that they might have found a way to emigrate, that against the odds they'd gotten themselves to some benign and distant place, Argentina or Australia or America; or, failing that, that the inspector might be able to lift them out of whatever hell they'd fallen into, might reunite them all in a neutral city where they would be safe. It wasn't an entirely baseless hope; the inspector had often used his position to arrange favors for his lovers and protégés. In fact, during the six months Polaner lived on the Behrenstrasse, those past favors took their toll: a series of irregularities came to the attention of the inspector's superiors, and the inspector fell under investigation. Fearing for his position and for Polaner's life, the inspector concluded that Polaner must leave the country at once. He promised to get Polaner a visa that would allow him to travel anywhere within the area of the Reich's influence. But what was Polaner supposed to do? Where was he supposed to go? News of his parents had failed to arrive; how was he to choose a destination?

Later that same week, the first week of January 1943, the inspector's inquiries about Polaner's family yielded answers at last. Polaner's parents and sisters had died in a labor camp at

Płaszow—his mother and father in February of 1941, and his sisters eight and ten months later. The Nazis had appropriated his family home and the textile factory in Kraków. There was nothing left.

The night he received the news, Polaner had removed the gun from his bedside table—the inspector insisted he keep a pistol for protection—and had gone out onto the balcony and stood there in his nightclothes, in a cataract of freezing wind. He put the gun to his temple and leaned over the balcony railing. The snow below him was like an eiderdown, he told Andras— soft-looking, hillocked, blue-white; he imagined falling into that clean blankness and disappearing beneath a layer of new snow. The gun in his hand was an SS officer's Walther P-38, a double-action pistol with a round in the chamber. He cocked the hammer and put a finger against the curve of the trigger, envisioned the bullet shattering the ingenious architecture of his skull. He would count to three and do it: *eins, tsvey, dray*. But as the Yiddish numbers sounded in his mind, he experienced a moment of clarity: If he killed himself with this gun, this Walther P-38—if he did this because the Nazis had killed his parents and sisters— then *they*, the Nazis, would be the ones who had killed him, the ones who had silenced the Yiddish inside his head. They would have succeeded at killing his entire family. He removed his finger from the trigger, reset the safety, and slid the round out of the chamber. It was the bullet, and not Polaner himself, that fell three stories to that eiderdown of snow.

The next morning he fixed upon Budapest as his destination, in the hope of finding Andras there. The high-ranking inspector provided Polaner with the letters and documents necessary to obtain legal residency in Hungary; he even got him a doctor's certificate declaring Polaner unfit for military service due to a chronic weakness of the lungs. He gave Polaner twenty thousand reichsmarks and put him into a private compartment on a train. When Polaner arrived, he made his way to the grand synagogue on Dohány utca, where he found an ancient secretary who spoke Yiddish; he communicated that he was looking for Andras Lévi, and the secretary had directed him to the Budapest Izraelita Hitközség, which provided him with Andras's address on Nefelejcs utca. Klara had taken him in, and here he'd remained ever since. Just a week ago he'd received his official Hungarian papers, which he produced now from a brown portfolio as if to prove to Andras it was all true. Andras unfolded Polaner's passport. *Teobald Kreizel. Permanent resident.* The photograph showed a thin hollow-eyed Polaner, even paler and more horror-stricken than the young man who sat across the kitchen table from Andras now. This passport was as crisp and clean as Andras's had been when he'd left for Paris; it lacked only the telltale *Zs* for *Zsidó.* The brown portfolio also contained a party identity card stamped with the ghost of a swastika, declaring Teobald Kreizel to be a member of the National Socialist Party of Germany.

"These papers will serve you well," Andras said. "Your German friend knew what he was doing."

Polaner shifted in his seat. "It's a shameful thing, a Jew posing as a Nazi."

"My God, Polaner! No one would begrudge you that protection. It'll keep you out of the Munkaszolgálat, at the very least, and I know what that's worth."

"But you've had to serve for years. And if the war goes on, you'll serve again."

"You did your time," Andras said. "Yours was far worse than mine."

"Impossible to weigh them," Polaner said.

But there were times when it was possible to weigh suffering, Andras knew. He, Andras, hadn't been raped. He hadn't lost his country or his family. Klara was asleep in the bedroom, their son beside her. Tibor and Ilana lay in each other's arms on a mattress on the sitting-room floor. Their parents were well in Debrecen. Mátyás might be alive still, somewhere beyond the borders of Hungary. But Polaner had lost everything, everyone. Andras

thought of the Rosh Hashanah dinner they'd eaten together at
the student dining club five and a half years earlier—how Andras
had marveled that Polaner's mother had let him return to school
after the attack, and what Polaner had said in reply: *She's never
glad to see me go. She's my mother.* That woman who had loved her
son was gone. Her husband was gone, and their daughters were
gone. And the young Andras Lévi and Eli Polaner—those boys
who had spent two years in Paris arguing about a war that might
or might not come, drinking tea at the Blue Dove, making plans
for a sports club at the center of the Quartier Latin—they, too,
were gone, grown into these scarred and scraped-out men. And
he lowered his head onto Polaner's sleeve and mourned for what
could never be returned.

All that spring they waited for news of Mátyás. When they celebrated Passover, Andras's mother insisted upon setting a place
for him; when they opened the door to welcome Elijah, they
were calling him home too. In the time since Andras had been
sent to Ukraine, his mother and father seemed to have grown
old. His father's hair had gone from gray to white. His mother's
back had acquired a curve. She curled into the tent of her cardi-
gan like a dry grass stem. Even the sight of Tamás and Ádám
failed to cheer her; it wasn't her grandchildren she longed for,
but her lost boy.

Polaner, who knew what it meant to wait for news, kept his
own mourning private. He never spoke of his parents or his sisters, as though a mention of his loss might bring on the tragedy
that Andras's family dreaded. He insisted upon going alone to
the Dohány Synagogue every afternoon to recite Kaddish. Tradition required him to do it for a year. But as the news continued
to drift in from Poland, it began to seem as though no one could
be exempt from mourning, as though no period of mourning
would ever be long enough. In April, the Jews of the Warsaw
ghetto had mounted an armed stand against the deportation of

the ghetto's last sixty thousand residents; no one had expected it to last more than a few days, but the ghetto fighters held out for four weeks. The *Pesti Napló* printed photographs of women throwing Molotov cocktails at German tanks, of Waffen-SS troops and Polish policemen setting buildings afire. The battle lasted until the middle of May, and ended, as everyone had known it would, with the clearing of the ghetto: a massacre of the Jewish fighters, and the deportation of those who had survived. The next day, the *Pesti Napló* reported that one and a half million Polish Jews had been killed in the war, according to the exiled Polish government's estimate. Andras, who had translated every article and radio program about the uprising for Polaner, couldn't bring himself to translate that number, to deliver that staggering statistic to a friend already in mourning. One and a half million Jewish men and women and children: How was anyone to understand a number like that? Andras knew it took three thousand to fill the seats of the Dohány Street Synagogue. To accommodate a million and a half, one would have had to replicate that building, its arches and domes, its Moorish interior, its balcony, its dark wooden pews and gilded ark, *five hundred times*. And then to envision each of those five hundred synagogues filled to capacity, to envision each man and woman and child inside as a unique and irreplaceable human being, the way he imagined Mendel Horovitz or the Ivory Tower or his brother Mátyás, each of them with desires and fears, a mother and a father, a birthplace, a bed, a first love, a web of memories, a cache of secrets, a skin, a heart, an infinitely complicated brain— to imagine them that way, and then to imagine them dead, extinguished for all time—how could anyone begin to grasp it? The idea could drive a person mad. He, Andras, was still alive, and people were dependent upon him; he couldn't afford to lose his mind, and so he forced himself not to think about it.

Instead he buried himself in the work that had to be done every day. The single apartment, which had been full even when the men were away in the Munkaszolgálat, proved unlivable now that they were home. Tibor and Ilana took a flat across the street, and József moved with his parents into another small flat in the building next door. Polaner remained with Andras and Klara, sharing a room with Tamás. For all those living spaces, rent had to be paid. Andras went back to work as a newspaper illustrator and layout artist, not at the *Magyar Jewish Journal* but at the *Evening Courier*, Mendel's former employer, where a new round of military conscriptions had decimated the ranks of graphic artists. He persuaded his editor to hire Polaner as well, arguing that Polaner had always been the true talent behind their collaborations in architecture school. Tibor, for his part, found a position as a surgical assistant in a military hospital, where the wounded of Voronezh were still being treated. József, who had never before had to earn a living, placed an ad in the *Evening Courier* and became a house painter, paid handsomely for his work. And Klara taught private students in the studio on Király utca. Few parents now could afford the full fee, but she allowed them to pay whatever they could.

In July, as Eisenhower's armies bombed Rome, Budapest stood on the banks of the Danube in an excess of summer beauty, its palaces and grand old hotels still radiating an air of permanence. The Soviet bombardments of the previous September hadn't touched those scrolled and gilded buildings; Allied raids had failed to materialize that spring, and the Red Army's planes hadn't returned. Now the clenched fists of dahlias opened in the Városliget, where Andras walked with Tibor and József and Polaner on Sunday afternoons, speculating about how much longer it might be before Germany capitulated and the war ended at last. Mussolini had fallen, and fascism had crumbled in Italy. On the Eastern Front, Germany's problems had multiplied and deepened: The Wehrmacht's assault on a Soviet stronghold near Kursk had ended in a disastrous rout, and defeats at Orel and Kharkov had followed soon after. Even Tibor, who a year earlier had cautioned against wishful thinking, voiced the hope that the war might be over before he or Andras or József could be called to the Munkaszolgálat again, and that the Hungarian prisoners of war might begin to return.

The Jews of Hungary had been lucky, Andras knew. Thousands of men had died in the Munkaszolgálat, but not a million and a half. The rest of the Jewish population had survived the war intact. Though tens of thousands had lost their jobs and nearly all were struggling to make a living, it was still legal at least for a Jew to operate a business, own an apartment, go to synagogue to say the prayer for the dead. For more than a year and a half, Prime Minister Kállay had managed to stave off Hitler's demands for more stringent measures against Hungary's Jews; what was more, his administration had begun to pursue justice for the crimes perpetrated earlier in the war. He had called for an investigation into the Délvidék massacres, and had vowed to punish the guilty parties as severely as they deserved. And General Vilmos Nagybaczoni Nagy, before he'd given up his control of the Ministry of Defense, had called for the indictment of the officers at the heart of the military black market.

But Andras had been schooled in skepticism not only by Tibor but by the events of the past year; despite the hopeful news, he found it impossible to shake his sense of dread. More events accrued to reinforce it. As he followed the black-market trial in the newspaper that fall, it became increasingly clear that the accused officers, if they were convicted, would carry only nominal sentences. And Hitler, whose Wehrmacht had looked so vulnerable during the summer months, had halted the Allied attack south of Rome and secured Germany's southern borders. In Russia he continued to throw his troops at the Red Army, as though total defeat were impossible.

Then there was the absence of news about Mátyás, who had been missing now for twenty-two months. How could anyone continue to believe he had survived? But Tibor persisted in believing it, and his mother believed it, and though his father wouldn't speak of it, Andras knew he believed it; as long as any of them did, none of them could claim even the bare comfort of grief.

The year's final act of aborted justice concerned the Hász family and the extortion that had drained its fortunes almost to nothing. Once György's monthly payments had dwindled to a few hundred forint, the extortionists decided that the rewards of the arrangement were no longer worth the risk. The Kállay administration seemed intent upon exposing corruption at all levels and in all branches of the government; seventeen members of the Ministry of Justice had already been indicted for financial improprieties, and György's extortionists feared they would be next. On the twenty-fifth of October they called György to a midnight meeting in the basement of the Ministry of Justice. That night, Andras and Klara kept a vigil with Klara's mother and Elza and József in the small dark front room of the Hász apartment. József chain-smoked a pack of Mirjam cigarettes; Elza sat with a basket of mending beside her, needling her way through the unfamiliar ravages of poverty upon clothing. The elder Mrs. Hász read aloud from Radnóti, the young Jewish poet Tibor admired, and whose fate in the Munkaszolgálat was unknown. Klara, her hands pinned between her knees, sat beside Andras as if in judgment herself. If her brother came to harm, Andras knew she would hold herself responsible.

At a quarter to three in the morning a key sounded in the lock. Here was György, soot-stained and breathless but otherwise unharmed. He removed his jacket and draped it over the back of the sofa, smoothed his pale gold tie, ran a hand through his silver-shot hair. He sat down in an empty chair and drained the glass of plum brandy his wife offered him. Then he set the empty glass on the low table before him and fixed his eyes on Klara, who sat close at his side.

"It's over," he said, covering her hand with his own. "You may exhale."

"What's over?" their mother asked. "What's happened?"

There had been a great immolation of documents, he told them. The extortionists had taken György to his office and made him gather all evidence of the ministry's illegal relationship with the Hász family—every letter, every telegram and payment record, every bill of sale and bank-deposit receipt—and had forced him to throw the lot into the building's incinerator, making it impossible for the Hász family ever to mount a case against the Ministry of Justice. In return, the ministry officials produced a new set of papers for Klara, restoring the citzenship she'd lost as a young girl. Then they took the file containing all the documents pertaining to Klara's alleged crime—the photographs of the murder scene and victims, the rapist's sworn testimony revealing Klara's identity, the depositions linking Klara to the Zionist organization Gesher Zahav, the police reports documenting Klara's disappearance, and Edith Novak's statement concerning Klara's return to Hungary—and fed it, too, to the building's central incinerator.

"You saw them burn those things?" Klara said. "The dossier, the photographs—everything?"

"Everything," György said.

"How do you know they didn't keep copies?" József said. "How do you know they don't have other documents?"

"It's possible, I suppose, but not likely. We must remember that any evidence they might retain would be evidence against *them*. That's why they were so eager to destroy those papers."

"But the evidence has always implicated them!" József said, rising from his chair. "That's never bothered them before."

"These men were frightened," Hász said. "They did a poor job of hiding it. The administration isn't on their side. They've seen seventeen of their colleagues fired, and a few imprisoned or sent to the labor service, for less than what they've done to us."

"And you destroyed everything?" József said. "Truly everything? You didn't keep a single copy? Nothing that would give us recourse later?"

György gave his son a hard and steady look. "They held a gun to my head as I emptied the files," he said. "I would like to say I had duplicates elsewhere, but it was risky enough to keep what I had. Anyway, it's finished now. They can't open Klara's case again. I saw the documents burn."

József stood over his father's chair, his hands clenched. He seemed ready to grab his father by the shoulders and shake him. His eyes flickered toward his grandmother, his mother; then his gaze fell upon Andras and rested there. Between them lay a history so terrible as to throw the moment's frustration into a different light; to look at each other was to be reminded what it meant to escape with one's life. József sat down again and spoke to his father.

"Thank God it's over," he said. "Thank God they didn't kill you."

In their bedroom that night, Andras held Klara as they lay awake in the dark. How many times over the past four years had he imagined her arrested and beaten and jailed, placed far beyond his reach? He could scarcely believe that the ever-present threat was gone. Klara herself was silent and dry-eyed beside him; he knew how keenly she felt the price of her own liberation. Her return to Hungary, a risk she had undertaken for his sake, had ruined her family. She was free now, but her freedom would never extend far enough to allow her to demand legal justice or the repayment of her family's losses. Her silence wasn't directed at him, he understood, but it lay between them nonetheless. Had he ever been close to her in the way married people were supposed to be close? he wondered. Of their forty-eight months married, he had spent only twelve at home. To survive their separation they'd had to place each other at a certain remove. Every time he'd been home, including this one, there had been the fear that he would be called up again; as much as they tried to ignore it, the fact was always there. And veiling all their intimacy, shadowing it like a pair of dark wings, was what they knew was happening in Europe, and what they feared would happen to them.

But here they were together, in their shared bed, out of the grasp of danger for the moment. They lived, and he loved her. It was folly in the French sense—madness—to keep her at a remove. It was the last thing he wanted. He touched her bare shoulder, her face, pushed a lock of hair away from her brow, and she moved closer against him. Mindful of Polaner sleeping on the other side of the wall—of his losses, and his loneliness—they made love in clenched and straining silence. Afterward they lay together, his hand on her belly, his fingers moving along the familiar scars of her pregnancies. They hadn't taken precautions against her becoming pregnant again, though neither wanted to imagine what it might mean if she were carrying a child when the Soviets crossed the Hungarian border. As they drifted toward sleep he described in a whisper the little house he would build beside the Danube when the war was over. It was the place he had envisioned when he'd been to Angyalföld the first time, a whitewashed brick house with a tile roof, a garden large enough for a pair of milking goats, an outdoor bread oven, a shaded patio, a pergola laced with grapevines. Klara slept at last, but Andras lay awake beside her, far from comfort. Once again, he thought, he had drawn a plan for an imaginary house, one in a long line of imaginary houses he had built since they'd been together; in his mind he could page through a deep stack of them, those ghostly blueprints of a life they had not yet lived and might never live.

On Saturday afternoons, when the weather was fine, Andras and Klara made a point of walking alone on Margaret Island for an hour or two while Polaner played with Tamás in the park. It was during those walks that they spoke of the things Andras could not write about in his brief and censored letters from Ukraine: the reasons for their deportation, and the role that *The Crooked Rail* may have played; the circumstances surrounding Mendel's death; the long struggle with József afterward; and the strange conjunctions of the journey home. On the first subject, Andras's greatest fear was that Klara herself might hold him responsible for what had happened, might blame him for keeping the family from attempting its escape. She had warned him; he hadn't forgotten it for a moment. But she was at pains to reassure him that no one held him responsible for what had happened. Such an idea, she said, was a symptom of the loss of perspective caused by the Munkaszolgálat and the war. The journey to Palestine might easily have ended in disaster. His deportation may have saved them all. Now that he had returned, she was at liberty to be grateful that they'd been spared the uncertainties of the trip. To the second subject she reacted with grief and dismay, and Andras was reminded that she, too, had been present at the death of her closest friend and ally; she, too, had been witness to the senseless killing of a man she had loved since childhood. And on the third subject, she could say only that she understood what it must have required for Andras to keep from doing some great violence to József. But the time in Ukraine, and with Andras, had changed József in some deep-rooted way, she thought; he seemed a different man since his return, or perhaps he seemed finally to have become a man.

For reasons Andras found difficult to articulate, the most difficult subject was that of Zoltán Novak's death. Months of Saturday walks passed before he could tell Klara that he had been with Novak on the last days of his life, and that he had buried Novak himself. She had read of Novak's death in the newspapers and had mourned his loss before Andras's return, but she wept afresh at that news. She asked Andras to tell her everything that had happened: how he had discovered Novak, what they had said to each other, how Novak had died. When he had finished, putting matters as gently as possible and omitting many painful details, Klara offered an admission of her own: She and Novak had exchanged nearly a dozen letters during his long months of service.

They had paused in their walk at the ruin of a Franciscan church halfway up the eastern side of the island: stones that looked as though they had risen from the earth, a rose window empty of glass, Gothic windows missing their topmost points. It was December, but the day was unseasonably mild; in the shadow of the ruin stood a bench where a husband and wife might make confession, even if they were Jewish. Even if no confessor was present except each other.

"How did he write to you?" Andras asked.

"He sent letters with officers who came and went on leave."

"And you wrote back."

She folded her wet handkerchief and looked toward the empty rose window. "He was alone and bereaved. He didn't have anyone. Even his little son had died by then."

"Your letters must have been a comfort," Andras said with some effort, and followed her gaze toward the ruin. In one of the lobes of the rose window a bird had built its nest; the nest was long abandoned now, its dry grass streamers fluttering in the wind.

"I tried not to give him false hope," Klara said. "He knew the limitations of my feelings for him."

Andras had to believe her. The man he had seen in the granary in Ukraine could not have been operating under the illusion that someone was nursing a secret love for him. He was a man who had been forsaken by everything that had mattered, a man who had lived to see the ruin of all he had done on earth. "I don't begrudge him your letters," Andras said. "I can't blame you for anything you might have written to him. He was always good to you. He was good to both of us."

Klara put a hand on Andras's knee. "He never regretted what he did for you," she said. "He told me he'd spoken to you at the

Operaház. He said you were much kinder than you might have been. He said, in fact, that if I had to marry anyone, he was glad it was you."

Andras covered her hand with his own and looked up again at the bird's nest shivering in the rose window. He had seen architectural drawings of this church in its unruined state, its Gothic lines graceful but unremarkable, indistinguishable from those of thousands of other Gothic chapels. As a ruin it had taken on something of the extraordinary. The perfect masonry of the far wall had been laid bare; the near wall had weathered into a jagged staircase, the edges of the stones worn to velvet. The rose window was more elegant for its lack of glass, the bones of its corolla scoured by wind and bleached white in the sun. The nest with its streamers was a final unbidden touch: It was what human hands had not brought to the building, and could not remove. It was like love, he thought, this crumbling chapel: It had been complicated, and thereby perfected, by what time had done to it.

His most melancholy times that year were those he spent alone with Tibor. Wherever they walked, whatever they did—whether they were occupying their usual table at the Artists' Café, or strolling the paths of the Városliget, or standing at the railing of the Széchenyi Bridge and looking down into the twisting water—when he was with Tibor, Andras understood acutely that they were at the mercy of events beyond their control. The Danube, which had once seemed a magic conduit along which they might slip out of Hungary, had become an ordinary river once more; Klein was in jail, their visas expired, the *Trasnet* no more than the memory of a name. Before, Tibor's will had seemed to Andras an inexorable force. He had always had a preternatural talent for making the impossible come to pass. But their escape had not come to pass, and now they had no secret plan of action to balance against their fears. Tibor himself had undergone a change; he had been in the Munkaszolgálat for three years now, and like Andras he had been forced to learn its difficult lessons. He had carried a great weight since his return from the Eastern Front, it seemed to Andras—the weight of dozens of human bodies, the living and the dead, every sick or wounded man he'd cared for in the labor service and in the hospital where he'd been working in Budapest. "We couldn't save him," his stories often ended. He told Andras in detail about bleeding that couldn't be stopped, dysentery that turned men inside out, pneumonia that broke ribs and asphyxiated its victims.

And the bodies continued to accumulate, even in Budapest, far from the front lines of the war. One evening Tibor appeared at the offices of the *Courier* and asked if Andras might want to knock off a bit early; a young man whom Tibor had tended had died a few hours earlier on the operating table, and Tibor needed a drink. Andras took his brother to a bar they had always liked, a narrow amber-lit place called the Trolley Bell. There, over glasses of Aquincum beer, Tibor told Andras the story: The boy had been wounded months earlier in the battle of Voronezh, had taken shrapnel in both lungs and hadn't been able to breathe properly since. A risky operation to remove the fragments had severed the pulmonary artery, and the boy had died on the table. Tibor had been present in the waiting room when the doctor, a talented and well-respected surgeon named Keresztes, had delivered the news to the boy's parents. Tibor had expected cries, protests, a collapse, but the young man's mother had risen from her chair and calmly explained that her son could not be dead. She showed Keresztes the jersey she had just finished knitting for the boy. It was composed of wool that had been immersed in a well in Szentgotthárd where the Blessed Virgin's face had appeared three times. She had just tied off the last stitch when the surgeon came in. She must be allowed to lay the jersey over her son; he was not dead, only in a state of deep sleep under the Virgin's watch. When Keresztes began to explain the circumstances of the boy's death, and the impossibility of his recovery, the young man's father had threatened to slit the surgeon's throat with his own scalpel if the mother were not allowed to do what she wished. The surgeon, weary from the long procedure, had escorted the parents to their son's bedside in a room near the operating theater and had left Tibor to oversee their visit with the dead boy. The mother had laid the jersey over the matrix of bandages on the boy's chest, and had commenced to pray the Rosary. But the Virgin's blessing failed to revive her son. The boy lay inert, and by the time she had reached the end of her line of beads she seemed to comprehend the situation. Her boy was gone, had died in Budapest after having survived the battle of Voronezh; nothing would bring him back now. When a nurse had come in to remove the body so the room might be used for another patient, Tibor had asked her to let the parents stay there with the boy as long as they wished. The nurse had insisted the room be cleared; the new patient would be out of surgery in a quarter of an hour. The boy's parents, understanding that they had no choice, shuffled toward the door. On the threshold, the mother had pressed the jersey into Tibor's hands. He must take it, she said, as it could no longer be of any use to her son.

Tibor opened his leather satchel now and took out the jersey, gray yarn knitted in close regular stitches. He laid it on his knees and smoothed the wool. "Do you know what the worst of it was?" he said. "When Keresztes left the room, he rolled his eyes at me. *What fools, these fanatics.* I know the mother saw him." He rested his chin on his hand, regarding Andras with an expression so laced with pain as to make Andras's throat constrict. "The worst of it was, all my sympathies lay with Keresztes at that moment. I should have wanted to beat him to a pulp for rolling his eyes at a time like that, but all I could think was, *My God, how long is this going to take? How soon can we get these people out of here?*"

Andras could only nod in understanding. He knew Tibor didn't need reassurance that he was a good man, that under different circumstances his sympathies would have lain with the parents instead of with the exhausted surgeon; he and his brother had perfect comprehension of each other's minds and inward lives. Simply to have heard the story was enough. A long silence settled between them as they drank their beer. Then, finally, Tibor spoke again.

"I had a piece of good news on my way out of the hospital," he said. "One of the nurses caught it on the radio. The generals from the Délvidék massacres, Feketehalmy-Czeydner and the others, are going to jail this Monday. Feketehalmy-Czeydner's in for fifteen years, I understand, and the others nearly as many. Let's hope they rot there."

Andras didn't have the heart to tell his brother the rest of that story, which he'd heard just before Tibor had arrived at the newsroom: Feketehalmy-Czeydner and the three other officers convicted in the Délvidék case, facing the start of their long prison sentences, had fled that very day to Vienna, where they'd been seen dining at a famous beer hall in the company of six Gestapo officers. The *Evening Courier*'s Viennese correspondent had been close enough to observe that the men had been eating veal sausage with peppers and toasting the health of the Supreme Commander of the Third Reich. The Führer himself, it was rumored, had extended the officers a guarantee of political asylum. But Tibor would read about it soon enough in the papers. For now, Andras thought, let him have a moment of peace, if that was the word for it.

"To rotting in jail," he said, and raised his glass.

CHAPTER THIRTY-EIGHT

Occupation

In March of 1944, not long after Klara had discovered she was pregnant again, the papers would report that Horthy had been called to Schloss Klessheim for a conference with Hitler. With him went the new minister of defense, Lajos Csatay, who had replaced Vilmos Nagy; and Ferenc Szombathelyi, chief of the General Staff. Prime Minister Kállay proclaimed to the newspapers that the Magyar nation had reason to be hopeful: What Hitler wanted to discuss was the withdrawal of Hungarian troops from the Eastern Front. Tibor speculated that this turn of events might bring Mátyás home at last when all else had failed to do so.

The evening of the Klessheim conference found Andras and József at the Pineapple Club, the underground cabaret near Vörösmarty tér where Mátyás had once danced on the lid of a white piano. The piano was still there; at the keyboard was Berta Türk, a vaudevillian of the old school, whose snaky coiffure called to mind a Beardsleyesque Medusa. József had received tickets to the show as payment for a house-painting job. Berta Türk had been an adolescent fad of his; he couldn't resist the chance to see her, and he insisted that Andras accompany him. He lent Andras a silk dinner jacket and outfitted himself in a tuxedo he had brought home from Paris five years earlier. For Madame Türk he had a bouquet of red hothouse roses that must have cost half his weekly earnings. He and Andras sat near the stage and drank tall narrow glasses of the club's special medicine, a rum cocktail flavored with coconut. Berta delivered her punning innuendoes in a low raw-honey voice, her eyebrows dipping and rising like a cartoon moll's. Andras liked that József-the-adolescent had fixed on this strange object of obsession instead of on some cold and voiceless beauty of the silver screen.

But he found he had little heart for Berta's jokes; he was thinking of Mátyás, feeling him present everywhere in that room—tapping out a jazz beat at the bar, or lounging on the lid of the piano, or laying a line of hot tin across the stage like Fred Astaire. At the break, Andras stepped outside to clear his head. The night was cool and damp, the streets full of people seeking distraction. A trio of perfumed young women brushed past him, heels clicking, evening coats swaying; from a jazz club across the way, "Bei Mir Bist Du Schön" filtered through a velvet-curtained entrance. Andras looked up past the scrolled cornice of the building to a sky illuminated by an egg-shaped moon, threads of cloud tracing illegible lines of text across its face. It seemed close enough for him to reach up and take it in his hand.

"Got a light?" a man asked him.

Andras blinked the moon away and shook his head. The man, a dark-haired young soldier in a Hungarian Army uniform, begged a match from a passerby and lit his friend's cigarette, then his own.

"It's true, I tell you," the man's friend said. "If Markus says there's going to be an occupation, there'll be an occupation."

"Your cousin's a fascist. He'd love nothing more than a German occupation. But he doesn't know what he's talking about. Horthy and Hitler are negotiating as we speak."

"Precisely! It's a distraction tactic."

Everyone had a theory; every man who had returned alive from the Eastern Front thought he knew how the war would unfold, on the large scale and the small. Every theory seemed as plausible as the last, or as implausible; every amateur military theorist believed just as fiercely that *he alone* could beat order from the chaos of the war. Andras and Tibor, József and Polaner, were all guilty of bearing that illusion. Each had his own set of theories, and each believed the others to be hopelessly misguided. How long, Andras wondered, could they keep building arguments based on reason when the war defied reason at every turn? How long before they all fell silent? It might even be true that the Germans were carrying out an occupation of Hungary that very moment; anything might be true, anything at all. Mátyás himself might be jumping from the mouth of a boxcar at Keleti Station, slinging his knapsack over his shoulder, and heading to the apartment on Nefelejcs utca.

Through a haze of coconut-scented rum, Andras drifted back inside and wandered toward their table beside the stage, where József had engaged Madame Türk's attention and was paying his compliments. Madame Türk, it seemed, was saying farewell for the evening; a piece of urgent news had made it necessary for her to leave at once. She suffered József to kiss her hand, tucked one of his roses behind her ear, and swept off across the stage.

"What was the piece of news?" Andras asked when she'd gone.

"I haven't the slightest idea," József said, afloat on his own delight. He insisted they have another round of drinks before they left, and suggested they take a cab home. But when Andras reminded him what he'd already spent that evening, József allowed himself to be led to the streetcar stop on Vámház körut, where a noisy crowd had gathered to wait for the tram.

By that time everyone seemed to have heard the same set of rumors: A transport of SS troops, somewhere between five hundred and a thousand of them, had arrived at a station near the capital, were marching east, and would soon breach the city limits. Armored and motorized German divisions were said to have advanced into Hungary from every direction; the airports at Ferihegy and Debrecen had been occupied. When the streetcar arrived, the ticket girl proclaimed loudly that if any German soldier tried to board *her* car, she'd spit in his face and tell him where to go. A bawdy cheer rose from the passengers. Someone started singing "Isten, áld meg a Magyart," and then everyone was shouting the national anthem as the streetcar rolled down Vámház körút.

Andras and József listened in silence. If the rumors were true, if a German occupation was under way, Kállay's government wouldn't last the night; Andras could well imagine the kind of regime that would replace it. For six years now, he and the rest of the world had been receiving a lesson in German occupation and its effects. But what could be the purpose of an occupation now? The war was as good as lost for Germany. Everyone knew that. On all fronts, Hitler's armies were close to collapse. Where would he even find the troops necessary to carry out an occupation? The Hungarian military wouldn't take kindly to the idea of German command. There might be armed resistance, a patriotic backlash. The generals of the Honvédség would never submit without a fight, not after Hitler had thrown away so many Hungarian lives on the Eastern Front.

At their stop, Andras and József got off and stood on the pavement, looking up and down the street as if for some sign of the Wehrmacht. Saturday night seemed to be proceeding as before. Cabs tore along the boulevard with their cargos of partygoers, and the sidewalks were full of men and women in evening clothes.

"Are we supposed to believe this?" Andras said. "Am I supposed to bring this news home to Klara?"

"If it's true, I'll bet the army will put up a fight."

"I was thinking that, too. But even if they do, how long can it last?"

József took out his cigarette case, and, finding it empty, drew a narrow silver flask from his breast pocket. He took a long pull, then offered it to Andras.

Andras shook his head. "I've had enough to drink," he said, and turned toward home. They walked up Wesselényi to Nefelejcs utca, then turned and said a grim good-night at the doorstep, promising to see each other in the morning.

Upstairs in the darkened apartment, Tamás had joined Klara in bed, his spine nestled against her belly. When Andras climbed into bed with them, Tamás turned over and backed up against him, his bottom needling into Andras's gut, his feet hot against Andras's thigh. Klara sighed in her sleep. Andras put an arm around them both, wide awake, and lay for hours listening to their breathing.

At seven o'clock the next morning they woke to a pounding at the door. It was József, hatless and coatless, his shirtsleeves stained with blood. His father had just been arrested by the Gestapo. Klara's mother had fallen into a dead faint moments after the men had taken György, and had struck her head on a coal fender; Elza was on the verge of nervous collapse. Andras must get Tibor at once, and Klara must come with József.

In the confused moments that followed, Klara insisted that it couldn't have been the Gestapo, that József must have been mistaken. As he pulled on his boots, Andras had to tell her that it could in fact have been the Gestapo, that the city had been burning with rumors of a German occupation the night before. Andras ran to Tibor's apartment and Klara to the Hászes'; a quarter of an hour later they were assembled around the bed of the elder Mrs. Hász, who had by then regained consciousness and insisted upon relating what had happened before her fall. Two Gestapo men had arrived at half past six that morning, had dragged György from his bed in his nightclothes, had shouted at him in German, and had pushed him into an armored car and taken him away. That was when she had lost her balance and taken a fall. She put a hand to her head, where a rectangle of gauze covered a gash from the fireplace fender.

"Why György?" she said. "Why would they take him? What did he do?"

No one could answer her. And within a few hours they began to hear of other arrests: a former colleague of György's from the bank; the Jewish vice president of a bond-trading company; a prominent Leftist writer, a non-Jew, who had authored a bitter anti-Nazi pamphlet; three of Miklós Kállay's closest advisors; and a liberal member of parliament, Endre Bajcsy-Zsilinszky, who had met the Gestapo with a pistol in hand and had engaged them in a firefight before he'd been wounded and dragged away. That night József took the risk of going to inquire at the jail on Margit körút, where political prisoners were held, but was told only that his father was in German custody, and would be held until it could be proved that he didn't constitute a threat to the occupation.

That was Sunday. By Monday the order had come for all Jewish citizens of Budapest to deliver their radios and telephones—*volunteer* was the word the Nazis used—to an office of the Ministry of Defense at Szabadság tér. By Wednesday it was decreed that any Jewish person who owned a car or bicycle had to sell it to the government for use in the war—*sell* was the word the Nazis used, but there was no money exchanged; the Nazis distributed payment vouchers that were soon discovered to be irredeemable for real currency. By Friday there were notices posted all over town notifying Jews that by April fifth they would be required to wear the yellow star. Soon afterward, the rumor began to circulate that the prominent Jews who had been arrested would be deported to labor camps in Germany. Klara went to the bank to withdraw what was left of their savings, hoping they might bribe someone into releasing György. But she found she could get no more than a thousand pengő; all Jewish accounts had been frozen. The next day a new German order required Jews to surrender all jewelry and gold items. Klara and her mother and Elza gave up a few cheap pieces, hid their wedding bands and engagement rings in a pillowcase at the bottom of the flour bin, and packed the rest into velvet pouches, which József carried to the Margit körút prison to plead for his father's release. The guards confiscated the jewelry, beat József black and blue, and threw him into the street.

On the twentieth of April, Tibor lost his position at the hospital. Andras and Polaner were dismissed from the *Evening Courier* and informed that they wouldn't find work at any daily paper in town. József, employed informally and paid under the table, went on with his painting business, but his list of clients began to shrink. By the first week of May, signs had gone up in the windows of shops and restaurants, cafés and movie theaters and public baths, declaring that Jews were not welcome. Andras, coming home one afternoon from the park with Tamás, stopped short on the sidewalk across from their neighborhood bakery. In the window was a sign almost identical to the one he'd seen at the bakery in Stuttgart seven years earlier. But this sign was written in Hungarian, his own language, and this was his own street, the street where he lived with his wife and son. Struck faint, he sat down on the curb with Tamás and stared across the way into the lighted window of the shop. All looked ordinary there: the girl in her white cap, the glossy loaves and pastries in the case, the gold curlicues of the bakery's name. Tamás pointed and said the name of the pastry he liked, *mákos keksz*. Andras had to tell him that there would be no *mákos keksz* that day. So much had become forbidden, and so quickly. Even being out on the streets was dangerous. There was a new five o'clock curfew for Jews; those who failed to comply could be arrested or shot. Andras pulled out his father's pocket watch, as familiar now as if it were a part of his own body. Ten minutes to five. He got to his feet and picked up his son, and when he reached home, Klara met him at the door with his call-up notice in her hand.

CHAPTER THIRTY-NINE

Farewell

THIS TIME they were together, Andras and József and Tibor; Polaner had been exempted, thanks to his false identity papers and medical-status documents. The labor battalions had been regrouped. Three hundred and sixty-five new companies had been added. Because Andras and József and Tibor lived in the same district, they had all been assigned to the 55/10th. Their send-off had been like a funeral at which the dead, the three young men, had been piled with goods to take into the next world. As much food as they could carry. Warm clothes. Woolen blankets. Vitamin pills and rolls of bandage. And in Tibor's pack, drugs pilfered from the hospital where he had worked. Anticipating their call-up, he had felt no compunction about laying aside vials of antibiotic and morphine, packets of suture, sterile needles and scissors and clamps: a kit of tools he prayed he wouldn't have to use.

Klara had not been with them at the train station for their departure. Andras had said goodbye to her that morning at home, in their bedroom at Nefelejcs utca. The first nine weeks of her pregnancy had passed without event, but in the tenth she was seized with a violent nausea that began every morning at three o'clock and lasted almost until noon. That morning she'd been sick for hours; Andras had stayed with her as she bent over the toilet bowl and dry-heaved until her face streamed with tears. She begged him to go to bed, to get some sleep before he had to face the ordeal of his journey, but he wouldn't do it, wouldn't have left her side for anything in the world. At six in the morning her strength broke. Shaking with exhaustion, she cried and cried until she lost her voice. It was intolerable, she whispered, impossible, that Andras could be here with her one day, intact and safe, and the next be taken away to the hell from which he'd come last spring. Given to her and taken away. Given and taken away. When so much of what she'd loved had been taken away. He couldn't remember a time when she had stated her fear, her sense of desolation, so plainly. Even at their worst times in Paris, she had held something back; something had been hidden from him, some essential part of her being that she'd had to guard in order to survive the ordeals of her adolescence, her early motherhood, her solitary young womanhood. Since they'd been married, there had been the necessary holding back imposed by their circumstances. But now, in the vulnerability of her pregnancy, with Andras on the verge of departure and Hungary in the hands of the Nazis, she had lost the strength to defend her reserve.

She cried and cried, beyond consolation, beyond caring whether anyone heard; as he rocked her in his arms he had the sense that he was watching her mourn him—that he had already died and was witnessing her grief. He stroked her damp hair and said her name over and over again, there on the bathroom floor, feeling, strangely, as if they were finally married, as if what had existed between them before had only been preparation for this deeper and more painful connection. He kissed her temple, her cheekbone, the wet margin of her ear. And then he wept, too, at the thought of leaving her alone to face what might come.

At dawn, just before he had to dress, he took her to bed and slid in beside her. "I won't do it," he said. "They'll have to drag me away from you."

"I'll be fine," she tried to tell him. "My mother will be with me. And Ilana, and Elza. And Polaner."

"Tell my son his father loves him," Andras said. "Tell him that every night." He took his father's pocket watch from the nightstand and pressed it into Klara's palm. "I want him to have this, when it's time."

"No," she said. "Don't do that. You'll give it to him yourself." She folded it into his own hand. And then it was morning, and he had to go.

* * *

Again the boxcars. Again the darkness and the pressure of men. Here was József beside him, inevitable; and Tibor, his brother, his scent as familiar as their childhood bed. This time they were headed, as if into the past, toward Debrecen. Andras knew exactly what was passing outside: the hills melting into flatlands, the fields, the farms. But now the fields, if they were worked, were worked by forced-labor companies; the farmers and their sons were all at war. The patient horses shied at the unfamiliar voices of their drivers. The dogs barked at the strangers, never growing accustomed to their scent. The women watched the workers with suspicion and kept their daughters inside. Maglód, Tápiogyörgy, Ujszász, those one-street towns whose train stations still bore geraniums in window boxes: They had been stripped of their Christian men of military age, and their Jewish men of labor-service age, and would soon be stripped of the rest of their Jewish inhabitants. Already the concentrations and deportations had begun—deportations, when Horthy had vowed never to deport. Döme Sztójay was prime minister now, and he was doing what the Germans had told him to do. Concentrate the Jews of the small towns in ghettoes in the larger towns. Count them carefully. Make lists. Tell them they were needed for a great labor project in the east; hold out the promise of resettlement, of a better life elsewhere. Instruct them each to pack a single suitcase. Bring them to the rail yard. Load them onto trains. The trains left daily for the west, returned empty, and were filled again; an unspeakable dread settled over those who remained and waited. The few, like Polaner, who had already been inside German camps and had lived to tell about them, knew there was to be no resettlement. They knew the purpose of those camps; they knew the product of the great labor project. They told their stories and were disbelieved.

For Andras and Tibor and József, the four-hour trip to Debrecen took three days. The train stopped at the platforms of the little towns; in some places they could hear other boxcars being coupled to their own, more work servicemen being fed into the combustion engine of the war. No food or water except what they'd brought. No place to relieve themselves except the can at the back of the car. Long before they pulled into the station at Debrecen, Andras recognized the pattern of track-switching that characterized the approach. In the semidarkness, Tibor's eyes met Andras's and held them. Andras knew he was thinking of their parents, who had withstood so many departures, who had already lost one son and whose two remaining sons were now headed toward the fighting again. Two weeks earlier, Béla and Flóra had been locked into a ghetto that happened to contain their building on Simonffy utca. There had been no way, no time, to say goodbye. Now Andras and Tibor were at Debrecen Station, not fifteen minutes' walk from that ghetto, if there had been any way to get off the train, and any way to walk through the city without being shot.

The boxcar sat on its track in Debrecen all night. It was too dark for Andras to read his father's pocket watch; there was no way to determine how late it was, how many hours until morning. They couldn't know whether they would leave that day or be forced to remain in the reeking dark while more cars were hitched to theirs, more men loaded aboard. They took turns sitting; they drowsed and woke. And then, in the stillest hour of the night, they heard footsteps on the gravel outside the car. Not the heavy tread of the guards, but tentative footsteps; then a quiet knocking on the side of the boxcar.

"Fredi Paszternak?"

"Geza Mohr?"

"Semyon Kovács?"

No one responded. Everyone was awake now, everyone stilled with fear. If these seekers were caught, they would be killed. Everyone knew the consequences.

After a moment the footsteps moved on. More seekers approached. Rubin Gold? György Toronyi? The names came in a steady stream; soft excited voices could be heard from a nearby car, where someone had found who they were looking for. And then, in the next wave of seekers, Andras Lévi? Tibor Lévi?

Andras and Tibor rushed to the side of the car and called to their parents in hushed voices: Anyu, Apu. The diminutive forms not used since childhood. Andras and Tibor made young again in their extremity, by the impossible closeness and untouchability of their mother, Flóra; their father, Béla. Inside the boxcar, men pushed aside to give them room, a measure of privacy in that packed enclosure.

"Andi! Tibi!" Their mother's voice, desperate with pain and relief.

"But how did you get here?" Tibor asked.

"Your father bribed a policeman," their mother said. "We had an official escort."

"Are you all right, boys?" Their father's voice again, asking a question whose answer was already known, and to which Andras and Tibor could only respond with a lie. "Do you know where they're sending you?"

They did not.

There was little time to talk. Little time for Béla and Flóra to do what they had come to do. A package appeared at the bars of the single high window, looped to a metal hook with a length of brown twine. The package, too large to fit through the window bars, had to be lowered again and broken down into its components. Two woolen sweaters. Two scarves. Tight-wrapped packages of food. A packet of money: two thousand pengő. How had they saved it? How had they kept it hidden? And two pairs of sturdy boots, which had to be left behind; no way to pass them through the window.

Then their father's voice again, saying the prayer for travel.

Flóra and Béla hurried through the darkened streets toward home, each carrying a pair of sturdy boots. Behind them, with a hand on their shoulders as though they were under arrest, was the bribed policeman, a former member of Béla's chess club, who had arranged for them to slip out through a cellar that joined two buildings, one inside the ghetto, one out. Others had slipped out in the same manner and returned safely, though some had failed to return and had not been heard from again. They were entirely at the mercy of this policeman with whom Béla had shared a few chess matches, a few glasses of beer. But they had little fear of what might happen now, little fear of being turned over to a less sympathetic member of the Debrecen police; now that they had delivered the food, the sweaters, the money, had exchanged a few words with the boys, had given them their blessing, what else mattered? What a waste it would have been to be caught with the packages in hand, but they'd been lucky; the streets had been nearly empty when they'd left the ghetto. Béla's intelligence sources, a rail-yard foreman of his long acquaintance and the bartender called Rudolf, had both proved reliable. The train was there, just where it was supposed to be, and the guards at the train yard engaged in a drinking party for which Rudolf had supplied the beer. Rudolf had remembered Andras from his visit to the beer hall, the evening when he had quarreled with his father over the choice of Klara. What a luxury it had been, Lucky Béla thought, to have had the time and inclination for a quarrel. He had admired his son's defense of his choice of wife. In the end he had been right too: Klara had been a good match for him—as good, it seemed, as Flóra had been for Béla. Lucky. Yes, he was lucky, even now. Flóra was there at his side, the policeman's hand on her shoulder—his wife, the mother of his sons, willing to risk her life for them in the middle of the night, despite his protests; unwilling to allow him to go alone.

At last the policeman delivered them to the courtyard that led to the cellar. With an antiquated and incongruous politeness, he held the door as they entered that tunnel back to their enclosed lives. Before long they had reached their own building and climbed the stairs to their apartment, where they undressed in the dark without a word. There would only be a few hours to sleep before they would rise to the circumscribed business of their day. In bed, Flóra pulled the coverlet to her chin and let out a sigh. There was nothing more they could say to each other, nothing more to do. Their boys, their babies. The little three, as they'd always called them. The little three adrift on the continent, like wooden boats. Flóra turned over and put her head on Lucky Béla's chest, and he stroked the silver length of her hair.

For another few weeks they would share this bed while the Jews of Hajdú County were massed in Debrecen. Then, on a late June morning, as the nasturtium vine opened its trumpets on the veranda and the white goats bleated in the courtyard, they would descend the stairs, each with a single suitcase, and walk with their neighbors through the ghetto gates, down the familiar city streets, all the way to the Serly Brickyards west of town, where they would be loaded onto a train almost identical to the one that had carried their sons to no one knew where. The train would roll west, through the stations with the window boxes full of geraniums; it would roll west through Budapest. Then it would roll north, and north, and farther north, until its doors opened at Auschwitz.

The train carrying Andras and Tibor and József rolled east to the edge of the country. There, in a Carpatho-Ruthenian town whose name would change twice as it became part of Czechoslovakia again and then part of the Soviet Union, they were escorted by armed guards to a camp three kilometers from the Tisza River. Their task would be to load timber onto barges for transport through Hungary and on toward Austria. They were assigned to a windowless bunkhouse with five rows of three-tiered bunks; outside, along the edge of the building, was a line of open sinks where they could wash. That evening at dinnertime they drank a coffee that was not coffee, ate a soup that was not soup, and received ten decagrams of gritty bread, which Tibor made them save for the next day. It was the fifth of June, a mild night redolent of rain and new grass. The fighting had not yet reached the nearby border. They were permitted to sit outside after dinner; a man who'd brought a violin played Gypsy tunes while another man sang. Andras could not know—and none of them would learn, not for months—that later the same night, a fleet of Allied ships would reach the coast of Normandy, and thousands of troops would struggle ashore under a hail of gunfire. Even if they'd known, they wouldn't have dared to hope that the Allied invasion of France might save a Hungarian labor company from the terrors of the German occupation, or keep their own bend of the Tisza from being bombed while they were loading the barges. Even if they'd known of the invasion, they would have known better than to attempt to determine one set of circumstances from another, to trace neat lines of causality between a beach at Vierville-sur-Mer and a forced labor camp in Carpatho-Ruthenia. They knew their situation; they knew what to be grateful for. When Andras lay down that night on his wooden bunk, with Tibor on the tier above and József below, he thought only: Today at least we're together. Today we are alive.

CHAPTER FORTY

Nightmare

IN THE END, what astonished him most was not the vastness of it all—that was impossible to take in, the hundreds of thousands of dead from Hungary alone, and the millions from all over Europe—but the excruciating smallness, the pinpoint upon which every life was balanced. The scale might be tipped by the tiniest of things: the lice that carried typhus, the few thimblefuls of water that remained in a canteen, the dust of breadcrumbs in a pocket. On the tenth of January, at the cold disordered dawn of 1945, Andras lay on the floor of a boxcar in a Hungarian quarantine camp a few kilometers from the Austrian border. The nearby town was Sopron, with its famous Goat Church. A vague childhood memory—an art-history lesson, a white-haired master with a moustache like the disembodied wings of a dove, an image of the carved stone chancel where Ferdinand III had been crowned King of Hungary. According to the legend, a goat had unearthed an ancient treasure on that site; the treasure had been buried again when the church was built, as a tribute to the Virgin Mary. And so, somewhere up the hill, beneath the church whose blackened spire was visible from where he lay, an ancient treasure moldered; and here in the quarantine camp, three thousand men were dying of typhus. Andras climbed into the swirling heights of a fever through which his thoughts proceeded in carnival costume. He remembered, vaguely, having been told that the quarantined men were supposed to consider themselves lucky. Those not infected had been shipped over the Austrian border to labor camps.

Some facts he could grasp. He counted these certainties like marbles in a bag, each with its twist of blood- or sea-colored glass. Their bend of the Tisza had, in fact, been bombed. It had happened on an unseasonably warm night in late October, nearly five months after they'd arrived at the camp. He remembered crouching in the darkness with Tibor and József, the walls shuddering as shock waves rolled through the earth; only by an act of grace, it seemed, had their building remained intact. Thirty-three men had been crushed in another bunkhouse when it collapsed. Six bargemen and half a company of Hungarian soldiers, quartered that night on the riverbank, had all been killed. The 55/10th, in tatters, had fled west ahead of the advancing Soviet Army. For weeks their guards had shuffled them from one town to another, quartering them in peasants' huts or barns or in the open fields, as the war rumbled and flared, always a few kilometers away. By that time Hungary had fallen into the hands of the Arrow Cross. Horthy had proved too difficult for Germany to control; under pressure from the Allies he had stopped the deportations of Jews, and on the eleventh of October he'd covertly negotiated a separate peace agreement with the Kremlin. When he announced the armistice a few days later, Hitler had forced him to abdicate and had exiled him to Germany with his family. The armistice was nullified. Ferenc Szálasi, the Arrow Cross leader, became prime minister. The news reached the labor servicemen in the form of new regulations: They were now to be treated not as forced laborers, but as prisoners of war.

Those things Andras remembered in detail. More confusing was what had passed between then and now. Through the haze of his fever he tried and tried to remember what had happened to Tibor. He remembered, weeks or months earlier, fleeing with Tibor and József along a road west of Trebišov on a bright day, pursued by the sound of Russian tanks and Russian gunfire. They'd been separated from their company; József had been sick and couldn't keep up. German jeeps and armored cars shot along the road beside them. Approaching from behind, an earthquake: Russians in their rolling fortresses, guns blazing. As they fled along the road, József had stumbled into the path of a German armored car. He'd been thrown into a ditch, his leg twisted into an angle that was—the fevered Andras grasped in darkness for the word—*unrealistic*. It was unrealistic; it did not represent life. A leg did not bend in that way, or in that direction, in relation to a man's body. When Andras reached him, József was open-eyed, breathing fast and shallow; he seemed in a state of strange exultation, as though in one quick stroke he'd been vindicated on a point he'd argued fruitlessly for years. Tibor bent beside him and put a careful hand to the leg, and József released an unforgettable sound: a grating three-toned shriek that seemed to crack the dome of the sky. Tibor drew back and gave Andras a look of despair: He was out of morphine, the supplies he'd hoarded in Budapest exhausted by now. Moments later, it seemed, an olive-colored van had appeared, Austrian Wehrmacht flags fluttering at its bumpers, a red cross painted on its side. Andras tore the yellow armband from his sleeve, from József's, from Tibor's; now they were just three men in a ditch, without identity. Austrian medics arrived, judged them all in need of immediate medical care, and loaded them into the van. Soon they were moving along the road at an incredible rate of speed—still fleeing before the Russians, Andras imagined. Then there was a burst of deafening noise, a brilliant explosion. The canvas of the van tore away, floor became ceiling, a tire traced an arc against a backdrop of clouds. A jolt of impact. A thrumming silence. From somewhere close by, József calling for his father, of all people. Tibor stood unharmed amid dry cornstalks, dusting snow from his sleeves. Andras, a wild white pain abloom in his side, lay in a furrow of the field and stared at the sky, an impossibly high milk blue stretching forever above him. In his memory a cloud took the shape of the Panthéon, a suggestion of columns and a dome. A moment later that milky blue, that dome, disappeared into an enfolding darkness.

Later he had opened his eyes to a vision so blinding he was certain he had died. Snow-white walls, snow-white bedstead, snow-white curtains, snow-white sky outside the window. He came to understand that he was lying on a hospital cot, under the excruciating weight of a thin cotton blanket. A doctor with a

Yugoslav name, Dobek, removed a bandage from Andras's side and examined a red-toothed wound that extended from beneath his lowest rib to just above his navel. The sight of it brought on a wave of nausea so deep that Andras looked around in panic for a bedpan, and the motion called forth a shearing pain inside the wound. The doctor begged Andras not to move. Andras understood, though the admonition came in a language he didn't know. He lay back and fell into a dreamless sleep. When he woke, Tibor was sitting in a chair beside the cot, his glasses unbroken, his hair clean, his face washed, his labor-service rags exchanged for cotton pajamas. Andras had been wounded, he explained; the medical van had hit a mine. He'd had to have emergency surgery. His spleen had been damaged, his small intestine severed near the terminal ileum; but all had been repaired, and he was recovering well. Where were they? In Kassa, Slovakia, in a Catholic hospital, St. Elizabeth's, under the care of Slovak nuns. And where was József? Recovering in a neighboring ward; his leg had been shattered, and he'd had a complicated surgery.

They lay in that Slovak hospital, he and József, for an indeterminate number of weeks; he lay there recovering from his terrible wound, and József from his complex fracture, while a war raged nearby. Tibor came and went. He was serving the nuns, the doctors, working at their side, assisting in surgery, triaging new patients who came in. He was exhausted, grim with the sight of bullet- and bomb-ravaged bodies, but there was a calm purpose in his expression: He was doing what he'd been trained to do. The Russians were making progress, he told Andras, slowly but steadily. If the hospital could survive the onslaught of the battle, they might all be safe soon.

But then the Nazis arrived to clear the hospital. *Evacuate* was the word they used, though the meaning wasn't the same for everyone. In that place where no patient had been asked his religion, no distinction made between gentile and Jew, the Jews were now identified and herded into a corridor. Andras and

Tibor supported József between them, his leg unwieldy in its plaster cast, and the three of them were marched to a train and loaded onto a boxcar. Again they rolled off into the unknown, south and west this time, toward Hungary.

For nearly a week they traveled across the country. Tibor gleaned what he could about their location from the shouts he overheard when the train stopped, or from the little he could see from the tiny window in the bolted door. They were at Alsózsolca, then at Mezőkövesd, then at Hatvan; there was a moment of wild hope that they might turn south toward Budapest, but the train rolled onward toward Vác. They skirted the border near Esztergom and traveled for a time along the ice-choked Danube, then through Komárom and Győr and Kapuvár, toward the western border. All that way, Tibor had cared for Andras and József, preserving their delicate recovery. When Andras vomited on the boxcar floor, Tibor cleaned him, and when József had to use the can at the back of the car, Tibor walked him there and helped him. He ministered to the other patients, too, many of whom were too sick to understand their luck. But there was little he could do. There was no food, no water, not a clean bandage or a dose of medicine. At night Tibor lay beside Andras for warmth, and whispered in Andras's ear as if to keep them both from losing their minds. *Let me tell you a story*, Tibor said, as if Andras were the son Tibor had left behind. *Once there was a man who could speak to animals. Here is what the man said. Here is what the animals said.* A vast deep itching spread over every inch of Andras's body, even inside the wound: the bites of lice. A few days later came the first tendrils of fever.

When the train stopped, it meant that they had reached the edge of the country. Again they were to be sorted into two groups: those who could cross and those who could not cross. Those who had typhus wouldn't be allowed to cross. They would be placed in a quarantine camp on the border.

"Listen to me, Andras," Tibor had said, just before the selection. "I'm going to pretend to be ill. I'm not going to be sent over the border. I'm going to stay with you here in the quarantine camp. Do you understand?"

"No, Tibor. If you stay, you'll get sick for certain." He thought of Mátyás, the long-ago illness, his own desperate night in the orchard.

"And if I go on ahead?"

"You have a skill. They need it. They'll keep you alive."

"They don't care about my skill. I'm going to stay here with you and József and the others."

"No, Tibor."

"Yes."

The boxcars became the barracks of the quarantine camp. At the station they were left on the switching rails, rows and rows of them, each with its cargo of dead and dying men. Every day the dead were hauled out of the cars and lined up beneath them on the frozen ground; it was impossible to bury them at that time of year. Andras lay on the floor of the boxcar in a rising fever, floating just inches above his dead comrades. He'd had no word from Klara in months, and no way to get word to her. Their second child would already have been born, or would not have been. Tamás would be nearly three years old. They might have been deported, or might not have been. He drifted in and out, knowing and not knowing, thinking and unable to think, as his brother slipped out of the quarantine camp and walked into Sopron for food, medicine, news. Every day Tibor returned with what little he could glean; he befriended a pharmacist who supplied him with small amounts of antibiotic and aspirin and morphine, and whose radio picked up BBC News. Budapest had been under a grave threat since early November. Soviet tanks were on the approach from the southwest. Hitler had vowed to hold them off at all costs. Roads were blocked. Food and fuel supplies were running short. The capital had already begun to starve. Tibor would never have delivered that grim news to Andras, but Andras overheard him speaking to someone outside the boxcar; his fever-sharpened hearing carried every word.

He understood, too, that he and József were dying. *Fleckty-phus*, he kept hearing, and *dizentéria*. One day Tibor had returned from town to find Andras and József with a bowl of beans between them; they'd managed to finish half of what they'd been given. He scolded them both and threw the beans out the boxcar door. *Are you mad?* For dysentery, nothing could be worse than barely cooked beans. Men died from eating them, but in the quarantine camp there was nothing else to eat. Instead, Tibor fed Andras and József the cooking liquid from the beans, sometimes with bits of bread. Once, bread with a slathering of jam that smelled faintly of petrol. Tibor explained: In his wanderings he'd come across a farmhouse that had been hit by a plane; he'd found a clay pot of preserves in the yard. Where was the clay pot? they asked. Shattered. Tibor had carried the jam in the palm of his hand, twenty kilometers.

As József got better on the food Tibor brought, Andras's fever deepened. The flux rolled through him and emptied him. The skeleton of reality came apart, connective tissue peeling from the bones.

A constant foul smell that he knew was himself.

Cold.

Tibor weeping.

Tibor telling someone—József?—that Andras was near the end.

Tibor kneeling by his side, reminding him that today was Tamás's birthday.

A resolution that he would not die that day, not on his son's birthday.

Rising through his torn insides, a filament of strength.

Then, the next morning, a commotion in the quarantine camp. The sound of a megaphone. An announcement: All who could work were to be taken to Mürzzuschlag, in Austria. Soldiers searched the boxcars and pulled the living into a glare of cold light. A man in Nazi uniform dragged Andras outside and threw him onto the railroad tracks. Where was Tibor? Where was József? Andras lay with his cheek against the freezing rail, the metal burning his cheek, too weak to move, staring at the frost-rimed gravel, at the moving feet of men all around him. From somewhere nearby came the sound of metal on dirt: men shoveling. It seemed to go on for hours. He understood. Finally, the burial of the dead. And here he was, waiting to be buried. He had died, had gone across. He didn't know when it had happened. He was surprised to find that it could be so simple. There was no *alive*, no *dead*; only this nightmare, always, and when the dirt covered him he would still feel cold and pain, would suffocate forever. A moment later he was caught up by the wrists and ankles and flung through the air. A moment of lightness, then falling. An impact he felt in all his joints, in his ravaged intestines. A stench. Beneath him, the bodies of men. Around him, walls of bare earth. A shovelful of earth in his face. The taste of it like something from childhood. He kept pushing and pushing it away from his face, but it came and came. The shoveler, a vigorous black form at the edge of the grave, pumped at a mound of dirt. Then, for no reason Andras could see, he stopped. A moment later he was gone, the task forgotten. And there Andras lay, not alive, not dead.

A night in an open grave, dirt for his blanket.

In the morning, someone dragging him out.

Again, the boxcar. And now.

Now.

Beside him was a bowl of beans. He was ravenous for them. Instead he tilted the bowl to his mouth, sipped the liquid. With that mouthful he felt his bowels loosen, and then, beneath him, heat.

Another day passed and darkened. Another night. Someone— Tibor?—tipped water into his mouth; he choked, swallowed. In the morning he crawled out of the boxcar, trying to escape the smell of himself. Unaccountably his head felt clearer. He paused, kneeling, and thrust his hand into the pocket of his overcoat, where, when there had been bread, he had carried bread. The pocket was sandy with crumbs. He pulled himself to a puddle where the sun had melted the snow. In one hand he held the crumbs. With the other he scooped water from the puddle. He made a cold paste, put his hand to his mouth, ate. It was his first solid food in twenty days, though he did not know it.

Sometime later he woke in the boxcar. József Hász was bending over him, urging him to sit up. "Give it a try," József said, and lifted him from beneath the shoulders.

Andras sat up. Black ocean waves seemed to close over his head. Then, like a miracle, they receded. Here was the familiar interior of the boxcar. Here was József kneeling beside him, supporting his back with both hands.

"You're going to have to stand now," József said.

"Why?"

"Someone's coming to gather men for a work detail. Anyone who can't work will be shot."

He knew he wouldn't be selected for a work detail. He could scarcely raise his head. And then he remembered again: "Tibor?"

József shook his head. "Just me."

"Where's my brother, József? *Where's my brother?*"

"They've been desperate for workers," József said. "If a man can stand, they take him."

"Who?"

"The Germans."

"They took Tibor?"

"I don't know, Andráska," József said, his voice breaking. "I don't know where he is. I haven't seen him for days."

Outside the boxcar, a German voice called men to attention.

"We're going to have to walk now," József said.

Tears came to Andras's eyes: To die now, after everything. But József took him from beneath the arms and hoisted him to his feet. Andras fell against him. József swayed and yelped in pain; his shattered leg, freed from its cast, could only have been half knit. But he caught Andras around the back and led him toward the door of the boxcar. Slid it aside. Took Andras down a ramp and out onto the cold bare dirt of the rail yard. Thin blades of pain shot up from Andras's feet and through his legs. In his side, along the surgical wound, a dull orange burning.

A Nazi officer stood before a row of labor servicemen, inspecting their soiled, ribbon-torn overcoats and trousers, their rag-bound feet. Andras's and József's feet were bare.

The officer cleared his throat. "All those who want to work, step forward."

All the men stepped forward. József pulled Andras, whose legs buckled. Andras fell forward onto his hands and knees on the bare ground. The officer came toward him and knelt; he put a hand to the back of Andras's neck, and reached into his own overcoat pocket. Andras imagined the barrel of a pistol, a noise, an explosion of light. To his shame, he felt his bladder release.

The officer had drawn out a handkerchief. He mopped Andras's brow and helped him to his feet.

"I want to work," Andras said. He had managed the words in German: *Ich möchte arbeiten.*

"How can you work?" the officer said. "You can't even walk."

Andras looked into the man's face. He appeared almost as hungry, almost as ragged, as the work servicemen themselves; his age was impossible to determine. His cheeks, slack and wind-burned, showed a growth of colorless stubble. A small oval scar marked his jawline. He rubbed the scar with his thumb as he looked at Andras contemplatively.

"A wagon will be here in a few minutes," he said at last. "You'll come with us."

"Where are we going?" Andras dared to ask. *Wohin gehen wir?*

"To Austria. To a work camp. There's a doctor there who can help you."

Everything seemed to have a terrible second meaning. Austria. A work camp. A doctor who could help him. Andras put a hand on József's arm to steady himself, pulled himself to his bare feet, and made himself look into the Nazi's eyes. The Nazi held his gaze, then turned sharply and marched off through the rows of boxcars. Exhausted, Andras leaned against József until the wagon arrived. The Nazi officer quick-stepped alongside the wagon, carrying a pair of boots. He helped Andras and József into the wagon bed, then put the boots into Andras's lap.

"Heil Hitler," the officer said, saluting as the wagon pulled away.

A hundred times it might have been the end. It might have been the end when the wagon arrived at the work camp and the men were inspected, if the inspector hadn't been a Jewish kapo who had taken pity on Andras and József—he'd assigned them to a work brigade rather than sending them to the infirmary, though they could scarcely walk. It might have been the end, again, on the day their group of a hundred men failed to meet its work quota: They were supposed to load fifty pallets of bricks onto flatbed trucks, and they'd only loaded forty-nine; as punishment, the guards selected two men, a gray-haired chemist from Budapest and a shoemaker from Kaposvár, and executed them behind the brick factory. It might have been the end when the food at the camp ran out, had not Andras and József, digging a trench for a latrine, come upon four clay jars buried in the ground: a cache of goose fat, a relic of a time when the camp had been a farm, and the farmer's wife had foreseen lean days ahead. It might have been the end if the men at the camp had had time to finish their project, a vast crematorium in which their bodies would be burned after they had been gassed or shot. But it was not the end. On the first of April, as the exhausted and starving men waited to be marched from the assembly ground to the brickyard for the day's work, József touched Andras's shoulder and pointed toward a line of vehicles speeding along the military road beyond the barbed-wire fence.

"See that?" József said. "I don't think we're going to work today."

Andras raised his eyes. "Why not?"

"Look." He pointed along the curve of the road as it bent away toward the east. A confusion of German and Hungarian armored vehicles bumped along the rutted track, some leaving the roadbed to pass, others getting mired in the deep mud of the road, or spinning out of control into the ditches. Behind them, as far as Andras could see, a line of sleeker, swifter tanks barreled in their direction: Soviet T-34s, the kind he'd seen in Ukraine and Subcarpathia. That explained why their work foreman still hadn't appeared, though it was half past seven: The Russians had come at last, and the Germans and Hungarians were running for their lives. At that moment the camp loudspeaker broadcast a command for all inmates to return to their quarters, gather their belongings, and meet at the camp gates to await orders for redeployment. But József sat down just where he was and crossed his legs before him.

"I'm not going anywhere," he said, "Not a step. If the Russians are coming, I'm going to sit here and wait."

The announcement raised a shout from the other men, some of whom threw their caps in the air. They stood in the assembly yard and watched their Nazi guards and work foremen flee the camp, some on foot, others in jeeps or trucks. No one seemed to take notice of the few men who'd gathered with their belongings near the gate. No further orders came over the loudspeaker; anyone who might have given orders had gone. Some of the inmates hid in the barracks, but Andras and József and many of the others climbed a low hill and watched a battle unfold in the neighboring fields. A battalion of German tanks had turned to meet the Soviets, and the cannons barked and roared for hours.

All day and into the night they watched and cheered the Red Army. After dark, gunfire made an aurora in the eastern sky. Somewhere beyond that peony-colored light was the border of Hungary, and beyond that the road that led to Budapest.

At dawn the next day, a Soviet detachment arrived to take charge of the camp. The soldiers wore gray jackets and mud-smeared blue breeches. Their boots were miraculously intact, and their leather straps and belts gleamed with polish. They stopped just outside the gates and their captain made an announcement in Russian over a megaphone. The men of the camp had anticipated this moment. They'd made white flags from the canvas sacks that held cement dust, and had tied the flags to slender linden branches. A group of Russian-speaking prisoners, Carpathians from a Slovak border town, approached the Soviets with the branches held high. The absurdity of it, Andras thought—those gaunt and grief-shocked men carrying flags of surrender, as though they might be mistaken for their captors. The Soviets had brought a cartload of coarse black bread, which they distributed among the men. They broke the locks of the storehouses from which the camp officers had supplied themselves; after they'd taken as much as their cart could hold, they indicated that the prisoners should take whatever they wanted. The men walked through the storehouse as if through a museum of a bygone age. There on the shelves were luxuries they hadn't seen for months—tinned sausages, tinned pears, tinned peas; slender boxes of cigarettes; stacks of batteries and bars of soap. They packed those things into squares of canvas or empty cement bags, hoping they might sell or trade them on the way home. Then the Soviets marched the men to a processing camp thirty kilometers away on the Hungarian border, where they lived for three weeks in filthy overcrowded barracks before they were given liberation papers and released. They were two hundred and fifteen kilometers from Budapest. The only way to get there was to walk.

* * *

They trusted nobody, traveled at night, evaded the last few fleeing Nazis, who would shoot any Jews they met, and the Soviet
liberators, who, it was rumored, could take away your liberation
papers and send you off to work camps in Siberia for no reason
at all. József's injured leg meant they had to travel slowly; he
could manage no more than ten kilometers before the pain
stopped him. From the direction of the city, reports of horrors
drifted across the rolling hills of Transdanubia: Budapest bombed
to rubble. Hundreds of thousands deported. A winter of starvation. The part of Andras's mind that he was accustomed to sending in Klara's direction had shriveled to a hard knot, like scar
tissue. He allowed himself to imagine nothing beyond the
moment's necessary work; he fixed his mind on his own survival.
He would not allow himself to remember the first weeks of the
year, that gray-blue blur of horror that was January 1945. The
surgical wound in his side had healed to a puckered pink seam;
the injured spleen, the torn intestine, had resumed their invisible
work. He would not think about his parents, about Mátyás;
would not think about Tibor, who had disappeared somewhere
beyond the Austrian border. With József at his side he slept in
the ruins of barns or dug into haystacks and bedded down in the
sweet-smelling dark, then woke to nightmares of being buried
alive. By night they walked in the thick brush beside a highway
that led toward Budapest. One evening, when they stopped at
the back door of a large country house to trade German cigarettes and batteries for eggs and bread, they learned from the
cook that Russian tanks had entered Berlin. She showed them
where they could conceal themselves in a stand of lilacs by an
open window and listen to that night's radio broadcast. Amid the
clusters of syringa they listened as a BBC announcer described
the events transpiring in the German capital. To Andras the
English words were a maze of sharp vowels and rapid-fire consonants, but József knew the language. The Russians, he translated,

had surrounded the Reichstag, where Hitler had chosen to make his last stand; no one knew what was going on within.

One morning a few days later, as they slept in a boathouse on Lake Balaton beneath a mildewed canvas sail, they were awakened by the sound of bells. Every bell in the nearby town, Siófok, rang balefully, as though a great emergency were at hand. Andras and József ran out of the boathouse to find the townspeople streaming into the streets, moving toward the center of town in a stunned procession. They followed the crowd to the town square, where the mayor—a war-starved grandfather in an ill-fitting Soviet jacket—climbed the steps of the courthouse and announced that the war in Europe was over. Hitler was dead. Germany had signed an agreement of unconditional surrender in Reims. A cease-fire would go into effect at midnight.

From the crowd, a single beat of silence; then they roared in celebration and threw their hats into the air. For that moment it didn't seem to matter that Hungary had been on the losing side, that its shining capital on the Danube had been bombed to rubble, that the country had fallen under Soviet control, that its people had nothing to eat, that its prisoners still hadn't returned, that its dead were gone forever. What mattered was that the war in Europe was over. Andras and József put their arms around each other and wept.

The hills east of Buda had come into their young leaves, insensate to the dead and the grieving. The flowering lindens and plane trees seemed almost obscene to Andras, inappropriate, like girls in transparent lawn dresses at a funeral. He and József hiked the ruined streets on the east side of Castle Hill; at the top they paused and stood looking out over the city in silence. The beautiful bridges of the Danube—Margaret Bridge, the Chain Bridge, the Elizabeth Bridge, all those bridges whose every inch Andras knew by heart, every one of them as far as he could see— lay in ruins, their steel cables and concrete supports melting into the sand-colored rush of the river. The Royal Palace had been bombed into the shape of a crumbling comb, a Roman lady's hair ornament excavated from an ancient city. The hotels on the far side of the river had fallen to ruins; they seemed to kneel on the riverbank in belated supplication.

In wordless shock, avoiding each other's eyes, Andras and József stumbled down through the streets of the old city toward the bridgeless river. They knew they had to cross, knew that whatever waited for them waited on the far bank, amid the remains of Pest. Near Ybl Miklós tér, the square named for the architect who had designed the Operaház, they found a slip where a line of boatmen waited to ferry passengers across. For their passage they traded their last six packages of cigarettes and a dozen large batteries. The boatman, a red-faced boy in a straw hat, looked exceptionally well fed. As the boat cut toward the opposite shore, the feeling in Andras's chest was like a hand raked through the tissue of his lungs; his diaphragm contracted with a spasm so painful he couldn't breathe. The boat, a leaking skiff, made a shaky downstream progress across the river, twice threatening to capsize before it delivered them sick and shaking to the shore of Pest. They climbed out onto the wet sand beneath the embankment, the water lapping their shoes. Then they ascended the stone steps and stared up into a corridor of ruined buildings. On either side, a few buildings stood intact; some had even retained the colored tiles of their decorative mosaics, the leaves and flowers of their Baroque ornamentation. But Andras and József's path toward the center of town led them through a museum of destruction: endless piles of bricks, splintered beams, shattered tiles, fractured concrete. The dead had been moved out of the street long before, but crosses stood on every corner. Signs of ordinary life presented themselves as if in total ignorance of this disaster: a clean shop window full of dough twisted into the usual shapes; a red bicycle reclining against a stoop; from far away, the improbable clang of a streetcar bell. Farther along, the skeleton of a German plane protruded from the top story of a building. A section of burned wing had fallen to the ground; the rust along its edges suggested it had lain there for months. A dog sniffed the blackened steel ribs of the wing and trotted off down the street.

They went along together toward Nefelejcs utca, toward the buildings where their families had lived—the building where József had said goodbye to his mother and grandmother; the building where Tibor and Ilana had moved after Andras's return; the building where Andras and Klara had crouched together on the bathroom floor the night before his departure. They turned the corner from Thököly út and passed the familiar greengrocer's, empty of green, and the familiar sweet shop, empty of sweets. At the corner of Nefelejcs utca and István út was a pile of wreckage, a mountain of plaster and stone and wood and brick and tile. Across the street, where József's family and Tibor and Ilana had lived, there was nothing at all. Not even a ruin. Andras stood and stared.

Later he would say of himself, "That was when I lost my head." It was the closest he could come to describing the feeling: His head had departed from his body, had been sent, like the evacuated children of Europe, somewhere dull and distant and safe. His body went to its knees in the street. He wanted to tear his clothing but found he couldn't move. He wouldn't listen to József, wouldn't consider that his wife and child, or children, might have left the building before it had been destroyed. He couldn't see anyone or anything. Passersby moved around him as he knelt on the pavement.

He might have stayed there an hour, or two, or five. József seated himself on an upturned cinderblock and waited. Andras was aware of him as a kind of fine tether, a monofilament connecting him, against his will, to what was left of the world. His eyes, unfocused on the ruin of the building, filled and drained and filled again. And then a familiar sound resolved from the nebula of his dulled senses: the sound of delicate hooves on pavement, the jingle of twin bells. The sound approached until it reached him, then went still. He raised his eyes.

It was the tiny grandmother of Klein, and her goat cart, newly painted white.

"My God," she said, and stared at him. "Is it Andras? Is it Andras Lévi?"

He took her hand and kissed it. "You remember me," he said. "Thank God. Do you know anything about my wife? Klara Lévi? Do you remember her, too?"

"Get up," she said. "Let me take you to my house."

The house in Frangepán köz stood in its ancient silence, in a haze of dust suspended in the viscous light of late afternoon. In the yard, a quartet of tiny goatlets nosed at a bucket of breadcrusts. Andras ran the stone path to the door, which stood open as if to admit the breeze. Inside, on the sofa where Andras had first waited to see Klein, lay his wife, Klara Lévi, asleep, alive. At the other end of the sofa was his son, Tamás, deep in a nap, his mouth open. Andras knelt beside them as if in prayer. Tamás's skin was flushed with sleep, his forehead pink, his eyes fluttering beneath the lids. Klara seemed farther away, scarcely breathing, her skin a luminous white film over her faintly beating life. Her hair had come out of its coil and lay over her shoulder in a twisted rope. Her arm was crooked around a sleeping baby in a white blanket, the baby's hand an open star on Klara's half-bare breast.

My polestar, Andras thought. My true north.

Klara stirred, opened her eyes, looked down at the baby and smiled. Then she became aware of another presence in the room, an unfamiliar shape. Instinctively she drew her blouse over her breast, covering that slip of damp white skin.

She raised her eyes to Andras and blinked as if he were the

dead. She pressed her eyes with a thumb and forefinger and then looked again.

Andras.

Klara.

They wailed each other's names into the ancient space of that room, into that dust-storm of antique sunlight; their little boy, their son, woke with a start and began to cry in panic, unable to distinguish joy from grief. And perhaps at that moment joy and grief were the same thing, a flood that filled the chest and opened the throat: This is what I have survived without you, this is what we have lost, this is what is left, what we have to live with now. The baby raised a high wet voice. They were together, Klara and Andras and Tamás, and this little girl whose name her father did not know.

CHAPTER FORTY-ONE

The Dead

KLARA HAD SURVIVED the Siege of Budapest in a women's shelter at Szabadság tér, under the protection of the International Red Cross. The Allies would not bomb it; the Germans had little interest in it. The inhabitants, young mothers and babies, were of no use to them. Klara had gone there in early December, a few weeks after the Russians had reached the southeastern edge of the capital. By that time Horthy had been deposed, the Arrow Cross had come to power, and seventy thousand Jews had been deported from Budapest. Those who had escaped deportation had had to move twice: first from their original homes to yellow-star buildings, Jewish-only apartments in neighborhoods all over the city; and then to a tiny ghetto in the Seventh District, in the streets surrounding the Great Synagogue.

In the first wave of displacements, Klara and Ilana, the children, Klara's mother, and Elza Hász had all been assigned to a building on Balzac utca, in the Sixth District. Polaner had gone with them. The diminutive Mrs. Klein, grandmother of Miklós Klein, had provided her goat cart to help them transport their things. Klara had seen Klein's grandmother on a last desperate visit to the Margit körút prison, where György was supposed to have been interned; Mrs. Klein had been there to inquire about Miklós. There had been no news of either man that day, but as the women had walked together afterward along the Danube embankment, trying to distract each other from their fear and grief, they'd talked of the practical difficulties of the upcoming move. On the day designated for their departure from Nefelejcs utca, Klara had awakened to an early-morning knock at the door. It was Miklós Klein's grandmother in her peasant skirt and black boots, with the news that her goat cart stood at the ready in the courtyard. Klara had looked over the balcony railing, and there was the cart beside the fountain, two white goats sniffing at the water. Miklós Klein's grandmother, it turned out, had been assigned to a building not far from Klara's own, and had already transported what she and her husband could salvage from their tiny homestead in Angyalföld. Seven goats had accompanied them to the inner district of the city: these two wethers, two milch does, three kids. Klara could see them herself that very afternoon, Klein's grandmother said; she'd hidden the goats in a carriage house behind the yellow-star building on Csanády utca.

Even with the aid of the goat cart, they'd had to leave almost everything behind. They were moving into a single room in a three-room apartment with a shared bath; one family lived there already and a third would join them. Klara and Ilana, the children, the elder and younger Mrs. Hász, and Polaner, carrying his loaded gun—the seven of them had crossed the city on foot, through crowds of thousands of Jewish men and women and children pushing their possessions in wheelbarrows or carrying them on their backs or leading them along in horse carts. It took four hours to make the journey of two kilometers. When they carried their things upstairs, they found that all the rooms were occupied; a fourth family had been assigned to the apartment at the last moment. But there was nowhere else for any of them to go, so they would have to share. And that was the beginning of five months in that apartment on Balzac utca. Soon it came to seem to Klara that she had always slept on a pallet on the floor between her mother and her child, had always shared a bath with sixteen others, had always woken to the sound of her elder sister-in-law weeping. Miklós Klein's grandmother arrived every few days with goat's milk for the children and for Klara, reminding Klara that she must keep up her strength for the sake of the baby in her womb. But Klara's pregnancy seemed a terrible irony, the mockery of a promise. As she waited in line for bread one day, two old women had spoken of her as though she weren't there, or couldn't hear: *Look at that poor Jewish pregnant woman. What a shame she's got no future.*

In fact, the aperture to any future beyond the war seemed to contract by the day. They lived in constant fear of deportation; from the outlying towns came news of thousands sent away in closed trains. In the capital itself there were horrors enough: frequent Arrow Cross raids on the yellow-star buildings, the displaced families' possessions stolen, men and women taken away for no reason other than that they happened to be home when the Nyilas men arrived. At times there was reason for hope, reason to think the nightmare might soon end; in July, Horthy stopped all deportations of Jews from Hungary. The Budapest Jews thought they were saved. Klara heard rumors in the streets of talks between Hungary and the Allies, plans for an armistice. Then in mid-October came Horthy's announcement that Hungary had concluded a separate peace with the Russians. For a few hours there were mad celebrations in the streets. Men tore down the yellow-star signs above their doorways, and women ripped the yellow-star patches from their children's coats. But then came the terrible double blow of the Arrow Cross coup and Szálasi's installation as prime minister. The deportations began again, this time in Budapest: Tens of thousands of men and women were taken from their houses and marched to the brickyards at Óbuda, then onward toward Austria. The actions of the Arrow Cross seemed dictated purely by cruel whim. A gang of Nyilas men had raided the building across the street from their own, and had deported nearly a dozen men and women, many of them too old for active labor; Klara had expected their own building to be raided at any moment, but the men had never returned.

All that time, the front lines of the war had been drawing closer and closer. Hitler, determined to keep the Russians from reaching Vienna, decided to delay them at Budapest as long as possible; as winter approached, Nazi and Hungarian forces dug in for what everyone already knew to be a futile struggle. Red Army forces encircled the city in a tightening ring. Air raids drove the terrified civilians underground every night. At times it seemed to Klara they were living in the air-raid shelter, that they spent their entire lives huddling in the dark. There were moments when she almost wished for the shuddering blast she'd experienced a thousand times in her mind, the crushing darkness after which there would be nothing at all. But one morning when Klein's grandmother came to deliver the goat's milk, she brought a slip of hope: A few women and children from her building had moved to an International Red Cross shelter at Szabadság tér, at the very center of the city. Klara and Ilana must go there as soon as possible, must try to get in while there was still space. If Klara was lucky, she might be able to have her baby there. Surely there would be a better chance of getting medical help if she were under the protection of the International Red Cross.

The next day the order came that the Jews must move again at the end of November, this time to the ghetto in the Seventh District. It was clear that there was no time to waste. Klara and Ilana went that afternoon to make inquiries at the International Red Cross offices at Vadász utca, and learned that Klein's grandmother had been correct: There was a shelter for women and babies at Szabadság tér. Klara and Ilana received papers that would allow them to bring the children there that very day. They went home and packed the last of their money and valuables, the children's diapers and clothing, a few sheets and blankets; they loaded the bundles into Tamás's and Ádám's baby carriages and dressed the children in their warmest coats. Then, for the last time, Klara said goodbye to Elza Hász and to her own mother—though she had not known it was to be the last time. Her mother had pressed her wedding band and engagement ring into Klara's hand.

"Don't be sentimental," her mother had said, her eyes calm and steady on Klara's. "Trade them for bread if you have to." She'd made Klara slip the rings onto her finger, had given her a brusque kiss of the kind she'd always given Klara in the mornings before school, and then she'd gone inside to pack what little she could take to the ghetto.

Polaner had volunteered to escort Klara and Ilana the fourteen blocks they would have to walk to the shelter. In his pocket he carried the Walther P-38 given to him by the officer who'd arranged his safe passage to Hungary, and in his arms he carried Tamás, who had become inseparable from Polaner during the turmoil of the past months. At the doorway of the Red Cross building on Perczel Mór utca, Tamás, faced with the prospect of Polaner's departure, raised such an uproar that the shelter director told Polaner he could stay the night to help the women and children settle in. The director was the mother of a little girl whom Klara had taught a few years earlier. The girl, who had died of scarlet fever, had been a favorite of Klara's, and her mother wanted to do whatever she could to help. In gratitude for her kindness, Polaner explained that his false papers and his Nazi Party identity card might allow him to be of help to the women and children of the shelter; at least until the Russians arrived, he would have a certain freedom of movement in the city. By morning he had taken an inventory of the many things the shelter's inmates needed. Milk for the babies was at the top of the list. So the first gift he brought to the shelter was half a dozen goats: the wethers, the does, and two of the three kids that had been living in the carriage house behind the yellow-star building on Csanády utca. Klein's grandmother had entrusted them to Polaner's care that morning when she and her husband had departed for the Seventh District ghetto, taking the last kid with them.

The Red Cross shelter was housed on the second story of the building, in three rooms of what had once been an insurance office. Mothers who had arrived in fur coats and custom-made shoes sat on desk chairs or on the floor, nursing their babies alongside those who had come with their feet wrapped in newspaper. Day and night the women filled the shelter with urgent talk and weeping and low infrequent laughter. They soothed the babies with songs, tried to distract the two- and three-year-olds with hand games and improvised toys. Pebble-filled pillboxes became rattles; dirty rags became pigtailed dolls. The mothers took turns washing their babies' diapers in a laundry room on the ground floor, their only source of running water. When bombs broke the windows and the building became so cold that the newly washed diapers froze, they wrapped the diapers around themselves at night and dried them with the heat of their bodies. Ten times a day, it seemed, they rushed down to the shelter beneath the building and huddled there while bombs fell all around Szabadság tér.

Polaner worked tirelessly for the women and children. He scrounged rags for diapers; he stole the women's own winter clothing back from the apartments they'd been forced to leave. At night, in violation of the citywide curfew, he gleaned fodder for the goats from abandoned stables and from the garbage that had begun to pile in the streets. On his travels through the neighborhood he discovered the secret Jewish hospital on Zichy Jenő utca, a few blocks from the shelter, where an Armenian doctor named Ara Jerezian had assembled forty Jewish physicians and their families. The Arrow Cross flag flew over the shelter entrance, and Jerezian wore the official Nyilas uniform. He had renounced his party membership years earlier, in protest against the Arrow Cross's anti-Jewish policies, but had taken it up again when he realized he might work secretly for the Jews from inside the party. Under the pretense of setting up a hospital for the Arrow Cross wounded, he'd assembled the Jewish doctors and their families and had laid in a store of food and medicine. Now, in those cramped apartments that had become a hospital, the doctors were treating the horrific casualties of the siege. Polaner brought sick women and babies from the Red Cross shelter to that hospital and took them back again when they were better. In return for the doctors' attention, he gave their hungry children what little goat's milk could be spared.

All over the city, people were beginning to starve. The first weeks of December the Red Cross shelter had been supplied with soup, which had to be transported on a cart from a kitchen on the other side of Szabadság tér. When the soup ran out there were soybeans and potatoes in their own cooking water; then just the soybeans; then, finally, nothing except what the goats produced on their own starvation diet. The women of the shelter pooled their jewelry and gave it to Polaner so he might trade it for food; Klara slipped her mother's wedding band and engagement ring into the bag with the rest. But Polaner returned empty-handed. The women's jewelry was worth nothing. There was no food to be had. Even the scant running water had ceased to run. Their only water now came from melted snow they'd brought in from the courtyard. The women became sick with hunger and thirst, and a drought of milk spread through the shelter. At first the children cried, but by the beginning of January they had become too weak to protest. One by one they went silent, their breathing a fluttering of wings beneath the breastbone. That was when Polaner did what Klein's grandmother had instructed him to do if the situation grew dire. That gentle textile-maker's son, the dovelike young man skilled with pen and protractor, killed the goats and their kids with his Walther P-38, then turned them over to one of the shelter's inmates, a woman whose husband had been a butcher and who knew what to do with Polaner's knife.

A week later, on the eighth of January, Klara's labor began. Ilana insisted that she must go to the hospital on Zichy Jenő utca; after two cesarean sections, she could hardly risk labor at the shelter. Ilana herself would care for Tamás. She kissed Klara and assured her that all would be well. Then Klara and Polaner struggled through a network of smoke-darkened alleys to Ara Jerezian's hospital. As the fighting drew closer, the halls of the hospital had become clogged with horrifically wounded soldiers; men lay crying and sweating and panting on cots along the walls, and the hallways were slick with blood. The doctors could scarcely pause to consider the situation of a healthy woman in labor, whatever her history. Klara and Polaner waited in a makeshift kitchen for three hours until a series of contractions brought her to her hands and knees. At last Polaner begged the help of Ara Jerezian himself, who took Klara to his office and made a pallet for her on the floor. Polaner brought water, sponged Klara's forehead, changed her soaked sheets as she labored. When it became clear that the baby was in the breech position, and that Klara couldn't deliver without a cesarean, Dr. Jerezian brought her to an impromptu operating theater—three metal tables lit only by a bank of high windows—and anesthetized her with morphine as the steadfast Polaner averted his eyes. Klara woke to learn she'd had a girl, whom she named Április in the hope that she would live to see the spring. And Polaner observed that the baby resembled her father.

For five days Klara recovered in Jerezian's office. Whatever food Polaner could find in the hospital, he brought to her. He tended her wound, cooled her forehead with wet cloths, held the baby while she slept. The baby, tiny at birth, gained weight on Klara's milk. When at last they carried her home to the Red Cross shelter, they found Tamás silent and glassy-eyed in the director's arms. Where was Ilana? they asked. Where was the boy's aunt, who was supposed to care for him? The director regarded them for a moment in silence, her mouth trembling, and then she told them.

Ádám Lévi had died of a fever on the twelfth of January. In a delirium of grief, his mother had run out into the street, where a Russian shell had killed her.

The fighting continued in Pest for six more days. The Russian forces drew close now to the center of the city, seeming to converge upon Szabadság tér itself; artillery fire shook the building day and night. Klara, in a shock of grief and fear, huddled in the bomb shelter with the baby while Tamás clung to Polaner. She would die without seeing her husband again; if he lived, how would he even learn of her death, of their children's deaths? It was possible he might never learn he'd had a daughter. *A shame she doesn't have a future.* What kind of future could be imagined after such a time? That night, when Polaner ventured out to get water at a standpipe across the street, he returned with the news that Nyugati Station was on fire, and that Hungarian soldiers were fleeing in the direction of the Danube bridges. That infernal glow along the Danube was the conflagration of the grand hotels. Flames climbed the dome and spire of Parliament. Civilians rushed toward the river with their dogs and bags and children, but the bridges were under bombardment. In the whole city there was nothing left to eat. Klara received the last piece of news with the understanding that she would watch her children die. Later that night, when a shallow panicked sleep overtook her, she dreamed of feeding her own right hand to the children; she felt no pain, only a relief that she had arrived at this ingenious solution.

In the morning she woke to an unaccustomed quiet. In place of gunfire there was a resonant stillness. Now and then a burst of shots cut through the morning air, and from the west bank of the Danube, where the fighting continued, came the faint echo of battle. But the battle for Pest was over. The bridges had all been destroyed; the Soviets held the city. The last Nazis in Pest had been taken as prisoners of war, or were cowering in buildings where they had made others cower. In the Red Cross shelter, the women waited for some sign of what to do. They were faint with thirst and hunger, sick with grief; though the building had withstood the night's bombing, two more babies had died. The children who had survived were quieter that day, as if they knew something had changed. By midday the shelter residents came out of the building and into the cold gray light of Szabadság tér.

What they saw seemed like an image from a newsreel or a dream: the American flag flying brazenly above the shuttered embassy. Two Arrow Cross soldiers lay dead on the embassy steps, the breasts of their overcoats tattered with bullet holes. A pair of Russian military policemen stood at the edge of the square and stared at the smoking dome of the Parliament building. The director of the shelter crossed the square toward the Russian men and fell to her knees before them; they could understand nothing she said, but they offered her their canteens.

That afternoon, the inhabitants of the shelter began to leave in search of food and water. Klara and Polaner lined the babies' carriages with extra blankets and packed them with what remained of what they'd brought. Into Ádám's empty carriage they put Tamás, who, for the past week, had had nothing to eat but the scant trickle of Klara's milk. Into the other carriage they put the new baby. Klara, blind with exhaustion, could scarcely walk. They made their way through the rubble of the city, not knowing where they were going; they steered the carriages around crashed planes, horse carcasses, exploded German tanks, fallen chimneys, piles of rubbish, bodies of soldiers, bodies of women. At the corner of Király and Kazinczy utca they came across a group of Russian soldiers shoveling rubble into the back of a truck. Their leader, a decorated officer, stopped Klara and Polaner and made a loud demand in Russian. They knew he wanted their papers, but Polaner's papers could only have gotten him arrested or shot; he replied in Hungarian that Klara was his wife and that they were bringing the children home. For a long time the officer looked at the gaunt, hollow-eyed Klara and Polaner, and peered into the carriages at the silent children. Finally he reached into the pocket of his coat and brought out a photograph of a round-faced woman with a round-faced child seated on her knee. While Klara held the photograph, the soldier went to the cab of the truck and took out a canvas rucksack. Kneeling, he drew out a paper bag that bulged as though it contained stones, then reached into the bag and withdrew a handful of wizened hazelnuts. These he passed to Klara. A second handful of nuts went to Polaner.

On those two handfuls of food, Klara would nurse both children for a week.

Because there was nowhere else to go, they went to the ghetto, which had been liberated by the Russians earlier that day. There, at the gates of the Great Synagogue on Dohány utca, they found Klein's grandmother holding the single goat kid she'd nursed through the siege. Klein's grandfather, that tiny bright-eyed man with his two uplifted wings of hair, had died of a stroke the first week of January. He'd been taken to the courtyard of the synagogue, where hundreds of Jewish dead lay waiting to be buried.

What about my mother? Klara had asked. What about my brother's wife?

And in the same grief-raked voice, Klein's grandmother delivered the news that Elza Hász and Klara's mother had been shot, along with forty others, in the courtyard of a building on Wesselényi utca. She spoke the words with lowered eyes as she stroked the head of the last surviving kid, the remnant of the urban flock that had saved the lives of thirty women and children at Szabadság tér.

In the courtyard of the synagogue at Bethlen Gábor tér, where the concentration-camp survivors were supposed to register when they returned, those who had remained in Budapest begged the camp survivors for news of those who hadn't come home. Nearly every day until Andras's return, Klara had gone to that synagogue. Though she feared the answers to her questions, she had asked and asked. One week she met a man who'd been in a camp in Germany with her brother; they'd been workmates at an armaments factory there. This man took her into the synagogue sanctuary, where he sat down with her in a pew, took her hands in his own, and told her that her brother was dead. He'd been shot on New Year's Eve along with twenty-five others.

For a week she sat shivah for him at the house on Frangepán kóz; as far as she knew, she was the only member of their family still alive. Then she went back to the synagogue again, hoping for news of Andras. Instead she learned something that she must tell him now. A woman from Debrecen had come to Bethlen Gábor tér to look for her children. Not long before, this woman had been in a camp herself; she had been in Oświęcim, in Poland. She had seen Andras's parents on a railroad embankment there, before she herself had been moved into a group of those who were well enough to work. Of the other group, the old and sick and very young, nothing more had been seen, nothing heard.

As Klara delivered the news, Andras began to shake with silent grief. József sat beside him in hollow-eyed shock. In a single day, in this strange small house filled with photographs of the dead, they had both become orphans.

For months after Andras came home, they went to the synagogue at Bethlen Gábor tér every day. Hungarian Jews were being exhumed from graves all over Austria and Germany, Ukraine and Yugoslavia, and, whenever it was possible, identified by their papers or their dog tags. There were thousands of them. Every day, on the wall outside the building, endless lists of names. Abraham. Almasy. Arany. Banki. Böhm. Braun. Breuer. Budai. Csato. Czitrom. Dániel. Diamant. Einstein. Eisenberger. Engel. Fischer. Goldman. Goldner. Goldstein. Hart. Hauszmann. Heller. Hirsch. Honig. Horovitz. Idesz. János. Jáskiseri. Kemény. Kepecs. Kertész. Klein. Kovacs. Langer. Lázár. Lindenfeld. Markovitz. Martón. Nussbaum. Ócsai. Paley. Pollák. Róna. Rosenthal. Roth. Rubiczek. Rubin. Schoenfeld. Sebestyen. Sebök. Steiner. Szanto. Toronyi. Ungar. Vadas. Vámos. Vertes. Vida. Weisz. Wolf. Zeller. Zindler. Zucker. An alphabet of loss, a catalogue of grief. Almost every time they went, they witnessed someone learning that a person they loved had died. Sometimes the news would be received in silence, the only evidence a whitening of the skin around the mouth, or a tremor in the hands that clutched a hat. Other times there would be screams, protests, weeping. They looked day after day, every day, for so long that they almost forgot what they were looking for; after a while it seemed they were just looking, trying to memorize a new Kaddish composed entirely of names.

Then, one afternoon in early August—eight hours before the *Enola Gay's* flight over Hiroshima, and eight days before the end of the Second World War—as they stood scanning the lists of dead, Klara's hand flew to her mouth and her shoulders curled. In that first moment Andras wondered only who she could have had left to lose; it didn't occur to him that her reaction might have anything to do with him. But he must have sensed unconsciously what had happened. When he looked at the list, he found he couldn't bring the names into focus.

Klara held his arm, trembling. "Oh, Andras," she said. "Tibor. Oh, God."

He moved away from her, unwilling to understand. He looked at the list again but couldn't make sense of it. Already people were stepping away from them, giving them a respectful space, the way they did when people found their dead. He stepped forward and touched the list where it bled from *K* to *L*. Katz, Adolf. Kovály, Sarah. László, Béla. Lebowitz, Kati. Lévi, Tibor.

It couldn't be his Tibor. He said this aloud: It's not him. It's someone else. It's not our Tibor. Not our Tibor. A mistake. He pushed his way through the crowd around the list, toward the door of the synagogue, up the stairs to the administrative offices, where an explanation would be found. He terrified a woman at a desk by roaring for the person in charge. She took him to an anteroom where, unbelievably, they made him wait. Klara found him there; her eyes were red, and he thought, *Ridiculous. Not our*

Tibor. And in the office of the person in charge, he sat in an ancient leather chair while the man leafed through manila envelopes. He handed one to Andras, labeled with the name LÉVI. The envelope held a brief typewritten note and a metal dog-tag locket, its clasp twisted. When Andras opened the dog tag he found the inner document still intact: Tibor's name, his date and place of birth, his height and eye color and weight, the name of his commanding officer, his home address, his Munkaszolgálat number. *Your dog tags might come home, but you never will.* The brief typewritten note stated that the tag had been found on Tibor's body in a mass grave in Hidegség, near the Austrian border.

That night Andras locked himself into the bedroom of the new apartment he shared with Klara and Polaner and the children. He sat on the floor, cried aloud, beat his head against the cold red tile. He would never leave that room, he decided; would stay there until he was an old man, and let the earth burn through its years around him.

Sometime in the night, Klara and Polaner came in and helped him to bed. In the vaguest way, he was aware of Klara unbuttoning his shirt, of Polaner sliding his arms into a new one; vaguely, through a veil, he saw Klara washing her face at the basin and getting into bed beside him. Her arm across his chest was a warm live thing, and he was dead beneath it. He couldn't move to touch her or respond to anything she said. He lay spent and exhausted and awake, listening as her breathing fell into its familiar rhythm of sleep. He saw Tibor in those last weeks, the nightmare of their life at Sopron: Tibor going to the village for food. Tibor overturning Andras and József's bowl of beans. Tibor bathing Andras's forehead with a cold cloth. Tibor covering him with his own overcoat. Tibor walking twenty kilometers with a handful of strawberry jam. Tibor reminding him that it was Tamás's birthday. Then he thought of Tibor in Budapest, his eyes dark behind his silver-rimmed glasses. Tibor in Paris, lying on Andras's floor in an agony of love for Ilana. Tibor hauling

Andras's bags to Keleti Station one September morning a lifetime ago. Tibor at the opera, the night before Andras's departure. Tibor dragging an extra mattress up the stairs to his own
small room on Hársfa utca. Tibor in high school, a biology book
open on the table before him. Tibor as a tall young boy, chasing
Andras through the orchard, throwing him to the ground. Tibor
pulling Andras from the millpond. Tibor bending over Andras
where he sat on the kitchen floor, tipping a spoonful of sweet
milk into his mouth.

He turned over and pulled Klara against him, cried and cried
into the damp nebula of her hair.

There was a funeral at the Jewish cemetery outside the city, a
reburial of Tibor's remains and the remains of hundreds of others, a field of open graves, a thousand mourners. Afterward, for
the second time that year, he observed a week of shivah. He and
Klara burned a memorial candle and ate hard-boiled eggs, sat on
the floor in silence, received a stream of guests. In accordance
with the ritual, Andras did not shave for thirty days. He hid
inside his beard, forgot to change his clothes, bathed only when
Klara insisted. He had to work; he knew he couldn't afford to
lose his new job as a dismantler of bombed buildings. But he performed the work without speaking to the other men or seeing
the houses he was taking apart or thinking of the people who had
lived in them. After work he sat in the front room of the apartment they'd taken on Pozsonyi út, or in a dark corner of the
bedroom, sometimes holding one of the children on his lap,
stroking the baby's hair or listening as Tamás described what had
happened at the park that morning. He ate little, couldn't concentrate on a book or newspaper, didn't want to go out for a walk
with József and Polaner. He said Kaddish every day. It seemed to
him he could live this way forever, could make a permanent
employment of grief. Klara, whose motherhood had prevented

her from sinking into an all-consuming mourning for her own mother and György and Elza, understood and indulged him; and Polaner, whose grief had been as deep as Andras's own, knew that even this abyss had a bottom, and that Andras would reach it soon.

He could not have anticipated how, or when. It came on a Sunday exactly a month after the funeral, the day Andras shaved his mourning beard. They were sitting at the breakfast table, eating barley porridge with goats' milk; food was still scarce, and as the weather turned colder they had begun to wonder whether, having survived the war itself, they would die of its aftermath. Klara spooned her own porridge into the children's mouths. Andras, who could not eat, passed his along to her. József and Polaner sat with the newspaper spread between them, Polaner reading aloud about the Communist Party's struggle to recruit members before the upcoming general election.

It was Andras who rose when they heard a knock at the door. He crossed the room, drawing his robe closer against the morning chill; he unlocked the door and opened it. A red-faced young man stood on the doorstep, a knapsack on his back. His cap bore the Soviet military insignia. He reached into the pocket of his trousers and drew out a letter.

"I've been charged to deliver this to Andras or Tibor Lévi," the man said.

"Charged by whom?" Andras said. With numb dispassion he noted how strange it was to hear his brother's name in this soldier's mouth. *Tibor Lévi.* As if he were still alive.

"By Mátyás Lévi," the man said. "I was with him at a prisoner-of-war camp in Siberia."

And so, Andras thought. The final piece of news. Mátyás dead, and this his last missive. He felt himself to be in a place so remote from human feeling, so far removed from the ability to experience pain or hope or love, that he did not hesitate to take the letter. He opened it as the young man stood watching, as his family looked at him for the news. And he learned that his brother Mátyás lived, and would be home the following Tuesday.

In the winter of 1942, just a month after he'd been sent to Ukraine, Mátyás Lévi had been taken prisoner by the Soviets, and along with the rest of his labor company had been sent to a mining camp in Siberia. The location was the region of Kolyma, bounded by the Arctic Ocean to the north and the Sea of Okhotsk to the south. They'd gone via the Trans-Siberian Railway to the end of its easternmost spike at Vladivostok, and then had been transported across the sea on the slave ship *Dekabrist*. The camp had two thousand inmates, Germans and Ukrainians and Hungarians and Serbs and Poles and Nazi-sympathizing French, along with Soviet criminals and political dissidents and writers and composers and artists. In the camp he'd been beaten with clubs and shovels and pickhandles. He'd been bitten by bedbugs and flies and lice. He'd been frozen almost to death. He'd worked seventeen-hour days at seventy degrees below zero, had received a daily ration of twenty decagrams of bread, had been thrown into isolation for disobedience, had nearly died of dysentery, had earned the respect of the guards and officers by painting bold Communist posters for the barracks walls, had been named official propaganda-poster designer and official snow sculptor of the camp (he had made ten-foot-high busts of Lenin and Stalin to preside over the parade ground), had learned Russian and had volunteered as a translator, had been called upon to interview Hungarian Nazis, had seen a hundred Arrow Cross members brought to trial and sentenced and in some cases executed, had been attacked by a secret coalition of Hungarian Arrow Cross members who broke both his legs, had convalesced in the infirmary for six months, and finally had been informed one morning that his time at the prison camp was through, and when he'd asked what had earned him the privilege of release, had been told that it was because his official designation, and that of five hundred twenty other prisoners, had been changed from Jewish Hungarian to Hungarian Jew, and that the prison camp was not in the business of detaining Jews, not after what the Nazis had done to them.

But nothing that happened to him those three cold years had prepared him for what waited at home. Nothing had prepared him for the news that four hundred thousand of Hungary's Jews had been sent to death camps in Poland; nothing had prepared him for the bombed ruin of Budapest with its six severed bridges. And nothing had prepared him for the news that his mother and father, his brother and his sister-in-law and his nephew, had all vanished from the earth. It was Andras who delivered the news. Mátyás, grown into a lean, hard-eyed man with a short dark beard, sat before him on the sofa and took it in without a sound; the only sign he gave of having understood at all was a faint trembling of the jaw. He got up and smoothed his pant legs, as if, having been given a military briefing, he was ready now to incorporate the news into his plans and move onward. And then something seemed to change beneath the skin of his face, as though his muscles had received the news on a long-distance telephone delay. He went to his knees on the floor, his features twisting with grief. "Not true," he cried, and moved his arms around his head as if birds were flying at him. It was the news, Andras thought, the unrelenting news, a troop of crows circling, their wings smelling of ash.

He knelt beside his brother and put his arms around him, held him against his own chest as Mátyás wailed. He said his brother's name aloud, as if to remind him of the astonishing fact that at least, he, Mátyás, still lived. He would not let go until Mátyás pulled away and looked around at the unfamiliar room; when his eyes came to rest on Andras's again, they were lucid and full of despair. *Is it true?* he seemed to be asking, though he hadn't said a word. *Tell me honestly. Is it true?*

Andras held Mátyás's gaze steady in his own. There was no

need to speak or to make any sign. He put his arm around Mátyás's shoulder again, drew him close and held him as he cried.

It was Andras who sat with him that night and the next and the one after that, Andras who urged him to eat and who changed the damp bedding on the sofa where he slept. As he did these things he felt the first thinning of the fog that had enveloped him since he'd learned that Tibor was dead. Over the past month he'd nearly forgotten how to be a man in the world, how to breathe and eat and sleep and speak to other people. He had let himself slip away, even though Klara and the children had survived the war, the siege; even though Polaner was there with him every day. On the third night after Mátyás's return, after Mátyás had fallen asleep and he and Klara had retreated to their bedroom, Andras took her hands and begged her forgiveness.

"You know there's nothing to forgive," she said.

"I vowed to take care of you. I want to be a husband to you again."

"You've never stopped," she said.

He bent to kiss her; she was alive, his Klara, and she was there in his arms. Nest of my children, he thought, placing a hand on her womb. Cradle of my joy. And he remembered her with an orange-red dahlia behind her ear, and the way her skin felt beneath a film of bathwater, and what it was like to meet her eye and to know they were thinking the same thing. And he believed, for the first time since he had seen Tibor's name on the list at Bethlen Gábor tér, that it might be possible to live beyond that terrible year; that he might look into Klara's face, whose planes and curves he knew more intimately than any landscape in the world, and feel something like peace. And he took her to bed and made love to her as if for the first time in his life.

CHAPTER FORTY-TWO

A Name

THE MORNING was crisp and blue, early December. From the window of their building on Pozsonyi út, Andras could see a line of schoolchildren being led into Szent István Park—gray woolen coats, crimson scarves, black boots that left herringbones of footprints in the snow. Beyond the park was the marbled span of the Danube. Farther still was the white prow of Margaret Island, where in the summertime Tamás and Április swam at Palatinus Strand. When, on a walk through the park last spring, he'd told them that the pool had once been closed to Jewish swimmers, Április had looked at him with pinched brows.

"I don't see what being Jewish has to do with swimming," she said.

"Neither do I," Andras said, and put a hand at the nape of her neck, where her little gold chain closed. But Tamás had looked through the fence at the pool complex, his hands on the green-painted bars, then turned to meet his father's eyes. He knew by now what had happened to his family during the war, what had happened to his uncles and grandparents. He had gone to Konyár and Debrecen with his father to see where Andras had lived as a boy, and where Andras's parents had lived; he had watched his father place a stone on the doorstep of the house in Konyár as if at a grave.

"I'm going to train for the Olympics here," he said. "I'll set a new world record."

"Me too," Április said. "I'll set a record in freestyle *and* backstroke."

"I have no doubt you will," Andras said.

That was before the escape had come to seem like a reality, before the children had begun to envision their future lives taking place on the other side of the Atlantic. It wouldn't be long now; only a few details remained, including the business Andras would conclude that morning at the Ministry of the Interior. Tamás had wanted to come along with Andras and Klara and Mátyás to pick up the new identification cards. Last night he'd stood before Andras in the sitting room with a grave expression on his face, his arms crossed over his chest. He had already prepared his lessons for the next two days, he announced. He'd miss nothing at all by going with them.

"You have to go to school," Andras said. He rose from his chair and put an arm around Tamás's shoulders. "You don't want the students in America to get ahead of you."

"I'm not worried about *that*," Tamás said. "Not if I miss just one afternoon. They get Saturdays and Sundays off *every week*."

"I'll leave your new papers on your desk," Andras said. "They'll be waiting for you when you get home from school."

Tamás sent a glance toward Klara, who sat at her writing desk by the window; she shook her head and said, "You heard your father."

Shrugging, sighing, declaring it all to be unfair, Tamás gave up the argument and loped off down the hallway to his room. "As if I'd *get behind*," they heard him say as he closed the bedroom door.

Klara lifted her eyes to Andras, trying to restrain her laughter. "He's been a grown man for years, hasn't he?" she said. "What on earth will he do in America, among those kids with their banana splits and their rock and roll?"

"He'll eat banana splits and listen to rock and roll," Andras predicted, which turned out, in fact, to be true.

Andras and Mátyás had taken the day off work to go to the Ministry of the Interior. They were employed at *Magyar Nation*, one of the secondary communist newspapers, where they directed the design department; they had been up late the previous night judging a contest of winter-themed drawings by gimnázium students. The winning drawing had depicted a skating race, athletics being a safe subject under the judging regulations, which disqualified any drawing that made reference to Christmas. That holiday belonged to the old Hungary, at least officially. Of course, people still celebrated it; they were relying on that fact, all of them—Andras and Mátyás, Klara and Tamás and Április. In a few weeks, on Christmas Eve, they would take a train to Sopron, and then they would walk six miles in the snow to a place where they might cross the Austrian border unnoticed; they would slip through while the border patrol drank vodka and listened to Christmas carols in their warm quarters. In Austria they would catch a train that would take them to Vienna, where Polaner had been living since his own border crossing in November. From there they would travel together to Salzburg, and then to Marseilles. On the tenth of January, if all went well, they would board an ocean liner for New York, where József Hász had secured an apartment for them.

But first they had to settle the business about the name change and the new identity cards. They had submitted the application eight weeks earlier, in October; it had gotten delayed, like all other government business, in the confusion surrounding the abortive revolution that fall. Even now, less than a month after it had been quelled, Andras found it difficult to believe the revolution had occurred—that the public debates of the Petőfi Society, a small group of Budapest intellectuals, had blossomed into vast student demonstrations; that the students and their supporters had unseated Ernő Gerő, Moscow's puppet, and had installed the reformist Imre Nagy as prime minister; that they had pulled down the twenty-meter-high statue of Stalin near Heroes' Square, and planted Hungarian flags in his empty boots. The demonstrators had called for free elections, a multiparty system, a free press. They wanted Hungary to disengage from the Warsaw Pact, and more than anything they wanted the Red Army to go home. They wanted to be Hungarian again, even after what it had meant to be Hungarian during the war. And at first, Khrushchev had conceded. He had recognized Nagy as prime minister, and began to call the occupying troops back to Russia. For a few days in late October it seemed to Andras that the Hungarian Revolution would be the swiftest, the cleanest, the most successful revolution Europe had ever known. Then Polaner came home one afternoon having heard a rumor that Soviet tanks were massing at the Romanian and Ruthenian borders. That evening, in the Erzsébetváros café where Andras and Polaner went to hear Jewish artists and writers argue long into the night, the item of hottest debate was whether the Western nations would come to Hungary's aid. Radio Free Europe had led many to believe it would be so, but others insisted that no Western nation would risk itself for a Soviet-bloc state. The cynics turned out to be correct. France and Britain, preoccupied with the Suez Crisis, scarcely cast an eye toward Central Europe; America was caught up in a presidential election, and kept to itself.

More than twenty-five hundred people were killed, and nineteen thousand wounded, when Khrushchev's tanks and planes arrived to crush the uprising. Imre Nagy had hidden himself in the Yugoslav embassy, and was imprisoned as soon as he emerged. Within days the fighting was over. In the weeks that followed, nearly two hundred thousand people fled to the West—among them Polaner, whose image had appeared in one of the many newspapers that had arisen during Hungary's fortnight of freedom. He had been photographed tending a young woman who'd been shot in the leg at Heroes' Square; the woman turned out to be a student organizer, and Polaner had been tagged as a revolutionary. Grim tales of torture had emerged from the Secret Police detainment center at 60 Andrássy út; rather than test their truth, Polaner had decided to risk the border crossing. To his good fortune, and that of the two hundred thousand refugees, the brief conflict had left the Iron Curtain riddled with holes: Many of the border guards had been called in to fight smaller uprisings in the towns and cities of the interior.

Those conflicts, too, had since been put down, but the border remained more permeable than it had been for years. It was decided that the rest of the family would follow Polaner. How long now had they been waiting for a chance to leave? There was no future for them in Hungary. They'd known it to be true before the revolution, and it was all the more apparent now. József Hász, who had made his own escape to New York five years earlier, had been at pains to convince them that they were fools to stay. He had found them the apartment and promised to help them find work. Tamás and Április were old enough to make the border crossing on foot; Christmas Eve would provide the aperture. So at last they decided to take the risk. They had written the news, in carefully veiled language, to József and Elisabet and Paul. And now, on the other side of the ocean, Elisabet was beginning to prepare the apartment, furnishing the rooms and laying in everything they would need. Andras had resisted thinking about the flat itself; such detailed imagining of their future lives seemed to invite bad luck. But he and Klara told the children about the junior high and high schools they would attend, the movie theaters with their pink neon-lit towers, the stores with great bins of fruit from all over the world. Elisabet had been writing to them about those things for years; by now they had attained the quality of images from a legend.

Even more fantastical to Andras was the prospect of returning to school himself, the prospect of finishing his degree in architecture. He and Polaner had made a pact to do it, and Mátyás had agreed to join them. For the past eleven years, exhausted by their daily work, Andras and Polaner had struggled to retain what they'd learned at the École Spéciale. They had set each other exercises, had challenged each other to solve problems of design. They had even attended a few night classes, but had been so dispirited by the dullness of Soviet architecture that they had found themselves unwilling to continue. New York presented a different prospect. They knew nothing of the schools there, but József had written that the city was full of them. He and Polaner had sworn their pact over glasses of Tokaji on the evening of Polaner's departure.

"We'll be old men among boys," Andras had said. "I can see us now."

"We're not old," Polaner said. "We're not even forty."

"Don't you remember what it was like? I don't know if I have the stamina."

"What's going to happen?" Polaner said. "Are you going to get a nosebleed?"

"Without a doubt. And that'll be just the beginning."

"Here's to the beginning," Polaner said, and two hours later he had disappeared into the uncertain night, carrying only his knapsack and a green metal tube of drawings.

Now, on this clear December morning, Klara stood beside Andras at the window, following his gaze toward the park and the river. After the war she had left off teaching and had turned her attention to choreography. The Soviets loved that she had been trained by a Russian and spoke the language; never mind that her teacher had been a White Russian who had fled St. Petersburg in 1917. The Hungarian National Ballet gave her a permanent position, and the state newspaper praised the strength and angularity of her work. *K. Lévi is a choreographer in the true Soviet style*, the official dance critic wrote; and Klara, who for years had been plotting her family's defection to the United States, sat at the kitchen table with the newspaper in her hand and laughed.

"Time to go," she said now. "Mátyás will be waiting."

Andras helped her into her gray coat and draped a cinnamon-colored scarf around her neck. "You're as lovely as ever," he said, touching her sleeve. "You used to wear a red hat in Paris. You'll have one again in America."

"As ever!" she said. "Has it come to that? Am I so old?"

"Ageless," he said. "Timeless."

They met Mátyás at the corner of Pozsonyi út and Szent István körút. In honor of the occasion he had worn a pink carnation in his buttonhole, a gesture that seemed to recall his younger self. He had returned from Siberia hardened and sharpened into a man, a fierce aggressive light radiating from his eyes. He had never returned to dancing, would never again wear a top hat, white tie, and tails. The part of him that had been inclined toward the physical expression of joy had been carved away in Siberia. But now, on the day of the name change, a pink carnation.

Klara pressed Andras's arm as they crossed Perczel Mór utca. "I brought the camera," she said. "I hope you're feeling photogenic."

"As ever," said Andras, who detested any photograph of himself. But Mátyás straightened the carnation in his buttonhole and struck a pose against a streetlight.

"Not yet," Klara said. "After we get the documents."

They arrived at the gray monolith that housed the Ministry of the Interior—a building, Andras recalled, that stood in the footprint of the eighteenth-century palace of a famous courtesan. The palace had been destroyed in the siege of 1944, but a single elm that appeared in engravings of the building still stood behind its low iron fence. Andras touched the bark as if for luck, trying to imagine what it would be like to live in a city where he would not see ghosts of buildings and people everywhere he looked, where what existed now was all there was for him. Then he and Mátyás and Klara climbed the steps and entered the glass-and-concrete cavern of the building. They waited for an hour while the man in charge of name changes fingered his way through an endless series of documents, each of which had to be stamped thrice and signed by elusive functionaries before it could be delivered. But finally their name was called—their old name, one last time—and they had the papers in hand: new identification cards and work cards and residency certificates. Documents, Andras hoped, that would soon be of no use to them at all. But it had seemed important to know that the new name had been recorded in Hungarian record books, important that it be made official.

Outside, the high blue sky had gone metallic gray, and they stepped into a cloud of falling snow. Klara ran down the steps to prepare the camera while Andras and Mátyás stood with the new documents in their hands. Andras had not expected the sight of the cards and papers to bring tears to his eyes, but now he found himself weeping. It had become real at last: this memorial, this mark they would carry all their lives and pass to their children and grandchildren.

"Stop that," Mátyás said, drawing the back of his sleeve across his own eyes. "It won't change anything."

He was right, of course. Nothing would change what had happened—not grief, not time, not memory, not retribution. But they could leave this place, would leave it in a few weeks. They could cross an ocean and live in a city where Április might grow up without the gravity that had marked her brother, without the sense of tragedy that seemed to hang in the air like the brown dust of bituminous coal. And Andras would become a student again—if not the young man who had arrived in Paris with a suitcase and a scholarship, then a man who knew something more of both the beauty and the ugliness of the world. And Klara would be with him—Klara, who stood before them now with her dark hair blowing, her hands raised, the camera hiding her face behind its glass eye. He put his arm around his brother and said, "Ready." She counted to three in English, a daring act in the shadow of the Ministry of the Interior. And she captured them, the two men on the steps: Andras and Mátyás Tibor.

Epilogue

IN THE SPRING, on afternoons when she didn't have soccer practice, she would skip her last class—orchestra—and take the 6 uptown to her grandfather's building. She thought of it that way, his building, though he didn't live there or own it. It was a four-story building set at an angle to the street; the façade was made up of hundreds of small rectangles of steel-framed glass, shunted skyward in a violent and asymmetrical upward thrust, like an exploding Japanese screen. Slim birches grew in the trapezoid of earth between building and sidewalk. The marble lintel above the door read AMOS MUSEUM OF CONTEMPORARY ART; her grandfather's name was chiseled into the cornerstone, above the word ARCHITECT. The building housed a small collection of paintings and sculptures and photographs she'd seen a thousand times. In its central courtyard was a café where she always ordered her coffee black. At thirteen she considered herself on the cusp of womanhood. She liked to sit at a table and write letters to her brother at Brown, or to her friends from camp in the Berkshires. She would sit for hours, almost until dinnertime, and then she would run to catch the express, hoping to make it back to the apartment before her parents got home from work.

Her grandparents didn't live in the city. They lived upstate, down the road from her great-uncle, and five miles away from the man whom she called uncle but who was her grandfather's friend. Sometimes she went to visit them on weekends. Three hours by train, which passed quickly if you had a window seat. Her grandfather had a barn he'd converted into a workshop, with high windows that let in northern light. They all worked there still, her grandfather and her great-uncle and her not-uncle uncle, though they were old enough to retire. They let her sit at their sloping desks and use their ink-stained tools. She liked to draw oblique entryways, fractured rooflines, curvilinear façades. They gave her books about architects they'd known, Le Corbusier and Pingusson. They taught her the Latin names of arches and showed her how to use the French curve and the beam compass. They taught her the single-stroke Roman lettering they used to label their plans.

They had lived through the war. Every now and then it drifted into their speech: *During the war,* and then a story about how little they'd had to eat, or how they'd survived the cold, or how long they'd gone without seeing each other. She'd learned about that war in school, of course—who had died, who killed whom, how, and why—though her books hadn't had much to say about Hungary. She'd learned other things about the war from watching her grandmother, who saved plastic bags and glass jars, and kept bottles of water in the house in case of disaster, and made layer cakes with half as much butter and sugar as the recipes called for, and who, at times, would begin to cry for no reason. And she'd learned about it from her father, who'd been hardly more than a baby at the time but who could remember walking with his mother through ruins.

There were strands of darker stories. She didn't know how she'd heard them; she thought she must have absorbed them through her skin, like medicine or poison. Something about labor camps. Something about being made to eat newspapers. Something about a disease that came from lice. Even when she wasn't thinking about those half stories, they did their work in her mind. A few weeks ago she'd had a dream from which she'd woken shouting in fright. She and her parents had been standing in a cold black-walled room, wearing pajamas made of flour sacks. In a corner her grandmother knelt on the concrete floor, weeping. Her grandfather stood before them, too thin, unshaven. A German guard came out of the shadows and made him climb onto a raised conveyor belt, something like the luggage carousel at the airport. The guard put cuffs around his ankles and wrists, then stepped to a wooden lever beside the conveyor belt and pushed it forward. A meshing of gears, a grinding of iron teeth. The belt began to move. Her grandfather rounded a corner and disappeared into a rectangle of light, from beyond which came a deafening clap that meant he was dead.

That was when she'd shouted herself awake.

Her parents had come running into the room. *What is it? What is it?*

You don't want to know.

Today she sat in the courtyard with her notebook and her bitter coffee, the first time she'd been there since the dream. It was a deep blue afternoon, sun slanting through the courtyard in a way that reminded her of the north woods and camp. But she couldn't stop thinking about the conveyor belt and that deafening shock of noise. She couldn't concentrate on writing to her brother. She couldn't drink her coffee, or even take a deep breath. She reminded herself that her grandfather wasn't dead. Her grandmother wasn't dead. And her great-uncle, and the uncle who wasn't her uncle—none of them were dead. Even her father had survived, and his sister, her aunt Április, who'd been born in the middle of it all.

But then there was the other great-uncle, the one who had died. He'd had a wife, and his son would have been her father's age now. They had all died in the war. Her grandparents almost never talked about them, and when they did, they spoke in lowered voices. All that was left of that uncle was a photograph taken when he was twenty years old. He was handsome, with a strong jaw and heavy dark hair, and he wore a pair of silver-framed glasses. He didn't look like someone who expected to die. He looked like he was supposed to live to be a white-haired old man like his brothers.

Instead there was just that photograph. And their last name, a memorial.

She wanted to hear the whole story: what that brother had been like as a boy, what he'd been good at in school, what he'd wanted to do with his life, where he'd lived, who he'd loved, how he'd died. If her own brother died, she would tell her granddaughter everything about him. If her granddaughter asked.

Maybe that was the problem: She hadn't asked. Or maybe even now they didn't want to talk about it. But she would ask, next time she went to visit. It seemed right that they should tell her, now that she was thirteen. She wasn't a child anymore. She was old enough now to know.

Any Case

It could have happened.
It had to happen.
It happened earlier. Later.
Closer. Farther away.
It happened, but not to you.

You survived because you were first.
You survived because you were last.
Because alone. Because the others.
Because on the left. Because on the right.
Because it was raining. Because it was sunny.
Because a shadow fell.

Luckily there was a forest.
Luckily there were no trees.
Luckily a rail, a hook, a beam, a brake,
a frame, a turn, an inch, a second.
Luckily a straw was floating on the water.

Thanks to, thus, in spite of, and yet.
What would have happened if a hand, a leg,
One step, a hair away?

So you are here? Straight from that moment still suspended?
The net's mesh was tight, but you? through the mesh?
I can't stop wondering at it, can't be silent enough.
Listen,
How quickly your heart is beating in me.

—Wislawa Szymborska
translated from the Polish by Grazyna Drabik and Sharon Olds

ACKNOWLEDGMENTS

Deepest gratitude to everyone who helped bring this novel to its final state. The National Endowment for the Arts, the MacDowell Colony, the Corporation of Yaddo, the Rona Jaffe Foundation, and the Dorothy and Lewis B. Cullman Center for Scholars and Writers at the New York Public Library provided invaluable gifts of time and freedom. The United States Holocaust Memorial Museum, the Mémorial de la Shoah in Paris, the library of the École Spéciale d'Architecture, the Budapest Holocaust Memorial Center, and the National Jewish Museum of Budapest gave me access to artifacts and documents that made the history tangible. Zsuzsa Toronyi of the National Hungarian Jewish Archives in Budapest led me to the Munkaszolgálat newspapers, and Gábor Nagy was a subtle and insightful translator. CUNY professor emeritus Randolph Braham documented the Hungarian Holocaust in his career-long study of the subject, and particularly in *The Politics of Genocide*, which was an infallible guide; on a snowy day in February he met with me to answer questions of geography and Hungarian military ranking. The USC Shoah Foundation Institute for Visual History and Education provided many hours of videotaped interviews. Killian O'Sullivan gave detailed architectural advice. Professor Brian Porter at the University of Michigan offered insight into twentieth-century Central European politics and history. Kenneth Turan answered my Yiddish questions. Alice Hudson at the New York Public Library unearthed wartime maps of Budapest and Paris. Professor Edgar Rosenberg at Cornell led me to Gerald Schwab's *The Day the Holocaust Began: The Odyssey of Herschel Grynszpan*.

Jordan Pavlin at Knopf offered unflagging patience, encouragement, and the most sensitive and painstaking editing. Kimberly Witherspoon championed this project from the beginning. Sonny Mehta gave me the great gift of his confidence. Mary Mount edited the novel from a European perspective. My copy editor, Kate Norris, went far beyond the call of duty. Leslie Levine responded with calm grace to every query.

Michael Chabon and Ayelet Waldman were dazzlingly generous readers, editors, and friends. Brian Seibert lent me his sharp editorial eye, guidance on matters of dance, and courage when my own flagged. Daniel Orringer was a tireless source of medical detail, and Amy Orringer was an excellent travel partner and a fearless, nonjudgmental early reader. Carl and Linda Orringer gave their love, support, and unwavering belief in this project. Tom Tibor sent his meticulously researched writings about our family's experience. Judy Brodt shared her memories and her knowledge of Jewish observance. Tibor Schenk described his wartime experiences at Bór and led me to Munkaszolgálat websites. Christa Parravani walked into a ruin with me to take photographs.

Above all, this book owes its existence to my grandparents Andrew and Irene Tibor, and to my great uncle and aunt Alfred and Susan Tibor. Deepest gratitude for your patience, belief, and generosity. To my uncle Alfred, thank you for taking the time to answer my questions, narrate our family's stories, and read the draft so carefully. To my grandmother, Anyu, most profound thanks: you read and edited with a poet's artistry, a dressmaker's exactitude, and a mother's sensitivity. The insight you provided could have come from nowhere else.

My husband, Ryan Harty, read this novel countless times, and offered his incomparably acute editorial insight, his deep understanding of character, and his flawless ear for language. At every stage he made me feel that finishing the book was possible and necessary. No words of thanks can ever be enough.

PERMISSIONS ACKNOWLEDGMENTS

Grateful acknowledgment is made to the following for permission to reprint previously published material:

Continuum International Publishing Group: The poem "D'Anne qui luy jecta de la Neige" from *Les Epigrammes* by Clément Marot (London: Athlone Press, 1970). Reprinted by permission of Continuum International Publishing Group.

New Directions Publishing Corp., Hamish Hamilton, and Carl Hanser Verlag GmbH & Co.: "It is," from *Unrecounted* by W. G. Sebald, translated by Michael Hamburger, copyright © 2004 by The Estate of W. G. Sebald. Copyright © 2003 by Carl Hanser Verlag Müchen. Translation copyright © 2004 by Michael Hamburger. Reprinted by permission of New Directions Publishing Corp., Hamish Hamilton, and Carl Hanser Verlag GmbH & Co.

ALSO BY JULIE ORRINGER

HOW TO BREATHE UNDERWATER

Nine brave, wise, and spellbinding stories make up this award-winning debut. In "When She is Old and I Am Famous" a young woman confronts the inscrutable power of her cousin's beauty. In "Note to Sixth-Grade Self" a band of popular girls exert their social power over an awkward outcast. In "Isabel Fish" fourteen-year-old Maddy learns to scuba dive in order to mend her family after a terrible accident. Alive with the victories, humiliations, and tragedies of youth, *How to Breathe Underwater* illuminates this powerful territory with striking grace and intelligence.

Fiction/Literature/978-1-4000-3436-9

VINTAGE CONTEMPORARIES
Available at your local bookstore, or visit
www.randomhouse.com

Meet with Interesting People
Enjoy Stimulating Conversation
Discover Wonderful Books

VINTAGE BOOKS / ANCHOR BOOKS ⊕

Reading Group Center

THE READING GROUP SOURCE FOR BOOK LOVERS

Visit ReadingGroupCenter.com where you'll find great reading choices—award winners, bestsellers, beloved classics, and many more—and extensive resources for reading groups such as:

Author Chats

Exciting contests offer reading groups the chance to win one-on-one phone conversations with Vintage and Anchor Books authors.

Extensive Discussion Guides

Guides for over 450 titles as well as non-title specific discussion questions by category for fiction, nonfiction, memoir, poetry, and mystery.

Personal Advice and Ideas

Reading groups nationwide share ideas, suggestions, helpful tips, and anecdotal information. Participate in the discussion and share your group's experiences.

Behind the Book Features

Specially designed pages which can include photographs, videos, original essays, notes from the author and editor, and book-related information.

Reading Planner

Plan ahead by browsing upcoming titles, finding author event schedules, and more.

Special for Spanish-language reading groups

www.grupodelectura.com

A dedicated Spanish-language content area complete with recommended titles from Vintage Español.

A selection of some favorite reading group titles from our list

Atonement by Ian McEwan
Balzac and the Little Chinese Seamstress by Dai Sijie
The Blind Assassin by Margaret Atwood
The Devil in the White City by Erik Larson
Empire Falls by Richard Russo
The English Patient by Michael Ondaatje
A Heartbreaking Work of Staggering Genius by Dave Eggers
The House of Sand and Fog by Andre Dubus III
A Lesson Before Dying by Ernest J. Gaines

Lolita by Vladimir Nabokov
Memoirs of a Geisha by Arthur Golden
Midnight in the Garden of Good and Evil by John Berendt
Midwives by Chris Bohjalian
Push by Sapphire
The Reader by Bernhard Schlink
Snow by Orhan Pamuk
An Unquiet Mind by Kay Redfield Jamison
Waiting by Ha Jin
A Year in Provence by Peter Mayle